PRAISE FOR SCOTT TUROW'S
ORDINARY HEROES

"Searching and heartfelt . . . ORDINARY HEROES has the conviction of utter sincerity . . . The author's anguish about war is unmistakably real . . . Storytelling drives his fiction."
— *New York Times*

"What Turow wrestles with is of a deeper and more complete nature [than legal thrillers]. The correct category for Turow is rather that of a major American novelist rising from the tradition of the Midwest, such as Theordore Dreiser, Sinclair Lewis, and James T. Farrell."
— *Los Angeles Times*

"An intricate combination of action and sentiment, with a dynamic, compelling plot . . . Best of all are Turow's characterizations, which are full, multilayered, and ring as true as a tuning fork."
— *Boston Globe*

"Turow's gift for smooth, suspenseful narrative and his skill in dissecting the vulnerabilities and desires that drive his characters' actions are apparent on every page."
— *San Diego Union-Tribune*

more . . .

"A first-rate mystery is meant to keep you guessing, but the enigmas and sorrows at the heart of ORDINARY HEROES do more; they keep you thinking and feeling."

—*Newsday*

"Scott Turow at the very top of his form ... ORDINARY HEROES is a beautifully wrought, finely achieved reconstruction of an elusive, clandestine life ... So be warned: a book to start on a Friday night."

—**ALAN FURST, author of *Dark Voyage***

"Poignant and gritty ... The author's action sequences do plenty to quicken the pulse."

—*Booklist*

"Beneath all the glorious, bloody, heartbreaking stories of wartime heroics and human frailties ... Turow makes his most pointed and incisive commentary on what it means to be human."

—*Oregonian*

"As engrossing as any of Turow's legal thrillers ... In a change of venue from contemporary courtroom to World War II battlefield, Turow further distinguishes himself from other lawyers turned bestselling authors."

—*Kirkus Reviews* **(starred review)**

"A complex, absorbing novel ... Readers of Turow's thrillers will find plenty to pull them into this more ambitious narrative."

—*Hartford Courant*

more . . .

"An extraordinary, unforgettable novel . . . a searing story . . . The book's emotional wallop more than justifies literary license, and should secure its place in the canon of World War II literature."

—*Library Journal* (**starred review**)

"Graphic and compelling . . . More than just a wartime thriller . . . A double detective story . . . Full of well-described action, sharp dialogue, and precise characterization."

—*Bergen County Record* (**NJ**)

"Turow makes the leap from courtroom to battlefield effortlessly . . . a fascinating page-turner."

—*Publishers Weekly* (**starred review**)

"Excellent . . . an extraordinary read . . . Turow has written a superb historical novel that is as vivid and powerful as his previous books. It has rich characters, an authentic feel, and enough twists and turns to keep you flipping the page."

—*Akron Beacon Journal* (**OH**)

"Powerful . . . Top marks to Turow for stepping outside what he's known for and giving his audience something extra."

—*Edmonton Journal* (**Canada**)

"Engrossing . . . Turow lives up to his reputation as a spellbinding teller of tales."

—*Charlotte Observer* (**NC**)

ALSO BY SCOTT TUROW

FICTION

Reversible Errors (2002)

Personal Injuries (1999)

The Laws of Our Fathers (1996)

Pleading Guilty (1993)

The Burden of Proof (1990)

Presumed Innocent (1987)

NONFICTION

Ultimate Punishment:
A Lawyer's Reflections on Dealing with the Death Penalty
(2003)

One L (1977)

SCOTT TUROW

ORDINARY HEROES

WARNER BOOKS

NEW YORK   BOSTON

Copyright © 2005 by Scott Turow
All rights reserved. No part of this book may be reproduced in any form or by any electronic or mechanical means, including information storage and retrieval systems, without permission in writing from the publisher, except by a reviewer who may quote brief passages in a review.

This Warner Books edition is published in arrangement with Farrar, Straus and Giroux.

Warner Books
1271 Avenue of the Americas
New York, NY 10020

Printed in the United States of America

First International Paperback Printing: May 2006

10 9 8 7 6 5 4 3 2 1

ATTENTION CORPORATIONS AND ORGANIZATIONS:
Most WARNER books are available at quantity discounts with bulk purchase for educational, business, or sales promotional use. For information, please call or write:

Special Markets Department, Warner Books, Inc.
1271 Avenue of the Americas, New York, NY 10020
Telephone: 1-800-222-6747 Fax: 1-800-477-5925

In memory of my father

ORDINARY HEROES

I.

Write the complete address in plain letters in the panel below, and your return address in the space provided on the right. Use typewriter, dark ink, or dark pencil. Faint or small writing is not suitable for photographing.

Miss Grace Morton
37 Wiberly Road
Kindle County 16, Iv.
USA

FROM 1Lt. David Dubin
0446192
Judge Advocate General's
Dept.
APO 403 c/o Postmaster
N.Y.
March 19, 1944
In the Atlantic 5th Day
aboard SS King Henry

CENSOR'S STAMP   SEE INSTRUCTION NO. 2

Dearest Grace--

My sickness is over, and I love you and miss you more than
ever! Yesterday I got up feeling fine and ran to breakfast and I
have been well ever since. I am beginning to know the routine
aboard this commandeered cruise ship, where much of the civilian staff remains on duty--including Indian wallahs who serve
the officers in our staterooms. We also have a wonderful band
that three or four times a day strikes up sentimental classical
numbers in the old first-class dining room, which is still turned
out with baubled chandeliers and red velvet drapes. The enlisted men below enjoy many fewer luxuries, but even they know
their accommodations are a marked improvement over what they'd
get on most of the Navy's old buckets.

With Tchaikovsky on the air, I sometimes forget we are in a
war zone and distinctly treacherous waters. Yet with time on my
hands, I suppose it's natural that thoughts of what may lie
ahead occasionally preoccupy me. During the four days of sickness after we sailed from Boston, I naturally spent long periods
on deck. For all the sophistication I like to think I acquired
at Easton College and in law school, I am still a Midwestern
hick. Until now, I have never been on a body of water broader
than the Kindle River, and there have been moments when I've
found the vastness of the Atlantic terrifying. Gazing out, I realize how far I have gone from home, how alone I am now, and how
immaterial my life is to the oceans, or to most of the people
around me.

Of course, with my transfer to the Judge Advocate General's
Department, I have much less to fear than when I was training
as an infantry officer. The closest I am likely to get to a German is to give advice about his treatment as a POW. I know you
and my parents are relieved, as I am, too, but at other moments I
feel at sea. (Ho ho!)

HAVE YOU FILLED IN COMPLETE
ADDRESS AT TOP?

HAVE YOU FILLED IN COMPLETE
ADDRESS AT TOP?

Print the complete address in plain letters in the panel below, and your return address in the space provided on the right. Use typewriter, dark ink, or dark pencil. Faint or small writing is not suitable for photographing.

To: Miss Grace Morton
37 Witerly Road
Kindle County 16, Iv.
USA

From: 1Lt David Dubin
0446192
Judge Advocate General's Dept.
APO 403 c/o Postmaster N.Y.
March 19, 1944
In the Atlantic, 5th Day
aboard HS King Henry
(Censor is not to note military clearances)

SEE INSTRUCTION NO. 2

I'm not sure why God sets men against each other in war—in fact, I'm no surer than ever that I believe in God. But I know I must do my part. We all must do our parts, you at home and us here. Everything our parents taught us—my parents and your parents, different though they may be—is at stake. I know this war is right. And that is what men—and Americans, especially—do. They fight for what is right in the world, even lay down their lives if that's required. I still feel as I did when I enlisted, that if I did not take up this fight, I would not be a man, as men are. As I must be. There are instants when I am actually jealous of the soldiers I am traveling with, even when I see them overcome by a sudden vacancy that I know is fear. They are imagining the bullets sizzling at them in their holes, the earthquake and lightning of bombs and artillery. But I envy who they will become in the forge of battle.

I promise you that such insanity passes fleetly and that I'll happily remain a lawyer, not a foot soldier. It is late now and they say there are heavy seas ahead. I should sleep while I can.

Good night, darling. I'll see you in my dreams!
With love forever,

David

1. STEWART: ALL PARENTS KEEP SECRETS

All parents keep secrets from their children. My father, it seemed, kept more than most.

The first clue came when Dad passed away in February 2003 at the age of eighty-eight, after sailing into a Bermuda Triangle of illness—heart disease, lung cancer, and emphysema—all more or less attributable to sixty years of cigarettes. Characteristically, my mother refused to leave the burial details to my sister and me and met the funeral director with us. She chose a casket big enough to require a hood ornament, then pondered each word as the mortician read out the proposed death announcement.

"Was David a veteran?" he asked. The undertaker was the cleanest-looking man I'd ever seen, with lacquered nails, shaped eyebrows, and a face so smooth I suspected electrolysis.

"World War II," barked Sarah, who at the age of fifty-two still raced to answer before me.

The funeral director showed us the tiny black rendering of the Stars and Stripes that would appear in the paper beside Dad's name, but my mother was already agitating her thinning gray curls.

"No," she said. "No war. Not for this David Dubin." When she was upset, Mom's English tended to fail her. And my sister and I both knew enough to keep quiet when she was in those moods. The war, except for the bare details of how my father, an American officer, and my mother, an inmate in a German concentration camp, had fallen in love, virtually at first sight, had been an unpleasantness too great for discussion throughout our lives. But I had always assumed the silence was for her sake, not his.

By the end of the mourning visitation, Mom was ready to face sorting through Dad's belongings. Sarah announced she was too pressed to lend a hand and headed back to her accounting practice in Oakland, no doubt relishing the contrast with my unemployment. Mom assigned me to my father's closet on Monday morning, insisting that I consider taking much of his clothing. It was nearly all disastrously out of fashion, and only my mother could envision me, a longtime fatso, ever shrinking enough to squeeze into any of it. I selected a few ties to make her happy and began boxing the rest of his old shirts and suits for donation to the Haven, the Jewish relief agency my mother had helped found decades ago and which she almost single-handedly propelled for nearly twenty years as its Executive Director.

But I was unprepared for the emotion that overtook me. I knew my father as a remote, circumspect man, very orderly in almost everything, brilliant, studious, always civil. He preferred work to social engagements, although he had his own polite charm. Still, his great success came within the mighty fortress of the law. Elsewhere, he was less at ease. He let my mother hold sway at home, making the same weary joke for more than fifty years—he would never, he said, have enough skill as a lawyer to win an argument with Mom.

The Talmud says that a father should draw a son close with one hand and push him away with the other. Dad basically failed on both accounts. I felt a steady interest from him which I took for affection. Compared to many other dads, he was a champ, especially in a generation whose principal ideal of fathering was being a 'good provider.' But he was elusive at the core, almost as if he were wary of letting me know him too well. To the typical challenges I threw out as a kid, he generally responded by retreating, or turning me over to my mother. I have a perpetual memory of the times I was alone with him in the house as a child, infuriated by the silence. Did he know I was there? Or even goddamn care?

Now that Dad was gone, I was intensely aware of everything I'd never settled with him—in many cases, not even started on. Was he sorry I was not a lawyer like he was? What did he make of my daughters? Did he think the world was a good place or bad, and how could he explain the fact that the Trappers, for whom he maintained a resilient passion, had never won the World Series in his lifetime? Children and parents can't get it all sorted out. But it was painful to find that even in death he remained so enigmatic.

And so this business of touching the things my father touched, of smelling his Mennen talcum powder and Canoe aftershave, left me periodically swamped by feelings of absence and longing. Handling his personal effects was an intimacy I would never have dared if he were alive. I was in pain but deeply moved every minute and wept freely, burbling in the rear corner of the closet in hopes my mother wouldn't hear me. She herself was yet to shed a tear and undoubtedly thought that kind of iron stoicism was more appropriate to a man of fifty-six.

With the clothing packed, I began looking through the pillar of cardboard boxes I'd discovered in a dim corner. There was a remarkable collection of things there, many marked by a sentimentality I always thought Dad lacked. He'd kept the schmaltzy valentines Sarah and I had made for him as grade-school art projects, and the Kindle County championship medal he'd won in high school in the backstroke. Dozens of packets of darkening Kodachromes reflected the life of his young family. In the bottom box, I found memorabilia of World War II, a sheaf of brittle papers, several red Nazi armbands taken, I imagined, as war trophies, and a curled stack of two-by-two snaps, good little black-and-white photos that must have been shot by someone else since my father was often the subject, looking thin and taciturn. Finally, I came upon a bundle of letters packed in an old candy tin to which a note was tied with a piece of green yarn dulled by time. It was written in a precise hand and dated May 14, 1945.

Dear David,

I am returning to your family the letters you have sent while you have been overseas. I suppose they may have some significance to you in the future. Inasmuch as you are determined to no longer be a part of my life, I have to accept that once time passes and my hurt diminishes, they will not mean anything to me. I'm sure your father has let you

*know that I brought your ring back to him last
month.*

*For all of this, David, I can't make myself be
angry at you for ending our engagement. When I
saw your father, he said that you were now being
court-martialed and actually face prison. I can
hardly believe that about someone like you, but I
would never have believed that you would desert
me either. My father says men are known to go
crazy during wartime. But I can't wait any longer
for you to come back to your senses.*

*When I cry at night, David—and I won't pretend
for your sake that I don't—one thing bothers me the
most. I spent so many hours praying to God for Him
to deliver you safely; I begged Him to allow you to
live, and if He was especially kind, to let you come
back whole. Now that the fighting there is over, I
cannot believe that my prayers were answered and
that I was too foolish to ask that when you returned,
you would be coming home to me.*

*I wish you the best of luck in your present
troubles.*

Grace

This letter knocked me flat. Court-martialed! The last
thing I could imagine of my tirelessly proper father was
being charged with a serious crime. And a heartbreaker
as well. I had never heard a word about any of these
events. But more even than surprise, across the arc of time,
like light emitted by distant stars decades ago, I felt pierced
by this woman's pain. Somehow her incomprehension al-
loyed itself with my own confusion and disappointment

and frustrated love, and instantly inspired a ferocious curiosity to find out what had happened.

Dad's death had come while I was already gasping in one of life's waterfalls. Late the year before, after reaching fifty-five, I had retired early from the Kindle County *Tribune*, my sole employer as an adult. It was time. I think I was regarded as an excellent reporter—I had the prizes on the wall to prove it—but nobody pretended, me least of all, that I had the focus or the way with people to become an editor. By then, I'd been on the courthouse beat for close to two decades. Given the eternal nature of human failings, I felt like a TV critic assigned to watch nothing but reruns. After thirty-three years at the *Trib*, my pension, combined with a generous buyout, was close to my salary, and my collegiate cynicism about capitalism had somehow fed an uncanny knack in the stock market. With our modest tastes, Nona and I wouldn't have to worry about money. While I still had the energy, I wanted to indulge every journalist's fantasy: I was going to write a book.

It did not work out. For one thing, I lacked a subject. Who the hell really cared about the decades-old murder trial of the Chief Deputy Prosecuting Attorney that I'd once thought was such a nifty topic? Instead, three times a day, I found myself staring across the table at Nona, my high-school sweetheart, where it swiftly became apparent that neither of us especially liked what we were seeing. I wish I could cite some melodrama like an affair or death threats to explain what had gone wrong. But the truth is that the handwriting had been on the wall so long, we'd just regarded it as part of the decorating. After thirty years, we had drifted into one of those marriages that never recovered its motive once our daughters were grown. Nine weeks before Dad's passing, Nona and I had separated. We had dinner once each week, where we discussed our business amiably, frustrated one another in the ways we always had, and exhibited no signs of longing or second thoughts. Our daughters were devastated, but I figured we both deserved some credit for having the guts to hope for better at this late date.

Nevertheless, I was already feeling battered before Dad died. By the time we buried him, I was half inclined to jump into the hole beside him. Sooner or later, I knew I'd pick myself up and go on. I'd been offered freelance gigs at two magazines, one local, one national. At five foot nine and 215 pounds, I am not exactly a catch, but the expectations of middle age are much kinder to men than women, and there were already signs that I'd find companionship, if and when I was ready.

For the moment, though, out of work and out of love, I was far more interested in taking stock. My life was like everybody else's. Some things had gone well, some hadn't. But right now I was focused on the failures, and they seemed to have started with my father.

And so that Monday, while my mother thought I was struggling into Dad's trousers, I remained in his closet and read through dozens of his wartime letters, most of them typed Army V-mails, which had been microfilmed overseas and printed out by the post office at home. I stopped only when Mom called from the kitchen, suggesting I take a break. I found her at the oval drop-leaf table, which still bore the marks of the thousands of family meals eaten there during the 1950s.

"Did you know Dad was engaged before he met you?" I asked from the doorway.

She revolved slowly. She had been drinking tea, sipping it through a sugar cube she clenched between her gapped front teeth, a custom still retained from the shtetl. The brown morsel that remained was set on the corner of her saucer.

"Who told you that?"

I described Grace's letter. Proprietary of everything, Mom demanded to see it at once. At the age of eighty, my mother remained a pretty woman, paled by age, but still with even features and skin that was notably unwithered. She was a shrimp—I always held her to blame that I had not ended up as tall as my father—but people seldom saw her that way because of the aggressive force of her intelligence, like someone greeting you in sword and armor. Now, Mom studied Grace Morton's letter with an intensity that seemed as if it could, at any instant, set the page aflame. Her expression, when she put it down, might have shown the faintest influence of a smile.

"Poor girl," she said.

"Did you know about her?"

"'Know'? I suppose. It was long over by the time I met your father, Stewart. This was wartime. Couples were separated for years. Girls met other fellows. Or vice versa. You've heard, no, of Dear John letters?"

"But what about the rest of this? A court-martial? Did you know Dad was court-martialed?"

"Stewart, I was in a concentration camp. I barely spoke English. There had been some legal problem at one point, I think. It was a misunderstanding."

"'Misunderstanding'? This says they wanted to send him to prison."

"Stewart, I met your father, I married your father, I came here with him in 1946. From this you can see that he did not go to prison."

"But why didn't he mention this to me? I covered every major criminal case in Kindle County for twenty years, Mom. I talked to him about half of those trials. Wouldn't you think at some point he'd have let on that he was once a criminal defendant himself?"

"I imagine he was embarrassed, Stewart. A father wants his son's admiration."

For some reason this response was more frustrating than anything yet. If my father was ever concerned about my opinion of him, it had eluded me. Pushed again toward tears, I sputtered out my enduring lament. He was such a goddamn crypt of a human being! How could Dad have lived and died without letting me really know him?

There was never a second in my life when I have doubted my mother's sympathies. I know she wished I'd grown up a bit more like my father, with a better damper on my emotions, but I could see her absorb my feelings in a mom's way, as if soaked up from the root. She emitted a freighted Old World sigh.

"Your father," she said, stopping to pick a speck of sugar off her tongue and to reconsider her words. Then, she granted the only acknowledgment she ever has of what I faced with him. "Stewart," she said, "your father sometimes had a difficult relationship with himself."

I spirited Dad's letters out of the house that day. Even at my age, I found it easier to deceive my mother than to confront her. And I needed time to ponder what was there. Dad had written colorfully about the war. Yet there was an air of unexpressed calamity in his correspondence, like the spooky music that builds in a movie soundtrack before something goes wrong. He maintained a brave front with Grace Morton, but by the time he suddenly broke off their relationship in February 1945, his life as a soldier seemed to have shaken him in a fundamental way, which I instantly connected to his court-martial.

More important, that impression reinforced a lifetime suspicion that had gone unvoiced until now: something had *happened* to my father. In the legal world, if a son is to judge, Dad was widely admired. He was the General Counsel of Moreland Insurance for fifteen years, and was renowned for his steadiness, his quiet polish, and his keen ability in lasering his way through the infinite complications of insurance law. But he had a private life like everybody else, and at home a dour aura of trauma always clung to him. There were the smokes he couldn't give up, and the three fingers of scotch he bolted down each night like medicine, so he could get four or five hours of sleep before he was rocked awake by unwanted dreams. Family members sometimes commented that as a younger man he had been more outspoken. My grandmother's theory, which she rarely kept to herself, was that Gilda, my mother, had largely taken David's tongue by always speaking first and with such authority. But he went through life as if a demon had a hand on his shoulder, holding him back.

Once when I was a boy, he saw me nearly run over as a car screamed around the corner, barely missing me where I was larking with friends on my bike. Dad snatched me up by one arm from the pavement and carried me that way until he could throw me down on our lawn. Even so young, I understood he was angrier about the panic I'd caused him than the danger I'd posed to myself.

Now the chance to learn what had troubled my father became a quest. As a reporter, I was fabled for my relentlessness, the Panting Dog School of Journalism, as I described it, in which I pursued my subjects until they dropped. I obtained a copy of Dad's 201, his Army personnel file, from the National Personnel Records Center in St. Louis, and with that fired off several letters to the Defense Department and the National Archives. By July, the chief clerk for the Army Judiciary in Alexandria, Virginia, confirmed that she had located the record of my father's court-martial. Only after I had paid to have it copied did she write back stating that the documents had now been embargoed as classified, not by the Army, but by, of all agencies, the CIA.

The claim that my father did anything sixty years ago that deserved to be regarded as a national security matter today was clearly preposterous. I unleashed a barrage of red-hot faxes, phone calls, letters, and e-mails to various Washington offices that attracted all the interest of spam. Eventually, my Congressman, Stan Sennett, an old friend, worked out an arrangement in which the government agreed to let me see a few documents from the court-martial, while the CIA reconsidered the file's secret status.

So in August 2003, I traveled to the Washington National Records Center, in Suitland, Maryland. The structure looks a little like an aircraft carrier in dry dock, a low red-brick block the size of forty football fields. The public areas within are confined to a single corridor whose decor is pure government, the equivalent of sensible shoes: brick walls, ceilings of acoustic tile, and an abundance of fluorescent light. There I was allowed to read—but not to copy—about ten pages that had been withdrawn from the Record of Proceedings compiled in 1945 by the trial judge advocate, the court-martial prosecutor. The sheets had faded to manila and had the texture of wallpaper, but they still glimmered before me like a treasure. Finally, I was going to know.

I had told myself I was ready for anything, and what was actually written could hardly have been more matter-of-fact, set out in the deliberately neutral language of the law, further straitjacketed by military terminology. But reading, I felt like I'd been dropped on my head. Four counts had been brought against Dad, the specifications for each charge pointing to the same incident. In October 1944, my father, acting Assistant Staff Judge Advocate of the Third Army, had been directed to investigate allegations by General Roland Teedle of the 18th Armored Division concerning the possible court-martial of Major Robert Martin. Martin was attached to the Special Operations Branch of the Office of Strategic Services, the OSS, the forerunner of the CIA, which had been founded during World War II (accounting, I figured, for why the Agency had stuck its nose in now). Dad was ordered to arrest Major Martin in November 1944. Instead, in April 1945, near Hechingen, Germany, my father had taken custody of Martin, where, according to the specifications, Dad "deliberately allowed Martin to flee, at great prejudice to the security and well-being of the United States." Nor was that just rhetoric. The most serious charge, willful disobedience of a superior officer, was punishable by execution.

A weeklong trial ensued in June 1945. At the start, the

count that could have led to a firing squad had been dismissed, but the three charges remaining carried a potential sentence of thirty years. As to them, I found another discolored form labeled JUDGMENT.

> The court was opened and the president announced that the accused was guilty of all specifications and charges of Charges II, III, and IV; further that upon secret written ballot, two-thirds of the members present concurring, accused is sentenced to five years' confinement in the United States Penitentiary at Fort Leavenworth at hard labor, and to be dishonorably discharged from the U.S. Army forthwith, notice of his discharge to be posted at the place of his abode.

I read this sheet several times, hoping to make it mean something else. My heart and hands were ice. My father was a felon.

Dad's conviction was quickly affirmed by the Board of Review for the European Theater—the Army equivalent of an appellate court—leaving General Teedle free to carry out the sentence. Instead, in late July 1945, the General revoked the charges he himself had brought. He simply checked off a box on a form without a word of explanation. But it was not a clerical error. The court-martial panel was reconvened by the General's order the next week and issued a one-line finding taking back everything they had done only a month and a half earlier. My father, who had been under house arrest since April, was freed.

The blanks in this tale left me wild with curiosity, feeling like Samson chained blind inside the temple. The Army, the CIA, no one was going to keep me from answering a basic question of heritage: Was I the son of a convict who'd betrayed his country and slipped away on some technicality, or, perhaps, the child of a man who'd endured a primitive injustice which he'd left entombed in the past?

I filled out innumerable government forms and crossed the continent several times as I pieced things together, visiting dozens of document storage sites and military libraries. The most productive trips of all were to Connecticut, where I ultimately acquired the records of Barrington Leach, the lawyer who'd defended my father unsuccessfully at Dad's trial before General Teedle revoked the charges.

Almost as soon as my travels started, I became determined to set down my father's tale. Dad was the only member of the Judge Advocate General's Department court-martialed during World War II, and that was but a small part of what made his experiences distinctive. I toiled happily in the dark corridors of libraries and archives and wrote through half the night. This was going to make not only a book, but *my* book, and a great book, a book which, like the corniest deus ex machina, would elevate my life from the current valley to a peak higher than any I'd achieved before. And then, like the cross-examiners in the criminal courtrooms I had covered for so many years, I made the cardinal mistake, asked one question too many and discovered the single fact, the only conceivable detail, that could scoop me of my father's story.

He had written it himself.

2. DAVID: REGARDING THE CHARGES AGAINST ME

CONFIDENTIAL
ATTORNEY-CLIENT COMMUNICATION

TO: Lieutenant Colonel Barrington Leach, Deputy
Associate Judge Advocate, Headquarters, European
Theater of Operations, U.S. Army (ETOUSA)

FROM: Captain David Dubin

RE: The Charges Against Me

DATE: May 5, 1945

I have decided to follow your suggestion to set down the major details I recall regarding my investigation of Major Robert Martin of OSS and the ensuing events which will shortly bring me before this court-martial. Since I have no desire to discuss this with another soul, including you as my lawyer, I find writing a more palatable alternative, even while I admit that my present inclination is not to show you a word of this. I know my silence frustrates you, making you think I lack a full appreciation for my circumstances, but rest assured that the prospect of a firing squad has caught my attention. Yet as a member of the JAG Department who has both prosecuted and defended hundreds of general courts-martial in the year or so I have been overseas, I am fully convinced that I have nothing to say for myself. General Teedle charges that last month in Hechingen I willfully suffered Major Martin to escape from my lawful custody. And that is true. I did. I let Martin go. I intend to plead guilty because I am guilty. The reasons I freed Martin are irrelevant in the eyes of the law and, candidly, my own business. Let me assure you, however, that telling the whole story would not improve my situation one whit.

I may as well start by expanding on some of the information I routinely request of my own clients. I am a Midwesterner, born in 1915 in the city of DuSable in Kindle County. Both my parents were immigrants, each hailing from small towns in western Russia. Neither was educated beyond grade school. My father has worked since age fourteen as a cobbler, and owns a small shop a block from the three-flat where they raised my older sister, my younger brother, and me.

I was a good student in high school, and also won the Kindle County championship in the hundred-yard backstroke. This combination led me to receive a full scholarship to Easton College. Easton is only about twenty miles from my parents' apartment, but a world apart, the longtime training ground of the genteel elite of the Tri-Cities. As a man whose parents' greatest dream was for their children to become 'real Americans,' I embraced Easton in every aspect, right down to the raccoon coat, ukulele, and briar pipe. I graduated Phi Beta Kappa, and then entered Easton's esteemed law school. Afterward, I was lucky enough to find work in the legal department of Moreland Insurance. My parents pointed out that I appeared to be the first Jew Moreland had hired outside the mail room, but I'd always endeavored not to look at things that way.

For two years, I tried small personal-injury lawsuits in the Municipal Court, but in September 1942, I enlisted. No one who cared about me approved. Both my parents and my sweetheart, Grace Morton, wanted me to wait out the draft, hoping against hope that I'd be missed, or at least limit my time in the path of danger. But I was no longer willing to put off doing my part.

I had met Grace three years earlier, when I fit her for a pair of pumps in the shoe section of Morton's Department Store, where I'd earned pocket money throughout college and law school. In her round-collared sweaters and tiny pearls and pleated skirts, Grace was the image of the all-American girl. But what most attracted me was not her blonde bob or her demure manner so much as her high-mindedness. She is the best-intentioned soul I have ever met. Grace worked as a schoolteacher in the tough North End and waited several months before letting on that her family owned the department store where I'd first encountered her. When I decided to enter the service, I proposed, so that we could remain together, at least while I was posted Stateside. She instantly agreed, but our marriage plans set off a storm in both families that could be calmed only by postponing the wedding.

After basic training at Fort Riley, I entered Officers

Candidate School in the infantry at Fort Benning in Georgia. I was commissioned a Second Lieutenant on April 6, 1943. Two days later, I was transferred forthwith to the Judge Advocate General's Department. I had just turned twenty-eight, making me eligible for JAGD, and some thoughtful superior had put me in for reassignment. In essential Army style, no one asked what I preferred, and I probably don't know the answer to this day. Still ambivalent, I was sent to the stately quadrangle of the University of Michigan Law School to learn about the Articles of War. My graduation in the upper half of my class made my promotion to First Lieutenant automatic.

When I entered the JAG Department, I had requested service in the Pacific, thinking I was more likely to get within the vicinity of active combat, but in August 1943, I was sent to Fort Barkley, Texas, for a period of apprenticeship, so-called applicatory training as the Assistant Judge Advocate at the camp. I spent most of my time explaining legal options to soldiers who'd received Dear Johns from their wives and, as an odd counterpoint, sorting out the many conflicting Dependency Benefit Claims the Army had received from the five women a soldier named Joe Hark had married at his five prior postings, each without benefit of any intervening divorce.

In March 1944, I was at last reassigned overseas, but to the Central Base Station in London, rather than the Pacific. I was fortunate, however, to come under the command of Colonel Halley Maples. He was in his early fifties, and the picture of a lawyer, more than six feet tall, lean, with graying hair and a broad mustache. He seemed to hold a high opinion of me, probably because I, like him, was a graduate of Easton University Law School. Sometime in July, only a few weeks after D-Day, the Colonel was designated as the Staff Judge Advocate for the newly forming Third Army, and I was delighted when he asked me to serve as his acting assistant. I crossed the Channel on August 16, 1944, aboard the USS *Holland*, finally coming within the proximity of war.

The staff judge advocates were part of Patton's rear-echelon headquarters, and we traveled in the General's wake as the Third Army flashed across Europe. It was an advantageous assignment. We did none of the fighting, but time and again entered the French villages and towns jubilantly celebrating their liberation after years of Nazi occupation. From atop the beds of half-ton trucks and armored troop carriers, the infantrymen tossed cigarettes and chocolates to the crowds while the French uncorked bottles of wine hidden from the Germans for years and lavished kisses on us, more, alas, from whiskery old men than willing girls.

In the liberated towns, there was seldom any clear authority, while dozens of French political parties squabbled for power. Locals clustered about the police station and our military headquarters, seeking travel passes or trying to find the sons and fathers who'd been carried off by the Germans. The windows of stores purveying Nazi goods and propaganda were smashed with paving stones, while the cross of Lorraine, symbol of the French resistance, was painted over every swastika that could not be removed. Collaborators were routed out by mobs. In Brou, I saw a barmaid set upon by six or seven youths in resistance armbands who cut off all her hair as punishment for sleeping with Nazis. She endured her shearing with a pliancy that might not have been much different from the way she'd accepted her German suitors. She said nothing, merely wept and sat absolutely still, except for one arm that moved entirely on its own, bucking against her side like the wing of some domesticated fowl engaged in a futile attempt at flight.

Patton was concerned that the chaotic atmosphere would affect our troops and looked to Colonel Maples and his staff to reinforce discipline. I and my counterpart, Anthony Eisley, a squat young captain from Dayton who had practiced law in his father's firm for several years, were assigned to try the large number of general courts-martial which were arising for fairly serious offenses—murder, rape, assault, major thefts, and insubordination—many of these crimes committed against French civilians. In other commands, these cases, especially the defense of the accused, were handled by line officers as an auxiliary duty, but Colonel Maples wanted lawyers trained in the Articles of War dealing with matters that could end in stiff prison sentences or, even, hanging.

The principal impediment in carrying out our assignment was that we had barely set up court when we were on the move again, as Patton's Army rampaged at an unprecedented pace across France. Columns raced through territory even before navigators could post the maps at headquarters. We tried men for their lives in squad tents, with the testimony often inaudible as bombers buzzed overhead and howitzers thundered.

I felt grateful to be at the forefront of history, or at least close to it, and appreciated Colonel Maples as a commander. In the Army officers corps, being built on the double, it was not uncommon, even in the upper ranks, to find commanders who had never so much as fired a rifle in combat, but Maples was not merely a distinguished lawyer who'd risen to the pinnacle of a famous St. Louis firm, but also a veteran of the Great War, which had taken him through many of these towns.

In early September, headquarters moved again to Marson, from La Chaume, bringing us across the Marne. The Colonel asked me to drive with him in search of the field where he had survived the most intense battle he'd fought in. It was a pasture now, but Maples recognized a long stone fence that separated this ground from the neighbor's. He had been a twenty-five-year-old second lieutenant dug into one of the slit trenches that ran across this green land, no more than one hundred yards from the Germans.

There had been more fighting here again lately. In the adjoining woods, artillery rounds had brought down many of the trees, and tank tracks had ripped into the earth. The dead personnel and spent matériel had been cleared away, but there were still several animals, cows and military horses, bloated and reeking and swarming with flies. Yet it was the battles of a quarter century ago which appeared to hold the Colonel. As we walked along the devastated field, he recalled a friend who had popped out to relieve himself and been shot through the head.

"Died like that, with his drawers around his knees, and fell back into the latrine. It was terrible. It was all terrible," he said and looked at me.

Beyond the fence on the neighbor's side, in a narrow culvert, we found a dead German soldier facedown in the water. One hand was on the bank, now withered with a bare leathery husk over what would soon be a skeleton. He was the first dead man I'd seen on a battlefield, and the Colonel studied the corpse for quite some time while I contended with my thumping heart.

"Thank God," he said then.

"Sir?"

"I thank the Lord, David, I shall be too old to come to this place again in war."

Back in the jeep, I asked, "Do you think we might have to fight another World War soon, sir?" Eisley, my courtroom colleague, believed that war with the Soviets was all but inevitable and might begin even before we'd mustered out. The Colonel greeted the idea with exceptional gravity.

"It must not happen, Dubin," he said, as if imparting the most consequential order. "It must not."

By the end of September, Patton's sprint across Europe had come to a virtual stop. Our armored divisions had outraced their supply lines, and the dusty tanks and half-tracks sat immobile awaiting fuel, while the weather turned from bright to gloomy, soon giving way to the wettest fall on record. The front stretched on a static line about ten miles south of the Vosges Mountains. In the interval, infantry replaced the armor and dug themselves into foxholes which, in an echo of the Great War, were only a couple hundred yards from those of the enemy. The Krauts reportedly hurled nighttime taunts. "Babe Ruth is Schwarz-black. Black niggers is at home fucking with your wife." We had plenty of German speakers in our ranks, kids from New York and Cincinnati and Milwaukee, who shouted out their own observations about the puniness of Hitler's balls, hidden under his dress.

The stall allowed the administrative staff, including the judge advocates, to make our first durable headquarters in

Nancy early in October. As a student of French in high school, I seemed to have acquired the impression that there was only one city to speak of in that country. But Nancy's center had been erected in the eighteenth century by a king without a country, Stanislas Leszczynski, later to become Duke of Lorraine, with a grandeur and panache equal to my images of Paris. Patton's forward headquarters was in the Palais du Gouverneur, a royal residence at the end of a tree-lined arcade that resembled pictures I'd seen of the Tuileries. Our offices, along with other rear elements, were about a fifteen-minute walk across town, in the Lycée Henri Poincaré, the oldest school in Nancy.

To process the backlog of cases that had collected as we were trying to keep up with Patton, Colonel Maples asked the personnel nabobs in G-1 to appoint two standing courts-martial. They ultimately assigned nine officers to each, allowing the members to attend to other duties on alternate days. Eisley and I, however, were in court seven days a week, ten hours a day. To break the routine we agreed to rotate roles as the prosecuting trial judge advocate, and as counsel for the accused.

The military tribunal was set up in the former party room of the school, where three dormitory dining tables had been pushed together. At the center was the most senior officer serving as president of the court-martial, flanked by four junior officers on either side. At the far left, Eisley or I would sit with our client, and on the opposite end whoever that day was the TJA. In the center of the room, a table of stenographers worked, taking down the testimony, while a single straight-backed chair was reserved for the witness. The president of one panel was Lieutenant Colonel Harry Klike, a bluff little prewar noncom who'd risen through the Quartermaster Corps and was determined to exhibit the cultivation he believed appropriate for an officer and gentleman. Each day's session ended with Klike officiously announcing, "The court-martial stands adjourned until zero eight hundred tomorrow, when we will reconvene to dispense with justice." No one, as I recall, had the heart to correct him.

We proceeded with dispatch and often finished two or even three cases in a day. In need of a break when court adjourned, Eisley and I often strolled down the rue Gambetta to the magnificent Place Stanislas, with its ornate state buildings and elaborate gates tipped in gold. At a café on the square we sipped cognac and eyed the good women of the town, with their wedgies and upswept hairdos. Tony, married but at full liberty three thousand miles away, praised the imagination of French women and their rugged lovemaking style. I listened without comment, while the *patron* tried to shoo the French kids who appeared beside our table with cupped hands, all of them the master of at least one line of English: "Some gum, chum?"

Out on the avenue, long military columns passed, coming from or going to the front. The hardest-hit units on the way back passed with little expression, grimy, embittered hangdog men, on whom the wages of war were posted like a sign. Cordons of ambulances sometimes raced through, carrying the wounded to the local field hospital. But the replacement troops headed for battle made the most unsettling sight. A hush often came over the streets while the soldiers stared down at us from the trucks. In their faces you could see their desperation and anger about the cruel lottery that left us secure and them facing mortal danger. At those moments, I often found myself thinking uneasily about the way the Third Army's successes were described around headquarters using the word 'we.'

Eventually, Tony and I would begin preparing for the coming day. When the crimes involved attacks on local residents we would go out to jointly interview the witnesses. With the benefit of my high-school French, I read well and could understand, but spoke with more difficulty. Nonetheless, I had improved considerably in my two months on the Continent, and allowing for the grace of hand gestures, we could usually make our way through these meetings without a translator.

The MP who drove us most days, Staff Sergeant Gideon Bidwell, was called Biddy, a shortened version of the nickname Iddy Biddy he'd been awarded by the usual boot-camp smart alecks. He was as wide at the shoulder as a bus seat and at least six foot two, with curly black hair and a pink face holding a broad nose and green eyes. Bidwell was highly competent, but in a cheerless way. He was one of those enlisted men who realize that they are the true Army, whose jobs consist of winning the war at the same time that they keep the officers from making fools of themselves. He hauled the gear, and drove the jeep, and turned the map so I had it going in the right direction, but with a sullen air that made him somewhat unapproachable. When he had picked me up in Cherbourg where I landed, I recognized the sounds of Georgia in his speech, after my time at Fort Benning, but in response to my questions, he said only that his folks had left Georgia several years ago. He remained generally closemouthed about himself, not outwardly insubordinate, but with a sour look tending to indicate he didn't care much for anyone. I sensed that sooner or later we were going to clash.

One evening, we stopped at the stockade so I could interview my client for the next day's proceedings. Biddy was with me as we entered the doubled-wire perimeter, where three long lines of pup tents were erected in abnormally tight formation. When my client shuffled out of the guardhouse in his ankle irons and manacles, Biddy buried a heavy groan in his chest.

"Why they always colored?" he asked himself, but loud enough for me to hear. Enough of Georgia seemed to have come North with Bidwell that I preferred not to hear his answer. I gave him a bit of a look, at which he stiffened, but he had the good sense to turn away.

Oddly, Biddy's remark provoked me to ponder his question, albeit from another angle. Given my sympathies for the French families who appeared so often as the victims in our courtrooms, it had not even struck me much at first that many of the soldiers being sentenced to long terms in disciplinary barracks were colored. Yet Biddy was right, at least about the pattern, and the next time I found myself alone with Colonel Maples, I asked why he thought Negroes appeared so frequently among the troops we prosecuted.

"Negroes?" Maples looked at me sharply. "What in the world are you suggesting, Dubin? There are plenty in the stockade who are white." There surely were. Lots of soldiers had ended up in the Army only because a sentencing judge had given them that option rather than prison. Men who were strong-arm robbers and drug fiends at home did not always change their stripes, even on the battlefield. "Do you doubt these boys are guilty?"

In most of the cases I handled, the soldiers were sober by the time I saw them and entered abashed guilty pleas.

And the crimes with which they were charged were seldom minor. A few days ago, I had been the prosecutor of a colored soldier who literally knocked the door down at a girl's house, when she refused him; he'd had his way with her only after beating both her parents brutally. It puzzled me that the colored troops had generally maintained such good order in England, but were losing discipline on the Continent.

"They're guilty, sir, no question. But thinking about it, I've found myself wondering, sir, if we're as understanding of the colored troops."

I did not need to mention any particular incidents, because that week we had evaluated the case of a decorated officer who'd been on the front since D-Day. As he'd watched a line of German prisoners marching past, he'd suddenly raised his carbine and begun shooting, killing three and wounding four others. His sole explanation was, "I didn't like the way they were looking at me." Colonel Maples had decided that we would seek a sentence of only three years.

"These Negro boys aren't in combat, Dubin, not for the most part. We can't treat them as we do the men who've been through that." I could have pointed out that the colored battalions weren't generally given the option, but I felt I had gone far enough. "It's liquor and women, Dubin," the Colonel added. "You're a smart man to stay clear of liquor and women."

I could tell my questions had troubled the Colonel, and I wasn't surprised two days later when he called me into his office. It was the former quarters of the school prefect, a room of tall antique cabinets in mellow oak.

"Listen, Dubin, I don't know how to say this, so I'll

just come out with it. About your remarks to me the other day? You'd best be careful with that sort of thing, man. You don't want people to think you're the wrong kind of Jew. Is that too plain?"

"Of course not." In truth, I received the Colonel's remark with the usual clotted feelings references to my heritage inevitably provoked. My parents were Socialists who disparaged religious practice. Thus for me, the principal meaning of being a Jew was as something people reliably held against me, a barrier to overcome. I had labored my whole life to believe in a land of equals where everyone deserved to be greeted by only one label — American.

The Army did not always appear to see it that way. I was a week into basic training before I found out that the 'H' on my dog tags meant 'Hebrew,' which irritated me to no end since the Italians and Irish were not branded with an 'I.' But the armed forces were awash in bias. The enlisted men could not talk to one another without epithets. Spic, Polack, dago, Mick, cracker, hick, Okie, mackerel-snapper. Everybody got it. Not to mention the coloreds and the Orientals, whom the Army preferred not even to let in. The JAG Department's officers, however, were primarily well-bred Episcopalians and Presbyterians with excellent manners who did not engage in crude insults. Colonel Maples had gone out of his way to make clear he harbored no prejudice, once saying to me that when we got to Berlin, he planned to march up to the Reichstag with the word '*Jude*' written on his helmet. But his remark now was a reminder that my colleagues' silence about my ancestry did not mean any of them had forgotten it.

A few days later, the Colonel again asked to see me.

"Perhaps you need a break from these courts-martial day in and day out," he said. "Quite a grind, isn't it?"

Given what the soldiers at the front put up with, I would never have taken the liberty to complain, but the Colonel was right. There was not much about my daily activities that would lift the spirits, sending boys who'd come here to risk their lives for their country to a military prison instead. But the Colonel had a plan to give all of us a breather. Eisley would switch places for a couple of weeks with Major Haggerty, the Deputy Staff Judge Advocate, who had been reviewing convictions and providing legal advice as the law member on one of the panels. As for me, I was to conduct a Rule 35 investigation, looking into the potential court-martial of an officer.

"There's a bit of a problem on the General staff. The Brits have a word: 'kerfuffle.' Lord, I miss the Brits. The way they speak the language! Fellows made me howl several times a day. But that's what there is, a kerfuffle. I assume you've heard of Roland Teedle." General Teedle was a virtual legend, often said to be Patton's favorite among the brigadier generals. His 18th Armored Division had been at the forefront of the charge across France. "Teedle's gotten himself into a state of high dudgeon about some OSS major who's been operating on his flank. How much do you know about the OSS, Dubin?"

Not much more than I'd read in the paper. "Spies and commandos," I said.

"That's about right," said the Colonel. "And certainly true of this particular fellow. Major Robert Martin. Sort of an expatriate. Fought in Spain for the Republicans. Was living in Paris when the Nazis overran it. OSS recruited him, apparently, and he's done quite well. He's been on the Continent since sometime in 1942. Ran an Operational Group behind German lines — a collection of Allied spies and French resistance forces who sabotaged Nazi operations. After D-Day, he and his people were placed under Teedle's command. They derailed supply trains, ambushed German scouts, gave the Nazis fits while the 18th was bearing down on them."

I said that Martin sounded brave.

"Damn brave," said Maples. "No doubt of that. A hero, frankly. He's won the Distinguished Service Cross. And the Silver Star twice. And that doesn't count the ribbons de Gaulle has pinned on his chest."

"Jesus," I said before I could think.

The Colonel nodded solemnly during the brief silence, one that often fell among soldiers when they faced the evidence of another man's courage. We all had the same thought then: Could I do that?

"But you see," the Colonel said, "it's one of those devilish ironies. Probably what's led to Martin's troubles. He's been a lone wolf too long, really. He has no fear. Not just of the enemy. But of his own command. The Army is not a place for individualists." I could tell that the Colonel had spent time thinking about this case. He smoothed the edges of his broad mustache before he continued. "I don't have the details. That's your job. But Teedle claims that Martin's defied his orders. Several times now. Says Martin is just sitting out in some château leading the life of Riley and thumbing his nose. Apparently there's a girl involved."

The Colonel paused then, presumably reconsidering his frequent reminders that women and warriors were a bad mix.

"At any rate," he said, "there's to be a Rule thirty-five investigation. Follow the manual. Interview Martin. Interview the General. Talk to the witnesses. Do formal examinations. Prepare a report. And be diplomatic. Formally, a junior officer shouldn't be interviewing his superiors. I'm trusting you, David, not to ruffle feathers. Remember, you act in my name."

"Yes, sir."

"G-1 is hoping that this Major Martin will see the light when he recognizes that matters are turning serious. An actual court-martial would be tragic, frankly. Teedle and this fellow Martin—both are very fine soldiers, Dubin. General Patton hates that kind of catfight. Bring Martin to his senses, if you can. But watch yourself. Don't forget that at the end of the day, Roland's the one who's going to have Patton's ear."

The Colonel came around his desk to put a hand on my shoulder, and with it I felt the weight of his avuncular affection for me.

"I thought you'd enjoy this break, David. Get you a little closer to the front. Something's bound to start happening there again any day. I know you'd like that. And there may not be much more chance. Word is that Monty's bet Ike a fiver that the war here will be over before the New Year. Now that would make a fine Christmas present for all of us, wouldn't it?"

He was beaming until something froze his features, the realization, I suspect, that Christmas meant far more to him than to me. But I answered, "Yes, sir," in my most enthusiastic manner and issued a brisk salute before going off to find out whatever I needed to about Major Robert Martin.

3. DAVID: THE GENERAL

The 18th Armored Division had made camp about twenty-five miles north and east of Nancy, not far from Arracourt, where they were enjoying a period of rest and recovery. When Biddy and I showed up at the motor pool for a jeep to proceed to our interview with General Teedle, we were told that because of severe supply discipline with gasoline, we would have to squeeze in four boys from the 134th Infantry who'd missed their convoy. The 134th was relieving troops on the XII Corps front and these soldiers, who'd already seen their share of combat, made glum traveling companions. A private sitting behind me, a boy named Duck from Kentucky, struck up a few verses of "Mairzy Doats," until his buddies finally became spirited about one thing — that Duck should shut the hell up.

The air remained sodden, and approaching the front the bleakness went beyond the weather, clinging to the soldiers trudging down the roads. The signs of the recent battles were all about. The earth was scorched and rutted, and the picturesque French farmhouses, with their thatched roofs that made them look like something out of "Hansel and Gretel," were mostly in ruins. Even the ones that had fared relatively well were usually open to the top, looking like a man without his hat. Timbers lay strewn on the ground and often all that remained of a structure that had been home to a family for decades, even centuries, was the whitewashed chimney or a lone wall. The debris had been bulldozed to the side of the road, but every now and then there were disturbing tokens of the civilian casualties, a decapitated doll, wounded like its human counterparts, or a coat without a sleeve.

Given the conditions of the roads, it took us several hours to reach the 18th. They had spread out across the drier ground on the downslopes of several vast bean and hay fields. Having dealt with the claims for the land our troops trampled in England, I could only imagine the joy of the French farmer who would now get compensation for the use of land on which his crops were already drowned.

The 18th Armored Division had been the heroes of every newsreel we'd seen for months, the troops who'd dashed across France and were going to chase Hitler into some hole in Berlin and shoot a mortar down it for good riddance. There was a bold air here and loud voices after having survived the front. While Patton waited for fuel, ordnance, and rations, he had ordered many of the infantry divisions into intensive training, but for the 18th, with its tanks and mobile artillery, the strict conservation of gasoline left them with little to do each day but clean their weapons and write long letters home.

Crossing the camp with our packs, looking for Teedle's HQ, Biddy and I drew resentful stares. Our uniforms were still fresh, not grease-stained or torn, and our helmets lacked the mottled camouflage nets handed out for combat. Once or twice we passed soldiers who made a chicken squawk behind us, but Biddy's sheer size was enough to stifle most of the insults I was used to hearing tossed down from the troop convoys that passed through Nancy.

Rather than commandeer a house in town for himself, as other generals might have done, Teedle had remained with his men in a large tent that served combat-style as both his billet and headquarters. The heavy blackout flaps had been raised in daytime. Inside, a board floor had been installed in sections, and there were several desks, two of them face-to-face, where a couple of corporals were pounding away at Remingtons. Another, larger desk was unoccupied beside a frame cot which was certainly the General's. Two footlockers were stacked there with a kerosene lamp atop them for nighttime reading.

I approached the first of the two corporals, who was working with a pencil clenched between his teeth, and gave my name and unit. He was a very thin fellow with a wry look and he began to rise. I said, "At ease," but he tossed off a quick salute from his seat.

"Corporal Billy Bonner, Paragraph Trooper in the Armchair Division."

"Oh, isn't that cute?" said the second corporal, without looking up from his work. "Bonner's going back to burlesque when the war is over." Bonner addressed the other corporal as 'Frank,' and told him to shut up. They bickered for a moment.

"Well, then just don't talk to me at *all*," Frank concluded. His voice was high and he gave his head a dramatic toss. I exchanged a look with Biddy, who had remained at the tent opening. No need to ask why that one wasn't in combat.

In frustration, Bonner arose and limped toward Biddy, waving me along. Bonner proved chummy enough that I felt free to ask about his leg. He'd been shot at Anzio, he said, and had opted to become a clerk rather than go home. The reward for his dedication, he said, was working beside Frank. "Welcome to the Army," he added. Listening to him, I remembered a sergeant in basic training who'd warned me not to tell anybody I could type, good advice as Bonner could now attest.

The Corporal had just finished explaining that Teedle was due back momentarily from an inspection of forward installations, when he caught sight of the General and scurried to his desk like a schoolchild.

I snapped to attention as Teedle stormed past us. A private from the Signal Corps was trailing him, hauling the body of a huge radio telephone while Teedle screamed into the handset, alternately venting at the poor fellow at the other end and at the signal man, whenever the sound faded.

"Tell him that I have two battalions down to one ration a day. No, damn it. *Two* battalions, one ration. *One* ration. An army moves on its stomach. Ask him if he's heard that one. If the Nazis kill these boys it's one thing, but I'll be damned before I see their country starve them to death." I'd heard that the frontline troops were often hungry. In the officers' mess in Nancy, food was plentiful — canned goods, pastries with honey, tea, Nescafé. Midday meals were often huge. The meat and poultry, requisitioned from the locals, swam in heavy gravies.

Teedle handed the phone roughly to the signal man and dismissed him, then plunged to his seat, looking unhappily at the papers stacked on his desk. He had yet to remove his helmet. The General barked suddenly at Bonner.

"Are you telling me that Halley Maples sent that pup to deal with Martin?" As far as I had noticed, Teedle hadn't even looked at me.

Bonner turned my way and said with his subversive smile, "The General will see you now."

When I'd first heard Teedle's name, I had expected some round little fellow who'd look at home in a Technicolor musical movie like *The Wizard of Oz*. But the General gave every impression of being a soldier, the kind who would have been happy to be referred to as a rough-and-ready son of a bitch. Teedle was a big red-faced man, with a chest as round as a cock robin's, and tiny pale eyes set off starkly within lids that appeared to have been rubbed raw, probably from exhaustion or perhaps an allergic condition, or even, I suppose, tears.

In front of the General's desk I came to attention again, gave name, rank, and unit, and explained that with his permission, I would like to take a statement from him, in connection with the Rule 35 regarding Martin. Teedle studied me throughout.

"Where'd you go to college, Dubin?"

"Easton."

"Uh-huh. I'm from Kansas. None of those fancy-ass schools in Kansas. How about law school?"

"Easton. If I may, General, I went on scholarship, sir."

"Oh, I see. A smart guy. Is that what you're telling me?"

"Not to suggest that, sir."

"Well, if you gad about telling everybody you meet first thing how bright you are, you're not very smart at all, are you, Lieutenant?"

I didn't answer. He had me pinned and that was the point anyway. Teedle was plainly another of those commanders who wanted his troops to know he was the match of any of them. He took a second to set his helmet on his desk. His hair, what little was left of it, was somewhere between red and blond, and stood up on his head like stray wires. He'd found his canteen and screwed off the cap. Even at a distance of six feet, I could smell the whiskey. He took a good solid slug.

"All right, so what do I need to tell you about Martin?"

"As much as you can, sir."

"Oh, I won't do that. You'll start thinking Martin's a wonderful fellow. You're likely to think he's a wonderful fellow anyway. I'll tell you something right now, Dubin. You're going to like Robert Martin a good deal better than you like me. He's charming, a sweet talker. And brave. Martin may be the bravest son of a bitch in the European theater. You seen combat, Dubin?"

"No, sir. I'd like to."

"Is that so?" He smirked and pointedly lowered his line of sight to the JAG Department insignia on the collar of my tunic. "Well, if you ever find yourself in the middle of a battlefield, Lieutenant, what you'll see around you is a bunch of fellows scared shitless, as they should be, and one or two sons of bitches jumping up and down and acting as if the bullets can't touch them. They get hit sooner or later, believe me, but it takes a hell of a lot longer than you'd think. Martin's one of those. Thinks he's invincible. I don't like that either. A soldier who's not afraid to die is a danger to everybody."

"Is that the problem, sir? The root of it?"

"Hardly. The problem, if you want to call it that, is that the fucking son of a bitch won't follow orders. He's gone off on several operations without my say-so, even though he's supposed to be under my command. Successful operations, too, I don't dispute that, sabotaging train lines, mostly, so those Nazi pricks can't get troops and supplies where we're heading. He's a whiz at that. Every railway worker in France seems to bow at Martin's feet.

"But twice I've sent troops to the wrong position because I didn't know he'd already blown the lines. I've had to hold off artillery because I got late word that Martin and his men turned up in the target area, without any prior communication to me. And I've slowed deployments several times because Martin was off screwing with the Germans, instead of finishing the recons he'd been assigned. And it's not just discipline that concerns me, Lieutenant, although I believe in discipline as much as any other general you've ever met. What makes my hemorrhoids ache is that men were in danger each time, men who didn't need to be killed. Not that day. Not in that place. And I take that personally."

My face must have reflected some doubt about his choice of words.

"You heard me, Lieutenant," he said, and stood behind his desk. "It's personal. I get up every goddamn morning knowing that young men under my command are going to die — even now with nothing special happening, I'm losing thirty men a day, and I'll carry their souls with me as long as I live, Dubin. I mean that. While I last on this globe, there will always be some shadow of grief. I wanted this star so bad I probably would have killed someone to get it, but I didn't realize that the dead stick with generals this way. I grieved for plenty who died under my command at lower ranks, but that burden departed, Dubin, and it doesn't now, and when I've asked others, all they can say is that this is just how it is."

He paused to see how I was taking this. His face, especially his large, lumpy nose, had gained even more color, and he helped himself to another snort from his canteen.

"That, in a few words, is what I don't like about Robert Martin. I've been a soldier my whole life, Dubin, I know how the game is played, and I realize I'd get nowhere with the General staff complaining about Martin's heroics. But I passed the word to OSS that he's outlived his usefulness here. And eventually they agreed. Told me I should order him back to London. And now we get the melodrama. Because Martin won't go.

"The prick won't go. I've given him his orders in writing three times, and he's sitting there like he's on vacation. I've tolerated the bastard when I had to, Dubin, but I've got him dead to rights now, and I'm not taking any more of his crap. All understood? So type that up, just the last part there, and I'll sign it."

"I thought there was something to do with a woman, sir. That's what Colonel Maples indicated."

Teedle laughed suddenly. He was so relentlessly intense that I nearly jumped at the sound. I would have bet the man in front of me laughed at nothing.

"Oh, that," he said. "I'll tell you the truth, Dubin. I don't give a dry turd about the woman. Patton's G-1 cares—they want the same rules for all personnel, naturally. Before D-Day, Martin commanded an Operational Group here on the Continent—Sidewinder, or some such name. They were spying and making the Nazis' lives difficult with little hit-and-run operations. He must have had thirty men under him, a few Allied spies who'd come ashore like him, but most of his command were members of the French and Belgian underground. The Frenchmen have all run home, the spoils of war and whatnot. I suppose the bastards are going to fight each other about who runs the show here.

"There are still a few odd ducks remaining with Martin, probably because they're not welcome anywhere else. And one of them's a woman, a beautiful little bit from what I hear. He recruited her in Marseilles a few years ago, and she's been beside him, helping with a lot of the ruses OSS is always employing. These OSS women have been damned effective, Dubin. Don't sell them short. You know the fucking Krauts, they think they're gentlemen, so they're never as suspicious of females as they should be. This girl claims to be a nurse sometimes. You can go just about anywhere in a nurse's uniform in the middle of a war.

"Now it's true, she's probably twenty years younger than Martin, and by all accounts he's been giving her the old one-two and maybe he's even in love with her or thinks he is. That's the theory in London, I suspect, about why he won't go back. My theory is that it just jollies him up to grind his finger in my eye.

"But as for the fact that he's stuck on the girl, or fighting beside his bed partner, they may not like that in the General staff, think it's bad for discipline when our troops catch on, but I couldn't care less. Soldiers always want sex. Do you know why?"

Because they were away from women, I answered. Their wives, their girlfriends.

"You think they'd hop their wives the way these boys go diving after these French girls? I don't. They think they're going to die, Dubin. The reasonable ones anyway. That's what *I* think. And if you get the time in combat you say you'd like, you'll be thinking that way, too. And when you feel death imminent, Dubin, you don't want to be alone. Isolation is the next stage, in the casket. You desire nothing more than contact with life, and life in its purest form. You want sex. And God. These boys want God, too. They want to fuck. And they want to pray. That's what a soldier wishes for when he doesn't wish he was back home. Forgive me for lecturing, but you're new to all of this and you're better off getting used to the truth.

"So I don't care if Martin's fucking this girl, or some calf he encounters on the road. We have a few troops doing that, too, I get the farmers in here complaining. Fuck who you want to as far as I'm concerned. But follow orders. So write up what I need to sign and then tell that son of a bitch to get the hell out of my area or he'll have an escort to the disciplinary barracks. That's all."

Yet again, Teedle lifted the canteen. It was his fifth or sixth drink. He should have been loaded, but his fury burned at such intensity that the liquor was probably vaporized on the way down his throat. I had no idea exactly what to think of General Teedle, especially the eagerness with which he'd invited me to dislike him. He seemed to have been one of those boys picked on all his childhood who grew up determined to be tougher than the bullies, yet who never overcame the hurt of being the odd man out. But his brusque honesty impressed me, especially since it even seemed to go so far as acknowledging his own unhappiness.

After seeing General Teedle, it made more sense not to return to Nancy, but rather to set out for Major Martin, who was nearby. The General directed his G-1 to assist us, and the personnel officer, Lieutenant Colonel Brunson, briefed us further and ordered maps. When we were done, we returned to the motor pool, where the sergeant in charge informed us that they'd dispatched our jeep and couldn't spare another until morning.

Biddy caught on immediately. "Burnin our gas, not theirs," he murmured to me. He was right, of course, but we still weren't going to get a vehicle. Instead we went off separately to seek billeting. The captain of the headquarters company found me a cot in a four-man tent and showed me where dinner would be in the officers' mess, formed from two squad tents. The meal, when it was served, was hot B ration reduced to a greenish mash, but no one around here was complaining, since even headquarters company, which usually wangled the best, was down to only two meals a day. One of my most embarrassing little secrets was that I had found during training that I did not mind field rations, even what came in tins in the B and C: meat and vegetables, meat and beans, meat and spaghetti. The typical lament was that it looked like dog food and tasted like it, too. But much of it struck me as exotic. My parents, for all their lack of formal religious practice, had never brought pork into our home. Pork and beans was not my particular favorite, but I regarded ham as a delicacy, so much so that even Spam was a pleasure.

Afterward, I wandered toward the staging area where the enlisted men were encamped to make sure Bidwell had found a place. There was a virtual tent city there encompassing several battalions. It had its own eye appeal. The ranks of pup tents were in perfect lines stretching out hundreds of yards, with the latrine slit trenches dug at regular intervals, all of it illuminated by the brightness of the fires the cooks were still tending. I walked along, exchanging salutes with the enlisted men who took notice of me, trying to find Division Headquarters Company, with whom Biddy was said to be quartered.

Now and then, when I asked directions, I'd also see if I could swap novels with some of the men. I had stuffed books in every pocket of my fatigues before we left Nancy, eager for new reading material. I sometimes felt I had read every novel in the city. I had been holding on to two of the most popular titles, *Lost Horizon* and *Sanctuary*, by William Faulkner, the latter much in demand because of Popeye's foul activities with a corncob. My hope was for more Faulkner, which I was lucky enough to find in the hands of a redheaded private from Texas. I also got a novel by James Gould Cozzens in exchange for *The Last Citadel*.

It would be hard to say how important the few minutes I spent reading each night were to me. Thoughts of my parents, of my brother and sister, or of Grace were fraught with emotion. I could not surrender to the comfort of imagining myself among them again, to the security of the life I had left, because I knew I could go mad with yearning and with regret that I'd been so determined to do my duty. But the chance to feel myself in another locale, neither here nor home, if only for a few minutes, was a special reprieve, an essential sign that life would again have the richness and nuance it holds in times of peace.

I never found Bidwell. But after I made my last literary trade, I bumped into Billy Bonner. He'd been tippling and was holding a cognac bottle, most of the contents gone now.

"Trying to become acquainted with native customs, First Lieutenant," Bonner said. "French might be onto something with this stuff." He hefted the bottle and missed his mouth at first. Half the off-duty soldiers I encountered in France were pie-eyed, fueled by stores of wine and newer treats like Pernod and Benedictine they'd never seen in the States. Not that the officers were any better. Those of us at headquarters were still receiving the garrison ration of liquor every month, and even officers in foxholes were supposed to get a quart of scotch, a pint of gin, two bottles of champagne, and a bottle of brandy, although it was rarely delivered, given the strains on the supply chain. I traded away most of what arrived. Even at Easton College, where Prohibition had made drinking an adventure, I tended to abstain, never caring much for liquor's loose feeling.

"You seem fairly deep into your exploration of local culture, Bonner."

"Yes, sir. Just so long as I can roll out in the morning."

Bonner saw the pocket book in my hand and we exchanged thoughts about novels for a moment. I promised to trade him *Light in August* on our next visit. I had turned away when Bonner said clearly behind me, "They've got you investigating the wrong one, Lieutenant."

I revolved to stare at him.

"Teedle and Martin?" he said. "You're investigating the wrong one. At least, as I see it. You oughta ask around."

"Then I'll start by asking you, Corporal. Tell me what that remark means."

Bonner peered at length into the mouth of the bottle, as if the answer were in there.

"It probably means I've had too much of this," he said after quite some time. He gave me that thin, conspiratorial smile and without waiting for a response slipped off into the dark camp.

II.

4. STEWART: MY FATHER'S LAWYER

According to the Record of Proceedings of my father's court-martial, a high-ranking JAG Department lawyer from Eisenhower's headquarters, Barrington Leach, had been Dad's attorney. His name rang a bell, and a search online reminded me why. In 1950, Leach took a leave from the prominent Hartford law firm in which he was a partner to become Chief Counsel to Senator Estes Kefauver in his investigation of organized crime. The televised Kefauver Hearings introduced many Americans to the Mafia and, not coincidentally, to the privilege against self-incrimination. From then on "taking the Fifth" inevitably brought to mind the line of dark gentlemen in expensive suits who answered every question by reciting their rights from index cards adhering to their palms. It was Leach, most often, who was up there making them sweat.

After returning to Connecticut, Leach in time became a judge, eventually rising to the Connecticut Supreme Court. His name actually turns up in a few news accounts in the Johnson era as a potential candidate for the U.S. Supreme Court.

I had started researching Leach during the months I was stalemated by the government in my efforts to pry loose the court-martial file. (I finally got it in June 2004, but only because I could demonstrate by then that I knew virtually all the information contained there.) I had assumed that Leach, an experienced trial lawyer in 1945 and thus quite a bit older than Dad, had to be dead, and I only hoped that his family had kept his papers. In late October 2003, I called the Connecticut Supreme Court to locate Leach's next of kin.

"Did he die?" the clerk asked me. He turned from the phone, inquiring of a colleague with alarm, "Did Justice Leach die?" I could hear the question ping-ponging across the room, until the clerk came back on the line. "No, sir. Happy to say Justice Leach is still with us." He declined to provide an address or phone, but promised to forward any mail. Within a week, I had received a response, with a return address at the Northumberland Manor Assisted-Care Facility in West Hartford, written in a craggy hand that brought to mind that enduring children's toy, the Etch A Sketch.

I surely recall representing your father. David Dubin's court-martial remains one of the most perplexing matters of my life as a lawyer, and I am willing to discuss it with you. In answer to your inquiry, I have retained some materials relating to the case that you would probably wish to have. As you can see, writing letters is a particular burden at this stage of my life. We could converse by telephone, if need be, but, if I may be so bold, I suggest that, if possible, you pay me a visit.

*While I am happy to provide you with my
recollections and these papers, doing so is a bit
sticky legally, inasmuch as your father was my
client. You would set an old man's mind at ease if,
when you came, you brought a letter from all your
father's legal heirs—your mother, if she remains
alive, and any siblings you have—stating that each
of you relinquishes any objections related to what I
share. I'd suggest you contact the lawyer who is
handling the estate to help you. I will be happy to
speak with him, if he likes.*

*Without being alarmist, I call your attention to
the fact that I am ninety-six years old and that I no
longer purchase green bananas. I look forward to
meeting you soon.*

*With all good wishes,
Barrington V.S. Leach*

Watching me dash around the country, passing hours in
dank library basements and talking about opposition from
the CIA, the members of my family were convinced that my
elevator had stopped between floors. Nona regarded it as
conclusive proof that she'd gotten out at the right time,
while my daughters offered a succinct explanation to anyone who asked: "Dad's on crack."

My mother said the least, but might have been the most
unhappy. Mom remained as fiercely possessive of Dad in
death as she had always been. She had picked his suit
and tie each day and had remained his principal coun-
selor on the wary maneuverings of the commercial world,
where he was often led astray by his native inclination to
see almost every issue as a question of principle. But in my

house, each of us depended on Mom's vitality and shrewdness, regarding it as a fact-established that my mother, as a camp survivor, had an extra measure of whatever living required. She took it as my single greatest fault that I had not been smart enough to marry someone like her.

In light of all of that, it was predictable that she wouldn't like me claiming a piece of my father on my own. There were no tirades, just occasional remarks indicating that she found it distasteful that I was making Dad's Army secrets a professional project. To her it was as if I were beating drums with bones I'd uncovered in the graveyard. And it was worse than cruel irony that I was digging into a period whose anguish they'd spent a lifetime trying to inter.

Which made Leach's letter a problem. My sister would do what Mom said. But it would take some talking to get my mother to sign off. I strategized for at least a week. Then one morning when I stopped in, as I did most days, I sat her down at the kitchen table, where important family discussions always have occurred, and made my pitch. She listened avidly, her small black eyes intent, and asked for a day or two to think. I left with hope.

But walking in a week later, I knew from my first breath that I was doomed. She'd baked. Rugelach, an all-time favorite, sat on the kitchen table. She might as well have used the pastries as blocks to spell out COMFORT FOOD. Being who I am, I ate, and being who she is, she waited until I was in the initial stage of near delirium before she started.

"Stewart," she said, "about this lawyer and his papers. Stewart, I have thought very hard. I tell you, with all my heart, I believe your father *alav hashalom*, would be moved to tears to know that you have made this effort to understand his life. And the one question I have asked myself for the last few days is whether that might have made him reconsider. Because I agree with what you said when Daddy died, Stewart, that he must have made a choice not to discuss this with his family. But in the end, you are asking me to set aside my loyalty to him. It is not for me to imagine new decisions for your father now, Stewart. He is entitled to my support in his judgments about what he wanted to say about his own life."

I whined, of course. I was his kid, I said. I was entitled to know. That remark provoked her.

"Stewart, where is it written that a parent is required to become your journalistic subject? Is giving life to a child, Stewart, like running for public office, where every piece of dirty linen is open to inspection? Is it not a parent's right to be understood on his own terms? Do you pretend that your daughters know every seamy detail of your youth?"

That was a low blow, but effective. I took a second.

"Mom, don't you want to know the story?"

"Stewart, I know the only story that matters, and I knew it from the moment I fell in love with your father in the concentration camp. David Dubin was kind. He was intelligent, educated. Jewish. I could tell at once he was a loyal person, a person of values. What more could matter to me, or to you? Then. Or now?"

Naturally, I phoned my sister. Mom could dress this up however she liked, I said, claiming she was bound by Dad's wishes, but it was really about her. And being in control.

"God, Stewie, why do you always make her the bad guy? So what if it's about her? She lived with the man for fifty-eight years. Now you come along to tell her that her husband was a convict? Of course she doesn't care to hear the details. Leave her alone. If you have to do this, do it when she's gone."

I reminded Sarah that Leach was ninety-six. "Look," I offered, "I swear I won't tell her anything I find out."

"Oh, Stew," my sister said, tart as always, "when was the last time you kept a secret? Haven't you figured out yet what you liked about being a reporter? I'll sign whatever you like after she's gone. But I don't want to hear another word about this now. Maybe you should spend some time asking yourself why you're hyperventilating to learn all this."

I already had. Every day and every night. But the simplest answer to Sarah was probably the best: he was my father. We can all dream up the hero we want to be when we're adolescents and spend our adult years trying to live out the ideal, but sooner or later we each realize that our options are limited by the raw materials, that dose of DNA we get and the imprinting of early childhood. As a young man, I did not see myself in Dad. Now when I go through the many photos I have assembled from his youth, there are moments when I cannot tell whether the fellow standing there is he or I. That body, which years ago stopped belonging to either of us, was fundamentally one: the same corrupted posture, sagging somehow from a point between the shoulder blades, the same dark-complected look like a warm tan, the same uncertain approach to the camera, unsure how much to surrender. I have his nose, they say, and at moments, his haunted eyes. From Dad I got my taste for salty things, and my acceptance of the Trappers' losses as a piece of fate.

In my research, I discovered many unacknowledged

debts I owed my father. Scouring his letters, and later, what he had written for Leach, I was struck that my old man could turn a phrase. My father spent two hours every night reading any novel he could get his hands on, a habit so unvarying that he actually wore two rawhide stripes into the leather ottoman where he perched his feet. Yet it had never clicked that Dad was probably the source of my own interest in writing, even though I'd always been heartened by his quiet pride in my bylines. Now, looking back, I realized that he must have intervened to get my mother to quit her pestering about law school.

Yet it was not the things I liked about myself that fed my hunger to find out what he'd done wrong. In the end, I fear it was probably more of the affliction that had made me a happy observer in criminal courtrooms for decades: I wanted to know Dad's failings, so I'd feel better about my own.

And given what happened next, you might say that self-acceptance is not all that it's cracked up to be. But I have always been a slave to impulse, and slow to face the fact. When I look in the mirror, I see a trim guy, inconveniently burdened with a few dozen pounds that belong to someone else. That's because the thinner fellow, with his good intentions, generally holds the rudder on my soul. On a perpetual diet, I'm the guy at the restaurant who orders the little salad that comes topped with a tiny pellet of poached salmon—before I eat the French fries off everybody else's plates. My eternal undoing arrives in these instants when my appetites are more than I can handle. My saddest turn as a courthouse reporter came in the early '90s as I was walking past the jury room and, with no planning whatsoever, pressed my ear to the door, hoping for a scoop on an important verdict. When a bailiff caught me, I was suspended from the paper for thirty days and, far worse, showered doubt on every honest success before and after. It's a lifetime pattern. I resist. I struggle. But I also succumb.

Which in this case means that when I wrote back to Barrington Leach, I not only set a date to visit, but formally released him from any legal responsibility for what he might reveal. How? I simply stated that my mother had died a few years ago and that I was an only child. Just like the crooks I covered for twenty years, I told myself that nobody would ever know.

5. DAVID: MAJOR ROBERT MARTIN

October 22, 1944

With the Third Army in France

Dearest Grace,

I have been sent to the front (where all remains quiet, so please don't worry) to do a little investigation, involving Army politics among the brass. Since I have been able to borrow a typewriter, I wanted to say hello and tell you I think of you always.

Yesterday was really a banner day, as I received four airmails and a V-mail from you. I've brought all of them with me to read a second (and third!) time. In your V-mail, dearest, you tell me of your cold--please take care of yourself. If you don't feel well, stay home from school. I don't want anything happening to you--you mean too much to me, and we have too much living together in the near future for you to take any chances.

Tonight, my bed will be a cot in a tent, a reminder of how embarrassingly good life is in Nancy. Eisley and I have found new quarters with Madame Vaillot, whose husband has been carted off by the Germans to God knows where. She greets us each morning at 6:30 a.m. with strong coffee and our laundry, for which she refuses to take any money. She says in cultivated French, "We are repaid enough by your keeping the Germans out and protecting us." So what can we say? Our room is nice, but cold with the constant rains, and fuel is in short enough supply that we start a fire only if we are going to be awake in the room for a while, which we seldom are.

I've been thinking about the nest egg I'll have when the day comes that I get back. With allowances, I should be making around $350 per month when my promotion comes through (November 1, they swear). I'm going to send $300 a month to Mom, by way of a Class E allotment, to put into my savings account. (Please tell my dad to make sure Mom uses a few bucks to buy a new frock or something as a birthday gift from me. They won't do it unless you insist on my behalf.) There will be $300 mustering-out pay plus the insurance policy of $250 I have, and fifteen or twenty war bonds. All in all, I'm thinking you're right and that I should open my own law office. There may even be enough left over to buy a jalopy. I wouldn't mind getting a little joy out of this money. Other boys have done more to earn it, but it's not a picnic being away from all of you. I still keep my house key in my wallet. Call it loony if you

like, but several times a day, I'll reach to my back
pocket and feel its impression against the leather,
and know that I have a place to return to.

    Well, I'm getting maudlin, so I'll stop.

Love forever,

David

Lieutenant Colonel Brunson, General Teedle's personnel officer, had said that Martin and the remainder of his Operational Group were quartered at the country estate of the Comtesse de Lemolland, west and south of Bezange-la-Petite, near the skirmishing edge of the front. Brunson couldn't explain how Martin had arranged such a scenic billet, but it was clear that many of Teedle's officers, camped in tents on wet ground, had taken notice.

It was nearly noon the next day before the 18th Division's motor pool surrendered a jeep to us, and I thought for a second that Bidwell was going to get into a fistfight with the private filling the tank, who might as well have been using an eyedropper.

"That ain't but a third of the gas we come with," Biddy told him.

"Sarge," the boy said, "this here's my orders. And you'd do better to look close at that map than keep your eye on me. Krauts are two miles from where you're headed. One wrong turn, Sarge, and your war might end early."

As we drove north into the hills, the sun arrived like a blast of horns, lighting up the isolated groves of trees in full fall color. This was rolling country, principally open fields, resembling southern Wisconsin, where my parents sometimes took us for long Sunday drives in my Uncle Manny's borrowed Model A when I was a boy. After a day together,

Bidwell had become more approachable and we laughed about the private who'd parceled out gasoline as if he expected us not to come back. Half an hour later, when we heard the echo of mortars and the pecking of rifle fire from the east, we grew a trifle more serious.

I asked Biddy if this was the closest he'd been to the front. A sardonic snort escaped him.

"D-Day," he said. "That count, Lieutenant? D plus one, actually. Landed my whole MP company on Omaha. Needed us to take custody of the POWs, but we had to scrap our way up that beach like everybody else."

"D-Day! My God, I bet this duty seems boring after that."

He found the idea amusing.

"Hell no, Lieutenant. That was the like of somethin I don't never wanna see again. Truth to tell, I didn't care much for it when they made me an MP. Basic, I put in for an engineering company, truck mechanic. I been fixing cars at home a couple years since I left high school, figured it'd only make sense. But this here is the Army. My orders come through sayin 'Provost Marshal Section,' I had to ask what all that was, and cussed when they told me. I don't hold nothin 'gainst po-licemen, Lieutenant, but it ain't what I ever had a mind to do. Turns out, though, it got its good side. Generally speaking, MPs don't get there till the shooting's over and Mama's little boy here, he promised her he's gonna do his best not to get hisself killed. You can keep combat, Lieutenant. All I care for is take a few pictures and go home."

Like half the soldiers I knew, who remained part tourist, Bidwell always had a camera in his hand. Given his size, he looked almost dainty when he put it to his eye.

Most troops took photos of the wreckage of war and of their buddies, but Biddy seemed more studious about it and, typical of his solitary ways, would go off at moments and fix on particular objects and scenes that didn't appear to hold much interest. Driving yesterday, we fell in with the convoy from the 134th and came to a halt when they did, so we could empty our bladders in a roadside ditch. The drivers were Negro troops, as was often the case, and six or seven of them had gathered for a little society, since the white boys as a rule would have nothing to do with them. From behind one of the trucks, Biddy snapped several photos of the colored men carrying on with one another over their cigarettes. It had disturbed me that he hadn't bothered to get their permission.

Recollected, the incident brought Biddy's Georgia roots to mind and I asked when his people had left there and where they'd ended up. He seemed to have no interest in answering. That was this man's army. From boot camp on there were guys who showed you photos of their ma and pa and sweethearts and told you every imaginable detail about them, right down to dress size, and others who wanted to keep home as far from this mess as possible. I was in the latter group anyway, but I prodded a bit now, because I wanted to be sure before criticizing Bidwell's manner with the coloreds that he'd actually had the chance to learn the difference between North and South.

"Daddy, he was a tenant farmer down there. His people been workin that patch, only God Hisself knows how long, hundred years, two hundred years, but it just didn't make no sense to him, when times got so bad. In 1935 he picked us all up and moved us North. He was thinkin to find somethin in a factory, I guess."

"Yes, but where did you settle, Bidwell?"

He smiled for a second while he looked over the road. "Ever hear of Kindle County?"

I actually cried out. "Dear God, Biddy! You must have heard me talk to Eisley a dozen times about home. Why didn't you say anything? I'm half a world away and it turns out I'm touring around with a neighbor."

"'Cause of just that, Lieutenant. Wasn't much way you and me was neighbors."

"Don't be so sure, Biddy. I don't come from the high and mighty. My father's a shoemaker." I rarely shared this detail, fearing it might undermine me, both among fellow officers and the troops, and as I'd anticipated, I could see I'd caught Bidwell by surprise. "Pop's been at that trade since he was a boy, right after he landed in the U.S. An uncle took him in and taught him. I grew up in a three-flat on Deering Road. The folks are still there. What about you?"

Biddy shook his head as if he didn't know.

"We was all over," he said. "You know how that goes when a man's scratchin for work. Come the end of the month, sometimes Dad and the landlord wudn't seein eye to eye. I must have been near to eighteen 'fore I stopped in askin why we didn't move in daytime like other folks." He smiled at the memory, but his green eyes drifted over to see what I made of that. As the son of a cobbler, though, I knew a lot about hard times. In the Depression, Pa had plenty of work because people wanted to make their shoes last. But many of them couldn't come up with the six bits once their footwear was mended. Some pairs left on credit, if Pa knew who he was talking to, even when it was all but certain he'd never get paid. But he'd let a man walk out barefoot rather than get cheated.

After hearing the gunfire, we stopped several times to check directions with the locals. In the end, a farmer on a horse trotted ahead of us and pointed out the Comtesse's narrow drive, which we might well have missed amid the heavy brush. The Lemolland property was bounded by an old stone fence, topped in the French way in red roofing tiles, but the gate was open and we headed up an incline beside the vineyards, where several workers were tilling among the stubby twists of the grapevines. The plants, hanging on long wire supports, looked to have been recently harvested.

At the top, we found a square formation of joined sand-colored buildings. I thought of a fort, but I suppose the arrangement was a small replica of a feudal manor. Each wing was several stories high, sporting long red jalousies folded back beside the deep windows and topped with a steep mansard roof. Huge wooden doors were thrown open on an arch that passed through the building facing us, and we drove into a vast cobblestone courtyard. At the far end stood the house. It incorporated a round tower that had to date from the Middle Ages, giving the residence the look of a little castle.

An unshaved worker with a hoe watched us warily as we stopped. Visible behind a corner of the Comtesse's château were a ramshackle chicken coop and a pasture, where two cows swished their tails.

At the house, I pulled several times on a bell rope until the door was parted by a large dark man, with the stub of a cigarette in the corner of his mouth and one eye closed to the smoke. He was a Gypsy, with a potato face and women's-length hair tied behind him. In French, I asked for Major Martin. The Gypsy took a second surveying our uniforms, then motioned us in and bellowed up a staircase at his right.

"Ro-bert," he called, giving the name the French pronunciation, without a 't.' "*Un moment*," he told us, then disappeared out the door we'd entered.

Biddy and I remained in the entry for several minutes. The old house had stone walls of monumental thickness. It was dark and still, except for the bright kitchen which lay ahead of us at the end of a hall. From there, I could hear voices and a pump handle squealing, and smell pleasant aromas—burning wood and something cooking. Standing here, I was reminded of waiting in the foyer of Grace's great stone house, when I would pick her up for the evening. They were excruciating moments for me, especially when her father was around, since he was convinced I was a fortune hunter. For my part, the distaste was mutual. Privately, I realized that Horace Morton would never accept my good intentions regarding his daughter, because he himself wouldn't have pursued any girl without first knowing all about her bank account.

With great pounding, a middle-sized man in a khaki Army officer's shirt bounded down the heavy stairs. He wore no tie or insignia but there was a trench knife on his belt, in addition to a bayonet in its scabbard. This, without question, was Major Martin.

Biddy and I saluted. Smiling, he tapped his forehead, but only to be polite.

"We don't do that around here," he said. The Operational Groups, as I was to learn, proceeded with a minimum of military formalities. There was a "leader" from whom all took direction, but the OGs included not only members of the armed forces of several nations, but civilians in the underground who had no duty to adhere to Army rules.

"Where from?" Martin asked, when I gave him my name. I repeated that I was with Staff Judge Advocate, Third Army, which brought a laugh. "No, I can see that wreath on your lapel, son. Where in the States? Where's the home this war has taken you away from?"

When I told him Kindle County, he brightened. "Oh, that's a swell place. I've had some swell times there." He shared a few memories of a Negro speakeasy in the North End, then asked about my education and my family. These were not the kind of questions a superior officer usually bothered with on first meeting, and I enjoyed his attention. He made similar inquiries of Biddy, who predictably retreated rather than offer much of a response.

Martin was no more than five foot ten, but remarkable to behold, dark haired, strong jawed, and vibrating with physical energy. Much like Grace, he had the all-American looks, with tidy, balanced features, that I, with my long nose and eyes shadowed in their sallow orbits, always envied. A single black curl fell across the center of Robert Martin's forehead, and even racing down the stairs he made an impression of unusual agility. Despite addressing me as "son," he did not look to be much more than forty.

He interrupted when I tried to explain my mission here.

"Oh, I've heard about that," he said with a brief smile, waving us behind him down the hall. When we entered the kitchen, a young woman was over the sink washing her hair beneath the cast-iron pump. She was small and striking, dressed in surplus camouflage fatigues far too large for her, and she glanced my way immediately to size me up. She had a tiny, almost childlike face, but it held an older, ruthlessly cool aspect. I could see at once that this was the woman who was the problem.

Finding herself unimpressed, she went back to wringing out her short wavy tresses over the copper basin. At the same time, she spoke to Martin.

"*Qui sont-ils?*" Who are they?

Martin answered her in French. "The Lieutenant is sent by Teedle."

"*Merde,*" she replied. "Tell them to go away." She reached beside her and lit a cigarette.

"By and by," he answered. He waited until she was done frisking a towel through her hair, then made introductions in English. She was Gita Lodz, a member of OG Stemwinder and the FTP, Francs-Tireurs et Partisans, one of the largest resistance organizations, union-oriented and supposedly red. When Martin gave Mademoiselle Lodz our names, she offered a smile as purely formal as a curtsy.

"*Enchanté,*" I answered, thinking that this might clue them that I had understood their conversation, but I saw no sign that either took it as more than a tourist courtesy.

"Excuse, pliss," Gita Lodz said in English, "I go." She had a heavy Slavic accent, undetectable to my ear when she had spoken French. Hastily she recovered her cigarette from the sink edge as she left.

A meal of some kind was under way and a servant in an apron was stirring a huge iron pot on the black stove. The kitchen, like the rest of the house, was rustic but the room was large and light. Copper pans with burned bottoms were suspended from the exposed timbers of the ceiling, and blue delft plates decorated the walls, a sure sign that this place had so far escaped the war.

"You've arranged charming quarters, Major," I said.

"Quite," he said. "Stemwinder is on R and R with the war at a standstill. Here it seems far away." He swept his arm grandly. "The Comtesse de Lemolland is a magnificent patriot and a great friend to our OG."

The house, he said, had been the country home of the Comtesse's family, bankers from Nancy, since the time of Napoleon. She had maintained it even after marrying the Comte de Lemolland after the First War, when her principal residence became a château in the Côtes-du-Nord. This property had not suffered as badly under the Germans as many others. Periodically, SS would take over the house as a resort for officers, and a German garrison would come each fall to confiscate crops and wine. Nonetheless, with the Comtesse's return, the vineyard and farm were already returning to life. The Comtesse herself, Martin confided, was not doing as well. Her son, Gilles, a member of another resistance group, Forces Françaises de l'Intérieur, FFI, had been confirmed captured and burned alive by the Nazis earlier this month. The old woman had largely kept to herself since then.

"Nonetheless," said Martin, "she would never forgive me if an American officer visited her home and I did not allow her to say a word of welcome. You will enjoy meeting her. She is a remarkable and gallant woman." Preparing to summon the Comtesse, Martin caught sight of Mademoiselle Lodz peeking into the kitchen, probably to see if we had yet been dispatched. She was now in country attire, a blouse with ruffled sleeves and a flowered dress with a bib and flouncy skirt.

"*Va leur parler*"—Talk to them—he told her, gesturing her in. To us he said, "If you chaps will excuse me just one minute, Gita will keep you company." He admonished her in a low voice as he breezed out, "*Sois plaisante.*"

Biddy had retreated to a corner, leaving me to face Gita Lodz in silence. She was narrow as a deer, and in that fashion, pleasingly formed, but with a second chance to observe her, I had decided it would be a stretch to call her beautiful. Dry, her hair proved to be a brass-colored blonde. Her nose was broad and her teeth were small and crooked. Given the darkness of her eyes, her complexion was oddly pale. But she had what the Hollywood tattlers liked to call "it," an undefined magnetism which began with a defiant confidence about herself, palpable even from across the room.

I attempted small talk.

"May I be so bold as to ask about your name, Mademoiselle Lodz? Do you hail from that Polish city? From Lodz?" I said this in very correct French, which drew a pulled-down mouth from her, a seeming acknowledgment that she had not given me that much credit. But she replied in the same language, clearly delighted not to struggle with English.

"I am Polish, yes, but not from Lodz. It is no one's name really. I am a bastard." She made that declaration with utter equanimity, but her small black eyes never left me. I always thought I'd learned a good poker face watching Westerns, but I feared at once that I'd reacted to her frankness, and I was grateful she went on. "My mother was Lodzka," she said—'Wodjka,' as she pronounced it—"from her first husband. She had not seen him in years, but it was convenient, naturally, for me to share her name. The French, of course, can only speak French. So it is easier here to be simply Lodz. And your name?" she asked. "How would it be spelled?"

"Doo-ban?" she said once I had recited the letters. I said it again, and she tried a second time. "Doo-bean?"

I shrugged, accepting that as close enough.

"But what kind of name is that? Not French, no?"

I answered simply, "American."

"Yes, but Americans, all of them come from Europe. Where in Europe was Doo-bean?"

I told her Russia, but she took my answer with mild suspicion.

"In what part?" she asked.

I named the village where both my parents had been born.

"Near Pinsk?" she said. "But your name does not sound Russian."

"It was Dubinsky, back then," I said after a second, still not acknowledging everything I might have. However, I had won a brief smile.

"Like 'Lodzka,'" she said. A second passed then, as we both seemed to ponder how to go forward, having found an inch of common ground. I finally asked where she was from in Poland, if not Lodz.

"Eh," she said. "Pilzkoba. A town. You put a thumbtack in a map and it is gone. *Que des crétins*," she added bitterly. All idiots. "I ran from there in 1940. After the Germans killed my mother."

I offered my condolences, but she shrugged them off.

"In Europe now we all have these stories. But I could not stay. I hated the Germans, naturally. And also the Poles, because they hated me. Bastards are not favorites in small Polish towns, Doo-bean. So I left. You see?"

"Yes," I said. In English, I quoted Exodus. "'I have been a stranger in a strange land.'"

She lit up. The phrase delighted her. "*Parfait!*" she declared and haltingly repeated as much as she could.

Martin reappeared just then and swept behind her.

"Ah, but no stranger to me," he said, and with his arms around her waist swung her off the floor. Once she was down she pried his hands apart to escape.

"I am enjoying this conversation," she told him in French.

"So you like this American?" Martin asked her.

"I like Americans," she answered. "That must be what interested me in you. *Pas mal*," she added—Not bad—a reference to my looks, then winked at me with Martin behind her. She clearly had no intention to let him know I understood.

"You think he has silk stockings and chocolate bars?" asked Martin.

"*Merde.* You are always jealous."

"Not without reason," he answered.

"Yes, but without right."

"Eh," he responded. It was banter. Both were grinning. He faced me and said that the Comtesse would be down momentarily.

With Martin's reappearance, I had taken a notebook from my fatigues and asked the Major if we might use the interval before the Comtesse's arrival to discuss my mission here. I presented him with an order from Patton's adjutant authorizing the Rule 35 investigation, but Martin did not read more than the first lines.

"Teedle," he said then, as if it were the most tiresome word in any language. "What does he say? No, don't bother. Mark it as true, whatever he says. All true. 'Insubordinate.' 'Mutinous.' Whatever the hell he wants to call it. Write down in your little book: Guilty as hell. The Army still doesn't know what to do with me." He laughed, just as he had when he recollected the Negro speakeasy.

I followed him across the kitchen. "I wouldn't make light of this, Major. Teedle has laid serious charges, sir." I explained his rights to Martin—he could give a statement himself or direct me to other witnesses. If he preferred to speak to a superior officer, he was entitled to do so. And certainly he could hear a specification of what had been said against him.

"If you must," he answered. He picked at a plate of grapes.

"General Teedle alleges that you've been ordered to disband your Operational Group and return to London. He says you've refused."

"'Refused'? What rubbish. I'm here under the command of OSS London, and London has directed me to continue as before. Gita and I and the others are going to finish our business in France, then continue on to Germany. I have built networks there, too, Dubin. We will see this to an end. Teedle can be damned with his nonsense about refusing orders."

"This is a misunderstanding, then?"

"If you wish to call it that."

I was somewhat relieved to find the matter could be settled quickly. I asked Martin to see his orders from OSS, which brought an indulgent smile.

"You don't know much about OSS, do you, Dubin?" In fact, I had tried to learn as much as I could, but except for an old propaganda piece in *Stars and Stripes* and what I gleaned at the 18th Division from Martin's sanitized 201 file, I was largely in the dark. "An OSS officer carries no written orders," he told me. "The Nazis have said forthrightly that they'll shoot any OSS member they capture. Teedle knows this. But mine are orders nonetheless."

"Well, if I may, sir, who gave those orders?"

"My operational officer in London. I was ordered back to see him the last week in September, as a matter of fact."

"And his name, if you please?"

Again, Martin smiled as he would with a boy.

"Dubin, OSS has strict rules of secrecy. It is not a normal military organization. Only London can reveal the information you're asking for. But feel free to check with them. They will confirm everything."

I frowned.

"Oh, pshaw, Dubin. You doubt me? Look around here. We live in the open in the French countryside, fed and housed by a noted French resister. If London didn't want this, don't you think they could inform the local networks, the Free French, with whom they've worked hand in glove for years now? Do you think the Comtesse would defy them? I am here only with the leave of OSS."

He was making some sense, but I knew I could not conclude this investigation merely by inference. However, I had lost Martin's attention. On the threshold was an older woman, very erect, very slim, very drawn. Her graying hair was swept back smoothly and she wore a simple dress, sashed at the waist, and no jewelry besides a cameo that hung between her collarbones. Biddy and I were introduced to the Comtesse de Lemolland. I bowed briefly, accepting her hand.

She addressed us in English.

"I owe to all Americans my deepest gratitude for your courage in behalf of my country."

"I am only a lawyer, Comtesse. Your thanks go to the likes of Major Martin, not to me."

Martin interjected, "The Comtesse herself is a great heroine."

"Not at all true," she answered.

"May I tell the story then, Comtesse, and allow Lieutenant Dubin to judge for himself?"

Leaning against a large cutting block in the center of the kitchen, Martin played raconteur, a role that clearly pleased him. He explained that when the Nazis arrived in 1940, they had commandeered the Comte de Lemolland's ancestral house in the Côtes-du-Nord, where the Comtesse, a widow of three years, had been residing. The Germans turned the château into a communications node. The Comtesse was forced to live as a guest in her own home, confined to an apartment of several rooms. Because the Germans adored rank, they accorded her some dignity, but they partied with prostitutes and nailed maps to the wainscoting in the parlor and abused her servants. Twice maids were raped.

One of the Comtesse's house staff was a member of the underground, and it was she who secretly introduced Agnès de Lemolland to Martin. The Comtesse agreed to the installation in her salon of a listening device, an induction microphone no larger than a button, which was attached by a filament to a tiny earphone that ran to her sitting room. There the Comtesse listened to the daily flow of information through the communications center downstairs, reporting what she'd overheard. When the plans were laid for D-Day, the Comtesse understood that it was from this very center that German reinforcements would be routed to Normandy. With no request from Martin, she designated her own house for bombing once the invasion began, fleeing with her servants only minutes before the first strike.

"Major Martin is quite correct in his assessment," I told the Comtesse. I bowed again, but felt pained to realize that this frail old woman had done far more to win the war than I ever would.

"I am no one," she said simply, "but if you insist that I am as important as all that, Lieutenant, I must take advantage and insist that you and your companion honor me by joining us at supper." Without awaiting a reply, she instructed Sophie, the servant who was at the stove, to set two more plates.

I went looking for Bidwell, whom I found outside, leaning on the jeep and shooting pictures. In the bright daylight, looking back at the Comtesse's little castle, I felt as if I'd just left an amusement park.

"Quite a bunch, aren't they?" I asked. They were all captivating, the gallant Comtesse, and fierce little Mademoiselle Lodz, and of course Martin. "I think the Major is the first actual war hero I've met," I said.

From Biddy I received one of his sour looks, a step from insubordination.

"No disrespect, Lieutenant, but ain't no way rightly to tell where all the malarkey ends in there, sir. Only it's plenty of it, this country boy knows that." He closed the snaps on the leather camera case. "Food smells just fine, though," he said and headed inside.

6. PRINCIPLES

Supper at the Comtesse de Lemolland's was an idyll. In an alcove beside the kitchen, we ate at a long table of heavily varnished wood, enjoying a savory stew. It might have been veal, although there was not much meat among the root vegetables that were the main ingredients. Nevertheless, the usual French hand with food prevailed and the victuals were far tastier, if less plentiful, than even the very good rations we had at HQ. Some of my appreciation for the meal might have been due to the Comtesse's wine, newly pressed, which was poured freely. But in time I realized that the principal charm was that at the Comtesse de Lemolland's I had left the military. A civil — and civilian — atmosphere prevailed. I sat next to the old woman while she shared reflections in English on the history of the region. When we started, Biddy lingered, uncertain if he was invading the officers' mess, but Martin waved him to a chair. Sophie, who had cooked, joined us, too. The Gypsy I had seen, called Antonio, was at the far end of the table speaking in French with Peter Bettjer, a ruddy blond Belgian, who was the Operational Group's communications expert.

Last to sit was Mademoiselle Lodz, who took the empty chair on my right. Midway through the meal, I felt the weight of her gaze. She was studying me unapologetically.

"I am reflecting about you, Doo-bean," she told me in French. It was clear already that she was never going to pronounce my name any other way.

"I am delighted to know I concern you at all. What exactly is it you are thinking, Mademoiselle?"

"If you are indeed Dubinsky from Pinsk"— she puckered her lips, then stared straight at me —"*vous êtes juif.*"

So that was it. In the little fantasia of the Comtesse's home, I felt especially scalded, which my face apparently betrayed.

"This is nothing to be ashamed of," she said in French. "In my town there were many Jews. I knew them well."

"I am hardly ashamed," I said quickly.

"There are many Jewish soldiers in the American Army?"

"Some."

"And they stay among the other troops?"

"Of course. We are one nation."

"But the dark ones I see — they drive and move the equipment. The Jews do not have separate battalions like the Negroes?"

"No. It is entirely different. The blacks were slaves to some of the Americans' grandfathers, who, regrettably, have not allowed the past to die."

"And these Jew soldiers. They look like you? You have no sidelocks. Are there *tsitsis* beneath your garments?"

"I am not a Jew in that way."

"In my town they had only one way, Dubin. *Red Yiddish?*" she asked. That made the third language in which she had addressed me, and her smile revealed a dark space between her front teeth.

"*Ayn bisel. Yich red besser am franzosich.*" My grandparents who had followed my father to the United States spoke Yiddish, but my mother and father used only English in the presence of their children, unwilling to risk hindering our development as Americans. My Yiddish was not even close to my French, as I had just told her.

"*Ach mir,*" she answered, "*ayn bisel.*" With me, too, a little bit.

Martin, across the table, asked her in French, "What language is that?"

"We are speaking Jewish, Robert."

"Jewish? I thought you disliked the Jews."

She looked at him sharply. "Wrong. Stupidly wrong. This is because you will never listen to anything I say about my home. My only friends as a child were Jewish. They alone would allow me in their houses. Why would I dislike them?"

"But they spurned you."

"For a bride, Robert. It is their way."

He turned away to ask Sophie for the bread, while Mademoiselle Lodz was left to explain.

"*C'est une histoire compliquée,*" she told me. It's a long story. "My mother, Dubin, wanted me to find a Jew to be my husband. She said, 'They are seldom drunks and rarely beat their wives.'" Mademoiselle Lodz's mother had clearly never met Julius Klein, who lived on the third floor above us when I was a child and whose wife and children often ran for their lives while his drunken rages shook the entire building. "But no Jew, of course, would marry me."

"You are a Catholic?"

"Only to a Jew. I have never set foot inside a church."

"So you felt, as the Major put it, spurned?"

She wagged her head from side to side, as if weighing the idea for the first time only now.

"The Poles were far worse. Those who regarded themselves as respectable would not even speak to my mother — including her own family. So we lived happily among the Jews. And if I'd had a Jewish husband, I would have been on the trucks beside him. For me, in the end, it was a piece of good fortune."

"The trucks?"

"*Vous m'étonnez!* You do not know of this? In my town, every Jew is gone. The Nazis took them away. They are in the ghetto in Lublin, held like livestock inside fences. This has happened everywhere. France, too. In Vichy, Pétain rounded up the Jews even before the Germans asked. As a Jewish soldier, you, especially, should be here fighting Hitler."

When I enlisted, my first choice was to battle Tojo and the sinister Japanese who had launched their sneak attack on Pearl Harbor. As for Hitler, I knew about his ruthless war against the Jews in Germany, smashing Jewish businesses and confiscating Jewish homes, and felt a stake in bringing him down, but it was not the same as the sense of direct attack I'd experienced from the Japanese bombs on American soil.

I was disinclined to try to explain any of this to Mademoiselle Lodz. Instead, I gave my attention to Martin,

who was across the table regaling Bidwell with tales of
the Operational Group during the years before the invasion. To introduce Antonio and Bettjer, Martin was detailing their most entertaining success against the Nazis,
which had come in a small town to the west. There vint-
ners sold *vin ordinaire* by hauling it through the streets in
a hogshead mounted on two wheels, from which the vil-
lagers would fill their carafes through a bunghole in the bottom. Together Antonio and Bettjer had inserted a wooden
partition in one of these casks, leaving wine in the lower
portion. In the upper half, Bettjer had crawled between
the staves. Looking out a tiny spy hole, he radioed information to Martin on the whereabouts of a German Panzer
division moving through the town, while Antonio rolled
the barrel down the street so their wireless was immune
to the German direction-finding trucks that crawled
around the area in search of resistance transmitters.

"It was all brilliant," said Martin, "except that poor
Peter literally got drunk on the fumes. When we opened
the cask, he had passed out cold."

Around the table, there was a hail of laughter and several jokes about Bettjer and alcohol, to which he'd clearly
become more accustomed. Right now he was bright red
with drink. I had been more careful with the wine, but the
same could not be said of most of the others and the level
of hilarity had increased as Martin went on recounting
their adventures.

"You appear, Major, to have been destined for this
life," I said to him eventually.

"Oh, hardly," he answered. "I was organizing for the
International Transport Workers around Paris, when the
Nazis decided to go marching. I had no desire to return to

war, Dubin. I'd had more than enough of it in Spain. I'd led other Americans in the Abraham Lincoln Brigade, then became a commando when the foreign troops were sent home. It was all quite dismal, to be frank. I had no desire to see more friends and comrades tortured and killed by Fascists. After Paris fell, I moved back to Madrid, where I was a transportation official with an oil company. Spain was a neutral country, and with a Spanish passport I could go anywhere, even Germany, which is why the OSS approached me. Originally, I thought I was to be a mere conduit for information. But one thing led to another. I had no interest in joining the Army, yet I could not refuse when they asked me to lead the OG."

Yesterday, at the 18th, I had reviewed a clip from *Stars and Stripes* in Martin's file, detailing how the Operational Groups had been formed. Colonel Donovan, the founder of the Office of Strategic Services, had corralled swashbucklers from everywhere, Russian émigrés, Spanish Civil War veterans like Martin, and a number of Italian speakers from New York, Boston, and Chicago. All of them had been trained at the Congressional Country Club outside D.C., where they had done conditioning runs on the famous golf course and received instruction in the black arts of silent assassination, demolition, secret radio broadcast, judo, cryptography, lock picking, safecracking, and installing listening devices. Martin's efficiency reports from that period were often marked out, but made clear he had been a star, except with Morse code, where he never succeeded in getting above twelve words a minute.

Following his training, according to Lieutenant Colonel Brunson, Teedle's G-1 who'd briefed me, Martin and two comrades, as well as eight supply chutes carrying radios, weapons, and necessities like currency, were dropped over France by a low-flying bomber in October 1942. Each man had a fake ID, a work card, and a cyanide capsule. Somehow, the Nazis had seen the drop. The Englishman with them was shot, while Martin and a French sergeant, who I believed was the Gypsy Antonio now at the end of the table, spent two days in the woods barely avoiding the Germans.

Over time, however, the OG was established. Because of his union activities before the war, Martin was able to build an active network among the rail workers, many of whom he had known for years. Together they sabotaged 370 trains in the succeeding months, destroying railheads and tracks, setting locomotives afire, igniting fuel dumps, and attacking German convoys on the run. After D-Day, as the Third Army advanced north, Stemwinder monitored German troop movements and brought down bridges along the Loire. In the file, there were several laudatory communications from grateful commanders. Leaving aside Teedle.

"And before Spain?" I said to him. "May I ask what you asked me, Major? Where is the home war has taken you from?"

He laughed, but the wine gave him a wistful look.

"Good for you, Dubin. That's the sixty-four-dollar question. But I left all that behind long ago." His smile had faded, when he added, "The answer is as lost to history as the ruins of ancient Greece."

After coffee—Nescafé, about which the Comtesse permitted herself one rueful remark over the lost pleasures of former days—I asked Martin to help me find evidence that would show that OSS had directed him to remain here. Very drunk now, he took a second to marshal himself, and in his confused expression I could see he was peeved by my determination. But in the end he laughed and patted my back.

"What a serious fellow you are, Dubin. Yes, of course."

The first thought was to show me the shortwave radio through which they received London's orders, but I needed something better than that. Martin frowned again at my doggedness but put the question in French to his Stemwinder colleagues who remained at the table.

"*Londres?*" asked Bettjer. "*Les documents des cons, non?*"

Martin laughed. "How wonderful. Yes." 'The papers of the idiots' referred to the Finance Officers in OSS, who were the same relentless penny-pinchers in that outfit they were everywhere else, demanding that Martin keep exact accounts of the funds advanced for the Operational Group. If I had not been in the Army, I might not have believed that Martin's orders to mount commando attacks were never reduced to writing, but that nickels and dimes required precise records. Mademoiselle Lodz said she kept the papers with the radio, and I followed her outside to find them. At 3:00 p.m. the daylight was still bright, and leaving the dim house, especially after the wine, I needed to shield my eyes.

"*Cela vous dérange si je fume?*" she asked. Does it bother you if I smoke? It was a meaningless courtesy since she already had the flame of her lighter, an American Zippo, to the tip. She had not lit up at the table in deference to the Comtesse, who did not approve of women with cigarettes. Otherwise, Mademoiselle Lodz had barely been without a Lucky Strike between her fingers. I took smoking as the source of her appealing cough-drop voice, like June Allyson's. I declined when she offered me one, telling her I'd never picked up the habit.

"The C rations are terrible," she said. "But the cigarettes? This is the best thing the American Army brought with them." She actually hugged her green pack of Luckys to her breast. "In Vichy, the women were banned from buying cigarettes altogether. Martin says that is why I had no choice but to join the resistance." She laughed at herself.

At supper, Martin had recounted several of Gita's adventures. On D-Day, for example, she had calmly turned the road signs at an intersection ninety degrees and stood there long enough to direct an entire Nazi tank battalion south rather than west. Later that afternoon, according to Martin, they had destroyed a large part of the same unit, when Gita and he herded dozens of sheep onto a bridgehead the Nazis were hoping to cross. While the German soldiers were shooing the livestock, Antonio slipped beneath the bridge and set detonators and dynamite, which they blew when the tanks moved forward.

"Martin's stories of your exploits are remarkable."

She smiled. "And even better if they were true."

I lost a step, which evoked another spirited laugh from her.

"Those of us with Martin," she told me, "have watched our lives grow larger when he describes our activities. But he is so good at it, we all believe him. That is Martin's way. At times, there's not a person here who knows whether he's speaking the truth. I am not even certain that his name is Martin. With the OSS, they all take noms de guerre. But it does not matter. Who are we, Dubin, but the stories we tell about ourselves, particularly if we accept them? My mother said that always."

I had never heard anyone declare such a notion aloud, that we somehow had the power to make ourselves up on the go. Yet it was an idea that attracted me, and I reflected a moment, trying to determine whether life allowed that kind of latitude and how far it might extend.

"Without disrespect to your mother, Mademoiselle, it is better, is it not, if those stories are also true?"

"But who is to tell the truth, Doo-bean? In my town, they said my mother was a tramp. She was a seamstress, but she had lovers among the well-to-do, and took their money. In her view, she was a nonconformist, an artiste at heart. She chose to believe that, and I did as well."

"I am sure that is so," I said, deferring to the reflective softness that had come over Mademoiselle Lodz as she spoke about her mother. "Her loss must have been terrible for you," I said quietly.

"Quite terrible. She remains with me every moment. If not for those assassins, she would have lived to be one hundred. In my family, all the women do. My mother said that was our problem, she and I. There is too much life in us. It makes us wild in youth. And for her that made enduring burdens." She smiled sadly as she touched her own blouse.

"And when she died and you ran from Poland, where did you go first?"

"I landed in Marseilles. I was seventeen. I envisioned myself as the new Bernhardt. Bold, eh? I could barely speak a word of French. I did what needed doing. My mother had taught me to sew, and I found a job mending sheets in a hospital laundry. Soon I was promoted and allowed to empty bedpans." Again, she permitted a husky laugh about herself. "I found my way. Come," she said, "I will show you the items you wish to see."

Walking briskly, she reached the cowshed at the far end of the courtyard, which, like all the connected buildings, had been built of thick stones clad in a coating of cement and sand. On the second floor were quarters for a staff. Judging from the line of curtained windows that surrounded us, the Comtesse once must have employed dozens more workers than now.

Inside the old barn, the air was dense with the ripe smells of animals and moldy hay. Entering a cow stall, Mademoiselle Lodz took hold of a weathered milking stool. With a screwdriver, she removed a metal plate from the bottom of the seat, revealing the radio and its battery.

"Peter says only a few years ago the radios were enormous. Ten, twelve kilos. But now." She withdrew the sleek transmitter and placed it in my hand. It was about six inches long and did not weigh even a pound. Before D-Day, she said, their orders came over the BBC in code with the 9:00 p.m. news. These days, messages were relayed back and forth once a week, when an OSS plane carrying a radio relay to London passed overhead. I nodded, but it was the papers that interested me and I mentioned them again.

"*Voilà*." Mademoiselle Lodz drew a wad from inside the stool. Included was the yellow duplicate of Standard Form 1012a, Martin's travel voucher, signed and stamped by the paymaster at Central Base Station in London, and containing the details of Martin's trip there and back between September 26 and 30. There were also receipts for two meals Martin had consumed on the way, and French war scrip. Martin's itinerary was exactly as he claimed: OSS had redispatched him here a little more than three weeks ago. When I asked to take the papers, Mademoiselle Lodz was reluctant, but I promised to have them back within a week. In return, she wanted to know what this was all about. I gave her the bare details of Teedle's complaint.

"London just sent Martin back," she said. "You can see yourself." The records didn't seem to leave much doubt of that. All in all, it had the look of a typical Army SNAFU. "Teedle would be eager to believe the worst," she said. "*Bon sang.* Teedle, Martin—that is a bad match. They have been unpleasant with each other from the start."

"Teedle is the superior."

"*Il a une dent contre lui.*" He has a grudge against him. "It is true Martin does not like to receive orders in the field," she said. "He prefers to reach concord with his commanders. Teedle wants only to be obeyed."

"There must be order in war. A chain of command."

"In war, order is no more than a good intention. Order is for generals. Not soldiers. *Tu te mets le doigt dans l'oeil.*" You are putting your finger in your eye, meaning I was fooling myself.

"I am a lawyer, nonetheless. I must defend the rules."

"Lawyers are functionaries. Little men. Are you a little man, Dubin? It does not seem so."

"I don't regard the law as little rules. I regard it as an attempt to impart reason and dignity to life."

"Justice imparts reason and dignity, Dubin. Not rules. Little rules and large wrongs are a bad mix. I don't know your rules. But I know what is wrong. As does Martin. The Nazis are wrong. Fight them. That is the only rule that should matter. Not whether Martin does Teedle's bidding."

"You argue well," I said to her. "If Martin has need of a lawyer, he should consider you."

At the idea, she laughed loudly, until giving way to a hacking smoker's cough. I was impressed by Mademoiselle Lodz's raucousness, which seemed bold compared to Grace, who literally raised her hand to her mouth when she was amused. We had reached the sun again. Mademoiselle Lodz flattened her small hand above her eyes as she regarded me.

"You interest me, Doo-bean."

"I am flattered, Mademoiselle. Is that because I am a lawyer, or an American, or a Jew?"

"*Ça ne rime à rien.*" That doesn't rhyme with anything, meaning there was no point. "Who you are, you are, no?"

"I suppose. And who, Mademoiselle Lodz, may I ask, are you?"

"Who do you take me for, Dubin?"

"You seem to be a soldier and a philosopher."

She laughed robustly again. "No," she said, "I am too young to be a philosopher. I spout, but you should pay no attention. Besides, I don't trust intellectuals. They place too much faith in ideas."

"I am probably guilty of that."

"It seems so."

"But principles matter, do they not?"

"*Mais oui*. But do they come before anything else?"

"I hope so. Certainly that is desirable, is it not, to care first about principles?"

"*C'est impossible*," she said.

I expressed my doubts, and she told me I was being naïve.

"Perhaps," I said, "but if I was being a lawyer—or a philosopher—I would tell you that a convincing argument requires proof."

"'Proof'?" She smirked. "Proving is too easy."

"How so?"

"Eh, Doo-bean. You are an innocent at heart. I will show you, if I must. *Un moment*." She disappeared into the barn again, but promptly called out, "Come."

I stepped back into the humid scents and darkness. At first, I saw no one.

"Here," she said behind me. When I turned, Gita Lodz had lifted her skirt to her waist, revealing her slim legs and her undergarment, a kind of cotton bloomer. It fit snugly, revealing her narrow shape and, with another instant's attention, the indentation of her female cleft and the shadow of the dark triangle around it.

"Is it principle you feel first, Dubin?"

I had long recognized that the hardest part of life in a war zone was that there was so often no routine, no order, nothing to count on. Every moment was a novelty. But this display exceeded even the limited boundaries that remained. I was literally struck dumb.

"*Touché*," I finally said, the only word I could think of, which brought another outburst of laughter while she smothered down her skirt. By pure chance, I had come off as a wit.

"We are primitive, Dubin. If we are not to be, then we require one another's assistance. But first know who we are."

I gave a simple nod. Satisfied she had made a potent demonstration, Mademoiselle Lodz strolled from the cowshed, looking back from the sunlight with a clever smile. I waited in the shadows. She would treat this as a prank, but free to watch from the darkness, I had a sudden vision of Gita Lodz and the riot of feeling that underlay her boldness. Her upbringing in scorn had left her with no choice but to defy convention, yet despite her confident airs and the stories she wished to believe, I sensed, almost palpably, that her personality was erected on a foundation of anger, and beneath that, pain. When I stepped back into the sun, some sadness must have clung to the way I looked at her, which I could tell was entirely unexpected. As we considered each other something fell away, and she turned heel immediately, headed toward the house.

I caught up, but we trudged back in silence. It was she who spoke finally, as we approached the little castle.

"Have I offended you, Dubin?"

"Of course not. I challenged you. You responded. Convincingly."

"But you are shocked."

"Pay no attention. I am easily shocked, Mademoiselle Lodz."

"Good for you," she said. "In France, no one will admit to being bourgeois."

I laughed. "In America, it is the universal aspiration. But I still must respect proprieties. I am sent to inquire of a man. The law might question my impartiality if I was interested instead in looking at his woman in her dainties."

"Not his woman. I am not with Martin in that way, Dubin. That is done between us. Long ago."

I thought of Martin embracing her in the kitchen.

"I have heard many refer to you as his woman."

"That is convenient for both of us. There are soldiers everywhere, Dubin. It is better to be known as spoken for. Do not be repelled for Martin's sake. Only your own." She gave me that sly smile. "À *la prochaine*," she said — Until next time — and breezed through the door, restored to her former self.

Biddy was waiting there. We needed to be back at the 18th before dark, but I was still reverberating like a struck bell. It had been months since I'd had anything to do with a woman, except with the clinical neutrality of a lawyer interviewing witnesses, and I had forgotten the pull that seemed to emanate from every cell. I had been resolutely faithful to Grace, even in the brothel atmosphere of London, where the joke went that every girl's knickers had the same flaw: one Yank and they were off. There I had known what to expect. Sex was everywhere — you could hear the moans when you passed a supposedly unoccupied air raid shelter, or walked in the dark through Hyde Park. The U.S. soldiers, with their Arrid and Odo·Ro·No, seemed rich and well-groomed compared to the poor beaten-down Brits, who had a single uniform and their noisy hobnailed boots. Now both Biddy and I were looking at the doorway through which Gita had gone.

"You have a girl at home, Biddy?" I asked.

"Nope. Had one, but let her get away. Joyce Washington. Courted with her all through high school. Was het up to marry, too. She got herself a job typing at the First National Bank. And there was some fella there, Lieutenant, I guess he just swept her off her feet. And her with my ring on her finger. She come to tell me and I said to her, 'How can you do this, go off with another man when you promised yourself to me?' And you know what she says? She says, 'Gideon, he's got a Hudson.' Can you imagine? I honestly got to say, Lieutenant, I really don't think it was the letdown that bothered me so much as wondering how in all get-out I could have been fool enough to love a woman like that." He fixed on the distance while the pain swamped him again, then shook it off.

"I done all right with those English girls," he said, "but I can't make head or tail of these Frenchies. All that ooh-la-la junk may go in Paris, but out this way, these are just country gals, Lieutenant, and it ain't no different than in Georgia, mamas tell them all their lives to keep their legs crossed till the day they say 'I do,' war or no war. What about you, Lieutenant? You been makin any time?" Unconsciously perhaps, his eyes diverted toward the doorway.

"I have a fiancée back home, Biddy." We both knew this was not a direct response. Eisley, with a wife in Ohio, could explain in utter seriousness how all formalities, especially marriage vows, were suspended during times of war. But I left it at that.

Martin had stepped out of the house, still flushed from the wine and smiling hugely. I took it that he'd had a word with Gita and had come outside to say goodbye to us.

"So I hear we actually found your precious papers. I could tell you came here with the wrong impression.

Mark my words, Dubin, Teedle is trying to stir things up. He's giving orders where he has no call to."

"Mademoiselle Lodz says he has a grudge against you."

"That would be one way to put it." His blue eyes went for a moment to the horizon, the first occasion when I had seen him measure his words. "Look, Dubin, sooner or later you're going to figure out what this is all about. You don't need my *j'accuse*."

"If you'd rather I not share your response with General Teedle—"

"Oh, I don't care a fig about Teedle. Look, Dubin, it's this simple. He thinks I'm a Communist. Because I fought in Spain. After the Axis, the Soviets are next. I'm the new enemy. Or so he believes."

"Are you?"

"An enemy of the United States? I should say not."

"A Communist, sir."

"I've been fighting too long, Dubin, to call myself anything. I believe in power for the powerless, food for the hungry, shelter for the homeless. Does that make me a revolutionary? Here, Dubin, it all comes down to this. The man is wasting your time and he knows it. I intend to fulfill my mission. And I won't allow Teedle to get in my way, or bog me down with Army folderol. I can melt into this landscape, or that of any other place from here to Berlin, if I choose."

He gave me a pointed look. I was startled by the openness with which he discussed insubordination, but there was no chance for rejoinder, because both of us were drawn to the buzz of planes overhead. Martin was immediately on alert, like a pointer in the field, squinting to search the sky. But the aircraft were ours.

"B-26s, I reckon," he said then. "They're going to take advantage of the break in the weather to bomb."

Just as he predicted, the heavy sounds echoed a few minutes later. At first, the distant bombardment was like oil popping in a skillet, but as the squadrons kept passing overhead, the noise came closer. A barrier of smoke and dust arose and drifted back to us, damming the light and ghosting over the Comtesse's fields, carrying along the odor of gunpowder. We could hear German antiaircraft fire. No more than a mile ahead, we saw a plane burst into flame and parachutes bloom in the sky.

A number of the farmworkers as well as Antonio had joined us on the cobbles as spectators. Martin asked the Gypsy about the position of the 26th Infantry to be certain they would be able to reach the downed fliers. While this discussion was under way, another squadron passed, flying lower. We had been trading around a pair of field glasses that someone had brought from the house and when I took my turn, I could see the bomb bays open beneath the planes. I had just remarked on this to Martin, when an explosion shook the air around us, and a column of fire rose on the next hill.

"Lord," said Martin. "We'll be lucky if they don't drop on us as well." He looked up one more time, then dashed into the little castle, yelling first to Gita, then everyone else. He emerged in seconds behind the Comtesse and her servants. In both English and French, he commanded everyone into the old stone cellar beneath the house. He stood at the door, shooing all of us down, ordering us to be quick. The workers came running out of the fields, some still in waders they had been wearing in the flooded lower grounds. I was already in the earthen-floored cellar when another detonation reverberated, closer than the first. I looked to the entrance to see about Martin, but he appeared in a moment, slamming the door behind him and thumping down the stairs. The cellar was no more than six feet high and there was now no light. I'd seen Biddy hunched in the corner, next to the shelves of jarred fruits and an adjoining wall racked with dusty bottles of wine. There must have been twenty people huddled in the dark. The air quickly grew close. There were the usual jokes. One of the women said, "Keep your hands to yourself," and a man responded, "You, as well." In a far corner, a cat was meowing.

"*D'ici peu, on va se sentir tous comme des cons,*" someone remarked across the room. In a moment we will feel like fools. He had barely spoken, when the atmosphere was rent by the fabulous concussion of an explosion directly overhead.

The Germans still had 280mm railway artillery pieces in the Vosges elevated over Nancy, and once or twice a day the cry of incoming fire would ring out and everyone in the court-martial session would scramble into the cellar of the Lycée, waiting for the big boom of the shells. But that was no preparation for being bombed. The air seemed to slam shut on me, then opened briefly only to pound me again, while the earth literally jostled beneath our feet. I felt the shock across my entire body — even my cheeks and eyeballs were compressed. And the sound was worse. I had never understood until that moment that noise alone, even when you knew its source, could be loud enough to inspire panic. My ears went numb, then revived, throbbing.

In the instant afterward, I assumed the house had been

struck and would collapse on us, but there was no sign of that. Instead there was light now. Eventually I realized that the wooden door of the cellar had been blown off. Martin went out first and in time called down that it was safe to emerge. Coming up into the daylight, I noticed that my boots were soaked with wine.

The crater of the bomb, the depth and the size of a small pond, had disturbed earth all the way to the house, but the actual point of impact seemed to have been about 150 yards away in the pasture. Everyone who had been in the cellar radiated off to inspect the damage. It was quickly determined there were no human casualties, although a number of those who had been near the cellar walls had been struck by falling bottles and several had been cut, including Biddy, who had pulled a shard the size of an arrowhead out of his arm.

Around the farm, the Comtesse's chicks and her one cow were nowhere to be found, and a horse was dead, keeled over like a life-size toy with his lips raveled back fearfully over his huge teeth. The family dog had literally been blown to bits. His leather collar was about a hundred yards from the house. I suspected that the blast that blew off the cellar door had been the end of the hound, who had probably been cowering there.

As for the little castle, the damage was moderate. All the rear windows had been blown out, and their shutters were gone. A piece of the roof had been ripped off like the corner of a sheet of paper. Inside, I saw that much of the crockery had shattered. For the Comtesse de Lemolland, this proved too much. She had withstood the death of a spouse and a son with dignity, and the destruction of her husband's château, but the loss of an old delft plate that her mother had hung on the wall sixty years ago somehow exceeded her meager abilities to carry on. She was on the wooden floor of the kitchen, her skirt billowed about her, while she gathered the chalky pieces in her hands and wailed in complete abandon. Gita held one shoulder to comfort her.

I fled outside, where Martin still searched the sky with the field glasses to be sure we were safe.

"Did they lose their coordinates?" I asked.

"Perhaps," said Martin, then erupted in a sharp laugh. "Perhaps not." He lowered the binoculars to look at me. "I rather suspect, Dubin, we've all had a greeting card from General Teedle."

III.

7. STEWART: BEAR LEACH

Northumberland Manor occupied a large campus in West Hartford, a collection of white clapboard buildings containing various facilities for the elderly, everything from independent housing to hospice, and the several other stages in between as decline rolls downhill to death. Arriving early, I awaited Justice Barrington Leach, my father's long-ago lawyer, in the front room of the Manor's nursing home. With its wall-to-wall robin's-egg carpeting and nice Ethan Allen furnishings, the place presented itself as far superior to the usual holding tank for the barely living.

Given everything it had taken to get to Leach, including passing myself off as a lately orphaned only child, I sat there with high expectations. Leach, after all, was a longtime legal hotshot, whose skills had somehow allowed him to erase his trial loss and persuade General Teedle to revoke my father's conviction and prison sentence. Thus, I couldn't help being disappointed when a nurse's aide pushed the old man into the room. Overall, Justice Leach

gave the physical impression of a fallen leaf crisped down
to its veins. His spotty bald head listed, barely rising above
the back of his wheelchair, and the hose from an oxygen
tank was holstered in his nose. He had been so whittled by
age that his sturdy Donegal tweed suit, perhaps older than
I am, was puddled around him, and his skin had begun to
acquire a whitish translucence which signaled that even
the wrapper was giving out.

Yet none of that mattered once he started talking.
Leach's voice wobbled, just like his long hands on which
the fingers were knobbed from arthritis, but his mind
moved along quickly. He remained fully connected to this
world. To say Barrington Leach still took great joy in life
would be not only hackneyed, but probably inaccurate.
The Justice's wife and his only child, a daughter, were both
dead of breast cancer. His three adult grandkids lived in
California, where they had been raised, and he had resisted their heartsore efforts to move him from Hartford. As
a result he was largely alone here, and he suffered from
Parkinson's, among several other ailments. I doubt he
found life either comfortable or amusing most of the time.

But none of this inhibited his intense curiosity about
human beings. He was a gentle wit, and full of a generous
acceptance for people's foibles as well as reverent wonder
at our triumphs. I come easily to envy, but with Barrington
Leach, when I mused, as I always did, about why I couldn't
be more like him, it was with pure admiration. He was in-
spiring.

My first order of business with Leach was to set the
record straight, not about my mother and sister, naturally,
but rather about what to call me. He had written to me as
"Mr. Dubin," but in 1970, I had reverted to the name my

grandfather had brought from Russia and have been known as Stewart Dubinsky throughout my adult life. The story of that change, too involved to repeat here now, made a fairly poignant introduction to my relations with my father. Leach asked several searching questions before going on to inquiries about my work, my parents, and the course of my father's life. He was so precise, and cautious in a way, that I feared at first he knew I'd lied about Mom, but it turned out he had something else in mind.

"You know, Stewart, I think you mean to honor your father's memory, but I would be remiss if I didn't issue a caveat. If you go forward, you could very well discover things that a loyal son might not enjoy finding out. I've always believed there is great wisdom in the saying that one must be careful what to wish for."

I assured him I had reflected about this. After hanging around courtrooms for a couple of decades, I knew that the odds were that my father had been convicted of a serious crime for a reason.

"Well, that's a good start," Leach said. "But the particulars are always worse than the general idea. And that assumes you even have a general idea. You may find, Stewart, you've been running headlong with blinders."

I told him I was resolute. Whatever happened, I wanted to know.

"Well, that's one problem," said Leach.

"What are the others, Justice?"

"'Bear' is fine." I was never sure if the nickname had to do with his physique as a young man—he was anything but bearlike now—or, more likely, was merely a convenient shortening of his given name, adopted in an era when being 'Bare' would have been too risqué. "I confess that I've spent quite a bit of time, Stewart, since you contacted me, wondering what call I have to tell you any of this. I feel a good deal of fondness for David, even today. He was a fine young man, articulate, thoughtful. And it was his wish not to speak about this with anyone, a wish he apparently maintained throughout his life. Furthermore, wholly aside from personal loyalties, I was his attorney, bound by law to keep his secrets.

"On the other hand, I have things of your father's, Stewart, a document of his, as I've mentioned, that belongs to you as his heir. I have no right to withhold it from you, and therefore, as to the matters disclosed there, I believe I am free to speak. That, at any rate, will be my defense when the disbarment proceedings begin." He had a prominent cataract in one eye, large enough to be clearly visible, but it could not obscure the light that always arose there with a joke. "But you and I must reach an understanding to start. I can't go beyond the compass of what's written. You'll find me able to answer most of your questions, but not all. Understood?"

I readily agreed. We both took a breath then before I asked what seemed like the logical first question, how Leach had been assigned my father's case.

"It was roundabout," he answered. "Throughout the war, I had been in the sanctuary of Eisenhower's headquarters, first in Bushy Park outside London, and then later in 1944 at Versailles. These days, I'd be referred to as a 'policy maker.' I had been the District Attorney here in Hartford and certainly knew my way around a courtroom, but my exposure to court-martials was limited to reviewing a few trial records that came up to Eisenhower for final decision, hanging cases most of them. However, your father's commanding officer, Halley Maples, knew my older brother at Princeton, and Maples made a personal appeal to my superiors to appoint me as defense counsel. I had very little choice, not that I ever regretted it, although your father as a client came with his share of challenges." That remark was punctuated with a craggy laugh.

At ninety-six, Bear Leach had been what we call an old man for a long time, at least twenty years, and he had grown practiced with some of the privileges and demands of age. He had been asked about his memories of one thing or another so often that, as I sometimes joked with him, his memoirs were essentially composed in his head. He spoke in flowing paragraphs. As we grew friendlier over the next several months, I brought him a tape recorder in the hope he would use it to preserve prominent stories of his life. But he was too humble to think he'd been much more than a minor figure, and the project didn't interest him. He was, as he always said, a trial lawyer. He preferred a live audience, which I was only too happy to provide.

"It was late April 1945 when I first came to Regensburg, Germany, to meet your father. Officers facing court-martial were traditionally held under house arrest pending trial, and your father was in the Regensburg Castle, where the Third Army was now permanently headquartered. This was a massive *Schloss* occupied for centuries by the Thurn und Taxis family, a palace as Americans think of palaces, occupying several city blocks. Its interior was somewhat baroque, with pillars of colored marble, Roman arches with lovely inlaid mosaics, and classical statuary. I walked nearly twenty minutes through the castle before getting to your father, who was restricted to a suite the size of this sitting room, perhaps larger, and full of marvelous antiques. In this splendor your father was going to remain jailed until the Army got around to shooting him. If you have a taste for irony, you can't do better than the United States military, let me tell you that." Leach smiled then in his way, a gesture restricted by age and disease, so that his jaw slid to the side.

"Your father was an impeccable man, nearly six feet as I recall, and the very image of an officer and a gentleman. He had a perfectly trimmed line mustache above his lip, like the film star William Powell, whom he resembled. From my initial sight of him, the notion that David Dubin had actually engaged in any willful disobedience of his orders, as was charged, seemed preposterous. But establishing that proved one of the most difficult propositions of my career."

"Because?"

"Because the man insisted on pleading guilty. Nothing unusual in that, of course. There are persons charged with crimes who understand they've done wrong. But your father would not explain anything beyond that. Any questions about the events leading up to his apparent decision to release Major Martin were met only with his declaration that it served no point to elaborate. He was very courteous about it, but absolutely adamant. It was a bit like representing Bartleby the Scrivener, except your father said solely 'I am guilty,' rather than 'I would prefer not to,' in response to any request for more information. I was forced to investigate the matter entirely without his cooperation. I learned quite a bit about your father's wartime experiences, but next to nothing about what had gone on between Martin and him.

"Eventually, I had an inspiration and suggested to your

father that if what had transpired was so difficult to speak about, he at least ought to make an effort to write it all down, while matters were fresh. If he chose not to show the resulting document to me, so be it, but in the event he changed his mind, I would have a convenient means of briefing myself. He did not warm to the proposal when I made it, but, of course, he had little to do with his days. He enjoyed reading—he soon had me bringing him novels by the armful—but I took it that he, like many other soldiers, had been an inveterate writer of letters and that that outlet was no longer very rewarding for him. As I recollect, he had disappointed his fiancée, and had then horrified his family with the news of his current predicament. Apparently, producing a written account of what had led to these charges provided an agreeable substitute, and after his initial reluctance, he took up the task with ardor. Whenever I visited him in quarters he was chopping away on a little Remington typewriting machine which sat on a Louis XIV desk, yet another priceless antique, that wobbled with his pounding. About a month along, during a visit, I pointed to the sheaf of pages stacked at his elbow. It was over an inch by now.

"'That's getting to be quite a magnum opus,' I said. 'Are you considering showing any of it to me?' I had been waiting for him to reveal the material in his own time, but with the hearing coming closer, I was concerned that I wouldn't be able to assimilate what clearly was turning into an imposing volume, especially if it opened up new avenues for investigation.

"'Some days I think yes, Colonel,' he said to me, 'and some days I think no.'

"'And why "no"?'

"'I don't believe it's going to help me.'

"'Because I'd think poorly of you? Or accept your judgment of your guilt? You know well enough, Dubin, that nothing would prevent me from making a defense for you.'

"'I do. Reading this, Colonel, might satisfy your curiosity. And it will prove I'm right to plead guilty. But it won't change the result. Or make things any easier for you. More the opposite.'

"In weaker moments, I sometimes considered sneaking in and stealing the pages, but he was right that it was his ship to sink. But I kept after him about letting me see it. Each time he seemed to give full consideration to my points, and then, after due reflection, rejected them. And so we went to trial. David tendered a plea of guilty at the start. The trial judge advocate, the prosecutor, had agreed to drop the most serious charge in exchange, but he still went on to prove his case, which was commonplace in serious court-martials. This, of course, was a decided contrast to the usual criminal matter, where a guilty plea avoids a trial, and I couldn't quite accommodate myself to the difference. I cross-examined with a fury, because none of the accounts were consistent in any way with a soldier who would willfully abandon his duties. Very often, I retired for the night, thinking how well I had done, only to recall that my client had already conceded the validity of the charges.

"The *Manual for Courts-Martial* at that time—and now, for all I know—gave the accused the right to make an uncross-examined statement to the panel, immediately preceding closing arguments. The night before the hearing came to an end, I made my last effort to get your father to share his written account, urging him to consider submitting his memoir, or portions of it, to the court. My heart leaped when he came to the proceedings the next morning with what I judged to be the manuscript under his arm in two portfolios, but he kept them to himself. He made a brief statement to the court, saying simply that in releasing Martin he had meant no harm to the United States, whose service remained the greatest honor of his life. Only when the evidence was closed did he turn the folders over to me. It was meant as a generosity on his part, I think, to repay me for my efforts on his behalf, so that I could accept the result with peace of mind. He told me to read it all, if that was what I liked, and when I was done to return it to him. He said forthrightly that he was then going to set fire to the whole thing.

"Even at that stage, I remained hopeful that I'd find something recorded there that I might use to reopen the case. The court was recessed on Sunday. I spent the whole day reading, morning to night, and finished only instants before I arrived for court at eight a.m. on Monday."

"And what did it say?" I was like a child listening to campfire tales, who wanted only to know what children always do: the end of the story.

Bear gave a dry laugh in response.

"Well, Stewart, there aren't many tales worth telling that can be boiled down to a sentence or two, are there?"

"But did you use it?"

"Most assuredly not."

"Because?"

"Because your father was right. He was a good lawyer. A very good lawyer. And his judgment was correct. If the court-martial members knew the whole tale, it would only have made matters worse. Possibly far worse."

"How so?"

"There were many complications," he said, "many concerns. As I say, I was fond of your father. That's not just prattle. But a trial lawyer learns to be cold-blooded about the facts. And I looked at this as trial lawyers do, the best case that could be made and the worst, and I realized that nothing good was going to come from revealing this to the court. Your father's cause, in fact, could have been gravely prejudiced."

"You're not being very specific, Justice. What was so bad?"

Bear Leach, not often short of words, took a second to fiddle with his vintage necktie, swinging like a pendant from the collar of his old shirt, which, these days, gapped a good two inches from his wattled neck.

"When I read your father's account, I realized he had been the beneficiary of an assumption that the trial judge advocate might well regard as ill founded, once the underlying facts were better known."

I tumbled my hand forward. "You're being delicate, Justice."

"Well, it requires delicacy, Stewart, no doubt of that. I'm speaking to a son about his father."

"So you warned me. I want to know."

Leach went through the extended effort it required to reposition the oxygen in his nose.

"Stewart, your father was charged with willfully suffering a prisoner to escape. The evidence, in sum, was that Robert Martin had last been seen by several troops of the 406th Armored Cavalry in your father's custody. Your father admitted he had allowed Martin to go, freed him from his manacles and leg irons and saw him out of the bivouac. The escape charge took it for granted that Martin had fled from there. But what your father had written suggested a far more disturbing possibility, one whose likelihood was enhanced, at least in my mind, by your father's rigorous silence."

"What possibility?"

"Now, Stewart, let me caution that this was merely a thought."

"Please, Bear. What possibility?"

Leach finally brought himself to a small nod.

"That your father," he said, "had murdered Robert Martin."

8. DAVID: TEEDLE'S SECRETS

By the time Biddy and I had returned to the 18th from the Comtesse de Lemolland's, we found no one in General Teedle's tent. The MP outside said that both orderlies were off duty, and Teedle was surveying battalions. With time, I wandered down to the enlisted men's area again. The bombing at the Comtesse's had revived my curiosity about Billy Bonner's remark that I was investigating the wrong man.

The skies had closed in once more, leaving no chance for further air traffic. Freed from blackout restrictions, the men had built fires and were enjoying themselves amid the usual barroom atmosphere. Somebody had run Armed Forces Radio through a loudspeaker. Harry James was on *Command Performance*, and I stopped to listen as he blew his way majestically through "Cherry." It suddenly hit me how much I missed music, for which I'd once felt a yearning as keen as hunger. These days, that longing was dampened under piles of law books and by the frantic concentration required for seven-day weeks in court.

Closing my eyes, for just one second, I caught the sure feel of Grace's waist beneath my hand while we were dancing.

I ran across Biddy unexpectedly. He was standing back with his camera, taking snaps of four men playing cards by lantern in a mess tent. They'd come inside to keep the invasion currency they were gambling with, French francs that had been printed in the U.S., from blowing off in the wind. Each man was straddling an empty cartridge case, while they used a crate emptied of bazooka rounds for a table.

"Jesus God almighty," one said. "Play a fucking card, won't you, Mickey. You're gonna be dead this time next month, and still wondering what you should have led for trump."

"Mortenson, don't talk like that."

"You think the Krauts are listenin?"

"No, but it's kind of like you're putting the evil eye on me."

"Oh, shut your damn swill hole, Krautbait, will you, and play a card."

"Don't be a sorehead, Witkins."

"Yeah, take a bite of this."

"Several soldiers in line in front of me for that pleasure."

"Fuckin Mickey still ain't recovered from striking out with that Frenchy. Only because half the platoon had some ass with her and she still wouldn't come across for him."

"Half the platoon are doggone liars. That girl was a nice girl. I just wanted to buy her a Coke."

"Coke ain't what you wanted her to swallow."

"Geez, Mort, what kind of pervert are you?"

"Listen, kiddo, these French girls use their mouths."

"Not on me. That's strictly perverted."

"Would youse guys shut the fuck up. It's gonna be fuckin reveille by the time this slowpoke plays a card."

I enjoyed Tony Eisley, but there was none of this raw camaraderie among JAG Department officers. Not that I shared in it here. Twenty-nine was old to most of these boys, and the presence of an officer was unsettling, even resented. My visits to the enlisted men's quarters reminded me of coming home to DuSable from Easton, when neighbors asked about the "college man" in a tone that was not altogether admiring. I was going to make money, they thought. I was going to move away from there, and them. In the enlisted ranks these days, there were a fair number of college boys because early this year Congress had put an end to the Army Specialized Training Program that had sent recruits to college classes full-time. On the other end, a few enlisted men from the premobilization Army had been commissioned. For the most part, though, you might as well have put up signs over the enlisted men's and the officers' sides of camp that said POOR and RICH. I had not figured out yet why the Army thought discipline or any other military purpose was advanced by these disparities. Yet I knew, much as I had in basic, that here I was among the real soldiers. The generals' names might be remembered by historians, but it was these men who would fight the true war.

Emerging from the tent, I wandered for some time before I caught sight of Billy Bonner around a fire with several other soldiers, each of them holding a dark bottle of wine. Bonner clearly regarded me as the law and stopped with his arm in midair, causing two or three of his buddies to turn away, until I said, "At ease."

We strolled off a few paces and I explained to Bonner that Teedle appeared to be gone.

"Oh, he'll be back. General likes his nights in his own tent." One of Bonner's smart-aleck looks accompanied the remark.

"Bonner, you don't seem to hold the General in high esteem."

"No, sir," he said. "He's as good a brass hat as this Army's got."

"But?"

Bonner shook his head and rolled his lips into his mouth, but I was persistent tonight. After quite a bit of cajoling, he finally motioned me farther from his companions.

"You didn't hear this here," said Bonner. He lifted the wine bottle again to stick his courage. "The bastard's a nelly."

"I'm sorry?"

"Teedle's a fruit, damn it."

"In what way?"

"In *that* way. Jesus, Lieutenant, don't you know what a queer is?"

"Good Lord, Bonner." I told him that if he wasn't potted, I'd have had the MPs take him off.

"Just remember you said that, Lieutenant. That's the reason no one does anything about him."

"About what?"

"I already told you. The man's a homo. You know, the General, he's got his billet right there in his tent. Makes like it's so he can work around the clock. But that's not why. Damn bugger gets himself rip-roaring — worse than normal — and then sends Frank for this enlisted man or that. Always some boy who looks like he rolled out from under a hay bale, too, strapping kids from the country, blond-haired. I'm dismissed when they get there. Now and then, I come back in the morning, those poor boys are still around. Some, God save them, they're sleeping like lambs. But there must have been a few to put up a fight, 'cause the General, he's had some damage on him, a shiner once that wouldn't go away for a week. I'll tell you, Lieutenant, I've been there, and two or three of those boys come out — there isn't a thing those Krauts could do to them that would be worse. His own damn CO. You can just see how bewildered these kids are. They don't know nothin anymore."

I wasn't sure I'd ever heard a more revolting story.

"Why, the bloody bastard," I said. "And haven't you brought this to the attention of an officer?"

"Well, I'm talking to you, Lieutenant. General Patton hasn't come by to chew the cud lately. But who's to say I didn't make this up? None of these boys care to discuss it, not the ones who like it, and especially not the ones who don't. I thought that the fellow who socked the General in the eye, soldier named Lang, I figured he might have a word to say, but his sergeant wouldn't even hear about it. Wasn't getting his private in a swearing match with that star, not about something like this, not in this man's Army. But maybe you fellas can loosen tongues. I don't know boo about Captain Martin," Bonner said. "But I'd say if Teedle wants a court-martial so bad, get started with him."

★★★

At 0730, when I came by, General Teedle was in his tent, speaking with his G-3 Major Michaels. As the operations officer, Michaels would not have had much to do lately, but today he had laid out several large battle maps on the General's desk. This was work, planning combat movements moment by moment, sequence by sequence, in which I'd excelled in infantry officer training at Fort Benning. At this stage, before the bullets flew, it was an exercise of pure intellect, a cross between chess and playing with tin soldiers, but the deadly reality of these decisions was manifest in the intensity of both men. Seeing them, it was obvious that new stores of fuel and ammo were finally on the way. The 18th's R & R was going to end shortly.

As I waited between the tent flaps, I found myself turning over Bonner's accusation while I scrutinized Teedle, with his cock-robin posture and his rosy drunkard's hue. The very notion of the General's conduct had wrenched me awake several times during the night. Eventually, I'd settled back to the practical problem of what to do. Because I liked Billy Bonner, I'd taken him at his word. But God only knew all the reasons he might be lying. Finally, near 4:00 in the morning, I resolved that I would simply wait for a private moment with Colonel Maples and pass the word to him. Sometimes the Army's long chain of command was not all bad. If a problem was big enough, you could hand it to somebody else.

Even so, I had no confidence that I wouldn't break into a visible sweat when Teedle was finally ready to see me. I was only grateful that Bonner was not yet on duty so I wasn't obliged to meet his eye.

"So how was Charming Bob?" Teedle asked me, when

I saluted before his desk. "Charming, eh? Did he entertain you like visiting royalty?"

"More or less."

"Have his girlfriend flirt with you, too? She's as clever as Martin, you know. She's batted her eyes at several folks I've sent down there. Anything that works, with those two." Bonner's remarks had been enough that my mind hadn't worked its way back very often to Gita Lodz. Nonetheless, Teedle had his intended effect of deflating me a bit, by revealing that I was not the first of his emissaries on whom Mademoiselle Lodz had settled her candid look and told them, one way or the other, how interesting they were. On the other hand, I was hardly surprised that a woman who'd raise her skirt for a debater's point wasn't shy around other men. For whatever reason, though, I felt some need to stick up for her.

"I wouldn't say she batted her eyes, General."

"That surprises me, Dubin, handsome young fellow like you." He gave me a wry look, chin lowered. Under the circumstances, Teedle's assessment nearly made me jump.

"I'm engaged, sir," I finally blurted.

"Good for you," he said, then asked what Martin had to say for himself. I had wondered how I was going to question General Teedle about Martin's claims—I had no right to demand answers from a general. But Teedle was far too voluble for that to prove a problem.

"That's horse hockey," he responded, when I explained that Martin said OSS had returned him from London late last month with directions to proceed into Germany. Showing Teedle Martin's papers stopped the General cold.

"I'll be a son of a bitch," he said, as he looked them

over. "First I heard of this, I admit. All I know is that two weeks ago OSS told me I was finally free to send him packing. I'd asked several times before. I can't tell you why they changed their minds."

"General, the only way to resolve this is to get written confirmation from OSS about whether they have or haven't given Martin other orders."

"Written?" Teedle frumped around in his chair. "Christ, so that's the game! What an operator this prick is. The Army has never been any match for a good operator, Dubin, and Martin's one of the best. OSS isn't going to put anything on paper about Special Operations and send it near the front. Soldiers are taken prisoner, Dubin, but spies are shot. Martin knows all that. Messages from OSS are coded radio transmissions and 'DAR.'" Destroy after reading. The General thought for a moment. "All right. I'll take care of this."

He made a note. It would have been better practice for Colonel Maples or me to communicate with OSS, rather than Teedle, the complainant, but the General didn't seem in any mood to hear about further legal technicalities.

"What else?" said Teedle. "Let's hear all Martin's folderol now, so I can deal with it at once. I'm sure he had a few choice words for me."

I described the bombing. Teedle, to his credit, asked first about casualties.

"I'd heard something about that," Teedle said then. "General Roy from 19th TAC sent a signal yesterday evening. Says he had a squadron that lost its bearings and might have dropped on our troops. He was damn apologetic. If I'd known it was Martin, I'd have sent back a thank-you note."

"Yes, sir, well, I was there, too."

Teedle shot me a look riddled with irony. I could not have understood much about being a general, this look said, if I expected him to be concerned about that. He called out to Frank to have his staff JAG expedite the Comtesse's damage claims.

"So now what mud was Martin slinging? That I have control of the Army Air Corps and arranged to bomb him?"

"He allowed how it was possible."

Teedle answered with a crude laugh. "There are plenty at my rank, Dubin, who wouldn't bother with a Rule Thirty-five investigation when they had an insubordinate officer. They'd send Martin out personally to scout a hilltop guarded by a full German company and never lose a wink. But if that was my idea, I wouldn't have bothered going to HQ, would I?"

"Quite right, sir."

"Oh, don't give me that 'quite right' horseshit. If you don't believe me, say so."

"I think you're making sense, General." I did, too, but Teedle seemed far too complex to expect all his actions to line up with reason. Having a minute to think, I didn't understand why General Roy had apologized to Teedle. The 26th Infantry, not Teedle's unit, was under Roy's bombs. Unless Roy forgot they had changed positions. Which was possible, too.

"Any other calumnies Martin spread to which you'd like a response?"

"May I speak freely, sir?"

"You just accused me of trying to bomb one of my officers. I think you're doing a pretty fair job of it already, Dubin, but help yourself."

I knew better than to debate Teedle by pointing out what had been said previously and by whom. He was amusing himself with the verbal fencing, knowing he had rank on his side. For all his bluster, though, I didn't have the sense that Teedle was baiting me to be cruel, so much as test me. He was an unusual man. Forthright. Opinionated. Harsh. It did not stretch credulity, watching his mobile face, the way he veered between imperiousness and collegiality, and the frankness with which he dared you to dislike him, to think that Teedle's peculiarities extended to far darker realms, as Bonner maintained. But not necessarily to cruelty. Cruelty was a part of human nature, I suspect he would say. We were all mean. But he was no meaner than most.

"Sir, he says your desire to get rid of him is all about the fact that you think he's a Communist."

When he heard that, Teedle put his feet up on his footlocker beside him, while he smiled and stroked his chin. It was the first time I'd seen him pause to reflect, much as Martin had shied away from the same subject. All the while, he tossed his head and the little bit of red steel wool on top of it, with what appeared to be admiration. He could never anticipate Martin. That seemed to be the meaning.

"Well, first of all, Dubin, I don't *think* Martin's a Communist. I *know* he's a Communist. He was a party member in Paris when he went off to fight in Spain. That's one of the reasons OSS wanted him in the first place. Because of his influence with the Communist unions.

"But put that aside. I'm not charging the man with disagreeable politics. I'm charging him with insubordination and endangering other troops. Even in Russia, despite calling me Comrade General, if I told him to get on his knees and kiss my ass, it's same as here, he'd have to do it."

Until that remark, I'd almost put Bonner out of my mind.

"Now whether his political background is the reason OSS agreed with me that it's time to send Martin elsewhere, nobody's said that, but frankly it's a pretty fair guess, and it makes sense. *Stars and Stripes* and the newsreels don't tell you everything our precious Russian allies are up to, Dubin. Do you know anything about what happened in Poland in August?"

I hadn't heard much and Teedle enjoyed filling me in. With the Soviet Army on their border, thousands of Polish patriots in Warsaw had risen up against the Nazis. Many on our side, Teedle said, believed that Stalin had encouraged the Home Army to think that the Soviets would storm into Poland and join them in expelling the Nazis. But the Russians held their ground. In fact, Stalin wouldn't even allow the Allies to assist the Poles by dropping arms and supplies. Instead the Home Army was crushed. Thousands were executed, shot on the spot or locked in buildings which were then set ablaze, while the Nazis leveled Warsaw's city center.

"And why, you might ask," said Teedle, "why would the Soviets do that? Why would the Russians not help the Polish resistance, since it could very well diminish their own losses in retaking Poland? Any ideas?"

Nothing came to me.

"Because, Dubin, a patriot who resists Nazi occupation is just as likely to resist the Soviets. Stalin got the Nazis to do his dirty work in Poland. At that point the Supreme Command, Roosevelt, Churchill, they all knew with absolute certainty what we are in for. Stalin might as well have let his air force put it in skywriting. They aim to conquer and occupy eastern Europe. They want to substitute Soviet rule for Nazi rule. And you're damn right, we don't need anybody operating in advance of our troops who might take the Soviets' side. Martin has many friends in the ranks of the Soviet Army. He fought for at least three different Soviet generals in Spain. And I'll wager a good sum that he'll give their orders a lot more heed than he's given mine. So yes, the fact that he's a Communist, that concerns me. It concerns me a good deal. Especially since he won't follow fucking orders. But if he weren't insubordinate, I wouldn't care if he went to sleep each night in red pajamas."

The General leaned forward with his fists on his desk. "Now, man to man, Dubin, tell me the truth, does that bother you? Because listening, I thought this asshole's complaint that I'm after him because of what he thinks about political matters—I had the impression that cut some ice with you."

I took my time, but I knew I wasn't going to back down from General Teedle. It wasn't required.

"General, there are a lot of Socialists who are loyal to the United States. And hate Stalin." Two of them happened to live in an apartment in Kindle County and had raised me. I didn't say that, as usual. Who I was and where I came from was my own secret. But Teedle was perspicacious enough to sense I spoke from experience.

"And are you one of them, Dubin? Is that what you're saying? Are you a loyal American Socialist?"

"I'm a loyal American, sir. I don't agree with the Socialists all the way. My problem with Socialists, sir, is that I've met quite a few who don't strike me as idealists. They hate the rich, because they envy them." Of course, socialism and how to react to it were topics of unending contemplation for me throughout high school and college. Easton had brought me into contact with many of the people my parents reviled, and Grace herself might belong in that category, even though she largely shunned her family's privileges. Between the two of us, one of our enduring discussions was about whether we were Socialists. There was so much that went wrong in the world that came down to being poor. But I never felt comfortable with the socialist morality of my parents, by which they were entitled to want more, while the rich were obliged to want less.

"Interesting, Dubin, very interesting." I had no doubt Teedle meant that. He flipped a pencil in the air and caught it. "You and I are polar opposites here. What I have against the Commies is what you seem to want more of. I dislike them, Dubin, because they're fools. *Fools.* Hapless idealists who want to believe that humans are inclined to share and think first about others, when that's never going to be the case. Never.

"And because they don't see us as we are, Dubin, don't see how brutal and selfish we are, because of that, Dubin, they think we can do without God. That's why I truly dislike them. Because they believe mankind can be good without His assistance. And once we go down that road, Dubin, we're lost. Utterly lost. Because we need God, Dubin. Every man out here needs God. And not to save his soul or keep him safe, Dubin, none of that guff. Do you know why we need God, why we must have Him, Dubin? Do you?"

"No, sir," I said. I was no surer of God than of social-ism, but it was one of those moments when Teedle was on the boil again, full of a locomotive fury that forbade me to get in his way.

"Well, I'll tell you, Dubin. Why we need God. Why I need God. To forgive us," he said then, and with the words his anger almost instantly subsided to sadness. His tiny eyes were liquid and morose, and any doubts I'd had about Bonner vanished. "Because when this is over, this war, that's what we'll need, all of us who have done what war requires and, worse, what war permits, that's what we'll need, in order to be able to live the rest of our lives."

Teedle went for his canteen for the first time since I'd been there. When he lowered it, he dragged the back of his hand along his lips like a tough in a beer hall, but his little birdie eyes rimmed in pink remained on me, full of his sorry knowledge of the excesses of war and the bleak mystery of a God who, before forgiving, allowed those things to occur in the first place.

9. FURTHER ORDERS

In the two weeks following our return to Nancy, it became clear that the pace of the war was again quickening. Stores of gasoline had finally been received. Other field supplies — tents, blankets, jackets, two-burner stoves — remained short, but the General staff had swapped ten thousand gallons of no. 10 motor oil with the Seventh Army for an equal amount of diesel fuel, and it was a good bet that Patton's push into Germany would start whenever it arrived.

Yet even with the changed atmosphere, life in Nancy still seemed as relaxed as a summer resort, compared to my three days near the front. As Colonel Maples had anticipated, I had relished the excitement, and even felt some awkward satisfaction about surviving a bombing, never mind that it had been inflicted by our own forces. On the whole, my encounters with Teedle and Martin and Gita Lodz were probably the first moments since I had enlisted that fulfilled some of my hopes.

On November 3 an orderly appeared in court to tell me

that Colonel Maples wanted me when we finished for the day. As soon as Klike promised to dispense with justice, I went upstairs, where the Colonel showed me documents that had been pouched from the 18th Armored Division. Teedle had ordered me to deliver them to Robert Martin.

HEADQUARTERS, 18TH ARMORED DIVISION

APO 403, U.S. ARMY

E X T R A C T

1. Major Robert P. Martin, 04264192, is relieved of duty with this Division at once and assigned to Central Base Station, London, England. WP w/o delay reporting upon arrival to CO thereat for duty. Govt. T is authorized. EDCMR: 1 November 1944 BY ORDER OF BRIGADIER GENERAL TEEDLE

Official:

James Camello

Major AC

Ass't Adjutant

cc:

Colonel Bryant Winters

U.S. Army

68 Brook Street

London

Except for the designation of a carbon copy to Colonel Winters, who I inferred was Martin's OSS commander, the order didn't differ noticeably from prior ones I'd seen. Attached, however, were travel documents identical to those Gita had produced on my visit to the Comtesse's. They, too, were issued by Central Base in London and directed Martin to return to England forthwith, even enclosing $20 in Army scrip for a per diem. Teedle had answered Martin in kind. Since OSS would not issue direct written orders to an operative, the travel authorization was the best proof that its commanders backed Teedle.

"Well, that explains it," Colonel Maples said, once I'd reminded him that I'd needed something from OSS to deal with Martin's claims that he had other orders. "When he rang, General Teedle passed a comment about you. I think he finds you a bit precise for his taste."

"I thought that's what lawyers are, Colonel. Precise."

"Teedle regards it as an impediment." Seated behind a large oak desk as substantial as a half-track, Maples was smiling, touching his mustache as he often did for comfort. "Not all that different, by the way, from my clients in private practice, who gritted their teeth before talking to their lawyer. For some it was akin to the discomfort of going off to Sunday prayers."

"I'm not trying to be difficult, Colonel, but when I think this over I still can't make top or bottom of it. Why would a decorated officer suddenly defy his commanders? The girl is rather emphatic that her romance with Martin is over."

"Perhaps Martin has had enough of war. He wouldn't be the first. But ours is not to reason why, David. I told you, Rollie Teedle is not an enemy you need. Get out there and finish this off. Teedle wants Martin packing and on to London before you leave."

"Yes, sir." Maples' renewed warning about Teedle banished any lingering thought of reporting Billy Bonner's accusations. I'd hesitated when I'd briefed the Colonel on my return, realizing once I was in his office that Maples would regard the charge as patent lunacy and be displeased with me for pulling the pin on this kind of hand grenade, then lobbing it on his desk. The truth was that in the presence of the Colonel, a person of gentle but unrelenting propriety, I had no idea even how to relate what Bonner had said.

With Teedle's order in hand, Biddy and I had no trouble securing a jeep and left not long after sunrise on November 4, headed again toward Bezange-la-Petite. There was now heavy traffic on the small roads with lines of trucks and armor moving out. We made slow progress and finally came to a complete halt behind a tank battalion stalled on its way north. The 761st was all colored, except for some of the officers. They were the first Negroes I had seen in combat, and they looked as apprehensive as everybody else did making the journey to the front.

After half an hour, I took the jeep and went to see about the holdup, which proved to be three convoys crossing paths. Two MPs had arrived on motorcycles and stood at the crossroads directing traffic, just like cops at the busy hours on the streets of Center City back home.

When I returned, Biddy and a colored soldier were having words. Biddy was shaking a finger and telling the soldier, another sergeant, not to talk to him. The fellow threw a hand in Biddy's direction and walked away as I came up.

"What was that about?"

"Just some boy from Georgia causing a ruckus. Said

he was from that town where I growed up." Biddy was still following the man with his eyes.

"Was he?"

"Mighta been. But I didn't need no strolls down memory lane, Lieutenant." The brooding air that overtook Biddy when he was dealing with the colored was evident. Whatever my reluctance about pulling rank, or disturbing our increasing amity, I felt I had no choice about speaking up.

"A colored man's as good as anybody else, Gideon." This was my parents' perpetual lesson. Once the goyim got done with the Negroes, we all knew who'd be next. "I had several colored friends in high school, men I played music with and studied with, as fine and smart as anyone I know. I realize you come from Georgia, Biddy. I can't change the way you think, but I don't want to see it or hear it. Clear?"

Gideon's green eyes remained on me for some time, but he seemed more startled than defiant.

"Yes, sir," he said eventually.

Ahead, the tanks were finally moving.

When we pulled into the courtyard in front of the little castle, Gita Lodz was there, just stepping out of the Comtesse's charcoal-burning Citroën, where Antonio was at the wheel. She was dressed like a city lady, in a plaid skirt, with her wavy bronze hair pulled straight in a bun.

"Doo-bean!" she cried, and greeted me in French. "So you return." She approached beaming and kissed me on each cheek. We were already old friends. I remarked that she did not appear to be dressed for combat. "For spying," she answered. "We have been to look in on some people in Strasbourg. Martin will need them soon. Antonio has fetched us from the train."

Strasbourg was nearly seventy miles away, far behind the German lines.

"My Lord! You just went?"

"*Pourquoi pas?* Our documents say we are from Arracourt, going to see Robert's *grandmère* who is near death. The Nazis are oxen. A snake with proper papers could board the train. This has been our life for years, Dubin."

Behind her, the Comtesse's house was under repair in the wake of the bombing. Heavy tarpaulins hung over many of the broken windows, although in the few instances where the shutters remained they had simply been closed. Either way, it would make for a cold winter. There had been talk after the blast that by December the Comtesse would have to abandon the house for the servants' quarters across the courtyard, which were undamaged.

On the other side of the vehicle, Martin had arisen. Until now, I had been too intent on Gita to notice. He was dressed in a suit and a fedora, looking proper and bourgeois. I saluted, which drew a faint smile, as he wandered up with far less enthusiasm than Gita had shown.

"Back so soon, Dubin?"

I reminded him of my promise to return his documents. "And I've brought you a few new ones."

He read for a while, nodding. "Very good," he said. He handed the orders back, with a bright grin. "I guess I've won this round."

"Sir?"

"Proves the point, doesn't it? Teedle has given up his claim to be my commanding officer. I'm under OSS direction. And London has ordered me to proceed here. That's my duty. All cleared up, I'd say."

"Major, these documents require you to travel to London at once."

"Yes, and I've done so and London sent me back. You're holding the proof of that in your other hand. Am I to be court-martialed because I have already carried out my orders?"

Martin gave another glowing smile, as if this weren't flimflam. On the other hand, there wasn't much here to prove him wrong. Nothing showed OSS's involvement or that some obliging paymaster hadn't simply sent the travel papers at Teedle's request, a prospect I hadn't considered until now.

"Major, I mean no disrespect, but even if there's a mistake, had you asked OSS to contact Third Army G-1 or Colonel Maples, this could have been resolved instantly."

"Well, it *is* a mistake, Dubin, quite clearly, because I received the go-ahead by radio yesterday on an operation that's been planned for months. And inasmuch as the one thing Teedle and I now agree upon is that I take my commands from OSS, I will carry out those orders. I'll deal with your papers straightaway when we return."

I asked the nature of this new operation, but Martin gave a strict shake of his head.

"I'm hardly at liberty to discuss that, Dubin. The other members of Stemwinder don't even have the details yet. We work strictly on a need-to-know basis. Capture is always a risk in this line of work, Dubin. And what difference would that make?"

"I'm just looking for a way to confirm your position, Major."

Standing by and listening, Gita suddenly interjected, "*Laisse-le venir.*"

Martin drew back. What Gita had said was, Let him come.

"*Très dangereux, non?*" he responded.

"*Demande-lui.*" Ask him. Martin reflected, then took on a look of revelation.

"My God, she's right. What a marvel you are, Gita, you never cease to amaze." He swung an arm around her waist and planted a paternal kiss atop her head. "You want evidence of my orders from OSS? Come watch me follow them. You say I get to present any proof I wish to your investigation, don't I?"

"Yes, sir." Those were surely the rules.

"Then this is it. Patton's going to be on the move again momentarily, and this operation is an essential prelude. You're more than welcome to observe, Lieutenant, to see once and for all that I'm under OSS direction and not sitting out here on Roman holiday, or whatever else it is that Teedle imagines. It will put an end to all questions. If you choose not to come, there's no more I can do."

I had no idea, of course, what I was being asked to say yes to. Except that I'd heard the word 'dangerous.' It was a dare, actually, the man of action's challenge to the deskbound bureaucrat, and Martin was probably betting I would never accept. But his logic was impeccable. If I refused, I'd have denied him the opportunity to offer the only evidence he had. In fact, reading the rules, I might even have been derelict. I told him I would have to consult Maples.

"As you wish. But we start this afternoon, Dubin. You'll have to be there and back before three."

That was impossible, especially with the movements on the roadways that could sidetrack us for hours. Martin, still with his hand on Gita's back, turned away, and she gave me a quick private frown before heading off beside him. I was being just the man of small points she'd ridiculed last week. Worse, I felt like a coward.

"I'll go," I told Martin.

Martin didn't flinch when he revolved my way, even though I'd probably called his bluff.

"Bravo, Dubin. I'll brief you shortly. Glad to have you," he said, and continued toward the house with his arm still around Gita's waist.

I found Bidwell with the Gypsy, Antonio, and several of the farmworkers, showing off the photos he had taken during our last visit. They were little two-by-twos and he was complaining about the supplies he'd had to work with.

"Can't get no bigger film. Damn lucky for what I have. Wanted my folks to send some six-twenty but they-all is hoarding silver on the home front."

Small or not, the images were striking. After the bombing, Biddy had shot through a broken window into the darkness of the house. Within, you could detect the form of a tall chifforobe, while the glass reflected uprooted trees outside leaned together like a tepee and, farther in the background, Antonio, with his long hair and dark intense eyes aimed right at the camera. Biddy had taken another photo inside the bomb crater looking up at two of the dead animals. There were also several pictures he'd snapped on our way here last time of haystacks being gathered in the open fields.

"Put me in mind of those paintings in the Museum of Art," he said. "You seen them?" I had. Famous Impressionist works in vivid hues, but the artist's name eluded me. "Same idea," Biddy said, "but in black and white. You think that's okay?"

They were beautiful photos. I asked what could be wrong.

"I don't know," he said. "Seems like if you make a picture you oughta rightly be thinkin about life, not other pictures. But I got those paintings in my head."

"Did you study art, Biddy?"

"Aw, hell, Lieutenant, my daddy, he'd probably just keeled over dead if I'd'a tole him I was going to art school. I just liked them paintings, seein what happened to our world when it went flat. I was over there whenever I could. A lot of that, the stuff folks are doin these days especially, they really talk to me, you know?"

My mother was always hauling me down to the museum, hoping something would rub off, but the truth was I couldn't make heads or tails of the works that excited Biddy.

"I think I'm too practical-minded for modern art, Gideon. Art and opera. My mother loves that, too. But I like your photographs."

He shook his head. "You see things through that lens, Lieutenant, you can't catch with your eye. And I like how I feel when I'm lookin, with that contraption between me and everything else. Here in this mess and able to stand back like that, I'm a million miles away sometimes." He looked at me. "I don't know what the hell I'm talkin about, you know."

"You're making plenty of sense, Biddy. Don't sell yourself short. Maybe you should think about art school."

"Maybe I should. We-all gotta live through this first."

That was the reminder I needed. I told him about my conversation with Martin. As his expression darkened, I could see he was resisting the impulse to stab me.

"No disrespect, Lieutenant, but what the heck is it you call yourself doin?"

I tried to explain the logic of the rules that required me to follow where Martin led.

"This here," said Biddy, "is how the law sure enough don't make sense. Figures Martin'd use it against you. Ain't no tellin what kinda trouble a huckster like that is gonna get us into, Lieutenant."

"This is my frolic and detour, Biddy. You're not required."

"Hell, I'm not. You think they send an MP sergeant out here with you, Lieutenant, just to drive? Ain't no way I can let you go do this whatever on your lonesome. Only I'd think a growed man would have the sense to ask what he was doin 'fore he said yes." Biddy had never been this direct with me, but after the scolding I'd given him on the way here, he apparently felt inclined to speak his mind. And there was no question of his loyalty. Still shaking his head, he walked beside me toward the little castle to see what was in store for us.

By 3:30, we had moved out. In a time of short provisions, Martin was remarkably well supplied. He may have been the scourge of General Teedle, but in these parts he was widely respected, and the Quartermaster with the Yankee Division had given the Major whatever he needed for this venture more than a month ago. Biddy and I had our choice of combat and cargo packs, cartridge belts and M1A1 carbines. I hadn't fired a weapon since training camp, and I spent some time handling the rifle to bring back the feel of it. We had come with our own raincoats, which we folded behind us over our belts, following the example of the rest of our party, which consisted of Gita, Martin, Antonio, and two locals, Christian and Henri. They were frumpy-looking farmers, a father and son, both shaped like figs. They trudged along in silence at Martin's side, acting as guides, with American rifles over their shoulders. Beside me, Gita was in farm overalls, but wore a surplus Army helmet with the liner tightened to the maximum so it fit her.

"Do you like battle, Mademoiselle Lodz?"

"No one should like battle, Dubin. It is much too frightening. But Martin's style is most successful when not a gun is fired. You will see."

"But it remains strange to me to think of a woman in combat."

She laughed, but not in good humor. "*Ça, c'est le comble!*" That's the last straw. "Men think only they can fight. With guns? With planes? With artillery. Who is not strong enough to pull a trigger, Dubin, or throw a grenade?"

"Yes, but a man who does not fight is called a coward. No one expects this of you. Quite the contrary. Do you think fighting is as much in a woman's nature as a man's?"

"Knowing what is right is in the nature of everyone. I

allow, Dubin, that I do not enjoy killing. But many men feel as I do, and fight nonetheless."

Martin had turned back to us with a finger to his lips, inasmuch as we were leaving the Comtesse's lands. I still had little idea where we were headed. Martin would brief us only when we'd made camp for the night. For the time being, he wanted to use the weakening daylight to move ahead. We proceeded due north, across adjoining farms. Knowing the fence lines and the old paths, Henri led us along at a good pace. The rains held off while we hiked, but the ground everywhere was soft and in the lowlands we splashed through standing water, soaking my wool trousers and the socks inside my shoepacs.

As darkness encroached, I was certain we were behind Nazi lines. Martin, Biddy, and I were in uniform and stood at least a chance, if captured, of being taken prisoner, rather than executed. The Frenchmen with us were all but certain to be shot on the spot. But there was no sign of Germans. In these parts, the locals were firmly committed to the Free French, and Martin regarded his intelligence on enemy positions as virtually faultless. Nonetheless, whenever possible, we remained on the other side of the shallow hills, so we were not visible from the road, and ducked into the trees if we were near a wooded draw. When there was no choice but to cross an open field, we ambled along in pairs, as if we were hikers.

At one point, as we stopped briefly to refill our canteens in a spring, Martin came back to check on me. Gita and Antonio were on lookout at the perimeter, apparently enough security for a quiet conversation.

"Holding up?"

I was hardly laboring with a full pack. I had a bedroll,

a canteen, a bayonet, and ammunition, but I hadn't been out on maneuvers since basic and Martin was right to suspect I was tired. I told him I was fine.

"Nothing like this in the past, I assume?" he asked.

"I was trained as an infantry officer, but aside from exercises, no."

"You'll have an exciting time. You'll be thanking Gita for suggesting this." He waited. "She seems to have taken a shine to you."

"Has she? I'm honored. She is very charming." Then as the only avenue to approach the lingering question, I added, "You have a charming woman."

"Oh, yes," he said, "very charming. Only I doubt that Gita would agree."

"That she's charming?"

"That she is my woman. Candidly, I wonder if Gita would ever choose but one man. Besides," he said, "she is much too young for me." He had raised his eyes to her up on the hill, where the wind tossed around the kinks of dark gold hair that escaped her helmet. "I have only one thing I want for her, really. Most of all, Dubin, I would like to see her safe. That would be my last wish. Were I permitted one. I owe her that." Catching Martin's eye as we were looking her way, Gita knotted her small face in an open frown.

"There, you see. She is always displeased with me." His glance fell to the ground. "Does she speak ill of me?"

I didn't understand the crosscurrents here, only that they were treacherous.

"On the contrary," I answered. "She is your admirer."

"Surely not always. She calls me a liar to my face."

"Does she?" I felt certain that Martin knew exactly

what Gita had said to me the last time I was here. "It is the nature of this life, Dubin. Somewhere, buried in the recesses of memory, is the person I was before I was Robert Martin." He pronounced his full name as if it were French: Ro-*bear* Mar-*tan*. "But I was trained to tell every tale but his. And it suits me well, Dubin. No soul in war is the same as she or he was before. You'll learn that soon enough."

He took a tiny humpbacked metal cricket from his pocket and gave its twanging steel tongue two clicks, calling an end to our respite. Scampering down from the prominence, Gita fell in at the head of our column but shortly worked her way back to me, as we were weaving through a small woods. She had heard her name and wanted to know what Martin had said. I tried to satisfy her with the most neutral remark I remembered.

"He told me he hopes you are safe. When the war ends."

"He lies. As always. That is not what he hopes. He would much prefer we die side by side in battle. *Tellement romantique.*"

Long ago I'd learned not to be the messenger in couples' disagreements, a lesson originally taken from childhood. The more I heard from both Gita and Martin, the less sure I was of the dimensions of their relationship. Nor did it seem that it was very clear to either of them. I was better off with another subject and asked her about Bettjer, the radioman, whose absence I had noticed.

"Peter? Peter is no good anymore. For some, bravery is like blood. There is only so much in your body. He was very courageous, very bold, but with a month to sit and think about all he has survived, every fear he did not feel before has rolled down on him like a boulder off a mountain. He will drink three bottles of cognac in the day we are gone. *Ainsi va la guerre*," she added in a tragic tone. So goes war.

This discussion of Bettjer and his anxieties somehow became a gateway to my own worries. I had felt my nervousness growing as we tromped along. Now, with the description of Bettjer as unmanned by fear, I was attacked full-on by shrieking doubts. Apparently, I did a poor job of concealing them.

"This is bad talk," said Gita. "I should have told you something else. Martin will watch out for you. He watches for all of us. And there is no need for you to be in the midst of things when the operation starts."

"If I can be helpful, I would like to take part. I'd feel as if I were a child, merely watching from safety."

"That is for Martin to say. But if so, you will do well, Dubin. You are a man of principles, no? Principles are the main ingredient of courage. A man with principles can get the better of fear."

"I thought you doubted the existence of principles."

"*Touché*," she answered, and gave me a fleet impish smile. "I do not doubt the power of principles, Dubin. I say only that it is an illusion that they are the first thing in life. It is an illusion we all crave — better principles than the abyss — but an illusion nevertheless. Therefore, one must be careful about what he deems issues of principle. I despise petty principles, obstinate principles that declare right and wrong on matters of little actual consequence. But there are large principles, grand principles most men share, Dubin, and you have them, as well." She showed a tidy smile, and actually patted my hand in reassurance.

Ahead, Martin had halted at the edge of another open field. He clicked the cricket again as a signal for silence, and Gita dispensed a quick wave before moving toward her assigned place at the head of the line. Antonio fell in behind me. We both watched her dash away, her legs tossed outward with unexpected girlishness, as she drew abreast of Martin. She was extraordinary. No doubt about that.

"What is she to him?" I asked Antonio suddenly.

He gave a rattling laugh and shook his long hair, as if I had asked an eternal question.

"I think she is his glory," he answered. "I think when he looks at her he remembers what he once believed."

10. LA SALINE ROYALE

November 5, 1944

Dearest Grace—

Tomorrow I will see my first action. It is too complicated to explain why (and the censors would black it out anyway). But please focus on the word "see." I am going only as an observer, for one day, and by the time you receive this, I will be back and safe and will have written you to say so. I'll mail both letters together, so you never have occasion for concern. I feel as I have always imagined I would in this circumstance, as if my skin might not contain me, and thus I doubt I'll sleep. But for better or worse, I remain eager.

We start very early in the morning, so I will close now. Just to let you know how much I love you and am always thinking of you.

David

★ ★ ★

November 7, 1944

Dear Grace—
   Back at HQ and safe. I am much too
disappointed in myself to say more. Will write
further later in the week.

David

La Saline Royale, the royal saltworks, had been opened in 1779 to put an end to fractious competition between bishops and lords for control of what was then a precious commodity. The King declared himself the owner of all the salt in France and auctioned it to European merchants from open-air barns here in Marsal, where the prized granules were mined.

After invading France, the Nazis had commandeered the saltworks, whose long radiating shafts made it ideal as a munitions dump, eventually becoming the largest in the Lorraine. The works had been built like a fortress, surrounded by both twenty-foot walls of limestone and brick, meant to repel thieves, and the river Seille, which formed a virtual moat at the northern border. With the armaments, mostly large-caliber artillery shells, stored more than six hundred feet under the earth, they were invulnerable to air attack, and a German garrison was stationed in the former mine offices as further protection.

Martin and his OG had been dispatched to this vicinity in early September to destroy the dump, but the operation had been put on hold when the pace of combat slackened. Now, Martin said, London wanted the mission completed. The Germans had fortified their stores in the interval, making La Saline Royale an even more inviting target.

We were gathered probably a mile from the saltworks, inside a small shepherd's hut in the field of a farmer who was a member of a local resisters' unit, or *réseau*. Sitting on the dirt floor, the six of us listened as Martin illustrated the operation's plan beside a Coleman lantern. From his field jacket, Martin had removed a pack of playing cards, peeling a backing off of each one and laying them out in rows, until they formed a map of the saltworks and the surrounding area. Biddy and I grinned at each other. The OSS's ingenuity was equal to its legend.

There were two breaches, Martin said, in the saltworks' fortifications. The only formal approach was from the north to the massive iron front gates, behind which the German troops waited. On the west, the walls parted a few meters where a railroad siding ran down into the mine. Laid for the shipment of salt, the tracks continued to be used to deliver and remove armaments, and emerged on an angled trestle over the Seille, meeting the railhead on the western bank.

A ground assault against the railroad gate also appeared unpromising. Fording the Seille without bridge work was nigh impossible. 'Seille' means 'pail,' the name drawn from the depth of the narrow gray river below its steep banks. Even in a season of record floods, the waters remained a good ten feet under the stone retaining walls, which were overgrown with moss and creepers. Worse, where the tracks passed through the mine wall, crews manned two MG42 high-caliber machine guns. Nonetheless, Martin laid his pencil tip there on the map and said this opening would be the point of attack for our party of seven.

"*Merde*," said Henri.

"*Tu perds la tête*," said Christian to Martin jovially. You've lost your mind.

"There is a way," said Martin, and in the sallow lantern light, looked about the circle like a schoolmarm to see if anyone who did not know the plan could guess.

"By train," I answered.

"Bravo, Dubin."

My clue was Martin's background. Members of his former union, the International Transport Workers, were so thoroughly committed to resistance that before D-Day the Germans had been required to take over the French railroads, importing nearly 50,000 rail men from Germany. As the Allies advanced, however, most of these civilian crews had been shipped home, or had simply deserted. While the rail yards remained heavily patrolled, the Nazis had had no choice but again to let Frenchmen run the trains in the corner of France the Germans controlled.

This evening, mechanics at the yard in Dieuze, a few miles farther east, would conclude that the arriving locomotive on a Nazi supply train needed repairs. It would be steered toward the mechanical facility at the distant side of the yard, and would slowly roll right through. A mile farther on, Antonio would board, replacing the engineer and the rest of the crew, and steam off toward the dump. In the morning, after the operation, the local *réseau* would tie up the crew members, leaving them in the bushes along the right-of-way, where, upon discovery, they would claim to have been set upon by dozens of saboteurs many hours before.

Martin expected no trouble with any of that. If there were to be problems, they were more likely to come at La Saline Royale. If the Germans here realized what was happening, they would blow or blockade the trestle leading to the mine, so stealth was essential. There were two guards at a switching point, set up roughly a mile and a half from where we were now, to keep unauthorized traffic off the spur. They had to be quietly subdued. After that, a distraction on the other side of the works would obscure the sounds of the approaching locomotive. That was Henri and Christian's task.

"Ever seen one of these?" Around the circle Martin handed an object about the size of an apple, Army green, with yellow stenciling that said T13. From the ring on top, I could tell it was a hand grenade, but twice as big as any other I'd seen.

"It's called a Beano. I have damn few left, too. Like a grenade but with one great advantage. Blows on impact. No one kicks this out of the way or throws it in the river. And if you have to hold on to it after you pull the ring, you can. I wouldn't walk around with it in my pocket, mind you, but I've carried one along for several minutes."

The Beano—actually two of them—were for Christian and Henri. We would all initially approach from the south, ascending the hills behind the saltworks, with Christian and Henri then fanning off toward the front gates. They had grenade-launcher attachments for their M1s, which, even firing something the size of the Beano, would have a range of one hundred yards. Their target was the gasoline tanks that serviced the garrison. If the fuel ignited, all troops would rush out there to extinguish the flames burning perilously close to the wooden entrance to the shafts and the tons of munitions below. But even if the father and son missed, the Germans could be expected to rouse off-duty troops to begin combing the overlooking hills. In the meantime, the locomotive would speed across the trestle, crash the railroad crossing gate, and hurtle down into the mine. There was a chance that the impact of the locomotive with the train cars loaded with shells might detonate them, but rather than count on that, Martin was packing a satchel charge whose fuse he would light before jumping from the train.

The explosion inside the mine would act more or less like a pipe bomb, with the shafts channeling the huge force of the blast from either end. If we made it back over and down the hill from which we'd come, we would escape unharmed. Martin didn't address his own safety, but I couldn't see how he'd get away, since he had to remain on the locomotive to steer it over the trestle. As for Biddy and me, Martin planned for us to wait on the hillside. We would have a clear view of his activities, but would need only a few seconds to get back over the top and down.

"But be alert for Krauts," Martin told us. "They may be out by then, looking for the saboteurs who fired the grenades."

We would start again at 5:00 a.m. That left about six hours to sleep, but I was much too excited to try.

Ready to turn in, Gita came to check on me. She remained concerned that she had told me too much with her stories about Bettjer.

"I am fine," I told her. "I am sure that before I sleep, I will think of those I have left at home and feel bad about that, as soldiers do. But I am pleased finally to know a little of what soldiers feel."

"I have that luck," she said. "No home." She dug a stick into the ground and pondered it. "Robert does not like talk of home," she said quietly. "He says it is not good for soldiers. But it would be unnatural to forget, no?"

"Of course," I said.

She did not look up, but smiled wistfully as she turned over clods.

"Did I tell you, Dubin, that my mother was killed for harboring Jews?"

"Certainly not. You have not mentioned she was a hero."

"No," Gita answered decisively. "She was no heroine. She did it for money. She hated the Nazis, naturally. She worried constantly that they would send me to Germany to be made German as had been done with dozens of the Polish children in my town. But a man, Szymon Goldstein, came to her when the Nazis began rounding up the Jews and deporting them to Lublin. Goldstein ran a tannery and had been rich before the war. And was once my mother's lover, as well. Their affair had ended badly, as my mother's affairs tended to do. They were gruff with each other, but she was the only Pole he knew who might be daring enough to take his money. It was a huge sum. And even so, Dubin, I was very much against this. But my mother always refused to do what other people considered wise.

"So in the middle of the night, Goldstein and his wife and his four children stole into our tiny house and lived in our little root cellar. For the month it lasted, it made for a strange household — my mother under the same roof with Madame Goldstein, who despised her, these six people whose noises we always heard from below like mice in the walls. Then they were betrayed. The Nazis found another Jew who had been hiding in the woods. To save himself, he told them about Goldstein. The SS came into the house and found my mother and all the Goldsteins and shot them. I was out trying to find coal that day. When I came back the bodies were piled in front of the door, as a warning to anyone who might do the same.

"I have always thought, if only I had come back in time I could have saved them. But I have no idea how. Naturally enough, people say I am lucky not to have died with them, yet how can one remember such a thing with any feeling of good fortune?" She had been driving the stick into the ground all the time she told this story. "So what do you think, Dubin?"

"I think it is a terrible story. It makes me very sad for you."

"Yes." She said nothing for a moment, then finally cast her stick aside. "So tonight we both think of home before we are soldiers." She grasped my hand for a second, before moving off to her bedroll.

I was grateful to hear Gita's story, a powerful reminder of why we were fighting, but it had not brought me any closer to sleep. Instead, I watched Martin pack the satchel charges. He had a bottle of brandy, which he offered to me, and I took a long pull in the hope that it would make me weary. Martin was clearly going to finish off the rest himself. That did not strike me as wise, but his hands were still nimble assembling the charge. It was essentially dynamite, sixteen square blocks of TNT fixed in sawdust, each weighing more than a pound. Martin would strap them around a blasting cap, but first he had to prepare the fuse. He stood outside, lighting and relighting varying lengths, recording how fast they were consumed. He planned to hang the satchel charges in the windows of the locomotive cab, so that the explosions had the maximum effect, but timing was essential. If the charges went too quickly, they'd drop the locomotive into the Seille; too late and the Germans might have time to extinguish the flame. I held the ends of the lines for him, watching the flame sparkle toward me. Nine feet, six inches, is what he ultimately figured. It would give him about four minutes to escape. When he was done, at last, he carefully slid the charges into a green canvas sack.

"Time to turn in," he told me. He clapped me on the shoulder. "Exciting, eh?"

"Major," I said, "I'd like to do more than watch."

"You're here as an observer, Dubin."

"Frankly, sir, if something goes wrong, I don't think the Germans will care why we're here. We might as well take part."

"We'll see. Sleep now." He smiled. "You can carry the satchel in the morning. Damn heavy, too."

Biddy had brought a pup tent for the two of us. There was a strange domestic order in that. I thought of myself as tidy, but Bidwell was downright precise: boots, weapon, pack, in perfect rank. As a boy who'd grown up sleeping with my brother in the kitchen of my parents' small apartment, I sometimes thought I'd feel more at home in the closeness of enlisted quarters. Crossing the ocean, while the officers lived in style in our staterooms, the enlisted men below slept in shifts on rows of canvas bunks suspended between the posts every two feet like shelving. Their deck was tight as a hive, which made the perpetual good cheer of the troops there more remarkable — and enviable.

I crept in now and found paper and a pencil in my field

jacket and stood outside to write quick letters to Grace and my parents by firelight. There was almost no chance the mail would be delivered if something went wrong, but it was a ritual I felt obliged to carry out. With that done, I crawled into the tent. Quiet as I'd been, I'd apparently roused Bidwell.

"Permission to speak, sir?" Biddy rarely invoked these formalities. "Lieutenant," he said, "you got me wrong today. And it's been weighin on my mind. About that Negro soldier I didn't talk to? I don't feel no better than him, Lieutenant. Not one bit. He knew my momma and daddy and there was some ruction at home I didn't want to hear tell about. But it wasn't 'cause I looked down at him for being colored. I swear."

There'd been too many incidents, but this was hardly the time for a debating society.

"I'm glad to hear that, Biddy."

"Yes, sir."

We said no more then.

11. ACTION

I awoke from a dream of music. Biddy was up already, organizing his pack, and we took down the tent together.

"I dreamed I was playing the clarinet, Biddy."

"Was that your thing, that old licorice stick?"

"It was. Not much of an embouchure left now. I thought I was Benny Goodman, Gideon. I just couldn't find anybody to agree."

He laughed and we talked about music. I asked which musicians he liked.

"Duke," he said. "Pretty niftic."

"I'll say."

"Did you have a group, Lieutenant?"

Here in the hills of Lorraine, about to take my first intentional risks since going to war, I felt the embrace of the summer nights when we played on Mo Freeman's front stoop. The neighbors had been less than enthusiastic when we were freshmen, but by the time we reached our senior year we used to draw a little crowd.

"Killer-diller," I said, repeating the compliment we

once gave one another on our improvisations. "Haven't played like that in years."

"What happened to you-all?"

"Oh, the world began to get in the way. I went off to Easton College. Mo deserved the scholarship more than me, but he was colored. He ended up okay, though. I saw him before I left. You know, that little tour we all made of the folks we wanted to remember us if anything happened? He went to medical school at the U. Two coloreds in his class, but he was past the rough part. He's done by now. He was laughing because the draft board didn't know what to do with him. They weren't going to take a colored doctor. If he's over here, it's as a damn private in the Negro troops. And that's not right, Biddy."

"No, sir, it ain't, it surely ain't." I had a hard time believing I'd made a convert overnight, but he sounded sincere.

Antonio had been gone for more than two hours now. The remaining six of us moved out a little after 5:30 a.m., careful as we climbed into the first hills. At one point when we stopped, Henri pointed to a stork's nest, the size of a harvest basket, on the roof of a farmhouse beside a small lake.

Halfway up the hill behind the saltworks, we parted with Henri and Christian. Each of us took turns wishing them well.

"*Merde*," answered Henri. I don't believe I'd heard another word from him in twelve hours. In the dark, they would assume positions on an adjoining hill to the north. The Germans walked the walled perimeter of the works in daylight, but at night, they relied on sentries posted in towers. If Henri and Christian were quiet, they could pitch down their grenades and be gone almost instantly. The wall would end up protecting them from the German forces, who would be a long time getting outside.

To signal Henri and Christian to fire, Martin would blow the locomotive whistle once, indicating that the guards at the switch had been dispatched. The Germans were unlikely to make much of the sound coming from the main line, but one minute later, the grenades would explode among the salt barns.

Without his guides, Martin touched a button on the tunic he wore beneath his field jacket and a compass popped open on his chest, mounted upside down so he could read the phosphorescent dial. Until now I'd been so absorbed with my own apprehensions that I had largely forgotten why I'd come. But witnessing the elaborateness of the plans, the ingenious OSS gizmos with which Martin had been supplied, and the extensive cooperation from local elements, it was beyond doubt that Martin was acting under OSS command. Whether it was political prejudice or egotism or simply miscommunication amid the smoke of war, Teedle was plainly wrong.

The separation from Henri and Christian had brought a new gravity to both Martin and Gita, who led us in heavy silence as we ascended. Every now and then Martin took a strip of cloth from his sack and tied it to the bough of a buckthorn or other small tree, marking the way back. I wasn't certain if the sky was brightening a trace, with perhaps an hour to dawn, or if my eyes had adjusted to the dark, but smoky puffs of fog were visible beneath the cloud cover. When we made the crest, Martin reached out to take the satchel charge from Bidwell. I'd labored with it, and Biddy had grabbed it from me, toting it along as if it were no heavier than a lunch bucket.

"Gentlemen," said Martin, "here we part. I suggest you continue down perhaps a hundred yards. You'll be able to see our activities clearly. Again, eye out for Krauts."

"And if we wish to help?" I asked.

Martin shrugged, as if it were no matter to him. "I'm sure Gita could use a hand in Bettjer's place."

I looked at Biddy. He had a straightforward analysis. "Seems to me we're a helluva lot better off, Lieutenant, stayin with folks who know what-all they're doin."

I could see Martin had anticipated these responses, not because there was anything special about Biddy, or me, but because there wasn't. It was a tribute to our soldiers, most of whom would have made the same choice.

Before saying goodbye, Martin loosened the chinstrap on my helmet.

"You don't want that around your neck when the dump goes, Dubin. It could garotte you. Follow Gita," he said. "She'll give you directions."

Our role was to cover Martin. We edged our way down the hill behind him. At the foot, we were on the plain beside the Seille, still a quarter mile south and east of the switching point. The train tracks lay before us, and we dashed across one at a time, plunging into the heavy growth on the riverbank. Gita followed Martin, and I followed her; Biddy was at my back. It was slow going. Martin pulled aside the branches as if parting a heavy curtain, but there were still thorns that grabbed my clothes and clawed my face, and I stumbled several times on the soft ground. We crept along this way for half an hour until Martin suddenly stopped, one hand aloft.

He had caught sight ahead of the two Germans guarding the switch. They were kids, of course. They sat on two ammunition crates, using a third as a table while they played cards, betting cigarettes and cursing fate with each hand. They were in full uniform, wearing their Dutch-boy helmets. Their rifles were slung across their backs and would be inaccessible just long enough to make it easy to overtake them, four soldiers on two. With hand signals, Martin drew a plan in the air. He was going to continue until he was behind the two sentries. When he erupted from the bushes, ordering them to surrender, the three of us would rush forward to surround them.

Martin had gone about ten paces, mincing through the underbrush, when he again stilled. The soldiers remained occupied with their game, but after another second, I heard what Martin had: the rising clatter of the locomotive.

The two Germans noticed the racket down the track at the same time, both standing and swinging their rifles into their hands. I would have thought they'd have an established drill with passing trains, but they had been taken by surprise and they shouted at each other while they tried to decide what to do. One galloped down the track, coming within a few feet of our hiding place in the brush as he raced toward the sound of the engine, which remained around the bend of the hill. The other watched over his shoulder as he wandered toward his radio. He was headed directly to the spot where Martin was hidden in the greenery along the bank.

Martin killed him quickly. He was as expert as his stories suggested. As soon as the soldier turned again to check on his comrade, Martin slipped from the bushes, loping in a peculiar side-to-side crouch, meant either to cushion his footfalls or to make him less visible if his sound was detected. When he neared the boy, he tossed a pebble to draw the soldier's attention forward. The German had raised his rifle in that direction when Martin caught him from behind, circling a length of wire around his windpipe. He snatched it taut, dumped the soldier on his seat, and braced his knee in the boy's back as he finished him. The only sound throughout was of the boy's heavy boots thumping on the ground, hardened by the native salt deposits.

I had watched the mangled, eviscerated, and limbless men who came off the Red Cross vehicles in Nancy, and I'd encountered corpses now and then, as on the day with Colonel Maples, but I'd seen a man die only once before, when I'd been sent as the departmental representative to a hanging. I had looked away immediately when I heard the trap sprung. But now the moment of death struck me as far more ordinary than I might have thought. Life was headed toward this instant and we all knew it, no matter how much we willed ourselves to forget. Wiping the wire on his gloves before returning it to the side pocket of his combat jacket, Robert Martin was the master of that knowledge. He appeared entirely unaltered by what he'd done.

Instead, he waved us forward, while he went flying down the track toward the locomotive. By the time we arrived, the other German soldier was on the ground with his face covered in blood. Antonio had stopped the engine on the young soldier's orders, then smashed the boy across the cheek with a wrench as soon as he tried to mount the ladder to the cab. He was moaning now, a low guttural sound from deep within his body. From the looks of it, I wasn't sure he was going to live, but Martin stuffed a handful of leaves into the long gash that was once the boy's mouth, and bound him with the laces of the low rawhide boots he'd worn under gaiters.

Then we stood in silence beside the enormous steam-driven machine that Antonio and the *réseau* had stolen. It was the height of at least four men and probably one hundred feet long, with six sets of steel wheels polished by the tracks, and a black boiler right behind its front light. Unlike American trains, the turbine was exposed. But there was little time to admire it. Martin's gesture set Gita running, and Biddy and I sprinted behind her. When I looked back, Antonio and Martin were leaning together to free the switch.

We retraced our path, running back along the river-bank as fast as the undergrowth would allow. A hundred yards on, behind a bend in the wall, we crossed the track again and headed up the hill, climbing on all fours to a path that rose steeply along the ridgeline.

Three or four minutes after leaving Martin, we heard the long lowing of the locomotive whistle. The train was on its way. I counted to sixty as we ran, and the detonations of Henri and Christian's grenades followed precisely. We were close enough to the saltworks to hear the cries of alarm go up in the German garrison — shouting and a siren pealing — and to see color against the low clouds. We continued upward until we could look down on the works and the trestle, two hundred yards from the railroad gate Martin was preparing to attack. Only one of the machine guns looked to be manned. Inside the high walls, the red flames were partially visible, and in that light, we could see the anthill swirl of soldiers pouring in that direction.

The locomotive lumbered around the bend then, moving at no more than ten miles an hour as it rocked on the old rail bed. The three machine-gun crewmen had turned to watch the fire, but the train sounds caught the attention of one of them. He stepped toward the trestle with his hands on his waist, an idle spectator for a lingering second, and then, with no transition, an image of urgent action waving wildly to his comrades, having suddenly recognized that the grenades and the locomotive bearing down on them were part of the same attack.

Watching from above, I briefly panicked when I realized what would happen if the gunners were smart enough to begin firing at the trestle. Delivering nine hundred rounds a minute, the MG42s probably could have damaged the ties enough to derail the train, maybe even to send it into the Seille. But they'd clearly given that alternative no forethought and prepared to take out their attackers more directly. One soldier steadied the MG42 on its tripod, while the gunner put on his helmet and the third crewman strung out the ammunition belt. Beside us, Gita raised her M1 and whipped her chin to indicate Biddy and I should move apart. Before the Germans could fire, we began shooting down at them. We did not have the range at first, and the gunners suddenly swung the MG42 in our direction. As the long muzzle crossed my plane of vision my entire body squeezed in fear and I started firing frantically, until one of our bullets, maybe even mine, took down the gunner. With that, the other two retreated inside the walls, dragging the fallen man behind them.

When I lowered the carbine, I found my heart banging furiously and my lungs out of breath. I was at war. In war. The momentousness of it rang through me, but already, with just this instant to reflect, I felt the first whisper of disappointment. Below, the locomotive went down the trestle like a waddling hen, the burning fuse of the satchel charge now visible in the cab window.

I caught sight of Martin then, rolling along the right-of-way between the river and the high wall of the saltworks. As the engine rumbled past him, he sprang back to his feet and sprinted down the track, taking advantage of the cover provided by the huge iron machine. Once he was beyond the curve of the wall, he swung his rucksack around him and removed two lengths of rope, both secured to grappling hooks, which he dug into the crotches of two small trees. Bracing himself that way, he backed to the edge of the river, and then, without hesitation, skidded down the concrete retaining wall on the bank, disappearing into the water.

Suddenly, a gun barked on my left. I flinched before I heard Biddy crying out. He was shooting, and Gita immediately joined him. A gunner had returned to the other MG42. I fired, too, the jolting rifle once escaping my shoulder and recoiling painfully against my cheek, but in a moment the man was back inside the walls. One of the Germans had closed the low iron gate, but it was thin and presented no obstruction to the locomotive that crashed through it, headed for its descent into the mine. With a little shout, Gita signaled us to run.

Once we were beyond the crest, Gita dropped to her knees and threw herself down the hill in a ball. I fell where she had started but ended up spinning sideways into a tree stump. Biddy came somersaulting by, bumping along like a boulder. I dashed several feet, then tripped and accomplished what I had meant to, rolling on my side down the hill, landing painfully and bouncing forward.

In the midst of that, I heard an enormous echo of screaming metal piped out of the tunnel and knew the locomotive had barreled into the loaded flatcars. In the reality of physicists, there were actually two detonations, the satchel charges and then the ordnance, but my experience was of a single sensational roar that brought full daylight and fireside heat and bore me aloft. I was flying through the air for a full second, then landed hard. Looking up, I saw giant pillars of flame beyond the hilltop, and nearby a corkscrew of smoking black iron, a piece of the locomotive, that had knifed straight into the earth, as if it were an arrow. My knee, inexplicably, was throbbing.

"Cover up," Biddy yelled. My helmet had been blown off. I saw it back up the incline, but a fountain of dirt and stone and hot metal began showering around me. Debris fell for more than a minute, tree boughs and shell pieces that plummeted through the air with a sound like a wolf whistle, and a pelting downpour of river water and the heavy mud of the bank. At the end came a twinkling of sawdust and the tatters of leaves. I had crawled halfway to my helmet when there was a second explosion that blew me back down to where I had been at first. The concussion was less violent, but the flames reached higher into the sky and the hot remains of what had been destroyed rained down even longer.

I still had my hands over my head when Gita slapped my bottom. I jumped instantly and found her laughing. "*Allons-y!*" She took off down the hillside. Biddy was already in motion and I sprinted behind them. He moved well for a man his size, but lacked endurance. I had retained some of the lung strength of a swimmer and eventually pulled past him, but I was no match for Gita, who flew along like a fox past the strips of cloth Martin had tied, stopping only when we reached the edge of the last open farm field we'd crossed this morning. At the margin of a small woods, Gita scouted for signs of the Germans, but we all knew that the blast that had roared out of the tunnel, as from a dragon's mouth, had to have devastated the garrison. Biddy arrived and laid his hands on his thighs, panting.

"What about Martin?" I asked her, when she signaled we were secure.

"We never worry about Martin," she said.

"Because he is safe?"

"Because it could drive one to lunacy. *Regarde*." Across the field, Henri and Christian were ambling toward us, both so thoroughly relieved of their prior grimness that I failed to recognize them at first. They had ditched their rifles to appear more innocuous, and approached in their muddy boots and soaked overalls, smiling broadly. Henri, it turned out, lacked most of his upper teeth. They hugged Gita first, then both embraced Biddy and me. Henri virtually wrested me from my feet, and isolated within his powerful grasp and his warm husky scent, I felt the first stirrings of pride at the magnitude of our achievement and my own small role in it.

"We showed them," Henri said in French. The way back to the shepherd's hut was safe, he said. There they had built a fire and filled a cistern with water from a nearby spring, and we all sat on the ground, drinking and warming ourselves, while we waited for Antonio and Martin. As we recounted the operation in a jumble of conversation, every spark of shared memory seemed to make each of us hilarious, but there was truly only one joke: we were alive.

When I was warmer, I hiked up my woolen pants leg to see what I had done to my knee. There was a gash, only an inch wide but deep, a smile amid a large purple welt. I had no clue how it had happened. Prodding the edges of the wound, I could feel nothing inside.

"For this a Purple Heart?" Gita asked Biddy in English, when she saw me toying with the injury. I had found my first-aid kit in my field-jacket pocket and Gita helped me wash the cut with a little of the gauze in there. Across the cut, she dumped a dusting of sulfa powder out of a packet, then skillfully fashioned a bandage from the remaining gauze. Wrapping my knee, she told me that it would be a week or so before I danced in the Follies again.

"Your nursing skills are impressive, Mademoiselle Lodz. How were you trained?"

"In Marseilles, in the hospital, I watched and learned."

"Is that what drew you to the hospital, a vocation for nursing?"

"Far from it. I wanted to steal opium." She smiled regally. More than anything, Gita Lodz enjoyed being shocking, and in me, she had easy prey.

"You were a drug fiend?"

"A bit. To dull the pain. Principally, I sold to opium dens. War is very hard on those people, Dubin. I survived on their desperation—until I met Robert. But I am a good nurse. I have what is required, a strong stomach and a soft heart. Even someone whom I would despise were he in good health moves me as an invalid."

"A bit of a paradox, is it not? To be a soldier and a nurse?"

Her small shoulders turned indifferently.

"I told you, Dubin, I do not fight to kill. Or conquer."

"So why, then?"

She pulled my pants leg down to my boot and smoothed it there. Then she sat back on her haunches.

"I will tell you how it has been with me, Dubin. I have fought because the Nazis are wrong and we are right and the Nazis must lose. But I also fight death. I see it in the barrel of every gun, in the figure of every Boche, and when they are defeated, I think each time: Today I may live. *Tu comprends?*" She finished off by giving her full brows a comic wiggle, but her coffee eyes had been lethally intent. I knew she thought she had told me something remarkable, but I did not really grasp it. Right now I felt the thrill of surviving in all my limbs, as if I'd acquired the strength of ten.

"I fear I am too dense to fully understand, Mademoiselle."

"No, Dubin, it does not mean you are slow-witted." She stood with a sealed smile. "It means you are lucky."

The plan called for us to remain in the shepherd's hut until we had all reassembled and the local *réseau* could assure safe passage. Christian wandered down to the farmhouse to see if there had been any warnings.

"All quiet," he said. Word was that Patton's Army was advancing. The Germans had more pressing business than to hunt a few stray commandos on friendly ground.

Antonio arrived about half an hour later and the same circle of embraces was repeated, despite the fact that his face and uniform were pasted with mud.

"*Nom de nom,*" he said. "What an explosion! I was

more than a kilometer away and it drove me into the riverbank so deep I thought I would suffocate. When I looked up there was not a tree standing for five hundred meters from the tunnel."

His account of the blast made me more concerned about Martin, but Gita refused to worry. Just as she said, an hour and a half along, Martin appeared. His pack and helmet were gone and the knee was torn out of his trousers. He was entirely soaked, but cheerful. Whistling, he came sauntering across the field.

When OSS had originally planned the operation in the fall, their engineers had calculated that Martin would survive the explosion by jumping from the trestle into the Seille and swimming away in a sprint. Knowing the timing, he would dive for the bottom just in advance of the blast, where the waters' depths would protect him from the plummeting debris.

But that scheme had been drawn up before the record rains of the autumn. The Seille, normally a slow-moving canal, was ten feet over its usual level and now a rushing river. That was why Martin had secured the ropes, so that he could use them to keep the current from carrying him back toward the tunnel. The theory was no match for reality when the shafts blew.

"Damn stupid," he said. "Lucky I didn't rip my arms off." With the explosion, the ropes tore through his hands, burning both palms despite his gloves, and lifting Martin from the water. He plunged back down farther on, but he was too dazed to get a footing or a handhold and was driven by the current at least a hundred yards until he was stopped by a dam of mud and rock that the explosion had dropped into the Seille almost directly opposite the point of attack. Swimming to the west bank, he crawled in a rush up the hill, expecting to be fired on any second, but from the top, he saw no soldiers moving amid the lingering smoke. The garrison appeared to have been wiped out to a man.

"What a beautiful locomotive," said Martin as we went over the events yet again. "Hochdruck by Henschel." In the midst of his recollection, his gaiety and wonder swiftly passed. "It was bad business about those boys," he said abruptly. No one added more about those deaths.

After walking through another field, we arrived at the road, where an old farmer rolled up on a horse-drawn flatbed loaded with newly harvested grapes. With their dusty skins, they looked like high clouds in a darkening sky. Martin instructed us to wade in and work our way down to the wagon bed to hide. Biddy and I went first. I could feel the grapes burst under my weight and their juice soaking my uniform. I positioned myself on my side to protect my knee, then heard Gita's rasp as she swam down through the bunches. Suddenly she was on top of me, her leg over mine, her face and torso some short distance away, the crushed fruit leaking out between us, but she made no effort to move, nor did I, and we remained that way all the time it took the wagon to clop back to the Comtesse de Lemolland's.

12. CELEBRATION

At the Comtesse de Lemolland's there was a celebration. The explosion had resounded even here and the giant flames, phosphorescent orange, shot a mile into the sky. In the house, the sole question was whether we had survived. The Comtesse would not consider the possibility that we had not, and once the lighting fixtures had stopped rocking, she ordered preparations for *une grande fête*. By the time we arrived, several dozen local residents, all with resistance affiliations, had gathered in the courtyard. It was the liberation scenes all over again — embraces, shouting, bottles of wine and cognac for each hand. A whole lamb was being roasted over an outdoor pit beside the stables. The seven of us — Biddy, Henri, Christian, Antonio, Gita, Martin, and I — stood shoulder to shoulder amid the grapes, waving our fists, praising France and America, to unending laughter and applause. It was 3:00 p.m. and Biddy and I might have reached HQ by nightfall, but I gave no thought to that. With my arm around Gita's slim waist, the other hand mounted on Biddy's wide shoulder, I felt an exhilaration and freedom that were new in my life.

The smell of the cooking meat woke an enormous hunger, but I desired even more to shed my uniform, mud-slimed, grape-stained, bloodied in spots, not to mention sopped and chafing. Gita sent the drunken Bettjer to fetch dry fatigues for both Biddy and me, and we changed in a room in the farmhands' bunkhouse over the barn. My knee was growing stiff, but in my present mood even the discomfort seemed a pleasant souvenir.

"Oh, now look at this," said Bidwell. His pants stopped midway down his shin. I offered to swap, but mine were the same length and Biddy was just as happy to be silly. The Frenchmen were delighted when he appeared in his 'culottes.'

I had never been one to enjoy parties, but it seemed that I hadn't ever before had so much to celebrate. When the rain began again the crowd moved inside, where I drank and repeated the story of the attack for little knots of Frenchmen who gathered around. Almost all of them had assisted somehow over the months the operation had been planned, surveillance agents who fished the Seille to reconnoiter the dump, or silent sentries who'd kept watch once we'd slipped behind the German lines. The size of the explosion was remarked on again and again, tangible proof of the risk and of the triumph.

Eventually, the talk turned to other developments in the war. Patton's principal force was said to be moving against Metz. Many of the French were convinced that the fight would end soon, that in a matter of months *la vie normale* would resume and the Americans would be returning to the States. In response to questions about my home, I pulled my Kodaks from my wallet and set them on the long planked dining table where I had taken a seat, a bit woozy from the cognac I'd been sipping. The little snaps were all somewhat disfigured from the impression of my house key that I kept beside them, but that did not seem to deter my audience, who made laudatory remarks as they examined the photos of my parents, sister, and baby brother, and of Grace.

I became aware of Gita leaning over my shoulder. She was dressed again as a civilian, in a simple blouse and skirt. She lifted Grace's photo from the table with her customary boldness. Everyone else had treated the pictures as if they were sacred relics that could not even be touched.

"*Ta soeur?*" Your sister?

"*Ma fiancée.*"

She gave me a direct look, finally a pursed grin. "*Mes félicitations*," she said and turned away.

A few minutes later, as I was about to replace the snapshots, Biddy plopped beside me, and asked to see them. Slowed by drink, he took a long time with each.

"Not your quality," I told him, "but it helps me remember their faces. You have Kodaks of your family, Biddy?"

He gave his head a solemn shake.

"Now, how could that be," I asked, "a picture-taker like you?"

"Just reckon it's better that way, Lieutenant. I got 'em here and here." He touched his heart, his head. Our exchange in English had isolated us from the Frenchmen. Gideon gathered the pictures up tenderly and handed them to me.

"You come from a big family, Biddy?"

"Not compared to some. Me, Momma, Daddy, two brothers."

"Brothers in the service?"

"No, sir. The older one, he's *too* old, and my middle brother, he just never got called."

"Volunteered for the Navy?" I knew several fellows who put in for the Navy and still hadn't gone in when I did.

"Nope. Just somethin 'bout him the draft board didn't never take to."

"Four-F?"

"Nothing wrong with his body, not so they ever said." He shrugged, as baffled as the rest of us over the Army's eternal unreason.

I asked if he heard from them.

"My momma. You know how moms are. I must get four letters from her every week. My middle brother, he ain't much for writing, same as my dad. But Daddy, he sends me stuff, you know, magazine clippings and what-not. It's hard on all of 'em my bein here. My folks got into a big tussle before I went into the service, and they ain't quite set that right yet. You know how families go."

"That I do. My folks still haven't forgiven me about this girl I'm going to marry."

"Now how's that, Lieutenant? She looks like a million bucks."

"And smarter and nicer than she looks. But Grace's family is Episcopalian and I'm Jewish, Biddy." I paused to wonder if I'd said that as frankly since I'd entered the service. "That difference didn't sit well in either house."

At the news of my proposal, Horace Morton had exploded. Grace related only that he had denounced me as 'conniving,' but I'm sure 'Jew' had been the next word.

Grace's mother, however, took my side, and in time the two women wore down Mr. Morton. Soon I was allowed to enter the great stone house to ask for his daughter's hand. Along the way, to help subdue the histrionics there, I had volunteered to become an Episcopalian so Grace could marry at her church.

Because of my parents' hostility to religious practice, I had convinced myself that this last detail would not greatly concern them. I knew that my mother did not favor my romance with someone so different, but I had dismissed that view as Old World. As I later learned, my father had persuaded Ma not to say more by pointing out that people as highly placed as the Mortons would never let their only daughter marry so far below her class. Now, when I told them about my proposal and my prospective conversion, my mother probably felt she'd been double-crossed. In any event, she stood straight up from the kitchen table, making no effort to contain herself.

"This is madness, Duvid," she said, pointedly using the Yiddish version of my name, as my parents sometimes did. "You think some priest can wave a magic wand and go poo, poo, poo so that instead of a chicken you are now a duck? To people like this, you will always be a shabby Jew and nothing else."

In answer, I described the church service Grace and her mother had envisioned, believing it evidenced their acceptance of me. My mother responded by sobbing.

"I don't go to a synagogue," she cried. "I should go kneel in a church so my son can forget where he comes from? Feh," she said. "Sooner dead. Not for all the gold in Fort Knox. If this is how you marry, you marry without me."

"She means it, Duvid," my father said, then added, "Me, too."

I hesitated even to tell Grace for days, because she would have no way to break this to her mother. Mrs. Morton had taken the side of love, but its culmination in her mind required an organ and afternoon light through the rose window in the nave. With little time to negotiate, we debated eloping, but I simply could not go off to war so deeply at odds with my family. Not quite knowing how it had happened, I shipped out for basic training with Grace still my fiancée, rather than my wife.

I told Biddy the story in shorter strokes, but drunk as he was, it seemed to move him.

"Ain't that terrible, Lieutenant, when folks get goin on like that? Someday people's just gonna be people." He looked pitiably confused and morose, his face contorted as he kept going "Mmm, mmm, mmm" in disapproval. I ended up putting my hand on his shoulder in consolation, and struck by that, Biddy smiled, eyeing me for some time.

"You are all right, Lieutenant. You gotta get outta your head and into the world, but you are definitely all right."

"Thank you, Biddy. You're okay yourself. And we were definitely in the world today."

"Yes, sir. We sure enough were. I ain't never gone see nothin like that again. This bird Martin, Lieutenant. Could be I had him wrong. I think he may be all right, too."

I knew the image of Martin dropping so gracefully into the quick waters of the Seille despite the many perils would retain a hallmarked spot in my memory.

Some of the Frenchmen were circulating now with dinner, which had been set out on a buffet in the kitchen, and I could not wait to eat. Even after the relative grandeur of my meals in Nancy, the lamb was a spectacular treat, even more so to the locals after years of wartime privations. The animal, I was told, had been hidden from the Germans. It had been slaughtered out of season, old enough to be closer to mutton, one farmer said, but still remarkably tasty as far as I was concerned.

Martin eventually arrived at the center of the kitchen by the huge iron stove and called for silence. He praised our success and the courage of everyone present and thanked the gallant Comtesse yet again for her bravery and magnificent hospitality throughout the weeks they had waited.

"I raise my glass last to those of you who were with me. To do what we do and live, one must be lucky. You were all my luck today."

There was applause, shouted congratulations, to which Gita's voice was eventually added from the back of the room.

"I am always your luck," she called. "It's boring. Every time, the same thing. Martin fights, I save him. Martin fights, I save him."

This was comedy, and her parody of the shrewish country wife evoked drunken laughter. Inspired by her audience's enthusiasm, Gita mounted a chair to continue, very much the girl who had seen herself as the new Bernhardt. Now she engaged in a dramatic retelling of the story of Martin's capture by the Gestapo early in 1943. The Nazis had not recognized him as an American. Suspecting instead that Martin was a Frenchman connected with the underground, they imprisoned him in the local village hall, while they investigated. Knowing there was little time, Gita stuffed her skirt with straw and arrived in the receiving area of the hôtel de ville, demanding to see the German commandant. At the sight of him, she dissolved in tears, decrying the son of a bitch who had left her with child and now was going to prison without marrying her. After twenty minutes of her ranting, the commandant was ready to teach Martin a lesson, and sent four storm troopers to bring him in chains to the local cathedral where the marriage could be performed. It never was, of course. The four soldiers escorting Martin and Gita were set upon by two dozen *maquisards*, resistance guerrillas, who quickly freed them both.

"I curse the fate that intervened," cried Martin in French, raising his glass to her. "I will marry you now."

"Too late," she cried, and on her chair, turned away, her nose in the air, an arm extended to hold him at bay. "Your horse has eaten *le bébé*."

Their tableau was received with more resounding laughter and clapping. A moment later, as the first of the crowd began departing, Martin took the chair beside me. I had barely left my seat. The cognac had me whirling.

"You did well today, Dubin."

I told him sincerely that I hadn't done much more than fire my M1 a few times, but he reminded me that we had all been in harm's way when the machine gun had swung toward us. He stopped then to ponder the circle of brandy in his glass.

"That was unfortunate with those young soldiers. I don't mind killing a man with a gun pointed at me, but I took no pleasure in that." I, on the other hand, had still given no thought to those deaths. I was aloft on the triumph and my reception as a hero. I was surely different, I thought, surely a different man.

"When I was their age," he said of the two Germans,

"I'd have thought they had met a good end. Foolish, eh? But as a young man, I woke up many days feeling it would be my last. Gita and I have this in common, by the way. I recognized the same fatalism when I met her. The bargain that I struck with myself to forestall these thoughts was that I would die for glory. So that at the moment that the bullet entered my brain, I could tell myself I had made this a better world. I was looking for a valiant fight for years until I found it in Spain. But it turns out I'm a coward, Dubin. I am still alive, and now an old warhorse."

"You are the furthest thing from a coward I have ever met, Major."

He made a face. "I tell myself each time I will not fear death, but of course I do. And I wonder what all of this has been for."

"Surely, Major, you believe in this war."

"In its ends? Without question. But I have been making war now for a decade, Dubin, give or take a few years off. I have fought for good causes. Important causes. But I mourn every man I've killed, Dubin. And not merely for the best reason, because killing is so terrible, but because there really is no point to so many of these deaths. This boy today? I killed him to save all of us at the moment. But I don't fool myself that it was indispensable, let alone the dozens, probably hundreds, we left dead or maimed in that garrison. We make war on Hitler. As we must. But millions get in the way and die for the Führer. What do you think? How many men do we truly need to kill to win this war? Ten? Surely no more than one hundred. And millions upon millions will die instead."

The tragedy of war, I said.

"Yes, but it's a tragedy for each of us, Dubin. Every moment of terror is a month of nightmares later in life. And every killing like today's is a mile farther from ever feeling joy again. You think when you start, 'I know who I am. At the core, I am inviolate. Permanent.' You are not. I did not know that war could be so terrible, that it would crowd out everything else in a life. But it does, I fear, Dubin."

I was startled by this speech, given my own buoyancy. But Martin was not the first man I'd met to find gloom in alcohol. To comfort him, I repeated the prediction I'd heard tonight that we were going to make short work of the Germans, and Martin answered with a philosophical shrug. I asked what he would do then.

"Wait for the next war, I suppose," he answered. "I don't think I'm good for much else, that's what I'm saying, unless I spare the world the trouble and put an end to myself. I really can't envision life in peacetime anymore. I talk about a good hotel room and a good woman, but what is that? And I am not so different, Dubin. Soon everyone will be driven into this lockstep. War and making more war."

"So you think we will fight the Russians, Major?"

"I think we will fight. Don't you see what's happening, Dubin? No one has choices any longer. Not here and not at home. I always thought that the march of history was forward, less suffering and greater freedom for mankind, the chains of need and tyranny breaking apart. But it's not what meets my eye when I look to the future. It's just one group of the damned making war on the other. And liberty suffering."

"You're in the Army, Major. This has never been freedom's Valhalla."

"Yes, that's the argument. But look at what's happened

on the home front. I get letters, I read the papers. War has consumed every liberty. There's propaganda in the magazines and on the movie screens. Ration books and save your tin cans. Sing the songs and spout the line. There's no freedom left anywhere. With one more war, Dubin, civil society will never recover. The war profiteers, the militarists, the fearmongers — they'll be running things permanently. Mark my words. Mankind is falling into a long dark tunnel. It's the new Middle Ages, Dubin. That's the bit that breaks my heart. I thought fascism was the plague. But war is. *War* is." He looked into his glass again.

As he spoke, Teedle came to mind. I wondered if Martin and he had had this argument face-to-face. Or simply suspected as much of one another. They both saw the world headed to hell in a handbasket. I gave them credit for worrying, each of them. For most of the men out here, me included, the only real concern was going home.

"May I assume I am quit of your charges?" Martin asked then.

I told him I'd certainly recommend that, but that the safest course, given the orders he'd received, would be for him to return to Nancy with me in the morning to sort it out. He thought it through, but finally nodded.

"I'll spend a few hours," he said, "but I have to get on now to the next assignment." That would be the operation in Germany he'd mentioned when I first arrived here, the one for which he'd been called back to London. "I think it will be the most important work I've done, Dubin. There's no counting the lives we may save." He lifted his eyes toward the bright light of that prospect, then asked when I wanted to start in the morning. Dawn, I said, would be best, given how long we'd been away.

That reminded me that I needed to retrieve my uniform. I stood hesitantly, my knee quite stiff, to seek Gita. She had been outside saying adieu to the locals. I met her in the parlor, where Bidwell had crawled up on one of the Comtesse's elegant red velvet divans and was fast asleep beneath a lace shawl from the back of the couch.

"Leave him," she said.

"I shall, but I can't take him back to headquarters in culottes."

Gita consulted Sophie, the maid who had washed our uniforms and left them to dry over the same fire, now banked, where the lamb was roasted. As we headed out, Gita threw her arm through mine companionably as I limped along between the puddles etched in the candlelight from the house. The rain had been heavy for a while but had ceased, although the eaves and trees still dripped. The Comtesse's other guests had gone down the road in a pack and their drunken uproar carried back to us in the dank night.

I told her about my conversation with Martin. "Is he normally so dour?"

"Afterward? Afterward, always. Have you known gamblers, Dubin? I have often thought that if there were not war, Martin would probably be standing at a gaming table. Many gamblers have moods like this. They exult in the game, in betting everything, but their spirit flags once they win. *Voilà la raison.* Martin speaks the truth when he says he is miserable without war. That was the case when I met him."

"In Marseilles?"

"Yes. I sold him opium, when he visited from Spain." I managed not to miss a step. I seemed to have prepared myself for anything from her. "He smoked too much of it, but he recovered a few months later once he agreed to go to the States to train as a commando."

"His new wager?" I thought of the way Martin had raised his eyes at the thought of his next assignment in Germany.

"Precisely," Gita answered.

The uniforms were by the barn entrance, now imbued with an intense smoky aroma, but dry. She helped me fold them and I placed them under the arm she had been holding.

"Martin says his remorse is over no longer being who he was," I told her.

"Does he?" She was struck by that. She squinted into the darkness. "Well, who is? Am I who I was when I ran to Marseilles at the age of seventeen? Still," she said, "it is true he suffers."

From what she'd told me, I said, it seemed as if Martin had suffered always.

"*D'accord*. But there are degrees, no? Now at night, he sleeps in torment. He sees the dead. But that is probably not the worst of it. There is no principle in war, Dubin. And Martin has been at war so long, there is no principle in him. I was not sure he recognized this."

"Ah, that word again," I said. We were standing in the open doorway of the barn, where the dust and animal smells breathed onto us in the wind. Her heavy brows narrowed as she sought my meaning.

"Principles," I said.

She grinned, delighted to have been caught again. "And here we debated," she added.

"You most effectively," I answered.

"Yes, I showed you my principles." She laughed, we both did, but a silence fell between us, and with it came a lingering turning moment, while Gita's quick eyes, small and dark and sometimes greedy, searched me out. She spoke far more quietly. "Shall I show you my principles again, Doo-bean?"

The hunger I felt for this woman had been no secret from me. Amid the peak emotions of the day, the increasing physical contact between us had seemed natural, even needed, and the direction we were headed seemed plain. But I had been equally certain that reason would intervene and find a stopping point. Now, I realized there would be none. I felt a blink of terror, but I had learned today how to overcome that, and I also had the tide of alcohol to carry me. Yet drink was not the key. Gita was simply part of this, this place, these adventures. I answered her question with a single word.

"Please," I said. And with that she took her thin skirt in her fingertips and eased it upward bit by bit, until she stood as she had stood two weeks ago, delicately revealed. Then she was in my arms. With her presence came three fleeting impressions: of how small and light she was, of the stale odor of tobacco that penetrated her fingertips and hair, and of the almost infinite nature of my longing.

For a second, I thought it would happen there in the barn, among the animals, a literal roll in the hay, but she drew me to the narrow stairs and we crept up together to the tiny room where Biddy and I had changed. Her blouse was open, one shallow breast exposed. She stepped quickly out of her bloomers, and with no hesitation placed one hand on my belt and lowered my fly, taking hold of me with a nurse's proficiency. We staggered toward the bunk and then we were together, a sudden, jolting, desperate coupling, but that seemed to be the need for both of us, to arrive at once at that instant of possession and declaration. My knee throbbed throughout, which seemed appropriate somehow.

Afterward, she rested on my chest. I lay on the striped ticking of the unmade bunk, my pants still around my ankles, breathing in the odor of the mildewed mattress and the barnyard smells of manure and poultry feathers rising up from below while I assessed who I really was.

So, I thought. So. There had been something brutal in this act, not between Gita and me, but in the fact it had happened. The thought of Grace had arrived by now to grip me with despair. It was not merely that I had given no consideration to her. It was as if she had never existed. Was Gita right? No principle in war and thus no principle in those who fight it? It was the day, I thought, the day. I conveniently imagined that Grace would understand if she knew the entire tale, although I harbored no illusion I would ever tell her.

Gita brought her small face to mine and whispered. We could hear the snores of the farmhands sleeping on the other side of the thin wooden partitions that passed for walls.

"À quoi penses-tu, Doo-bean?" What are you thinking?

"Many things. Mostly of myself."

"Tell me some."

"You can imagine. There is a woman at home."

"You are here, Dubin."

For the moment that would have to be answer enough.

"And I wonder, too, about you," I said.

"Vas-y. What do you wonder?"

"I wonder if I have met another woman like you."

"Does that mean you have met such men?"

I laughed aloud and she clapped her small hand over my mouth.

"That is your only question?" she asked.

"Hardly."

"*Continue.*"

"The truth?"

"*Bien sûr.*"

"I wonder if you sleep with all the men you fight with."

"Does this matter to you, Dubin?"

"I suppose it must, since I ask."

"I am not in love with you. Do not worry, Dubin. You have no responsibilities. Nor do I."

"And Martin? What truly goes on between Martin and you? You are like an old married couple."

"I have told you, Dubin. I owe much to Robert. But we are not a couple."

"Would he say the same thing?"

"Say? Who can ever tell what Martin might say? But he knows the truth. We each do as we please."

I did not quite understand, but made a face at what I took to be the meaning.

"You do not approve?" she asked.

"I have told you before. I am bourgeois."

"Forgive me, but that cannot be my concern."

"But Martin is mine. And you intend to stay with Martin."

"I am not with him now, Dubin. I am with you."

"But I will go and you will stay with Martin. Yes?"

"For now. For now, I stay with Martin. He says he dreads the day I go. But I stay with Martin to fight, Dubin. Will the Americans allow me to join their Army?"

"I doubt it."

She sat up and looked down at me. Even in the dark, I could see she was narrow and lovely. I ran my hand from her shoulder to her waist, which did nothing to diminish the intensity with which she watched me.

"How many women, Dubin. For you? Many?"

I was shy of this subject, not the doing, but the talking. At twenty-nine, my sexual history remained abbreviated. Some love for sale, some drunken grappling. It was best summarized by the phrase a college friend had applied to himself that fit me equally: I had never gotten laid with my shoes off. Tonight was another example.

"Not so many," I said.

"No? You forgive me, but I think not. Not from the act, Dubin, but from how you are now. And how is it with this woman of yours at home?"

I recoiled at that, then realized the question was not all that different from the ones I'd been asking her.

"It has not occurred, as yet."

"Truly?"

"She is my fiancée, not my wife."

"This was her choice?"

It was mutual, I supposed. Not that there had ever been much discussion. Grace and I had the same assumptions, that there was special meaning in the union of man and woman.

"I worship Grace," I said to Gita. That was the perfect word. 'Worship.' It had not dawned on me until this moment that I could not say in the same way that I craved her.

"She should have insisted, Dubin. She had no idea what she was sending you to."

I could see that much myself.

Gita went down to the barn to attend to herself. A pump handle squealed. Most single men I knew talked a tough game about the women they slept with. But my experience had always been the opposite. In the wake of sex, I inevitably felt a bounty of tenderness, even when I paid a local lunatic called Mary Quick Legs $4 for my first encounter. Now that Gita had left my side, I longed to have her back there. I lay there wondering if I had ever known people like Martin and Gita who had so quickly altered my understanding of myself.

Her small tread squeaked up the stairs and she crept in, standing near the bunk. Seeing her dressed, I reached down and drew up my trousers.

"I must go, Dubin," she whispered. "They will be looking for me shortly. Au revoir." She peered at me, albeit with some softness. "Doo-bean, I believe we shall have other moments together."

"Do you?" I had no idea if I wanted that, but I told her that I would probably return one more time to give Martin the final papers on my investigation.

"Well, then," she answered. She hesitated but bent and pressed her lips to mine lightly. It was more of a concession than an embrace. She said au revoir again.

I had been so raddled by emotion all day that I would have thought my nerves would be too unsettled for sleep, but as with every other expectation of late, I was wrong. I had purposely not drawn the wooden shutters outside and woke at 7:30, as I intended, with the livid sunrise firing through the clouds. Coming to, I recognized my knee as the discomfort, which, like a leash, had seemed to drag me up from sleep periodically throughout the night. The leg was swollen and stiff and I eased myself up slowly, then put on my uniform, refastening the insignia. As I went back toward the house to rouse Bidwell and to see about Martin, I could hear mortars pounding. The 26th Infantry Division, as it turned out, was about to seize Bezange-la-Petite. I was standing there, trying to make out the direction of the booming guns, when Bettjer, still with a cognac bottle in his hand, stumbled into the courtyard.

I asked if he knew where Bidwell was. Peter answered in perfect English.

"Inside. Just now awake. The rest are gone for several hours."

"Who?"

"Martin. Antonio. The girl. Packed and gone for good. They have left me behind. After all of that, they have left me behind."

"Gone?"

"They went in darkness. Hours ago. They tried to creep away, but the Comtesse wept terribly. You must have slept soundly not to hear her."

"Gone?" I said again.

Bettjer, the very image of a sot, whiskered and disheveled in his brown Belgian uniform with half a shirt-tail out, lifted his bottle to me. He had fallen during the night and bloodied his nose and now when he smiled, I could see he had lost half a tooth as well, from that stumble or from one before. Still, he was having a fine time at my expense.

"I see," he said. "I see."

"What do you see, Peter?"

"Why, they have left you behind, too."

IV.

13. SWIMMING

My father had learned to swim as a child in Lake Ellyn, a man-made lake that was actually a large retaining pond in the South End, dug to keep the Kindle River from overflowing its banks in wet seasons. His parents apparently liked the water, too, because there are many photos of the whole family in the ridiculously full bathing costumes of that era, cavorting at the lake, or in the Garfield Baths, a giant teeming indoor swimming pool which was a favorite diversion for Kindle County's working families until the baths' role as a polio breeding ground led them to be closed in the 1950s.

Watching my father swim was always mesmerizing to me. His grace in the water, and the carefree way he splashed around, was inconsistent with the guy who existed on dry land. And so was the physique revealed in his bathing suit. He was a fair-sized person, five foot eleven, and while not exactly Charles Atlas, pretty muscular. Whenever I saw the solid body concealed beneath the shirt and tie he wore until he went to bed each night, I was amazed. So this was who was here. I felt simultaneously reassured and baffled.

Eventually, when I was around fourteen, my father, never much for boasting, admitted in response to my questions that he had been the Tri-Cities high-school champion in the hundred-yard backstroke. Even then, I was hungry for any morsel about who he was, and so one day when my duties on *The Argonaut*, the high-school paper, required me to visit the U High Athletic Association, I decided to look in the archives to see if I could find my father's name.

I did. Sort of. The backstroke champion of 1933 had been called not 'David Dubin,' but 'David Dubinsky.' I knew, of course, that immigrants of all kinds had Americanized their names. Cohens had become Coles. Wawzenskis had become Walters. But it did not sit well with me that he had made this alteration just before starting on his scholarship at Easton College, that gentile bastion. It was a bitter hypocrisy to disown your past and, worse, a capitulation to the happy American melting pot that had marginalized many citizens, especially those with darker skin, whom it could not fit into the blender. When I discovered that Dad had talked his parents into following this example, so he wouldn't be undermined in his new identity, I couldn't keep myself from confronting him.

He defended himself in his usual fashion, with few words. "It seemed simpler then," he said.

"I am not hiding my heritage," I told my father. "However you felt, I'm not ashamed." This was a fairly cheap shot. In our home, my mother had insisted on Jewish ritual and Jewish education. There was a Sabbath meal on Friday night, Hebrew school, and even a quaint form of kosher in her kitchen, in which *traife* of all kinds, including the ham sandwiches she loved, could be consumed, but only if they were served on paper plates and stored on a single, designated shelf in the Frigidaire. Dad had never seemed adept with any of that, probably because he had absolutely no religious training in his own home, but on the other hand, I never doubted that my mother had his full support. Nonetheless, in my final year of college, in 1970, I did my father one better and legally changed my name back. I have been known as Stewart Dubinsky ever since.

Nature, of course, has this way of getting even. Daughter Number 1, since the age of six, has told me she hates Dubinsky (which first-grade meanies turned into 'Poopinsky') and has vowed to take the last name of whomever she marries, even if it's Bozo A. Clown. And I didn't do my father much worse than he'd done his own dad. My grandfather, the cobbler, was in his last years when I made the change, and actually seemed pleased. But as I labored throughout 2003 to recover what my father had never seen fit to share, there was always a little sore spot in my heart whenever I recalled how I had shunned the one thing of my father's I'd had.

This, then, was the story I told Bear Leach immediately after first meeting him in the front sitting room of Northumberland Manor. Bear extracted the complete tale with adroit questioning and accepted my rueful second thoughts about the change with a sage smile.

"Well, Stewart," he said, "I sometimes think that's everything that goes wrong between parents and children. What's rejected. And what's withheld."

In the latter column I could count my father's manuscript, which I eventually thought to ask Leach about. At that point,

I assumed Dad had carried through on his threat to burn it. When I said as much, Leach struggled to his left and right, muttering until he located a Redweld he'd rested against the chrome spokes of his wheelchair. Inside the expandable folder he handed over was at least an inch and a half of jumbled papers, but thumbing through them I instantly recognized my father's lovely cursive hand on several interlineations. Big goof that I am, I sat there on the little love seat where I was perched and cried.

I'd read every line by the time I returned home, finishing by spending three hours in the Tri-Cities Airport after stepping off my plane, unable to endure even the thirty-minute drive to my town house before reaching the culmination. I was a sight, I'm sure, an economy-size fiftysomething guy bawling his eyes out in an empty passenger lounge, while travelers on the concourse cast worried glances, even while they went on hustling toward their gates.

The day Bear had given the typescript to me, I eventually asked how he had ended up with it.

"I have to say, Stewart, that I've always regarded my possession of this document as the product of ambiguous intentions. As I told you, your father said he was intent on burning it after my reading, and once I finished, I felt strongly that would be a terrible loss. I held on to the manuscript for that reason, claiming that I needed it in order to clarify little matters connected to his appeals. Then in late July 1945 your father was released quite unexpectedly and left Regensburg in haste, with other things on his mind. I expected to hear from him about the document eventually, but I never did, not in Europe, and not when we returned to the U.S. I thought of looking him up from time to time over the years, especially as I moved the manuscript from office to office, but I concluded that your father had made a choice he deemed best for all of us, and certainly for himself, that he go on with his life without the complications and memories our renewed contact would raise. The typescript has been in storage at the Connecticut Supreme Court among my papers for several years now, with a note informing my executors to locate David Dubin or his heirs for instructions on what to do with it. I was quite pleased to hear from you, naturally, since it saved my grandchildren from making that hunt."

"But why burn it?" I asked. "Because of this stuff about murdering Martin?"

"Well, of course that was my suspicion, at least at first." Bear stopped then, something clearly nagging him, perhaps a thought about how close he was to the boundaries of what he could properly disclose. "I suppose all I can say for certain, Stewart, is what David told me."

"Which was?"

"Oddly, we never had a direct conversation, your father and I, about what he had written. Even once I'd read it, he was clearly disinclined to discuss the events he'd described, and I understood. The closest we came was a day or two after the sentencing. Your father was going to remain under house arrest during the pendency of his appeal, but he was beginning to accommodate himself to the idea of five years at hard labor. I told him what criminal lawyers always tell their clients in this predicament, that there was going to be another day, a life afterward, and that he might look back on all of this, years from now, with different eyes. And in that connection I brought up the manuscript, which at the moment I'd conveniently left in the safety of my new office in Frankfurt.

"'I think you should save it, Dubin,' I said to him. 'If nothing else, it will be of great interest to your children. Surely, you can't pretend, Dubin, you wrote something like this just for me. And certainly not to reduce it all to ashes.' He pondered that, long enough that I thought I'd struck a chord, but in the end he stiffened his chin and gave his head a resolute shake. And at that point, Stewart, he gave me the only explanation I ever heard about his determination to destroy what he'd put on paper.

"'My most desperate hope,' he said, 'is that my children never hear this story.'"

14. STOP

Dearest Grace—

Sorry for the silence. As you can tell from the
news reports, the troops are on the move again,
and the pace of our work has picked up, too. There
are battlefront incidents that by their nature
are often urgent, and we know that the move to a
new HQ may not be far off. Our hope is that it
will be in Germany—better yet, Berlin.

I'm feeling more myself now than when I last
wrote. You must be wondering about those letters
I dashed off a couple of weeks ago, bracketing my
little detour into "action." With the distance of
time, I have decided to put the entire experience
behind me. That is what the old soldiers tell you
to do: take the past as gone, and realize the
chasm between war and normal life is wider than
the Grand Canyon and not to be crossed. Darling,
believe me, one day when this thing is over, I

want you sitting beside me, so I can stroke your hair while I think over some of this. But please don't mind if it turns out that there's not much I care to say.

On a happier note, your most recent package, no. 15, arrived today. Only two of the sugar cookies were in pieces and I enjoyed them that way, too, believe me. Even better was the bottle of Arrid you sent, which I know is in short supply and thus made me the envy of many. Because of the lack of fuel, hot water is a rarity, meaning few showers and baths. Let your brother know how much I appreciated the deodorant. Say what you like, but sometimes it is an advantage having your own department store. On that score, I'd like to request a favor. If George sees any film pack, size of 620, I'll take whatever he can find. My sergeant, Biddy, is quite the photographer and is having trouble getting film. He's probably the best fellow I've met in the service and I'd love to help him out.

Winter has come. The weather has gone from dank to bone-chilling. It is still raining, at least in name, but what falls now are icy pellets that sting the skin and freeze solid within hours. I wear my woolen gloves when I am sitting at my desk, although the courtroom has a little heat. The cycles of rain and ice are far worse for the boys in the foxholes. Trench foot has become a plague. Estimates are that a third of the troops are suffering from it, many with cases so severe they have to be hospitalized. Patton has ordered

85,000 extra pairs of socks and is rumored to
have lectured troops that in war, foot hygiene is
more important than brushing your teeth.
Overshoes are coveted. The boys out there
continue to amaze me with their courage and
determination.

Their hardships are at great remove from me, as
I continue with the safe but dreary life of a
lawyer in court. I do have one piece of news. My
promotion came through yesterday (only four months
overdue). I am now Captain Dubin, with the word
"acting" removed from my title as Assistant Staff
Judge Advocate. I put on my silver bars immediately
and walked around all day feeling great
satisfaction every time a lieutenant saluted
as I passed.

Have a wonderful Thanksgiving, my love. I
expect to be with you, by the fire, this time next
year.

I love you and think of you always,
David

One afternoon in the second week in December a
clerk dropped my mail call on my desk, three letters
and a card. I was stuffing them inside my tunic, to
be savored in privacy later, when the postcard grabbed my
attention. On one side was a black-and-white photo of a
gabled structure, with narrow variegated spires and two
concentric arches over the door. The tiny legend on the
reverse identified the building as the synagogue at Arlon,
the oldest in Belgium. But I was more astonished by the
handwritten note there.

Dubin—
Am sorry we fool you. Robert says was no choice.
You is good fellow. Please not to think bad of me.
Perhaps we meet again when is not war. For Jew
is ok to say Joyeux Noël?

G.

Gita Lodz's handwriting was pointed and not particularly tidy, just as I might have guessed. She had used English, knowing that a message in French might be months getting past the Army censors.

I read the postcard perhaps twenty times in the next day, trying to determine if it had any larger meanings. Why did she bother? Did I actually care? Eventually I began to wonder whether she was truly in Belgium or if this was another ruse, designed by Martin. I asked a postal clerk if he could tell the mailing location of the card, which bore the purple circled stamp of the Army post office. A three-number code at the center was from the First Army Headquarters near Spa, Belgium.

After pondering, I sent a teletype to Teedle's headquarters at the 18th Armored Division, stating that I'd had a communication indicating where Martin might be. By now, the 18th had returned to combat, moving past Metz into Luxembourg where they were skirmishing with the Germans as they fell back toward the heavy concrete fortifications of the Siegfried line, ringing Germany. With the approval of General staff, only days after Martin had disappeared, Teedle had issued an order for Martin's arrest, bringing a formal end to my investigation. Thus relieved, I had been doing my best not to think about either Robert Martin or Gita Lodz, both of whom had misled me to my serious detriment. On my hangdog visit to Teedle the day Martin had decamped, I'd gotten the hiding I expected, but not simply for losing track of the Major. Patton was incensed about the explosions at La Saline Royale, and in Teedle's words, wanted "Martin's balls for Thanksgiving dinner." The raid on the dump had been planned by OSS in the fall, but, as it turned out, no one had given Martin permission to proceed now. Apparently, it was an adventure he just couldn't stand to miss before absconding. Without coordination, it proved a tactical disaster. The Germans' 21st Panzer Division had been spooked by the massive fireball and curtailed its advance on the region near Marsal, unwittingly avoiding three American antitank battalions Patton had had lying in wait.

My message to Teedle brought a quick response. Late the same day, I was hauled out of court for an urgent phone call. Dashing upstairs, I found Billy Bonner on the other end. Teedle was apparently in range of an Antrac phone relay and wanted to talk to me personally. The sound quality on the field telephone was static-scratched and thin, and when Bonner went to get the General, the thunder of artillery resounded down the line.

"I have your goddamn teletype, Dubin," said Teedle without preliminaries, "and it's too fucking lawyerly, as usual. I need some details in order to contact VIII Corps. What kind of communication was it you received?"

"A card, sir."

"A postcard? The son of a bitch sent you a postcard? Who does he think he is, Zorro?"

"It was from the girl, sir."

"His girl?"

"Yes, although I don't think she's really his girl, sir."

"Is that so? Dubin, you're turning out to be more interesting than I imagined. Well, whatever you call her, she's stuck to him like glue, right?"

"Oh, I expect she's with him, sir. I just doubt she'd do anything to jeopardize him. That's why I wasn't sure if I should bother you with this. I realize you've got your hands full, General, but the arrest is under your command."

"You did right, Dubin. And don't worry about us. We're kicking the shit out of these pricks. Not that it wouldn't be going even better if our President stopped mousing around with the Russians. We should be in Saarbrücken, but FDR's afraid if we move into Germany too fast Stalin will go batty." Teedle held up there, clearly reconsidering the wisdom of his remarks over an open telephone line. The heavy guns went off again in a second and the connection was lost.

A few days later, on December 15, I was in the officers' mess at about 7:00 a.m., eating a breakfast of powdered eggs with Tony, when a pimply young orderly, a new recruit who took virtually every development as an occasion for hysteria, flew in to tell me that I was wanted in the signal office. It was Teedle, this time at the other end of a coded teletype writer. Once the signalman indicated I was present, the machine began spitting tape, which the code reader transferred with intense chattering onto the yellow bale in the machine.

"Bastard located," Teedle wrote. "Up near town of Houffalize in the VIII Corps sector. Robin Hood now. Whole merry band with him. Told VIII Corps command was sent by OSS to reconnoiter German positions. Wish you proceed to Houffalize to arrest."

"Me?" I said this to the signalman, who asked if I wanted to transmit that response. I chose something more diplomatic, suggesting the duty might be better suited to the Provost Marshal.

"Negative. You will recognize subject," he wrote back. "Also know entire background. MPs here have combat responsibilities with POWs. We are fighting a war FYI."

I considered my alternatives, but ultimately responded that I understood my orders.

Teedle wrote, "Subject due back in 72 hours. Presently scouting behind enemy lines."

"How likely to return?"

"Very. Left girl behind. Proceed at once. Will notify London of imminent arrest."

I went immediately to Colonel Maples. With Teedle, I had been reluctant to raise technicalities, knowing he would not tolerate them, but there was a fundamental problem. I opened a copy of the *Manual for Courts-Martial* on the Colonel's desk to Rule 20.

20. COURTS-MARTIAL PROCEDURE BEFORE TRIAL—ARREST AND CONFINEMENT—WHO MAY ORDER: METHOD—THE FOLLOWING CLASSES OF PERSON SUBJECT TO MILITARY LAW WILL BE PLACED IN ARREST OR CONFINEMENT UNDER ARTICLE OF WAR 69, AS FOLLOWS:

OFFICERS—BY COMMANDING OFFICERS ONLY, IN PERSON, THROUGH OTHER OFFICERS, OR BY ORAL OR WRITTEN ORDERS OR COMMUNICATIONS. THE AUTHORITY TO PLACE SUCH PERSONS IN ARREST OR CONFINEMENT WILL NOT BE DELEGATED.

In other words, Martin could only be arrested by someone directly under Teedle's command, a member of the 18th Armored Division. After some debate at the time the arrest order was issued, our staff had concluded that Teedle, rather than Winters at OSS, remained Martin's commander, because Martin had disobeyed the very order transferring him back. But surely I wasn't under the General. If so, I couldn't arrest Martin without jeopardizing the ensuing court-martial.

Maples pinched his thumb and forefinger through his long mustache, which had gone completely white in the last few months and now resembled a smear of shaving lather. As usual, he remained reluctant to buck Teedle and came up with a lawyerly solution. He would get Third Army G-1 to designate me to the 18th solely for the purpose of carrying out Martin's arrest.

"We'll have to button up the paperwork. But you best get up there, David. Patton won't be amused if Martin slips away again. What a peculiar situation." The Colonel wobbled his hoary head. "Human misconduct, David. There's more imagination and mystery there than in the world of art."

"May I take Bidwell, Colonel?"

"Yes, of course." He sent me off to find a replacement in court for the day.

By noon, Biddy and I had our papers and were once more on the road. It was dank, with fog again gathered like smoke over the hills, and we had full side panels mounted to the canvas top on the jeep. Houffalize barely showed up on the maps, but it was somewhere in the vicinity of Saint-Vith, about 150 miles away. We'd be approaching areas of serious fighting and figured we'd do well to make it there

by sunset the next day. Not knowing exactly what we'd encounter, we traveled with full packs and winter overcoats.

As we neared Metz and the territory the Americans had
taken in recent weeks, we encountered signs reading
ACHTUNG MINEN, left behind by the retreating German
Army. I was not sure if these were warnings for their own
troops, or a form of psychological warfare. When we made
a stop, I checked with units from the Sixth Armored Division, who reported that minesweepers had been over the
roads, but otherwise to proceed with care. "You wouldn't be
the first guy, Captain, who walked behind a bush to take a
leak and got a leg blown off instead," a sergeant told me.

Proceeding north, we passed occasional lines of ambulances heading to the local field hospitals. For lack of Red
Cross trucks, jeeps had been commandeered, with the
wounded strapped on stretchers over the hoods and back-
seats. Near 4:30, after we began thinking about settling
down someplace for the night, we encountered an MP roadblock. A squint-eyed policeman pushed his head all the way
inside our vehicle. I removed our orders from the inside
pocket of my overcoat, but the MP didn't bother with them.

"Where does Li'l Abner live?" he asked me.

"Are you sober, soldier?"

"Answer the question, Captain."

"Dogpatch."

"And what's the name of Brooklyn's baseball team?"
He was pointing to Biddy at the wheel.

"The Dodgers," he answered grumpily. "And they ain't
no kind of a team neither." Amazingly, that response drew
a laugh from the MP and immediately solved the problem. All day, the policeman told us, they'd had reports of
German impostors in American uniforms who'd crossed

our lines to engage in sabotage, cutting phone connections, removing signs, and occasionally pointing our units toward German forces, the same stuff Gita had done to them on D-Day.

"This happens again," the MP said to me, "show them your ID card. Theirs all say 'For Identification Only.'" Our officers' IDs bore a typo, 'Indentification,' quickly noted among the newly commissioned as a token of the value of their promotion. Some stone-headed Kraut had been unable to resist correcting the Americans on their English.

We crossed into the First Army zone and spent the night in Luxembourg City, in a hotel being used as rear-echelon headquarters by elements of the Ninth Armored Division. We had gotten farther than we expected, and it looked as if we would reach Houffalize by the next afternoon. I was awakened at about 5:30 a.m. by heavy shelling to the north. We would be headed straight that way, and I asked the major who'd arranged our billet what was happening.

"No worries. The Germans like to fire their guns while they still have them. They're not going anywhere. Bradley's pulled VIII Corps back for the time being. We're thin up on the front lines, but the Krauts know they'd just be running right into a huge force if they pushed forward. All this banging won't last more than an hour."

On our way out of town a young bazooka man with a strange accent asked if he could hitch a ride to his unit about ten miles north and climbed in back next to our packs. From a small town in Pennsylvania where they still spoke a German dialect, he was an amazingly cheerful kid, utterly indifferent to the war. He sang us several songs he'd learned at home in a strong, if not always perfectly pitched, tenor, and was in the midst of a ballad about a young lass pining for her lover gone to battle, when the jeep suddenly vaulted through the air aboard a tidal wave of sound and dirt. Next thing I knew, I was in a wet ditch at the roadside. When I looked up, there was a smoking pit in the farm field beside me, probably from a heavy mortar. The jeep was several yards ahead, canted at a thirty-degree angle with the front and rear right wheels also in the ditch. The canvas coverings I'd been thrown through flapped uselessly in the wind, while the young Pennsylvania Dutch boy was nearby in the field, still smiling as he got to his feet. I yelled to him to watch for mines, but promptly discovered that the rocket had fallen out of his bazooka and landed in the mud alongside me. I looked at the shell in a little pool of still water, afraid even to touch it for fear it would arm itself. I was edging away when another shell hit about a quarter mile ahead, leaving a crater that had taken out the road from side to side. The Germans had to be closer than anyone figured.

I yelled twice for Bidwell. He turned out to have been thrown only to the vehicle floor, and he poked his head up, none the worse for wear. The jeep was still running, but Biddy looked it over and announced that because of the angle at which the vehicle was pitched, the differential wouldn't let the rear wheels turn. We swore at the thing as if it was a spavined horse, and tried to shoulder it back up to the road, well aware that another shell could land any instant.

A small convoy arrived behind us. The gold-bar lieutenant in charge jumped down from the truck to help, while he sent his sergeant ahead to try to figure how they were going to get past the crater in the road.

"Some hellacious fighting up ahead, Captain," he told me, when I explained where we were headed. "You picked the wrong day for legal work. Looks like Hitler's decided to make his last stand." He suggested we proceed west.

With the help of several of his troops, we got the jeep out of the ditch and fixed a flat on the right rear tire. The bazooka man put his weapon together and climbed onto one of the convoy's trucks, while Biddy and I headed in the direction of Neufchâteau. Two of the canvas panels had torn and flapped as we drove, admitting a frigid breeze.

The sky was too low and bleak for aircraft and thus for bombs, but the pounding of heavy artillery was constant. About an hour later, we reached a crossroads, where the roads wagon-wheeled in all directions, beside signs for Aachen, Luxembourg, Düsseldorf, Neufchâteau, and Reims. Two MPs stood at the center of the intersection, holding up every vehicle. When one reached us, he asked for our papers, which he examined for quite some time.

"If you're headed north, how come you're going west?"

I told him about the shelling.

"Uh-huh," he said. "And how long you been stationed in Nancy?" When I'd answered that, he said, "What's the name of the main square there?"

I answered again, but pulled my ID card from my wallet. "See here." Biddy pointed out the word 'Indentification' but the MP stared as if we'd chosen another language.

"Sergeant, aren't you trying to make sure we're not German impostors?" I asked.

"Captain, all due respect, but I'm trying to make sure you're not a deserter."

"Deserter!" I was offended by the mere notion.

"Believe you me. Yes, sir. If you don't mind my saying so, Captain, those RTC boys," he said, referring to the replacement troops, "they don't know what the fuck to do when the shells start flying. Over in the 28th it seems like half the division has taken off for the rear. I found several hauling along dead bodies, making like they were looking for the medics. Another one told me he was a messenger, only he couldn't recall what he was going to tell anybody. And plenty waving their hankies and giving themselves up to the Krauts with barely a bullet fired. I hear close to ten thousand boys from the 106th surrendered to the Germans already. And not just enlisted men, not by any means. We got plenty of officers running from the bullets today, saying they were going to check with battalion."

"Are we talking about Americans?" I asked. "What in the hell is going on?"

"Heavy woods up north. Apparently the whole fucking SS Sixth Panzer was hidden in the trees. Von Rundstedt busted out of there with tanks and artillery, going through our lines like grease through a goose. The VIII Corps is getting a pretty good pasting right now. I'm hearing a lot of crazy stuff. Some guys are claiming there are German tanks fifty miles west of here already. We had an antiaircraft battalion in retreat come through twenty minutes ago, and some of the enlisted guys were saying rumor is their orders are to fall all the way back and defend Paris. I'll tell you one thing, Captain, this fucking war ain't over yet."

We turned north from there, but within half an hour, as the MP had warned, the road was choked with trucks and armored vehicles streaming south in full retreat. Many of these units were in complete disarray, separated from command and driving on only to find safety. We came upon an armored battalion stopped on the side of the road, completely out of gas. A young boy, a buck private, was sitting on a wheel well, crying with abandon, wailing and looking around as if he expected someone else to tell him how to stop. Every minute or so, another soldier gave him a few pats on the shoulder. A sergeant explained that the boy's best buddy had been blown to bits not three feet from him this morning.

Back in the jeep, Biddy said, "Sir, this here ain't no time to be arresting somebody, not in the middle of a battlefield."

"We have orders, Biddy." I really didn't know what else to do.

"I'm just saying, sir, gotta have a way to carry out your orders. Better to hold back here for a day or two till the smoke clears. Wherever the hell Martin was, Captain, he's gotta be on the move now, probably comin right this way."

He was making sense. We headed west again, where we were stopped twice more by MP patrols pushing back deserters. Near dark, we finally arrived in Neufchâteau. It was a postcard of a town, with a crush of pretty, narrow buildings and steep streets of cobblestone, but there was an air of chaos. We reported to the rear-echelon head-quarters for VIII Corps, in the columned Palais de Justice, where they were receiving grim reports from forward command in Bastogne. Men seemed to be rushing in and out of every office, shouting information that someone else immediately screamed was wrong. Several regiments had given up under white flags, while many other units were unaccounted for. Whenever I could get someone's brief attention, his eyes seemed to wander to the windows, expecting to see the German Panzers out there any second. Clerks were in the halls boxing papers, separating what needed to be carried along so the remainder could be burned at the inception of the retreat.

After a long wait in the signal office, I finally got a young corpsman to send a wired message to General Teedle, giving our current position and asking for further direction. Then I conducted a reconnaissance for a billet. I was directed to officers' quarters that had been set up two blocks away in the city hall. As I passed down the corridors, looking for an empty bunk, I encountered little knots of off-duty officers, huddled and often passing around whiskey as they talked in suppressed murmurs. No one seemed able to accept what was happening. There hadn't been a day since I'd landed in Europe that the Germans had made progress across a broad front. A fellow who claimed to have seen the latest maps said we'd been suckered too far east, that the Nazis were about to split the Twelfth Army group, dividing the First Army from the Third, and the Ninth from the other two, with pincer actions to follow on the northern and southern flanks. No one knew the limits of today's German advance, but it was clear they had the upper hand, and several of these officers remarked about earlier reports of Nazi movements that General Bradley had ignored. Every face reflected the same thoughts: We were not going home soon. We were not going to win the war by Christmas, or New Year's, or even Valentine's Day. When I bedded down, I finally asked myself the question that nobody would utter: Were we going to win the war at all?

We were, I thought then. We had to. We had to win this war. I would give my life in order to stop Hitler. And I knew, despite whatever panic gripped the replacement

troops who'd deserted on the front, that most of the sea-
soned officers sleeping in this building felt the same way.
I turned off the light and realized only then that I'd forgotten to eat. There was a K ration in my pack, but I was
too tired and disappointed to bother.

Light across my eyes woke me a few hours later. My
first thought was another explosion, and as I gathered myself I couldn't understand how I had missed the sound.
Instead, I found the young corporal from the Signal
Corps who'd taken my message to Teedle holding the
flashlight against his face so I could recognize him. My
watch said 2:10 a.m. He whispered to avoid waking the
other five officers snoring around me in the old office, and
led me into the hall, still in my briefs.

"Captain, this signal just came through, sir, labeled
'Immediate Attention.'" I could see from the boy's face
he had read the telegram in the envelope and thought immediate attention was warranted. It was from Teedle, and
had arrived in code, the boy said, requiring deciphering
by the cryptographers.

```
Classified Information/Top Secret/Destroy After
Reading
        OSS states man you seek Soviet spy STOP
Arrest top priority STOP Further instruction by
radio 0600 STOP
```

15. JUMP

Teedle never got through on December 17. Many of the Allied communications centers around Saint-Vith had been cut off by the Germans. Although we were south of there, the remaining lines and relays were dedicated to signal traffic more important than the fate of one man, even a spy, and I spent approximately forty hours on a bench in the VIII Corps signal office, waiting to hear from the General.

In Neufchâteau, like many other places, the Signal Corps had established its headquarters in the dusty offices of the PTT—Postes, Télégraphes et Téléphones—which was housed in a narrow pinkish building on a corner. Topped by a strange iron cupola, it looked as if it were wearing a helmet. From my seat inside, I could watch the young women, with their bright lipstick and the sleek hairdos required to fit under their headsets, plugging and unplugging the lines in the tall switchboards. American enlisted men strolled back and forth to keep an eye on them, just as the Germans had been doing a few months ago. Every now and then, civilians would enter to mail a letter or package, which the dour clerks accepted with no assurance that the item would ever get through.

The one compensation in my wait was that this was probably the most informative location in Neufchâteau. I asked no questions, but overhearing the messengers and aides who rushed up the stairs made it possible to piece things together. The news was almost completely dismal. Sepp Dietrich's 6th Panzers were rolling steadily in our direction, overrunning the thinly manned VIII Corps positions. Nor was it clear yet if any force could come to their aid, since the 5th Panzer Division was advancing south to hold off Patton.

Listening from my outpost on the bench, it was difficult not to admire the Nazi strategy, however reluctantly. Given the salient Dietrich was cutting, Runstedt's plan seemed aimed at severing the American forces, then crossing the Meuse and driving on toward Antwerp. If the Nazis succeeded, the Allied troops in Holland and northern Belgium would be cut off entirely, without avenue for retreat. Dunkirk would look like a minor setback by comparison. With a third of the Allied forces held hostage, Hitler might be in a position to negotiate an armistice. Or, if his madness prevailed, he could destroy them and then turn south, with other forces roaring out of Germany in one last effort to reconquer western Europe. The betting in the signal office was that, insane or not, Hitler would make peace, if only to give himself time to rebuild his military. On the bench, I thought repeatedly about Martin's predictions of war and more war. It was hard to believe a victory that had seemed inevitable could be imperiled in only days. Every few minutes the same simple resolve lit up in me like a flashing sign, as it had since I arrived here. We had to win this war. I had to help.

Now and then, in mild desperation, I would cross the street to the rear headquarters in the Palais de Justice, a vast columned building of orange stone, to see if my orders had been misdirected there. Biddy also visited on occasion, and we walked in circles up and down Neufchâteau's tiny sloping streets, although the cobbles proved icy and treacherous on the steeper grades. It snowed both days, heavy flakes descending from a sky so low it seemed only a few feet over our heads. Hitler had either planned well or been lucky, since the cloud cover made it impossible for us to put planes in the air, unless they wanted to fly right over the barrels of the German antiaircraft guns.

I hesitated at first to share Teedle's highly classified message with Biddy, but decided I had to tell him, so he would understand whatever happened next.

"A spy!" I was ready for Biddy to say he'd always had suspicions about Martin, but he seemed to have the same difficulties I had in accommodating himself to the idea. "Cap, how in the world's that make any sense after what we seen?" I'd pondered that and one of the most disconcerting thoughts to invade me in the last two days was that the operation at La Saline Royale, which we'd so proudly joined, had been undertaken in reality to hinder the U.S. Army for the benefit of the Soviets. Despite Patton's outrage about the timing of the explosions, I couldn't quite make the notion add up, but then again, I realized, that was how spies succeeded, by making themselves appear to be patriots. OSS was bound to have had reasons for its conclusion.

At 4:00 a.m. on December 19, the same corporal, Lightenall, shook me awake on the bench where I'd been sleeping. Teedle had gotten through, once more using the encrypted teletype. I sat down in front of the keyboard myself. I'd had time to learn how to use the machine while I waited.

"Confirm receipt of my signal of 12/16/44."

I did.

"Not even I thought that," Teedle continued. "London insists there is evidence." Without fears of interception, the General proved expansive. I imagined him after a day of battle, his canteen in hand while he shouted at the teletype operator and, in the midst of another sleepless night, diverted himself with one more duel with me. The dialogue was stranger than ever because of the eerie interval before his response emerged with a sudden violent clatter.

In a gauged way, I asked what had been on my mind, whether the operation we'd taken part in at La Saline Royale was somehow in service of Martin's new allegiance.

"No idea. London still talking riddles. Seems our man not working against good guys in current game. Instead, getting ready for next one, moving ahead so he can inform red team re our team's movements, also try to slow them. If our team, red team don't come to blows, red team gets bigger piece of what's been taken when this game ends. Following?"

"Roger."

"London desperate for arrest, but per usual won't put in writing. Prefer not to explain to 531 fans in D.C. how star began playing for other team. Continue proceeding on my order. Our man still believed in VIII Corps sector. Contact General Middleton to make arrest."

I explained the problems with that directive. By now, Middleton had decided to abandon Bastogne as a forward HQ. His artillery, six or seven battalions of 155mm guns and eight-inch howitzers, had already begun a staged withdrawal, but none of them had been able to occupy their prepared rearward positions because the Panzer elements were upon them so quickly. They were basically on the run back here. A faster-moving Airborne Division, the 101st, was going to take over and was trucking up from Reims. I told the General it was chancy for any communication to get through. More important, there were legal issues. As I had discussed with Colonel Maples, only someone under Teedle's direct command could arrest Martin. Teedle reacted as I expected.

"Goddamn Army's been fucked up since they put Washington on a horse."

"Rules, General. We would have to free him."

There was a long wait for an answer. I was sure Teedle was contemplating how he would explain it to both the OSS and Patton, when Martin waltzed off through a legal loophole.

Finally Teedle wrote, "You volunteering to go?"

My fingers faltered on the keys. But I understood the logic. Bidwell and I were the nearest soldiers for 150 miles who were even arguably under Teedle's command. I couldn't imagine how two men in a jeep were supposed to move on terrain under assault by Panzer forces, but what I'd been thinking for three days remained close to my heart. I would do what I had to to win this war.

I wrote, "Yes, sir."

"Good," he fired back in a moment.

"Sir, will need better information on our man's whereabouts. Unlikely still at Houffalize." Biddy had told me an astounding story, which he swore he'd heard from the MPs who'd been at Houffalize on December 17. American and German military police had stood back to back at an intersection in the town directing traffic, both sides too busy and too lightly armed to bother battling one another. The Americans pointed their forces toward retreat, while the Germans waved on the reconnaissance and mine-clearing crews that were making way for the Panzers only a few miles behind them. By now, Houffalize had fallen.

"London already contacted Supreme Headquarters, which understands utmost priority. Will seek their assistance. Stand by for further orders."

I thought we were done, but a second later the keys flew again.

"How bad up there?"

"Fine here," I typed. "Hell on wheels a few miles forward."

"Tell them, hold on. Cavalry's coming. Will see you at the Siegfried line. Expect that SOB in chains. Out."

It took two more days before further orders came by cable.

Confirmed officer you seek commanding battalion
NW of Bastogne STOP Proceed RAF airstrip Virton
for transport to make arrest STOP

Late in the day on December 21, Biddy and I drove due south. Snow so solid that it looked like someone emptying a box of baking powder had been coming down all night, letting up only with the arrival of a cold front that felt just like the Canadian Express that bore down on Kindle County in the worst of winter.

The so-called airstrip at Virton proved to be no more than a wide dirt path recently bulldozed through a snowy field, but we found the small ground crew, mostly flight mechanics, expecting us. There were no hangars, because it would have been mad to house airplanes this far east in the face of the offensive, but the Brits had been landing in the dark here for a few days, hauling supplies cadged from Montgomery's forces, which were then trucked to our troops. Our soldiers, once expected to slice through the Germans in no time, were now short of everything, except, ironically, fuel, which had been stockpiled for their lightning advance.

"You the one going to Bastogne, then?" a flight sergeant asked me. "Place is damn near surrounded, you know, sir. Germans battering the hell out of everything. All the big roads go right through there, so Jerry can't go rolling on without taking the town." The Ardennes had provided an excellent hiding place for the Panzers, but one reason Bradley and Middleton had discounted the reports that the German tanks were massing there was because a forest was such an unpromising locale for a tank assault. It was easier to run over men than thousands of trees. Once the Panzers had crawled from the woods, they still were not able to maneuver freely, because the fall we'd been through had left half the fields swamps. I'd heard often about our tanks sinking. The Panzers were regarded as better machines — our Shermans were so likely to ignite that the troops called them Ronsons — but German treads got stuck in the muck same as American, and the weight of the biggest of Panzers, the King Tigers, would literally bury them in the wet ground. Because the Panzer forces were confined to the existing roads, holding on to the paths and byways for as long as possible was the key to slowing the Germans and allowing the Americans to reassemble for a counteroffensive. Patton reportedly had outflanked the 5th Panzer and was still speeding north to help out.

"Sounds like it's going to be a difficult landing there," I said to the sergeant.

"Landing?" He had a wrench in his hand and was toying with an engine part, but now he turned full around, a craggy English face. "Crikey, mate. Don't you know you're getting dropped?"

"Dropped?"

"Parachute. You know, big bedsheet in the sky?" His smile faltered. "You're a paratrooper, then, sir, ain't you?"

"I'm a lawyer."

"Oh, Lord Jesus."

His reaction said it all. It was so absurd, I laughed out loud. As I left to tell Biddy, I heard the sergeant explaining my situation to his crew. "Poor sod," he said, "thought he was going to Bastogne in the royal carriage."

Biddy couldn't even manage a pained smile.

"Parachute? Shit, Captain, my knees are lard when I get up on the roof of our tenement. I don't know about no parachute. You got any parachute training?"

I'd had none. Yet I had told myself for three days that I would do whatever I had to to win this war. It was a vow I'd taken and now would keep. If Martin was really intent on impeding our troops in Germany, I had to do this.

"Biddy, there's no need for both of us to go."

"Aw, hell, Captain. You know I'm just blabbing. Ain't no way I'm gonna let loose of you now, so let's not bother with that talk."

The plan, as it was explained to us, was essentially an experiment. For the moment, there was no way to resupply the troops in Bastogne. The main road from Neufchâteau had been cut off and in Hitler's weather, flyers could not navigate by sight to make airdrops at heights safe from antiaircraft fire. The RAF pilots had agreed to try one low-altitude night flight, thinking that if it worked, more planes would do the same tomorrow evening. Three pallets of medical supplies were going to be parachuted in with us. If Biddy and I made it, doctors might follow.

There were a couple of hours before the plane was due and in that time we got what would pass for jump instructions: toes down, knees and feet together, eyes straight ahead. We made dozens of efforts to practice rolling as our boots struck the ground. The knee I'd cut when the dump exploded had healed well and had given me no pain for weeks, but now there were little phantom throbs each time we reenacted the landing. After the first half hour, it was clear to me that our instructors, with all but one exception, had never jumped themselves. Nonetheless, they made a good case that if the chute released, we didn't have much to do but hang on and try not to break our legs. Real training, which addressed maneuvers in the event the chute ripped or inverted, or the suspension lines or risers snarled, would do us no good anyway from five hundred feet. None of those problems could be fixed before we hit the ground.

"Telling you the truth, Captain, t'ain't the jump what

ought to concern you. Hanging like an apple on a tree, if Jerry works out you're there—that's a worry, sir."

The crew packed our chutes for us, then bundled our overcoats and cinched them beneath our val-packs, which would come down behind us with the medical supplies. We donned jumpsuits over our wool outdoor uniforms, and traded our headgear for paratroopers' helmets with their leather chin cups, the better to absorb the shock of the chute opening. Then we waited. Every ten minutes, I wandered outside to pee. My body temperature was about the same as marble. I simply could not imagine the circumstances under which I might be alive in another two hours.

Nearing 8:30, the truck convoys that would carry off the supplies on the arriving aircraft began to form in the field, but there was still no sign of the planes. By 9:00, I began to suspect they would not get here and wondered if I could pretend to be disappointed, when the mere thought flushed me with relief.

And then they came. The initial drone might have been insects if it were another season. The ground crew ignited dozens of Coleman lanterns and ran them out to illuminate the borders of the strip, and the planes came down with barely thirty seconds between them. The convoy crews rushed forward to unload.

The flight sergeant who'd been assisting me helped me into the rest of my parachute gear. First was a Mae West, the life vest required because there was no guarantee we wouldn't settle in a lake or pond, then I stepped into the harness, a web of straps and buckles that were tightened on each side of my crotch.

"Not exactly comfy knickers, but your nuts might still

be rattling round once you land, Captain." What I had on already was cumbersome, but it turned out I'd just made a start. Since we could put down on enemy ground, the sergeant inserted a Thompson submachine gun under the waist web, and clipped on two five-pound boxes of machine-gun ammo, then strapped a fight knife on my leg and, for good measure, a small Hawkins mine, looking like a can of paint thinner, against my boot. He turned my woven waist piece into a combat tool belt, hanging off it a trenching shovel and a canteen, my pistol in its holster, a skein of rope, a pair of wire cutters, and a folding knife. An angle-headed flashlight went under a band on my chest. Then, when I thought he was done, he put a reserve chute across my belly. I expected to topple any second. Even Biddy, huge as he was, looked weighed down.

"You're traveling light, mate, 'cause you're first-timers. Paratroops usually carry a Griswold bag under one arm."

Biddy and I were jeeped to our plane, a light bomber called a Hampden. It had two engines, a silvery fuselage, and a low glass nose that made it appear like a flying turtle. We stood with difficulty on the car's hood and with two men steadying us from below climbed a ladder through the bomb bay into the bare sheet-metal belly of the plane.

There was a four-man crew there—pilot, bombardier, gunner, and radioman—but their attitude toward us seemed slightly standoffish, even for Brits. I wondered if the RAF would have been trying this run without Teedle's—or the OSS's—insistence at Supreme Headquarters on the paramount importance of Biddy and me reaching Bastogne. Perhaps, I decided, these four were just exhibiting a natural reluctance to develop attachments to the doomed.

With all the gear on, we could get only the rear edge of our butts onto two fold-down seats bolted to the fuselage, but the radioman harnessed us in with the strapping that had secured the unloaded cargo. The pilot, a Flying Officer, came rear to brief us. We would reach Bastogne in twenty minutes, he said. As soon as the joe hole, the bomb bay in the silver floor in front of us, opened, we should hook our rip cords to the line above and get out on the double. Our drop area was in open fields just west of Bastogne, near a town called Savy. If the Germans figured out we were in the air, the gunner and radioman would put down covering fire with the Vickers machine guns on turrets in the gun wells in front of us. However, the pilot thought the Nazis would never see the chutes in the dark, because the sound of the plane would draw all the fire. He was businesslike but made it plain that if there was a fools' contest here, they were probably the winners. I understood then why we'd received such an unenthusiastic greeting.

Sitting there in the instants before the plane took off, I felt completely detached from myself. I thought I had given up on life, but as soon as the engines triggered, a sharp whinny of protest rose straight out of my heart. This is crazy, I thought. Crazy. Men down there are going to try to kill me, men who have never met me, men I've never tried to harm. Suddenly, I could not remember why that made any sense.

We built speed, enduring that second of weightlessness when we left the ground. I looked to Biddy, but he was staring at the floor, clearly trying to contain himself.

As we climbed, I remembered that I'd passed all that time waiting without writing to my family or Grace, but I couldn't think of what I would have said besides 'I love you, and I am going to leave you for the sake of madness.'

As we flew, the interior grew unbearably hot, but I was principally preoccupied with trying to ignore the urgency of my bladder and my bowels. The bombardier came over and crouched beside me. He was a Sergeant, a handsome dark-haired kid.

"First jump, then?" He had to repeat himself several times because the throbbing buzz of the engines filled the entire belly of the plane.

I nodded and asked for last-minute pointers.

He smiled. "Keep a tight arsehole."

Almost on cue then, Biddy vomited in front of himself and sat there shaking his head, manifestly ashamed. "It's the heat," I yelled. The interior of the Hampden was like a blast furnace, and fouled with the sickening fumes of the plane's exhaust. I felt woozy myself. The bombardier acted as if he'd seen it all before.

"You'll feel better now," he told Biddy.

When the phone beside the hatch flashed, the bombardier grabbed it, then motioned to fix our chinstraps.

"All right, then," he yelled, "who's first?"

We hadn't discussed this, but Biddy raised a hand weakly, saying he had to get out. He hooked on, then crawled to the edge of the joe hole. The doors fell open slowly, emitting a frozen gale. Some part of my brain was still working, because I realized the plane had been overheated in anticipation of the cold. The bomb bay was not even fully extended when Gideon lowered his head and suddenly disappeared without a backward glance.

After hooking overhead, I tried to stand, but my legs were like water, and it would have been difficult anyway given all the equipment I was wearing and the shimmying of the plane. Like Biddy, I went on all fours, remembering too late to avoid the puddle he had left behind. The instant he was gone, I was at the edge, leaning into the great rush of icy air. My face went numb at once, as I looked down to the vague form of the land moving below in the darkness. In the white leather jump gloves, my hands were clamped to the edge of the bomb bay. The bombardier placed his face right next to mine.

"Captain, I'm afraid you must be going. Otherwise, sir, I'm going to have to put my boot in your bum."

Ma, what am I doing? I thought. What am I doing? And then I thought, I must do this, I must do this, because it is my duty, and if I do not do my duty, my life will be worth nothing.

But still, my body would not surrender to my will. I shouted to the bombardier, "I'll take that kick in the ass."

It was like diving into a pool, the shock of cold, the sudden distance from sound. I did a complete somersault in the air and came upright with my heart pumping nothing but terror, while one thought leaped at me with startling clarity. As my chute snapped open and I was slammed against the sky, a white pain ignited in my arms. I had forgotten to grip the harness, falling with my hands spread before me like a child taking a spill, and I feared for one second that I had dislocated my shoulders. But even that was not enough to distract me. Because in the instant of free fall, I had realized I hadn't really come to find Martin. The form I'd seen as I tore through space was Gita Lodz.

For half the descent there was no sound or sensation except the racing cold. I saw only the earth, black on black, a swimming form without perspective. And then it was as if the night, like the shell of a hatching egg, was suddenly pecked by light. Volleys of antiaircraft fire came from at least three sides and the rockets tore by like massive lethal bugs. Then, without warning, a squeal of red flares brought day to the sky. I caught sight of Biddy's chute, mushroomed below me, and took heart for just a second, knowing I was not alone here, but that was replaced at once by another spasm of terror when I realized that the Germans were firing at us. The AA was still blasting, but smaller rounds also ripped by like shooting stars. In the instantaneous glow, I actually saw one make a hole in the canopy of Biddy's chute, whose descent accelerated. It would be a good thing for him, though, assuming he survived, to get out of the barrage.

Paying my nickel on a Saturday afternoon, I'd heard the shots whanging past Tom Mix in the movie-theater speakers. But the real sound of a round that misses is just a sinister little sizzle and a wake of roiled air, a bee farting as it passes, followed instantaneously by the sharp report of the rifle the bullet came from. The German infantry, thank God, hadn't practiced shooting falling objects. A dozen shots missed by only a few feet. But as the ground came near, my ear was bored by an intense pain.

My next memory is of lying in the snow. Under my nose, Biddy was waving an ammonia ampoule he'd extracted from the first-aid kit on the front of his helmet. I flinched from the driving odor.

"C'mon, Captain. Those 88s will be on us any minute." I continued to lie there while I put things together. Somewhere along, I realized he'd already cut me free of my chute. "You passed out, Cap. Maybe a concussion." He wrestled me to my feet. I reached to grab my pack, which he'd also collected, then stopped dead, astonished by what I felt against the back of my thigh. I retrieved the sensation at once from the remote memories of childhood. I had shit in my pants.

Behind Bidwell I ran in a half crouch through a farm field where the snow was up to our knees until we reached a wooded border. All that worry about parachute training and it turned out we were landing on a pillow. After the flares, we knew American forces would be looking for us, assuming we'd come down in an area they controlled. While Biddy struggled in the dark to read the compass strapped to his arm, I shed my parachute harness and pushed farther into the brush, where I dropped both pairs of trousers. It could not have been more than ten degrees but I still preferred to stand there naked, rather than go on with crap trailing down my legs. I cut my briefs off with the jackknife from my belt, cleaned up as best I could, and hurled away my underwear, which ended up snagged on one of the bushes. Biddy was watching by now, but asked for no explanation.

A recon group arrived five minutes later. We raced with them to gather up the medical bundles before the German artillery turned on us, then clambered into the backs of a pair of two-ton trucks from an ordnance unit that had pulled up. As the vehicles rolled out, Biddy, beside me, reached up to touch my helmet. Removing it, I saw a dent in the steel above my right ear, and a fracture running down two inches to the edge. That was from the round that had knocked me out. I shook my head, as if I could take some meaning from the nearness of the miss, but nothing came to me. There was alive and there was dead. I wasn't dead. Why or how close really meant nothing compared with the elemental fact.

We had ridden half a mile before I picked up on the radio traffic blaring from the cab. Someone had not been found.

"The Brits," Biddy said. "The Hampden went down right after you landed." The Kraut AA had caught it in a direct hit, a giant ball of fire and smoke, he said, but they were east of us by then, over the Germans. I thought about the four men we'd flown with, but I could make no more of their demise than I had of my own survival. Instead I turned to Biddy to complain for a second about the cold.

The soldiers who had collected us were elements of the 110th Infantry Regiment of the 28th Infantry Division who had been cut off in their retreat and ended up here, formed up with the 101st Airborne, which was the principal force defending Bastogne. They drove us back to their command post set up in the hamlet of Savy. The town consisted of a few low buildings constructed of the native gray stone. In the largest of them, a cattle barn, the acting combat team commander, Lieutenant Colonel Hamza Algar, had established his headquarters.

Algar was working at a small desk set in the center of the dirt floor, when we came in to report. The orderlies had done their best to sweep the place clean, but it was still a barn, with stalls on both sides and open beams above, and the residual reek of its former inhabitants. Four staff officers were standing around Algar, as he went over lists and maps beside a lantern. They were in field jackets and gloves, shoulders hunched against the cold. It was better in here, because there was no wind, but there was still no heat.

Algar stood up to return my salute, then offered his hand.

"How much training did you have for that jump, Doc?" he asked me. "That was damn brave. But, Doc, you came to the right place. Unfortunately." This made the third or fourth time since we'd landed that I'd been addressed as 'Doc.' Perhaps it was the concussion, or the numbness of surviving, but I realized only now that this greeting wasn't being offered in the fashion of Bugs Bunny.

"Begging your pardon, Colonel, but I'm afraid you have a misimpression. I'm a lawyer."

Algar was small, five foot six or seven, and perhaps in compensation was plainly attentive to his good looks. He had a narrow split mustache over his upper lip, carefully trimmed even on the battlefield, and his hair was pomaded. But he was clearly bewildered.

"I was told you were dropped with medical supplies. Sulfa. Bandages. Plasma." Algar sat down and turned to his aides. "We get lawyers by parachute," he said. "What about ammunition? Or reinforcements? Jesus Christ." In a second, he got around to asking why I was there. He stared at me even longer than he had when I'd said I wasn't an M.D., once he heard my explanation.

"Martin?" he asked. "Bob Martin? They've sent you to

arrest Bob Martin? Don't they know what the hell is
going on here? We've got everybody firing a weapon, including the cooks. I have three companies under the command of NCOs. I've got two second lieutenants who
between them have a total of one week's experience in
Europe. And they want you to arrest one of my best combat officers?"

"Those were my orders, sir."

"Well, I'll give you different orders, Captain. You arrest Major Martin or anybody else who's able-bodied and
firing back at the Germans and I won't bother arresting
you. I'll shoot you, Captain Dubin, and don't take that for
jest."

I looked to the circle of officers for help.

"Three days from now," Algar told me, "four, whatever
it takes to deal with the Krauts, we can sort this out.
McAuliffe can talk to Teedle. They can take it up with
Patton if they like. Or even Eisenhower. They'll hash it
out at the top. Right now we're all trying to save this
bloody town. And ourselves. Understood?"

I didn't answer. There was a silent moment of stand-
off, before Algar spoke again.

"Just out of curiosity, Dubin, what is it exactly that
Martin's supposed to have done?"

I took a second evaluating what I could say, then asked
to speak to him alone. It was too cold for Algar to ask his
officers to step outside, but he shooed them to a corner.

"Colonel," I said in a whisper, "there's a question of
loyalty."

Algar leaned forward so quickly I thought he meant to
hit me.

"Listen, Dubin, Bob Martin has been fighting with the

110th for almost a week now, leading a combat unit, and doing one heck of a job. As a volunteer. He's been through hell, like the rest of us, and he's just taken on another mission that requires more guts than common sense. I'll stake my life on his loyalty."

"Not to the Allies, sir. It's a question of which one."

Algar watched me, once more trying to figure me out. He betrayed his first sign of nervousness, nibbling at the mustache over his lip, but that, it turned out, was only as a means to control his anger.

"Oh, I see," he said, "I see. More red-baiting? Is that it? I've been watching the brass give the cold shoulder to a lot of the French resisters whose politics they don't care for, men and women who risked everything for their country, while half of France was kneeling down in Vichy. Well, I've got no use for that, Dubin. None.

"I'll tell you the truth, Captain. I feel sorry for you. I do. Because that jump took some guts. And it was for a bunch of silly crap. And now you're not just out of the frying pan into the fire, but straight into a volcano. The Germans have us surrounded. We have damn little food, less ammunition, and the only medical supplies I've seen are the ones that fell with you. So I don't know what the hell you're going to do with yourself, but I promise you this — you're not arresting Bob Martin. Ralph," he said, "find Captain Dubin and his sergeant a place to sleep. Gentlemen, that's all I can do for you. Dismissed."

16. NIGHT VISIT

Biddy and I were transported about a mile to the town of Hemroulle and a small stone church that stood amid a clutch of dark farm buildings, where we put up for the night with an infantry unit under Algar's command. I slept on an oak pew, better than the cold floor, but too narrow to be comfortable. Between that and the reverberations of jumping and deflecting bullets, I could not really manage much sleep and I woke easily at the sound of two men, Americans, shouting at each other in the back of the sanctuary. Somebody else hollered to take the row outside. The radiant dial on my watch showed nearly 3:00 a.m. I lay there a second longer determined to sleep, then suddenly recognized both of the quarreling voices.

When I bolted up, Biddy was visible in the light of a candle beside the door, dragging Robert Martin along by the collar of his field jacket, looking like a parent with an unruly boy. I took just an instant longer to convince myself I was awake, then grabbed my tommy gun and rushed back there. Biddy's woven belt was tied around Martin's hands. The Major was furious.

"Why is it when you tell even a good man that he's a policeman, he turns into a thug?" Martin asked as soon as he saw me.

According to Bidwell, Martin had driven up only a moment ago, while Bidwell was on his way back from the outhouse.

"Smiles like he was my auntie come to visit and asks for you," said Biddy. "My orders say arrest him and that's what I done."

I knew Biddy had laid hands on Martin just for the pure pleasure of it, given what we'd been through. Nor did I blame him. But Algar would treat this as mutiny.

"Let him go, Gideon."

He looked at me in his way. "Hell, Captain," he said.

"I know, Biddy. But untie him. We need to get things straightened out first."

One of the men from the platoon sleeping behind us sat up on his pew and called us jerk-offs and told us again to take it outside.

We passed into the church's narrow entry, just beyond the sanctuary. Two candles had been placed in the corners for the benefit of those using the outhouse. As soon as Biddy untied Martin, he banged out the old wooden doors. I assumed he was leaving, but the Major returned in an instant with his steel flask. Apparently he'd lost it after offering it to Bidwell. Martin's knowledge of judo might have given him a fair chance, even against Gideon, but Biddy had fallen on him without warning, while Martin was offering him a drink.

I remained astonished to see Martin. If he knew we were here, he had to know why.

"Come to taunt us, Major?"

"More to pay my respects and clear things up. That is, until I ran into Primo Canera here. I understand it was you two we saw being shot at in the sky last night. What kind of training did you have for that, Dubin?"

I was not sure I wanted to answer, but shook my head a bit.

"Quite heroic," said Martin. "I hope you weren't patterning yourself after me." He found the comment amusing. Martin was dressed as he was at La Saline Royale, in a field jacket and combat fatigues, with a vest full of equipment. He was dirty and unshaved and rubbing at one of his wrists, which must have been a little sore after his tussle with Gideon. Every now and then he reached down to swipe off more of the snow that had collected on his trousers when Bidwell had pinned him out on the church steps.

"I don't fancy myself a hero, Major. It's not a label I deserve. Or that I'd exult in."

"Is that a personal remark, Dubin?"

It was, but I wouldn't admit it. "I admire what you've done, Major."

"Is that why you've come to arrest me?" He said he'd heard about my orders from Ralph Gallagher, Algar's Exec. I still had a copy of Teedle's written directive in the inside pocket of my tunic, now wrinkled and still moist with my sweat. Unfolding it, Martin walked closer to one of the candles to read, his shadow looming enormously behind him. Biddy was crouched down along the paneled wall opposite. His hand was on his tommy gun and his eyes never left Martin.

"Seems like everybody's quite vexed with me, Dubin," said Martin as he handed the paper back. "Including you."

"You lied to me, Major. And stole away in the dead of night."

"I told you I was about to depart on a mission, Dubin, when you arrived that day at the Comtesse's."

"You were referring to blowing the dump at La Saline Royale."

"Was I? Your misunderstanding. I'm sorry. Have you spoken yet to OSS? What is it they've told you about my current orders?" I realized then that was why Martin had come around. He wanted to know what OSS surmised about his disappearance—whether they thought he'd gone mad, or had deserted, or if, more critically, they'd figured out that he was working for the Soviets. I was determined to give him no answers to that.

"London has approved your arrest, Major."

"Rubbish. I'd wager a large sum, Dubin, you have not heard that personally from anyone at OSS. They're the ones who sent me this way. Don't you recall? I told you several times I was being dispatched to Germany." To link up with his old network and save lives, he had said. There was no doubt OSS would want German supporters at this stage.

Across the entryway Bidwell's eyes had jumped from Martin to me to be certain I wasn't going to be taken in again, but he had no need for concern. The motto of the law remained with me. *Falsus in uno, falsus in omnibus.* False in one thing, false in all. One lie was enough to deprive any witness of credibility and Martin's fabrications were beyond tolling. Whatever the irony, I reposed considerable faith in Teedle's veracity by now. He was too direct to lie. I simply shook my head at Martin.

"You make it your business to get to London, Dubin, and to speak with Colonel Winters. You'll see I'm telling the truth."

"For your sake, I hope you are, Major. But there is no ambiguity in the orders I have. You are to be arrested. Whenever we can make safe passage to the west, Bidwell and I will escort you back to Third Army Headquarters. As an officer you'll be held under house arrest until your trial."

"'House arrest?'" He chuffed some air after the words. "That sounds like my childhood. And won't Teedle be satisfied?" That thought wilted him. He slumped against the wall across the entryway from Bidwell, and opened up his flask. He offered me a slug, which I declined. I wanted no more of Robert Martin's generosity.

"Do you read Nietzsche, Dubin?" Martin asked after a moment.

"I have."

"Yes, I have, too. General Teedle has read Nietzsche, of that you can be certain. 'Life's school of war: what does not kill me makes me stronger.' It's all rot," he said. "And Teedle is not Superman. Do you know why the General wants the world to think he's a great man of action, with his arms across his chest? Have you seen him strike that pose in the newsreels? The General is a fruit," Martin said. "Have you learned that yet?"

I said nothing.

"I don't mind faggots," said Martin. "There've been several who've done some damn good stuff for me over the years. One of them was a waiter in Paris. Can't imagine what a waiter overhears, Dubin. But he was one of those wispy queers who made no bones about it. The General thinks he's just a man who sleeps with men."

"Are you saying that feeds his grudge against you, Major?"

"Who knows? Probably not. For Teedle it's probably all about me supposedly being a Communist. Have you asked him about that?"

I took a second to consider what I should say. I couldn't entirely surrender my curiosity now that he'd raised the subject.

"Teedle says you were a party member, Major. In Paris."

Rarely given to laughter, Martin managed a short high-pitched cackle. "Well, I've always liked a good party," he said. "And for that I'm to be arrested?"

"You're to be arrested for insubordination, Major. But General Teedle would probably tell you to your face that he suspects that when our armies meet, you'd follow the orders of Russian generals rather than his." Given my experiences with Martin, I wouldn't have placed much faith in his denials. But I was still taken aback when he made none. Instead, he chuckled again.

"You can lay good money on that, Dubin. I'd sooner take directions from a squawking parrot than Teedle. But fortunately I'm here under a fine commander. I have no problems with Algar, you'll notice."

"The Lieutenant Colonel said you were about to undertake some new operation, Major?"

"Indeed. We start about an hour from now." I expected him to invoke the privileges of required secrecy, but apparently the mission was common knowledge. The military situation around Bastogne was even worse than the flight mechanics at Virton had suggested. The Germans had cut the last roads yesterday and fully encircled the area. Now they would tighten their grip until they could blast the American troops into submission. Our position was tenuous, but the men I'd encountered, including those with Algar, and Martin now, remained calm. Patton was on the way, supposedly, but the troops all felt that what they needed was bullets and equipment so they could break out themselves. That was what Martin's operation was about.

On December 19, as the Germans had flanked Bastogne to the south and west, they had cut off an American supply train near Vaux-les-Rosières, blocking the tracks with tanks and leaving the train there, probably waiting to determine if they could make any use of its contents themselves. Along with some of the men from the 110th Regiment whom he'd been commanding for a week now, Martin aimed to reach those railcars full of ammunition. The bet was that when his troops and his three Hellcat tank destroyers cut into the thin German lines, the Nazis would fall back to consolidate their position, thinking this was the spearhead of a concerted American effort to pierce the encirclement. Martin and his men would probably have an unimpeded path to the train. If Martin could get the locomotive moving, they would steam into Bastogne. If not, they would off-load as much as they could of the 75mm ammunition and the bullets for smaller arms and then dash back before the Germans closed in again.

The only difficult part, Martin thought, might be getting through in the first place.

"The infantry's thin," he said. "We'll go right past them. The Panzer Lehr are roaming out there somewhere, but even McAuliffe thinks it's a solid plan," he said, referring to the commander of the 101st who was directing the defense of Bastogne. "Even if the Lehr show up, we can fall back. And if we make it through, our chances of success are very high."

"Trains and ammunition," I said. "You seem to have a motif, Major."

"Old dog, old tricks," he answered. "It's damn boring to be a specialist. I never wanted to specialize in anything when I was a boy. But then I fell in love with the railroad."

I asked if he was the kind who ran model locomotives around a track decorated with miniature trees and stations.

"Never had patience for that. I was somewhat frenetic as a child. I suppose you can still see that. No, trains for me came at a later point. I left home for a spell when I was seventeen. Hopped a freight car. First taste of freedom I'd had in my life was when that car went hurtling out of Poughkeepsie. I decided at that moment that the railroad was the greatest of mankind's inventions. I loved being around trains. When I went to my mother's people in Paris after I dropped out of college, that was the work I sought. Started as a porter. Ended up as an engineer. The idea that I was a common workingman appalled my father, but it delighted me."

"I don't think I've heard you mention your parents before, Major."

"No accident in that, Dubin." He nipped at his flask again and looked at the candles. "My father's a professor of Romance languages at Vassar College. Met my mother when he was at the Sorbonne. Very distinguished fellow, my father. And the meanest man walking God's green earth. I agree with him about everything. Politics. Music.

I don't like his attire, I suppose, I don't like his hats. But it goes to show you beliefs aren't everything. He's a complete son of a bitch."

"Hard on you?"

"Very. And harder on my mother. She couldn't get away by hopping a train. So she blew her head off with his shotgun when I was sixteen."

As the wind came up outside, the wooden doors knocked and the candles guttered, but he didn't take his gaze from the corner. I expressed my sympathies.

"Well," he said. "It was hard, of course. Horrible. But it wasn't a picnic before then. My mother was always in bed, an impossibly beautiful woman, but utterly morose. I can barely remember her features because I rarely saw her anywhere but a dark room." He drank and looked at the wall. "These aren't stories I often tell, Dubin."

I could understand that. But I recognized Martin's instinct always was to master the moment however he could. His charm had been undermined by his lies. So now he would prey on my sympathies. Or parade out Teedle's perversions.

"I think I should come along on this operation with you tonight, Major." I had been considering that for a while. Across the entryway, Biddy could not contain himself.

"Jesus Christ crucified," he moaned. I found a pebble on the floor and tossed it at him, then repeated my request of Martin.

"Afraid I'll run away, Dubin?"

"That would not be without precedent, Major."

"Well, right now you have the Germans to ease your mind. Every road has been cut. And the snow is high. And I've got a team to bring back."

I said I still wanted to come.

"Don't be an ass, Dubin. You won't be there for the mission. You'll be there to keep an eye on me. Which means you'll be a danger to both of us. And damn certain to get in the way."

"We didn't get in the way at the salt mine."

"At the salt mine, Dubin, you stayed in one place. This is a mobile operation. In armored vehicles on which you've never been trained."

"I'll speak to Algar."

"It's not Algar's choice. It's mine. And I don't want you there."

The chance that Algar would overrule Martin was minimal, but given the situation I needed to try. I asked if Martin was willing to drive me back to Algar's headquarters so I could make my case to the Lieutenant Colonel. He wound his head disbelievingly, but smiled brightly at my doggedness, as usual.

"I have to get ready, Dubin, but I'll drop you there. Come along."

I told Biddy to stay and sleep. He seemed unconvinced.

"He's got a tommy gun with him, Sergeant," said Martin. "I think he'll have a fair chance against me." Martin called Gideon "Bruiser" when he gestured goodbye.

As soon as we were under way in his jeep, Martin said, "Aren't you going to ask me about Gita?"

I took a second. "I hope she's well."

"As do I."

"I understand she's near Houffalize."

"You won't find her if you look there, Dubin." Martin turned from the road with a tart, narrow look and we stared at each other. It was the first instant of actual hardness between us, undeflected by irony. He wanted me to ask where she was, and I wouldn't give him the pleasure. Even so, this friction reminded me yet again what a terrible mistake I'd made with her.

"If you have a complaint with me, as far as Mademoiselle Lodz is concerned, Major, feel free to lodge it."

"No complaints," he said quickly. "She wouldn't stand for it. Her life is her own. Always has been and always will be." This was a disciplined answer, like a soldier taking orders. "She's in Luxembourg. At least I hope she is. Roder. Overlooking the German border. We both sent reports to Middleton that the Germans were massing tanks, but nobody wanted to hear that. God bless the United States Army." He tossed his head bitterly, as he pulled the vehicle in front of the barn where Biddy and I had been with Algar a few hours earlier. When Martin's hand came forward, I lifted my own to shake, but instead he pointed at my side.

"I wouldn't mind having use of that tommy gun, Dubin. We don't have anything like that around. It might come in handy and you have my word it will be returned. I'll swap you my M1 for a few hours."

I looked at the submachine gun. I was glad Bidwell wasn't here, so I didn't have to hear the sounds he would make at the idea of giving Martin anything.

"Will you promise to surrender yourself to me, Major, when we're capable of moving out?"

Martin laughed. "Oh, Dubin," he said. In the darkness, he looked out to the snow. "Yes, I'll surrender myself. On the condition that you reach OSS personally before turning me over to Teedle."

We shook on that and I handed him the gun and the one ammo box I had with me.

"You'll have it back in a few hours," Martin promised before he drove off.

He was barely out of sight when the sentry outside the barn told me that Algar had gone up to the staging area to go over the maps one last time with Martin and his team. He said that Martin and Algar had set that meeting only half an hour ago when Martin first stopped here. I stood there in the wind. I would never be sharp enough to deal with Martin. I was not even angry at myself. It was simply the nature of things.

I considered walking back to Hemroulle, but I had a faint hope Algar might return before Martin's team set off. There was a hay locker attached to the barn, a platformed area raised so that the fodder could be tossed in from the back of a cart or truck through an opening outside. The sentry told me troops had slept in there the last two nights. He promised to rouse me as soon as Algar came back.

Only a little hay remained in the height of winter, but its sweet smell lingered. My predecessors had swept up the remnants and mounded them into a couple of beds and I lay down on one and fell soundly asleep. My dreams seemed rough and desperate, the kind that make you cry out in the night, but I stayed for many hours in that world, rather than this besieged circle in Belgium.

My name roused me. Hamza Algar, looking weary and nibbling at his mustache, was a few feet below me in the barn. He shoved my tommy gun across the board floor of the hay locker.

"Martin told his men to make sure this got back to

you," he said and turned away. As I crawled out, Algar walked to his desk at the center of the barn. There was daylight visible in the seam between the stone walls and the tin roof of the building. Sitting, Algar rested his face in his hands.

"How did they do?" I asked Algar.

He sighed. "Poorly. The Krauts pinned them down and then blasted the shit out of them at first light. The men who made it back came on foot."

"And Martin?"

"Gone," Algar said.

That was the same word Bettjer had used when I'd awoken at the Comtesse's after we blew the dump. I'd known it would happen. I reviewed in my mind what I'd been through—the terror of the jump, the shot, and the enduring indignity of fouling my trousers—only for Martin to have run from me again. Sisyphus came to mind.

"Any idea where he headed?" I asked.

I received another fixed uncomprehending look from Algar. So far all our conversations had somehow devolved into a competition in provoking speechlessness. The Lieutenant Colonel sighed deeply again.

"Well, if there's anything to your arrest order, Captain, he's probably headed to hell. Captain Dubin, you didn't understand me. Bob Martin is dead."

17. CHAMPS

Since December 16, Robert Martin had been in command of units that had been isolated from the 110th Infantry Regiment during its retreat from Skyline Drive in Luxembourg in the early hours of that day. Regrouping here with the remains of the regiment, Martin's two rifle companies and two towed guns from a tank destroyer battalion had been teamed with a platoon of M18 Hellcats. It was these troops Martin had led toward Vaux-les-Rosières, where the ammunition train was marooned. North and west of the town of Monty, they had crossed our lines and encountered thinly manned German positions, which they quickly pushed through.

Half a mile on, however, they were engaged by the Panzer Lehr, the tank division formed from Nazi training units. Less brazen forces might have fallen back to form a stronger line, as McAuliffe and Algar had anticipated, but the Panzer Lehr prided themselves on backing off from no one and had spread out to take on Martin's team. During the protracted firefight that resulted, Martin and his men moved to the top of a knob, which allowed them to destroy a number of the German tanks. Near daybreak, the Panzer Lehr withdrew. Martin and his unit leaders had gone up to the second floor of a small lodge on the hill to assess whether they still had a chance to reach the ammunition train. From there, they saw what had provoked the Germans' retreat, a battalion of American tanks emerging like specters through the falling snow. Patton had arrived.

Even when the first rocket came screaming toward Martin from a turret of the approaching armor, no one in his command had caught on that the tanks they saw had been captured by the Nazis from the 9th Armored Division. Never mustering a defense, Martin's unit had been left with only isolated survivors. The Major himself had gone down when the initial tank shell flew in the window at which he stood. At least four other shells hit the building, reducing it to a bonfire.

All of this was related to me the morning after we jumped into Savy by a boy named Barnes. He was perhaps five foot two, and slight as a butterfly. His nose was dripping the entire time I spoke to him, and he flinched whenever a shell exploded in the distance. For the moment, the fighting seemed to be a couple of miles off, to the north and east.

"Captain, we was blown to shit, there just ain't no other way to put it. I mean, those was American tanks. How was we supposed to know any different?"

Algar had corralled this boy, and one of the few other survivors of Martin's team, Corporal Dale Edgeworthy, and the two of them sat with Biddy and me, on wooden chairs in a corner of the empty barn.

"Martin got it right at the start of the attack," said Edgeworthy. "That's what came over the radio. We all saw the building go, Captain. It was the only thing standing out there. Sort of looked like when you toss a melon out of a truck and it hits the road. Pieces everywhere. The tech sergeant had command after that. But that couldn't have been more than fifteen minutes. Soon on, Captain, it was just run like hell and scatter, run for your life. There wasn't any choice, sir, but to leave the dead and wounded behind."

Edgeworthy, a tall man close to thirty, began to cry then. He kept saying there wasn't any choice about running.

I was ready to dismiss them, when one more question occurred to me. I told myself not to ask, then did anyway. These men had been with Martin nearly a week.

"What about the woman? I heard there was a woman with Martin originally."

Barnes and Edgeworthy looked at each other.

"I don't know, Captain," said Barnes. "When the offensive started on the sixteenth, we was up near Marnach in Luxembourg. The first night, when Major Martin took over after Colonel Gordon got it, the Major led us around to this farmhouse after dark. There was three people there, this farmer and this round old doll and their daughter. Seemed like they knew Martin, at least I thought so, 'cause the Krauts was a pretty good bet to take that ground, but they was still letting us in, a few soldiers at a time, so we could warm up while we ate our rations. But that was just a couple of hours. The Krauts never stopped fighting that night. They had their tanks painted white to match the snow and bounced them klieg lights off the clouds and they come right up that hill. They've got all that territory now."

"How old was the daughter?"

"Young, I guess." Barnes dragged his sleeve across his nose. "You know, Captain, I'm like any other fella, but I was pretty grateful to be out of the cold, I wasn't gonna give that girl the hairy eyeball. She was small," said Barnes, and smiled for the first time in the half hour we'd been with him. "You know, I'm kind of always watching out for short women. That's about all to tell you. I remember she was the right size."

Once they were gone, Biddy and I waited for Algar to return, shooting the breeze with the troops and officers who passed through the headquarters. The shelling continued in the mid-distance. It had begun at daybreak and started and stopped intermittently. Reports on Patton's progress were mixed. For each man who'd heard the Third Army was gaining, there were two bearing rumors that its divisions were stalled. In the meantime, the shortages of food and ammunition were past critical, not to mention the complete lack of medical items. This was not the moment to get wounded. The 101st's Division Clearing Station, and the eighteen doctors who manned it, had been captured on December 19. Yesterday, American artillery units south of the German troops had tried to cannon in bandages and plasma in howitzer shells, but the firing charge had blown all of it to smithereens. Everybody we encountered thanked us for the medical supplies that had fallen with us.

However, what the men here really craved was a few more degrees on the thermometer. They had stopped referring to the town as Savy. Everyone, officers included, usually called the village 'Save Me,' with salvation from the cold being their chief desire. Tank turrets and gas lines had frozen, and the soldiers routinely found their M1s inoperable until the bolts were freed by beating them with hand grenades. Some of the men who'd started suffering frostbite a couple of days ago claimed that they'd been cold so long that the intense burning sensations had ceased. The troops called themselves 'doggies' and everybody made the same joke: "This doggy can't feel his paws."

Algar came in, stamping the snow off his boots. He asked if I was satisfied after the interviews.

"Not to be grisly or cynical, Colonel, but I'm going to have to view the remains when they're recovered. Martin's been fairly slippery and there are people in London who'll want proof positive. I'd like to be certain myself."

I had irritated Algar again. He told me I'd know better than to say that if I'd ever seen a wooden building hit by four tank rockets. But he promised that as soon as the skies cleared and supplies came, we'd all be back on that hill, not so much for my sake but so that the men who'd died there, including Martin, could receive a proper burial. At his desk, Algar spent a minute shooting fire into the bowl of his pipe.

"And have you had a chance to consider what kind of duty Teedle's orders foresee for you now, Captain?" Algar asked this neutrally, as if it were not a loaded question. Biddy and I had discussed the answer at length this morning once Gideon had walked up here.

"Well, sir, Bidwell and I called a Yellow Cab so we could get back to Nancy, but they say there will be a delay picking us up, so we thought we might be able to serve with you, sir, in the meantime." Biddy had grumped around when I told him we had to volunteer for combat, but by now I understood that for him that was simply a prelude to bravery. He knew the score. If we didn't volunteer, Algar would have to order us into action. And there was no choice, anyway. The town was surrounded. It was a matter of fighting for our own survival.

"I don't suppose you two have any combat experience, Captain."

I said that Bidwell had gone up Omaha Beach. Algar had been there, too.

"That was a bitch," he said to Biddy.

"Hell on earth, sir."

"That's about the size of it. And what about you, Dubin?"

I told him I had only been shot at twice, including last night. "But I was trained as an infantry officer before I went to JAG school, sir."

Algar actually jumped out of his seat.

"A trained infantry officer? Ho my God," he said. He turned to his Exec, Ralph, who'd just arrived. "A trained infantry officer fell out of the sky, Ralph. Christmas has come early."

The 110th Infantry Regiment, what little was left of it, had been aggregated in a combat unit which Algar and his officers had named Team SNAFU. They were now under the 101st Airborne, plugging gaps as General McAuliffe designated, working in coordination with the 502nd Infantry Regiment. I was placed in command of a reformed rifle company in a re-formed battalion. Given my lack of experience, I would have been challenged as a platoon leader, but on the other hand, G Company, which at full complement would have numbered around 193 troops, was all of 98. I had no lieutenants, just three sergeants, including Biddy, in charge of three platoons, and sparse support personnel.

On the afternoon of December 22, the newly re-formed G Company was assembled at the center of Savy. By daylight, Save Me was no more than it had seemed at night, a cluster of farm buildings composed of small slate-toned stones with thick joints of yellowish mortar. The tin-roofed structures had been added on to over centuries, and the windows and doors were all different sizes and varying heights, making them look as if they'd been thrown onto the buildings.

My first sergeant, named Bill Meadows, functioned for all purposes as my first lieutenant. Meadows greeted me when we met as if we were going out together for a night of drinking.

"Whatta you know, Captain?" He smiled widely and seemed on the verge of delivering a comradely poke in the shoulder. Bill Meadows was a stocky man in his early forties, wearing metal-framed specs. Like every other soldier I had, he was unshaved and his face after nearly a week of fighting was grayed by perspiration, gunpowder, and the airborne debris of shell bursts. "All right, boys," he called out to the troops. "Bend an ear. Captain Dubin's going to give us our orders."

Outmanned and outgunned by virtually everyone, Team SNAFU had been positioned here on the west of Bastogne because it was the least likely point of attack. Most of the German tanks and artillery remained north and east. Given the difficulties of moving over the snowy hills, particularly with the remaining softness in the bottomlands, the odds were against the Germans mounting a major offensive from this direction. The fact was they didn't have to. Due to the thinness of the western defenses, Team SNAFU had been unable to prevent the Germans from working their way around us, flanking south toward the town, where they were now positioned.

For all of that, no place around Bastogne was secure. There had been a skirmish outside Champs earlier yesterday, when a German grenadier team and one half-track had briefly appeared there. But just as McAuliffe situated Algar to be less in harm's way, so Algar was locating G where we were not as likely to suffer attack. We were assigned to seal off a narrow farm road that came down from the west through Champs and Hemroulle and joined the main byway at Savy. Algar wanted G to go out after dark and dig in, in a wooded draw just north of Champs, on high ground that looked down on the road and the railroad track and a cow path directly to the west. The Germans, in theory, could come from any of those approaches. We were relieving E Company, who had been closer to Hemroulle and were taking a shellacking from German artillery which had gotten a fix on their position. E, which was down to seventy-two men, would serve as Headquarters Company, waiting as reinforcements if there was an assault.

Algar was certain that yesterday's encounter near Champs was a diversionary feint. If the Germans launched a significant western attack, they were far more likely to come at Savy, which was on one of the main roads to Bastogne. It ran north to Longchamps, and was big enough to make it vulnerable to the King Panzers. For that reason, Algar kept what little armor he had with him. Naturally, if the Krauts sent an armored column toward Champs, he would use his tanks and half-tracks and tank destroyers to reinforce us. Our job would be only to hold the road for a short time until the cavalry arrived, but that was a formidable assignment given our lack of ammunition. Algar ordered us not to shoot, even when fired on, unless we could see a human target. I was with Algar when Colonel Hunt, the 502nd's commander, called, and Algar described his intended defense of the Champs road as consisting of "a couple of empty muskets." It was something less than a vote of confidence.

I sent the men to pack up, ordering them to be in formation at 1615. Meadows drew what few rations we were allowed and gathered the maps. At 4:15 p.m., as dark was falling, I walked down the line for inspection, greeted every man by name and checked his equipment. Not one had an overcoat. They were dressed only in field jackets, sometimes more than one. All of them looked dirty, grim, and sleep deprived, but I was already proud to be their CO. They were prepared to fight, and that, I recognized, was what I'd really wanted to know in all my fretting about combat — what was worth fighting for.

The feelings of admiration were far from mutual. Most of the men hated me on sight and were sullen at best when I addressed them. For one thing, I had warmer clothes and a Thompson submachine gun, neither of which I was about to surrender, even after I learned that the undersupplied 101st had been instructed to shoot anyone in an overcoat, on the theory they were German impostors. Envy, however, was not the primary motive for my troops' discontent. They knew they were under the command of a man with no combat experience, and might as well have been led by a crawling infant.

I had little appreciation at that point for what these boys had been through, since nobody ever talked about the beating the 110th had sustained in the last week. After my time in the VIII Corps signal office, I knew that the LVII Panzer Corps had literally swept the entire 28th Infantry Division, of which the 110th was part, from the map. But positioned with only two of its three battalions along Skyline, the paved highway that paralleled the border between Luxembourg and Germany, the 110th had absorbed the worst of the initial assaults, when the Panzer infantries had crossed the Our River in rubber boats in darkness and overwhelmed them at dawn.

In the desperation of the first hours, with no Americans behind them, the 110th had been ordered not to surrender and had forced the Germans into house-to-house fighting in towns like Clervaux, Consthum, and Holzthum. Most of the men I commanded were alive only because they had run when their lines finally broke, and, given their orders, probably didn't know how to regard their survival. The majority of my troops had been replacements themselves, with less time on the Continent than I'd had, but they all seemed to feel they had unfinished business with the Germans, whatever the perils.

At 1630, Meadows called out, "Drop your cocks and grab your socks, gentlemen, we're heading out." We marched south a few blocks to the crossroads, then turned north and west out of town, proceeding a little more than a mile. Despite the cold, nobody complained, knowing they were warmer than they'd have been traveling in the back of an open truck. Halfway to our position, we passed E Company marching in. A sergeant was in command, because the other officers were dead, and he and I exchanged salutes. The enlisted men were less formal. Some wished us good luck. Several suggested my troops should write their wives and sweethearts now and tell them to forget about having a family. "The only good your nuts will be is for ice cubes." Meadows put an end to the banter. We were on foot because it was imperative to arrive unnoticed. Yesterday's skirmishing had made it clear the Krauts were nearby. The intelligence officers in McAuliffe's G-2 believed the grenadiers were hidden north and west of us in the trees.

When we reached the place the maps called for us to set up, we found a zigzagging network of foxholes already there, each of them set about five yards apart. They had almost certainly been dug in the late summer by the Germans, rearguard units protecting the retreat from Allied forces coming up from the south. After consulting with Meadows, I ordered most of the men to shovel out these holes, rather than digging our own. Each of the three platoons had a Browning water-cooled machine gun, a cumbersome high-caliber piece manned by a three-soldier crew, and I directed the Brownings to be set up on three strongpoints running around the curved edge of the woods. Then I ordered two squads to scout defensive positions at our perimeters, forward and rear. The squad moving back discovered an old pump house, good news since the closed structure would provide a few men at a time some relief from the biting wind.

Shoveling the snow out of the holes revealed the Germans' debris — empty rations and rucksacks, spent ammunition, rusted rifles and canteens. Despite the severe cold, there was a distinct odor. This area had been liberated in mid-September by the V Corps, First Army, and I had no memory of hearing about any major action at Hemroulle. The Nazi company that had preceded us here—probably SS given the difficulty of their assignment—had to engage the Allies and slow them, knowing that there were no reinforcements behind them. Two of the foxholes in the group had been hit by Allied artillery, reducing them to half circles twice the depth of the others. I suspected that what we smelled was the German soldiers who had been in there, literally blown to bits that had moldered through the wet fall and now were sprinkled under several inches of snow.

When we were done digging, we cut boughs from the surrounding fir trees and laid them in each hole to form a base. A few pine branches were left at the edge, to be used, when the men were allowed to sleep, as a roof to catch the snow. There was no question that German forces were out in the woods, because when the winds bore down from the north, we could smell their fires, a luxury I couldn't allow if we hoped to maintain the element of surprise.

Each platoon had responsibility for a flank in our three main perimeters, and we set up a watch schedule and ordered the men to turn in, which many were eager to do, because they were still warm from digging. As I was to learn, it was possible to be too cold to sleep.

Biddy and I took the same hole, which appeared to have been the former command dugout, its architecture a tribute to German precision. It had been cut in a perfect trapezoid that allowed two men to fire side by side, but left more room for living behind them. The face was reinforced by a log retaining wall into which a ledge had been cut for personal possessions. I put books, some hand grenades, and my razor there, not that there was much chance of running water. It seemed odd to be unpacking as if this was a hotel room, but that thought was cut short by Biddy's cursing.

"Left my toothbrush in town," he said. "No shave, no bath. Least you can brush your teeth. Damn." I understood at once that the toothbrush was an emblem of the security we'd relinquished on this quest for a man who'd turned up dead, and I offered him mine.

"We can share it," I said. "It won't be the worst of what we share in this hole." With orders to remain out of sight, we weren't going to be making any trips to the latrine during the day. And Biddy and I were past the point of pride or privacy. The last of that had passed when he scraped me off that snowy field with a load in my pants.

Biddy, though, seemed struck by the gesture. He stared at the brush as if it was burning, before he took it.

Near 9:00 p.m., when most of the men had settled in, I heard the rumble of motors behind us, and one of the machine gunners on the point demanding the password. I had motioned Biddy and one of his squads forward, but he came back explaining that it was Signal Corps. They had driven up the road without lights, a fairly daring maneuver in the heavy darkness left by the thick clouds. The signal team was here to extend lines for field telephone connections for me running to Algar, and to each platoon. I was relieved not to be out here alone, but the signalmen reminded me to use the phones sparingly and only in code. Communications by ground wire were subject to interception sometimes a mile away, a radius that almost certainly included the Germans in the woods. We also had a backpack radio, the SCR-300, in the event we were forced to move.

Before turning in, Biddy and I both inspected positions. He went to look after his platoon, while I checked the forward strongpoints manned by the Browning crews.

"Flash," a gunner called.

"Thunder," I answered, the password G had been using all week, according to Meadows. The Browning crews' holes were dug deeper and rounder than the rest of ours. In the most visible location, the men needed to be entirely below ground level but able to swing the gun in a full circle in the event of an assault. I found each of the three crews pretty much exhausted. The men lay in the holes with their feet sole to sole with the boots of their mates, a device to keep them from falling asleep.

Returning to our hole before Biddy, I could feel at once that my pack was not where I'd left it. By flashlight, I found it had been ransacked. An extra pair of field pants was gone and my second gloves, too. I had already decided to give up what I wasn't wearing, but I regretted that a thief was the beneficiary. He'd taken personal effects, too, including three of the letters from Grace I had been carrying. And the card from Gita.

The adjoining holes, where I'd heard voices when I was coming up, now had fir boughs and ponchos drawn over them. I debated my options, then ran down to Sergeant Meadows to tell him someone had 'acquired' some of my gear. He said it had been going on in G Company from the beginning.

"Don't ask me to make it sensible, Captain. Stand and die beside a man then steal his stuff, I know it's crazy. I'm just trying to tell you that you're not the first."

"But this didn't happen unnoticed, Sergeant."

"Probably not, sir." He looked away and back. "They don't like anybody new, Captain, and new officers most of all."

"Because?"

"Because you don't understand, Captain. Listen, these men will fight for you. I've seen them. They're good men, every one of them, and they'll fight because they know they'll die otherwise. They hate you because they hate being here. Only way out of a rifle company is dead or wounded. It's like those turnstiles that only go in one direction. They let you in, but you can never get out. There ain't a man here, sir, who doesn't start praying at some point, God, please let me get wounded so I can go home. Plenty of them would give up an arm or a foot. I'm telling you what every soldier thinks. And what you're going to be thinking, too. And I can see just looking at you that you don't believe it. And that's why they hate you, Captain. Because you hold a better opinion of yourself than they have of themselves, and they know they're right. But don't worry about it, Captain. None of this will matter much, if we don't have battle. And if we do, they'll be fine with you afterward."

I spent two hours too riled to sleep, and then got up for night guard. As an officer, I wasn't required to take this duty, but we were too shorthanded to stand on formalities, and I thought it would be good for morale. On the way, I stopped in the pump house, a brick box dug into the hill that flanked our rear, fully embedded in the earth to keep the hydroelectric pump from freezing. There were no windows on the single exposed wall, just a half-size wooden door, which my men had broken open. Inside, I found most of the soldiers in the second squad from Meadows' platoon, who'd chosen to play cards by the light of a Coleman lantern rather than sleep. They jumped up and I put them at ease. The pump, an old black hunk of iron, reached down into a well hole, and the men had fanned out around it. I took a moment to ask each of the eight soldiers where he was from, but I got the same surly responses, and headed out.

"You a Yid, Captain?" When I turned back, nobody in the pump house was looking at his cards. The speaker, staring hardest at me, was a Mississippi boy, a private named Stocker Collison.

Every candidate in OTS learns the same thing. Rule one, make sure they respect you. If they like you, that's okay. But if they don't, fear will do.

"Is that a Southern term?" I asked Collison.

"Just askin."

"Does the answer matter to you, Collison?"

Of course it did. It probably mattered to half the men in the company, maybe more.

"No, sir."

"Good. What time you stand guard, Collison?"

"At oh three hundred, sir."

"Why don't you walk the perimeter now to be sure everything's okay."

He spent a long time looking at me before departing. The other men remained silent. I had been better at this than I'd imagined, but I knew whose manner I'd instinctively assumed. Teedle's. I would have to think about that.

I had drawn guard with the platoon of Sal Masi, a shrewd little guy from Boston who was my third sergeant. He'd been promoted from corporal on the battlefield and still had the doglegs on his uniform. Along with two of Masi's soldiers, I had watch on the rear hill, a position I'd assigned myself because it was at the highest point we occupied, and thus the most exposed to the wind.

My spot was about fifteen yards from the pump house, and the tin chimney that poked through the roof was designed to vent the pump's heat in the summer, but now it funneled the sound from within as if it were being broadcast. On their first night here, the men inside clearly didn't realize that. As a result, I spent much of my two hours on watch listening as the north wind carried along the squad's conversations, including their commentary about me, which began when Collison got back from his snowy trip around the perimeter.

"Jesus fucking Christ, Collison. Why didn't you just ask him to stick out his pecker so you could check?"

"Man oughta say what he is. He ain't got no call to hide it."

"Hell, man, you're white trash and I don't see you wearing a sign."

"Aw, go soak your head, O'Brien. The thing with the damn Jews is you don't never know when you got one."

"That's bull, Collison," said somebody else. "You can tell by lookin. You just haven't seen any 'cause you're an ignorant Mississippi peckerwood."

"You got no call to talk to me like that, Marshall."

"Whatsa matter, Collison, did he hurt your feelings? I'm gonna cry, I'm not kidding. I'm crying already. I ain't cried like this since I read *My Friend Flicka.*"

The line, from O'Brien, a thin sharp-faced kid from Baltimore, provoked a storm of laughter inside the pump house. Encouraged, O'Brien took off on Collison.

"Know the difference between a zoo in the North and a zoo in the South?"

Collison didn't answer.

"In the South, they don't just write the name of the animal on the cage. There's also a recipe." The uproar rocked out again. "Know what they call a Mississippi farmer with a sheep under each arm? Huh? A pimp."

Apparently O'Brien decided Collison had had enough. The men went back to playing poker, largely silent except for the grousing when somebody won. Without that distraction, and with nothing to see in the farm field that lay ahead of me, I worried. I worried mostly about whether fear would paralyze me in the midst of combat as it had when I jumped, and what would happen then to the men I was supposed to lead. The moment in the plane had drifted with me all day, like the lingering weakness from a fever. It had taken something away from me, from everything I saw and every breath I drew. I was a coward. I didn't expect myself to be unafraid. But I had been dashed to discover that I could not overcome it. The man who had volunteered to jump, the American who believed in the right things, had no control over the other part of me. It was as Gita had been trying to tell me when she lifted her skirt. Everything except instinct was a pretense.

Hoping for other thoughts, I began searching the sky. The clouds to the south did not look quite as thick. If I was right, that would mean air support, supplies, maybe even reinforcements. I hung, yet again, in that uncertain zone, not knowing if I wanted to be replaced before the Germans attack. At least a demotion to platoon leader would let me pull duty I'd prepared for. If Meadows went down, I'd literally have to call Algar every hour for instructions.

As 5:00 a.m. approached, somebody else who'd gotten up for night guard entered the pump house, clearly another squad member, who received a full account of the evening, including the ungodly amount Bronko Lukovic had won, and Collison's encounter with me.

"Oh, Collison, you sure know your oats. Way to impress the new CO."

"I just like orders better comin from a Christian, is all," said Collison. "We're already fightin this fuckin war to save the Jews."

"Jesus, button your flap, Collison. You sound like Father Coughlin."

"Says you. Wasn't them Nazis that attacked us at Pearl Harbor. What the hell we care what ole Hitler's doin? I'm tellin you, it was all them Jews around Roosevelt. That's why we're here fightin."

"Collison, we're all fighting for the same damn reason. Because we have to. Because nobody gave us a choice."

"This platoon," answered Collison, "we got to be the worse-off bunch of doggies on the front. We been gettin nothin but screwed. I'm not kiddin. Two-thirds of our men dead and now they send us this Jew officer when we're surrounded."

"Shit, Collison. Don't snap your cap about Dubin. We've lost every officer we've had. And they knew what the heck they were doing. How long you think it's gonna take before this one stops a bullet? He's still looking around the woods for the men's room."

They all laughed. A minute later, I heard a familiar voice. Biddy had gotten up to spell me on night guard.

"Pipe down in here, y'all. Sound come outta that hole up top like cheers at a football game. Hear y'all fifty yards away." There was silence then. I'd wager some were wondering for the first time how far off I was. "And let me tell you something else. The Captain's a good man, y'all gone see that."

I could hear O'Brien ask, "Is he hep? I just can't take these officers who don't know nothing but what they read in the rule book."

"He's hep," Biddy said. He arrived at my position a minute later. He said nothing, but offered a cut-down salute when I left him to go back to sleep.

18. COLD TRUTH

Bill Meadows shook me awake a little after 7:00 a.m., as the faintest light was leaking into the sky. He wanted to go over orders for the day. To conceal our position, we couldn't risk contact with the men on point or relieve them once the sun was up. Meadows wanted to replace the crews who'd been out there freezing all night and I told him to proceed.

Before he left, we took a moment to inspect the terrain. The open, rolling hills — hayfields or grasslands grazed by beef cattle — were now deep in snow with no animals in sight. Most, I imagined, had been killed or eaten long ago. North of us, beyond the railroad tracks and the drifts mounded here and there on the road, several fields undulated, separated only by stone markers. With my field glasses, I saw that the land had already seen combat. The Germans who had once occupied our holes had been hit hard before retreating. The blackened form of a Panzer was out there, with snow heaped on the tracks and the turret, and I also could make out the axle and fenders of a truck. My guess was that there had been more wreckage, which our engineers had towed off to assemble the crude roadblock that stood a couple hundred yards from us. It was comprised of commandeered tractors and two burned-out tanks, one ours, one German.

To the west, in the distance, lay dense green woods of tall pines, where the German grenadiers were probably hiding. Even in daylight the forest appeared black and impenetrable. I thought of the Brothers Grimm, and their goblins and spooks stealing from the trees to snatch souls and visit curses.

The last thing Meadows pointed out was the stand we occupied, a mixture of the same skinny, thick-branched pines that were across the way and deciduous trees, most of them beeches still wearing some of their coppery leaves. The Germans were delivering daily artillery barrages across a broad sector, wherever they figured Americans might be positioned to protect the roads, often utilizing their 20mm antiaircraft guns, which had proven effective as offensive weapons, or the dual-purpose 88s. Fixed on quad mounts and half-tracks, the guns were tilted forward and fired into the treetops. The result was a little like a bomb exploding in midair, raining shrapnel down on everyone below. Algar had sent us north of E's holes in hopes that the Germans might not have been aiming here, but up high the trees were ragged, as if they had been eaten away by moths. Several of the beeches had most of their boughs blown away, the remaining trunks standing like solitary amputees, blackened by the shell bursts. In other words, we were going to get it. The Germans had been firing in the hour after dawn and just before sunset, periods when they could be certain that our planes, which could navigate only by daylight in this weather, would never be in the air.

"I want to tell the boys to stay low when that starts," said Meadows. "Or else get out and go hug the trees."

"Right."

"But the sergeants need to keep watch. It'd be a good time for that Panzer infantry to come out of the woods, with us hunkered down."

"Right," I said again. Commanding with Bill Meadows as your top NCO was a little like driving with a chauffeur. He and I exchanged salutes, but Meadows hung back.

"Captain, I hear you had a hard time with Collison last night."

"It was a short conversation, Bill. Nothing to be concerned about."

"Don't let Collison bother you, Captain. He's not a bad Joe, especially once he gets used to you. We got a lot of country boys in this man's Army just like him, and it don't matter if they're from Mississippi or the North Woods. First time he lived with indoor plumbing was in basic training. They've been through a lot, Captain, these boys. Sometimes they just talk a little bunk."

When Meadows left, Gideon crawled into his boots and coat to inform his platoon about today's orders. He'd been back in the hole only a few minutes, using my toothbrush for the first time, when the shelling began. If nothing else, the Krauts were punctual.

In the midst of combat, I was to discover that certain phrases would become lodged in my head, as if my brain was a Victrola stuck on a scratch. That day, the saying was "Forewarned is forearmed," mostly because it proved completely untrue. The Germans were employing a technique

I'd learned in infantry school called TOT, or time on target. The idea was that their shells would fly at several areas at once, before anyone could scramble back to his hole. Not knowing precisely where we were, the Germans calibrated each gun at intervals of roughly thirty yards.

The first rounds were screaming meemies, rocket-propelled shells that bore down with a constant heart-stalling screech like a car's tires when its clutch is popped, and that proved to be nothing compared to my dread when the ordnance started landing. I had thought it couldn't be worse than the bombing at the Comtesse's, but there was no way to anticipate the emotional effect of being under sustained bombardment. I will never hear anything louder—ears simply can't absorb more sound—and combined with the way the earth rocked, I was soon rattled with a primitive panic whenever I detected the sound of the 88s. It was distinctive as somebody's cough, to which it bore a thunderous resemblance. The shells exploded with a magnificent bouquet of flame and snow and dirt, raining down hot shrapnel, pieces often a foot or two long that ricocheted off the trunks, while huge limbs crashed around us. The closest blast to me, about fifty yards away, made my eyes throb in their sockets and squeezed my chest so hard I thought something was broken. After each detonation, just as a way to hold on, I promised myself it was the last, trying to believe that until I heard the throaty rumble of the artillery firing and the keen of the next shell heading in to knock us flat.

And then after almost an hour on the dot, it stopped, leaving the air hazy and reeking of cordite. In the sudden silence, you could hear only the wind and the thud of branches that continued to fall from the trees. After the first few minutes of the shelling, between explosions, a scream had gone out for medics and that shouting resumed now. I phoned Second Platoon. Masi told me that two men in the same hole had been struck by a tree burst. I didn't know what the CO should do, but I couldn't believe hiding was the answer, and I scrambled up there, weaving between the trees. The Krauts couldn't see much anyway, with all the smoke and dust in the air.

Arriving, I found a red-haired kid named Hunt dead from a piece of shrapnel that had descended like an arrow from an evil god and penetrated the soft spot beside his clavicle, plunging straight into his heart. He was lying in the hole, his eyes open and still. I was most struck by his arms, thrown back at an angle no one could have maintained in life.

The other man was being attended by a medic. His leg below the knee was a red mash. The bone was shattered and he was crying from the pain, but the medic thought he would live. They would move him out, once night fell, for what little good it would do. At this stage, this man, Kelly, was facing roughly the same chances for survival as soldiers wounded during the Civil War. The medics were using some sulfa powder, which they had been pilfering from the aid kits of the dead for days, in hopes of disinfecting the wound. Kelly would be transferred to an aid station Algar had set up yesterday at the church where we'd slept in Hemroulle. Back in my own hole, I took reports from the other platoons by phone. Only two casualties. Doing the arithmetic, I knew we had come through rather well.

During the barrage, it had started to snow. I had thought it was too cold to snow—we used to say that at home—but apparently the weather in Belgium didn't adhere to

Midwestern rules. It was not a storm of great intensity. Instead the large flakes drifted down almost casually. Like most little boys, I had grown up regarding snow as a thrill. It was pretty. It was fun. But I had never endured it in a foxhole. The snow danced down for more than two hours. As soon as Biddy and I shook it off, it collected again. Eventually, we were soaked and frozen. And it kept snowing. With overcoats, Biddy and I were better off than many of our troops, who were sitting in their holes wrapped in their ponchos and blankets, with their cold M1s held next to their bodies to keep the trigger mechanisms from freezing. But I had no feeling in my hands and feet, and I was increasingly amazed that the blood didn't just go to ice in my veins.

Dealing with the cold proved a matter of will. I was desperate for distraction, and on pure whim decided to light one of the cigarettes that had come in my rations. Cigarettes were probably the one thing not in short supply, although the men complained relentlessly about the fact that the cheaper brands — Chelsea, Raleigh, Wings — had been sent to the front.

The skies had remained so dim that it seemed as if the light was oil being poured in by the drop. Now I found myself keeping track of the birds. It was hard to believe any were left. The artillery barrages must have killed most of them, and during the German occupation food had been scarce enough that I'd heard of the locals routinely eating sparrows. A few crows scavenged in the forest, and some swift long-tailed magpies darted by. I pointed out a hawk to Biddy, but he shook his head.

"Ain't no hawk, Cap," he said. "That there is a buzzard."

By midday, we knew there was little chance an attack would come. The offensives were taking place around us — the air spasmed from artillery rounds, and the sputtering of machine guns and the sharp crack of rifle fire a mile this way or that carried distinctly through the cold. In considering things, I'd decided that our most likely role would be as reinforcements if the Germans attacked Savy. But if that happened at all, it would be tomorrow or the day after. While the sun was up, there was little to do but stay out of sight in the hole and battle the cold.

"You think it ever gets this cold in Kindle County?" I asked Bidwell.

"As I recollect, sir, yes. Colder. I still have in mind, Cap, walking up to high school eight blocks, and the mercury stuck clear at the bottom of the thermometer. Colder than twenty below."

I'd made those trips myself and laughed at the memory. Insane with adolescent vanity, I'd refused to wear a hat. I could recall my mother screaming at me from the back porch and the feeling once I'd reached the high school's hallways that if my ears grazed something hard, they'd break straight off my head.

In the middle of the day, there were suddenly shouts from within our midst. I jumped out with my tommy gun, certain the Germans had somehow snuck up on us, only to find that two men in Biddy's platoon had uncovered a discarded Luger in their hole — the breach mechanism had seized up — and a fistfight had broken out between them about who would get the souvenir. I put both men on discipline — meaningless now — and said the Browning crews, who'd been on the strongpoints without communication for hours, could draw straws for the pistol when they were relieved. We had to reassign the two soldiers to other holes, and even though I demanded silence,

I could hear both calling one another "motherfucker" as I left. That wasn't a word used much among the officer class, who usually adhered to a certain gentility.

"You ever know of anybody who actually fucked his mother?" I asked Biddy.

"Had a friend in high school who fucked one of my buddy's mothers. I heard of that."

"Well, that's not the same thing."

"No sir, not at all." We fell silent for a while.

"Biddy, where in the world did you go to high school, anyway?" He'd told me before that he hadn't quite made it to graduation. His family needed money.

"No place you'd know, sir."

"Don't bet on that. I think I swam against every school in Kindle County."

"You didn't never hear of Thomas More, sir. Wasn't no swimmers there."

"Thomas More? In the North End? Wasn't that all colored? I didn't know there were any white men in that school."

"Wasn't," he said. "Two white girls. No white men."

I had been looking at the sky, just realizing that blue was starting to edge past the dirty gray masses. That meant the planes would be flying. When I finally processed Gideon's words, I was sure I'd misunderstood. He had removed his helmet and, big as he was, I found him staring down at me, unconsciously drumming one finger on the MP stenciled in white on the front.

"You heard me, Captain."

"What the heck are you telling me, soldier?"

"I'm trusting you is what I'm doing. Against my better judgment."

A hundred things fell into place. After the artillery barrage, I was too drained to feel shock, but I was lost in some fundamental way.

"Now what're you thinking?" he asked me.

"Truthfully? I don't think I believe you."

"You better. Because this here's no off-time jive." He was sullen and probably more astonished with himself than I was. His choice of words, however, went to make his point.

Now that he'd said it, of course, now that I was actually looking, appraising his nose, his hair, I suppose I could see how he might have been colored. But there were men in the next hole, Rapazzalli and Gomez — not to mention me — who were probably darker complected, and none of us with eyes as light as Biddy's green peepers.

"I got my draft notice," he said. "I went down there. I didn't never say one way or the other. They just looked at me and put me in. You know, I'd always had that, folks saying as how I could pass. When I was a kid in Georgia, and we was away from home, I always knew I could go strolling free as a bird into places my brothers couldn't. It didn't seem to matter all that much once we got North. But there I was now. I come home and told my folks.

"'Did you lie?' my daddy asked me.

"'Not a solitary word.'

"My mom and he really got going. She wanted me to head straight down there and tell the truth. If the Army didn't want me doin no fighting, she was in no mind to quarrel. But Daddy wudn't hear none of that. 'What truth is that? That even though he looks every bit as good as any other man, even though he *is* every bit as good as any other man, he ought not get treated like it 'cause he's actually colored. Is that the truth? The day ain't dawned yet where I'll let a child of mine say that. Not yet.' I'm not sure the two of them have patched it up completely even now.

"But how it was really, Captain, I went along with it mainly because I was just like you. I wanted to fight. I wanted to be like Jesse Owens and rub old Adolf Hitler's face in the dirt so hard that that damn mustache come off his face. And I knew they wouldn't see hide of many colored troops near the front.

"Once I got in the middle of Omaha Beach, I gave that another think, all right. I'd'a been just as happy to set 'em straight and go back to England. It's full crazy, what I got myself into. Ain't a day that passes I don't think once or twice I should have listened harder to my mom. Times I feel like I'm not being true to my own, even though I never said a false word to nobody. And I'm always tellin myself I gotta get home alive, just so ain't nobody there sayin how it's a mistake for a colored man to think he can do the same things as white folks. It's just all one hell of a mess."

He peeked over at me again and reached onto the ledge for my toothbrush, which he'd pulled from his mouth and thrown in there as the shelling began.

"You want this back?"

The word 'yes' was halfway to my lips, but I retrieved it without a flicker.

"Yeah, damn it, I want it back," I said then and snatched it from him, jamming it into my mouth. The toothpowder had frozen hard on the bristles. "I didn't get a chance to use it this morning. And tomorrow I'm first. You can be first the day after that."

He looked at me for a while.

"Yes, sir," he said.

19. THE SKIES

Late in the day, American C-47s passed overhead. Looking back toward Savy, we could actually see the chutes and supplies drifting down out of the big Gooney Birds, and the glowing trails of the German anti-aircraft fire darting at them like malign june bugs. The parachutes, red, yellow, and blue, resembled blossoms, a lovely sight in the clean sky, but not one we enjoyed for long. Nazi bombers and fighters appeared from the other direction, and the fierceness of the AA soon cleared the skies. Once our planes were gone, the Germans repositioned their guns and another artillery barrage began. They clearly feared that with their AA occupied, the Americans might have moved out ground forces, and the new volleys seemed to go on twice as long as they had in the morning. As we huddled in the hole, I felt my teeth smash against each other so hard I thought I might have broken one of my molars.

Once it was over, the field telephone pealed. It was Algar, who'd chosen the code name Lebanon.

"What's the condition out there, Lawyer?"

We'd sustained two more wounded from the last barrage, both relatively minor injuries. One man would need to be moved back to town, along with the young fellow with the leg wound. Algar promised that the ambulances would be there after dark.

"I'm hearing that your Army commander has broken through to the south," Algar said. "Punched a hole, they're saying. We should start seeing reinforcements. Make sure your men know. We had a hundred sixty supply drops here, now. Not enough. But there's some ammo. Medicine."

"Yes, sir." The news about Patton was welcome, but my men would believe only what they saw. Everything was rumor until then.

"How's the mood?"

The mood, I said, was good, considering. The men realized there was nothing to do about the cold, but they were complaining often about not being allowed out of the holes in daylight, especially to relieve themselves. Orders were to shit in your hat if you had to, but since nobody was going to abandon his helmet with two tree bursts every day, the directive put the troops to a ridiculous choice.

Sunset came shortly after that, a moment of great solemnity, as it signaled a lessening of the dangers. The Panzers wouldn't come at night in these conditions when they could get stuck so easily if they veered off the roads. And the Germans, after the huge push that drove us back from the Ardennes, were too short supplied to engage in the harassing artillery fire they normally would have ordered up in darkness. We had to be alert for Kraut scout teams, who could sneak across the field in an effort to assay our position, but we all knew we had survived and would soon be able to move around. The sun, which had edged in and out for hours, knifed through in the distance, breaching the clouds with an intense coppery shaft blazing on the forest across the field. Biddy grabbed his camera, somehow seeing a black-and-white picture in all that color.

Meadows called and we made night assignments. Bill also had a request. The men wanted to make a fire in the pump house. There would be no light. The issue was the smoke, which might betray our position. But the wind was still coming from the north, which would carry the odor back toward town. It was a calculated risk, but we decided it was worth it. I doubted that even if the wind shifted the Germans would be able to tell our smoke from their own. Each squad would be allowed in the pump house for half an hour to eat their rations, as well as fifteen minutes before and after night guard. The gunners who'd been out on the strong-points all day without communication would get stretches twice as long and go first.

The ambulance arrived near 6:00 p.m., accompanied by a supply truck. The quartermasters were supposed to be bringing tomorrow's rations, but they had only two C ration containers. It meant I was going to be able to feed the men just once tomorrow.

"Colonel hopes for better Christmas Day," said the quartermaster sergeant. I knew he was husbanding whatever he had for a Yule treat, but starving the troops in advance seemed like a poor way to enhance their appreciation. "He did send these, though. Requisitioned them from a local café in Bastogne. Owner beefed something terrible, but hell, he ain't doing much business these days anyway."

I stuck my field knife into one of the soft pine boxes and

found table linens. It took me a moment to catch on, then I summoned my three noncoms, Meadows and Biddy and Masi, to distribute them to their platoons.

"What the hell?" Meadows asked.

I explained that the men could use the white table-cloths as camouflage, if they needed to leave their holes during daylight. We were lucky the linens had been starched. Otherwise they would have been shredded for bandages.

Once he'd handed out the cloths and napkins, Meadows returned. He wanted me to know this had elevated me in the eyes of the men, an effect that would undoubtedly be lost when they got hungry tomorrow. Nevertheless, I appreciated the fact that Meadows was looking out for my morale, too.

"If Algar had any sense, Bill, he'd have made you the company commander."

"Tell you a secret, Captain, he offered. But I don't see myself as officer material. Second lieutenant, frankly, that's the worst job in the Army. At least in the infantry."

Biddy, across the hole, grumbled in agreement. I'd heard the statistics, but I answered, "The food is better at headquarters."

"Suppose that's so," said Meadows. "I'm just not the one to give orders, sir. Not in combat."

"Because?"

"Because if you live through it and your men don't, that's something I don't want to deal with. All respect, sir."

It was another problem I'd never considered, because I was too green, and I dwelt on it in silence while Meadows went on his way.

As captain, I'd assigned myself the last stretch in the

pump house, and I decided to try to sleep before then. I took off my overcoat. The snow had frozen it solid and it actually stood up by itself, leaned against one wall in the foxhole. I was too cold to fall off. Instead, near the end, awaiting my turn in the pump house, I actually started counting to myself. When I finally walked in, the heat was one of the sweetest sensations of my life, even though my hands and feet burned intensely as they thawed. The men of Meadows' Second Squad were in there again, taking as long as they could to consume their rations. I knew they'd overstayed by the speed with which they all jumped up when I entered.

"As you were, gentlemen."

O'Brien told me to go slow approaching the fire. These men were familiar with the hazards of frostbite.

"Captain," said O'Brien. "Can I ask you a question? You ever heard of a fella getting frostbite of the dick? Collison's worried that his dick will fall off."

I'd never heard of that. I thought back to high-school biology and explained that what imperiled the extremities was their distance from the heart.

"I told you, Collison," said O'Brien. "You're so dumb, you know what they call the space between your ears? A tunnel. You know what you got in common with a beer bottle, Collison? You're both empty from the neck up."

Collison, on his haunches, looked toward the fire as O'Brien laid into him. I suspected that O'Brien was giving him the treatment for my benefit, after last night.

"Take it easy, O'Brien. Save a few cracks for the rest of the war."

Saved by an unexpected source, Collison looked my way briefly.

"How's he even remember all these? I can't never remember no jokes."

"That's because you're a marching punch line, Collison," said O'Brien.

Meadows came in then to send the squad back to their holes. First Squad was on the way up. I crept closer to the fire and Meadows stayed with me a minute to warm his wire-framed glasses, which were frosting over. The little red dents stood out beside his nose.

"So, Bill, what was your racket before this started?"

"Me? I was on hard times, Captain, if you want to know the truth of it. I grew up in California, close to Petaluma. My folks were farmers but I got myself down to Frisco, worked as a longshoreman and made a good buck, too. But there was no work come '34 or '35. It didn't go right between me and my wife, then. I was drinking. Finally, she took herself and my two boys back to Denver where her people was from, put up with her folks. I just started hopping freight cars, looking for work. But there were lots of chappies like me sittin' 'round fires in every freight yard in every city. Those were bad times, Captain. I was first in line at the Army recruiter when the mobilization started in '40. This damn war was a piece of luck for me. If I live through it. Wife remarried but it didn't work out and she's all lovey-dovey now when she writes me. I really want to see those boys. Oldest is sixteen. I sure as hell hope this war ends before he can join up. I don't know how I'd keep my senses if I had to worry about him being in this mess, too. You think it's gonna be over soon?"

I'd thought so, just a week ago. At the moment it looked as if there was more fight in the Nazis than any of us had expected. Still, it seemed important to tell the men I believed victory was not far off. Meadows looked at me hard to see if I really believed it.

I ate a cracker out of today's K ration and decided to save the rest for morning. I caught two hours' sleep, then warmed up again in the pump house before my watch. The men of Masi's platoon, too small to be divided into squads, began filing in. Meadows and I were on the same schedule and headed out together.

"Gee whiz," said Meadows, putting his gloves on again, "how do you figure they took a fella from California and sent him to the European theater?"

"Man, you ain't countin on the Army to make any sense, are you, First Sergeant?" asked one of the men coming in.

We all laughed. I stood outside listening to my men for a minute as their talk rose into the night through the chimney.

"You figurin it's some bad luck we're here rather than the Pacific?"

"Lot warmer in the Pacific, I know that."

"Every letter I get from my brother," said someone else, "is about how damn hot it is. But it's not how that's a blessing or nothing. They get every kind of rash. He says he got stuff growin on him, he didn't even know a man's skin could turn that color. And a boy's got to have some absolute luck to get himself a drink. Ain't like here in Europe with all this wine and cognac, nothing like that. Best that happens is somebody with an in with the quartermaster gets hold of some canned peaches and sets himself up a still, makes something tastes like varnish. Guys is drinkin so much Aqua Velva, quartermaster's never got any in stock. And they-all's fighting among themselves to get it."

"But it ain't cold there."

"Yeah, but I'd rather get killed by a white man, I really would."

"Now what kind of fucking sense does that make?" another asked.

"That's how I see it. I ain't askin you to feel that way, Rudzicke."

"Don't be a sorehead."

"Just how I feel is all. Think it would be a little easier to go out like that. Just don't want the last face I see to be brown."

"I can understand that," said another man.

"I tell you another thing," said the first man, called Garns, "them Japs is savages. They're like the wild Indians, eat a man's heart. They think we're some inferior species like monkeys. They really do."

"They're the ones look like monkeys. Don't they? The Krauts at least, they'll treat you okay if they take you prisoner. Buddy of mine wrote me how he was fighting on this island, Japs caught one of their men. They sliced this guy's backbone open while he was still alive, then they poured gunpowder in there, and lit the poor son of a bitch. Can you imagine? And the rest of his platoon, they're hidin out and listening to this shit."

There were plenty of hideous stories from the Pacific. I'd heard several times that the Japs cut the ears off living prisoners.

"Yeah, but it's warm," said someone. That drew a laugh.

"I don't figure war's much good wherever you are," somebody else said.

"You hear about these Polynesian dames. Buddy wrote me they landed in a couple of places, girls didn't even have no shirts on when they got there. And they fuck sort of like saying hello."

"Ain't no women fuck like saying hello. Ain't no woman do that lest she's gettin somethin out of it. My daddy tole me that and I ain't never seed how he was wrong."

"Yeah, but I still hear these dames in the Pacific, they're something else. This buddy said one of these dolls, she could pick up a silver dollar with her you know what. Finally, somebody got the idea of taking out his business and laying the dollar on there and this girl she took up both. That musta been a sight."

"You think it's true what they say?"

"How's that?"

"That the Nazis travel with whores. They bring them along."

"Sounds like Nazis."

"Yeah, we're goddamn Americans. We believe in freedom. The freedom not to get laid."

Meadows came crunching back through the snow. He gave me a wink, then opened the door to tell the men to keep it down.

"Krauts are still there," he said.

When I left, a soldier named Coop Bieschke was carving his name in a copper beech about halfway to my guard position. He'd been at it both nights, using up his sleeping time for this enterprise. I thought to ask him what was so important, but I wasn't sure Coop could explain it. Maybe he was planning to come back here after the war ended, or perhaps he wanted his people to know the spot where he'd died. Maybe he simply hoped to leave a mark on the earth that was definitively his. I watched him at work with his jackknife, oblivious to me and everything else, then continued up the hill.

After guard, I returned to the pump house, then rushed back to our foxhole before my boots could freeze again, placing them under my legs, in the hopes that my body warmth would keep them from hardening overnight. It was a wasted effort. When I woke up, my pants legs had actually frozen together and it was a struggle even to get back on my feet.

The morning of December 24 was cloudless and our Air Corps was in the sky not long after first light. As the formations of bombers, and the P-47s to protect them, roared overhead, my men waved from inside their foxholes. The German antiaircraft was intense, especially as our planes penetrated German territory. We could see the red trails of the AA rising, and several times aircraft suddenly becoming a star of flame. But the ranks of bombers and supply planes kept appearing for nearly five hours, vapor trails behind each motor, making the sky look a little like a plowed field. The escorts weaved up and down, on the lookout for German fighters, while the chutes on the supply drops continued to unfurl in the skies near Savy. Occasionally, when the wind died down, we could hear the rumble of the trucks fetching the medicine and food and ammunition back into Bastogne.

The men remained in their holes, but now with the camouflage, I was able to move out every hour or so to check our positions. I dashed through the woods, wrapped in a tablecloth, with a linen napkin knotted beneath my chin like my grandmother's babushka. When I ran up to their holes, several soldiers looked at me and said, "Trick or treat."

For the most part, I was in the hole with Biddy, trying to tell myself that I had borne the cold yesterday, so I could make it today. Today would be easier, I told myself, because now I knew there would be a fire in the pump house later. But perhaps that made it worse, since I could recall now what it felt like to be warm.

Every hour, I lit a cigarette. In the interval, I took to sniffing the odor of the tobacco on my gloves. I couldn't understand the odd comfort it seemed to bring me, until I thought of Gita Lodz and the strong scent of her hair and clothing. I wondered if I'd ever see her again. Or if I cared to. Then I asked myself the same thing about Grace. And my parents. If I had to choose only one of them to be with last, who would it be?

"Lord, Biddy," I said suddenly, "doing nothing but standing in this hole and thinking is enough to make a man stark raving mad."

He grunted as a form of agreement.

"I wonder if we'd be better off if the Germans just came and we got it over with."

"Captain, you don't want to say that. Take it from me."

I asked him to tell me about Omaha Beach.

"I don't know, Captain. It ain't nothing like whatever we-all gonna get ourselves into here. The thing of D-Day was the size of it. I was there D plus one. And it was war everywhere, sir. Them battleships was behind us firing at the Germans on the cliffs, and the Germans was shooting down. Our bombers was up above and the Kraut AA batteries were roaring. And you had thousands of soldiers running up that beach, shooting whatever there was to shoot at. It was fighting everywhere, men giving battle cries, and all that moaning and screaming of the wounded. When the troop carrier dropped us and we sloshed up through the water there, even the sand was red from the blood, and I couldn't see how we'd ever get to the rendezvous point. There were bodies all over. You couldn't pick a straight line up that beach without tromping on the dead. And each step, I looked at them and thought: This here is my last step, the next one, it's going to be me. When I got my squad assembled, I turned back and I realized it was just like I'd imagined it. I'd imagined this my whole life."

"War, Biddy?"

"No, sir. Hell. It was the devil's hell, all right. Sitting in church, having the preacher tell me where the sinners was gonna find their ugly selves, and thinking so hard about it, that was what I'd seen. The banging, the screaming, the pain. Even the smells of the bombs and the artillery rounds. That's a saying, sir, you know, war is hell, but it's a truth. The souls screaming and sinking down. And the skies falling. When I get to thinking about it, sometimes I wonder if I'm not dead after all." He shook his head hard as if to empty it of thought. "I don't like going on about this, Captain."

I told him I understood. He was silent for a second.

"You know, Captain, about Martin?"

"What about him?"

"Men like that who've been at war for years now. I understand why they keep doin it. Because it's the truth, sir. It's hell. And it's the truth, too. Ain't nothin else so real. Can you figure what I'm saying?"

I couldn't really. But the idea frightened me as much as the thought of the Germans waiting to attack.

We were an hour from sunset when there was a little aimless putt-putting overhead. My first thought was that it was German buzz bombs, the V-1s that I'd heard about, but when I got my binoculars, I followed the sound to a little single-engine plane. The field telephone growled at once. It was Meadows, telling me the aircraft was a Nazi scout and that we should yell to all the men to get their tablecloths on and hunker deep in their holes. But about five minutes later, the plane circled overhead again. When I heard the engine nearing for a third pass, I knew we'd been observed. I raised Meadows.

"Any question he's seen us?"

"No, sir."

"Well then, let's try to shoot him down."

"We don't have bullets to waste, Captain."

We agreed that the Browning crews had the only real chance of hitting a target at five hundred feet and we both dashed forward to the strongpoints to issue that instruction. It seemed to take the three-man crews forever to get the unwieldy machine guns elevated, but even at that, one round took a piece out of the plane's left wing, before the craft climbed out of range.

I called Algar.

"Shit," he said. "Any chance the plane didn't make it back?"

There was a chance, but it was still in the sky when we'd last seen it. If it made it, we'd be sitting ducks for the Kraut artillery. We had to move out, but not until we had another defensive position as good as the one we were giving up. Algar also wanted to see if our recon had provided any clues about where the Germans were in the woods. Putting down the phone, I thought the same thing all my men would. Another position meant giving up the pump house.

Algar was back to me in a few minutes. Both intelligence and operations thought that the Germans were repositioning much of their artillery in light of the morning overflights. If so, they were probably not ready yet to fire on us, and both G-2 and G-3 doubted that the Germans would risk a barrage at night, which would pinpoint their guns' new positions to air surveillance, inviting bombing at dawn.

"It's your choice," Algar said about staying put for the moment. "We'll reposition you by morning, either way."

This was my first real decision as a commander. For the sake of the pump house and the fire, I decided to remain here, but in the next thirty minutes, every creak of the trees in the wind seemed to be the first sound of incoming shells. I stood up in the hole, examining the skies, hoping to smell out the artillery like a pointer. The field telephone rang as soon as darkness began to settle over us. It was Meadows.

"Captain, a lot of these men, they'd like to get that fire going. It's Christmas Eve, sir. They want to have a little service. I guess they figure that if God's gonna protect them, it has to be tonight." I gave permission.

Having gone last to the pump house the night before, I was entitled to an early trip and I took it, before the prayer service began. As Meadows had predicted, coming up with the table linens had broken the ice for me with some of the men, and I found one of Biddy's squads in there anyway, troops better disposed to me for his sake. A lanky Texan,

Hovler, had taken a place on a stone near the fire, and looked up at me as I warmed my hands beside him.

"Captain, you married?"

"Engaged," I said, although life in a foxhole made that seem more chimerical every minute. Home was so far away.

"Pretty," Hovler allowed, when I found my wallet. "This here is my Grace," he said.

"Grace. Why, that's my girl's name, too." We marveled at the coincidence. His Grace was sunny and buxom. In the snapshot, her hair was flowing behind her in a wind that also formed her dress against her.

"Fine-looking."

"She shore is," he said. "Shore is. Only thing is, that works on my mind. You think your Grace is gonna wait for you?"

Eisley and I had bunked at the Madame's with two different fellows in Nancy whose women had Dear Johned them. I wondered how it would feel, if Grace got some intimation of my fling with Gita and abandoned me. I'd excused myself because of the excesses of war, but what if she didn't? Grace had two suitors left at home, boys she had been going with before me, one a 4-F because of a glass eye, and the other running a factory critical to the war effort. Now and then, when I listened to men like Hovler worry that their gals could two-time them, the idea that Grace might take up with one of these boys would pierce me like an arrow, and then, like an arrow pass through. I did not believe she would do it. It was that simple. Boredom, longing, loneliness — even jealousy and anger — were not forces capable of conquering Grace's virtue. Until I met Gita, I might have called it principle. But even by Gita's view, even if she were correct that every man and woman was a story they had made up about themselves and tried to believe, that was Grace's — that she was a person of virtue so lightly borne that it did not really touch the earth. She could never do that to me. Because, in the process, she would destroy herself.

"I hope so," I answered.

"Sitting out here, it kinda gets in my mind that she can't possibly wait for me. She got any sense, she'd know I'm three-quarters of the way to dead anyhow, being out here surrounded. And likely to come back with some piece of me missin, if I make it. Why should she wait? There all those 4-Fs and smart guys and USO commandos at home, makin good money 'cause there ain't many men left. Why shouldn't a dame get herself a beau?"

I still had the picture in my hand.

"She doesn't look like the kind of girl to do that, Hovler."

"I hope not. I'd hate to live through all this just to come home to a broken heart. I don't know what I'd do. I'd mess her up, I think." The thought made him so unhappy that he left the fire and went back to his hole.

At 9:00 p.m., a jeep came creeping up the road. I'd been summoned into town to see Algar. He was at the same desk where I had met him, now trimmed out with pine boughs. His pipe was in hand, but I could tell from the aroma that he'd been reduced to filling it with tobacco from cigarettes.

"Merry Christmas, David." He offered his hand. He and his staff had been contemplating my company's situation and the way it fit into the overall picture. Creeping ever closer, the Krauts had issued an edict today to McAuliffe to surrender and he'd reportedly said "Nuts" in reply. There was reason to think he'd made a good decision. Patton's forces were said to be advancing down the Assenois road on Bastogne now, and more than 1,200 loads of supplies had fallen by parachute today. As a result, General staff was convinced that the Germans had no choice but to mount an all-out attack tomorrow. They could not position their tanks to take on Patton without control of Bastogne. And they knew that with every hour, supplies were being distributed to peripheral forces, meaning the longer they waited, the stiffer the resistance.

Given the scout plane, Algar figured there was now some chance that one of the Kraut attacks might come from the west, perhaps through Savy. Perhaps even through Champs. There was no telling. And in any event, whatever force was in the woods would move on us, at least for a while, to keep the company in place. So Algar and his staff still wanted us in position to hold that road. They were just going to move us a little, into the woods on the eastern side, in order to lessen the chances of the German guns fixing on us. If the first attack came at us, we were to move north and contact the enemy. With luck, we'd catch them by surprise and be able to flank the Panzer grenadiers. Either way, we were better off attacking than waiting for the Germans to mass and pin us down. If we did get the first attack, Algar would send tanks and reinforcements, even call in air support if the weather held. It was more likely that we'd get called to reinforce Savy. Those were the orders.

Ralph, the Exec, came in to report on a conversation with McAuliffe's staff in Bastogne, who were suddenly disheartened about Patton's progress.

"Ham, I don't know what to make of this, but this guy

Murphy, he was sort of implying that maybe Bastogne is bait."

"Bait?"

"That Ike wants to draw as many of the German assets as possible tight around the town, and then bomb it to all hell. Make sure there's never another offensive like this. Better in the long run."

Algar thought about that, then gave his head a solid shake.

"Patton might bomb his own troops. Never Eisenhower. We want to keep that one to ourselves, Ralph."

"Yes, sir."

When Ralph left, Algar looked at me. "Here's another thing to keep to ourselves, David. A couple of things. I don't like to say either of them, but we're all better off being plain. Don't let your men surrender to the Panzer forces. Name, rank, and serial number won't get them very far. After the job we've done on the Luftwaffe, most of their intelligence comes from what they can beat out of our troops. Once they've got what they want, the buggers have no means to keep prisoners. And they don't. Word is they flat-out shot dozens of our troops at Malmédy. But understand what I mean. I was with Fuller at Clervaux, when Cota wouldn't let us retreat. I'm never going to issue that command. I don't want to lose that road. But I don't want a bunch of soldiers with rifles trying to stop tanks. Fight like hell, as long as you can, but protect your men. Those are your orders."

I saluted.

I passed through our strongpoints, giving the password. Walking up, I encountered another member of Masi's platoon, Massimo Fortunato, a huge handsome lump, on guard duty. An immigrant, Massimo claimed to have lived in Boston "long time," but he spoke barely a word of English. Even Masi, who said he knew Italian, generally communicated with Massimo by hand signals like everybody else. Fortunato had come in as a replacement, but one with combat experience, which meant that he was not subject to the usual ridicule. He had fought through North Africa and Italy, until a sympathetic commander transferred him to Europe, following an incident in which Fortunato believed he was firing at a boy he'd grown up with.

I asked Fortunato if all was quiet.

"Quite," he answered. "Good quite."

I went back to the pump house to find Meadows. O'Brien was helping Collison with a letter home, writing down what Stocker told him, sometimes framing the words for him. Bill and I agreed that he'd send a scout team across the road to assess our new position. After that, we'd give the men orders to pack up. Bill went out to make the assignment, as Biddy's platoon was filtering in.

"Think we'll ever have a worse Christmas, Captain?" Biddy's second-in-command, a PFC named Forrester, asked me.

"Hope not."

"Nah. Next Christmas, we'll be dead or the war'll be over. Right?"

"It'll be over. You'll be home. That'll be your best Christmas, then."

He nodded. "That'd be nice. I'm not sure I ever had a best Christmas." I didn't say anything, but I'm sure my face reflected my curiosity. "I was adopted, Captain. Old man got it at Verdun. My mother, she ran out of gas somehow. Some friends of my aunt's took me in. They had six other kids in that house. I don't know what made them do it. Good sods, I guess. Irish, you know. Only Christmas, somehow, that was always strange. They were Catholic, went to midnight Mass. My family was Scotch-German, Presbyterians. Not such a big deal, but Christmas would get me thinking. These here ain't my real brothers. Ma and Pa ain't my real ma and pa. Adopted like that, Captain, at that age, it didn't seem there was anything real in my life. Not like for other people." He looked at me again. I couldn't think of anything to do but clap him on the arm, yet the gesture drew a smile.

When I returned to our forward position, I wrote letters to my parents and to Grace, as I had in the hours before we'd attacked La Saline Royale, just on the chance the messages might somehow reach them if worse came to worst. Writing to Grace was getting harder. I knew what to say, but I seemed to mean less of it each day. It was not my stupidity with Gita Lodz, either. Instead, there was something about my feelings for Grace that seemed to suit me less and less. After standing there with Hovler, thinking about whether Grace could do me wrong, I now experienced a pinch of regret that stepping out was beyond her, since it might even have been for the best.

While I was writing, I gradually became aware of music. The German troops were in the woods singing Christmas carols, the voices traveling down to us on the wind. Many of the tunes were familiar, despite the foreign tongue, whose words I could make out here and there because of my limited Yiddish. "*Stille Nacht*," they sang, "*Heilige Nacht*." Rudzicke scrambled up to my hole.

"Captain, I was going to sing, too," he said. "A lot of us wanted to. Seeing as how we're moving out anyway."

I debated, undertaking the unfamiliar arithmetic of pluses and minuses that an experienced combat officer probably had reduced to instinct. Would I mislead the Germans about our position in the morning, or give something away? With an assault in the offing, could I deny the men one meager pleasure of Christmas? And how to cope with the ugly worm of hope that this demonstration of fellowship might make the Krauts less savage at daybreak?

"Sing," I told him. And so as we packed up, G Company sang, even me. Christmas was nothing in my house, a nonevent, and I felt as a result that I was not a participant in the festival of fellowship and good feeling that Christmas was everywhere else. But now I sang. We sang with our enemies. It went on nearly an hour, and then there was silence again, awaiting the attack which all the soldiers on both sides knew was coming.

V.

20. DON'T TELL THE CHILDREN

Long after I first read what my father had written for Barrington Leach, one question preoccupied me: Why had Dad said he desperately hoped his kids would never hear this story? Granted the tale ended with what I viewed as an episode of heartbreaking gullibility, not to mention dead-bang criminality. But there were oceans of valor before that. What did Dad want to protect us from? I would have thought he'd learned too much to believe that anybody could be harbored from the everlasting universe of human hurt at human hands. Instead, Dad's decision to suppress everything could be taken only as the product of his shuttered character, and one more occasion for regret. God knows, it would have meant the world to me at a hundred points as I grew up to know even a little of what he had written.

Like every boy my age, soaked during the 1950s in World War II epics on TV and in the movie houses, I had longed to know that my daddy had done his part—best if he were another Audie Murphy, but at least someone who'd brought his rightful share of glory to our household. Instead my questions about the war were perpetually rebuffed by both parents.

The silence was so complete that I didn't even know whether Dad had seen action. I believed he had, because of the profound stillness that gripped him when battle scenes from WWII appeared on *The Way It Was*, my father's favorite show. It was TV's first video history, hosted by the sage and solemn Eric Sevareid. I would watch the black-and-white images leap across my father's unmoving eyes. There were always artillery pieces firing with great flashes, their barrels rifling back and mud splattering as the massive armaments recoiled into the ground, while aircraft circled in the distance overhead. The grimy soldiers, caught in the camera's light, managed fleeting smiles. It became an article of faith to me that Dad had been one of them, a claim I often repeated when my male friends matched tales of their fathers' wartime exploits.

Yet all I knew for sure was that both my parents regarded war as a calamity which they often prayed would never be visited on Sarah and me. No one was more determined than my father and mother that I not go to Vietnam when my number came up in 1970. They were ready to hire lawyers, even leave the country, rather than allow me to be drafted. The sight of Richard Nixon on TV inspired Dad to a rare sputtering fury. He seemed to feel a basic deal America had made with him was being broken. Simply put, he had gone to war so that his children would not have to, not so they could take their turn.

But that period might have been less unsettling for me if I'd known a little more about my father's wartime experiences. At the U., among the antiwar types, there were occasional debates about the ethics of avoiding the draft. Logic said that some kid, working class or poor, was going to take my place. Four decades later, I still accept my rationale for wiggling out with a medical exemption due to a deviated septum, a breach between my nasal passages, which, in theory, might have led to breathing problems on the battlefront. My first responsibility was for my own actions. Understanding how misguided Vietnam was, I faced a clear moral imperative against killing—or even dying—there.

But for those of us who didn't go, there was always a lurking question. Granted, we were privileged, moralistic, and often ridiculously rude. But were we also cowards? Certainly we had planted our flag in new ground. Before 'Nam, the idea had been handed down since the Revolution, like some Chippendale heirloom, that braving death in defense of the nation was the ultimate measure of a true-blue American guy. Knowing a few details of how my father had passed this fierce test of patriotism and personal strength might have given me some comfort that I could do it, too, if need be, and made me more certain I was standing up, rather than hiding.

Instead, the only story about my father's war I ever heard came from his father, my grandfather the cobbler. Grandpa was a wonderful raconteur in the Yiddish tradition and, when Dad was not around, he told me more than once the colorful tale of how my father had entered the service. In 1942, after Dad had decided he could no longer wait to do his part, he had gone for his induction physical and been promptly rejected because of the deviated septum I ended up inheriting from him (and which, when I faced the draft, he wisely suggested I ask an ENT to check for).

My father was so upset at being turned down that he finally persuaded my grandfather to go with him to visit Punchy Berg, the local Democratic committeeman, who was able to influence the course of most governmental affairs in Kindle County. Punchy received entreaties in the basement of a local county office, where boxes of records were stacked on steel shelving. There beneath a single lightbulb, Punchy sat among his henchmen at a teacher's desk while he pondered requests. He either said no, or nothing at all. In the face of silence, one of Punchy's sidekicks would step forward and whisper a price—$5 to allow a child to transfer to a better school, $15 to get a driver's license after failing the exam. Favorable verdicts in the Kindle County courts were also available, but at costs beyond the means of workingmen.

My father stood before Punchy and poured his heart out about not being allowed to serve his country. Punchy had expected something else, a request, of which there were a number, that a draft notice be delayed or, better yet, forgotten. My grandfather said that Punchy, a former boxer whose nose was flattened on his face like the blade of a shovel, spent a minute shaking his head.

"I'll tell you, kid. Maybe you want to think about this. I know your old man a long time. Schmuel, how long it's been you fixed my shoes?"

My grandfather could not remember that far back.

"A long time," Punchy said. "You're the firstborn son. That makes you an important guy to your folks."

This remark provided the only encouragement my grandfather needed to let fly with his own opinions about what my father wanted. It was pure craziness to Grandpa's way of thinking. He had come here to America, like his brothers, so that they did not get dragooned for the Tsar's army, as Jews so often were. And now his son wanted to go back across the same ocean and fight, beside the Russians no less?

"Your old man's got a point," Punchy allowed.

My father was adamant.

"Well," said Punchy, "this is hard to figure. How I hear tell, it's costing families twelve hundred to keep their sons out. But gettin in?" Punchy rubbed his chin. "All right, kid," he said. "I gotta tell you. I'm pretty red, white, and blue myself. Half the time I'm cryin that I'm too old to go over there and take a bite out of Hitler's dick. In you want, in you get." And then Punchy proved what a true patriot he was. "Kid," he said, "it's on the house."

21. COMBAT

12/24/44—At the front

Dear Grace—

    I am writing to wish you and your family a wonderful Christmas holiday. I imagine all of you together, cozy around a fire, but perhaps that's just to comfort myself, because right now I'm colder than I have ever been in my life. At the moment, I'm convinced we should honeymoon in Florida and I am trying to warm myself up by imagining that.

    I assume news of the German offensive has reached you, but the commanders here are encouraging. This is magnificent, scenic country, tremendous hills of trees, deep with snow, and beautiful little towns nestled between, but combat has blown many of them to smithereens. I arrived as part of the investigation I have mentioned now and then, and given the circumstances have actually been pressed into combat as the leader of

*a rifle company. Finally, a chance to put that
training to good use! At last I'll have a little story
or two to tell you and our children.*

*Please give my warm regards to your family. I
assume you will be praying tonight. I'm not much
of a prayer-sayer myself, so please put in a few
extra for me, fortissimo. I want all the help we can
get.*

*Well, that's enough blabbing for tonight.
Remember I love you, darling.*

David

At 2:00 a.m., we moved out on the route the scout
team had traced along the edge of the forest, following their tracks in the snow. Orders went down
the line in a whisper. "Scouts out first in each squad. Patrol discipline. Silence. Move fast and low. Don't lose
sight of the man in front of you."

In all, we advanced about four hundred yards to another incline on the eastern side of the road, settling in a
small notch in the forest. It was not as good a position as
the one we had deserted. We were about thirty yards from
the roadside here, and even when we fanned out, we
could not really see well to the north. A small creek was
east of us, however, a good defensive perimeter. It must
have been fed by an underground spring, because it was
still running, even in the intense cold.

There had been no prior encampment here, which
meant the men had to dig in through the snow and the
frozen ground. It was hard work and we agreed we'd as-
sign four soldiers to each hole, and let them sleep in
shifts. Bidwell and I were still shoveling with our en-

trenching tools when Masi came up. He turned his angle-necked flashlight on to show me a German ration can. There was no rust on it, and the streaks of the meat that had clung to the side hadn't frozen yet.

"There was a pile of shit no more than ten yards away from it, Cap. Hot enough to have melted a little hole in the snow, and still soft when I put a stick to it."

I took the can to Meadows.

"Where are they?" I asked Bill.

"Back there somewhere," he said, pointing to the woods half a mile off. "Probably just following up on the scout plane, Captain. Good thing we changed position."

I wasn't as confident. The Krauts were paying a lot of attention to us, if they didn't intend to come down this road. We agreed we'd send out scouts at first light to follow the tracks and get a fix on the German forces. We also doubled tonight's guard. That was better anyway, given our shortage of deluxe accommodations.

Despite my concerns, I was calm. I seemed to have simply worn out my nervous system, subsiding to the resignation true soldiers acquire. If it happens, it happens. I slept for an hour or so, until heavy booms woke me, and I saw the light dancing up from Bastogne. The Germans were bombing there, giving General McAuliffe a Christmas present after the warm greetings he had sent them. The air assault went on about twenty minutes.

I fell off again before Biddy shook me awake for guard duty an hour later. I had been dreaming of home. There, it was the usual chaos. I was knocking at the front door and could not get in. But through the window I had a clear view of my parents and my sister and brother around the kitchen table. My mother, stout, voluble, enveloping, was ladling soup, and through the glass I could somehow enjoy the warmth and fragrance from the bowls she placed on the table. When the image returned to me now, I emitted the minutest moan.

"What?" asked Biddy. He was climbing into his bedroll. There was already some light in the sky, but we'd all been up most of the night. In the distance, the German artillery was pounding already. The Krauts were at work early.

I told him I had been dreaming of home.

"Don't do that," he said. "Best I can, sir, I try to never let my mind go runnin off in that direction. Just makes a body feel badly." That had been Martin's reasoning with Gita.

"You figure you'll go back home, Biddy? I mean afterward. You know. To stay?" I'd been deciding whether to ask this question for the last couple of days.

"You mean, am I gonna go back home and be myself? Who I was? Or go any other place and be who I am to you?"

That was what I meant. His big body swelled up and deflated with a long sigh.

"Captain, I been thinking on that so long, I'm just plain sick of it. Truth, Cap, I don't mind this here at all, not being every white man's nigger. It's okay — most of the time. Over there in England, lot of those English girls preferred the colored soldiers, said they was more polite, and I was trying to make time with one and she slapped my cheek when I said I was a Negro. Aside from that, it's been all right.

"But I can't go home and not claim my own. I can't go walking down the street pretending like I don't know the fellas I do, men I played ball with and chased around with, I can't do that. That boy I was having words with last week — that's what it was about, and I wanted to crawl into a hole after you lit into me. I can't hardly do that. And I can't turn tail on the folks who love me neither. I'll go back. That's what I reckon. But no matter what, Captain, it ain't gonna feel right."

"It won't make any difference, Biddy. You go back, get some more schooling for your photography. It won't make any difference."

"Captain, you don't really believe that."

"I do indeed, Biddy. I know what it's been like. But we can't take up the same stupidity now. Here we've had Southerners and Northerners, rich and poor, immigrants from every nation, fighting and dying for this country. People can't go back home and tell themselves we're all different when we're not. You be your own man, Biddy, nobody's ever going to judge you, white or colored."

"Captain," he said. He stopped to think, then started again. "Captain, I want you to know something. You're a good man, all right, you truly are. You're as straight and honest an officer as I've met. And you ain't hincty — you don't get up on yourself too much. But Captain, you don't know what the hell you're talking about now. That's the last we-all gonna say on this."

I had no chance to argue further because the first artillery shell came wailing in then. It landed about two hundred feet away, rocking the earth and igniting a plume of flame that irradiated the near darkness. I rose, still without my boots, and hollered for everyone to get down, just in time to witness another detonation that hurled a private at the perimeter into a thick tree, shoulder first. It was Hovler, the Texan who'd worried about his girl stepping out on him. The sheer force threw his arms and legs behind his back so hard that they wrapped around the trunk, before he slithered down in dead collapse.

What followed was twice the intensity of the TOT barrages. This was not random shelling at thirty-yard intervals from converted light AA or mortars. This was fire from bigger German guns, the 88s and even the heavy loads of Nebelwerfers, all precisely targeted and seeming to cover every inch of the forest incline we occupied. On impact, the ordnance spit up flames and snow and soil in the dark like giant Roman candles. Slumping back, tying my boots, listening to the outcry all around me, I realized that the Germans knew exactly where we were, despite our move. The earth rocked and things went flying the way they did in the newsreels of tornadoes — rifles, soldiers, and tree trunks zooming through the air in the orange light of the explosions and the resulting fires. Chunks of steel sizzled as they sank into the trees, from which smoke, like blood, leaked forth. But the noise, as ever, was the worst of it, the whistling metal raining down, the titanic boom of the shells, and the seconds in between when the panicked voices of my men reached me, shrieking in anguish, yelling for medics, begging for help. Peeking out, I saw direct hits on two holes at the far perimeter and the soldiers, already dead, flying toward me. In the uneven light, one of them, Bronko Lukovic, the poker champion, seemed to break apart in descent. He landed twenty yards from me on his back. His arms and legs were spread as if he was floating in a pool in the sun, but his head was gone, a bloody mess sprouting from his neck like the teased ribbon on a gift box.

"Move 'em out," I started screaming. I clambered from the hole, waving my arms, giving orders to Biddy and Masi, and Forrester. Bill Meadows, unaccountably, was nowhere to be found. I located him, blundering around in his hole on his hands and knees.

"Lost my specs, Captain, I'm blind without those specs." I jumped in, groping with him for an instant, then climbed back out, running from hole to hole to get the men in his platoon moving. By now I knew that if we didn't go, most of us would be blown to bits, and the remainder killed in the ground assault that was sure to follow. Even so, a couple of soldiers had lost control of themselves in the relentless bombardment. In one hole, a private named Parnek was on his knees, sobbing hysterically, as he tried to claw a hole in the frozen ground with his fingers. Another man in his squad, Frank Schultz, wouldn't leave because he couldn't find his helmet.

"Where's my hat," he yelled, "where's my hat?" I grabbed him by the shoulders to tell him it was on his head. He touched it and fled.

With the creek behind us, we could only go toward the road, and as we tumbled off the incline, I could hear the roar of tanks approaching. My men dashed forward, including the wounded who were mobile. O'Brien, the wiseacre from Baltimore, was hobbling behind me. His whole lower leg was gone, even the trousers, and he was using his MI as a crutch. As we broke into the clearing, I was following Biddy and his platoon, and his troops were suddenly falling to their bellies in front of me. My instinct was to order them back to their feet until I found myself facing the black mouth of a 75mm tank gun aimed at us from no more than one hundred yards. As I crushed myself against the snow, a rocket went right over our heads, exploding in the midst of the holes we'd just left. Most of Meadows' platoon was still back there and I could hear the shrieking. On our left, a machine gun began barking, joined almost immediately by rifle fire from the foxholes we'd abandoned last night across the way. There were two tanks in the road now, both Mark IVs that had been painted white, their big guns flashing and recoiling as they spit shells into the woods. About fifteen infantrymen were riding on each tank and firing their rifles at us.

It was havoc. Fortunato was on his feet, looking on like a spectator, with the SCR-300 on his back. Who had given the radio to the man who couldn't speak English? Several of our soldiers were on the ground, doing nothing. "Shoot," I yelled, and raised my Thompson. I was sure no one could hear me, but on one of the tanks, a grenadier was struck and pitched forward into the snow. Ten feet to my left, Rudzicke, who'd wanted to sing Christmas carols, was hit in the back. The bullet left a clean hole that looked like it had been sunk by a drill bit. From the way he jerked forward, I was afraid he'd been shot by one of my troops, but the Germans had fallen upon us from all directions and the men had no idea even where to aim. Behind us, in the woods, grenades exploded, and in the fires burning back there, I recognized Volksgrenadiers, regular infantry who'd been able to sneak close in white snow-combat suits. They were cleaning out those of Meadows' men who'd remained in their foxholes. Amid the machine-gun and small-arms fire, there was a great jumble of voices, buddies crying out directions, but also men screaming in pain and terror.

Stocker Collison teetered by, blood-soaked hands over his abdomen. I had the impression that he was holding a cauliflower against his uniform until I realized that the blue-white mass was his intestines.

Biddy had his bazooka team taking aim at the tanks, but they got off no more than one round before a grenade landed in their midst. I wanted Masi to return with his platoon to attack the grenadiers in the trees to our rear, but he went down as soon as I reached him. It was a leg wound, but a bad one. Blue-black blood surged forth with every heartbeat. He cast me a desperate look, but by the time I thought of applying a tourniquet he had fallen backward. There were two final feeble squirts and then it stopped completely.

When the crossfire had started, probably two-thirds of the company had emerged from the woods, strung out over forty yards. At least half had gone down in no more than a minute. Amid the great tumult, I turned full circle. The sun was coming up and in the first hard light the world was etched with a novel clarity, as if everything visible was outlined in black. It was like that moment of impact I'd felt once or twice in a museum, but more intense, for I was beholding the gorgeousness of living.

Somehow, in that instant, I understood our sole option. Algar had told me not to surrender, a point proven by the slaughter behind me in the woods. Instead I dashed and rolled among the men, yelling one command again and again, "Play dead, play dead, play dead." Each of them fell almost at once, and I too tumbled down with my face in the snow. After a few minutes the firing stopped. I could hear the explosive engine roar of Panzers thundering by and orders being shouted in German. Not surprisingly, Algar seemed to have been good to his word. The rocking blast of mortars was nearby. I gathered that Algar had brought his armor up fast and had apparently engaged the Panzers a mile farther down, where machine-gun fire and the boom of the tank rockets was audible. Near us, I could make out different engines, probably armored troop carriers, into which the unit that had killed most of my men seemed to climb to join the battle up the road. Even as the shouts sailed off, two grenades exploded in the broad clearing where we lay, rattling the earth and leaving more men screaming.

That was the principal sound now, men moaning and crying. Stocker Collison was calling out, "Mama, Mama," a lament that had been going on for some time. The wounded were going to die fast in this weather. Soaked in their own blood, they would freeze soon, a process that would accelerate due to their blood loss. When the last German voice disappeared, I hoped to find the radio.

I was about to get up, when a single shot rang out, a parched sound like a breaking stick. The pricks had left a sniper behind, at least one, who'd probably fired when somebody else moved. I thought of calling out a warning, even though it would have given me away, but that would reveal that many of the others lying here were alive. I could only hope the men would understand on their own.

Instead, to betray no sign of life, I worked on slowing my breathing. The smell, now that I was aware of it, was repulsive. No one ever told me there is a stench of battle, of cordite and blood, of human waste, and as time goes on, of death. I had chosen a terrible position — I was lying on the submachine gun and after only a few minutes the stock had begun to sink into my thigh, so that I was being bruised under my own weight. But I would have to bear it. In some ways I welcomed the pain as my just deserts as a failed commander. I wondered how the Germans had found us. Their scouts must have been out in the darkness and followed our tracks through the snow. They may even have seen us cross the road. I reviewed my decisions repeatedly. Should I have recognized there was such a large force out here? Would we have been better off, in the end, remaining in the first foxholes and fighting from there? Could we have held the Krauts off longer, inflicted more losses? After days of suffering in the cold, we had not detained the Germans more than a few minutes as they came down the road.

I was freezing, of course. I had been freezing for days, but lying in the snow without moving was worse. My limbs burned as if my skin had been ignited from inside. Near me, someone moaned now and then for water and Collison was still asking for his mother. He went on for at least another hour and then a single sniper's bullet rang out and the calling stopped. I wondered if they'd shot him out of mercy or contempt. But within a second, there were several more bullets and a haunting punctured sound emerging from each man they struck. The snipers — I now thought there were two — seemed to be systematically picking off our wounded. I awaited my turn. I had gone through the entire battle, the few minutes it all had lasted, with no conscious fear, but now that I realized they were killing any man showing signs of life, I felt the full flush of terror. A thought struck through to the center of me like an ax: I was going to find out about God.

But I did not die. After five or six shots, the firing ceased. The wounded, at least those moaning or begging for water or help, had gone still, and there was now a harrowing silence in the clearing. I could hear the noises of the morning, the wind in the trees and crows calling. The submachine gun was still beneath me. From the last shots, I believed the snipers were across the road in the same woods we'd left. I had no idea how many men who lay here were still alive. Ten perhaps. But if we all stood and fired, we'd have a chance to kill the snipers before they killed us. Those would be my orders if the sharpshooting started again.

With no voices here, the fighting down the road was more audible. The rumbling explosions echoed and re-echoed between the hills. Late in the morning, the drone of aircraft joined it and bombs shook the air. I hoped we were dropping on the Panzers, but couldn't be certain.

Several hours along, I opened my eyes briefly. Near me Forrester, who'd been abandoned by his widowed mother, was jackknifed. A ragged bullet hole was ripped in the back of his neck. His carotids had emptied through it, staining his jacket, and he'd messed his trousers as he was dying, an odor I'd smelled for quite some time. But I hadn't looked out to count the dead around me, or even the living. With the planes aloft, I knew the sky was clearing, and I longed for one last sight of that fresh blue, so full of promise. I looked while I dared, then closed my eyes. I missed the world already.

By now, my bladder was aching. Urine, however, would eat through the snow and potentially give me away to the snipers. More important, I was likely to soak myself and freeze to death. For a while, I decided to count, only to know time was passing. Finally, I thought about the people at home. Lying there, I was full of regret about Gita. For weeks, I had been too confused to feel the full measure of shame that visited me now. It was the images of my morning dream that haunted me, a tender rebuke. I wanted home. I wanted a warm place that was mine, a woman within it, and children, too. I saw that spot, a neat bungalow, from outside, as clearly as if I were at the picture show. The light, so bright through the broad front window, beckoned. I could feel the warmth of the house, of the fire that burned there, of the life that was lived there.

Someone broke through the trees. Had the Germans come to finish us? But the tread was lighter, and too quick. Eventually I concluded an animal was lingering among us, some carrion eater, I feared, meaning I would have to lie here while it gnawed the dead. At last the footfalls reached me. I recognized the heat and smell of the breath on my face instantly, and had to work to hold off a smile as the dog applied his cold snout to my cheek. But my amusement quickly sluiced away in fear. I wondered if the Krauts were using the animal for recon. Could the dog tell the quick from the dead or was he sent to test our reactions? I refused to move although I could feel the mutt circling me. He lowered his muzzle yet again for a breath or two, then suddenly whimpered in that heartbreaking way dogs do. I could hear him padding around, nosing among the men. He cried out one more time, then went off.

Late in the afternoon, the battle appeared to shift toward us. I reasoned it through. We were winning. We had to be winning. There was gunfire only a few hundred yards away, on the western side of the road where we'd been yesterday. That meant Americans were nearby. An hour later, I heard English on the wind and debated whether to cry out. As soon as it was dark, I decided, we'd move.

When I opened my eyes again, it was dusk. Forty minutes later, the light was gone and I began to drag myself on my elbows through the clearing. I wanted to crawl toward the Americans, but the snipers' shots had come from there, and so I crept back to the woods where so many members of G Company had been slaughtered this morning. I was slithering on my belly into a black maze, through the snow and blood and shit and God knows what else, thinking in my brain-stuck way about the serpent in Eden.

I touched each body I passed. It was easy to tell the living, even with a gloved hand that was like lead. In the dark, I could see eyes spring open, and I pointed to the woods. I reached a form I recognized as Biddy's and hesitated. Please, I thought. He was alive.

I dragged myself around for nearly an hour, gathering the men who were able to move, and sending them scraping toward the woods, like a nighttime migration of turtles. Covered in sweat now, I'd worn the skin off my elbows and knees. I could make out the trees ahead of me, but stopped when I suddenly heard voices. Germans? After all of this we were crawling back into the arms of the Krauts? But I was too miserable to devise alternatives. Nearing the border of the woods, I realized someone was creeping toward me. I grabbed my gun while the other form continued forward on his belly. Then I saw the Red Cross on his helmet.

"Can you make it?" he whispered.

When I reached the trees, two more medics swept forward to grab me. As I stood up, the urge from my bladder overwhelmed me and I barely made it to a beech where I relieved myself, savoring the warm fog rising in the cold. I had a terrible cramp in one leg, and feared I would fall over and look like a fountain.

The medics explained the situation. The Germans who had passed by here had been routed. McAuliffe had brought up reinforcements and the firefight went on long enough for American bombers to get here and blow all of the Panzers off the road. More than one hundred grenadiers had surrendered, but one band had fallen back into the trees on the other side of the road. Algar was going to call in artillery, but he'd demanded that the medics first try to collect the survivors of G Company. The corpsmen had driven jeeps down the cow path from the west, then walked in nearly a quarter of a mile before they made out the dozen or so of us bellying our way through the snow.

Here, in what remained of the foxholes we'd been in this morning, the medics moved among the dead with gruesome efficiency, checking wrists and throats for the sign of a pulse, and when that was lacking, as it almost always was, pulling the dog tags through the shirtfronts to make work easier for those in the Quartermaster Corps Graves Registration Detail. With the medics, I talked about how to bring in the wounded still out in the open. We had to figure there were Germans in the woods across the road, but the medics understood I couldn't leave without the eight men I'd found in the clearing, still breathing but unable to move. Biddy and I crawled back out with two corpsmen. We formed litters by retying each man's belt under his arms, then peeling his field jacket back over his head and folding his rifle within the fabric. One of the medics gave a signal and I stood up first and began dragging the man I had, O'Brien, toward the trees. I waited to die, yet again, but after even a few yards, it was clear there was no one on the other side now, at least no one willing to give himself away by shooting. As I dragged O'Brien along, the dog followed.

From the woods, the corpsmen radioed for a convoy and ambulances, which met us on the other side of the creek where the cow path joined the woods. In the lights of the vehicles, I caught sight of a C ration cracker in cellophane lying unharmed in the snow. I broke it in pieces and passed it out to the three other men who were waiting with me. We ate this morsel in total silence.

"Damn," one of them, Hank Garns, finally said.

We were back at Algar's headquarters in minutes and ushered into the cold barn. There were thirteen of us. Counting the wounded, twenty-two men in G Company had made it, out of the ninety-two we'd had at the start of the day. Meadows and Masi were dead.

"Jesus, that was rough," said a dark man named Jesse Tornillo. "We came in on our chinstraps."

"Yeah," said Garns. "Guess you're right. Hadn't noticed till you mentioned it." Garns was smiling and seemed to take no notice that his entire body was rattling as if he had a mortal chill.

"Captain," said Tornillo, "it might be that mutt of yours saved our lives." I had not registered that the animal had followed me inside but he was looking around the circle as if he could follow the conversation, a black mongrel with a brown star on his chest and one brown paw. "When he started in with that whimpering, maybe he made those snipers think we were all of us dead." Tornillo bent to scratch the dog's ears. "Saved our lives," he said. "How you like that? I was laying there, listenin to him scratch around. Soon as I figured out it was a dog, hombre, I was praying for just one thing. 'Oh, Lord,' I kept sayin, 'if these Krauts gotta shoot me, please don't let this damn pooch piss on my head before that.'"

We laughed, all of us, huge gusts of laughter, full of the sweet breath of life. As for the dead, there was no mention of them now. They were, in a word, gone. I didn't doubt that these men, some of whom had been together for months, mourned. But there was no place in our conversation for that. They were dead. We were alive. It wasn't luck or the order of the universe. It was simply what had happened.

Algar came in then and I gave him my report.

"Good thinking, good thinking," Algar kept saying when I admitted how we'd survived by playing dead.

"It was an ambush, Colonel."

By now we both knew that G Company had been given a suicidal assignment. We did not have enough men or firepower to hold that road, no matter what our position. I didn't say that, but I didn't have to.

"Dubin," Algar said, "I'm sorry. I am the sorriest son of a bitch in the Army."

I went to the battalion aid station to check on the wounded from G, but they were already on the way back to the field hospital by ambulance. There were doctors in Bastogne now, four surgeons who'd landed this morning by glider.

When I returned, Algar had found the cooks and ordered them to reopen the mess to serve us Christmas dinner. We had fried Spam and dehydrated potatoes, with dehydrated apples for dessert. As a treat, there were a few fresh beets. We'd eaten one meal in the last two days, and I felt the full measure of my hunger as the heat and aroma of the food rose up to my face. I count that Christmas meal in that cold mess eaten off a tin plate as one of my life's culinary highlights.

Biddy sat down beside me. We didn't say much while we ate, but he turned to me once he was done.

"No disrespect to the dog, Captain, but it was you that saved our lives."

A couple of the other men murmured agreement. But I wanted no part of being treated as a hero. There were isolated instants when I had actually led my men, scrambling from hole to hole amid the initial artillery barrage, even when I waved them so disastrously into the clearing. In those moments, a tiny voice trapped somewhere in my heart had spoken up in utter amazement. Look at me, it said, I'm commanding. Or more often: Look at me, I didn't get hit. But I held no illusion that was fundamentally me. We can all play a part for a few minutes. But I was not like Martin — and it was he I thought of — able to do it again and again.

The real David Dubin had fallen to the earth and played dead, where he had eventually surrendered to terror. I had given my men saving advice mostly because it was what I had wanted to do, to lie down like a child and hope that the assault — the war — would be over soon. True, it was the wiser course. But I had taken it because at the center of my soul, I was a coward. And for this I was now being saluted. I was grateful only that I did not feel shocked at myself or overwhelmed with shame. I knew who I was.

The men began to talk a little about what had happened, especially the eight or nine hours we had lain in the snow.

"Praise God, man, these are the shortest days of the year."

"Lord, poor fucking Collison, huh? I ain't gonna sleep for three nights hearing that."

But as I sat there, finishing off my dinner, my will, indeed all that remained of my being, was summoned in a single desire: I was going to make sure I never set foot on a battlefield again.

22. THE REMAINS

My wish to avoid combat, like so many other wishes I made, did not come true. There were more battles, but never another day like Christmas. Patton's forces continued pushing on Bastogne from the south, and more and more supplies made it through. Like an eager audience, we cheered the sight of every truck carrying cases of C rations bound in baling wire, the brown-green ammo boxes, or the gray cardboard tubes containing mortar and bazooka rounds.

On December 27, the 110th was re-formed with elements of the 502nd Parachute Infantry Regiment. Algar became battalion commander. G Company was now E Company, but I remained in charge. With six days in combat, I was one of the more experienced field officers Algar had. A second lieutenant named Luke Chester, literally a month out of OCS, became my second-in-command. He was a fine young soldier, a serious man, who spent most of his free time reading the Bible. But he was not Bill Meadows.

We pushed farther down the road through Champs, where so many of my men had died, then swung north and east into Longchamps. Although it did not seem possible, the weather was worse, less snow, but the kind of brittle, devastating cold that had seemed liable to snap the ears off my head in high school. However, our assignments allowed us to be quartered indoors for a portion of most nights. Algar protected my company. We were not the forward element on many operations. Instead, we generally followed armored infantry, covering the flanks. We fought brief battles, two or three times a day, knocking back smaller German units, repelling commandos, securing positions other forces had already overrun, and often taking prisoners, whom we'd hold until the MPs arrived.

But it was war. We still entered scenes that, as Biddy had characterized them, seemed to have come from the *Inferno*: the dead with their faces knotted in anguish, weeping soldiers immobilized by fear, vehicles ablaze with the occupants sometimes still screaming inside, soldiers without limbs lying within vast mud-streaked halos of their own blood, and others careening about, blinded by wounds or pain.

Every morning, I awoke to the same sick instant when I realized I was here fighting. I thought the same things so often that they were no longer thoughts at all. The questions simply circulated through my brain with the blood.

Why was I born?

Why do men fight?

Why must I die now, before living my life?

These questions had no answers and that fact often brought pain. It was like running full tilt again and again at a wall. The only comfort — and it was a small one —

was that I saw these thoughts passing behind the eyes of every man I knew. They danced, like skinny ballerinas, across the thin membrane that separated everything from a molten surface, which was my constant fear.

I nearly did not make it to 1945. We were throwing the Germans back, inch by inch, but the control of terrain remained extremely confused. The Nazi lines, once drawn so tight around Bastogne, had been shredded, but not always with sufficient force to fully subdue the Krauts. On the maps, the intermingled American and German positions looked like the webbed fingers of joined hands.

On December 31, Algar sent us out to secure a hill on the other side of Longchamps. Our artillery had rained down already, and the enemy figured to have retreated, but as the first platoon started up, shots snapped in from above. Two men died and two were wounded. I was in the rear, but I scrambled forward to order everyone to dig in. A shot rang off a stone near my feet. I saw the German who had been shooting. He was up the hill, perhaps two hundred yards from me, peeking out from behind an outhouse in his large green coat with its high collar and the helmet that I still thought made every Kraut look half comic, as if he was wearing a coal scuttle. As he watched me through his rifle sight, I could see that killing me was a crisis for him. I had the nerve somehow to nod in his direction, and then scurried off on all fours, leaving the German infantryman little time to think. When I looked back, he was gone. I promised myself that I would spare one of them when the shoe was on the other foot. I tried to work out how fast the phenomenon of troops giving grace to one another would have to spread before the men in combat had made an armistice of their own.

I killed, of course. I remember a machine-gun nest we had surrounded, pouring in fire. A German soldier literally bounced along on the ground every time my bullets struck him, almost as if I was shooting a can. Each of these deaths seemed to enhance the power of the Thompson .45 submachine gun with which I'd parachuted, and which Robert Martin had borrowed, so that I sometimes felt as if I'd lifted a magic wand when I raised the weapon.

By now, I also thought I was developing animal senses. I knew the Germans were nearby even when they could not yet be seen or heard. In that instant before combat began, I passed down a bizarre passageway. Life, which had seemed so settled, so fully within my grasp, had to be renounced. I would now shoot my way across a bridge between existence and nonexistence. That, I realized mournfully, was what war was. Not life-essential, as I'd somehow believed, but a zone of chaos between living and dying. And then the bullets would fly and I would fire back.

On New Year's Day, after we'd turned east toward Recogne, we came upon a few advance scouts, Waffen troops. There were only four of them. They'd been hiding behind a crisscross of felled pines in the forest, and should have let us pass whatever their intentions, whether to ambush us or simply to report our whereabouts. Instead one of them spooked and fired at first sight of our uniforms. The four were no match for a company. Three were dead after less than a minute of fighting, while several of my men saw the fourth scout stumbling off into the brush. Reaching the three corpses, we could see the blood trail the fleeing German had left, and I dispatched

Biddy's platoon to find him before the man got back to his unit.

When Bidwell returned half an hour later, he was morose.

"Bled to death, Cap. He was just laid out in the snow, with his blue eyes wide open, lookin at this here in his hand." Biddy showed me a tiny snap the size of the ones he was always taking, but this was of the German soldier's family, his thin wife and his two little boys, whom he'd been staring at as he died.

On January 2, 1945, E Company received reinforcements, nearly thirty men, all newly arrived replacements. I hated them, with the same intensity my men had hated me only a few days ago. I could barely stand to command these troops. I hated being responsible for them and knowing how much danger they were destined to expose us to. One of them, Teddy Wallace from Chicago, told anybody who'd listen that he had a family at home. Fathers had been the last drafted and he worried aloud about what would become of his sons if something happened to him, as if the rest of us didn't have people who loved us and needed us, too. His first action required his platoon to clean out a German mortar team. Two squads had surrounded the position and then tossed in a grenade. When I arrived, I found Wallace on the ground. After falling on a rock, he had pulled his pants leg up to study the bruise, rubbing it repeatedly, while two men with bullet wounds groaned within feet of him.

He died the next day. We were trapped in the woods, while inching our way north and east toward Noville. The

artillery again had devastated the German position, but
two snipers had climbed into the trees, trying to shoot
down on us as if they were hunting deer. In the process,
they made themselves insanely vulnerable, but rather
than trying to lob bazooka rounds at them, I radioed for
tank support, and ordered my men to dig in on the other
side of one of those thick-walled Belgian farmhouses.
Suddenly, Wallace stood up, as if it was a new day and he
was getting out of bed. I don't know what he figured, that
the snipers were disposed of, or perhaps the battlefield
had simply gotten to him. In the instant I saw him, he
looked as if he had a question in mind, but a shot ripped
all the features off his face. A buddy pulled him down. I
thought Wallace was now going back to his family, albeit
without a nose or mouth, but when I crawled up later,
he was gone. I wrote to his wife and sons that night,
describing his bravery.

In the wake of battle, one of the principal preoccupa-
tions of my company, like every fighting band, was collecting souvenirs. German firearms, Lugers and Mausers,
were most prized, and everyone, including me, eventually
acquired one. One of the men found a good Zeiss photo-
graphic lens and gave it to Biddy. My troops also removed wristwatches, flags, pennants, armbands — and
cut off ears, until I put a stop to that. I understood this tro-
phy hunting, the desire to have some tangible gain for
what they had been through.

The day that Wallace went down, after two Sherman
tanks had arrived and blown up the trees where the German snipers had perched, I watched another replacement
soldier, Alvin Liebowitz, approach Wallace's body. I
hated Liebowitz most among my new men. He was a lean

boy, red-haired, with that New York air of knowing every angle. During several of the brief firefights we'd had, he'd seemed to disappear. Wallace and he had come over together, and I thought Liebowitz was reaching down to pass some kind of blessing. I was shocked when the sun gleamed before his hand disappeared into his pocket.

I came charging up.

"What?" Liebowitz said, with ridiculous feigned innocence.

"I want to see your right pocket, Liebowitz."

"What?" he said again, but pulled out Wallace's watch. He could have told me he was going to send it to Wallace's family, but then he might have had to hand it over. Alvin Liebowitz wasn't the kind to give up that easily.

"What the hell are you doing, Liebowitz?"

"Captain, I don't think Wallace here's going to be telling much time."

"Put it back, Liebowitz."

"Shit, Captain, there're guys over in the woods picking over the Krauts' bodies right now. Germans, Americans, what's the difference?"

"They're your dead, Liebowitz. That's all the difference in the world. That watch may be the only thing Wallace's sons ever have of their father's."

"Hell, this is a good watch, Captain. It'll disappear a long time before that body finds its way home."

That was Liebowitz. Smart-ass answers for everything. The Army was full of Liebowitzes, but he got under my skin to a degree unrivaled by any other man I'd commanded, and I felt a sudden fury that did not visit me even in battle. I lunged at him with my bayonet knife, and he barely jumped out of the way as he yelped.

"What the fuck's wrong with you?" he asked, but put the watch down. He went off, looking over his shoulder as if he was the aggrieved party.

Biddy had witnessed the incident. When we were settling in the empty train car where we billeted that night, he said, "That was dang good, Cap. Lot of the men liked seeing you put Liebowitz in his place, but it looked for all the world like you was actually gonna cut him."

"I meant to, Biddy. I just missed."

He gave me a long look. "I guess we all harder on our own, Captain."

By January 8, the battle had turned. Every day we were securing large chunks of the ground the Germans had taken back with their offensive. I woke that morning with a dream I'd had once or twice before, that I was dead. The wound, the weapon, the moment — I felt the bullet invade my chest and then my spirit hovering over my body. I watched the Graves Detail approach and take me. Fully awake, I could only say as everybody else did: Then that is what will happen.

It was Bidwell who had roused me inadvertently. He had my toothbrush sticking out of the corner of his mouth. We were quartered in a church school and Biddy, without apology, had taken a little water from a sacramental font.

"I dreamed I was dead, Biddy. Have you done that?"

"Captain, it ain't any other way to be out there but that." Then he pointed to the doorway, where a young private stood. He'd come to tell me that Lieutenant Colonel Algar wanted to see me on the other side of Noville.

Algar, as ever, was at his desk, looking at maps. He'd acquired a supply of narrow black cheroots and had one in his mouth whenever I saw him these days. He answered my salute, then pointed me to a canvas-back chair.

"David, I got a teletype this morning from a Major Camello. He's General Teedle's adjutant, or assistant adjutant. They were trying to determine your whereabouts. When I answered you were here, he wrote back wanting to know when you could resume your assignment. They're concerned for your welfare."

They were concerned about Martin, at least Teedle was. I asked if he'd told them Martin was dead.

"I thought I'd leave that to you. Besides, you said you needed to see a body. I asked General Teedle for your services for one more week. We're going to be a long way toward kicking Dietrich out of the Ardennes by then. If things go well, I hope to be able to relieve your entire unit."

I found the thought of Teedle, still up in the middle of the night, still incensed as he thought about Martin, richly comic. I would have laughed, except that I knew I was going to get killed in the next seven days. That was a certainty. If I didn't, then it would be Biddy. But I said, "Yes, sir."

"You've done your part. There's a first lieutenant in A who's ready to take over a company. So I'm relieving you, effective January 15. You and Bidwell. You're to follow your prior orders and, when complete, report to General Teedle." The 18th Armored had met the 6th Panzers and contained them, and was now pushing them back. They were south of us in Luxembourg.

Algar said he'd have written orders in the morning.

With them, we'd find he had put Bidwell and me in for medals. The Silver Star, he said. For our jump and for volunteering for combat.

"A Section Eight would be more appropriate," I said.

He said he felt a Distinguished Service Cross was actually in order, but that required an investigation which might reveal the condition of my trousers when I'd hit the ground in Savy.

We laughed and shook hands. I told him what a privilege it had been to serve under him.

"I'm going to look you up, if I get to Kindle County, David."

I promised to do the same when I was in New Jersey, another wish that went unfulfilled. Hamza Algar was killed in July 1945 in Germany, after the surrender, when his jeep ran over a mine. By then, 4,500 soldiers out of the 5,000 men in the 110th Regiment which had faced the first German assault of the Ardennes campaign along Skyline Drive were dead or wounded. So far as I know, Hamza Algar was the last casualty.

On the morning of January 15, Luke Chester assembled E Company and First Lieutenant Mike Como formally took command. It had been a hard week. The Germans seemed to be resisting Patton and the 11th Armored Division, behind whom we'd been fighting, with much greater ferocity than the armies of Montgomery and Hodges coming down from the north. I think Dietrich was unwilling to abandon his dream of capturing Bastogne, or perhaps he simply wanted to waste his last fury on the forces that had stopped him. My company lost six more men that week, and suffered thirteen wounded, all but four seriously. But there would be no casualties now for a few days. Most of the infantry elements in the 502nd, including E Company, were being relieved by the 75th Infantry Division. My men would head for Theux for a week's R & R, battlefront style, which meant nothing more than warm quarters and running water. Nonetheless, I told them they would have my enduring envy, because each man was guaranteed a bath. It had been a month since any of us had washed, other than what was possible by warming snow in a helmet over a camp stove, which generally meant a fast shave once a week when we were housed indoors. The smoke and grease from our guns had more or less stuck to our skin, turning all of us an oily black. We looked like a minstrel troupe, which made for a few private jokes between Bidwell and me. Now standing next to Como, I told the men that it had been the greatest honor of my life to command them and that I would remember them as long as I lived. I have never spoken words I meant more.

The dog, whom the men had named Hercules, presented a problem. Hercules was deaf, probably as the result of getting caught too close to an explosion. He fled yelping at the first flash of light on the battlefield, and we speculated that that was why whoever owned him had turned him out. Despite his handicap, he had made himself increasingly popular in the last two weeks by proving to be an able hunter. He'd snatch rabbits in the woods which he would deposit at my feet several times a day. We packed them in snow until he had caught enough for the cooks to give a ribbon of meat to each man as a treat with his rations. Hercules would sit at the fire and make a meal of the viscera, and, once he'd finished, the soldiers came by to ruffle his ears and praise him. I regarded him as a company mascot, but because Biddy and I fed him, he jumped into our jeep after I'd transferred command. We pushed him out at least three times, only to have him leap back in, and finally gave up. Half the company came to bid Hercules farewell, exhibiting far more affection than they'd shown Gideon and me.

Then we drove south and west, beyond Monty, to find out what had happened to Robert Martin and his team. The hill where they'd fallen had been retaken only in the last thirty-six hours and the bodies of the men who had died there were yet to be removed. Graves Registration Detail had arrived, but most of the GR troops were at work on a hillock to the west. In their gloves, they rooted for dog tags in the shirtfronts of the dead, bagging any possessions they found on a body and tying it to the man's ankle. Then they sorted the corpses by size, so that the cordon they were going to assemble would be stable. Quartermaster Salvage was with them, picking over the inanimate remains. During the stillborn portion of the war in September, Salvage went over some battlefields so closely you couldn't find a piece of barbed wire or a shell casing afterward. But right now they were interested in weapons, ammunition, and unused medical supplies. Even before GR got to most of the corpses, I noticed they had been stripped of their jackets and boots. It was probably the Germans who'd done that, but it could have been our troops, or even locals. I didn't begrudge any of them whatever it had taken to survive the cold.

Biddy and I walked up the hill. Most of the men in the team Martin had led here had been mowed down as they fled by the machine guns mounted on the Panzers. The corpses were frozen solid like statues. One man, on his knees in an attitude of prayer, had probably died begging for his life. I walked among the dead, using my helmet to clear off enough of the snow that had drifted over them to make out their features, giving each man a moment of respect. By now, their flesh had taken on a yellowish color, although I uncovered one soldier whose head had been blown off. The frozen gray brain matter, looking like what curdles from overcooked meat, was all around him. Somehow the back of his cranium was still intact, resembling a porcelain bowl, through which the stump of his spinal cord protruded.

Biddy and I passed several minutes looking for Martin. Four weeks ago I had seen nothing like this. Now it remained awful, but routine. And still, as I often did, I found myself in conversation with God. Why am I alive? When will it be my turn? And then as ever: And why would you want any of your creatures treated this way?

The lodge which had been Martin's observation post was about fifty yards west. According to Barnes and Edgeworthy, it had gone down like a house of cards. Everything had fallen in, except the lower half of the rear wall. The crater from the tank shells reached nearly to the brick footings and was filled with the burned remains of the building—cinders and glass and larger chunks of the timbers, and the blackened stones of the outer walls. We could see the view Martin had as he looked west where the American tanks had emerged like ghosts from the morning blizzard. He had died in a beautiful spot, with a magnificent rolling vista of the hills, plump with snow.

I summoned the GR officer and he brought over a

steam shovel to dig through the stony rubble, but after an hour they were unable to find a whole corpse. In the movies, the dead die so conveniently — they stiffen and fall aside. Here men had been blown apart. The flesh and bone, the shit and blood of buddies had showered over one another. Men in my company had died like that on Christmas Day, and among the burdens I carried, along with the troubled memory of the gratitude I'd experienced that it had been them and not me, was the lesser shame of feeling revolted as the final bits of good men splattered on me. Here, of course, if anything remained of Robert Martin, it probably had been incinerated in the burning debris. Biddy motioned toward a tree about twenty yards off. A ribbon of human entrails hung there, ice-rimed, but literally turning on the wind like a kite tail.

Edgeworthy and Barnes had placed Martin at the second-floor window, surveying the retreating Germans, when the first tank shell had rocketed in. Working from the foundation, it was not hard to figure the spot, but his remains could have blown anywhere within two hundred yards. The sergeant had his men dig in the area of the west wall for close to an hour. A pair of dog tags turned up, neither Martin's.

"They don't usually burn up," the sergeant said, meaning the tags. He expected eventually to identify Martin somehow. Dental records, fingerprints, laundry marks, school rings. But it would take weeks. As we were getting ready to leave, a hand and arm were discovered, but there was a wedding ring on the third finger. It wasn't Martin.

"Panzers didn't take many prisoners," said the sergeant, "but the Krauts are the Krauts. They'd have treated an officer better, if they found him alive. Only thing is, anybody who made it through this didn't live by much. Have to be in a POW hospital, wouldn't you think? And the Krauts don't have medicine for their own. I wouldn't think your man would be doing too well."

I sent a signal to Camello reporting on our findings and asking for the Third Army to contact the Red Cross, which reported on POWs. At this stage, it could take a month at least to be sure the Germans didn't have Martin, and even that wouldn't be definitive. General Teedle had another suggestion on how to fully investigate Martin's fate. The idea had occurred to me, but I had been unwilling. Lying in that snowy field on Christmas Day seemed to have put an end to my curiosity. Now I had a direct order, a three-word telegraphic response.

Find the girl

23. REUNION

I gave no credence to what Martin had told me in Savy about Gita's whereabouts, even though it had been vaguely corroborated by the little private, Barnes, and his memory of the girl with the farm family Martin contacted near Skyline Drive. Instead, we decided to retrace the initial intelligence which had placed Gita near Houffalize. After several signals, we were advised to see the leader there of the Belgian resistance, the Geheim Leger, the Secret Army, a woman named Marthe Trausch.

Traveling took two days, because Houffalize was not fully liberated until January 16, when the First Army's 84th Infantry and Patton's 11th Armored met at the town and began driving east. Like so much of the Ardennes, Houffalize sat handsomely in a snowy forest valley carved by the Ourthe River, a narrow tributary of the Meuse, but the town itself was now all but obliterated. The American bombers had leveled every structure large enough to be used by the Germans as a command center, killing hundreds of Nazis, but dozens of Houffalize residents as well. We rode in to indifferent greetings. For these people, when it came to war and warriors, the sides were less and less consequential.

Madame Trausch proved to be a seventy-year-old tavern keeper, a fleshy widow with a bright skirt scraping the floor. She had taken over her husband's role in the resistance when he died, her saloon providing an excellent site both for eavesdropping on the Nazis and for passing information. About half of the old stone inn had survived and I found her calmly clearing debris with two of her grandchildren. Her native tongue was Luxembourgian, a kind of Low German, and her accent made her French hard for me to follow, but she responded promptly when I mentioned Martin and Gita.

For once, Robert Martin appeared to have told the truth. Madame Trausch said Martin had been intent on getting into southern Germany, and asked for help setting up Gita in Luxembourg near the German border. The Luxembourgers had not put up the same fight against the Nazis as the Belgians, but a loose network existed there of residents who assisted the Geheim Leger when they could. More than a month ago, Gita had been placed with one of these families on a small farm in sight of the Our-the River, on the steep hills beneath Marnach. Gita posed as a milkmaid, taking the family cows to pasture and back each day. These rambles allowed her to watch the movement of the German troops from the heights over the river, leading to her unheeded warnings about tank activity near the German town of Dasburg.

"In war, it is all noise, no one listens," said Madame Trausch. She had no idea whether Gita or the farmer or their house had survived the battles. No one had yet been heard from, but it was unclear whether the Germans had even been pushed back there. We started east, were road-blocked by combat, and did not get to the hamlet of Roder until the afternoon of January 19. By then the fighting was about two miles east.

Here, as in Belgium, the ocher farmhouses and barns, rather than being scattered over the landscape, were arranged in the feudal manner around a common court-yard with each family's land stretching behind their abode. The medieval notion was common protection, but now this clustering had made all the structures equally vulnerable to modern explosives. Every house was damaged, and one had fallen in entirely, with only two walls of jointed stone partially standing in broken shapes like dragon's teeth. The round crosshatched rafters of the roof lay camelbacked between them, beside a heap of timber and stone over which a family and several of their neighbors were climbing. Apparently searching for any useful remains, they proceeded in a determined and utterly stoic manner. At the top of the hill of rubble a man picked up scraps of paper, sorting them in a fashion, some in his trouser pockets, others in his coat. Another fellow was already at work with a hammer, knocking loose pieces of mortar from the stones, probably quarried a century ago, and stacking them so that they could be used to rebuild.

But I sensed this was the place I was looking for, due not so much to Madame Trausch's information as to what I'd heard from Private Barnes. He'd described the lady of the house as "a round old doll," and there would never be better words for the woman wobbling along near the top of the pile.

I had started toward her, when I heard my name. On

the far side of the heap, Gita held a hand to her eye. She was dressed in a makeshift outfit — a headscarf, a cloth overcoat with fur trim on the sleeves, and torn work pants.

"Doo-bean?" She seemed only mildly surprised to see me, as if she presumed I'd been searching for her for weeks. She climbed up grinning and struck me on the shoulder, speaking English. It was only my physical appearance that seemed to inspire her wonder.

"You soldier!" she cried.

Despite all the vows I had made on the battlefield, I found myself enjoying her admiration. I offered her a cigarette. She shrieked when she saw the pack and dragged on the smoke so hungrily that I thought she would consume the butt in one breath. I told her to keep the package, which she literally crushed to her heart in gratitude.

We reverted to French. I said I was looking for Martin.

"*Pourquoi?* Still all this with Teedle?"

"There are questions. Have you seen him?"

"*Moi?*" She laughed in surprise. The round old doll teetered over to see about me. Soon, the whole family was describing the last month. In Marnach, like everywhere else, collaborators with the Germans had been severely punished when the Allies took control, and thus, once the Germans returned, those known to have aided the Americans were endangered, less by the SS than by their vengeful neighbors. Gita and the Hurles had endured many close calls. For several days, they had scurried like wood mice through the forest, eventually stealing back here and remaining in the woodshed of family friends. No one had food, and there was little way to know which side would bomb or shoot them first. The Hurles still had no idea who had destroyed their house, nor did it matter. All was lost, except two of their twelve cows. But the father, the mother, and their two married daughters were safe, and they all continued to hold out hope for their sons, who like most of the young men in Luxembourg had been forced into the German Army and sent to the eastern front. Madame Hurle remained on the Americans' side, but wished they would hurry up and win the war.

"*Qu'est-ce qu'ils nous ont mis!*" The Germans, she said, had beaten the hell out of them.

"But no sign of Martin?" I asked Gita. She had not really answered the question.

"*Quelle mouche t'a piqué?*" she answered. What's eating you? "You are angry with Martin, no? Because he played a trick. And me, too, I suppose."

"I received your postcard," I answered.

"Robert was very put out when I told him I wrote. But I owed you a word. I was afraid you would be hurt when you woke."

"And so I was."

"It was a moment, Dubin. An impulse. War is not a time when impulse is contained."

"I have had the very same thoughts in the days since."

"Ah," she said. "So between us, peace is declared."

"Of course," I said. We were both smiling, if still somewhat shyly. "But I must know about Martin. Tell me when you last saw him."

"A month, I would say. More. Since I am with the Hurles. When the battle is done, he will find me here. He always does." She was blithe, even childish in her conviction. Assaying her reactions, the question I had been sent here to pose seemed answered. Martin had made no miraculous escape, had sent no secret emissaries.

"Then I am afraid Martin is dead," I said.

"*Qu'est-ce que tu dis?*"

I repeated it. A tremor passed through her small face, briefly erasing the indomitable look that was always there. Then she gave a resolute shake to her short curls and addressed me in English to make her meaning clear.

"Is said before. Many times. Is not dead."

"The men in his company saw him fall, Gita. Tank shells struck the building where he was. He died bravely."

"*Non!*" she said, in the French way, through the nose.

I had watched myself, as it were, throughout this exchange. Even now, I could not completely fight off the fragment in me that was dashed that she took Martin so much to heart. But I felt for her as well. When I wondered where she would go next, I recognized much of the motive for her attachment to him. She was again a Polish orphan in a broken country. Even her time as warrior was over without Martin.

"I had very faint hopes, Gita. Hope against hope, we say. That is why I came. If he survived, I knew he would have contacted you."

She agreed with that in a murmur. I had toyed with the truth in my role of interrogator, and she might well have shaded her answers to me. After all, she wanted to be Bernhardt. But her grief looked genuine. She wandered down the mound by herself. She was not crying, though. Then again, I wondered if Gita ever wept. She stood alone, looking out at a field where a dead cow was frozen in the snow.

I asked Biddy how she appeared to him.

"Bad off," he answered. "I don't take her for foolin."

In a few minutes, I skirted the rubble heap to find her.

"You should come with us," I told her. She had nowhere else to go. "Even the cows you herded are gone. And my superiors may have questions for you. Best to deal with them now." I suspected OSS would want to glean what they could from her about Martin.

She nodded. "I am another mouth to them," she said looking back to the Hurle family.

We headed for Bastogne. Biddy drove and Gita and I sat in the back of the jeep, smoking cigarettes and chatting while she stroked Hercules, who took to her quickly. We all agreed his prior master must have been a woman.

For the most part, we talked about what we had been through in the last few weeks. I described our airborne arrival in Savy, including the condition of my trousers. Every story with a happy ending is a comedy, one of my professors had said in college, and our tale of parachuting without training into a pitched battle had all three of us rolling by the time we'd finished.

"But why so desperate to reach Bastogne?" she asked. I had given away more than I wanted to, but had no way out except the truth. "'Arrest Martin'!" she responded then. "These are foolish orders, Dubin. Martin played a trick. That is not a terrible crime. He has done nothing to harm the American Army."

I told her Teedle thought otherwise.

"*Merde. Teedle est fou. Martin est un patriote.*" Teedle is nuts. Martin is a patriot.

"It does not matter now," I said somberly.

With that her eyes were glued closed a moment. I offered her another cigarette. I'd acquired a Zippo along the way and lit hers before mine. She pointed to me smoking.

"This is how I know for sure you are a soldier now."

I showed her the callus I'd worn on the side of my thumb in the last month with the flint wheel of the lighter.

"You see, in the end, Martin was good for you, Dubin. You should be grateful to him. No? To fight is what you craved."

I was startled I had been so transparent. But that illusion was all in the past. I had not yet found a way to write to Grace or my parents about Christmas Day, but I told Gita the story now, quietly. Biddy stopped and got out of the jeep. He said he needed directions to Bastogne, but I suspected he wanted no part of the memories. I told her about lying in the snow in that clearing waiting to die, while the men nearby preceded me, and about feeling so shamed by my desperation to live.

"I thought all my last thoughts," I told her. "Including, I must say, about you."

Her full eyebrows shot up and I hurried to clarify.

"Not with longing," I said.

"Oh? What, then? Regret?" She was teasing, but remained attentive.

"I would say, with clarity," I said finally. "Our moment together had given me clarity. I longed for home and hearth. A normal life. To gather my family around a fire. To have children."

She had taken the Zippo and held its flame to the tip of a new cigarette for a long time. Through the blue scrim, she settled a drilling look on me, so intense my heart felt like it skipped.

"And I am what, Dubin? A vagabond? You think I care

nothing for those things? The fire, the warm meal, the children underfoot?"

"Do you?" I answered stupidly.

"You think I do not wish to have a place in the world, as other persons have a place? To want what you or any other person wants? To have a life and not merely to survive? You think I have no right to be as weary of this as everyone else?"

"I hardly meant that."

"No," she said. "I heard. I am not fit for a decent life."

She suddenly could not stand to look at me. She released the car door and jumped outside, where I felt I had no choice but to pursue her. Her dark eyes were liquid when I caught up, but her look was savage. She swore at me in French, and then, as an astonishing exclamation point, hurled the pack of cigarettes at me.

I was flabbergasted. Men always are when they sacrifice a woman's feelings, I suppose. But I had known better. I had glimpsed the fundamental truth of Gita in the instant she had raised her skirt in that barn. She would always be the spurned offspring of the town pariah. Everything about her character was built over an abyss of hurt.

I followed her farther out into the snow. She was already attracting attention from some of the soldiers on their guard post nearby. Her face was crushed on her glove and I touched her shoulder.

"I mourn Martin," she said. "Do not think your chatter about yourself has upset me."

"I had no such thought." I knew better than to tell her she wept for herself. "But I am sorry. I should not have said that. About what I thought. That I felt no longing. I am sorry."

"'No longing?'" She pivoted. If possible, she was even more furious. "You think I care about *that*? You think *that* damaged my pride?" She smashed the last of her cigarette underfoot and stepped toward me, lowering her voice. "It is your poor opinion of me I revile, not your desires. You know nothing, Dubin. You are a fool. No longing," she huffed. "I do not even believe it, Dubin." Then she lifted her face to me, so that there was only a hairbreadth between us. "Nor do you," she whispered.

She was an iceberg, of course, on the remainder of the ride, tomb-silent except to the dog, to whom she spoke in whispers he could not hear. I sat in front with Biddy, but he could tell there had been a personal eruption and said little. As we approached Bastogne, Gita announced that she wanted to be taken to the military hospital, where she would find work as a nurse. Trained assistance was never spurned in a war zone. In so many words, she was saying she needed no help from me.

Arriving in Bastogne, I was startled by its size. It was hard to believe thousands of men had died for the sake of such a small place. The town had only one main street, rue Sablon, although the avenue sported several good-size buildings, whose fancy stone façades were now frequently broken or scarred by shrapnel and gunfire. Iron grates framed tiny balconies under windows which, for the most part, had been left as empty black holes. Here and there one of the steep peaked roofs characteristic of the region lay in complete collapse as a result of an artillery strike, but in general the poor weather had kept Bastogne from more severe destruction by air. The cathe-

dral had been bombed as part of the Germans' Christmas
Eve present, a crude gesture meant to deprive Bastogne's
citizens of even the meager comfort of a holiday prayer,
but the debris from the buildings that had been hit had already been shoveled into piles in the streets, and was
being removed by locals in horse-drawn carts. Last night
there had been yet another heavy snowfall, and soldiers
on foot slogged along while the jeeps and convoys thick
on rue Sablon slid slowly down the steep avenue.

I had no way to temporize with Gita. Instead we simply asked directions to the American field hospital, which
occupied one of the largest structures of the town, a four-
story convent, L'Établissement des Soeurs de Notre
Dame de Bastogne. Despite the fact that the roof was
gone, the first two floors remained habitable, and the Sisters had given up their large redbrick school and the rear
building of their compound to the care of the sick and
wounded. The snow from the street had been pushed onto
the walks and sat in frozen drifts, some the height of a man.
Between them, several ambulances were parked, the same
Ford trucks that served as paddy wagons at home, here
emblazoned with huge red crosses. Gita snatched up the
small parcel she had gathered from the remains of the
Hurles' home and marched inside. I followed in case she
needed someone to vouch for her.

At the front desk sat a nun whose face, amid a huge
starched angel-wing habit, looked like a ripe peach in a
white bowl. She made an oddly serene figure in the entryway, which had been strafed. There were bullet holes in the
walls and in the somewhat grand wooden rococo
balustrades leading to the upper stories, while some kind
of ordnance had blown a small crater in the inlaid floor,

leaving a hole all the way to the cellar. After only a few moments of conversation, Gita and the nun appeared to be reaching an agreement.

Watching from a distance, I was surprised to hear my name from behind.

"David?" A doctor in a green surgical gown and cap had both arms raised toward me, a short dark man who looked a little like Algar. Once he removed the headgear I recognized Cal Echols, who had been my sister's boyfriend during his first two years in med school. Everyone in my family had loved Cal, who was smart and sociable, but he'd lost his mother as a four-year-old, and Dorothy said his clinging ultimately drove her insane. We'd never seen that side of him, of course. Now Cal and I fell on each other like brothers.

"Jeepers creepers," he said, when he pushed me back to look me over, "talk about the tempest tossed. I thought you lawyers knew how to worm your way out of things."

"Bad timing," I said.

He figured I had come to the hospital to visit a soldier, and I was immediately embarrassed that my preoccupation with Gita had kept me from realizing that several of the wounded men from my company were probably here. Cal had finished his surgical shift and offered to help me find them. When I turned to the front desk to attempt some awkward goodbye with Gita, she was gone.

Once Biddy had found a place for the jeep, he and I went over the hospital roster with Cal. Four of our men were still on hand. A corporal named Jim Harzer had been wounded by a mortar round during a hill fight near Noville. He was another of the replacement troops, the father of two little girls, and when I'd last seen him he was on the ground, with the corpsmen attending him. They had a tourniquet above his knee; down where his boot had been it was primarily a bloody pulp. In spite of that, Harzer had beamed. 'I'm done, Cap,' he said. 'I'm going home. I'm gonna be kissing my girls.' I found him in a similarly buoyant mood today. He'd lost his right foot, but he said he'd met several fellas missing their lefts and they planned to stay in touch so they could save money on shoes.

In the convent, all the class space had been converted to hospital wards. The long wooden desks at which students once sat facing the blackboards were being used as beds, with more cots placed in between. The valuable classroom equipment, bird exhibits for science, chem lab beakers, and microscopes, had been preserved in the closets.

Almost every patient had had surgery of some kind, the best-off only to remove shrapnel from nonmortal wounds. But on the wards were also the limbless, the faceless, the gut-shot, who too often were only days from death. The cellar that ran the length of the building now served as a morgue.

At the far end of the second floor, an MP stood outside a full ward of German POWs here as patients.

"We give them better than our boys get, that's for sure," said Cal. Indeed, several of the Germans waved when they recognized Cal in the doorway. "Nice kid, from Munich," said Cal about one of them. "Speaks good English, but both parents are Nazi Party members."

"Does he know you're Jewish?"

"That was the first thing I told him. Of course, all of his best friends at home were Jewish. All. He gave me a whole list." He smiled a little.

Cal had been here since the day after Christmas, and I began asking about the other men from my company who'd left the front in ambulances. He remembered a number. Too many had died, but there was some good news. Cal himself had operated on Mike O'Brien — the joker who'd enjoyed giving it to Stocker Collison — whom I'd dragged from the clearing on Christmas Day. He had lived. So had Massimo Fortunato, from whose thigh Cal had removed a shrapnel piece the size of a softball. He had been transferred to a general hospital in Luxembourg City, but Massimo had done so well that Cal thought he would be sent back to my former unit in a month or two.

Cal offered us billets in the convent, which we eagerly accepted, since it saved me from a problematic reconnaissance in the overcrowded town. The enlisted men, medical corpsmen for the most part, were housed in a large schoolroom converted to a dormitory. Their quarters were close, but the men weren't complaining, Cal said. The building had electricity from a field generator and central heat, coal-fired, although there was not yet running water in the tiled baths and shower rooms. Better still, the enlisted men were right next to the mess hall and on the same floor as the nuns and nurses, a few of whom were rumored to have dispensed healing treatments of a nonmedical variety. True or not, the mere idea had revived the men.

The docs were boarded on the second floor in the nuns' former rooms, which the Sisters had insisted on surrendering. These were barren cubicles, six feet by ten, each containing a feather mattress, a small table, and a crucifix on the wall, but it would be the first privacy I'd had for a month. Cal's room was two doors down. He had received a package from home only a day ago and he offered me a chocolate, laughing out loud at my expression after the first bite.

"Careful," he said. "You look close to cardiac arrest."

Afterward, in officers' mess where we had dinner, I again recounted Christmas Day. Despite all the fighting I'd seen following that, my stories never seemed to get any farther.

"This war," said Cal. "I mean, being a doc — it's a paradox, I'll tell you, David. You try like hell to save them, and doing a really great job just means they get another chance to die. We had a young medic who came in here yesterday. It was the third time in a month. Minor wounds the first couple of times, but yesterday just about his whole right side was blown away. What a kid. Even in delirium, he would reply to all of·my questions with a 'Yes, sir' or 'No, sir.' I stayed up all day with him, just trying to coax him to live, and he died not ten minutes after I finally went off." Cal peered at nothing, reabsorbing the loss. "A lot of these boys end up hating us when they realize they're going back. You know the saying. The only thing a doctor can give you is a pill and a pat on the back and an Army doc skips the pat on the back."

It was nearly 8:00 p.m. now, and Cal's surgical shift was about to begin. He would operate until 4:00 a.m. The surgical theater was never empty. Before he went back to work, he brought a bottle of Pernod to my room. After two drinks, I passed out with my boots still on.

I woke in the middle of the night when my door cracked open. At first, I thought it was the wind, but then a silhouette appeared, backlit by the brightness from the hall.

"*Ton chien te cherche*," Gita said. She slid through the door and closed it and flicked on the light. She had hold of Hercules by the woven belt that one of the men in my company had given him as a collar. Her hair had been pinned up under a white nurse's bonnet and she was dressed in a baggy gray uniform. The dog, which Biddy had left outside in the convent's one-car garage, had been found trotting through the wards. Harzer and a couple of others recognized him and swore that Hercules had come to pay his respects before moving on in his apparent search for Biddy or me. When she let him go, the dog bounded to my side. I scratched his ears, before I faced her.

Cal's stories about nurses scurrying through the halls at night had briefly sparked the thought that Gita might arrive here. It seemed unlikely given her mood when we parted, but before falling off I'd had a vision so clear I had actually deliberated for an instant about whether I would tell her to stay or to go. Yet in the moment there was no choice. As always, she presented herself as a challenge. But I doubted her boldness was only to prove her point about my longing. Her need was as plain as my craving for her, which just like my paralyzing fears in the air over Savy was not subject to the control of preparation or reason. I beckoned with my hand, the lights went off, and she was beside me.

As I embraced her, I apologized for my grime and the odor, but we met with all the gentleness our first time together had lacked, softened by what each of us had endured in the interval. Even as I savored the remarkable smoothness of her stomach and back, the thrill of touching a human so graceful and compact, something within me continued to wonder if this romance was a fraud, merely the overheated grappling of the battlefront. Perhaps it was just as Teedle had told me. When a human is reduced to the brute minimum, desire turns out to be at the core. But that did not matter now as we lay together in the tiny convent room. In the tumult of emotion Gita consistently provoked in me, there was a new element tonight. I had been fascinated from the start by her intelligence and her daring; and my physical yearning for her was greater than I'd felt for any woman. But tonight, my heart swelled also with abounding gratitude. I pressed her so close that I seemed to hope to squeeze her inside my skin. I kissed her again and again, wishing my appreciation could pour out of me, as I, David Dubin, recovered, if only for a fragment of time, the fundamental joy of being David Dubin.

24. ALIVE

We remained in Bastogne two more days. I had signaled Teedle that Gita was here if OSS wished to interview her, and awaited his order to formally abandon the effort to arrest Martin. Pending a response, I worked on a long report about the past month for Colonel Maples, who had moved to the new Third Army Headquarters in Luxembourg City. I also spent a couple of hours both days with the men from my former command who were hospitalized here. But every minute was only a long aching interval, waiting for dark and the end of Gita's shift, when she would slip into my room.

"You are an unusual woman," I had told her again that first night after she had come to me, as we lay whispering in the narrow bed.

"You notice only now?" She was laughing. "But I do not think you mean to praise me, Dubin. What do you find so uncommon?"

"That you mourn Martin and are with me."

She thought a moment. "No soldier in Europe more

eagerly sought death, Dubin. I knew that, no matter how often I tried to say otherwise. Besides, if my father died or my brother, would it be unusual, as you say, to find comfort in life?"

"Martin was not your father or your brother."

"No," she said and fell silent again. "He was both. And my salvation. He rescued me, Dubin. When I met him I was on the boil, furious at all moments except those when I simply wanted to die. He said, 'If you are angry, fight. And if you wish to die, then wait until tomorrow. Today you may do some good for someone else.' He knew the right things to say. Because he had said them to himself."

"But you do not mourn him as your lover?"

"*Qu'est-ce qui te prend?*" She raised her head from my chest. "Why does that matter so much to you — me with Martin? Do you fear that I liked Martin better this way than I like you?"

"You think that is the issue?"

"It is the issue with every man at times. And it is stupid. With each person it is different, Dubin. Not better or worse. It is like a voice, yes? No voice is the same. But there is always conversation. Does one prefer a person for the voice, or the words? It is what is being said that matters far more. No?"

I agreed, but pondered in the dark.

"Doo-bean," she finally said, more emphatically than usual, "I have told you. With Martin and me that aspect was long over. It became impossible."

"Because?"

"Because this is no longer an activity for him."

I finally understood. "Was he wounded?"

"In the mind. He has not been good that way for some

time. He punishes himself perhaps, because he likes the killing too much. He has clung to me, but only because he believes there will not be another woman after me. *Comprends-tu?*"

Surprisingly, something remained unsettled. I looked into the dark seeking the words, as if attempting to lay hold of a nerve running through my chest.

"When I think of Martin," I said then, "I wonder what interest I could have to you. I am so dull. My life is small and yours with him has been so large."

"*Tu ne me comprends pas bien.*" You do not understand me well.

"'Well'? You are the most mysterious person I have ever met."

"I am a simple girl, with little education. You are learned, Dubin. Occasionally humorous. Brave enough. You are a solid type, Dubin. Would you drink and beat your wife?"

"Not at the same time."

"*Tu m'as fait craquer.*" I cracked, meaning, I couldn't resist. "Besides, you are a rich American."

"My father is a cobbler."

"*Evidemment! Les cordonniers sont toujours les plus mal chaussés.*" The shoemaker's son always goes barefoot. "I have miscalculated." Once we had laughed for some time, she added, "You have a conscience, Dubin. It is an attractive quality in a fellow in a time of war."

"A conscience? Lying here with you when I have promised myself to someone else?"

"Eh," she answered again. "If you and she were destined for each other, you would have married before you departed. What woman loves a man and allows him to leave for war without having him to her bed?"

"It was not solely her choice."

"More the point, then. You are not so scrupulous here, when there are no expectations." She laid her fingertip directly on the end of my penis to make her point. "You chose to be free, Dubin. No? *Qui se marie à la hâte se repent à loisir*." Marry in haste, repent at leisure.

Gita's observation, made in her customary declarative fashion, seemed too stark to be true, but there was no avoiding it. I yearned for the aura that surrounded Grace like a cloud—her gentility, her blonde hair and soft sweaters, the way she glided through life, her pristine American beauty. But not enough to separate myself from my parents in the irrevocable way our marriage had called for. My sudden decision to enlist, rather than wait out my fortunes with the draft, seemed highly suspect from the distance of a convent bed in Belgium. But so did the balm these conclusions gave to my conscience.

"At any rate, Dubin, you are here with me now. Even though you felt no longing." She stroked now where she had left her finger, and I responded quickly. "Aha," she said. "Again, Dubin, you are betrayed."

"No, no, that is merely to save your feelings."

"Then, perhaps I shall stop," she said.

"No, no, I am much too concerned for you to allow that."

Afterward, we slept, but in time I was awakened by growling. I had heard it in my dreams for a while, but it grew insistent and I stirred, ready to scold Hercules. Instead, I found Gita snoring. Her constant smoking had apparently done its work on her sinuses. From an elbow, I studied her in the light borrowed from the hall. Lying there, she seemed, as we all do in slumber, childlike, her small sharp face mobile in sleep. She suckled briefly; an arm stirred protectively, and her eyes jumped beneath her lids. I was impressed by how small she appeared when the current, as it were, was turned off on her imposing personality. I watched several minutes. As she had been trying to tell me, she was, at heart, a far simpler person than I supposed.

After Gita had snuck back downstairs the first night we'd arrived in Bastogne, I met Cal for breakfast at the officers' mess, as planned. He had been in surgery until 4:00 a.m., then had made rounds to see his patients. He was still in a bloody gown, gobbling up something before he grabbed a few hours' sleep. Apparently, it was he who had directed Gita and the dog to my room, and he let me know promptly that he'd guessed the score.

"So how did your quarters work out? Bed a little tight?"

I could feel myself flush, and then, like a switchboard operator plugging in the lines, I made a series of connections which, when complete, brought me up short. Cal would write home that he had seen me. He would say I had a woman here. Grace, in time, would hear.

"Oh, don't worry," he said, when he saw my expression. He made that zipper motion across his lips.

But somehow I was caught up in a vision of Grace reacting to this news. Would she rely on some bromide about how men will be men? Or take comfort from the extremities of war? My mind continued tumbling down the staircase, descending into various images of what might occur when word reached Grace, until I finally crashed and came to rest at the bottom. In a figurative heap, I checked myself and was shocked to find myself frightened but unhurt — no bruises, no broken bones — and thus I knew at that moment, absolutely and irrevocably, that I was not going to marry Grace Morton. I cared intensely about Grace. I still could not imagine being the brutal assassin of her feelings. But she was not a vital part of me. Gita's role in this seemed incidental. It was not a matter of choosing one woman over the other, because even now I continued to doubt that Gita's interest would last. But, in the light of day, what I'd recognized lying beside Gita remained. Grace was an idol. A dream. But not my destiny.

With some bemusement, Cal had watched all this work its way through my features.

"Who is this girl, anyway, David? I asked the nuns about her. They say she knows her bananas, bright, works hard. Bit of a looker," said Cal, "if you'll forgive me. Every man in this hospital will be pea green with envy, even the ones cold down in the morgue."

I smiled and told him a little about Gita. Runaway. Exile. Commando.

"Is it serious?" he asked.

I shook my head as if I didn't know, but within a distinct voice told me that the correct answer was yes. It was gravely serious. Not as Cal meant. Instead it was serious in the way combat was serious, because it was impossible to tell if I would survive.

Gita's nursing duties included washing bedridden patients. Imagining her at it made me nearly delirious with envy, although I admitted to her that I was uncertain if I was jealous of her touch or of the chance to bathe. When she arrived on the second night, she swung through the door with a heavy metal pail full of hot water. It had been boiled on the kitchen stove, the only means available in the absence of working plumbing.

"You are an angel."

"A wet one." The sleeves of her shapeless uniform were black.

"So you can no longer tolerate the smell of me?"

"You smell like someone who has lived, Dubin. It is the complaining about it I cannot stand. Get up, please. I will not bathe you in your bed like an invalid."

She had brought a cloth, a towel, and another bowl. I removed my clothes and stood before her, as she scrubbed and dried me bit by bit. My calf, my thigh. There was a magnificent intermezzo before she went higher to my stomach.

"Tell me about America," she said, once she continued.

"You want to know if the streets are lined with gold? Or if King Kong is hanging from the Empire State Building?"

"No, but tell me the truth. Do you love America?"

"Yes, very much. The land. The people. And most of all the idea of it. Of each man equal. And free."

"That is the idea in France, too. But is it true in America?"

"True? In America there was never royalty. Never Napoleon. Yet it is still far better to be rich than poor. But it is true, I think, that most Americans cherish the ideals. My father and mother came from a town very much like Pilzkoba. Now they live free from the fears they grew up with. They may speak their minds. They may vote. They may own property. They sent their children to public schools. And now they may hope, with good reason, that my sister and brother and I will find an even better life than theirs."

"But do Americans not hate the Jews?"

"Yes. But not as much as the colored." It was a dour joke and she was less amused than I by the bitter humor. "It is not like Hitler," I said. "Every American is from somewhere else. Each is hated for what he brings that is different from the rest. We live in uneasy peace. But it is peace, for the most part."

"And is America beautiful?"

"*Magnifique*." I told her about the West as I had glimpsed it from the train on my way to Fort Barkley.

"And your city?"

"We have built our own landscape. There are giant buildings."

"Like King Kong?"

"Almost as tall."

"Yes," she said. "I want to go to America. Europe is old. America is still new. The Americans are smart to fight on others' soil. Europe will require a century to recover from all of this. And there may be another war soon. *Après la guerre* I will go to America, Dubin. You must help me."

"Of course," I said. Of course.

By the next morning, it seemed as if every person in Bastogne knew what was occurring in my quarters at night. Gita had made a clanging commotion dragging her pails up the stairs. I worried that the nuns would evict both of us, but they maintained a dignified silence. It was the soldiers who could not contain themselves, greeting me in whispers as "lover boy" whenever I passed.

Third Army had established a command center in Bastogne, and Biddy and I walked over there every few hours to see if Teedle's orders had come through. For two days now, no shells had fallen on the city, and the civilians were in the streets, briskly going about their business. They were polite but busy, unwilling to repeat their prior mistake of believing this lull was actually peace.

As we hiked up the hilly streets, I said, "I find I'm the talk of the town, Gideon."

He didn't answer at first. "Well, sir," he finally said, "it's just a whole lot of things seem to be moving around in the middle of the night."

We shared a long laugh.

"She's a remarkable person, Biddy."

"Yes, sir. This thing got a future, Captain?"

I stopped dead on the pavement. My awareness of myself had been growing since my conversation with Cal at breakfast yesterday, but trusting Biddy more than anyone else, things were a good deal clearer in his company. I took hold of his arm.

"Biddy, how crazy would it sound if I said I love this woman?"

"Well, good for you, Captain."

"No," I said, instantly, because I had a clear view of the complications, "it's not good. It's not good for a thousand reasons. It probably conflicts with my duty. And it will not end well." I had maintained an absolute conviction about this. I knew my heart would be crushed.

"Cap," he said, "ain't no point going on like that. They-all can do better telling you the weather tomorrow than what's gonna happen with love. Ain't nothing else to do but hang on for the ride."

But my thoughts were very much the same when Gita came to my bed that night.

"Your phrase has haunted me all day," I told her.

"*Laquelle?*"

"'*Après la guerre.*' I have thought all day about what will happen after the war."

"If war is over, then there must be peace, no? At least for a while."

"No, I refer to you. And to me. I have spent the day wondering what will become of us. Does that surprise you or take you aback?"

"I know who you are, Dubin. It would surprise me if your thoughts were different. I would care for you much less."

I took a moment. "So you do care for me?"

"*Je suis là.*" I am here.

"And in the future?"

"When the war began," she said, "no one thought of the future. It would be too awful to imagine the Nazis here for long. Everyone in the underground lived solely for the present. To fight now. The only future was the next action and the hope you and your comrades would survive. But since Normandy, it is different. Among the *maquisards*, there is but one phrase on their lips: *Après la guerre*. I hear those words in my mind, too. You are not alone."

"And what do you foresee?"

"It is still war, Dubin. One creeps to the top of a wall and peeks over, I understand, but we remain here. If one looks only ahead, he may miss the perils that are near. But I have seen many good souls die. I have promised myself to live for them. And now, truly, I think I wish to live for myself as well."

"This is good."

"But you told me what you see, no? The hearth, the home. Yes?"

"Yes." That remained definitive. "*Et toi?*"

"*Je sais pas.* But if I live through this war, I will be luckier than most. I have learned what perhaps I most needed to."

"Which is?"

"To value the ordinary, Doo-bean. In war, one feels its loss acutely. The humdrum. The routine. Even I, who could never abide it, find myself longing for a settled life."

"And will that content you? Is it to be the same for you as me? The house, the home, being a respectable wife with children swarming at your knees beneath your skirt? Or will you be like Martin, who told me he would soon look for another war?"

"There will never be another war. Not for me. You said once that a woman has that choice, and that is the choice I will make. 'A respectable wife'? I cannot say. Tell me, Dubin"— she smiled cutely —"are you asking?"

Lightly as this was said, I knew enough about her to recognize the stakes. She would chuckle at a proposal, but would be furious if I was as quick to reject her. And at the same time, being who she was, she would chop me to bits for anything insincere. But having left one fiancée behind for little more than a day, I was not ready yet for new promises, even in banter.

"Well, let me say only that I intend to pay very careful attention to your answer."

"You sound like a lawyer."

We laughed.

"Martin once said you will never be content with just one man."

"Eh, he was consoling himself. Believe me, Dubin, I know what I need to know about men. And myself with them. But one person forever? For many years that sounded to me like a prison sentence."

"May I ask? Was that perhaps your mother's influence?"

"I think not. My mother, if she had any influence, would have told me to find a fellow like you, decent and stable, and to stand by him. 'One craves peace,' she said always." She sat up into the borrowed light. Gita was more physically shy than I might have expected and I enjoyed the sight of her, her small breasts rising perfectly to their dark peaks.

"But she did not succeed herself."

"She had tried, Dubin. When she was seventeen, her looks attracted the son of a merchant, a wool seller from the city. She thought he was rich and handsome and a sophisticate and married him on impulse."

"This was Lodzka?" I tried to pronounce it correctly.

"Lodzki, yes. He was a cad, of course. He drank, he had other women, he was stingy with her. They fought like minks, even battled with their fists, and naturally she took the worst of it. One day she left him. She returned to Pilzkoba and announced that her husband was dead of influenza. Soon she had suitors. She had been married again for a month, when it was discovered that Lodzki was still alive. It was a terrible scandal. She was lucky they did not hang her. She always said she would have left, but it would have given everyone in Pilzkoba too much satisfaction." Gita stopped with a wistful smile. "So," she said.

"So," I answered, and drew her close again. One craves peace.

★★★

The next day, late in the afternoon while I was on the wards visiting, a private from the signal office found me with a telegram. Teedle had finally replied.

> Seventh Armored Division captured Oflag XII-D
> outside Saint-Vith yesterday a.m. STOP Confirms
> Major Martin alive in prison hospital STOP
> Proceed at once STOP Arrest

I had been with Corporal Harzer, the soldier who had lost his foot, when the messenger put the yellow envelope in my hand.

"Captain, you don't look good," he said.

"No, Harzer. I've seen the proverbial ghost."

I located Bidwell. We'd head out first thing tomorrow. Then I walked around Bastogne, up and down the snowy streets and passageways. I knew I would tell Gita. How could I not? But I wanted to contend with myself beforehand. I had no doubt about her loyalties. She would desert me. If she did, she did, I told myself again and again, but I was already reeling at the prospect. I concentrated for some time on how to put this to her, but in the event, I found I had worked myself into one of those anxious states in which my only goal was to get it over with. I waited for her to emerge from the ward on which she was working and simply showed her the telegram.

I watched her study it. She had left the ward smoking, and as the hand that held the cigarette threshed again and again through her curls, I wondered briefly if she would set fire to the nurse's bonnet on her head. Her lips moved as she struggled with the English. But she understood enough. Those coffee-dark eyes of hers, when they found me, held a hint of alarm.

"*Il est vivant?*"

I nodded.

"These are your orders?"

I nodded again.

"We talk tonight," she whispered.

And I nodded once more.

It was well past midnight before I realized she was not coming, and then I lay there with the light on overhead, trying to cope. My hurt was immeasurable. With Martin alive, she could not bring herself to be with me. That was transparent. Their bond, whatever the truth of their relationship, was more powerful than ours.

In the morning, as Bidwell packed the jeep, I sought her out to say goodbye. I had no idea whether I could contain my bitterness, or if I would break down and beg her to take me instead.

"Gita?" asked Soeur Marie, the nun in charge, when I inquired of her whereabouts. "*Elle est partie.*"

How long had she been gone, I asked. Since dark yesterday, the Sister told me.

It took nine hours to reach Saint-Vith and I realized well in advance what we would find. The MP at Oflag XII-D said that a Red Cross nurse, accompanied by two French attendants, had come hours ago to transport Major Martin to a local hospital. We followed his directions there, where, as I had anticipated, no one knew a thing about the nurse, the attendants, or Robert Martin.

VI.

25. WRONG DISH

When I was a senior in high school, I was desperately in love with Nona Katz, the woman I finally married six years later. The mere thought of parting from her for college left me desolate. I had been admitted to the Honors Program at the U., here in Kindle County. Nona, on the other hand, was never much of a student. She had been lucky to get into State, originally called State Agricultural College, which was not an institution in the same circle of heaven as the more famous university to the north. Not to be overlooked either was the fact that my admission to the U. Honors Program included a tuition waiver and a $1,500 stipend for room and board. My parents used endless ploys to get me to go there. From Kindle County, it was no more than a five-hour drive to State, they said, even in winter weather. They promised to help me buy a used car and pay my phone bills.

"You don't understand," I told them. "You don't understand what this feels like."

"Of course not," said my mother. "How could *we* understand? Ours must have been an arranged marriage."

"Ma, don't be sarcastic."

"It is you, Stewart, who does not understand. I met your father at perhaps the darkest time humanity has ever known. We fully comprehend the wonder of these feelings. That is not, however, all there is to consider."

"Ma, what else matters? What's more important than love?"

My father cleared his throat and took a rare part in our debates.

"Love in the form you are talking about, Stewart, does not remain unchanged forever. You cannot lead your life as if you will never have other concerns."

I was thunderstruck by this remark. First, because my mother looked on approvingly. And second, by the sheer notion that Dad was asserting so coolly. Nona—the discovery that there was some complementary principle in the world—had lifted the stinking fog from my morbid adolescence. My father's blasé assertion that love would somehow evaporate was like telling me I was going to be thrown back into a dungeon.

"You're wrong," I said to him.

"Well, consider that I may be right. Please, Stewart. Love in time takes a form more solid but less consuming. And thank the Lord! No one would ever leave the bedroom. There is work to do, families to raise. It changes, Stewart, and you have to be prepared for what happens next in life."

I did not hear much after that. It was the "thank the Lord" that always stuck with me, evidencing my father's frank relief that he had been able to escape from something as messy and demanding as passion.

And yet it was that selfsame guy I had to contemplate in the arms of Gita Lodz, so nuts with lust that he was rutting in a barn with the farm animals, and then, even more sensationally, getting it on in the bed of a nun. Yet I didn't feel as much discomfort with these scenes as I might have expected. For one thing, when you're big enough to think, on bad days, of replacing your bathroom scale with the ones they use at highway weigh stations, you accept one of life's most cheerful truths. Everybody fucks. Or at least they want to. Notwithstanding American advertisers, it's a universal franchise. The bald truth was that after several months of separation, Gita Lodz struck me as a pretty hot dish. Like my father, I've always been attracted to small women—Nona is barely five feet.

More to the point, I knew the end of the story. Mademoiselle Lodz was just a pit stop on Dad's voyage from Grace Morton to my mother. Irony being the theme song of life, middle-aged Stewart sat in the passenger lounge of the Tri-Counties Airport reading the end of Dad's account and warning young David to think twice. It was only going to turn out badly, I told him. Anticipating a train wreck, I was not surprised to see one at the end.

When I made my second visit to Bear Leach in November 2003, five weeks after our first meeting at Northumberland Manor, I wanted to know the aftermath of all the characters in my father's story. This led into the region where Bear had told me he might not be free to go, and at moments he chose his words carefully. As it turned out, there was plenty he could say about the fate of Robert Martin, and even a little about General Teedle. But asking what had happened to Gita Lodz stopped him cold. I'd brought Dad's manuscript along to illustrate my questions and Bear actually thumbed through the pages in his lap briefly, as if trying to refresh his memory when I mentioned her name.

"Well," he said finally, "perhaps it's most helpful if I give you the sequence, Stewart. I initially made an effort to locate Miss Lodz, believing she could be an important witness to mitigate your father's punishment. That was to be the principal issue at trial, of course, in light of David's intended guilty plea. Your father's service near Bastogne remained my ace in the hole; it was amply documented in his service record, especially in the papers recommending him for the Silver Star, which was approved, by the way, in the War Department, but never awarded as a result of the court-martial. However, I also wanted to show, if I could, that David had fought beside Martin. It would not excuse letting Martin go, but any soldier worth his salt who sat on the court-martial panel would understand an act of mercy toward a comrade-in-arms.

"Accordingly, I hoped to offer a first-person account of the incident in which your father had helped destroy the ammunition dump at the Royal Saltworks, which I learned of when I interviewed Agnès de Lemolland. I pressed the Army for the whereabouts of all the persons who had worked on that operation.

"When I informed your father about that, he became extremely agitated. 'Not the girl,' he said. Since he still refused to tell me anything about what had actually transpired, this frustrated me to no end and I said so.

"'It's beyond discussion,' he said. 'It would be a complete disaster.'

"'For your case?' I asked.

"'Certainly for my case. And personally as well.'

"'And what is the personal stake?' I asked.

"He yielded slightly in his usual adamantine silence and said simply, 'My fiancée.'"

I interrupted Bear. "Grace Morton?"

"Surely not. That was long over by then."

"My mother?"

Leach took his time before finding his way to a dry smile.

"Well, Stewart, I wasn't present when you were born, but you say your mother was an inmate at the Balingen camp and that was certainly the residence of the woman whom your father by then intended to marry."

He studied me with his perpetual generous look to see how I assembled this information.

"So he said, my dad said, it would be a disaster if Mom met Gita Lodz? Or found out about her?"

In a typically aged gesture, Bear's mouth moved around loosely for quite some time as if he was attempting to get the taste of the right words.

"David said no more than what I have stated. I drew my own conclusions at the time. Naturally, I had a far fuller picture when I eventually read what your father had written, which you now have done, too. The personal aspects, I ultimately decided, were best left without further inquiry. But, as a lawyer, I was relieved that your father had prevailed on this point. As I have said, his judgment as a trial attorney was first-rate. Calling Miss Lodz to testify and subjecting her to cross-examination would have been very damaging for his cause."

Having read the whole story by then, I understood. Had Mademoiselle Lodz told her story, Dad's decision to let Martin go could not have been made to look like an act of charity toward a buddy from combat, not even by a trial lawyer as skilled as Leach. In fact, as Bear had said last month, it could have raised the specter of murder in the mind of an imaginative prosecutor.

But that, I figured, was the least of it. Dad might have wanted to shield my mother from the details of his recent love affair. But I was sure the person he most wanted to protect was himself. Having gone on with his life, the last thing Dad needed was to see Gita Lodz. It would have made for a moment of unequaled bitterness, sitting there, knowing he was on the express for Leavenworth, while he looked across the courtroom at the woman who'd used every trick to abet Martin's countless escapes, including, as it turned out, dancing on my father's heart.

I was aware that Bear was watching me closely, but I was in the full grip of the illusion that I finally had some insight into my father, and had suddenly harked back to Dad's advice when I was eighteen. In telling me to base my college choice on something besides the bulge that arose in my trousers at the first thought of Nona, Dad, I saw, was speaking from experience, rather than his native caution. He wanted to keep me from taking my own helping of a dish that had been served cold to him decades ago by Gita Lodz.

26. CAPTURED

Outside the former French Army garrison building which had been used as a civilian hospital in Saint-Vith, Biddy and I awaited the organization of a posse of MPs, while I smoked in the cold. The fighting had taken an enormous toll on this town, too. Almost nothing remained standing. The hospital had survived only because of the huge red crosses painted on its roof.

The Provost Marshal Lieutenant who had surrendered Martin to the nice-looking little nurse was abject when he learned that the Major was a wanted man, but he insisted they could not have gotten far. The explosion in December that had leveled the lodge had also blown off Martin's left hand and a piece of his thigh, as well as layers of hair and flesh on the side of his head. A month later, he still had open burn wounds and had departed from the hospital in a wheelchair.

"If we don't find them," I told Biddy, "Teedle will court-martial *me*. Mark my words. Showing my orders to the known consort of a spy — what was I thinking?"

Biddy cocked a brow at the word 'consort.'

"Cap," he said finally, "let's just get 'em."

My grief over my professional failures seemed trivial, however, compared to the personal devastation. I had assumed Gita would disappoint me, but I'd never imagined she would play me entirely false. One question seemed to peck at my mind like an angry crow. Was she really the new Bernhardt? Had everything she'd exhibited toward me been part of a role? Even while my heart struggled for some other solution, I could not reason my way to any answer but yes. Martin and she were the worst kind of people, I concluded, manipulators willing to prey on the softest emotions. If I saw either, I might reach for my pistol.

According to the U.S. personnel who'd taken over at Oflag XII-D, Martin had been driven off in a horse-drawn cart with a long-haired Gypsy holding the reins. A team of six MPs was gathered to search the town. Biddy and I went to the rail yard, but there were no trains moving yet, not even military ones, and it seemed impossible that Martin could have escaped via his favorite route. I took a point from that. Here in Belgium, Martin had feeble alliances. His chances were better in France — or Germany, where he could rely on what remained of his old network. Heading that way would also allow Martin to continue doing his work for the Soviets. Whichever direction he went, he would need medical attention — or at least medical supplies. And the only reliable source for them was the U.S. Army. Overall, he figured to follow Patton's forces, some of whom would remain friendly to him, especially since, at OSS's insistence, the fact that Martin was wanted was not widely known.

I cabled Camello, stating that Martin had escaped and that we wanted authority to pursue and arrest him. We received a one-word response from Teedle: "Proceed." I was still not sure which of the two I was actually searching for.

Although it was a little like playing pin-the-tail-on-the-donkey, Biddy and I chose to follow the 87th Infantry as it moved out of Saint-Vith toward Prüm. We had encountered battalion commanders of the 347th Infantry Regiment in town and they had agreed to let us accompany them.

Virtually all the territory lost in the Ardennes offensive had been regained and some of Patton's elements were now mounting assaults against the massive concrete fortifications of the Siegfried line at the German border. The battle was progressing inch by inch, an advantage to Biddy and me, since it would make it hard for Martin to get far. Bidwell and I drove along just behind the fighting, going from one medical collecting company to another. By the third day, we had twice received reports of a little Red Cross nurse who'd presented herself at battalion aid stations. She'd helped minister to the wounded briefly and then disappeared with an armload of supplies.

On the front, the battle lines were constantly shifting, with each side making swift incursions and then drawing back. Several times Biddy and I found ourselves driving into firefights. However slowly, though, the Americans were gaining position and our troops were in a far different mood here than they'd been in during the Bulge. They were not simply more confident, but also hardened by being on enemy soil. Late on our third day, Biddy and I encountered an infantry platoon that had just taken a high point dominated by the house of a prosperous burgher.

A sergeant came out to greet us. "You figure this here is Germany?" he asked. I didn't know from hour to hour if we were in Belgium, Germany, or Luxembourg, but we compared maps and I agreed with his estimate. He then issued a hand signal to his troops and they rushed into the house, emerging with everything of value they could find. China. Candlesticks. Paintings. Linens. Two soldiers struggled through the door with an old tapestry. I had no clue how they even imagined they could get it back to the U.S. The homeowners had made themselves scarce but an old maid had remained and she followed the troops out, shrieking about every item, trying once or twice to grab them from the men's arms. When she would not desist, a thin private pushed her to the ground, where she lay weeping. A corporal delivered a set of silver wine goblets to the sergeant, who offered a couple to Biddy and me.

"I don't drink wine," Biddy said, which was untrue.

"Learn," the sergeant told him, and insisted on heaving them into our jeep.

We stayed the night in the house, where every man in the platoon seemed determined to consume the entire store of liquor they had discovered in the cellar. One literally drank himself into a coma. When a buddy tried to revive him by throwing schnapps in his face, the liquid splattered into the wood-burning stove in the center of the room and the flame leaped up into the bottle, which exploded. Several men were pierced by flying glass, and the couch and the carpet caught fire. The troops were so drunk they howled in merriment while they stomped out the flames, but the lieutenant in charge was irate, inasmuch as four soldiers had to be removed to the aid station.

In the morning, Biddy and I headed south. We were in American-held territory, no more than half a mile from the house, when half a dozen Germans, dressed in black leather coats and armed with Schmeisser machine pistols, leaped up from the ditches on either side of the road and surrounded the jeep. I could see they were SS, rather than Wehrmacht, because of the silver death's-heads over the bills of their caps and the Nazi runes on their coats.

My instinct was to shout out a stupidly casual remark like "Our mistake," and head the other way, but as the six came forward to disarm us, the full gravity of the situation settled on me. I had been off the battlefield ten days now, but I found it had never left me, as I suppose it never will. Within, my spirit shrunk to something as small and hard as a walnut and piped out its familiar resigned message: So if you die, you die.

They ordered us out of the jeep and drove it into a wayside of heavy bushes, marching Biddy and me behind it. As we walked through the snow, Hercules sat in the back of the vehicle, Cleopatra on her barge, surveying the scene with a struggling curiosity like the RCA hound staring into the trumpet of the Victrola. "Look at that dog," Biddy muttered, and we managed a laugh.

Once the jeep was out of sight, the Germans searched us, taking anything useful we had. Compass. Trench knives. Grenades. Watches. And, of course, Bidwell's camera. One of the soldiers looked at the lens and recognized it as German.

"*Woher hast du die?*" he asked Biddy.

Biddy acted as if he did not understand and the SS man raised his Schmeisser and asked the question again. Fortunately, he was distracted when the others found our store of K rations. They each tore through several boxes, tossing aside the cardboard covers with their wavy designs as they ate with feral abandon.

"Cut off from their unit?" I asked Biddy.

He nodded. They clearly hadn't seen food for days.

"Run for it?" he asked. I was still debating, when the German lieutenant came back our way and began to question me in terrible English. "Vhere Americans? Vhere Deutsch?" They obviously wanted to get back to their side.

I answered with my name, rank, and serial number. The Germans were far too desperate to be bothered with the Geneva Convention. The lieutenant motioned to two of his men, who took me by the shoulders while the lieutenant kicked me three times in the stomach. I was brought back instantly to the schoolyard, the last time I'd survived this panicked breathless moment when the diaphragm stops functioning after a blow to the gut. To make matters worse, when the air finally heaved back into my lungs, I vomited my breakfast on the lieutenant's boot. In reprisal, he struck me in the face with his gloved fist.

My vomiting seemed to catch Hercules' attention. Up until now, the deaf dog had been more interested in the discarded ration tins, but when I was hit this time, he bounded forward and started an enormous racket. He did not attack the German lieutenant, but came within a few feet, rocking back on his paws with his hot breath rising up in puffs, almost like punctuation, as he barked. The Germans immediately began glancing down the road while they futilely attempted to quiet the animal, raising their fingers to their lips, shouting at him, and finally reaching out to subdue him. When the men came after him, Hercules snapped at one and caught his hand, biting right through the leather glove as the German yelped somewhat pathetically.

There was then a single gunshot. The same SS man who'd been questioning Biddy had his pistol out. A little whiff of smoke curled up over the barrel and the dog lay in the snowy road motionless, with a bloody oval like a peach pit where his eye had been. Several of his comrades began shouting at the soldier who'd fired, afraid of the attention the shot would attract. In the confusion, Bidwell joined in.

"What the hell you'd go and do that for?" he demanded. The German soldier with the drawn Schmeisser appeared to have no idea how to respond to the berating he was receiving from all sides. When Biddy strode forward, intent on looking after the dog, the German recoiled slightly and his pistol ignited again in a short automatic burst. Gideon toppled, rolling to his back with three clean bullet holes in his stomach. It had happened so simply, with no preparation at all, and was so pointless, that my first reaction was that it could not be true. How could the world, which has always been here, undergo such a fundamental transformation in two or three seconds?

"Oh my God!" I yelled. I screamed again, one long lament, and for an instant broke away from the two men who were holding me, but they, along with the lieutenant, dragged me down into the ditch. I twisted, cursing them until the lieutenant put the pistol barrel straight to my forehead.

"*Schrei nicht. Schweigen Sie. Wir helfen deinem Freund.* We helf." I quieted to see if they'd aid Biddy as promised, and one of them scrambled up to the road. He was back in a second.

"*Er ist tot*," he said.

The lieutenant could see I understood and immediately placed the icy pistol muzzle to my forehead again. The idea of some vain act of resistance passed through my mind like a weak current. But I'd already learned on the battlefield the desperate, humiliating secret of how badly I wanted to live, and I said nothing, allowing the Germans to drag me along in despair.

With any kind of luck, we'd have encountered American troops, but it was, simply put, not a lucky day. The Germans nearby were mounting an offensive action and my captors moved toward the sounds of the battle. Near nightfall, they hooked up with a German antitank unit, which turned out to have taken a number of Allied prisoners. The unit was being redeployed and we marched at the end of their column, with our hands behind our heads. As the only officer, I was separated from the dozen or so enlisted men by the buffer of a single guard.

We were clearly inside Germany, because at one point we passed through a tiny village where several locals came out to observe us. An old woman rushed from her little house and spat on the first American in line. She was followed by another, younger woman who began to scream, while several more people stepped from their houses. Perhaps to pacify them, one of the German officers ordered us to surrender our coats to the residents. I couldn't see exactly what had happened in this town. Probably nothing different than in any other town. There were still bodies of American and German soldiers pushed to both sides of the road.

We slept that night in an open field. Another prisoner thought we were somewhere near Prüm. We were each issued a worn army blanket but no food. One man, a Brit, had been a prisoner for two days now. He said this was the second time he'd been captured. The first was during Market Garden, the invasion of the Low Countries, and he'd been shipped back to a German stalag in Belgium, not all that far from here, from which he and everyone else had escaped when it was bombed. As the only veteran of captivity, he did his best to remain sunny. If I'd been in a mood to like any human being, I probably would have liked him.

"POW ain't the end of the world, mate, not by my lights. Cuisine ain't the Savoy, but there been days when I ain't et in my own army. It's those blokes out there gettin shot at are 'avin the rough time, if you ask me. This 'ere, it's just boring."

One of the enlisted men asked what the former prison camp had been like.

"Jerries are completely crackers. All day long, they was counting us, mate. Stand up. Sit down. *Eins, zwei, drei.* Not like they were going to give us anything. Food was bread once a day, and couple times this awful potato stew. One day the commandant comes in. 'I have goot news and bat news. Goot news. Today each man will get a change of underwear. Bat news. You must switch with the man next to you.' Only a joke," he added.

Our laughter attracted the German guards, who stomped among us, demanding silence. Nonetheless, the talk resumed shortly. Sooner or later, we were going to be handed off to the Kraut equivalent of the MPs. The Brit didn't think we were going to a stalag. Before his capture, he'd heard that they were housing prisoners in the German cities which the Allies had begun to bomb.

This time, when the two guards heard us talking, they didn't bother with more warnings. They charged around, knocking heads with their rifle butts. I barely ducked when the soldier came at me and I took the blow with little reaction. The pain resounded. But I did not care much. Sooner or later, I realized, they'd take a proper inventory of us and notice the 'H' on my dog tag. At that point, things for me were likely to get considerably worse. But I could not hold on to any concern about that. I did not feel part of this world any longer. It was as if I had sunk one foot inside myself. I often wonder if I will ever fully return.

The Germans woke us a little before daybreak. We were issued our ration for the day, a roll to be split between two men.

"Eat it now," the Brit said. "Someone will steal it, if you try to save it."

As the guards got us to our feet, the SS lieutenant who'd put the gun to my head passed by. He looked at me and then came over.

"*Wie geht's?*" he asked, manifestly more at ease now that he was back among his own. He thought I spoke more German than I did. I'd been muddling along with my grandparents' Yiddish, and I answered only with a shrug. Even at that, I felt I was a coward. He had perfect blue eyes and he looked at me a moment longer. "*Bald schiessen wir nicht mehr,*" he whispered and gave me a weary smile. He was saying that the shooting was going to be over soon, and didn't seem to hold any illusion he would be on the winning side.

We marched most of the morning. I don't know where the Germans thought they were headed, probably to bolster more of the troops we could hear fighting, but they never got there. As we passed a wood, an American armored cavalry unit appeared out of nowhere. Six Shermans rolled in literally from every direction with their big guns leveled. The German commander surrendered without a shot. Apparently, he had the same view of the war's progress as the lieutenant.

The American troops rushed forward. The Germans who'd been our captors were forced to their knees with their hands behind their heads, while we were greeted like heroes. Two of the men who'd been prisoners had minor wounds, and they were whisked off for medical attention. The rest of us were loaded on a truck and transported to the regimental headquarters, while the Germans marched at gunpoint in the rear. This was the 66th Tank Regiment of the 4th Armored Division. While most of the division had been allowed a respite in Luxembourg after Bastogne, these tankers had been brought in to flank the 87th Infantry. They were doing one hell of a job as far as I was concerned.

Their mobile headquarters, about two miles behind the lines where we'd been captured, consisted of an array of squad tents in a snowy field. Each of the freed Americans was interviewed by regimental G-2. Since I had been the lone officer in captivity, the staff G-2, Major Golsby, interviewed me personally in his tent. He was confused about my orders, which I still had in my pocket, the only thing the Germans hadn't taken.

"I have to go back to Third Army JAG," I told him. If the MPs hadn't found Martin and Gita by now, there was no point in pursuing them now that they had another two days' lead time. More important, I had lost all interest in the mission. I knew as a matter of historical fact that it was my fault Bidwell was dead. My adolescent fascination with both Martin and Gita had led, as tragic errors always must, to tragedy — to combat, capture, and now Biddy's grave.

When I told Golsby what had happened to him, I realized I sounded remote. "I bawled my eyes out yesterday," I added. It was an absolute lie. I was yet to shed a tear. Instead, all my grief about Biddy had energized another of those circling thoughts, this one about why I'd never gotten around to telling him to call me David.

"They shot a POW?" he asked me, repeating the question a few times. "Unarmed? Stay here." He returned with Lieutenant Colonel Coleman, the deputy regimental commander. He looked like a former football player, big and stocky and quick to anger, and he was angry now, as he should have been, at my account of how Biddy died.

"Who did this to your sergeant? Are the men here who did this? Did we capture them?"

Coleman ordered a second lieutenant and a sergeant to accompany me through the camp to look for the SS men. The sergeant was carrying a Thompson submachine gun. The weapon was uncommon enough that I wondered if it was mine, reacquired from the Germans who'd taken it. The captured Krauts had just arrived on foot and were seated in rows with their hands clasped behind their heads. The MPs had made them remove their boots to safeguard against any effort to run. I walked up and down the rows. I had no illusions about what was going to happen.

The SS man who'd killed Bidwell saw me coming. Our eyes had found each other's almost mechanically several times in the last two days. I would steal hateful glances at him, but when his gaze caught mine, I hurriedly looked away, knowing he was easily provoked. Now it was he who turned in the other direction. He wasn't very old, I realized, perhaps twenty-one.

"This one," I told the second lieutenant.

"Get up." The second lieutenant kicked the German's foot. "Get up."

The German was not going to die well. "*Ich habe nichts getan.*" I have done nothing. He shouted it again and again.

The second lieutenant told him to shut up.

"Were there others with him?" I looked down the rows. I found three more, including the German lieutenant who had told me the shooting would end soon. He raised his perfect blue eyes to me, a single look of dignified entreaty, then cast his glance down. He had been at war too long to believe in much.

The four were marched, shoeless in the snow, back to the Lieutenant Colonel. Two of the Germans were virtually barefoot, their socks worn through at the toes.

"Which one did it?" Coleman demanded.

I pointed.

Coleman looked at the man, then withdrew his pistol and put it to the German's temple. The young SS soldier wept and shouted out in his own language yet again that he had done nothing. But he was too frightened to withdraw his head even an inch from the gun barrel.

Coleman watched him blubber with some satisfaction, then holstered his sidearm. The German went on heaving, his protests continuing, albeit in a reduced voice.

"Take them in back," Coleman said to the second lieutenant. I followed along, entirely a spectator, suddenly uncertain about what was to occur. I had been afraid that the Lieutenant Colonel was going to offer me the gun, but I had been disappointed when he decided not to pull the trigger. Now it seemed for the best.

The second lieutenant led the men behind Coleman's tent at the boundary of the camp and ordered the four to turn around with their hands behind their heads. He looked toward me, not long enough to allow much in the way of a reaction, then pointed to the sergeant with the tommy gun, which seemed to have begun firing almost before the weapon was aimed. Afterward, I figured that the sergeant had just wanted to get it over with. A thought arose to say a word for the German lieutenant, but I didn't. The machine gun's spastic bark resounded in the quiet camp and the four Germans went down like puppets cut from their wires.

At the sound, the Lieutenant Colonel came around the tent. Coleman walked along inspecting the four bodies. "Rot in hell," he told them.

I had watched all of this, there and not there. I had been unable to move since the Germans fell. I had been so pleased by the SS man's terror. Now it was as if I was groping around within myself, trying to find my heart.

27. LONDON

February 5, 1945

Dear Folks—

R & R in London. I have a chance at last to describe what we have been through, but at the moment I am in no mood to relive any of it. The war goes well, and I have done my part. But in thinking over everything I have seen, I cannot imagine how I will return home anything but a pacifist. Military calculations are so tough-minded—they must be, clear-eyed determinations of how to win and who must die. But employing the same kind of unsentimental reasoning, it is hard to understand how war—at least this war— has been worthwhile. The toll of daily oppression Hitler would wreak on several nations, even for years, cannot equal the pain and destruction that is being caused in stopping him. Yes, Europe would be in prison. But it is in rubble instead. And is a matter of government worth the millions upon

millions of lives lost to this carnage? I came
thinking that freedom has no price. But I know
now that it is only life about which this may truly
be said.

I send my love to all of you. I cannot wait to be
with you again.

David

I returned to Third Army Headquarters in Luxembourg City on February 1, 1945. Because the Luxembourgers were regarded as inappropriately accommodating to the Germans, Patton had treated them with little sympathy and had literally turned out the elderly residents of the national old people's home, the Fondation Pescatore, taking it for his headquarters. It was a castle-size structure of orange limestone squares and, with its two projecting wings, vast enough to accommodate both the forward- and rear-echelon staffs. Colonel Maples had been favored with a third-floor salon, where invalids formerly sunned in the banks of high windows, and he was extremely pleased with his surroundings. He walked me to the glass to ensure that I saw his view of the dramatic gorge that plunged several hundred feet, bisecting Luxembourg City. The furnishings in his office, like those of others in the senior staff, had been provided by a cousin of the Grand Duc's, whose generosity only enhanced the suspicion that he had collaborated with the Germans. The Colonel took a moment to point out the gold-mottled tortoise-shell inlay on his desk and credenzas, priceless heirlooms created in the time of Louis Quatorze by the cabinetmaker Boulle. Logs blazed in the marble fireplace, beside which the Colonel and I drew up two damask-covered chairs. The contrast to the frozen holes in which I had been dwelling only weeks ago was unavoidable, but my mind seemed incapable of making anything from it. There were no conclusions, except that life and, surely, war were absurd, something I already felt as palpably as the bones within my body.

The Colonel leaned forward to clasp my shoulder.

"You look a little worse for wear, David. Thinner and perhaps not the same bright look in your eye."

"No, sir."

"I've seen some papers for medals. You've done quite remarkably."

I recounted my failures for the Colonel. I'd lost the best man I'd met in the service and let Martin get away as the result of my own cupidity. This candor was characteristic of my exchanges with virtually everyone. I steadfastly rejected the fawning of colleagues like Tony Eisley, even while I became quietly furious with one or two people who treated me as if I'd been AWOL or, worse, on vacation. The truth was that no one's reactions pleased me. But because Colonel Maples had fought across the trenches a quarter century ago, a bit of my perpetual bitterness eased in his presence. If anything, my respect for him, never insubstantial, had increased, knowing he had volunteered to return to war. I would never do that. Nor could I imagine acquiring his avuncular grace. Today I could only picture myself as an irascible old man.

The Colonel, with his soft gray eyes, listened for a while.

"You are grieving, David. No one ever mentions that as an enduring part of war. You need some time."

I was given two weeks R & R. Most officers on leave

retreated to Paris, where the joy of liberation was enshrined in an atmosphere of guiltless debauchery, but that hardly fit my mood. I chose London, where I found a tiny hotel room off Grosvenor Square. I had made no plans other than to sit in a hot tub for hours, and to review the foot of mail that had awaited me in Luxembourg City. I wanted to sleep, read a few novels, and when I was able, write several letters.

In retrospect, I suppose I had crossed the Channel with the unspoken thought of again being whoever I was before I'd set foot on the Continent. But the war followed me. I'd barely slept longer than two or three hours in a row since Biddy and I had first been dispatched to arrest Martin. Now I was startled to find that I could not sleep at all. I had not spent a night entirely alone within solid walls for months, and I had the feeling they were encroaching. Often I couldn't even stand to close my eyes. The second night I bought a bottle of scotch. But several belts did not make things any better. The ghouls of war took control. Each time I drifted off some panicked sensory recollection raced at me—the keening of incoming artillery, the sight of Collison with his intestines in his bloody hands, the three holes in Biddy's stomach, the earthquake and thunder of the 88s, or the unbearable cold of Champs. And always there were the dead and, worse, the dying, screaming to be saved.

In the aftermath of all that, I guess I expected to feel some gratitude for being alive. But life had been a far sweeter affair without being confronted by the dread of extinction. I had become so accustomed to being afraid that fear was now a second skin, even in the relative safety of London. I awaited artillery blasts in the parks, snipers in every tree. I was ashamed of my fear, and frequently angry. I wanted to be alone, because I was not sure I could treat anyone else decently.

The letters I expected to write came hard. So much seemed beyond words. I wrote to Biddy's family for more than two days, draft after draft, and ended up with something barely longer than a note. I found it impossible to describe the bathos of his death, hoping to comfort a dog, after summoning such valor on so many prior occasions. The only solace I could offer was to enclose hundreds of his photographs which I'd gathered from his belongings. I promised to visit the Bidwells, if I was lucky enough to return alive. In the days that I had composed and recomposed this letter, I had envisioned putting the pen down at the end and, in utter privacy, finally sobbing. But I had never been a weeper, even in the later years of childhood, and tears still would not come, leaving me in a state of constipated agitation.

Then there was Grace. In my two days of German captivity, when the combination of Biddy's death and Gita's desertion had left me feeling certain that I was going to die of heartbreak, I'd had second thoughts about Grace. She was beautiful and brilliant and steady. The one thing I could say with utmost sincerity was that I wished that I could see her, because I had learned that presence meant everything. But without a photo in my hand I could barely bring her to mind. If we were together, if Grace were in my arms, then I might have had some chance of retrieving our life. "Here, here, here," I kept repeating to myself whenever I thought of her, feeling largely enraged that something so dignifying and eternal as love could be defeated by distance. Yet the memory of Gita, of her bare skin and the moments when we'd seemed to fuse souls, easily withstood whatever had been left behind for thousands of miles and many months. By now, I was willing to say only to my most private self that I did not fully regret Gita. I had told Biddy that I was in love with her. That seemed ludicrous. I had been the kind of fool men often were for sex. But even so, I found certain images of her recurrent and fabulously arousing. Again and again I saw her looming over me naked, stimulating me with unashamed intensity. Fantasies of how I might come to find her again in the burning ruins of Europe revolved through me, even as I sometimes begged myself not to abandon the decent life I knew I could make with Grace. But it was not a time for logic. I desired Gita against all reason, and my inability to control my passions seemed part and parcel of the harsh season I was experiencing within the narrow cold confines of my room.

I made it a point to walk as much as I could, but even on the London streets I found my thinking little more than a procession of spotlighted theater scenes, in which various figures, the dear and the dead and the dreaded, made unpredictable leaps onto center stage. Often I saw Robert Martin and Roland Teedle there. In most moods, I hated both of them for letting loose the torrent of events in which I was now drowning. In better moments, I realized that one of the barriers to righting myself was the fact that I still did not know which of them to believe. I despised Martin for his deceptions, but I remained unconvinced at the deepest level that the man I had seen swing down into the Seille like a real-life Jack Armstrong would stoop to spying. Even at this late date, some part of what I'd been told seemed untrue, and that in turn seemed to emanate somehow from the core of uncontrolled excess I'd always sensed in Teedle. Amid all the disgraces I'd suffered, my doubts about the bona fides of the commands that had led me to peril and ruin seemed intolerable.

My tours around the West End took me several times down Brook Street. I recalled the address from Teedle's order to Martin to return to London. What I found at number 68, a block from the U.S. Embassy and across the street from Claridge's, was an ordinary West End row house, with a dormered fourth floor, a limestone exterior on the ground level, and a roofed entryway. This presumably was the OSS, or at least one arm of it. There was no plate identifying the building's occupants, but after passing by a few times I noticed enough foot traffic in and out to convince me that an organization of one kind or another was housed there, and on my fifth or sixth morning in London, I unlatched the iron gate and walked up to the door. Inside, I asked the tidy middle-aged receptionist if I could speak to Colonel Bryant Winters. I gave her my name.

"Regarding?"

"Major Robert Martin." The faintest lick of reaction trickled into her bland face. I was directed to a straight-backed chair across the way. She had other business to occupy her, but eventually spoke into her phone.

I'd had very little notion of the OSS before I'd been assigned to Martin's case, but its mythology had grown in my mind and those of most other soldiers in the European theater. The stories of derring-do in France, Italy, and Africa were, even if untrue, greatly entertaining, and had become staples in the constant gossip and apocrypha that provided important diversions in a soldier's day-to-day life: OSS had wiped out a battalion of German artillery to the man by poisoning their rations. Special Services agents had dropped from the sky, surrounded Rommel's tent, and spirited him back to Rome, where he was being questioned.

Within the inner sanctum, however, the atmosphere was anything but swashbuckling. It was, rather, very much like the Yale Club, which I'd once visited in Manhattan, where everyone seemed to speak with his jaw tightened and where I sensed that Jews or Catholics would always be treated with a courtesy that would never embrace complete welcome. NOK, as some of the more genteel fraternity boys at Easton were apt to put it — not our kind. The men here had good American names and many had eschewed military attire in favor of tweed jackets. Something about the milieu appalled me, especially the degree to which I knew I had once hungered after this like a hound perched beside a table. Whatever had happened to me, I was well beyond that now.

I was absorbed with these reflections when a tall man in a uniform presented himself. I jumped up to salute. This was Colonel Winters. He smiled like a graceful host.

"Captain, we had no word you were coming. My aide is back there thumbing through the cables, but I recognized your name. Judge Advocate, right? I take it it's the usual signal foul-up?"

I shrugged, the familiar gesture of eternal helplessness that was part of life in the Army.

"Well, come along." He had a small office with full bookshelves among the freshly painted white pilasters and just enough room for two small ebony chairs, on which we sat facing each other. His large desk was columned with bound reports. As he closed the door, he permitted himself a well-behaved laugh. "That was a bit of a stir you created. We don't have soldiers wandering in off the street to talk about our operatives."

"No, of course not. But it's official business." I tried to avoid outright lying, yet I said nothing to dispel the idea that Maples had signaled ahead of me. I simply indicated that as long as I was in London, I had decided it was best to formalize certain matters in my investigation, which had to be completed if Martin's court-martial were ever to proceed someday.

"Of course, of course," answered Winters. He was impeccable, with a long handsome face and brilliantined hair sharply parted. But he had an easy air. Despite Winters' uniform, I didn't feel as if I were in a military environment. No colonel, not even Maples, would have come to greet me, and we chatted amiably about London and then the war. He asked what I could tell him about the front. We were going to win, I said. That conviction had returned to me. I told him about the German lieutenant who had expected an end to shooting soon, but made no mention of his death.

"Good, good," said Winters. "And tell me, then, Captain, what information is it you wish from us?"

I named several points on which direct confirmation from OSS was still required, reciting all of it in a drone meant to suggest my regrets about the punctiliousness of the law to which I was a slave. First, we needed to confirm that Martin had been ordered back to London by OSS. Second, that he had not been directed by OSS to blow the Saline Royale ammo dump when he had. Third, that Major Martin was a Soviet spy.

At the last request, Winters frowned noticeably.

"That's Teedle's word, then. That he is a Soviet spy?"

When I said yes, Winters reached down to fuss with his trouser cuff.

"I can confirm for you," he said, "that Martin has been insubordinate. That he has disobeyed direct orders, and conducted important military operations without final authorization. And that OSS supports his apprehension."

"And his court-martial?"

"In all likelihood. After we've spoken with him."

"But not charges as a spy?"

Winters raised his eyes to a window and the trees on Brook Street.

"Correct me, Captain. Are you the one who parachuted into Bastogne?"

"There were actually two of us," I said. "My sergeant and me. And no one had to kick Bidwell in the behind to get him out of the plane."

Winters smiled. Throughout the war, OSS operatives had done things like we had. Those acts were, in fact, the calling card of the agency, and I found it a bitter irony that so many of these mild, bookish types defined themselves by those exploits. If I hadn't made that jump, Winters probably would have left me in his reception area, never bothering to receive me. But I didn't feel like a member of their club. The soldiers at the front had few illusions about what they had endured. These men, with their self-congratulations and sense of noblesse oblige, lived on their own myths and probably refused to share with one another the essential information that those who carried out their operations did so in terror. In that, Winters appeared slightly different, and was seemingly pleased I was not seeking to impress him.

"And you jumped because Teedle told you Martin was a Soviet spy?"

I no longer remembered why I had done that. Probably because I did not yet understand how terrible it was to die. But I knew a leading question when I heard one, and nodded. Colonel Winters drew his hand to his mouth.

"I have great regard for Rollie Teedle. He's a magnificent commander. There's no other brigadier general in the Army bearing that kind of responsibility. He should have had his second star long ago, but for all the rumor-mongering."

I didn't bother asking what the rumors were.

"I have no doubt that someone here offered Teedle that surmise about Martin," said Winters. "That's surely the prevailing opinion. But it's only an opinion. Candidly, Captain, no one knows precisely what Martin is up to. Certainly it's not anything we've told him to do. Which lends itself to the idea that he's serving someone else's commands. And the Russians, given his background—that's the logical conclusion. Clearly, we can't have him out there on the loose. It's a very dangerous situation."

Even I could see that. "Were there prior signs he was disloyal?"

"No, but the truth is that he'd never been put to the test. This fall Martin was given a top secret briefing back here in London concerning a project we wanted him to undertake in Germany. And the information he learned then would be of special consequence to the Soviets. He made some remarks at the time which unsettled folks here. That's why, after some second thoughts, he was ordered to return. Wrong man for the job, we decided. It wasn't until he ran off that it occurred to anyone that he'd head into the Russians' arms. But if you knew the details, you'd agree it's the most reasonable conclusion. I'm sorry, Dubin, to be so cryptic. I can't say more."

I told him I understood.

"Personally," said Winters, "I hold to a sentimental belief that these conclusions are wrong. But it's a view I keep to myself, because, frankly, I have no other explanation for his behavior."

"Anyone having any better luck finding him than I did?" I'd relinquished the search for Martin when I got back to Luxembourg City and had had no news since. Robert Martin had made nothing but misery for me. Revenge being what it is, I might have relished the sight of him in handcuffs. But I felt that the best homage I could make to Biddy was to give up the quest, without which he'd be alive.

"We'll catch up with him in time. We don't want the Provost Marshal posting an all-points bulletin that might tip the Russians. We'd like to pull Martin in quietly. But he recruited many of the contacts we have in Germany, and a lot of them are leftists, union people, whose leanings these days, as between the Soviets and the other Allies, are a matter of doubt. And beyond that, it's a difficult proposition to tell them to turn their back on the man whom they've always seen as the face of this organization. It's all rather delicate. We've had several reports after the fact. Martin's been in touch with some of his old contacts, but only asks assistance in making his way. He presents himself as on a very sensitive mission. Once or twice, he's asked to be hidden. Him and the girl."

"The girl is with him?"

"I take it you've met her. Beguiling as they say?"

"In her way," I answered.

"I've never had the pleasure. She has her own legend around here. Martin recruited her out of a Marseilles hospital where she was working as an aide. A genius at playing her parts, whatever they are, and willing to do anything. Made the ultimate sacrifice, if you know what I mean, to get information out of a German officer a few years back, fellow who'd been a patient and continued to pursue her. Critical information about the bombing of London. She deserves a medal, if you ask me, but people in this building get squeamish about acknowledging those kinds of activities. Oldest trick in spying, really, sleeping with the enemy, but that's one of our dirty little secrets." He smiled, enjoying his double entendre.

He continued by telling the story I'd heard before about Gita rescuing Martin from the Gestapo by feigning pregnancy. It was fortunate Winters had gone on speaking, because I was not able to. Sleeping with the enemy. I stared at the intricate weave of the Colonel's carpet, which probably had been trod on for a century, trying to calculate what all of this meant for me. Every time I thought I'd absorbed the last from this woman there was more.

"And is she, the girl — is she with the Soviets, too?" I asked.

Winters shrugged. "Unclear. If Martin is really in this game, he might have shared his goals with no one. And then again —" He lifted a hand with elegant understatement. "Anyway, we're a bit astray."

I stood. He offered to buy me dinner one night while I was here, but I doubted, after hearing this information, that I'd have the heart to see him. I remained vague, and said I'd ring if I found a break in my schedule.

Bad as the period before had been, Winters' news about Gita drove me into a turmoil that was even more intense, making my efforts to focus on the outer world increasingly tenuous. I walked toward Green Park and found, half an hour later, that I was still standing at the edge of one of the paths, with my hand on the cold iron railing, beleaguered by what tumbled inside me. When I looked in the mirror I saw a man of normal appearance, but it was as if that outer self was the backside of a moving-picture screen. On the reverse a movie marathon played, a never-ending splash of imagery and sound, all of it tortured. Often, as I plunged along the streets, I thought, I am having a nervous breakdown, and was propelled back to the present only by the panic that accompanied the thought.

With three days to go on my leave I packed up. Before I left, I wrote briefly to Grace. Dashed by Gita, I still could not rebound toward Grace. I would never explain why deluding myself about one woman had meant a death to my love for the other, but that was clearly the case. Grace was estimable in every way. But she was a piece of a life I would never return to. That much was concluded. And so was my time away from the service. Any further idleness would rot me. I needed work. I would head back to Luxembourg City. There would be cases to try. Men to hang.

But I sensed that even the drama of the law might fail to preoccupy me. If I remained in this abyss, there could be only one choice. I knew instantly and found not the remotest irony in my decision. I would apply for transfer to the infantry and return to combat. The desperation to remain alive, to kill rather than die, was the only reliable distraction from what was rocketing around my mind.

Only as I closed the door of the hotel room, with my duffel slung across my back, did the full import of my plans strike home, and somehow it was Gita who addressed me. I listened to her voice in the same state of fury and surrender that had tormented me for days, wanting not to hear it and hearing it nonetheless.

"You are Martin," she said.

February 11, 1945

Dear Grace,

I have spent the last week in London, attempting to recover from what has transpired. After months of sharing so many impressions with you, I know how sparse I've been with details of the fighting. But there is no point to saying more. Imagine the worst. It is more awful than that. I came across the ocean, regretting that I was to be but a pretend soldier. I have been a soldier in earnest in the last months, and I regret that far more.

I now know, Grace, that I will not be able to come home to you. I feel myself damaged in some essential way I will never fully repair. I thought when I arrived here that love would survive anything. But that was one of many fabrications I carried along. For me, our sweet world has ended.

I know what a shock this letter must be. And I am crippled with guilt and shame when I imagine you reading it. But I am in a mood that seems to require me to cast off all illusions, and that includes the notion that I could return to be a loving husband to you.

I will carry you with me eternally. My regard and admiration are forever.

Please forgive me,

David

VII.

28. VISITING

For several years when Sarah and I were little, my mother would dress us up once each summer and put us in our Chevy with my father. There was a touch of foreboding about these trips, probably because Dad didn't take us many places without Mom, except for baseball games, which she regarded as permanently incomprehensible. It was summer, and Sarah and I were not in school, and this little automobile trip was the last thing either my sister or I wanted to do. Before getting very far, Sarah or I would claim to be carsick. But Dad continued, driving about twenty minutes into the heart of the black belt, proceeding through the most blighted streets until reaching a tidy block of three-flats. There he extracted my sister and me from the auto, notwithstanding our complaints.

Inside, we visited briefly with a soft-spoken light-toned black lady named Mrs. Bidwell. These meetings were palpably painful to everyone. After we'd come all that way, neither my dad nor Mrs. Bidwell seemed to have a clue what to say. In fact, even as a child, I realized that my sister and I had been hauled along principally as conversation pieces, so that the old woman could exclaim over how we had grown and Dad could agree. Race was not the issue. My parents lived in University Park, one of the earliest and most successfully integrated neighborhoods in the U.S., and they were comfortable socializing with black neighbors.

In Mrs. Bidwell's living room, we drank one glass of excellent lemonade, then went on our way. When I asked each time why we had to stop, my father said that Mrs. Bidwell was the mother of a boy he used to know. Period. I didn't even think of her when I started reading Dad's account because she was black, unlike Gideon Bidwell—yet another boat I missed.

Years ago, I broke a story about one of the supervising lawyers in the Kindle County Prosecuting Attorney's Office, whose gambling habit left him indebted to local loan sharks. My source was an FBI agent who was understandably concerned about the perils of having an Assistant P.A. in the pocket of hoodlums, and the Bureau guy even showed me the federal grand jury transcripts so I could reassure my editors before we went to press.

It was a great coup for me. The only problem was that the prosecutor involved, Rudy Patel, was a pretty good friend of mine. Both serious baseball fans, Rudy and I were part of a group that shared season tickets to the Trappers' games. We'd often sit side by side, cursing the Trappers' perpetual misfortunes, high-fiving homers as if we'd hit the balls, and berating the players for strikeouts and errors. Bleeding for the Trappers is a Kindle County ritual and it became a bond between Rudy and me. I gave him good coverage on his trials. And then cost him his job.

Fortunately for Rudy, he got into an impaired lawyers program, enrolled in Gamblers Anonymous, and avoided getting disbarred or prosecuted. Naturally, though, he had to be fired, and was required to live with the ignominy of being outed by me. He ended up as a professor at a pretty good local law school and has gone on with his life, albeit with none of the promise that radiated around him earlier. I took care of that.

Rudy and I still live on the same bus line to Nearing and every now and then in the station we'll see each other. Every time I do, I can feel myself light up instinctively with the affection of our old friendship, and even see him begin to brighten, until his memory returns and he retreats into loathing. Over the years, his look of pure hatred has abated a little. He must know I was doing my job. But the fact is that there's nowhere to go. Even if he forgave me wholeheartedly, our friendship would be part of a past that he's both set aside and overcome.

I mention this because it reminds me a little of my father's visits with Mrs. Bidwell. These brief meetings clearly upset Dad. Driving home, he had a look of quick-eyed distraction, gripping and regripping the steering wheel. I don't know what illusion had brought him to the North End. That he was obliged to keep faith and memory? That by showing us off he could restore just a shred of the stake in the future Mrs. Bidwell had lost with the death of her son? But after the last of these trips, when I was about ten, Dad looked at my mother as soon as we returned home and said, "I can't do that again." My mother's expression was soft and commiserating.

I'm sure Dad kept his vow and didn't go back. As I have said, there was never a living place for the war in my father's life. It was not life. It was war. Loyalty could not overcome that.

Nor, frankly, do I imagine that Mrs. Bidwell ever tried to contact him again. Looking back, I'm struck that neither Mr. Bidwell nor Biddy's brothers were ever there. For them, there was probably never any accommodating themselves to the intolerable irony of losing a son and a brother whose only equal opportunity involved dying.

In the end, Mrs. Bidwell and Dad were a lot like Rudy and me. There was a shared history, but it was a history they were impotent to change. Fate, inexplicably, had favored one and not the other. There was no erasing that inequity, or any other. And because they were powerless in these ways, they could only regard what the past had dished up with great sadness and then move on to the very separate lives that remained.

29. WINNING

From *Don't Be a Sucker in Germany!*, a pamphlet published by the 12th Army Group, found among my father's things:

The facts in this booklet were compiled by the Provost Marshal of the Ninth U.S. Army as a guide for troops in Germany. Nothing here was "dreamed up" by someone behind a desk. This booklet is a summary of the experiences of the French, Dutch, and Belgian underground workers now serving with the American armies. They know the tricks and the answers. That's why they are alive to pass this information on to you.

DON'T BELIEVE IT

Don't believe there are any "good" Germans in Germany. Of course you know good Germans back home. They had guts enough and sense enough to break from Germany long ago.

Don't believe it was only the Nazi government that brought on this war. Any people have the kind of government they want and deserve. Only a few people bucked the Nazis. You won't meet them; the Nazis purged them long ago.

One Belgian major, wounded twice in two wars with Germany, was stationed in Germany from 1918 to 1929. He says:

"A German is by nature a liar. Individually he is peaceful enough, but collectively, Germans become cruel."

If a German underground movement breaks out, it will be merciless. It will be conducted by SS and Gestapo agents who don't flinch at murder. They will have operatives everywhere. Every German, man, woman, and child, must be suspected. Punishment must be quick and severe. This is not the same thing as brutality. Allied forces must show their strength but must use it only when necessary.

We won the war. In February and March, the Allies ground forward. The Germans finally seemed to realize they were overwhelmed—depleted by the Battle of the Bulge (as people were now calling what had happened in the Ardennes), outmanned in the skies, and facing massive Russian forces attacking on their eastern front. "*Bald schiessen wir nicht mehr.*"

For the Third Army, the principal problems were weather and terrain. The worst winter in fifty years abated with an early thaw, swelling the rivers and streams in the mountainous landscape on which the Siegfried line had been erected. Waterways that our forces once could have forded on foot now required bridging by the engineers while the troops waited. But Patton, as always, advanced.

Nineteenth Tactical Air Command provided comprehensive support for the forward columns. On March 22, Patton defied Supreme Headquarters and secretly mounted a massive assault across the Rhine, thereby depriving Montgomery of the intended honor of being the first general into the German heartland. The fur was flying around HQ for weeks afterward, and I have no doubt that Patton's little mutiny provided much of the impetus that led to him being relieved of command as general of the Third Army by May.

Even with the end in sight, our progress brought none of the jubilation that had accompanied the liberation of France. Our men had been at war too long to celebrate combat, and, far more important, there was the daily evidence of what our victory meant to the local populations. A relentless parade of Germans driven from their homes by the fighting flowed back into our path, marching along with their most valued possessions on their backs. They lived in the open in unhappy packs that were soon breeding grounds for typhus. Some waved the Stars and Stripes as we passed, but we had killed their sons and fathers, and exploded or plundered their houses. For the most part, there was a miserable sulking suspicion between them and us, especially since we knew that many German soldiers had ditched their uniforms to hide among the throngs of the displaced.

Despite mass German desertions, the Third Army alone took 300,000 German POWs in those weeks. They were trucked to the rear, dirty, hungry, defeated men, herded into barbed-wire cages, many of whom, when addressed, prayed for the end of the fighting, which, under the Geneva Conventions, would allow them to go home.

As for me, I remained desolate and occasionally temperamental. I never carried through on my threat to myself to volunteer for combat. Instead, I went through the routines of a military lawyer with proficiency and disinterest. Reports describing thefts, rapes, and murders of Germans arrived on our desks in a tide and were generally ignored. We proceeded only with investigations of serious crimes against our own troops. It was not simply that the Germans were our enemies. Many military commanders, including General Maples — he was promoted April 1 — expressed the view that a nasty occupation in Germany was justified, not so much in the name of revenge, but so that the Germans saw firsthand what they had unleashed on the rest of the world. I never contested that point of view.

But I contested little. For me, the war was over. Like the cities and towns of western Europe, my steeples lay in ruins. I wanted only to go home and find time to pick through the rubble. It was the downcast civilians, as much as our own troops, with whom I often felt a bond.

From home, I continued to receive heartsore entreaties from Grace Morton, who refused to accept my judgment that our marriage would never occur. *My darling*, she wrote, *I know how awful this time has been for you and the tragedies you have witnessed. Soon, we will again be together, this madness will be forgotten, and we will be one.*

I wrote back with as much kindness as I could muster, telling her she would save us both continued anguish by abiding by my decision. In response, her letters grew more openly pleading. When they went unanswered, her magnificent dignity wore away. One day I would receive a diatribe about my disloyalty, the next a rueful and lascivious contemplation of how wrong we had been not to sleep together before my departure. I forced myself to read each note, always with pain. I was stunned by the extraordinary contagion bred by war, which had somehow conveyed my madness across the ocean to infect her.

The Third Army moved its forward HQ twice within a week, ending up in early April in Frankfurt am Main, which had been bombed unceasingly before our arrival. Blocks of the city were nothing but hillocks of stone and brick above which a little aura of dust lingered whenever the wind stirred. In the area close to the main train station, a number of the older buildings remained standing and the Staff Judge Advocate set up in a former commercial building on Poststrasse. I was given a spacious office that had belonged to an important executive, and was still unpacking there on April 6 when a chubby young officer came in, twirling his cap in his hands. He was Herbert Diller, an aide to the Assistant Chief of Staff of the Third Army, who wished to see me. I was rushing down the block with him toward the General staff headquarters before he mentioned the name Teedle.

I had not seen the General in person since the day I had slunk back from the Comtesse de Lemolland's to report Martin's initial disappearance. As far as I knew, Teedle had received my written reports, although I'd gotten no response. Now, from Diller, I learned that on April 1, General Teedle had been relieved of command of the 18th Armored, which was being cycled into a reserve position for the balance of the war. With that, Roland Teedle had become Patton's Assistant Chief of Staff. As Diller and I hurried down the broad halls of this former government ministry, I could hear Teedle yelling. His target turned out to be his corporal Frank, who'd been transferred with him.

General Teedle looked smaller and older in the office where I found him, a somber room with high ceilings and long windows. He was on his feet, facing, with evident bewilderment, a desk on which the papers looked as if they'd simply been dumped. I was surprised to feel some warmth for the General at the first sight of him, but I suppose after my visit to OSS in London, I'd come to recognize that he had been right about most things. Whatever else, Robert Martin was both disingenuous and a subversive force in the military. Not that I'd completely forgotten Bonner's accusation. It occurred to me for a second that Teedle might have been moved to HQ so someone could keep an eye on him. But I'd never know for sure, not whether Bonner spoke the truth, or had misperceived other conduct, or, even if correct, where Teedle's misbehavior should rank among the war's many other travesties.

I congratulated the General on his new posting. Another star had come with it. As usual, he had no interest in flattery.

"They're already replacing the warhorses, Dubin. They think diplomats should be in charge. The next phase of the war will be political. I'd rather be feeding cattle than sitting behind a desk, but at least there's some work left to do. Patton wants to be in Berlin before the end of the month, and I believe we will be. So how did you like war, Dubin? A bitch, isn't it?"

I must have betrayed something in response to his scoffing, because Teedle focused on me with concern.

"I know you had a bad time, Dubin. I don't mean to make light of it."

"I don't think I'm the only one with sad stories to tell."

"There are three million men here with nightmares to take home with them, and a million or so more half a world away. Makes you wonder what kind of country we can ever be. So much of civilization, Dubin, is merely the recovery periods between wars. We build things up and then tear them down again. Look at poor Europe. Some moments I find myself thinking about all the fighting that's gone on here and expect blood to come welling out of the ground."

"You sound like Martin, General." As ever, I was surprised by my forwardness with Teedle. But he seemed to expect it.

"Oh, hardly, Dubin. I'm sure Martin wants to put an end to war. I take it as part of the human condition."

My expression, in response, was undoubtedly pained, but in retrospect I am unsure whether that was because I resisted Teedle's view, or regarded it as a harrowing truth. Observing me, Teedle leaned back and drummed a pencil on the thigh of his wool trousers.

"Do you know what this war is about, Dubin?"

Teedle had made Diller wait outside and I could hear voices gathering, meaning another meeting was about to take place, most likely involving officers superior to me. But I wasn't surprised that the General wanted to take time for this discussion. There had never been any question that Teedle found something essential in his contest with Martin. He opposed everything Martin stood for — the solitary adventurer who thought he could outwit the machines of war; a spy who favored deception over hand-to-hand assault; and, of course, a Communist who would give to each man according to his need, as opposed to the fathomless will of God.

I asked if he was referring to the Treaty of Versailles.

"Fuck treaties," he said. "I mean what's at stake. In the largest terms."

I knew Teedle valued my seriousness, and I tried not to be flippant, but the fact was that I had no idea anymore and I said so. Teedle, naturally, had a view.

"I think we're fighting about what will unite people. I think that all of these machines we've fallen in love with in this epoch—the railroad, the telegraph and telephone, the automobile, the radio, the moving-picture camera, the airplane, God knows what else—they've changed the compass of life. A shepherd who tended his flock or a smith at his forge, folks who knew only their fellow townsmen, now contend with people a thousand miles away as an immediate presence in their lives. And they don't know exactly what they have in common with all those distant companions.

"Now, along come the Communists, who tell the shepherd the common interest is the good of man, and maybe he should give up a few sheep to the poor fellow a few towns over. And then we have Mr. Hitler, who tells his citizens that they should be united by the desire to kill or conquer anyone who doesn't resemble them. And then there's us—the Allies. What's our vision to compete with Mr. Stalin and Mr. Hitler? What are we offering?"

"Well, Roosevelt and Churchill would say 'freedom.'"

"Which means?"

"Personal liberty. The Bill of Rights. The vote. Freedom and equality."

"For what end?"

"General, I have to say I feel as if I'm back in law school."

"All right, Dubin. I hear you. I think we're fighting for God, Dubin. Not Christ or Yahweh or wood elves, no God in particular. But the right to believe. To say that there is a limit to this big collective society, there's something more important for every human, and he will find it on his own. But we're trying to have it two ways, Dubin, to be collective and individual at the same time, and it's going to get us in trouble. We can't tolerate Fascists *or* Communists, who want the same answer for every person. Or the capitalists either, if you want to know the truth. They want everyone to stand up for materialism. And that's a collectivism of its own and we have to recognize it as such."

"There's quite a bit of collectivism in religion, General, people who want you or me to do exactly as they believe."

"That's the nature of man, Dubin. And very much, I think, as God expects. But it's the human mission to welcome all reasonable contenders."

I wasn't following and said so. Teedle circled around his desk, coming closer in a way that felt strangely unguarded for him.

"I believe in democracy," he said, "for exactly the same reason Jefferson did. Because God made each of us, different though we may be. Human variety expresses His infiniteness. But His world still belongs to those who will struggle to do the mission He has chosen for them, whether it's the Trappist contemplating His will in silence, or the titan astride the globe. If God made a world with a billion different human plans, He must have expected struggle. But He couldn't have intended a world where one vision prevails, because that would mean only a single vision of Him, Dubin."

"Is war what God wants then, General?"

"We all think about that one, Dubin. I can't tell you the answer. All I know is He wants us to persevere." He picked up a paper off his desk. "I've been getting reports for a day now from a place called Ohrdruf. Heard anything about that?"

"No, sir."

"Three thousand political prisoners of one kind or another lying in shallow graves, starved to death by the Nazis. The few who remain alive survive in unimaginable squalor. The communiqués keep repeating that words can't describe it. God must want us to fight against that, Dubin."

I shrugged, unwilling to venture onto that ground, while the General continued to scrutinize me. I understood only then what my attraction had been to Teedle from the start. He cared about my soul.

"All right, Dubin. So much for the bright chatter. I have an assignment for you, but I thought we should have a few words first. I heard about your visit to London, checking up on me."

"I did what I always told you I had to, General. Confirm the details."

"You were checking up on me. I don't mind, Dubin. I suspect at this stage you hate Robert Martin more than I do."

"I've come to feel rather neutral, to tell you the truth, sir. I can't really make out what his game is. He might just be mad in his own way."

"He's a spy, Dubin. Nothing more complicated than that. He's on the other side."

There was no question that Martin and the General were on different sides. But so were Teedle and I. Not that I could name any of these camps.

"As you wish, General, but I wasn't trying to be in-subordinate. I simply wanted to see matters to a logical end."

"Well, you haven't done that, have you, Dubin? The son of a bitch is still cavorting around."

"He could be dead for all I know, sir."

"That, unfortunately, he is not." Teedle thumbed through the papers on his desk, finally giving up in exasperation and yelling for Frank, who was apparently away. "To hell with it," Teedle announced. "About forty-eight hours ago, a reserve battalion of the 100th Infantry Division en-countered a man with one hand who claimed to be an OSS officer. This was down near the town of Pforzheim. He said he was on a special operation and in need of sup-plies. An officer there with good sense contacted OSS, but by the time they'd alerted the MPs, Martin was with the four winds.

"So he's gone yet again. Amazing. Any idea how the hell the girl found out he was in that hospital last time? I've been wondering for months."

"I told her. It was rather stupid."

He made a face. "I thought that was possible. That's more than stupid, Dubin. Get into your pants, did she?"

I didn't answer.

"You should have known better than that, too, Dubin." But his pinched eyes contained a trace of amusement at my folly. Whatever his complex morality, Teedle was good to his word. Sex, like war, was something God expected humans to succumb to.

"I didn't do very well, General. I'm aware of that. It cost a very good man his life. I'll rue that to the end of my days."

He gave me a kinder look than I expected and said, "If you had the pleasure of being a general, Dubin, you'd be able to say that ten thousand times. It's not much of a job that requires other men to die for your mistakes, is it?"

"No, sir."

"But that's what it entails."

"Yes, sir."

He took a moment. "Here's where we stand. I've been doing the Dance of the Seven Veils with OSS for a couple of months now. Donovan hasn't wanted any Army-wide acknowledgment that one of their own has gone astray. They say that's so they can save a chance to use Martin against the Russians, but it's all politics, if you ask me, and I've put my foot down now. A bulletin is going to all MPs, Third Army, Seventh Army, the Brits, everybody in Europe. And I'd like you in charge, Dubin. You have experience that can't be spared. You know what Martin looks like. More important, you've seen his tricks. I could never tell somebody else to be wary enough. Besides, it will give you a chance to clean up whatever mess you made. That's a fair deal, isn't it?"

I didn't answer. Fair wasn't the point and we both knew it.

"I know you've had enough of this assignment, Dubin. And given what you've said — or haven't said — I can understand why. You did the right thing stepping out. But it's a war and we need you. I've discussed it with Maples.

And we agree. Those are your orders, Dubin. Get Martin." The General delivered his edict with his head lowered, enhancing the warning glare from his light eyes. There was no doubt the General meant to teach me a lesson. Running Martin to ground was going to convert me entirely to his point of view. And in that, I suspected he might even have been right. "I assume I don't have to add any cautions here about keeping your other gun in its holster, do I. Once burned, twice wise, correct?"

I nodded.

"Dismissed," he said.

30. BALINGEN

I drove south to interview the infantry officer who'd detained Martin at Pforzheim. The little towns I passed through brought to mind cuckoo clocks, with small narrow buildings set tight as teeth on the hillsides, all with painted wooden decorations along the steep rooflines. The officer who'd detained Martin, Major Farell Beasley, described him as robust in spite of his visible injuries and insisting that in Special Operations he could still be useful with only one hand. Beasley, like so many others before him, had been quite taken with Martin's sparkle and seemed puzzled to think such a fine soldier could have done anything wrong. In fact, Martin had provided excellent intelligence about the German units a mile ahead who were attempting to keep the 100th from crossing the Neckar River. As for his own objectives, Martin had declined to discuss them, except to say that he would be launching a small operation in the vicinity. I did not ask if there was any sign Martin was traveling with a woman.

I remained near Pforzheim for twenty-four hours to coordinate the MPs' search. The local Germans were only marginally cooperative and Martin was presumed to have melted into the surrounding hills, moving on behind the fighting.

On my return to Frankfurt, I found for the next several days that the teletype Teedle had initiated to MPs throughout the European theater brought numerous reported sightings of one-handed men. None of them, however, had the extensive burns on his left side Major Beasley had seen on Martin. Then late on April 11, I received a telegram from Colonel Winters at OSS in London, with whom I'd visited.

```
Our man captured STOP Will communicate 0600
tomorrow by secure channels.
```

He phoned on the dot. For the last three or four days, he said, Seventh Army forces outside Balingen in southwest Germany had been negotiating with the commandant of a German camp holding political prisoners. The Nazis had hoped to exchange them for their own POWs, but the Americans had simply waited out the Krauts and they had finally surrendered control yesterday. Entering the camp, the Americans found an infernal scene of sickness and starvation.

"They say it's quite awful. Most of the SS escaped, of course. But when the intelligence officers went nosing around, inmates pointed out a fellow with one hand who'd appeared in their midst only a few days ago. They all assumed he was a German guard who couldn't get away because of his injury. He claimed to be another internee, a Spanish Jew, who'd been working in Germany when he

was deported to another slave camp, but that was plainly
a lie. He was too well nourished, for one thing, and spoke
terrible German. And when they made him lower his
drawers, it was clear he wasn't Jewish. He told several
more stories, the last of which was that he was an American OSS officer named Robert Martin. That one was
wrung from him only when his interrogators threatened
to turn him over to the inmates, who've torn several
guards apart with their bare hands. Literally, Dubin. Literally. I can't even imagine what the hell is going on
down there. But I guarantee you one thing: Martin won't
be getting away. They have him chained to the wall. He
will be surrendered only to you."

I asked if Winters had any clue what had brought Martin there.

"I would say, Dubin, that the people around here who
took Martin for a traitor are the ones smiling a little more
broadly. Once you have him back in Frankfurt, we'd like
to send our people to interrogate him at length." He ended
the conversation with the familiar apologies for not being
able to say more.

I ordered up an armed convoy to transport the prisoner,
and immediately headed south in advance to take custody
of Robert Martin.

And so, driven by a new MP sergeant to whom I barely had
the heart to speak, I traveled to Balingen. It was April 12,
1945, a sweet morning with a spotless sky and a swelling,
vital aroma in the air. There had been many reports about
the German concentration camps, including one or two
published accounts by escapees. But the authors had gotten

away months ago, before matters turned dire for Hitler's regime. And even the claims made by the few survivors of the slave camp at Natzweiler in France, which several of us had heard of, tended to be dismissed as propaganda or yet another of the improbable, ultimately baseless rumors of disaster that circulated routinely among U.S. troops: The Russians had given up and Stalin had killed himself. Two hundred kamikaze pilots had flattened large stretches of L.A. Montgomery and Bradley had engaged in a fistfight in front of the troops. The Nazis were exterminating political prisoners by the thousands. The last of these stories had cropped up after the Soviets in Poland captured a supposed Nazi death camp called Auschwitz at the end of January, but these days nobody put much stock in what the Russians were saying.

From outside, the camp at Balingen was unremarkable, a sizable former military post at the margin of town, set on a high knoll amid the larches and pines of the Black Forest. The entire site was encompassed by a tall barbed-wire fence topped by brown electrification nodes, with the yellow-brick administration buildings standing in sight of the entrance. There the swinging gate was open and a lone apple tree was in bloom beside a young soldier, probably an SS guard, who lay dead, facedown, beneath a wooden sign reading ARBEIT MACHT FREI. Work makes freedom. Our troops had simply driven around the corpse — we could see the tanks and half-tracks within — and we followed.

We had not traveled far when my driver tromped on the brake, suddenly overpowered by the stench — excrement, quicklime, decaying flesh. It was crippling, and only grew worse when we finally drove on. That smell still revisits me without warning, usually propelled by a shock of some kind. At those instants, I imagine that the odor was so potent it somehow burned itself permanently into my olfactory nerves.

The first soldiers to enter the camp yesterday had come from the 100th Infantry Division, the same outfit whose reserve regiments had briefly seized Martin at Pforzheim. There were a few officers from divisional G-3 present now, but most of the troops I saw were with associated armored cavalry units and, a day later, still seemed at a loss over the scene. They stood beside their vehicles while perhaps a dozen of the former inmates in their threadbare striped uniforms teetered around near them, frightful otherworldly creatures. Many were more emaciated than I'd believed human beings could become, veritable skeletons with skin, whose wrists and knuckles bulged hugely within their hands, and whose eyes were sunk so far into their skulls they looked sightless. Several were barefoot, and a number had large spots of feces and urine on their clothing. All of them moved with almost inanimate slowness, staggering inches at a time, with no apparent destination. One of them, a man with arms like mop handles, turned to me as soon as I alighted from the jeep and lifted both hands in a shameless plea.

I still do not know what he wanted, food or just understanding, but I froze there, shocked again to my battered core, and gripped by revulsion. This man, and those around like him, frightened me more fundamentally than the dead on the battlefield, because I recognized them instantly as unmistakable tokens of the limitless degradation a human would endure in order to live.

It was some time before I noticed a lieutenant who'd

ventured forward to greet me. A tall, sandy-haired young man from divisional G-3, he gave his name as Grove and told me he had received a signal I was on the way. He motioned where I was looking.

"These are the lucky ones," he said. "Still on their feet."

"Who are they?" I asked.

"Jews," he answered. "Most of them. There are some Polish and French slave workers in one sub-camp. And a few of the Germans Hitler hated in another, mostly Gypsies and queers. But the greatest number of the folks here seem to be Jews. We've hardly sorted them all out. There's so much typhus here, we're afraid to do much."

I gasped then, choked almost, because I'd suddenly recognized the nature of a pearly mound a hundred yards behind the Lieutenant. It was made up of corpses, a nest of naked starved bodies, wracked and twisted in death. Instinctively, I moved a few steps that way. Grove caught my sleeve.

"You'll see a lot of that, if you care to."

Did I?

"I'd take a look," Grove said. "You'll want to tell people about this."

We began walking. Grove said there were probably 20,000 people held here now, many of them having arrived in the last few days. Some had been marched on foot from other concentration camps, with thousands dying along the way. Others, especially the sick, had been dumped here by the trainload. All had been crowded into makeshift wooden barracks, each about 150 feet long, in which there were only empty holes where the doors and windows were intended to be. I could not imagine what the savage winter had been like for the people already here, most of whom had had no more than their thin uniforms to protect them from the cold.

Outside the huts, there were open latrines, all over-flowing with human waste because they were plugged intermittently by corpses. American bombing of a pumping station a few weeks ago had put an end to running water, and the prisoners had not been fed with any regularity since early March, when the German commandant had cut off most meals as a cruel means of controlling the plagues of dysentery and typhus that had broken out. For the last week, while the camp was surrounded, those interned here had received nothing at all. Some of those we passed, with their scraps of clothing and impossibly vacant looks, begged for crumbs. Grove warned me not to oblige them. The troops who arrived yesterday had given candy and tinned rations to the first inmates they saw. Rioting had broken out and then several of the prisoners who'd won the grim struggle that ensued had died when their intestinal systems revolted as a result of their gorging.

The huts that had housed these people were miserable, dark and reeking. Piles of feces stood here and there on the straw-covered floors, and in the wood bunks, stacked like shelving, the sick and starving lay side by side with the dead. You could tell the living only by their occasional moans and because the lice were so numerous on the deceased that the bugs appeared to be a moving wave. Hundreds of inmates had died since yesterday, Grove said. The division's docs had arrived this morning but were at a loss for a treatment plan that had any chance of success for those already so sick or that would afford a sanitary means to avoid spreading the typhus, especially to American troops.

As a result, Grove said, we really had only marginal control of the situation. As a case in point, we came upon the remains of a female guard Grove had seen killed earlier this morning. A group of female internees had found her hiding under one of the buildings and had pulled her out by the hair. The guard had screamed and called the prisoners filthy names, while they stomped and spat upon her. Ultimately, several men arrived with discarded pieces of wood to beat her to death. The killings of the kapos — most of them thugs sent here from German penitentiaries — and the Wehrmacht guards the SS had deserted had been going on for a day now, Grove said. A water tower had been converted to a makeshift gallows yesterday, and several of our troops had volunteered and helped with the hangings.

Back near the yellow-brick administrative cluster, out of sight of the huts, was a square building that contained an enormous brick furnace at its center. Using two hands, Grove pried open the giant cast-iron doors, revealing two half-burned bodies. The eyeholes in one skull faced straight my way, and I flinched at the sight. In front of the oven was a huge butcher block, which some of the interrogated guards had admitted was used to crush the gold fillings from the teeth of the dead.

But death had come too swiftly of late for far too many in Balingen to dispose of them in one furnace. Everywhere — between the huts, along the camp's roads, around every corner we turned — were the bodies, ghastly grayish-white mounds of dead human beings in various states of decomposition, every body stripped naked and pitted by the appetites of vermin. The piles here were nothing, Grove said. At the edge of the camp, there was a giant pit full of human remains that the inmates still standing had been forced to drag there in the last few days. Someone from G-3, trying to find a way to communicate the scene to superiors, had begun counting the corpses heaped about the camp and had quit after reaching 8,000. For me, again and again, as I stared at these hills of human beings, so pathetic in their nudity, with their stick-figure limbs and exposed genitalia, I experienced the same panic, because I could not tell where one person began and ended in the pile.

Several times I noticed that the uppermost bodies in these mounds were marked with bloody gashes in their abdomens.

"Why?" I asked Grove. "What was in their stomachs that anyone wanted?"

The Lieutenant looked at me. "Food," he said.

My war without tears ended at Balingen. A moment after entering the only hut I visited, I rushed behind the building and vomited. Afterward, I found I was weeping. I tried for several minutes to gain control and eventually gave up and continued walking beside the Lieutenant, crying silently, which made my eyes ache in the strong sun. "Cried like a babe myself," he said at one point. "And I don't know if it's worse that I've stopped."

But it was not simply the suffering that had brought me to tears, or the staggering magnitude of the cruelty. It was a single thought that came to me after my first few minutes in the camp, another of those phrases that cycled maddeningly in my brain. The words were "There was no choice."

I had been on the Continent now for six months, half a year, not much longer than a semester in school, but it was impossible to recall the person I had been before. I had fought in terror, and I had learned to despise war. There was no glory in the savagery I saw. No reason. And surely no law. It was only brutality, scientifically perfected on both sides, in which great ingenuity had been deployed in the creation of giant killing machines. There was nothing to be loyal to in any of this and surely no cause for pride. But there in Balingen I cried for mankind. Because there had been no choice. Because knowing everything now, I saw this terrible war had to happen, with all its gore and witless destruction, and might well happen again. If human beings could do this, it seemed unfathomable how we could ever save our-selves. In Balingen, it was incontestable that cruelty was the law of the universe.

Amid all of this, I had lost any recollection of why I was there. When Grove walked into one of the yellow buildings near the gate, I expected him to expose another horror. Instead he led me down a cool stone stairway, into a rock cellar where an MP guarded an iron door. I could not imagine what the Germans had needed with a jail in a place like this, until I remembered that the camp had originally been a military post. This, apparently, was the stockade. There were eight cells here, each with stone walls and a barred front. Josef Kandel, the former camp commandant, today known as the Beast of Balingen, sat in one, erect in a spotless uniform but wearing no shoes, his legs chained. There were two SS officers in adjoining cells who'd been through rough questioning. One was in a heap on the floor; the other was largely toothless, with fresh blood still running down his chin. And in the far-thermost cell, on a small stool sat United States Army Major Robert Martin of the Office of Strategic Services. The lousy clothes which he'd stripped from one of the corpses as a disguise had been burned following his capture and replaced with a fresh officer's uniform, a russet shirt, under a sleeveless wool sweater, his oak leaves still on the right point of his collar.

Confronting him, I knew my features were swollen by weeping, but he was surely more changed than I. On the left side of his face, the skin shone, pink as sunrise, and his ear was a gnarly remnant melted to the side of his head, above which no hair grew for several inches. The end of his left sleeve was empty.

"Major," I said, "by the order of General Roland Tee-dle, you are arrested and will appear before a general court-martial as soon as it may be convened."

He smiled in response and waved the one good hand he had.

"Oh, come off it, Dubin. Get in here and talk to me."

His power of attraction was durable enough that I nearly did it before thinking. Even with one hand, Martin probably could subdue me and engineer yet another escape.

"I think not."

He laughed, shaking his head at length. "Then pull up a chair out there, if you must. But we should have a word."

I looked at Lieutenant Grove, who asked to brief me. As we walked down the dim hall, he whispered about what had transpired with the detail that had locked up

Martin yesterday. While they were escorting him to the cell, he had informed his jailers about a mountain two hundred miles from here, where he claimed the Germans had stored all the stolen treasures of Europe. Thousands of gold bars and jewels were hoarded in the caverns, including American ten- and twenty-dollar gold pieces. A U.S. Army detachment, he said, could fake its way in and out just by saying they had come to take custody of the American tender and head home with every man a millionaire. Martin had offered to lead the way. Informed of this story, Grove had regarded it as preposterous. Instead, when he'd contacted OSS, Winters had confirmed that only a few days ago the 358th Infantry Regiment had taken a salt mine at Kaiseroda in the Harz Mountains, where they discovered a vast booty stored in the underground channels. Paintings, gems, rooms full of currency and coins. Billions' worth. Grove's theory was that Kaiseroda had been Martin's objective all along.

"What does OSS think?"

"Those fellows never say what they think."

I weighed the possibility. It remained appealing to believe that Martin hadn't ever been intent on spying. Rather, he would resign from war and make himself rich forever. Perhaps. But I'd become reconciled to the fact that I'd never really understand Martin's motives. Only he could explain them, and no one could accept a word he said.

A few minutes later, at Grove's order, an MP lugged a heavy oak chair down the stone hall for me. I sat outside Martin's cell, and he brought his small stool close to the bars. He still appeared chipper, even though his steps were mincing in his leg irons.

"So," said Martin. "As you've long wanted. You have me in chains. I knew that was poppycock about house arrest."

"You are far better off than any other prisoner here, Major."

He accepted my rebuke with a buttoned-up smile. "Even down here, there's the smell." He was right, although it was remote enough that I could also detect the familiar rot bred by cellar moisture. "I had no idea what I was headed to. But your dogs were on my heels, Dubin. And with the camp about to be surrendered, I thought I'd mingle and depart. Once I was here, of course, it was plain that I'd have trouble passing as an inmate, even with my injuries. But I couldn't stand to leave. In three nights, Dubin, I killed four SS. They were easy pickings, trying to skulk out the back gate in the middle of the night. I just laid a trip wire." He gave a kind of disbelieving snort. "There won't be any killings that lie easier on my conscience."

As ever, I had no idea whether to believe him.

"And what about your plan to make yourself the new Croesus?" I asked. "Were you going to abandon that?"

"You don't believe that, do you, Dubin? It was a ploy, I admit. I was happy to make those boys think I could make them each into a Rockefeller. But we're two hundred miles away. If I was heading for Kaiseroda, I'd have been there by now."

"So where *were* you heading, Martin?"

"You want to know my plan? Is that why you're sitting here? Well, I shall tell you, Dubin. Gita knows, she'll tell you anyway when you find her. You do want to find her, don't you?" His hostility about Gita got the better of him, and he showed a quick vulpine grin. I was surprised and somewhat relieved by Martin's pettiness — it was a crack in his perfect edifice — but I felt little other reaction when he mentioned her name. Not today. "You can tell my friends in OSS what I was up to and save them some time. I'd rather talk to you anyway."

I gave him nothing by way of response.

"You know, Dubin, you needn't be so peeved with me. I'd have kept my word to you in Savy. About surrendering? I had every intention. You don't think I prefer this, do you?" He lifted his handless arm, so that the bright red stump, a distorted knobby shape, crept out of the sleeve. I could have debated with him about dropping me off when he knew I wouldn't find Algar at his headquarters, or the last two and a half months that Martin had spent on the run since Gita helped him flee from Oflag XII-D. But I discovered that I had one enduring gripe with Robert Martin over and above all the others.

"You took advantage of my regard for you, Major. You made me think you were a bright shining hero and used my admiration as the means to escape."

"All for the right reasons, Dubin."

"Which are?"

"I was doing a good thing, Dubin. You'll understand that. The Nazis, Dubin, have been working on a secret weapon that can destroy the world—"

I erupted in laughter. It was a starkly inappropriate sound given where we were and the noise ripped along the rock corridor.

"Laugh if you like, Dubin. But it's the truth. It's the one way the Germans could have won the war, even now may still hope to. The Allies have long known this. The Germans have had their best physicists laboring feverishly.

Gerlach. Diebner. Heisenberg. In the last several months, their principal workplace has been at a town called Hechingen, only a few miles down the road. Their efforts are rooted in the theorems of Einstein and others. They want to build a weapon, Dubin, that will break apart an atom. There's enough power there to blow an entire city off the map."

As usual, Martin seemed in complete thrall of his own entertaining nonsense. I was not much of a scientist, but I knew what an atom was and understood its infinitesimal size. Nothing of such minute dimension could conceivably be the killer force Martin was pretending.

"There is a race taking place now, Dubin. Between American intelligence and the Soviets. They each want to find the German scientists, their papers, and their matériel. Because whoever holds this weapon, Dubin, will rule the world. Ask your chums at OSS. Ask if this isn't true. Ask if there is not a group of physicists in Germany right now, working hand in glove with OSS. The code name is Alsos. Ask. They'll tell you they're going after these physicists even while we speak."

"This is where you were headed? Hechingen?"

"Yes. Yes."

I leaned back against the hard chair. Martin's dark hair was tousled over his brow and he had an eager boyish look, despite the relative immobility of the features on the florid side of his face. I was amazed at the magnitude of what he was confessing, probably unwittingly.

"If what you're saying is so, if all this Buck Rogers talk about a secret weapon bears any speck of truth, they'll hang you, Major. And well they should."

"Hang me?"

"Surely, you aren't working for OSS. Of that I'm certain. So it's quite obvious you were going to Hechingen to capture these scientists for the Soviets and spirit them off to the Russians."

"That's false, Dubin. Entirely false! I want neither side to prevail. I want neither Communists nor capitalists to stand astride the globe."

"And how then is it that you know all this, Major? The plans of the Americans? And the Soviets? If you are not at work for the Russians, how do you know their intentions?"

"Please, Dubin. I was informed of all of these matters by OSS last September. When I returned to London. But certainly not by the Soviets. I've told you, Dubin. I belong now to neither side."

"Would the Soviets say that?"

"I have no idea what they'd say. But listen to me. Listen. I was going to Hechingen, Dubin. But not for any country. My goal was destruction. Of the whole lot. The matériel. The papers. And the men. Let their dreadful secret die with them. Don't you see? This is a second chance to contain all the grief in Pandora's box. If this weapon survives, no matter who has it, there will be constant struggle, the victor will lord it over the vanquished, the vanquished will plot to obtain it, and in the end it is no matter which side has it, because if it exists, it will be used. There has never been a weapon yet invented that hasn't been deployed. Men can call that whatever they care to, even curiosity, but this device will be released on the globe. Let the world be safe, Dubin."

He was clever. But I'd long known that. No one — not Teedle, not me — would ever be able to prove he was working for the Soviets rather than for the sake of world peace. He and Wendell Willkie. It was, as I would have predicted, a perfect cover story.

"Dubin, find Gita. Find Gita. She will tell you that what I am saying is true. These are my plans. And there is still time to carry them out. No more than a few days. American forces will reach Hechingen shortly, depending on how the fighting goes. It's only a few miles up the road. Find Gita, Dubin."

How artful it was. How inevitable. Find Gita. She will persuade you to join my cause. And open the door to yet one more escape.

"She is here, Dubin. In the Polish sub-camp. There are Jews there from her town. She is nursing them. Go to the Polish camp. You'll find her. She will tell you this is true."

"No." I stood. "No more lies. No more fantasies. No more running away. We're going to Frankfurt. As soon as the armored vehicle arrives. Tell your story there, Martin. You must think I'm a child."

"I speak the truth to you, Dubin. Every word. Every word. Ask Gita. Please."

I turned my back on him while he was still assailing me with her name.

31. GITA LODZ, OF COURSE

This woman, Gita Lodz, is, of course, my mother.

I have no slick excuse for the months it took me to catch on, or for the elaborate tales I told myself during that period to hold the truth at bay. I guess people will inevitably cling to the world they know. Bear Leach's eventual explanation was more generous: "We are always our parents' children."

But sitting in the Tri-Cities Airport, reading the last of what my father had written, I had understood the conclusion of his account this way: Deceived yet again by Gita Lodz, Dad had proceeded to his final ruin and let Martin go. And then somehow, even while my father was absorbing the desolation of his most catastrophic mistake, he must have met this other woman at Balingen, Gella Rosner, and been transformed. It was love on the rebound, a lifeline to the man drowning.

In retrospect, all of that seems laughable. But for months I accepted it, and was frustrated and confused by only one omission: Dad never mentioned the courageous young

Polish Jewess I'd been brought up to believe he instantly fell in love with in the camp.

As for Barrington Leach, from the time I asked him what had become of Gita Lodz, he had realized how misled I was. Yet he made no effort to correct me, although I often visited with him, trying to glean every detail he recalled about my father's story. Bear was a person of gentleness and wisdom, and, given all his caveats at the start, clearly had promised himself that he would tell me only as much as I seemed willing to know. He presented me with the recorded facts. It was up to me to reach the obvious conclusions. Bear kept his mouth shut, not so much for my parents' sake as for mine.

One day in April 2004, my sister phoned me at home to discuss our mother's health, which was declining. Sarah wanted my views on whether she should accelerate her plans to visit in June around the time of my parents' anniversary, which had been an especially hard period for Mom in 2003 in the wake of Dad's death. I knew my parents' marriage had lasted almost fifty-eight years. They'd made no secret of their wedding date, June 16, 1945. Yet until that moment, I'd never connected the dots. I stood with the telephone in my hand, jaw agape, while Sarah shouted my name and asked if I was still there.

By then, it had become my habit to see Barrington Leach once a month. I went mostly for the pleasure of his company, but my excuse to write off the expenses was that Bear was helping me edit Dad's typescript for publication. (Because of the scam I'd run on my mother and sister, my plan, at that point, was to tell them Dad's account was actually my work, based on my lengthy research.) When I saw Bear, I'd hand over the most recent pages and receive his comments about what I'd done the previous month. Not long after he was wheeled into the front room for our visit in late April, I told him what had occurred to me while I was on the phone with my sister the week before.

"I just realized a few days ago that my parents got married right before Dad's court-martial. Did you know that?"

"I should say so," answered Bear. "I'm the one who arranged it."

"Arranged the wedding?"

"Not their meeting," said Bear. "But getting the military authorities to allow them to wed, yes, that was my doing. Your father was concerned, quite rightly, that when he was convicted, as was inevitable, he would be transferred immediately to a military prison in the U.S. He was therefore desperate to marry before the proceedings, so that your mother, as a war bride, would have the right to immigrate to the States. She had remained an inmate in a displaced persons camp that had been erected after burning down the Balingen huts. The conditions were far better, of course, but she was anything but free. It required countless petitions to the Army and the Occupation Authorities, but eventually your mother and a rabbi, also held at Balingen, were allowed to visit your father for half an hour at Regensburg Castle for their wedding. I was the best man. In spite of the circumstances, it was quite touching. They appeared very much in love."

Bear said only that and glanced down to the pages I'd handed him, allowing me to work my way through this information in relative privacy. Despite the horrors of the camp, or Mom's unfamiliarity with the military, or even her limited English at the time, someone as innately canny as she was couldn't possibly have failed to grasp the essentials of Dad's situation. She knew he was under arrest, and as such, had to be gravely concerned for her new husband. Clearly, then, Mom recalled a great deal more about Dad's court-martial than she'd been willing to acknowledge to me. Yet even at that moment, my first impulse was to accept her reluctance as a way of honoring Dad's desire for silence.

But somehow my mind wandered back to the question that had perplexed me for half a year now. Why did Dad say he desperately hoped his children would never hear his story? Out the paned windows of Northumberland Manor's sitting room, there was perfect light on the red maple buds just showing the first sign of ripening, and beholding them with the intense museum attention Dad wrote of, a moment of concentrated sight, I found the truth hanging out there, too. It was simple. My father's remark about keeping this from his children was not philosophical. It was practical. Dad had not wanted the truth to emerge at his trial, or to survive it, because it would have imperiled his wife and the lie she was to be obliged to live. That is why it would have been a disaster to call Gita Lodz as a witness. That is why he hoped we never heard the story—because that silence would have meant they had made a life as husband and wife.

Bear's head was wilted in his wheelchair while he read, and I reached out to softly clutch his spotted hand and the fingers crooked with disease.

"She's my mother. Right? Gita Lodz?"

Bear started, as if I'd woken him. His cloudy eyes that still reflected the depth of the ages settled on me, and his lower jaw slid sideways in his odd lopsided smile. Then he deliberated, an instant of lawyerly cool.

"As I have said, Stewart, I was not there when you were born."

"But the woman you saw my father marry—that was Gita Lodz?"

"Your father never said that to me," he answered. "Anything but. It would have compromised me severely to know that, inasmuch as I had spent months begging the military authorities for permission to allow David to marry a concentration camp survivor of another name. I would have been obliged to correct the fraud being perpetrated. I believe that was why he never contacted me once we were back in the U.S.A.—so that I didn't have to deal with any second thoughts about that."

Despite failing on the uptake for months, I now bounced rapidly along the path of obvious conclusions. I instantly comprehended why Gita Lodz, hero of the French underground, came here pretending to be the former Gella Rosner (whose name was Americanized as Gilda), David Dubin's war bride, allegedly saved from the Nazi hell called Balingen. In the spring of 1945, my parents had every reason to believe that OSS would never have permitted the sidekick of Robert Martin, suspected Soviet spy, to enter the United States. Indeed, as someone who had repeatedly abetted Martin's escapes, Gita stood a good chance of being prosecuted if OSS and Teedle had gotten their hands on her. A new identity was the only safe course. One that could never be disproved amid that ocean of corpses. One more role to add to the many the would-be Bernhardt had already played flawlessly. And one that guaranteed that Gilda would be welcome in David's family. A Jewish bride. As his parents wished. And as Gita herself, when she was younger, had once wanted to be.

And, probably not insignificantly, it was also a weighty declaration for my father. When I had changed my last name in 1970, Dad had never really responded to my implication that I was reversing an act of renunciation from decades before. There was only one thing he cared to be clear about.

"Do not doubt, Stewart," he said to me once, "that Balingen made me a Jew." Since I knew he would never describe what he'd witnessed there, I did not pursue the remark. On reflection, I took it as one more way of telling me how devoted he was to my mother. And even now I'm not completely certain of the precise nature of the transformation he was alluding to. I don't know if he meant that he had realized, as had been true for so many in Germany, that there was no escape from that identity, or, rather, as I tend to suspect, that he owed the thousands annihilated there the reverence of not shirking the heritage that had condemned them. Certainly, there was a touching homage in Gita's new persona, which allowed one of the millions who perished to be not only remembered, but revived. But I see that Dad was also making an emphatic statement about himself, about what an individual could stand for, or hope for, against the forces of history.

I, on the other hand, who had proudly reclaimed Dubinsky, who sent my daughters to Hebrew school and insisted we have shabbas dinner every Friday night, I now reposed in the nouveau-Federal sitting room of a Connecticut nursing home realizing that by the strict traditions of a religion that has always determined a child's faith by that of his mother, I am not really Jewish.

★★★

These are the last pages of my father's account:

I emerged again from the dungeon darkness into the brilliant day and terrible reek of Balingen. I suppose that humans recoil on instinct from the rankness of decaying flesh and I had to spend a moment fighting down my sickness again.

Grove was waiting for me. I thought he wanted to know how it had gone with Martin, but he had other news.

"Roosevelt is dead," he said. "Truman is President."

"Don't be a card."

"It's just on Armed Services Radio. They say FDR had a stroke. I kid you not." I had been raised to worship Roosevelt. My mother, who regarded the President as if he were a close relation, would be devastated. And then I looked to the nearest mound of broken corpses. At every one of these instants of paradox, I reflexively expected my understanding of life to become deeper, only to find myself more confused.

I asked the MP who'd accompanied me if we had an estimated arrival time on the half-track that would carry Martin back, but the news about Roosevelt's death seemed to have brought everything to a halt for a while. Nonetheless, I wouldn't countenance the idea of spending the night within Balingen. Whatever hour the convoy arrived, I said, I wanted Martin transferred. We could bivouac with the 406th Armored Cavalry a mile or two away, nearer Hechingen.

An hour or so later, vehicles reached the camp, but not the ones I awaited. They carried the first Red Cross workers. I watched with a certain veteran distance as these men and women, accustomed to working tirelessly to save lives, began to absorb the enormity of what they were confronting. A young French doctor passed out when he saw the first hill of bodies. Inexplicably, one of the wraiths moving vacantly through the camp, an elderly man who had somehow lived to liberation, fell dead only a few feet from the unconscious doctor. As with everything else, we all seemed bereft of the power to react. If the sky fell, as Henny Penny feared, we might have had more to say.

Many of the American infantrymen were standing in little groups, speculating about what the President's death might mean with regard to the Nazis' final surrender and the war in the Pacific. I could see that the shock of the news was welcome in its way, a chance to put where they were out of their minds for a while.

The half-track I awaited, a captured German 251 that had been repainted, finally appeared at 2:30 in the afternoon. Only a minute or so after that, Grove came to find me. We were preparing to load Martin. He would be in leg irons with at least two guns trained on him at all times.

"There's an inmate looking for you," Grove said. "She asked for you by name."

I knew who it was. A shamed and exhausted fantasy that Gita might appear had circulated through my mind, in just the way it had for months, even as I'd tried to banish it.

"Polish?" I asked.

"Yes, from the Polish camp. She looks quite well," he added, "but there are several young women here who look all right." He made no further comment on how these girls might have managed.

She was in the regimental office that had been established in the largest of the yellow buildings the SS had abandoned earlier in the week. The room was empty, paneled to half height in shellacked tongue-and-groove, with a broken schoolhouse fixture hanging overhead from a frayed wire. Beneath it, Gita Lodz sat on a single wooden chair, the only furnishing in the room. She sprang to her feet as soon as she saw me. She was still in the gray uniform the nuns had given her in Bastogne, although it was frayed at both sleeves and soiled, and bore a yellow star pinned above the breast.

"Doo-bean," she said, and with the name, more than the sight of her, my poor heart felt as if it might explode. I had no need to ask how she knew I was here. She would have maintained her own surveillance on the building where Martin was jailed.

I dragged another wooden chair in from the hall, taking a seat at least a dozen feet from her. We faced each other like that, with no barrier between us but distance, both of us with our feet flat on the worn floor. I was too proud to lose my composure, and waited with my face trembling, until I could drag out a few words.

"So we meet again in hell," I said to her in French. I felt my heart and mind pirouetting again with the unaccountable extremes in life. Here I was with this gallant, deceitful woman, full of wrath and anguish, while I was still reeling from the reek of atrocity, sitting where some of history's greatest monsters had been in charge only a week ago. Roosevelt was dead. I was alive.

Although I did not ask, she told me about the last several days. Martin and she had snuck in through the same breach in the rear fence the SS guards were using to slip away. After only a matter of hours, she recognized four people she had known in Pilzkoba and last seen on the trucks the Nazis had loaded for deportation to Lublin. One of them was a girl a year younger than Gita, a playmate, who was the last of a family of six. Two younger siblings, a brother and a sister, had been snatched from her parents' arms when they arrived at a camp called Buchenwald and were never seen again. There the next year her father had been beaten to death by a kapo right in front of her, only a few weeks after her mother had succumbed to pneumonia. But still this girl from Pilzkoba had survived. She had marched here hundreds of miles with no food, her feet wrapped in rags, a journey on which another of her brothers had perished. Yet she had arrived at Balingen in relative health. And then yesterday she had died of one of the plagues raging through the camp.

"In Normandy, Dubin, when we helped to direct the Allied troops through the hedgerows, I saw battlefields so thick with corpses that one could not cross without walking on the bodies. I told myself I would never see anything worse, and now I see this. And there are souls here, Dubin, who say the Germans have created places worse yet. Is that possible? *N'y a-t-il jamais un fond, même dans les océans les plus profonds?*" Is there no bottom even to the darkest ocean?

With that, she cried, and her tears, of course, unleashed my own. Seated a dozen feet apart, we both wept, I with my face in my hands.

"There is so much I do not understand," I finally said, "and will never understand. Here looking at you, I ask myself how it can seem possible, amid this suffering, that the worst pain of all is heartbreak?"

"Do you criticize me, Dubin?"

"Need I?" I answered with one of those French sayings she loved to quote. "*Conscience coupable n'a pas besoin d'accusateur*." A guilty conscience needs no accuser. "But I am sure you feel no shame."

She tossed her bronze curls. She was thin and sallow. Yet unimaginably, she remained beautiful. How was that possible either?

"You are bitter with me," she said.

"You decimated me with your lies."

"I never lied to you, Dubin."

"Call it what you like. I told you secrets and you used them against me, against my country. All for Martin."

"*Entre l'arbre et l'écorce il faut ne pas mettre le doigt.*" One shouldn't put a finger between the bark and the tree. In our parlance, she was caught between a rock and a hard place. "This is not justice. What you were about to do — what you will do now. Martin placed in chains by his nation? He has risked his life for America, for the Allies, for freedom, a thousand times. He is the bravest man in Europe."

"The Americans believe he is a spy for the Soviets."

She wrenched her eyes shut in anguish.

"The things they have asked you to accept," she murmured. "*C'est impossible*. Martin despises Stalin. He was never a Stalinist, and after Stalin's pact with Hitler, Martin regarded him as the worse of the two. He calls Stalin and Hitler the spawn of the same devil."

"And what then is it he has been doing all these months, defying his orders, running from OSS, from Teedle, and from me? Has he told you his goal?"

"Now? Lately, he has, yes. Up to the time of the Ardennes, I believed what he told you—that he was on assignment for OSS, as he has always been. He would not say where he was to go, but that was not unusual."

"And do you believe him now?"

"I think what he says is what he believes."

When I asked her to say what that was, she looked down to her small hands folded in her lap, clearly reluctant even now to disclose Martin's secrets. And still, I cautioned myself that the reaction I saw might be another pose.

"Since I took him from the hospital at Saint-Vith," she finally said, "he has maintained the same thing. Martin says that the Nazis are making a machine that can destroy the world. He wants to kill all who understand its workings and bury their secret with them forever. It is madness, but it is madness in Martin's style. It is glorious. He claims this is his destiny. For the most part, I have felt like, what is his name, the little one who walks beside Don Quixote?"

"Sancho Panza."

"Yes, I am Sancho Panza. There is no telling Martin this is lunacy. And I have stopped trying, Dubin. The scientists are at Hechingen. Martin has established that much. But a single device that could reduce London to cinders? It is fantasy, like so much that Martin tells himself. But it will surely be the last."

"Because?"

"Because he will die trying to do this. A man with one hand? His left leg is still barely of any use. The pain is so severe at night from the nerves that were burned that he sheds tears in his sleep. And he has no one to help him."

"Except you."

"Not I. I will have no part of this, Dubin. He does not ask it. And I would not go. I have been a member of the resistance, not a vigilante. He has no allies in this, no organization. But it is paramount to him nonetheless."

"But not because of the Soviets?"

"Dubin, it is how he wishes to die. Whether or not he admits as much to himself, death is clearly his goal. He is maimed and in unending pain. But now when he dies, as he surely will, he will believe he was doing no less than assuring the safety of the world. It is a glory as great as the one he has always wished for. That is what you would deny him. He says that the Americans will hang him instead, if he is caught. True?"

I had told Martin as much a few hours earlier, and with time to calculate, I had decided it was no exaggeration. The story Martin had told me would be enough to send him to the gallows. Whether he was working for the Soviets, as most of his superiors would believe, or as the new Flash Gordon, he had admitted that he was an American soldier trying to undermine American forces and deny them a weapon regarded as essential to the security of the United States. That would, at a minimum, make him a traitor and a mutineer. The law would need to sift no finer.

"And is that just, Dubin?" she asked, once I'd nodded.

"Just? Compared to anything that has happened in this place, it is just. Martin disobeyed orders. He brought this on himself."

"But is that what you wish to see, Dubin? Martin trembling at the end of a rope?"

"That is not my choice, Gita. I must do my duty."

"So the guards are claiming here. They did as ordered."

"Please."

"I ask again if that is what you would choose for him."

"I dare not choose a destiny for Martin, Gita. The law does not allow it. It would say I am hopelessly biased by jealousy. And in that, the law is surely wise."

"Jealousy?" She looked at me blankly until my meaning reached her. "Dubin, I have told you many times, you have no need to be jealous of Martin."

"And that proved to be another lie. You slept with me to learn what I would find out about Martin and then deserted me to rescue him. Jealousy is the least of it."

She had drawn herself straight. The black eyes were a doll's now, hard as glass.

"You think that is why I slept with you?"

"I do."

She looked askance and made as if to spit on the floor. "I misjudged you, Dubin."

"Because you thought I was more gullible?"

She actually lifted a hand toward her heart, not far from where the star was pinned.

"What do you believe, Dubin? That I am a statue and cannot be hurt? I value your esteem, Dubin. More, apparently, than you can understand. I cannot tolerate your scorn."

"I admire your strength, Gita. I still admire that."

She closed her eyes for a time.

"Be angry, Dubin. Be hurt. Think I was too casual with your feelings. But please do not believe I would make love to you with such ugly intentions. Do you see me as a harlot? Because I am a harlot's daughter?"

"I see you as you are, Gita. As someone who knows how to do what she has to." I repeated Winters' story about the German officer in Marseilles to whom she'd succumbed in order to win details of the London bombing. And even as I recounted the OSS's sniggering about her sleeping with the enemy, I realized I had awaited this moment for months so that she would tell me it was untrue. She did not.

"*Qui n'entend qu'une cloche n'entend qu'un son.*" He who hears one bell hears only one sound. There were, she meant, two sides of the story. "Something like that, Dubin, is so easy to judge from a distance."

I mocked her with another proverb. "*Qui veut la fin veut les moyens?*" He who wants the ends wants the means.

"Is that not true? In this place, Dubin, there are thousands who have done far worse to save just their own lives, let alone hundreds of others. Thousands probably were spared because of what I did. There are many mistakes I have made, Dubin, for which I forgive myself less freely. I was young. It was a poor idea only because I did not understand that even when the soul wears armor, it remains fragile. I thought, a cock is just another thing, Dubin. And Martin, by the way, knew nothing of this in advance and begged me never to consider such an act again, for my own sake as much as for his. But let me tell you, Dubin, what was the most confounding part. This man, this Nazi, this officer, he was kind to me. He was a man with some goodness in him. And to learn that about him on false pretenses — that was the most difficult part."

"As I am sure you have said the same of me."

"It is not the same, Dubin! I will not leave this place with you believing that." She continued to sit tall, her face folded in fury. "I care for you, Dubin. Greatly. You know that. Look at me here. You cannot tell me that even four meters away from me, you cannot feel that? I know you can."

"And that is why you crushed my heart. Because you cared for me?"

"My only excuse is one you must acknowledge as true. I left you before you left me."

"As you say. That is an excuse. I believed I loved you."

"You never spoke to me of love."

"You were gone before I could. But please do not pretend that would have made any difference. What I felt and what I showed could not have been clearer with a name applied. You rewarded my love with lies. Until I came here, I thought that was the cruelest thing in life."

"Yes," she said. "Such a thing is unkind. But understand, Dubin, please understand. Could I have stayed and loved you and watched as you took Martin off in chains to be hanged? He gave me back my life, Dubin. Should I have quietly condemned him for the sake of my own happiness?"

"I do not believe that is how you thought of it."

"How I thought of it, Dubin, is that a man like you, a proper bourgeois gentleman, would never make your life with a Polish peasant with no schooling. That is how I thought of it. You would return to your America, to your law books, to your intended. That is how I thought of it. I dream of children, as you dream. I dream of being as far from war as a happy home is. For me that is a dream that will probably never come true."

"These are excuses."

"This is the truth, Dubin!" She shook her small hands at me in rage, again in tears. "You say I would not forsake

Martin for you. But you surely have your own idols. If I had stayed and begged you not to do your duty with Martin, would you have refused?"

"I would like to believe that my answer is 'Yes.' But I doubt it. I am afraid, Gita, I would have done anything for you."

"And who would you be after that, Dubin, without your precious principles?"

"I do not know. But it would be who I had chosen to become. I could tell myself that. I could tell myself I had chosen love and that in a life as harsh as ours, it must come first."

She was motionless, staring at me in that way she had, a look so intense I thought it might turn me to flame. Then she asked if I had a cloth, meaning a handkerchief. She took it from me and returned to her chair to clear her nose. Finally, she sat forward and clasped her hands.

"Do you mean this? What you have just said? Do you speak from the heart, Dubin, or is this merely a lawyer's argument?"

"It is the truth, Gita. Or was. It is in the past."

"Must it be? We have our moment, Dubin. Here. Now. It can all be as you would like. As I would like. We will have love. We will have each other. But let him go, Dubin. Let Martin go and I will stay with you. I will tend your hearth and cook your meals and bear your brats, Dubin. I will. I want to. But let him go."

"'Let him go'?"

"Let him go."

"I cannot even imagine how I could do that."

"Oh, Dubin, you are far too clever to say that. You would not need an hour's reflection to concoct a scheme that would work. Dubin, please. Please." She walked to my chair and then put one knee on the floor. "Please, Dubin. Dubin, choose this. Choose love. Choose me. If you send Robert to the hangman, it will stand between us forever. Here in hell, Dubin, you can choose this one good thing. Let Quixote fight his windmill. Do not make him die in disgrace. He has lived to be a hero. It would be worse than torture for him to die known as a traitor."

"You would do anything for him, wouldn't you?"

"He saved my life, Dubin. He has shown me the way to every good thing I believe in. Even my love for you, Dubin."

"Would you pledge your love to me, give up your life, just to see him die one way rather than another?"

"Dubin, please. Please. This is my life, too. You are precious to me. Dubin. Please, Dubin." Slowly she reached for my hand. My entire body surged at her touch and even so, I thought: Once more, she will engineer his escape. But I loved her. As Biddy had said, it was pointless to try to reason about that.

With my hand in hers, she wept. "Please, Dubin," she said. "Please."

"You have the personality of a tyrant, Gita. You wish to turn me into a supplicant so you will think better of yourself."

Despite the tears, she managed a smile. "So now you know my secret, Dubin."

"You will mock me for being bourgeois."

"I shall," she said. "I promise to. But I will be thrilled, in spite of myself." She lifted her face to me. "Take me to America, Dubin. Make me your wife. Let Martin go. Let Martin be the past. Let me be the future. Please." She kissed my hand now, a hundred times, clutching it between hers and embracing every knuckle. What she proposed was mad, of course. But no madder than what I had watched men do routinely for months now. No madder than parachuting into a town under siege. No madder than combat, where soldiers gave up their lives for inches of ground and the grudges of generals and dictators. In this place, love, even the remotest chance of it, was the only sane choice. I pulled her hands to my mouth and kissed them once. Then I stood, looking down on her.

"When you betray me, Gita, as I know you will, I will have nothing. I will have turned my back on my country, and you will be gone. I will have no honor. I will believe in nothing. I will be nothing."

"You will have me, Dubin. I swear. You will have love. I swear, Dubin. You will not be betrayed. I swear. I swear."

Gita Lodz is my mother.

32. BEAR: END

When I first read Dad's account, the end had seemed
disappointingly abrupt. Not only did I think there
was no mention of my mother, there was also no
recounting of what had happened with Martin. Supposedly
writing to explain things to his lawyer, Dad was silent
about whether Martin fled, as Dad claimed, or had been
murdered, as Bear feared.

According to the testimony at the court-martial, late on
April 12, 1945, Martin had been loaded at gunpoint into
the armored vehicle Dad had awaited. In convoy with the
MPs, they traveled only a mile or two beyond the perimeter of Balingen toward Hechingen, to the bivouac of the
406th Armored Cavalry. There Martin was chained to a
fence post before a tent was erected around him. At
roughly 3:00 a.m., my father appeared and told the two
MPs guarding the Major that Dad could not sleep and
would spell them for two hours. When they returned Dad
was there and Martin was gone. My father told the
guards, without further explanation, he had let Martin go.

A day later he was back in Frankfurt to admit the same thing to Teedle.

The first time I came back to visit Leach in Hartford, in November 2003, I got right to the point.

"What Dad wrote doesn't answer your question."

"My 'question'?"

"Whether my father murdered Martin once he freed him."

"Oh, that." Bear gave his dry, gasping laugh. "Well, what do you think, Stewart?"

Before I'd read the pages Bear gave me, his suspicions were astonishing, but once I understood that Dad had abandoned everything for Gita Lodz, I comprehended Leach's logic. As my father had told her, if she betrayed him again, he would have had nothing. With Martin dead, on the other hand, she could never rejoin him. Certainly, Dad had no need to fear discovery if he murdered Martin. There was virtually no chance one more body would ever be identified among the thousands decomposing in the massive pit at the edge of Balingen. Dad was armed, of course. And after combat, he was sadly experienced in killing.

In other words, Dad had motive and opportunity, which I'd listened to prosecutors for years label as the calling cards of a strong circumstantial murder case. But my faith in my father's decency, which even now seemed as tangible to me as his body, remained unchanged. Realizing everything I hadn't known about his life, murder still seemed beyond him, and I told Leach that. Bear was very pleased to hear it, favoring me with his funny sideways smile.

"Good for you, Stewart."

"But am I right?"

"Of course. It became critical for me to determine the answer to my own question, especially after the verdict and sentence. Quite frankly, Stewart, if there was a worse crime to be discovered, I might have thought twice about pressing ahead with appeals. Five years for the murder of another officer, even a wanted one, was not a disappointing result, if that's what had actually occurred."

"But it turned out Martin was alive?"

"When your father last saw him? Without doubt. Where are my papers?" The Redweld folder, Bear's treasure chest, as I thought of it, rested against the chrome spokes of his wheelchair, and I handed it up. Leach's bent fingers stumbled through the pages. He would touch a paper several times before he could grab it and then bring it almost to his nose to read. "No," he'd say, and the process would begin again, with his apologies to me for the agonizing pace. "Here!" he said at last.

LABORATORY

60TH EVACUATION HOSPITAL

APO #758, U.S. ARMY

APO

May 16, 1945

REPORT OF AUTOPSY

C-1145

NAME: (Name, Rank, Unit & Organization Unknown)
AGE: Approx. 42   RACE: White   SEX: Male
NATIVITY: Unknown
ADMITTED: Not admitted to this hospital
DIED: Approx. May 9, 1945
AUTOPSY: 1230, May 13, 1945

CLINICAL DIAGNOSIS

1. Malnutrition, dehydration, severe

PATHOLOGICAL DIAGNOSES

MISCELLANEOUS: Malnutrition, dehydration, severe burns, third degree, partially healed

PRESENT ILLNESS: This patient was found dead sitting on a divan in the Hochshaus Hotel in Berlin, Germany (Grid Q-333690), upon the arrival of U.S. troops in that sector on or about May 11, 1945. He was dressed in the uniform of a United States Army Officer, with oak leaf cluster on his right shirt collar, but otherwise without insignia or identity tags. He evidently had been held as a prisoner for a period of time and had starved to death.

PHYSICAL EXAMINATION: Examination at the cemetery revealed no fresh external wounds. Patient appeared to be recovering from third-degree burns several months old; his left hand is missing.

AUTOPSY FINDINGS

The body is that of a well-developed but markedly emaciated male, about 40 years of age, measuring 70 inches long and weighing approximately 105 pounds. Rigor and livor are absent. The head is covered with long black hair, except for an area of scarring above the left ear,

upon which most of the helix has been lost,
apparently due to burning. The anterior portion
of his deeply sunken eyes is below the lateral
portion of the orbital margin. A beard, several
weeks' growth, covers his face and contains some
gray hairs in front of each ear. All of his teeth
are present. The rib markings are very prominent
and the thin anterior abdominal wall rests only
slightly above his spine.

Evidence of recent third-degree burns also
appears on the distal portion of the leg and
thorax; scar tissue remains livid and taut, and
appears abraded in several places. The left hand
is absent below the wrist. The uneven stump
reveals similar burn scarring, suggesting
the hand may have been lost in an explosion or
amputated thereafter. Suture scars indicate
recent surgical reparation.

PRIMARY INCISION: The usual incision reveals
one millimeter of subcutaneous adipose tissues,
thinning muscles, normally placed organs in the
smooth abdominal cavity, and normal pericardial
and pleural cavities.

GASTROINTESTINAL TRACT: The stomach
contains only a slight amount of light mucus, the
bowel is empty, and a minimal amount of fecal
material is in the colon. All the mesenteric
vessels are prominent on the colon.

NOTE: Nearly all of the adipose tissue
throughout the body has disappeared, and is
diminished even around the kidneys and heart.
The tissues display lack of turgor indicative of
severe dehydration. The absence of recent
external trauma and only mucus in the
gastrointestinal tract would seem to indicate
that this man died of malnutrition and
dehydration.

s/ Nelson C. Kell
Captain,
Medical Corps
Laboratory Officer

"I received that in June 1945," Bear said, "from your father's doctor friend, Cal Echols, only a few days after the court-martial concluded. Cal had been transferred to headquarters hospital in Regensburg and visited your father often before and after the trial. Since I had been on the lookout for Martin from the start, I had asked Cal to inform me discreetly if he ever heard reports of a one-handed burn victim. My thought was that Martin might seek medical treatment. Instead, this autopsy had come across Cal's desk as the object of considerable curiosity.

"When U.S. troops entered Berlin on May 11, the Soviets had directed the Americans to this body, citing it as another German atrocity. But you'll note the pathologist's conclusion that death had occurred within the last seventy-two hours. The Germans had surrendered Berlin to the Russians on May 2. This man didn't die until a week later. The American doctors suspected that the Russians, not the Germans, had had custody of him."

"The Russians killed Martin?"

"Well, that certainly was how it appeared. After several weeks Graves Registration still had had no success in identifying the remains. But the circumstances of the death, particularly the involvement of the Soviets, spurred continuing interest and finally had led the autopsy to be passed up the line in the Medical Corps. After a good deal of thought, I decided to report this development to General Teedle."

"Teedle?"

"I'd had contact with him now and then. We did not get off on a particularly good foot. I thought he was going to get out of his chair and throttle me during his cross-examination. But Teedle had remained preoccupied with your father's case, regarding it as totally enigmatic. He had let me know that he would always hear me out if I came up with any extenuating evidence. And I'll give Teedle credit. He recognized the prime significance of the autopsy at once."

"Which was?"

"Well, it was hard to believe that the Soviets would have killed a loyal agent, especially by starving him to death. There were many alternatives—perhaps Martin had fallen out with his Soviet masters—but with your father now under a prison sentence, Teedle recognized that the autopsy raised plausible doubts that Martin was a spy. After he turned it over to the OSS, they dispatched a team to identify the body. As usual, OSS wanted to keep the results of its subsequent investigation to themselves, but Teedle would not stand for that.

"As it developed, everything Martin had said to your father about the Alsos Mission was essentially true. OSS had recruited teams of physicists who were racing across

Germany, hoping to reach the German atomic scientists before the Soviets. And Hechingen, where the top German physicists had been sent from Berlin, was indeed Alsos' foremost target. There's been a good deal of writing about it."

Out of his folder, Bear handed me photocopied sections from several histories explaining the Alsos Mission, which I scanned. Hechingen was in the sector of Germany where the Free French were leading the combat effort, but because of the atomic secrets that rested with the German scientists, a large American force cut in front of the French without permission and entered Hechingen on April 24, 1945. They seized Werner Heisenberg's laboratory, secreted in a former wool mill on Haigerlocherstrasse above the town center, where they found several of Germany's foremost physicists, including Otto Hahn, Carl von Weizsäcker, and Max von Laue, along with two tons of uranium, two tons of heavy water, and ten tons of carbon. Hunting around, the Americans also located the records of the scientists' research secreted in a cesspool behind Weizsäcker's home.

"Heisenberg," Bear said, "the foremost physicist in the group, and Gerlach, were missing. Under OSS interrogation, their colleagues soon explained that Heisenberg and Gerlach had fled about ten days earlier, in the wake of a strange incident. A lone one-handed man had been apprehended about to detonate an enormous explosive charge, which would have brought down the brick mill building, killing everyone inside it. The would-be bomber had discarded his dog tags and claimed at first to be French, but when the SS arrived, they identified his uniform, which bore no insignia, except for an oak leaf cluster, as that of an American officer. Given his mission, and the fact that he had slipped into town well in advance of American forces, the SS concluded he could only be OSS.

"The German scientists at Hechingen had foreseen that the Allies, including the Soviets, would want to capture them to learn about their research. This was disheartening on one level, because they knew they were doomed to a lengthy captivity, but they had assumed that whoever caught them—and they much preferred the Americans or the British—was bound to keep them alive in order to absorb their knowledge. The implication of this attempted bombing was far more distressing, since it suggested that the Americans instead were intent on killing them all. Hahn and Weizsäcker and Laue decided to remain with their families and accept their fate. But Heisenberg and Gerlach and one or two others literally ran for their lives, only to be tracked down by the Americans within ten days."

Bear's photocopies described Heisenberg's apprehension. Naturally none of the scientists were killed. Instead, as they'd originally anticipated, all were removed to the British intelligence facility at Farm Hall in England, where a lengthy debriefing established that Heisenberg's team was far behind the Manhattan Project.

"And did OSS realize this one-handed soldier was Martin?" I asked.

"Immediately."

"So that was late April, right? Before the court-martial hearing. And did they tell you about this attempted explosion?"

"Not one word. Bear in mind, Stewart, the A-bomb remained America's deepest secret. OSS wouldn't say anything concerning that or Alsos—not to Teedle, the trial judge advocate, or least of all me. But their mania to suppress all knowledge about anything to do with the bomb worked to our advantage. The prosecuting TJA on David's case was a lawyer named Meyer Brillstein, who seemed far angrier at your father than Teedle. One may suppose why. But early on—I'm sure at the insistence of OSS—Brillstein offered to dismiss the capital charge against your father in exchange for David's guilty plea and a mutual agreement not to seek discovery or offer proof of any of Martin's OSS-related activities, aside from those David had witnessed firsthand. Both your father and I saw this offer as the proverbial gift horse, since it meant that the court-martial panel would never know that David deliberately released a suspected Soviet spy. If they had, there's no telling how much longer your father's prison sentence would have been.

"Of course, we can see now that Martin knew much less than he thought he did. He had been briefed for Alsos in London in September 1944, with the idea that he would lead the team of American physicists into Germany. Although Martin necessarily was informed about the German atomic program, in that need-to-know world, no one told him about the Manhattan Project. He had no inkling that the U.S.A. was close to perfecting the bomb on its own, and thus no foresight that in less than four months, Pandora's box, as he called it, would be opened over Hiroshima and Nagasaki. Of course, Martin's superiors at OSS became even more determined to keep him in the dark once he began openly expressing doubts about whether a weapon like the Bomb should be in the hands of any nation. By October 1944 he'd passed one comment too many. London decided to pull him in. And Martin decided to defy them.

"At OSS, when they learned in April 1945 about Martin's attempt at Hechingen, the meaning was regarded as patent: the Soviets had recognized that they would not get to Hechingen first and had dispatched Martin to destroy the facility to prevent the scientists and their research from falling into American hands. Game, set, and match on the issue of whether Martin was a spy. Within the agency, a small faction led by Colonel Winters maintained that it was dubious to believe the Soviets would have supported such an improbable effort. According to the physicists at Hechingen, Martin had assembled a jerry-rigged device made of unexploded artillery shells, was traveling in an American jeep with a short-circuited ignition, had no visible collaborators, and was done in because he'd not yet mastered the striking of a match with one hand.

"When the autopsy turned up in June, showing that Martin had suffered a cruel death in Soviet custody, it renewed the controversy within OSS concerning Martin's loyalty. Winters began to theorize that Martin might have been on a solitary crusade to enforce his expressed belief that this new weapon ought to belong to no nation. As a result, the agency redoubled its search for the SS officers who'd taken custody of Martin at Hechingen. Early in July, two of them were located in their hometowns on opposite sides of Germany, both with their uniforms burned and lengthy cock-and-bull stories about how they'd never served in the German Army. The Americans quickly loosened their tongues, and the two officers told roughly parallel tales.

"The SS installation which had been guarding Hechingen had been delighted to lay hands on Martin, but not for his intelligence value. By mid-April, they knew the war was over. However, an American OSS officer figured to make a valuable bargaining chip in securing the SS men's freedom, once the Americans got there.

"For that reason, they claimed they did not interrogate Martin. Rations were short and at first when he refused food or water, they thought nothing of it. He claimed to have a severe intestinal infection and they took that at face value, because it made no sense to think the man would prefer starvation to being returned to his army."

"But Martin knew we'd hang him, right?" I asked.

"Certainly that's what your father had told him. At any rate, the SS abandoned Hechingen a day before the Americans entered, and carried Martin off with them. German forces were falling back from the Oder in hopes of breaking the Soviet siege of Berlin which had begun. The SS men followed, and once they were surrounded by the Soviets, decided to see if they could buy their freedom with the same prize they were going to offer the Americans: a U.S. OSS officer.

"Many historians have puzzled about why Stalin was willing to lose the thousands and thousands of troops he did in besieging and conquering Berlin without the assistance of the Allies, especially since he eventually honored his promise to share the city after it fell. Some speculate that the Soviets wanted the unfettered right to wreak vengeance on the Germans, which they surely took. One hundred thousand German women were raped during the Russians' first week in Berlin, Stewart." Bear took a second to wobble his old head over one more of the war's disgraceful facts.

"But the foremost theory today, bolstered by documents found in KGB archives, is that Stalin wanted to reach Berlin alone because the Kaiser Wilhelm Institute there held the only pieces of the German nuclear program that the Americans had not already laid hands on. Indeed, the Soviets discovered stores of uranium oxide at the Institute with which they ultimately revived their flagging atomic program.

"Once the SS officers made contact with the Soviets, and revealed the circumstances under which they had captured Martin, they found Soviet Army intelligence quite willing to let the SS men go in exchange for telling all they knew about Hechingen and turning over the American. Upon learning he was being handed off to the Soviets, Martin, who was now very weak, asked the Germans, as gentlemen, to shoot him. When they refused, he attempted to escape, despite his condition. He never got through the door. That was the last the SS officers saw of Martin. In the custody of the Soviets, sixty miles outside Berlin."

"And why would Martin prefer to die in German rather than Soviet hands?"

"One can only assume. Given what he'd said to your father, it's clear that Martin realized the Soviets would be desperate to learn whatever they could about American knowledge and suspicions concerning the A-bomb. For Martin, it would not be an appealing prospect to die while having every American secret he knew extracted by torture." Bear and I both were silenced for a second, contemplating that.

The other thing that puzzled me at that moment was how Bear had learned all this. Some, he answered, had come through Teedle. More of what he knew was the product of his lingering curiosity about my father's case. He had read the histories as they emerged over the years. But he had also stayed in touch with Colonel Winters, Martin's OSS commander, who eventually became a senior intelligence officer at the CIA.

"After Bryant retired from the Agency in the early 1970s, I saw him for a drink at the Mayflower. Winters told me he'd had an intriguing exchange a few years earlier with a Soviet counterpart who said he'd been involved in Martin's interrogation in Berlin, an event which the Russians officially deny to this day.

"Martin had refused to talk, of course. This Soviet officer acknowledged that they would have tortured him, but Martin was so weak from his hunger strike that they suspected his heart would stop. The only way they found to pry more than Martin's name, rank, and serial number from him was purely accidental, when they called in a doctor, who proposed putting Martin on intravenous. At that point, the Major agreed to answer questions, if they would allow him to die. They interrogated Martin for an entire afternoon. Two days later he was gone. And, of course, it turned out that every word Martin had spoken, while compelling, proved an absolute lie."

Bear stopped to wipe his lips. I thought this might have been too much talking for him, but he insisted on continuing. He'd worked too long to learn all of this not to pass it on.

"Over the years," he said, "I've thought often of Martin at the end. He was disfigured and in great pain from his burns, while the nation in whose service he had suffered these wounds was intent on hanging him. Yet he would not betray us. Instead, he accepted death as his only honorable option. Dying in the hands of the Soviets, ironically, ended up reestablishing his bona fides at OSS, especially once they'd heard from the SS officers. They now saw Martin as lost on a frolic and detour, but not a Soviet spy, one of many men who'd broken under the strain of war rather than a true turncoat determined to aid America's enemies."

I sat awhile digesting what Bear had told me. It was interesting as far as it went, but I had a hard time connecting any of this to my principal remaining curiosity, namely how my father had escaped his prison sentence. I said as much to Bear, who responded with his abbreviated off-kilter nod.

"I understand that it's far from obvious, but these events in fact paved the way for your father's release. OSS had learned of all of this—the autopsy and the SS account of Martin being handed over to the Soviets—by July 1945, only a few days before Truman, Stalin, Churchill, and Attlee met to discuss postwar arrangements at Potsdam. Robert Martin ended up figuring in those discussions, because our diplomats had realized they could use his fate to our advantage. It was an incendiary notion that our Soviet allies would hold an American OSS officer and, rather than repatriate him, interrogate him about our secrets and starve him to death. It showed that Stalin was not an ally at all, but was in fact preparing for war with us. The Russians continued to officially deny that Martin had died in their hands, but the medical evidence was clear and the circumstances of the Major's death kept the Soviets on the defensive. Furthermore, the proof of their desire to acquire the A-bomb pointed the way for the ultimate revelation of Potsdam, Truman's announcement to Stalin that America had in fact perfected the weapon. I don't want to exaggerate the importance of Martin's death, but it was a clear note in an Allied chorus aimed at forcing Stalin to observe the agreements of Yalta about national boundaries and troop demarcations—and thus, ironically, in avoiding another war.

"However, in order to engage in a diplomatic dance in which the tune was our indignation over Martin's fate, it was essential that Robert Martin be portrayed as a great American hero, and certainly not a rogue agent. The inconvenient details about Martin's insubordination, the order for his arrest, and his many escapes from American hands had to be quickly blotted from community memory, which necessarily meant that the court-martial of David Dubin was required to swiftly become a historical nonevent.

"On July 26, 1945, I was called to Third Army Headquarters by Teedle, who informed me that the case was being dropped. He was forthcoming with the little he knew, but the General himself had been given only spare details. He was, however, all for anything that provided an advantage versus the Soviets. And from his perspective, the case against your father was far less meaningful now that OSS was saying that Martin had not been working for the Russians. Teedle was, frankly, quite chagrined by the about-face, and seemed to feel he'd been seriously misled.

"In court, I had learned never to question a favorable ruling. I thanked Teedle heartily and prepared to leave with the papers recalling the charges in my hand, but Teedle would not dismiss me. Instead, he came around his desk and bore down on me.

"'Why the hell did he do this, Leach?' he asked, referring to your father. There was a tremendous animal ferocity in Teedle. He was not an enormous man, but when the General became intent, it was frightening because you felt he was on the verge of assault. It made for an uncomfortable moment when I had to outline the bounds of lawyer-client confidentiality. But it turned out the General had a theory.

"'I think Dubin was convinced Martin was not a Soviet spy, and was afraid that between OSS and me, the man would hang for it anyway. Is that close?'

"I knew I wasn't leaving without telling the General something, and what he had posited was true, as far as it went. I thought I'd satisfy him by saying his guess was accurate, but instead he grew solemn.

"'I've long suspected this whole damn thing with Dubin was my fault,' he said. He was a very sad man, Roland Teedle, fierce and thoughtful, but morose at the core and full of a sense of his own shortcomings, which he felt had led him to eagerly accept a false view of Martin. I don't know if you realize this, Stewart, but after the war Teedle went on to get a degree in theology and achieved quite a bit of renown in those circles. He published several books. His main theory, as much as I understand these things, was that faith was the point of existence, even while sin was life's overwhelming reality. Society's goal was to lower the barriers to faith, since faith was all that could redeem us. Very complex. As a warrior theologian, Teedle even attracted two biographers after his death. One book was completely unsparing—alcoholism, wife-beating, bar fights into his seventies, but not a whiff of the kind of scandal your father had heard about from Billy Bonner. I wouldn't be surprised if you checked your father's bookshelves and found one or two of Teedle's works there." In fact, when I looked, every book written by or about Teedle was in Dad's library, each, from the feel of the pages, well-read.

"There was not much I could say to Teedle," Bear said, "when he claimed the whole episode was his fault. It was consummately Teedle. The willingness to accept responsibility was admirable, while the egotism that made him think he was the motive force for everything that had occurred was ironic, at best. But on the other hand, the fundamental quarrel between your father and Teedle had always been about Martin's core intentions, whether Martin, in a few words, was a good man or a bad one. In the end, the General seemed willing to grant the point to your father, and with that finally let me go to bring this news to my client."

"Who was delighted, I assume?" I asked.

"Very much so. There'd been so much intense scurrying about once the autopsy had turned up that we'd known some change was in the wind, but neither your father nor I ever dared to hope the entire case would be revoked. David responded appropriately. He jumped to his feet and pumped my hand, he read the discharge paper for himself several times, and once he realized that his house arrest was over, he insisted on buying me a drink. I expected him to ask about his manuscript, which I had yet to return, but he never did. Perhaps, at some level, he was willing to see me do what I'd urged, namely preserve it for his children. That, at least, is the excuse I have given myself, Stewart, in sharing all of this with you.

"Your father enjoyed the summer air on the way over to the café, but by the time two glasses of champagne were placed before us he had grown quite somber. I was sure it was remorse for the many losses he'd suffered in chasing

Martin, but that was not what preoccupied him at the moment.

"'I drink to you, Bear,' he said, 'and you should drink to me. Wish me luck.'

"Naturally, I did, but he let me know I had missed his point.

"'I must go to Balingen,' he said, 'to see how my wife reacts when I tell her I am free to be her husband.'"

33. ORDINARY HEROES

If you asked my mother, as I did now and then during my childhood, she would describe my father as the love of her life, the hero who, like Orpheus, had retrieved her from Hades and whose passion brought her back to the realm of the living. That was her story, as they say, and she was sticking to it. And I think, at heart, it was true. Despite the doubts my father expressed to Leach when he was freed, my mother remained loyal to him always, and he to her. There were the usual daily frictions, but my parents treated each other with appreciation and kindness. Whatever the other improvisations in their histories, the intensity of their bond remains an enduring reality for me. It was like the mystical forces that unite atoms and was the very center of the household in which I was raised. They always had each other.

My inch-by-inch discovery of the wartime travails of young David Dubin, so resolute, high-minded, and frequently unwise, eventually made some of my father's shortcomings as a parent easier to bear. Tenderness came hard to Dad, like so many other men in his generation, but I understand now that, very simply, he'd exhausted his capacity for daring in Europe. He'd bet everything on my mother and, having won, never put all his chips down anywhere else. The terror of the battlefield, the cruelty he'd witnessed, and the damage to his proudest beliefs were a weight always holding him a step back from life. Yet I grant him the one grace we can ask as humans: he had done his very best.

But the revelation of my mother's identity shook me to the core. How could she have done this? How could she have deceived my sister and me about our heritage? How could she have denied her own past? I barely slept for weeks. The world, as I knew it, seemed as dramatically changed as if I'd found out I was the offspring of an amphibian.

I had always accepted that there was an element of mild deceit in my mother's character. She was essentially a straightforward person, but she could lie like a champ when required. I was quite a bit older when I realized my parakeet, whose cage I had constantly failed to clean, did not simply fly away when I was seven. And she was very good at sticking up for utter implausibilities that she thought were good for us—like the alleged bout of childhood pneumonia she'd contracted because she had gone outside without a jacket.

But the autobiography she'd passed off was no little white lie, especially laying claim to the hallowed status of a survivor. How could she have done this? The words were buzzing through my mind at unexpected moments for months.

But time slowly began to leach away my anger. All parents keep secrets from their children. I eventually realized that neither she nor my father could have anticipated the abiding reverence the Jewish community ended up paying to those who had suffered in their names. True, that purported legacy allowed my mother at times to exert considerable emotional leverage over my sister and me, as well as my father's family, but she explicitly rejected any effort to celebrate her for what she had supposedly endured, always insisting without elaboration that she had been far, far luckier than most.

More important, I accept now that my parents really had no choice. They had started down this road before the revelations of Martin's death in Soviet hands and were stuck with it when Dad was released. Admitting they'd falsified Gita's identity would have been foolhardy; he'd risk renewed prosecution, and she, in all likelihood, would never have been admitted to the U.S. Once here, the legal perils remained real, both for him, as a licensed attorney, and for her. Ironically, every time our government pounced on a former Nazi and tossed him out of the country for lying his way in, I'm sure their fears were reinforced. Certainly no one would choose to reveal a secret so dangerous to loose-tongued creatures like small children. The years passed. And their joint refusal to speak about the war stiffened their resolve not to tell Sarah or me. The anguish and disorientation I felt when I discovered the truth was, oddly, testimony to the fact that they had been sparing us pain.

Nor do I think they made anything easier for themselves. Everyone who has so much as nodded toward therapy knows that the turmoil of the past is never wholly forgotten. Unresolved, it seeps through even the strongest foundation. My mother was warm, strong, and courageous. She was a venerated champion of the needy, who could count hundreds of persons rescued through the Haven, the relief agency she ran. But I never had the illusion she was happy. As the past receded, she grew more brittle and dwelled closer to her anger. Some of that fury, I think now, might have been easier to set aside if she'd been free to acknowledge the shame of being the town bastard, instead of pretending to come from a tragic but loving Jewish family. Yet my parents had taken to heart the lesson of Orpheus and could return to the world of light only by never looking back.

I do not judge. I still cannot fathom enduring or witnessing what they and millions of others had. My mother referred so frequently to the "darkest time humanity has ever known" that the phrase lost any power for me—she might as well have been saying, "Things go better with Coke." But my excavations finally brought me nose to nose with the staggering truth she had been trying to impart. More human beings were killed in Europe from 1937 to 1945 than in any epoch before or since. Yes, six million Jews. And also twenty million Russians. Another three million Poles. A million and a quarter in Yugoslavia. Three hundred and fifty thousand Brits. Two hundred thousand Americans. And, may a merciful God remember them, too, more than six million Germans. Forty million people in all. Mom had called it right. Not merely dark. Black.

In June 2004, my sister made her intended trip home to look in on Mom, who was declining. Caged by my own lies, I had debated for months what I would tell Sarah. By rights, our parents' story was as much hers as mine. I just didn't think I'd get much credit for sharing it. Still, the day she was leaving, I buttoned up my courage and gave her a copy of Dad's typescript, and a handwritten summary of what Leach had added. She read that letter in my presence and, despite the labored apology it contained, responded in the spirit of our era.

"I'm going to sue you," my sister said.

"And what good will that do?"

"Hire a lawyer, Stewart."

I did, my high-school pal Hobie Tuttle, but no papers were served. Sarah called two weeks later. She was still boiling—I could literally hear her panting in the phone—yet she admitted that she'd been moved reading Dad's account.

"But the rest of it, Stewart? About Mom being this other woman? You're making it up. The way you've always made things up. Reality has never been good enough for you. Dad didn't write one word saying that."

I reasoned with her for just a moment. Leave Leach aside, whom she dismissed as an addlepated ninety-six-year-old. Why else would Dad have let Martin go? What other woman could Dad have married, given the fact that Teedle had him in custody a day or two after freeing Robert Martin? By then, I'd sorted through dozens of Gideon Bidwell's two-by-twos, copies of photos which Dad had kept after sending everything else to Biddy's family. I found one showing my father in uniform, conversing with a woman who is indubitably my mother. They stand in a courtyard in front of a small château constructed around a medieval turret, a "little castle" if ever there was one. Sarah had a duplicate of the picture, but she claimed it might have been taken at another time and place.

"Believe what you want," I said.

"I will," she answered. "I will. But here's my bottom line. Leave Mom in peace. If you show her one page of this, I'll never speak to you again. And if you so much as talk to anyone else about this while she's alive, I swear to God, I really will sue you."

Mom, by then, was suffering. Within a year of my father's death, in an eerie reprise, she began to develop symptoms of most of the diseases that had killed him. There was a spot on her lung and serious vessel damage around her heart. The body contains its own brutal mysteries. How could an organic illness be aggravated, as it clearly was, by Dad's absence? The surgeons took a lobe from her left lung. Cancer showed up on the scans again within two months. We'd been down this path with my father. She was brave and philosophical—as he had been. But her time was dwindling. She had good days and bad. But having watched Dad slide over the cliff, I knew that if I was ever going to say anything to her, it had better be soon.

I checked on her every day, bringing groceries and other necessities. She resisted a caretaker, but we had someone coming in for a few hours each afternoon. One morning, when Mom and I were alone in the kitchen, having our usual daily discussion, which wandered between family gossip and global affairs, I brought up my book about my father.

"I've decided to put it aside for a while," I told her.

She was next to the white stove, where she'd been making tea, and faced me slowly.

"Oh, yes?"

"I think I've gotten what I wanted to. Maybe I'll go back to it someday. But I'm doing a lot of freelance stuff now and I don't really have time to get to the end."

"This, I think, is wise, Stewart."

"Probably so. There's just one thing I'm curious about. You may not remember."

She was already shaking her gray curls, the same stark refusal to be quizzed I'd dealt with for nearly two years now.

"Well, just listen, Mom. This might be something you want to know."

Sighing, she seated herself at the old oak kitchen table, where the history of our family was written in the stains and scratches. She was shrinking away inside her skin, a small person now reduced to the minuscule. I recited the one paragraph my sister, after months of my begging, had given me clearance to utter, my prepared statement as it were.

"There was a woman Dad knew," I said, "named Gita Lodz. She was amazing, Mom. Brilliant, beautiful, a commando who worked underground with the OSS. She'd been orphaned in Poland and made her way to Marseilles. She was like Wonder Woman. She was ten times braver than most of the soldiers who won medals. I think she was probably the most remarkable person I learned about."

Mom peered across the table, the same obsidian eyes my father often described.

"Yes?" she asked. "What is your question?"

"I just wondered if Dad ever talked about her?"

"She must have been someone he knew before he came to Balingen. I never heard her name from him once we were together there."

Disowning herself, she remained utterly serene, the same would-be Bernhardt who had saved Martin a hundred times. But the truth, as I'd recognized, was that the life she'd claimed was the life she'd lived. Who are we, she'd once asked, but the stories we tell about ourselves and believe? She had been Gilda Dubin now since 1945, nearly sixty years, far longer than she had been Gita Lodz, the firebrand and ingénue who'd cast her spell over my father. Gita, like millions of others, had been incinerated in Europe. As Mrs. David Dubin, she had raised me and loved me. She'd been to hundreds of Holocaust remembrances and synagogue services, had worked tirelessly at the Haven to aid Jews in need, most of them survivors or Russian immigrants. Her identity was assumed as a matter of necessity, but she was loyal to it, just as she had been to my father.

True to what Sarah and I had resolved in advance, following that brief excursion I let the subject go. I'd said what I meant to. I checked her pill counter to be certain she'd taken her medications, and prepared to leave. As usual, she asked me about Nona, whose past-tense status Mom refused to accept, even though I'd begun seeing someone else.

When I moved toward the door, she spoke up behind me again.

"Stewart," my mother said. "You know Emma Lazar?"

"Naturally, Ma." Emma was my mother's closest friend, a survivor of Dachau.

"Emma remembers every day. Every day she recounts something. She walks down the street, she is remembering—someone who was raped by a guard, a man who died from eating a scrap of rotten meat he'd found, the moment she last touched her father's hand as they were pulled apart. This is what she lives. She must, of course. I do not blame her. But that is a crippled life. To go no farther. That is the brutal scar the Nazis laid upon her.

"When I came here, I promised myself a new life. A life that would not look back. *This* is life." She touched the wood of the table and then reached for a perfect orange atop the mounded fruit bowl that was always there. "Right now. *This* is life. You know the philosophers? The present never stops. There is only the present. You cheat life to live in the past. Isn't that so?"

"Of course."

"The past is beyond change. Good or bad. I am your mother, Stewart. That is the present and the truth. And your father was your father. That, too, is the truth. Whom he knew, or didn't know, I never dwelled upon. He saved me. He chose to love me when that was the bravest possible choice. From there, we both vowed to go forward. For me he was a hero."

"To me, too, Mom. More today than ever. I see him as a hero. But you were a hero, too, Ma. An amazing hero. You are both my heroes. I just want you to know that."

When the word 'hero' was applied to my mother as a camp survivor, she rigidly refused to hear it, citing the greater bravery of millions. And she rejected the title again today.

"I knew people, Stewart, who aspired to be heroes, to live beyond human limits because they found routine life a misery, and who were therefore doomed to disappointment. But I am an ordinary person, Stewart, who was fortunate enough to realize she wanted an ordinary life. Your father, too. In unusual circumstances, we did what we had to in order to preserve our chances to return and live normally. We all have much more courage than is commonly imagined. Every day, Stewart, as I get older, I marvel at how much bravery it takes to go on, to bear the blows existence so often delivers. I bore mine and was lucky enough to survive to have the ordinary life I desired with your father and Sarah and you, a life that means far more to me than anything that went before. Does that," she asked, in a way that made me think she actually expected an answer, "does that make me a hero?"

They are both gone now. To quote a favorite author, "Death deepens the wonder."

As I have acknowledged, over many months I edited, reshaped, and occasionally rewrote many of the passages in Dad's account for the sake of publication. At this stage, with the manuscript having been put aside while I waited for my mother to make her rocky passage from this world, I frequently cannot remember whose lines are whose when I turn the pages.

I could go back to my father's original manuscript to sort that out, but, frankly, I don't care to. I've done my best. This is as real as I can make my parents, as fully as I can imagine them, as honest as I can stand to be with others, or myself. There are inevitably limits. When our parents talk about their lives, they relay what they think is best, for their sake or ours. And as their children, we hear what we want, believe what we can, and, as time lengthens, pry and judge and question as our needs demand. We understand them in that light. And when we tell our parents' tales to the world, or even to ourselves, the story is always our own.

A NOTE ON SOURCES

This book is a work of imagination, inspired by the historical record, but seldom fully faithful to it. Although I began from reported events, the action throughout the novel is my embroidery, undertaken by characters who, except for the largest historical figures, are entirely fictitious.

My principal imaginative starting point was stories about World War II, which I heard from my father when I was a boy, before he put away those experiences and retreated into silence. My dad, Dr. David D. Turow, trod much of David Dubin's path through Europe as commanding officer of the 413th Medical Collecting Company, which was attached to the Third Army after October 1944. From my father, who was a field surgeon at the Army hospital established in the Sisters of Notre Dame convent at Bastogne, I heard many tales that stayed with me: about that loose-sphinctered parachute jump into Bastogne; being taken captive by German troops who needlessly executed his driver; the horror experienced by the initial medical teams to enter Dachau and Bergen-Belsen.

My father's stories are grossly transmogrified in *Ordinary Heroes*; they provided only a point of departure. David Dubin is in no way a portrait of my dad. For those who might wonder, my mother, Rita Pastron Turow, was a schoolteacher in Chicago during World War II. I owe profound thanks to her for lending me my father's files and photographs and letters (from which I borrowed several lines appearing in the letters in the novel), since they inevitably revealed many things a child would never otherwise know, including the depth of Dad's devotion to my mother as a young husband. To Peggy Davis, who added the photos and memories of her father, Technical Sergeant Donald Nutt, my dad's clerk, I owe special thanks.

After a television appearance in which I said that my next novel would concern World War II, Mr. Robert Freeman of Tequesta, Florida, contacted me at the urging of his wife, Julie Freeman, to offer me free use of a variety of materials he had retained relating to his cousin Carl Cohen, an infantryman who was found starved to death in a building in Ludweiller, France, at the war's end. I am grateful to Mr. and Mrs. Freeman, and to Carl Cohen's sister, Dottie Bernstein of Bennington, Vermont, for sharing these materials with me, even though I have contributed nothing to solving the mystery of how Cohen fell into Nazi hands, or why his death was misreported by comrades who said they saw him die on the battlefield.

On slender historical footings like these, the novel was then imagined. All of Robert Martin's activities, for example, are invented, although they occasionally hark back to reported operations of the OSS. There was no ammunition dump at La Saline Royale, which is actually situated a few miles from the site I describe. A team of U.S. soldiers made unsuccessful efforts around December 22, 1944, to rescue a stranded ammunition train outside Bastogne, but not in the precise manner set forth in the novel. Heisenberg did run from Hechingen, but not because anyone had attempted to blow up the secret location of the Kaiser Wilhelm Institute on Haigerlocherstrasse. FDR's death was announced near midnight overseas, not in the afternoon of April 12, 1945. *Und so weiter*. A concentration camp was situated at Balingen, but it was much smaller and not as heartless as what I have portrayed, which is drawn instead from accounts of Bergen-Belsen.

With all of that said, I have tried to be mindful of the larger historical record, especially the chronology of the war, and the movement of forces, and to accurately reflect the individual experiences of American soldiers. A bibliography of the sources I consulted is posted at www.ScottTurow.com.

My research was enormously aided by several persons whom I must thank. Colonel Robert Gonzales, U.S. Army, Ret., a former Army JAG officer now employed at Fort Sam Houston, Texas, shared with me the manuscript of his excellent history of the JAG Department during World War II, which incorporates interviews of numerous JAG Department members of that period. I reached Colonel Gonzales at the end of a lengthy bucket brigade of helpful hands that began with Carolyn Alison, Public Affairs Officer for the Office of the Judge Advocate General of the Department of the Navy. With the grace of her boss, Rear Admiral Michael F. Lohr, the Navy's Judge Advocate General, Ms. Alison put me in contact with a number of able Army historians, starting with Colonel William R. Hagan, U.S. Army, Ret., another former Army JAG Corps member, who is now a civilian employee at Camp Shelby in Mississippi and who was of continuing aid. Bill Hagan went far out of his way to acquaint me with a number of his colleagues, to whom I am indebted, including Mitch Yockelson of the National Archives and Records Administration. Dan Lavering, the Librarian at the Army's JAG School Library in Charlottesville, Virginia, was particularly generous in providing me with materials, including copies of *The Judge Advocate Journal*, the JAG Department's newsletter during World War II, and the 1943 revision of *A Manual for Courts-Martial, U.S. Army*. Mary B. Dennis, Deputy Clerk of Court for the Army Judiciary, responded to my requests to obtain a court-martial record as an exemplar. Alan Kramer, Director at the Washington National Records Center at Suitland, Maryland, was a kind host and guide when I visited. I also must acknowledge research assistance from my friends at the Glencoe (Illinois) Public Library and the Western New England College of Law. Great thanks to Henri Rogister and Roger Marquet of the Center of Research and Information on the Battle of the Bulge (CRIBA) for responding to my questions. And to Michel Baert, formerly of the

Belgian Tourist Office, who guided me on a trip in 2004 along David Dubin's route, I am especially grateful. He was both remarkably well informed and a congenial traveling companion.

Several veterans of the European campaign offered comments on the initial drafts of this novel that kept me from making even more mistakes: my law partner Martin Rosen of New York; Sam L. Resnick of Bayside, New York, President of the 100th Infantry Division Association; and Harold Tauss of Wilmette, Illinois. Thanks, too, to Bill Rooney and the other members of the World War II Round Table, as well as the librarians at the Wilmette Public Library.

I had incisive literary comments from several early readers: Rachel Turow, Jim McManus, Howard Rigsby, Leigh Bienen, Jack Fuller. Dr. Carl Boyar answered medical questions, as he has often before. My assistants, Kathy Conway, Margaret Figueroa, and Ellie Lucas, kept me on my feet, with Kathy making a number of special contributions, ranging from proofreading to compiling the posted bibliography. My agent at CAA, Bob Bookman; my law partner Julius Lewis; Violaine Huisman; and my French publisher, Isabelle Laffont, each contributed many corrections to my ersatz French, for which I'm sure I still owe apologies to French speakers around the world. Thanks to Sabine Ibach for correcting the tattered remains of my high school German. Robert Marcus was chief consultant on Things Jewish. Eve Turow was a valued sounding board about many questions connected to the book's presentation. And of course the edifice stands only with my three pillars — my editor, Jonathan Galassi; my agent, Gail Hochman; and, at the center, my wife, Annette.

I will not even begin the mea culpas for the errors I must have made, notwithstanding my substantial efforts to avoid them. I hope none of these mistakes are taken to diminish my admiration for the men and women who fought that horrible and necessary war. I can only paraphrase the remark of my old mentor, Tillie Olsen, which is quoted at the novel's end: Time deepens the wonder.

S.T.

ABOUT THE AUTHOR

SCOTT TUROW is the acclaimed author of such best-selling novels as *Presumed Innocent, The Burden of Proof, Pleading Guilty, The Laws of Our Fathers, Personal Injuries,* and *Reversible Errors;* and the memoir *One L.* A former federal prosecutor, he is currently a partner in the law firm of Sonnenschein Nath & Rosenthal. He lives outside of Chicago with his family.

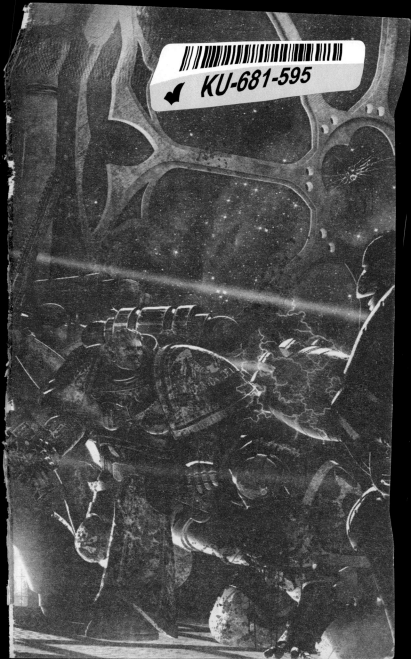

The Horus Heresy series

ABOUT THE AUTHOR

ROBERT SHECKLEY is the author of over fifty books in science fiction, fantasy, and mystery. His novel *Immorality, Inc.* was recently made into the movie *Freejack*. The cult classic *The Tenth Victim* was made from his original short story. Mr. Sheckley is a New Yorker currently residing in Portland, Oregon, with his wife and children.

THE HORUS HERESY

Ben Counter

BATTLE FOR THE ABYSS

My brother, my enemy

With special thanks to Nick Kyme.

A BLACK LIBRARY PUBLICATION

First published in Great Britain in 2008 by
BL Publishing,
Games Workshop Ltd.,
Willow Road, Nottingham,
NG7 2WS, UK.

10 9 8 7 6 5 4 3 2 1

Cover and page 1 illustration by Neil Roberts.

A CIP record for this book is available from the British Library.

ISBN 13: 978 1 84416 657 2
ISBN 10: 1 84416 657 0

See the Black Library on the Internet at
www.blacklibrary.com

Find out more about Games Workshop
and the world of Warhammer 40,000 at
www.games-workshop.com

Printed and bound in the UK.

THE HORUS HERESY

It is a time of legend.

Mighty heroes battle for the right to rule the galaxy. The vast armies of the Emperor of Earth have conquered the galaxy in a Great Crusade – the myriad alien races have been smashed by the Emperor's elite warriors and wiped from the face of history.

The dawn of a new age of supremacy for humanity beckons.

Gleaming citadels of marble and gold celebrate the many victories of the Emperor. Triumphs are raised on a million worlds to record the epic deeds of his most powerful and deadly warriors.

First and foremost amongst these are the primarchs, superheroic beings who have led the Emperor's armies of Space Marines in victory after victory. They are unstoppable and magnificent, the pinnacle of the Emperor's genetic experimentation. The Space Marines are the mightiest human warriors the galaxy has ever known, each capable of besting a hundred normal men or more in combat.

Organised into vast armies of tens of thousands called Legions, the Space Marines and their primarch leaders conquer the galaxy in the name of the Emperor.

Chief amongst the primarchs is Horus, called the Glorious, the Brightest Star, favourite of the Emperor, and like a son unto him. He is the Warmaster, the commander-in-chief of the Emperor's military might, subjugator of a thousand thousand worlds and conqueror of the galaxy. He is a warrior without peer, a diplomat supreme.

As the flames of war spread through the Imperium, mankind's champions will all be put to the ultimate test.

~ DRAMATIS PERSONAE ~

The Ultramarines Legion

CESTUS	Brother-captain and fleet commander, 7th Company
ANTIGES	Honour Guard, Battle-brother
SAPHRAX	Honour Guard, Standard Bearer
LAERADIS	Honour Guard, Apothecary

The Word Bearers Legion

ZADKIEL	Fleet Captain, *Furious Abyss*
BAELANOS	Assault-captain, *Furious Abyss*
IKTHALON	Brother-Chaplain, *Furious Abyss*
RESKIEL	Sergeant-commander, *Furious Abyss*
MALFORIAN	Weapon Master, *Furious Abyss*
ULTIS	Battle-brother

The Mechanicum of Mars

KELBOR-HAL	Fabricator General
GUREOD	Magos, *Furious Abyss*

The Space Wolves Legion

BRYNNGAR	Captain
RUJVELD	Battle-brother

The Thousand Sons Legion

MHOTEP   Brother-sergeant and fleet
captain, *Waning Moon*

The World Eaters Legion

SKRAAL   Brother-captain

The Saturnine Fleet

KAMINSKA   Rear Admiral, *Wrathful*

VENKMYER   Helmsmistress, *Wrathful*

ORCADUS   Principal Navigator, *Wrathful*

ONE

Bearers of the Word/Let slip our cloaks
The death of Cruithne

OLYMPUS MONS BURNED bright and spat a plume of fire into the sky. Below the immense edifice of rock lay the primary sprawling metropolis of Mars. Track-ways and factorums bustled with red-robed acolytes, pursued dutifully by lobotomised servitors, bipedal machine-constructs, thronging menials and imperious skitarii. Domed hab-blisters, stark cooling towers and mono-lithic forge temples vied for position amidst the red dust. Soaring chimneys, pockmarked by millennia of endeavour, belched thick, acrid smoke into a burning sky.

Hulking compressor houses vented steam high over the industrious swell like the breath of gods from arcane blasting kilns carved into the heart of the world; so vast, so fathomless, a labyrinthine conurbation as intricate and self-involved as its fervent populous.

Such innumerate, petty meanderings were as inconse-quential as a fragment of coal in the blast furnaces of the mountain forges, so great was the undertaking of that day. Few knew of its significance and fewer still witnessed the anonymous shuttle drone launch from the hidden caldera in the Valles Marineris. The drone surged into the stratosphere, piercing cloud-like crimson smog. Through writhing storms of purple-black pollution and wells of geothermal heat that hammered deep bruises into the sky, it breached the freezing mesosphere, the drone's outer shell burning white with effort. Plasma engines screaming, it drove on further into the thermosphere, the rays of the sun turning the layer into a blazing veil of relentless heat. Breaking the exosphere at last, the shuttle's engines eased. This was to be a one-way trip. Preset tracking beacons found their destination quickly. It was far beyond the red dust of Martian skies, far beyond prying eyes and questions. The shuttle was headed for Jupiter.

THULE HAD ORBITED the shipyards of Jupiter for six millennia. Suspended high above the gaseous surface of its patron planet, it dwelled innocuously beyond the greater Galilean moons: Callisto, Ganymede, Europa and Io. It was an ugly chunk of rock, its gravity so weak that its form was misshapen and mutated.

Such considerations were of little concern to the Mechanicum. What place did appearance and the aesthetic have in the heart of the machine? Precision, exactness, function, they were all that mattered.

Though of little consequence, Thule was to become something more than just a barren hunk of rock. It had been hollowed out by massive boring machines and filled with conduits, vast tunnels and chambers. Millions of menials, drones and acolytes toiled in the subterranean labyrinth, so great was the deed that they

were charged to perform. In effect, the dead core of
Thule had become a giant factorum of forge temples
and compressors, a massive gravity engine its beating
heart. This construction extended from the surface via
metal tendrils that supported blister domes, clinging
like limpets to the rock, and pneumatic lifter arrays.
Thule was no mere misshapen asteroid. It was an orbital
shipyard of Jupiter, and one that had guests.

'WE STAND UPON the brink of a new era.' Through the
vox-amplifier built into his gorget, Zadkiel's voice resonated powerfully in the gargantuan chamber. Behind
him, the exo-skeletal structure of Thule shipyard
loomed large and forbidding against the cold reaches of
space. Here, within one of the station's blister domes,
he and his charges were protected from the ravages of
the asteroid's surface. Solar winds scoured the rock,
bleaching it white, the inexorable erosion creating a
miasma of nitrogen-thick rolling dust.

'A red dawn is rising and it will drown our enemies in
blood. Heed the power of the Word and know it is our
destiny,' Zadkiel bellowed as he delivered the sermon,
animated and fervent upon a dais of obsidian. Scripture
carved into his patrician features and bald skull added
unneeded gravitas to Zadkiel's oratory. His grey, turbu-
lent eyes conveyed vehemence and surety.

His fists encased in baroque gauntlets, Zadkiel
gripped the edge of the lectern and assumed an insistent
posture. He wore his full battle armour, a fledgling suit
of crimson ceramite yet to bear the scars of conflict.
Replete with the horns of Colchis, in honour of the primarch's home world and the symbol of a proud and
distinguished heritage, it represented the new era of
which Zadkiel spoke.

The Word Bearers Legion had been denied their true nature for too long. Now, they had shed the simulacra of obedience and capitulation, the trappings of compromise and denial. Their new power armour, fresh from the forges of Mars and etched with the epistles of Lorgar, was a testament to that treaty. The grey-granite suits of feigned ignorance were destroyed in the heart of Olympus Mons. Clad in the vestments of enlightenment, they would be reborn.

A vast ocean of crimson stretched before Zadkiel, as he stood erect behind his pulpit of stone. A thousand Astartes watched him dutifully, a full Chapter split into ten companies, each a hundred strong, their captains to the fore. All heeded the Word.

The Legionaries were resplendent in their power armour, bolters held at salute in their armoured fists, clutched like holy idols. Zadkiel's suit was the mirror-image of those of his warriors, although sheaves of prayer parchment, scorched trails of vellum writ over with litanies of battle, and the bloodied pages ripped from sermons of retribution were affixed to it. When he spoke, it was with the zealous conviction of the rhetoric he wore.

'Heed the power of the Word and know this is our destiny.'

The congregation roared in affirmation, their voices as one.

'We have our lance of vengeance. Let it strike out the heart of Guilliman and his weakling Legion,' Zadkiel bellowed, swept up by his own vitriolic proclamations. 'Long have we waited for retribution. Long have we dwelt in shadow.'

Zadkiel stepped forward, his iron-hard gaze urging his warriors to greater fervour. 'Now is the time,' he said, smashing his clenched fist down upon the lectern to punctuate the remark. 'We shall cast off falsehoods and the shackles of our feigned obeisance,' he snarled as if the words left a bitter taste in his mouth, 'let slip our cloaks and reveal our true glory!

'Brothers, we are Bearers of the Word, the sons of Lorgar. Let the impassioned words of our dark apostles be as poison blades in the hearts of the False Emperor's lapdogs. Witness our ascension,' he said, turning to face the great arch behind him.

A vast ship dominated the view through the hardened plexi-glass of the blister dome. It was surrounded by massively over-engineered machinery, as if the scaffold supporting the hordes of menials and enginseers had been built around it, and thick trails of reinforced hosing bled away the pneumatic pressure required to keep the gargantuan vessel elevated.

Cathedra soared from the ship's ornate hull, their spires groping for the stars like crooked fingers. So armoured, it could withstand even a concerted assault from a defence laser battery. In fact, it had been forged with that very purpose in mind.

Its blunt bullet prow, and the way its flanks splayed out to encompass the enormous midsection, spoke of strength and precision. Three massive crenellated decks extended from it like the sharpened prongs of a stygian trident. Twin banks of laser batteries gleamed in dull gunmetal down its broadsides. A single volley would have annihilated the loading bay and everyone in it. Cannon mounts sat idle on angular blocks of metal filled with viewpoints that hinted at the myriad chambers within. The rapacious bristle of the defensive turrets along the dorsal and ventral spines, and the dark indentations of the torpedo tubes, shimmered with violent intent.

Spiked antenna towers punched outward from multitudinous sub-decks, interspersed with further weapon arrays and torpedo bays. The ship's ribbed belly shimmered like oil and was replete with dozens of fighter hangars.

At the stern, the huge cowlings of the exhausts flared over the deep glow of the warming engines, primed to unleash enough thrust to force the warship away from Thule. Like chrome hexagons, the engine vents were so vast and terrible that to stare into their dormant hearts was to engulf all sense and reason in a fathomless darkened void.

Finally, sheets of shielding peeled off the prow, revealing a massive figurehead: a book, wreathed in flame, wrought from gold and silver. Words of Lorgar's choosing were engraved on the pages in letters many metres high. It was the greatest and largest vessel ever forged, unique in every way and powerful beyond reckoning.

Such was the sight of it, like some creature born from the depths of an infinite and ancient ocean, that even Zadkiel fell silent.

'Our spear is made ready,' Zadkiel said at last, his voice choked with awe. 'The *Furious Abyss*.'

This ship, this mighty ship, had been made for them, and here in the Jovian shipyards its long-awaited construction had finally reached an end. This was to be a blow against the Emperor, a blow for Horus. None could know of the vessel's existence until it was too late. Steps had been taken to ensure that remained the case. The launch from little known, and even less regarded, Thule was part of that deceit, but only part.

Zadkiel turned on his heel to face his warriors.

'Let us wield it!' he extolled with vociferous intensity. 'Death to the False Emperor!'

'Death to the False Emperor,' his congregation replied like a violent blast wave.

'Horus exultant!'

Discipline broke down. The assembled throng bellowed and roared as if possessed, smashing their fists against their armour. Oaths of hatred and of devout loyalty were shouted fervently and the building sound rose to an unearthly clamour.

Zadkiel closed his eyes amidst the maelstrom of devotion and savoured, drank deep of the zealotry. When he opened his eyes again, he faced the archway and the landscape of the *Furious Abyss*. Smiling grimly, he thought of what the vessel represented, and he imagined its awesome destructive potential. There was none other like it in all of the Imperium: none with the same firepower; none with the same resilience. It had been forged with one deliberate mission in mind and it would need all of its strength and endurance to achieve it: the annihilation of a Legion.

IN THE DARKER recesses of the massive loading bay, now an impromptu cathedra, others watched and listened. Unfeeling eyes regarded the magnificent array of soldiery from the shadows: the product of the Emperor's ingenuity, even perhaps his hubris, and felt nothing.

'Curious, my master, that this Astartes should exhibit such an emotional response to our labours.'

'They are flesh, Magos Epsolon, and as such are governed by petty concerns,' remarked Kelbor-Hal to the bent-backed acolyte stooped alongside him.

The fabricator general had purposely taken the long journey from Mars to Thule aboard his personal barge. He had done so under the pretence of a tour of the Jovian shipyards, overseeing atmospheric mining on the surface of Jupiter, reviewing the operations on Io, and observing vehicle and armour production within the hive cities of Europa. All of which would explain his presence on Thule. The truth was that the fabricator general wanted to witness this momentous event. It was not pride that drove him to do it, for such a thing was beyond one so close to absolute communion with the Omnissiah, rather it was out of the compulsion to mark it.

One endeavour was much like any other to the fabricator general, the requirements of form and function outweighing the need for ceremony and majesty. Yet, here he stood swathed in black robes, a symbol of his allegiance to the Warmaster and his commitment to his cause. Had he not sanctioned Master Adept Urtzi Malevolus to forge Horus's armour? Had he not also allowed the commissioning of vast quantities of materiel, munitions and the machines of war? Yes, he had done all of this. He had done it because it suited his purposes, the burgeoning desire, or rather intrinsic programming, within the servants of the great machine-god to gradually become one with their slumbering deity. Horus had unfettered Mars in its pursuit of the divine machine, countermanding the Emperor's chastening. For Kelbor-Hal the question of his allegiance and that of the Mechanicum was one of logic, and had required mere nanoseconds of computation.

'He sees beauty where we see function and form,' the fabricator general continued. 'Strength, Magos Epsolon, strength made through fire and steel, that is what we have wrought.'

Magos Epsolon, also robed in black, nodded in agreement, grateful for his overlord's enlightenment.

'They are human, after a fashion,' the fabricator general explained, 'and we are as far removed from that weakness as the cogitators aboard that ship.'

Immensely tall, his ribcage exposed through the ragged edge of his robes with ribbed pipes and tendril-like servos replacing organs, veins and flesh, Kelbor-Hal was anything but human. He no longer wore a face, preferring a cold steel void implanted with a curious array of sunken green orb-like diodes in place of eyes. A set of mechadendrite claws and arms stretched from his back, like those of an arachnid, replete with blades, saws and other arcane machinery. His voice was devoid of all emotion, synthesised through a vox-implant that droned with artificial coldness and indifference.

As Kelbor-Hal watched the phalanx of Astartes boarding the ship through the tube-like umbilical cords that snaked from the vessel's loading ramps to the blister dome, their bombastic leader swelling with phlegmatic pride, the internal chron within his memory engrams alerted him that time was short.

Dully, the *Furious Abyss's* thrusters growled to life and the great vessel strained vertically against the lifter clamps. A low, yet insistent hum of building power from the awakening plasma engines followed, discernible even through the plexi-glass of the blister dome. With the Astartes and their crew aboard, the *Furious Abyss* was preparing to launch.

A data-probe snicked from the end of one of the fabricator general's twitching mechadendrites and fed into a cylindrical console that had emerged from the hangar floor. Interfacing with the device, Kelbor-Hal inputted the code sequence required to launch the ship. A series of icons upon the face of the console lit up and a slowly building hum of power resonated throughout the launch chamber.

Lead Magi Lorvax Attemann, part of the coterie of acolytes and attendant menials who had gathered to observe the launch, was permitted to activate the first sequence of explosions that would release the *Furious Abyss*. He did so without ceremony.

Lines of explosions, like stitches of fire, rippled along the side of the dock. Lifters, assembly arrays and webs of scaffolding fell away into the darkness, where magnetic tugs waited to gather the wreckage. Slabs of radiation shielding lifted from the ship's hull. The last dregs in the refuelling barges ignited in bright ribbons of fire.

The plasma engines roared, loud and throaty, scorching a blue swathe of fire and heat across the surface of Thule. A new star was rising in the darkling sky, so terrible and wonderful that it defied expression. It was a thunderous metal god given form, and it would light the galaxy aflame with its wrath.

At last the *Furious Abyss* was underway. As Kelbor-Hal watched it lift majestically into the firmament and registered the heavy thrum of its engines, a single tiny vestige of emotion blinked into existence within him. It was an ephemeral thing, barely quantifiable. Accessing internal cogitators, interfacing with his personal memory engrams, the fabricator general found its expression.

It was awe.

THE DRONE SHIP waited deep within the heart of Thule, accessed through a series of clandestine tunnels and lesser-known chambers. As it made its approach, the still toiling menials and servitors paid it no notice, programme wafers ensuring that they remained intent on their work. So, the shuttle passed them by slowly, unchallenged, unseen. Once through the myriad tunnels, the drone waited for several hours docked in a small antechamber that fed off the vast gravity engine at the asteroid's core.

An hour earlier, Fabricator General Kelbor-Hal's personal barge had departed the station, the head of the Mechanicum leaving his subordinate, Magos Epsolon, to organise the clean up after the launch of the *Furious Abyss*. It was to be the last vessel that left Thule.

Pre-programmed activation protocols abruptly came on line in the servitor pilot slaved to the drone shuttle. A mix of chemicals, separated within the body of the servitor pilot became merged as they were fed into a shared chamber. Once combined, the harmless chemicals became a volatile solution capable of incredible destructive force. A second after the solution became fully merged a small incendiary charge ignited their fury. The immediate firestorm engulfed the ship and spread out, the growing conflagration billowing down tunnels and through access pipes, incinerating labouring menials. When it struck the gravity engine the resultant explosions began a cataclysmic chain reaction. It took only minutes for the asteroid to break into flame-wreathed fragments. There was no time to flee to safety and no survivors. Every adept, servitor and menial was burned to ash.

The debris field would spread far and wide, but the asteroid was far enough away, locked at the farthest point of its horseshoe orbit, not to trouble Jupiter. It would not escape notice, but it was also of such little consequence that any investigation would take months to effect and ratify. None would discover the thing that had been wrought upon the asteroid's surface until it was much, much too late.

Much technology was lost in Thule's destruction. It was a steep price to pay for absolute and certain secrecy. In the end, the fabricator general's will had been done. He had willed the death of Thule.

TWO

Hektor's fate/Brothers of Ultramar/In the lair of the wolf

IT WAS DARK in the reclusium. Brother-Captain Hektor kept his breathing measured as he prosecuted another thrust with his short-blade. He followed with a smash from his combat shield and then twisted his body out of the committed attack to make a feint. Crouching low, blackness surrounding him in the chapel-like antechamber, he spun on his heel and repeated the manoeuvre in the opposite direction: swipe, thrust, block, thrust; smash, feint, turn and repeat, over and over like a physical mantra. With each successive pass he added a flourish: a riposte here, a leaping thrust there. The cycles increased in pace and intensity, the darkness enveloping him, honing his focus, building to an apex of speed and complexity, at which point Hektor would gradually slow until at peace once more.

Standing stock-still, maintaining control of his breathing, Hektor came to the end of the training regimen.

'Light,' he commanded, and a pair of ornate lamps flared into life on either wall, illuminating a spartan chamber.

Dressed in only sandals and a loincloth, Hektor's body was cast in a sheen of sweat that glistened in the artificial lamplight. The curves of his enhanced muscu-lature were accentuated within its glow. Indulging in a moment of introspection, Hektor regarded the span of his hands. They were large and strong, and bereft of any scars. He made a fist with the right.

'I am the Emperor's sword,' he whispered and then clenched his left. 'Through me is his will enacted.'

Two robed acolytes waited patiently in the shadows, cowls concealing their augmetics and other obvious deformities. Even without being compared to the tall slab of muscle that was an Astartes, they were bent-backed and diminutive.

Hektor ignored their obsequiousness as he released the straps affixing the combat shield to his arm and handed it over along with his short-blade to the acolytes. He looked at the ground as his attendants retreated silently into the shadow's penumbra at the edge of the room. An engraved 'U' was carved into the centre of the chamber, chased in silver on a circular field of blue. Hektor stood in the middle of it, in exactly the position that he had started.

He allowed himself a smile as he beckoned his atten-dants to bring forth his armour.

A great day was fast approaching.

It had been a long time since he had seen his fellow Ultramarines. He and five hundred of his battle-brothers had been far from their native Ultramar for three years, as they helped prosecute the Emperor's Great Crusade to bring enlightenment to the galaxy and repatriate the lost colonies of man by fighting the

Vektates of Arkenath. The Vektate were a deviant culture, an alien overmind that had enslaved the human populous of Arkenath. Hektor and his warrior brothers had shattered the yoke that bound their unfortunate human kin and in so doing had destroyed the Vektates. The human populace owed fealty to the Imperium, and demonstrated it gladly when they were free of tyranny. It had been a grim war. The *Fist* had been involved in a brutal ship-to-ship action against the enemy, but had prevailed. Repairs had been conducted on Arkenath, as well as the requisitioning of a small tithe of men, eager to venture beyond the stars, to help replenish elements of the ship's crew. Once the war was over, Hektor and his battle-brothers had been summoned to the Calth system and the region of space known as Ultramar. At long last, they would be reunited with their brothers and their primarch.

Hektor was full of pride at the thought of seeing Roboute Guilliman again, his gene-father and noble leader of the Ultramarines Legion. The deciphered messages from the *Fist of Macragge*'s astropaths had been clear. The Warmaster himself, mighty Horus, had ordered the Legion to the Veridan system. Guilliman had ratified the Warmaster's edict and instructed all disparate Ultramarine forces to muster at Calth. There they would take on supplies and rendezvous with their brothers in preparation to launch a strike on an ork invasion force besieging the worlds of neighbouring Veridan. A short detour to the Vangelis space port to take on some more battle-brothers stationed there and the campaign to liberate Veridan would be underway.

FULLY ARMOURED, HEKTOR strode down an access tunnel and headed towards the bridge. His ship, the *Fist of*

Macragge, was a Lunar-class battleship, named in honour of the Ultramarines' home world. Deck hands, comms-officers and other Legion serfs bustled past the Astartes down the cramped confines of one of the vessel's main thoroughfares.

The faint hiss of escaping pressure greeted Hektor's arrival on the bridge as the automated portal allowed him entry, before sliding shut in his wake.

'Captain on the bridge,' bellowed Ivan Cervantes, the ship's helmsmaster. Cervantes was a human, and despite being dwarfed by the mighty Astartes, he remained straight-backed and proud before the glorious countenance of his captain. Cervantes snapped a sharp salute with an augmetic hand; his original body part had been lost on Arkenath, together with his left eye, during the boarding action against the Vektates. The bionic replacement glowed dull red in the half-light of the bridge.

Screen illumination from various consoles threw stark slashes into the gloom, the activation icons upon them grainy and emerald. Crewmen, hard-wired directly into the vessel's controls from access ports bolted into their shaved scalps worked with silent diligence. Others stood, consulting data-slates, observing sensor readings and otherwise maintaining the *Fist of Macragge*'s smooth and uninterrupted passage through real space. Lobotomised servitors performed and monitored the ship's mundane functions with precise, circadian rhythm.

'As you were, helmsmaster,' Hektor replied, climbing a short flight of steps that led to a raised dais at the forefront of the bridge, and sitting down at a large command throne at its centre.

'How far are we from Vangelis space port?' Hektor asked.

'We expect to arrive in approximately–'

Warning icons flashed large and insistent on the forward viewport in front of the command throne, interrupting the helmsmaster in mid-flow.

'What is it?' Hektor demanded, his tone calm and level.

Cervantes hastily consulted a console beside him. 'Proximity warning,' he explained quickly, still poring over the data that had started churning from the console.

Hektor leaned forward in his command throne, his tone urgent.

'Proximity warning? From what? We are alone in real space.'

'I know, sire. It just… appeared.' Cervantes was frantically consulting more data as the organised routine of the bridge was thrust into immediate and urgent action.

'It's another ship,' said the helmsmaster. 'It's huge. I've never seen such a vessel!'

'Impossible,' barked Hektor. 'What of the sensorium, and the astropaths? How could it have got so close to us, so quickly?' he demanded.

'I don't know, sire. There was no warning,' said Cervantes.

'Bring it up on the viewscreen,' Hektor ordered.

Blast shields retracted smoothly from the front viewscreen, revealing a swathe of real space beyond. There, like black on night, was the largest ship Hektor had ever seen. It was shaped like a long blade with three massive decks that speared out from the hull like prongs on a trident.

Points of intense red light flared in unison down the vessel's port side as it turned to show the *Fist of Macragge* its broadside. The light illuminated more of

the ship, so that it stretched the entire length of the
viewscreen. It was even larger than Hektor had first
assumed. Even several kilometres from the *Fist of
Macragge*, it was rendered massive in the glow of its laser
batteries

'Name of Terra,' Hektor gasped when he realised what
was happening.

The terrible vessel that had somehow foiled all of
their sensors, even their astropathic warning systems,
was firing.

'Raise forward arc shields!' Hektor cried, as the first
impact wave struck the bridge. A bank of consoles on
the left suddenly exploded outward, shredding a
servitor with shrapnel and all but immolating one of
the deck crew. The bridge shuddered violently. Crewmen clutched their consoles to stay upright. Servitor
drones went immediately into action dousing sporadic
fires with foam. Hektor gripped the arms of his command throne as critical warning klaxons howled in the
tight space, and crimson lightning shone like blood as
emergency power immediately kicked in.

'Forward shields,' Hektor cried again as a secondary
impact wave threw the Astartes from his command
throne.

'Helmsmaster Cervantes, at once!' Hektor urged, getting to his feet.

No answer came. Ivan Cervantes was dead, the left
side of his body horribly burned by one of the many
fires erupting all across the bridge.

What was left of the crew worked frantically to reroute
power, close off compromised sections and find firing
solutions so that they might at least retaliate.

'Somebody get me power, lances, anything!' Hektor
roared.

It was utter chaos as the carefully drilled battle routines were made a mockery of by the sudden and unexpected attack.

'We have sustained critical damage, sire,' explained one of Cervantes's subordinates, blood running freely down the side of his face. Behind him, Hektor saw other crewmen writhing in agony. Some were prone on the bridge floor and not moving at all. 'We're dead in the void.'

Hektor's face was grim in the gory glow of the bridge, a burst of sparks from a shorting console casting his features in stark relief.

'Get me an astropath.'

'A distress call, sire?' asked the crewman, fighting to be heard above the chaotic din. The silhouettes of his colleagues rushed back and forth to stem the damage, desperately trying to restore order in spite of the fact that it was hopeless.

'We are beyond help,' Hektor uttered with finality as the *Fist of Macragge*'s systems started failing. 'Send a warning.'

CESTUS KNELT IN silent reflection within one of the sanctums in the Omega quarter of Vangelis space port. The vast orbital station was built into a large moon and based around several hexagonal blisters into which docks, communion temples and muster halls were housed. A labyrinthine tramway connected each and every location of Vangelis, which was organised into a series of courtyards or quarters to make navigation rudimentary.

The bustling space port was crammed with traders, naval crewmen and mechwrights. A large proportion of its area had been given over to the Astartes. Vangelis was a galactic waymarker and small numbers of Astartes involved in more discreet missions used it as a gathering point.

Once their objective was completed, they would congregate at one of the many muster halls designated for their Legion and await pick-up by their battleships. Though little more than a company from any given Legion would be expecting transit at any one time, sectors Kappa through Theta were at the complete disposal of the Legions. Few non-Astartes were ever seen there, barring ubiquitous Legion serfs and attendants, though occasionally remembrancers would be granted brief access in concordance with maintaining good relations with the human populous.

Cestus drank in the darkness of the sanctum and used it to clear his thoughts. He was fully armoured, and pressed his left gauntlet against the sweeping, silver 'U' emblazoned on the cuirass of his power armour, symbol of the great Ultramarines Legion, whilst keeping his head bowed.

Soon, he thought.

He and nine of his battle-brothers had been on Vangelis for over a month. They had been acting as honour guard for an Imperial dignitary at nearby Ithilrium and were consequently separated from the rest of their Legion. Their sabbatical had passed slowly for Cestus. At first, he had thought it curious and enlightening to mix with the human population of the space port, but even bereft of his power armour and swathed in Legionary robes he was greeted with awe and fear. Unlike some of his brothers, it wasn't a reaction that he relished. Cestus had kept to Astartes quarters after that.

The fact that transit was inbound to extract them from Vangelis and ferry him and his brothers to Ultramar and their primarch and Legion filled Cestus with relief. He longed to embark on the Great Crusade again, to be out on the battlefields of a heathen galaxy, bringing order and solidity.

Word had reached them that the Warmaster Horus had already departed for the planet of Isstvan III to quell a rebellion against the Imperium. Cestus was envious of his Legion brothers, the World Eaters, Death Guard and Emperor's Children who were en route with the Warmaster.

Though Cestus craved the esoteric and was fascinated by culture and erudite learning, he was a warrior. It had been bred into him. To deny it was to deny the very genetic construct of his being. He could no more do that than he could go against the will and patriarchal wisdom of the Emperor. Such a thing could not be countenanced. So, Cestus sought the seclusion of the meditative sanctum.

'You have no need to genuflect on my account, brother.' A deep voice came from behind Cestus, who was on his feet and facing the intruder in one swift motion.

'Antiges,' said Cestus, sheathing his short-blade at his hip. Normally, Cestus would have rebuked his battle-brother for such a disrespectful remark, but he had formed an especially strong bond with Antiges, one that transcended rank, even of the Ultramarines.

It was a bond that had served the battle-brothers well, their whole much more than the sum of their parts as it was for the Legion in its entirety. Where Cestus was governed by emotion but prone to caution, Antiges was at times choleric and insistent, and less intense than his brother-captain. Together, they provided one another with balance.

Battle-Brother Antiges was similarly attired to his fellow Astartes. The sweeping bulk and curve of his blue power armour reflected that of Cestus, together with the statutory icons of the Ultramarines. Pauldrons, vambrace and gorget were all trimmed with gold, and a gilt brocade hung from Antiges's left shoulder pad to the right breast of his armour's corselet. Neither Astartes wore a helmet; Antiges's fastened to a clasp at his belt, whilst Cestus's head was framed by a silver laurel over his blond hair, his battle helm cradled beneath his arm.

'A little on edge, brother-captain?' Antiges's slate-grey eyes, the mirror of his closely cropped skull, flashed. 'Do you desire to be out amongst the stars, commanding part of the fleet again?'

As well as a company captain, Cestus also bore the rank of fleet commander. During his sojourn on Ithilrium that aspect of his duty had been briefly suspended. Antiges was right, he did desire to be back with the fleet, fighting the enemies of the Emperor.

'At the prospect of you lurking in the shadows, waiting to reveal yourself,' Cestus returned sternly and stepped forward.

He managed to maintain the chastening expression for only a moment before he smiled broadly and clapped Antiges on the shoulder.

'Well met, brother,' Cestus said, clasping Antiges's forearm firmly.

'Well met,' Antiges replied, returning the greeting. 'I have come to take you away from here, brother-captain,' he added. 'We are mustering for the arrival of the *Fist of Macragge*.'

IT WAS A short journey from the sanctum of Communion Temple Omega to the dock where the rest of

Cestus's and Antiges's battle-brothers awaited them. A narrow promenade, lined with ferns and intricate statuettes, quickly gave way to a wide plaza with multiple exits. The Ultramarines, who spoke with warm camaraderie, took the western fork that would eventually lead them to the dock.

Turning a corner, at the lead of the two Astartes, Cestus was hit square in the chest. The impact, though surprising, moved the Astartes not at all. He stared down at what had struck him.

Quivering amidst a bundle of tangled robes, a lithoslate clasped reassuringly in his hands, was a scholarly-looking human.

'What is the meaning of this?' Antiges demanded at once.

The pale scholar cowered beneath the towering Astartes, shrinking before his obvious power. He was sweating profusely, and used the sleeve of his robe to wipe his head before casting a glance back in the direction he had come from in spite of the monolithic warriors in front of him.

'Speak!' Antiges pressed.

'Be temperate, my brother,' Cestus counselled calmly, resting his hand lightly on Antiges's shoulder pad. The gesture appeased the Ultramarine, who backed down a little.

'Tell us,' Cestus urged the scholar gently, 'who are you and what has put you in this distemper?'

'Tannhaut,' the scholar said through ragged breaths, 'Remembrancer Tannhaut. I only wanted to compose a saga of his deeds, when a madness took him,' he blathered. 'He is a savage, a savage I tell you!'

Cestus exchanged an incredulous look with Antiges, who turned back to fix the remembrancer with his imperious gaze once more.

'What are you talking about?'

Tannhaut pointed a quivering finger towards the arched entrance of a muster hall.

A stylised rendering of a lupine head was etched into a stone panel beside it.

Cestus frowned when he saw it, knowing full well who else was on the space port with them at that time.

'The sons of Russ.'

Antiges groaned inwardly.

'Guilliman give us strength,' he said, and the two Ultramarines strode off in the direction of the muster hall, leaving Remembrancer Tannhaut quailing behind them.

BRYNNGAR STURMDRENG'S BOOMING laughter echoed loudly around the muster hall as he felled another Blood Claw.

'Come, whelplings!' he bellowed, taking a long pull from the tankard in his hand. Most of the frothing, brown liquid within spilled down his immense beard, which was bound in a series of intricate knots, and swept over the grey power armour of his Legion. 'I've yet to sharpen my fangs.'

In recognition of the fact, Brynngar displayed a pair of long incisors in a feral grin.

The Blood Claw Brynngar had just knocked prone and half-conscious crawled groggily on his belly in a vain attempt to get clear of the ebullient Wolf Guard.

'We're not done yet, pups,' Brynngar said, clamping a massive armoured fist around the Blood Claw's ankle and swinging him across the room one-handed to smash into what was left of the furnishings.

The three Blood Claws left standing amongst the carnage of broken chairs and tables, and spilled drink and victuals, eyed the Wolf Guard warily as they began to surround him.

The two facing Brynngar leapt in to attack, their shorter fangs bared.

The Wolf Guard drunkenly dodged the swipe of the first and hammered a brutal elbow into the Blood Claw's gut. He took the punch of the second on his rock-hard chin before smashing him to the floor with his considerable bulk.

A third Blood Claw came from behind, but Brynngar was ready and merely sidestepped, allowing the young warrior to overshoot, before delivering a punishing uppercut into his cheek.

'Never attack downwind,' the bawdy Wolf Guard told the Blood Claw rolling around on the floor. 'I'll always smell you coming,' he added, tapping his flaring nostrils for emphasis.

'As for you,' Brynngar said, turning on the one who had struck him, 'you hit like you're from Macragge!'

The Wolf Guard laughed out loud, before stomping a ceramite boot in mock salute of his triumph on top of the last Blood Claw, who had yet to stir from unconsciousness.

'Is that so?' a stern voice from the entrance way asked.

Brynngar swung his gaze in the direction of the speaker, and his one good eye brightened at once.

'A fresh challenge,' he cried, swigging from his tankard and delivering a raucous belch. 'Come forth,' Brynngar said, beckoning.

'I think you've had enough.'

'Then let us see.' The Wolf Guard gave a feral grin and stepped off the inert Blood Claw. 'Tell me this,' he added, stalking forward, 'can you catch?'

* * *

CESTUS HURLED HIMSELF aside at the last moment as the broad-backed chair flew at him, smashing into splinters against the wall of the muster hall. When he looked up again, he saw a broad and burly Wolf Guard coming towards him. The Astartes was an absolute brute, his grey power armour wreathed in pelts and furs, numerous fangs and other feral fetishes hanging from silver chains. He wore no helmet, his long and ragged hair swathed in sweat together with a beard drenched in Wulfsmeade, swaying freely about his thick shoulders.

'Stay back,' Cestus advised Antiges as he hauled himself to his feet.

'Be my guest,' the other Ultramarine replied from his prone position.

Adopting a crouching stance as dictated by the fighting regimen of Roboute Guilliman, Cestus rushed towards the Space Wolf.

Brynngar lunged at the Ultramarine, who barely dodged the sudden attack. Using his low posture to sweep under and around the blow, Cestus rammed a quick forearm smash into the Space Wolf's elbow, tipping the rest of what was in the tankard over his face.

Brynngar roared and came at the Ultramarine with renewed vigour.

Cestus ducked the clumsy two-armed bear hug aimed at him and used Brynngar's momentum to trip the Space Wolf hard onto his rump.

The manoeuvre almost worked, but Brynngar turned out of his trip, casting aside the empty tankard and using his free hand to support his body. He twisted, using the momentum to carry him, and landed a fierce punch to Cestus's midriff when he came back too swiftly for the Ultramarine to block. An overhand blow followed as Brynngar sought to chain his attacks, but

Cestus moved out of the striking arc and unleashed a fearsome uppercut that sent Brynngar hurtling backwards.

With the sound of more crushed furniture, the Space Wolf got to his feet, but Cestus was already on him, pressing his advantage. He rained three quick, flat-handed strikes against Brynngar's nose, ear and solar plexus. Staggered after the barrage, the Wolf Guard was unable to respond as Cestus drove forward and hooked both arms around his torso. Using the weight of the attack to propel him, Cestus roared and flung Brynngar bodily across the muster hall into a tall stack of barrels. As he moved backwards, Cestus watched as the rack holding the barrels came loose and they crashed down on top of Brynngar.

'Had enough?' Cestus asked through heaving breaths.

Dazed and defeated, and covered in foaming Wulfs-meade, a brew native to Fenris and so potent that it could render an Astartes insensible should he drink enough, Brynngar looked up at the victorious Ultramarine and smiled, showing his fangs.

'There are worse ways to lose a fight,' he said, wringing out his beard and supping the Wulfsmeade squeezed from it.

Antiges, standing alongside his fellow battle-brother, made a face.

'Up you get,' said Cestus, hauling Brynngar to his feet.

'Fair greetings, Cestus,' said the Wolf Guard, when he was up, crushing Cestus in a mighty bear hug. 'And to you, Antiges,' he added.

The other Ultramarine backed away a step and nodded.

Brynngar put his arms down and nodded back with a broad smile.

'It has been a while, lads.'

It was on Carthis during the uprising of the Kolobite
Empire in the early years of the crusade that the three
Astartes had first fought together. Brynngar had saved
Cestus's life that day and had been blinded in one eye
for his trouble. The venerable wolf had fought the Kolobite drone-king single-handed. The mighty rune axe,
Felltooth, which Brynngar wielded to this day, had part
of its blade forged from the creature's mandible claw by
the rune-priests and artificers of Fenris in recognition of
the deed.

'Indeed it has, my noble friend,' said Cestus.

'Drunk and brawling? Are the drinking holes of this
space port insufficient sport, Brynngar? Did you build
this muster hall for just such a purpose, I wonder?' said
Antiges with a hint of reproach.

Lacquered wood panelled the walls, and a plentiful
cache of barrels, filled with Wulfsmeade, were stationed
at intervals throughout the hall. Huge, long tables and
stout wooden benches filled the place, which was
empty except for Brynngar and the groaning Blood
Claws. Tapestries of the deeds of Fenris swathed the
walls. The muster halls of the Ultramarines were austere
and regimented; this one, fashioned by the artisans of
Leman Russ's Legion, looked more like a rustic long-
house from the inside.

'A pity you could not have joined in sooner,' Brynngar
remarked. 'Perhaps tomorrow?'

'With regret, we must decline,' Cestus replied, secretly
relieved; he had no desire to go a second round with the
burly Space Wolf. 'We leave today for Ultramar. War is
brewing in the Veridan system and we are to be reunited
with our brothers in order to prosecute it. We are heading to the space dock now.'

Brynngar smiled broadly, clapping both Astartes on the shoulder, who both felt the impact through their armour.

'Then there is only one thing for it.'

Antiges's expression was suspicious.

'What is that?'

'I shall come to see you off.'

With that, the Wolf Guard turned the two Ultramarines and, putting his massive arms around their shoulders, proceeded to walk them out of the muster hall.

'What about them?' Cestus asked as they were leaving, indicating the battered Blood Claws.

Brynngar cast a quick look over his shoulder and made a dismissive gesture.

'Ah, they've had enough excitement.'

THREE

God of the *Furious Abyss*/Psychic scream/Visions of home

CORALIS DOCK WAS one of many on Vangelis. A wide, flat plain of plate metal stretched out from its many station houses and listening spires, ending in a trio of fanged docking clamps where the various visiting craft could make harbour and take on or drop off cargo.

Arriving at the main control hub of Coralis, the three Astartes found themselves in a tight chamber that overlooked the dock. Thick, interwoven cables looped from the ceiling and dim, flickering halogen globes illuminated the bent-backed menials and cogitator servitors working the hub. A backwash of sickly yellow light thrown from numerous pict screens and data-displays fought weakly against the gloom.

An azure holosphere was located in the centre of the chamber, rotating above a gunmetal dais. It depicted Vangelis space port in grainy, intermittent resolution and a wide arc surveyor net that projected several thousand metres from the surface.

A large, convex viewport confronted the Astartes at the far wall through which they could see the magnificent vista of real space. Distantly, writhing nebulae patterned the infinite blackness with their iridescent glory and fading suns. Starfields and other galactic phenomena were arrayed like the flora and fauna of some endless obsidian ocean. It was a breathtaking view and stole away the fact that the recycled air within the control hub was sickly and stifling. A machine drone accompanied it from the space port's primary reactor located in the subterranean catacombs of Vangelis. The insistent hum of latent power could be felt through the reinforced plasteel floor. It was hot, too, the stark industrial interior barely shielded against the dock's generatorium.

Saphrax was already on the command deck of the control hub, consulting with the hub's stationmaster, when the other Astartes arrived. Saphrax was the honour guard squad's standard bearer, and the Ultramarines honour banner was rolled up in its case slung over his back. The rest of Saphrax's battle-brothers were below at the hub's gate, preparing for their imminent departure.

'Greetings, Saphrax. You know Brynngar of the Space Wolves,' said Cestus, indicating the brutish Wolf Guard who gave a feral snarl.

'What news?' the brother-sergeant asked his banner bearer.

'Captain, Antiges,' said the Ultramarine to his battle-brothers. 'Son of Russ,' he added for Brynngar's benefit. Saphrax was a bald-headed warrior with a long scar that ran from his left temple to the base of his chin: another souvenir from the Kolobite. Cestus often mused that none in the Legion were as straight-backed as Saphrax, so much so that he seemed permanently at attention. Dependable and solid, he was seldom given to great emotion and wore a stern expression like a mask over chiselled stone features. Pragmatic, even melancholic, he was the third element to the balance that existed between Cestus and Antiges. Even so, the banner bearer's mood was particularly dour.

'We have received an astropathic message,' Saphrax informed them.

There were three astropaths in residence at the hub, and more in the space port at large. They were sunk into a deep, circular vestibule, just below floor level, and swathed in shadow. Dim lights set into the edge of the vestibule cast weak illumination onto their faintly writhing forms. A skin of translucent, psychically conditioned material was draped over the trio of astropaths like a clinging veil. Beneath it, they looked like they were somehow conjoined, as if feeling each other's emotions as one being. Other, less obvious, wards were also in place. All were designed to safeguard against the dangerous mental energies that could be unleashed during the course of their duties.

Withered and blinded, the wretched creatures – two males and a female – like all of their calling had undergone the soul-binding ritual; the means by which the Emperor moulded and steeled their minds, so that they might be able to look into the warp and not be driven insane. Astropaths were vital to the function of the Imperium; without them, messages could not be communicated over vast distances, and forces could not be readied and co-ordinated. Even so, it was an inexact science. Messages both sent and received by the Astra Telepathica were often nought but a string of images and vague sense-impressions. Wires and thick cables snaked from the vestibule, slaving the astropaths to the control hub, where their 'messages' could be logged and interpreted.

'It started fifteen minutes ago,' said the stationmaster, an elderly veteran of the Imperial Army with cables running from under his shaved scalp, plugged into the command ports of the consoles set above the astropathic chamber. 'We've only received fragments of meaning, so far. All we know for certain is that they come from a distant source. Thus far, only part of the message has reached us. Our astropaths are endeavouring to extract the rest as I speak to you.'

Cestus turned to regard the stationmaster and in turn the gibbering astropaths. Beneath the protective psyskin, he could see their wasted bodies, swaddled in ragged robes. He heard the hissing of sibilant non sequiturs. The astropaths drooled spittle as they spoke, their sputum collecting against the inner material of the skin enveloping them. Their bone-like fingers were twitching as their minds attempted to infiltrate the empyrean.

'Falkman, sire,' said the stationmaster by way of introduction with a shallow bow. His right leg was augmetic and, judging by his awkward movements, most of his right side, which was probably why he had been sidelined to age and atrophy at Vangelis, no longer fit to taste of the Imperium's glory on the battlefield. Cestus pitied his fragility and that of all non-Astartes.

'Could it be a distress beacon sent from a ship?' Antiges broke through Cestus's thoughts with his assertive questioning.

'We have been unable to discern that yet, sire, but it is unlikely,' said Falkman, his face darkening as he turned to Saphrax.

'The nature of the message was... broken, more like a psychic cry delivered with extreme force. With the warp in tumult the energy used to send it was unpredictable,' said Saphrax, 'and it was no beacon. There was a single message; the pattern does not repeat. We think perhaps it was an astropathic death scream. 'And that is not all.'

Cestus's gaze was questioning.

Saphrax's face was grim.

'We have yet to receive word from the *Fist of Macragge*.' The banner bearer of the honour guard let the words hang there, unwilling to voice what was implied.

'I will not make any negative conclusions,' Cestus replied quietly, unwilling to give in to what he feared. 'We must believe that–'

The three astropaths slaved to the control hub began convulsing as the full force of the psychic scream made its presence felt. Blood spurted inside the psy-skin covering them and looked hazy and bright viewed from outside it. The wasted limbs of the astropaths pressed against the material, forcing it tight, their muscles held in spasm as they writhed in agony. Cogitators set around the hub above them were spewing reams of data as the astropaths fought to control the visions rushing into their minds.

Smoke clouded the already hazy interior of the psy-skin as it rose from their decrepit bodies. Consoles sparked and exploded as wrathful electricity arced and spat. It earthed into the wizened frames of the astropaths, carried by the wires and cables, now little more than human conductors for its power. As one, they threw their heads back and a backwash of pure psychic force was unleashed in a terrible death scream that resonated throughout the room. The astropaths became a conduit for it, the strength of the psychic emission made many times more powerful by the volatile state of the warp.

Walls shuddering against the onslaught, the lights of Vangelis space port went out.

THE BRIDGE OF the *Furious Abyss* was like a sprawling city in miniature. The banks of cogitators were like hive-stacks rising above the streets formed by the exposed industrial ironwork of the deck. The various bridge crews sat in sunken command posts like arenas or deep harbours. Three viewscreens dominated one end of the bridge, while a raised acropolis at its heart was formed by the captain's post. A strategium table stretched out before it from which he could raise an orrery display, showing the ship and its foes wrought in rotating brass rings.

High above the sprawling bridge was a decked clerestory where the astropathic choir of the mighty warship were slaved. The vaulted space was shared by the Navigator's sanctum, concealed in an antechamber so as to be secluded whilst traversing the perils of the warp.

The command throne, raised upon a hard-edged pentagonal dais, was the seat of a god.

Zadkiel was that god, looking down upon a city devoted to him.

'Listen,' Zadkiel bade those kneeling before him in supplication. The dulcet roar of the *Furious Abyss*'s plasma engines, even dulled by the thick adamantium plating surrounding the ship's hull and interior, was like a war cry.

'Listen and hear the sound of the future...' Zadkiel was on his feet, sermonising, '...the sound of fate!'

Three warriors, true devotees of the Word, heeded Zadkiel's rhetoric and stood.

'We pledge our service to you, Lord Zadkiel,' said the tallest of the three. He had a voice like crushed gravel and one of his eyes was blood-red, surrounded by a snarl of scar tissue. Even without the injury, his granite slab of a face would have made him a figure of fear even among his fellow Word Bearers. This was Baelanos, assault-captain and Zadkiel's private terror weapon. A potent warrior, Baelanos lacked imagination, which made him the perfect follower in Zadkiel's eyes. He was obedient, deadly and fiercely loyal, all fine qualities in an underling.

'As do we all,' Ikthalon interjected blithely. Another Astartes, Ikthalon was a company chaplain, demagogue and expert torturer. Unlike Baelanos, he wore his helmet in the presence of his commander, a skull-faced piece of armour with a pair of discreet horns on either side of the temple. Even through it, Ikthalon's thinly veiled contempt was obvious. 'Perhaps we should address the matters at hand, brother,' he counselled, lingering sarcastically on the last word.

Zadkiel sat back down in the command throne. It was sculpted to accept his armoured frame, as if he had been born to take command of this bridge, to be the god of this warship.

'Then let us tarry no further,' he said, his viperous gaze lingering on Ikthalon.

'Sensorium reports that the *Fist of Macragge* was destroyed and all weapon's systems tested successfully, sire.' It was Reskiel who spoke. He was a youth compared to the other Astartes on the command dais, gaunt of face with a keening hunger in his black eyes, a strange quirk of his birth. Reskiel was a veteran of many battles, despite his age, and he wore the newly fashioned studded armour of his Legion proudly, keen to baptise it

with the scars of war. He was widely regarded as Zadkiel's second, if not in an official capacity – that honour
fell to Baelanos – and made it his business to know all
the happenings aboard the *Furious Abyss* and report
them to his master. Where Baelanos was the dutiful lap-
dog, Reskiel was the eager sycophant.

'It was as expected.' Zadkiel's response was terse.

'Indeed,' said Ikthalon, 'but our astropaths also suggest that the stricken ship, though smitten by our
righteous fury, managed to send out a distress call. I
would not like to think that all our caution at commissioning the vessel's construction in the Jovian shipyards
has been undone so swiftly and needlessly.'

Zadkiel allowed a flutter of emotion to cross his features for a moment at the news. He considered drawing
his power mace and staving in Ikthalon's skull for his
persistent insubordination, but in truth, he valued the
chaplain's council and his Word. Though he was a barb
in Zadkiel's side, even since the Great Crusade had been
in its infancy, he did not couch expressions with syco-
phantic frippery as Reskiel was prone too, nor was he so
singled-minded that he was unable to convey subtlety
and the need for delicacy when required like Baelanos.
Zadkiel did not trust him, but he trusted his Word and
so he was tolerated.

'It is possible that a message reached a way station, or
some isolated listening spire at the edge of the segmentum, but we are well underway and there is little that
any vessel can do to prevent our destiny. So it is written,'
Zadkiel said at last.

'So it is written,' the assembled commanders intoned.

'Reskiel, you will maintain a close watch on the sensorium. If anything should stray into surveyor range, I
want to know immediately,' Zadkiel ordered.

'It will be done, my lord.' Reskiel bowed obsequiously and retreated from the dais.

'Baelanos, Ikthalon, you have your own duties to attend to,' Zadkiel added, dismissively, not waiting to watch them depart as he turned to regard the viewscreens before him.

'Engines,' said Zadkiel, and at once the central viewscreen blinked into life, the bridge lights dimmed and the image on the screen lit the miniature city in hard moonlight. It showed the *Furious Abyss*'s cavernous engine room, the prostrate cylinders of the plasma reactors dwarfing the crewmen who scrabbled around them in their routine duties. The crew wore the deep crimson of the Word Bearers; they were servants of Lorgar just as the Word Bearers were, devoted to the primarch's Word and grateful for such a certain place in the universe.

They did not know the details of the Word, of course. They were ignorant of the web of allegiances and oaths that Lorgar had created among his brother primarchs, or of the mission that would seal the inevitability of the Word Bearers' victory. They did not need to know. It was enough for them that they laboured under the wishes of their primarch.

Amongst the piteous menials, a tall figure stood out. Looming from the darkness, he was swathed in black robes and bore the cog symbol of the Mechanicum around his neck on a chain of bolts.

'Magos Gureod, you are to keep us at a steady speed, but be ready to increase our plasma engines to maximum capacity.'

'It will be done,' the magos replied, his artificial voice relayed through a series of synthesisers. Gureod's face was hidden by the massive cowl over his head, but a pair of blinking red diodes was vaguely discernible in the void where his eyes should have been. Odd protrusions in the sweep of his long robes suggested further augmetics, and his withered hands, crossed over his abdomen, offered the only clue that Magos Gureod was indeed human. At the order, he withdrew into the shadows again, doubtless heading for the sanctum and deep communion with the machine spirit.

Turning to another screen, Zadkiel uttered, 'Ordnance.'

The crowded munitions deck was displayed there. Weapon Master Malforian was in residence, barking harsh commands to crews of sweating orderlies and gang ratings, toiling in the steam-filled half dark of the cluttered deck. Full racks of torpedoes stood gleaming, fresh from the Martian forges. The ordnance deck stretched across the breadth of the *Furious Abyss* beneath the prow, and like the rest of the ship it was wrought in a bare industrial style that had an elegance of its own.

Realising he was being summoned, Malforian attended to his captain at once.

'Keep broadsides primed and at ready status, Master Malforian,' Zadkiel instructed him. 'The test against the *Fist of Macragge* was to your satisfaction, yes?'

'Yes, my lord. Your will shall be done.' The lower portion of the weapon master's face was supplanted by a metal grille and he spoke in a tinny monotone as a result; most of his jaw and chin had been destroyed during the early years of the Great Crusade while he was aboard the *Galthalamor*, fighting the ork hordes of the Eastern Fringe. The vessel, an ancient Retribution-class battle cruiser, was all but annihilated in the conflict.

Zadkiel dismissed the weapons master and blanked the pict screens. Coding a sequence into his command throne, Zadkiel felt the hydraulic pistons at work in the dais as he was slowly, majestically, raised above the bridge and brought level with the massive viewport overlooking the vessel's prow. The endless expanse of real space stretched beyond it. Somewhere within that curtain of stars was Macragge, home world of Guilliman's Legion. It was the stage of his destiny.

'Navigator Esthemya,' said Zadkiel, staring into the infinite.

'My lord,' a female voice chimed through the vox set into the command throne.

'Take us to Macragge.'

'Vectors are locked, captain,' Esthemya informed him from the secluded cocoon in the clerestory, a hard-edged blister that was surrounded by spines of data medium like the spires of a cathedral.

Zadkiel nodded, turning to face the viewscreen in front of him as the Navigator went to her duties.

The infinite gaped before him, and Zadkiel was acutely aware of the power that lay beyond the veil of real space and the pacts he had made to harness its limitless strength. Before the countenance of his enemies, aboard this mighty vessel, he would be god-like. There was no other ship in existence that could do what the *Furious Abyss* was destined to do. It alone had the power to achieve the mission that Kor Phaeron had charged them with. Only the *Furious Abyss* could get close enough, could endure the awesome defences of Macragge to unleash its deadly payload.

Icons in his command throne lit up with the acquisition of their new heading, bathing Zadkiel in an aura of his own personal heaven.

'Like a god,' he whispered.

* * *

EVERY EMERGENCY KLAXON had gone off at once in the control hub of Coralis Dock at Vangelis space port. Cestus could barely hear the thoughts in his head. Light flickered sporadically from the warning readouts on every command surface, casting the darkened control hub like some monochromatic animation. The astropathic choir bucked and kicked, and spat blood beneath the psy-skin in a collective seizure.

'Station captain, report,' bellowed Cestus.

Falkman was reeling, trying to tear the cables from his skull as they pumped a screaming torrent of information into his mind.

Brynngar went to the side of the human at once, preventing Falkman from ripping out more cables, determined that the station master would do his duty.

'The hub reactor is overloading,' the station captain snarled through gritted teeth, trying desperately to hold on. 'The psychic jolt must have started a chain reaction in our electrical systems. The reactor must be shut down or it will destabilise.'

Cestus's face, lit up intermittently in readout flares and the bursts of warning strobes, held a question.

'The resulting explosion will vapourise the station, this dock and all of us.'

The Ultramarine captain turned to the assembled Astartes in the control hub.

'Saphrax, stay here and maintain control over the situation,' he ordered with a meaningful glance at Falkman. 'Try to salvage whatever you're able to from the astropathic choir.'

'But my captain–'

'Do it!' Cestus would not be argued with, even with a battle-brother so seldom disposed to querying orders as

Saphrax. 'Whatever was in that message was important; I can feel it in my very marrow. It must be recovered.'

'What of the rest of us?' asked Antiges, barley registering the flying embers of sparks spitting across the chamber.

'We're going to save the dock.'

'YOU ARE NO Techmarine. How do you plan on shutting down the reactor?' Brynngar shouted against the din, sparks showering him from cogitator cables above.

Although the Space Wolf's face was almost next to Cestus's ear, the Ultramarine could only just hear him. The droning reactor was a thunderous pulse in the subterranean access tunnels. After verbally guiding the Astartes to an antechamber below the control hub and a reinforced access portal that would lead them to the reactor, Falkman had neglected to provide them with the necessary instruction to shut the device down, the fact of his passing out from shock a major contributing factor to the oversight.

Usually, this area of the dock would be thronging with menials and engineers, but the rapid outflow of escape reactor radiation had prompted an evacuation alert. The Astartes had passed a number of fleeing tech adepts as they'd made their way down to the reactor. Those that were left were either dead or critically injured. The Astartes ignored them all, immune to their pleas for help with the safety of the entire dock at stake.

'I am hoping a solution will present itself,' Cestus replied as they made their way through the cramped tunnel. The corridor the Astartes were in spiralled around the main reactor shell down to the power source at the base of the station.

'To think the Legion of Guilliman are regarded as master strategists,' said Brynngar with bellowing laughter.

'Directness is a valid strategy, Space Wolf,' Antiges reminded him, shouting to be heard above the horrendous noise of lurching metal, as if an inner storm was at play within the conduit. 'I would have thought one of the Sons of Russ would find it familiar.'

Brynngar's amused response was raucous and deafening.

Shouldering past the last of the surviving crewmen and panicked tech adepts as they fled, Cestus led the Astartes to the reactor chamber. Only one of the Emperor's Angels, replete in his power armour, could hope to survive the reactor's intense radiation at such close range. Like his battle-brothers, Cestus had donned his helmet before entering the tunnel. Extreme radiation warning icons flashed insistently in the lens display. Time was running out.

Atmospheric pipes fractured and sprayed freezing gas across a pair of gargantuan blast doors closing off the interior of the reactor shell from the rest of the station. Doubtless, they'd been activated as soon as the psychic power surge from the astropaths had hit. The servos on the massive door had shorted and were a tangled mass of wires and machinery.

'Prepare yourselves,' cried Cestus, ignoring the sub-zero gas. He seized the edge of the blast door in an effort to prise it open.

'Stand back,' snarled Brynngar, using his bulk to muscle the Ultramarine aside. He hefted Felltooth with practiced ease, sweeping the rune axe around in a lazy arc.

'No sport when the enemy stays still,' he growled and split the blast door in two with one mighty swing, sparks cascading from the blade.

Stowing the weapon, Brynngar peeled back the rent metal with both hands, making a space wide enough for the Astartes to enter.

The reactor was a swirling mass of glowing blue-green energy, rippling in on itself as it drew in power from the plasma conduits looping around it like eccentric orbits around a star. It pulsed, streaked with black and purple, and chunks of scorched machinery tumbled into it. A hot blast of air, tingling with radiation, washed over them in a back-draught. More warning runes flickered against Cestus's helmet lens, transmitted through onto the display from the acute sensor readouts on his armour.

'Now what?' shouted Antiges above the howl of the reactor.

Cestus watched the writhing mass of energy, taking in the confines of the small chamber that housed it and the control console, all but destroyed by its wrath.

'How many charges do you have?'

'A cluster of fragmentation and three krak grenades, but I don't understand, captain,' Antiges replied, his perplexity concealed by his helmet.

'A full belt of krak,' Brynngar growled. 'Whatever you are planning, lad, we'd best be about it,' he added. Being blown to smithereens by a malfunctioning reactor was not the death saga he wanted for his epitaph.

'We prime the chamber with set charges, everything we've got,' said Cestus with growing conviction, 'and bury it.'

'That would cause catastrophic damage to the station,' Antiges countered, turning to regard his captain.

'Yes, but it would not destroy it,' said Cestus. 'There is no other choice.'

Cestus was about to detach the grenades from his clip harness when the reactor abruptly collapsed like a dying star imploding into a black hole. In its place a glowing sphere of deep purple blossomed, flickering like an image on a faulty pict screen. Purple lightning licked from the surface, playing over Cestus's armour. He took a step back.

Yowling static flared suddenly into life and the Astartes were floored by the wave of noise. A bright flash lit the entire chamber, overloading their helmet arrays in an instant. There, amidst the intense flare of light, Cestus saw an image, so fleeting and indistinct that it could have been an illusion from the overwhelmed optics in his helmet. He blinked once, seeing only white haze, and shook his head, trying to recapture it. The flare died down and when Cestus's vision returned the afterglow haunted the edge of his retinas, but the image was gone and the reactor was dead. The core had turned dark. Cracks of static electricity glowed over its surface. It shrank and became abruptly inert. The warning lights inside the reactor shell dimmed and went out.

Elsewhere on the station, secondary and tertiary reactors, registering the loss of the primary reactor, diverted power to the dock, allowing the tech-seers time to make the necessary repairs. The storm had howled itself out.

'What in the name of Terra just happened?' asked Antiges, a cluster of frag grenades still in his hand.

'Mother Fenris,' Brynngar breathed at what he had just witnessed.

'Did you see that?' asked Cestus. 'Did you see it in the blast flare?'

'See what?' Antiges replied, relieved that they didn't have to collapse the reactor chamber after all.

Cestus's posture displayed his shock and disbelief as sure as any facial expression disguised by his armour.

'Macragge.'

SHARDS OF BROKEN images flashed on the psy-receiver, what was left of the astropathic transference from the psychic scream.

Falkman, looking gaunt and haggard from his earlier experience, but otherwise intact, pored over them, running analysis protocols and clarity procedures with what little machinery still worked in the hub. Saphrax stood pensively beside him, awaiting the return of his captain.

'Brother-captain!' he said with no small amount of relief as Cestus and the others emerged from the tunnel, their armour scorched black in several places.

When Cestus removed his helmet, his face was ashen and a cold sweat dappled his brow.

Saphrax was taken aback; he had never seen a fellow Astartes, certainly not his captain, look so afflicted.

'The astropathic message,' Cestus stated coldly, going to the psy-receiver before Saphrax could verbalise his concern. 'What's left of it?'

'All is well, brother,' said Antiges, following in his captain's wake and placing his hand on the banner bearer's shoulder, though his tone was anything but reassuring.

Brynngar waited further back, deliberately distancing himself, and stony silent as if processing what had happened in the reactor. He touched a fang totem attached to his cuirass with an inward expression.

'There is little left,' confessed Falkman, who, though he had managed to restore lighting and some of the basic functions of the hub, had failed to recover the entire astropathic message. 'I need to get one of the logic engines functioning if I'm to decipher it with any degree of certitude, but this is what we have.'

Cestus glared at the pict-slate of the psy-receiver as the broken images cycled slowly: a gauntleted fist wreathed in a laurel of steel, a golden book, what appeared to be the hull of a ship and a cluster of indistinct stars. Cestus knew of a fifth image. Though his rational mind told him otherwise, in his heart, the Ultramarine knew what he had seen – the range of mountains, the lustrous green and blue – it was unmistakable. He also knew what he had felt: a sense of belonging, like coming home.

'Macragge,' he whispered, and felt suddenly cold.

FOUR

Divine inspiration/A gathering/Contact

MHOTEP STARED INTO the water, so still and clear its surface was like silver. The face that stared back at him had hard and chiselled features with a handsome bone structure, despite the velvet cowl that partly concealed it. Hooded eyes spoke of intelligence, and skin, so tan and smooth that it was utterly without imperfection, suggested the nature of his Legion: the Thousand Sons.

Mhotep was dressed in iridescent robes that pooled like deep red liquid around him as he knelt with head bowed. Stitched in runes, his attire suggested the arcane. He was at the heart of his private sanctum.

The ellipse-shaped chamber had a low ceiling that enhanced the sense of claustrophobia created by the sheer volume of esoteric paraphernalia within. Stacks of scroll cases and numerous shelves, replete with well-thumbed archaic tomes, warred for space with crys-glass cabinets filled with bizarre arcana: an oculum of many hued lenses, a bejewelled gauntlet, a plain silver mask fashioned into an ersatz skull. Upon a raised dais, there was a planetarium in miniature, rendered from gold, the stellar bodies represented by gemstones. Gilt-panelled walls were swathed in ancient charts in burnished metal frames, cast in the azure glow of eldritch lamps.

A red marble floor stretched across the entire room, engraved with myriad paths of interlocking and concentric circles. Runes of onyx and jet, etched into the stone, punctuated the sweeping arcs without regularity. Mhotep was at the nexus of the design, at the point where all of the interweaving circles converged.

A chime registered in a vox-emitter built into the sanctum's entry system, indicating a guest.

'Enter, Kalamar,' said Mhotep.

A hiss of escaping pressure accompanied the aide as the door to the sanctum opened and he shuffled into the room.

'How did you know it was I, Lord Mhotep?' asked Kalamar, his speech fraught with age and decrepitude.

'Who else would it be, old friend? I do not need the prescience of Magnus to predict your presence in my sanctum.'

Mhotep bent towards the bowl, plunging both hands into the water to lightly splash his face. As he came back up, he withdrew his cowl and the lamp light reflected from his bald scalp.

'And I need no sophisticated augury to divine that you bring important news, either,' Mhotep added, dabbing his face with his sleeve.

'Of course, sire. I meant no offence,' said Kalamar, bowing acutely. The serf was blind, and wore ocular implants; the augmetic bio-sensors built into his eye cavities could not 'see' as such, but detected heat and provided limited spatial awareness. Kalamar supplemented his somewhat unorthodox visual affliction with a silvered cane.

'My lord, we have docked at Vangelis,' he added finally, confirming what his captain already knew.

Mhotep nodded, as if possessed of sudden understanding.

'Have the Legion serfs prepare my armour, we are leaving the ship at once.'

'As you wish,' Kalamar said, bowing again, but as he was retreating from the sanctum he paused. 'My lord, please do not think me impertinent, but why have we docked here at Vangelis when our journey's end lies at Prospero?'

'The paths of destiny are curious, Kalamar,' Mhotep replied, looking back down at the bowl.

'Yes, my lord.' Even after over fifty years in his service, Kalamar did not fully understand his master's cryptic words.

When the Legion serf had gone, Mhotep rose to his feet, his voluminous robes gathering up around him. From within the folds of his sleeves, he produced a stave-like object, no longer than his forearm and covered in arcane sigils.

Stepping away from the circle, a single eye was revealed at its centre as he took a bizarre course through the labyrinthine design of the room. It represented the wisdom of Magnus, Primarch of the Thousand Sons Legion and gene-father to Mhotep. Locked in his cabalistic route, Mhotep arrived at an ornate, lozenge-shaped vessel and reverently placed the stave within it. The vessel was much like a gilded sarcophagus, similar to that in which the rulers of ancient Prospero had once been entombed. The item secured, Mhotep sealed the vessel shut, a vacuum hiss of escaping pressure emitting from its confines, and inputted a rune sequence disguised within the sarcophagus's outer decoration.

'Yes,' uttered Mhotep, the task done, absently caressing a scarab-shaped earring, 'very curious.'

'IT IS A low turn out,' muttered Antiges beneath his breath.

Within the stark, grey ferrocrete austerity of the Ultramarines muster hall three Astartes awaited Cestus and his battle-brothers. The three were seated around a conference table inset with a single arcing 'U'. A huge tapestry, depicting the auspicious day when the Emperor came to Macragge in search of one of his sons, framed the scene. Clad in glorious armour of gold, a shining halo about his patrician features, the Emperor stretched out his hand to a kneeling Roboute Guilliman, who reached out to claim it. That day, their primarch had been truly born and their Legion's inception cemented.

Even now, and rendered as mere artistry, Cestus could not help but feel his heart lift.

'With such short notice, I had expected less,' the Ultramarine confessed, approaching the gathering with Antiges. Cestus's battle-brother had briefed his captain on the attendees. Brynngar he knew, of course, but the two others, a Thousand Son and a World Eater, he did not.

Cestus and Antiges were joined by four more of their brothers – Lexinal, Pytaron, Excelinor and Morar, for the sake of appearances. The rest, Amyrx, Laeradis and Thestor, were with Saphrax on a separate duty. The Ultramarines had called the gathering, so it was only proper that they arrived at it in force to show their commitment.

'Greetings brothers,' Cestus began, taking his seat alongside his fellow Ultramarines. 'You have the gratitude of Guilliman and the eighth Legion for your attendance here this day.'

'As is well,' said a bald-headed Astartes with richly tanned skin, 'but we beseech you to illuminate us as to your plight.' His voice was deep and powerful. Clad in the panoply of the Thousand Sons Legion, a suit of lacquered dark red and gold power armour, as angular and proud as the monuments of Prospero, he cut an intimidating figure. Antiges had already informed Cestus that the Thousand Son was Fleet Captain Mhotep.

Darkly handsome, bereft of the usual battle scars and functional facial bionics wrought by years of unremitting warfare, this Mhotep had a curious, aloof air. His shining eyes seemed to bore into Cestus's very soul.

Not all of the assembly were so respectful of his obvious power.

'The Great Wolf values silence over idle chatter, so that he might heed wise words otherwise lost in needless interrogation,' snarled Brynngar, the animosity he felt towards the son of Magnus obvious.

It was the Wolf Guard, already pledged to Cestus's cause, together with Antiges, that had summoned the Legions on Vangelis to this meeting. They had done so with passion and curt request, divulging little of what Cestus needed of them. The Space Wolf had at first railed against the inclusion of the Thousand Sons to be their potential sword-brothers in this deed. The conflicting character of the two Legions did not lend itself to a ready accord, but Cestus had reasoned that they needed every soul, and Mhotep had answered the call. What was more, he also had his own ship, a fact that only served to bolster the small fleet he was trying to assemble.

The captain of the Thousand Sons ignored the Space Wolf's thinly veiled insult and leant back in his seat with a gesture for Cestus to proceed.

The Ultramarines captain told the assembly of his squad's scheduled extraction from Vangelis by the *Fist of Macragge*, and of the astropathic message that had very nearly wrecked the control hub of Coralis dock. He even confided in them his fears that some unknown enemy had destroyed the ship, but he did not mention his experience in the reactor core. Cestus was still processing what he had seen. Visions were the province of sorcery and to divulge that he, an Ultramarine, had witnessed one would undermine his credibility and arouse suspicion as to his motives.

'Perhaps this deed was committed by an alien ship. Ork hulks have been fought and crushed by my Legion as far as the Segmentum Solar,' said a voice like iron. Skraal was a World Eater, an Astartes of the XII Legion, and the third of the invited warriors, including Brynngar.

He wore battered Mark V power armour, rendered in chipped blue and white, the colours of his Legion, clearly eschewing the Corvus pattern suits worn by his battle-brothers. The armour was heavily dented in several places, sporting numerous replacement parts, and the battlefield repair work was obvious. Formed of basic materials, the plates were held together by spikes, the manifest studs clearly visible on the left pauldron, greaves and gorget. The helmet rested on the table next to the warrior. It was similarly adorned and bore a fearsome aspect of blade and ballistic damage that revealed bare, grey metal beneath.

Skraal's face was the mirror of his armour, cross-hatching scar tissue a map-work of pain and suffering. A thick vein across his forehead throbbed as he spoke. His bellicose demeanour, coupled with a nervous tic beneath his right eye, gave him the outward appearance of being unhinged.

The World Eaters were a fearsome Legion. Much like their primarch, Angron, they were a primal force that fought with fury and wrath as their weapons. Each and every warrior was a font of rage and barely checked choler, bloody echoes of the battle-lust of their primarch.

'That is possible,' said Cestus, deliberately holding the gruesome warrior's gaze, despite Skraal's obvious belligerence. 'What is certain is that a ship of the Emperor's Astartes has been attacked by enemies unknown and for some nefarious purpose,' he continued with building anger and got to his feet. 'This act cannot go unreckoned!'

'Then what would you have us do, noble son of Guilliman?' asked Mhotep, ever the epitome of calm.

Cestus spread his hands across the table, laying his palms flat as he regained his composure. 'Astropathic decryption revealed a region of space that has been identified by the station's astrocartographer. I believe this is where the *Fist of Macragge* met its end. I also believe that since the ship was headed for the Calth system and a rendezvous with my lord Guilliman, it is possible that their attacker was heading in the same direction.'

'A substantial leap of logic, Ultramarine,' Mhotep countered, unconvinced by Cestus's impassioned arguments.

'It cannot believe that the very ship carrying five companies of my battle-brothers and en route to Calth was destroyed before reaching Vangelis in a random act of xenos contrition,' Cestus reasoned, his need for urgency fuelling his frustration.

'How are we to find this slayer vessel, then?' asked Skraal, thumbing the hilt of his chainaxe, the urge for carnage obvious. 'If what you say is true, and the distress call you received from the vessel is old, the prey will be far from that location.'

Cestus sighed in agitation. He wished dearly that he could make his brothers see what was in his heart, what he knew in his gut. For now, though, he dared not, at least, not until he could make some sense of what he had seen. There was no time for delay.

'Our position on Vangelis bisects the route of the *Fist of Macragge*; the route it would have taken to Calth. In short, it is ahead of the site of its demise. If we make ready at once, it is possible we may be able to catch the enemy's trail.'

Silent faces regarded him. Even Brynngar did not look certain of the Ultramarine's reasoning. Cestus realised that it was not logic that guided him on this course, but instinct and inner belief. The image of Macragge seen for an instant in the flash of the reactor burned fresh in his mind, and he spoke.

'I do not need your aid in this venture. I have already sent one of my battle-brothers to commandeer a vessel from this very station and I will take it to the site of the *Fist of Macragge's* last transmission. With luck we can pick up a trail to follow and find whoever is responsible for what happened to it. No, I do not *need* your aid, but I *ask* for it, humbly,' he added, pushing the seat back and kneeling reverently before his fellow Astartes with head bowed.

Antiges was aghast at first, but then he too left the table and kneeled. The other Ultramarines followed his

lead, and soon all six of Guilliman's sons were genu-
flecting before the rest of the council.

'The sons of Russ do not refuse an honour debt,' said
Brynngar, getting to his feet and laying Felltooth upon
the table. 'I will join you in this endeavour.'

Skraal stood next and set his chainaxe with the Space
Wolf's rune blade.

'The fury of the World Eaters is at your side.'

'What say you, son of Magnus?' Brynngar growled, his
savage gaze falling upon Mhotep.

For a moment, the Thousand Son sat in calm reflection, considering his answer. He laid his ornate scimitar
with the other weapons, its gilded blade humming with
power as he unsheathed it.

'My ship and I are at your disposal, Ultramarine.'

'Bah! This council's greatest opponent; I should like
to know why,' said Brynngar.

Mhotep smirked with amusement at the Space Wolf's
rancour, but refused to be baited.

'You all know of the events at Nikea concerning my
primarch and Legion, and the sanctions placed upon us
that day,' the Thousand Son said plainly. 'I am keen to
foster improved relations with my fellow Legions and
where better to start than the vaunted sons of Roboute
Guilliman.' Mhotep nodded respectfully at the final
remark, a deliberately weak attempt to cover the slight.

Cestus cared little for the discord between the two
Astartes and arose, Antiges following his example.

'You do me great service this day,' Cestus said with
genuine humility. 'We meet at Coralis dock in one
hour.'

THE SATURNINE FLEET had existed before the Great Crusade, carving out a miniature empire among the rings of

Saturn. Its strength and longevity had been based on a tradition of navigational skill, essential to negotiate the infinitely complex puzzle of the rings. Its rolls of honour noted the first time it had encountered the warships of the fledgling Imperium. Its admirals saw a brother empire, based on the demonstration of power and not just empty words or fanaticism, and signed a treaty with the Emperor that still held pride of place in the Admiralty Spire on Enceladus. Its ships had accompanied the Great Crusade to all corners of the galaxy, but their spiritual home had always been in the rings, the endless circle of Saturn boiling above them.

The *Wrathful* was a fine ship, Cestus admitted to himself as he stood upon the bridge alongside Antiges. It was old and lavish, panelled and decorated with the heritage of a naval aristocracy that pre-dated the Imperial Army and its fleets. Its bridge looked like it had been lifted from a naval academy on Enceladus, all dark wood map tables and glass-fronted bookcases, with only the occasional pict screen or command console to break the illusion. A ring of nine viewscreens was mounted on the ceiling, where they could be lowered to provide an all-angles view of what was happening outside the ship. The command crew were in the dark blue brocaded uniforms of the Saturnine Fleet, all starch and good breeding.

In commandeering this vessel, Saphrax and his battle-brothers had performed their task well.

'Rear admiral,' said Cestus as he approached the captain's post, a grand throne surrounded by racks of charts.

The throne rotated to reveal Rear Admiral Kaminska. Cestus could almost see the proud heritage etched upon her face: strong jaw, fine neck, high cheekbones, with a slight curl to the lip that suggested acute arrogance.

'Captain Cestus, it is an honour to serve the Emperor's Astartes,' she responded coolly. Saphrax had described the admiral's reaction to the acquisition of her ship to Cestus as he and the rest of the Ultramarine honour guard had boarded. It was prickly and vociferous.

She gave a near imperceptible nod by way of acknowledgement. The gesture was all but lost in the high collar of her uniform and the thick, furred mantle that hung around her shoulders. Admiral Kaminska was a stern-faced matriarch. A monocle over her left eye partly obscured a savage scar that cracked that side of her face. The monocle's sweeping chain was set with tiny skulls and pinned to the right breast of her jacket. She carried a control wand at her waist, secured by a loop of leather, and a naval pistol sat snugly in a holster at her hip. Gloved hands bore a lightning flash emblem made from metal; they were tense and gripped the supports of her command throne tightly.

'The *Wrathful* is an impressive ship,' said Cestus, attempting to dispel the fraught atmosphere. 'I am glad you could respond to our summons.'

'Indeed it is, Lord Astartes,' Kaminska said in clipped tones. 'It would be a great pity to sacrifice it upon the altar of futile vengeance. As for your summons,' she added, face pinching tight with anger, 'it was hardly that.'

Cestus held his tongue. As an Astartes fleet commander, it was within the remit of his authority to take command of the ship. For now, he decided he would allow the admiral some leeway. He was sketching a suitable reproach in his mind, when Kaminska continued.

'Captain Vorlov of the *Boundless* has also requested to accompany us, although you'll find he is of a more placid demeanour.'

Cestus had heard of the vessel, and of Captain Vorlov. It was a warhorse ship of the fleet, its combat scars too numerous to count. Its star was in decline, as better, more powerful ships made their presence felt in the greater galaxy. Cestus suspected that the *Boundless* had been docked at Vangelis for some time, its role in the Great Crusade somewhat diminished, and that Captain Vorlov did not wish to submit to atrophy just yet.

'Very well,' said Cestus, deciding against rebuking the admiral. He had, after all, taken her ship for a mission of dubious reasoning. Her attitude, he told himself, was to be expected.

'You have your heading, admiral. There is little time to lose.'

'The *Wrathful* is the fastest vessel in the Segmentum Solar. If your enemy is out there in the void then we will catch him,' Kaminska assured him, and whirled her command throne back around to her instrument panels.

ADMIRAL KAMINSKA BRISTLED furiously as the Astartes departed the bridge. She had come to Vangelis to effect repairs and take on supplies and replacement crew. She had been looking forward to a week or so of recuperation. Yet, at the word of the Emperor's Angels, lord regents of the galaxy it seemed, she and her ship were pressed back into service with barely a moment's notice. 'By the authority of the Emperor of Mankind', those words were an unbendable edict that Kaminska could not refuse. It was not that she resented serving – she was a dutiful soldier of the Imperium who had distinguished herself on numerous occasions for its greater glory – no, she took umbrage at the fact that this particular mission was fostered on hunches and, as far as she could tell, whimsy. It did not sit well with Kaminska, not at all.

'Lord admiral, the escort squadron is in position,' said Helmsmistress Athena Venkmyer. Her long hair was tied up severely, and her shoulders were forced to attention by the brocade of her uniform.

'Good,' Kaminska replied. 'Screens down!'

The ring of viewscreens descended and glowed to life. The bright, hard gleam of Vangelis was visible from the assembly point, surrounded by a fuzzy shoal of lesser lights: satellite listening spires, fleets at anchor and orbital debris. A distant sun was a brighter point, automatically dimmed by the viewscreens' limiters.

Icons blinked onto the screens, showing the positions of the other ships in the makeshift fleet. The four escorts – *Fearless*, *Ferox*, *Ferocious* and *Fireblade* – were flying in a slanted diamond around the *Wrathful*. The vessel of the Thousand Sons and Captain Mhotep, the *Waning Moon*, was a short distance away. Even at this distance, the Astartes craft was impressive, a sleek dart of red and gold. The *Boundless*, a cruiser like the *Wrathful*, but fitted out with decks for attack craft, was further out, still making its approach.

Satisfied that they were about ready to disembark, Admiral Kaminska flicked a control stud on the arm of her throne and the bridge vox-caster opened up. 'Loose escort pattern, keep the *Waning Moon* in our lee. Advance to primary way point, plasma engines three-quarters.'

'Three-quarters!' came the yell from Helms-mate Lodan Kant at the engine helm.

'Mister Orcadus, the Terraward end of the Tertiary Core Transit if you please,' said Kaminska, having opened up a line to her principal Navigator.

'At your word, lord admiral,' was the dour response from the Navigator's sanctum.

The Tertiary Core Transit was the most stable warp route from Segmentum Solar to the galactic south-east. It would take them to their destination expediently, and hopefully allow the *Wrathful* to gain some ground on whatever foes, real or imagined, awaited them in the void. It was also the route that any void-farer, if he or she did not want to take a four to five year detour, would take to arrive at the Calth system. The Astartes had been very specific about that. Admiral Kaminska would have liked to question it, but there was no bringing the Emperor's Angels to account on such a triviality. She would defer to the Astartes's order, since he was in charge. It would have been unseemly to do otherwise. Kaminska resolved to discover the truth later.

The *Wrathful*'s engines kicked in, banishing the admiral's thoughts to the back of her mind. She could feel the vibration through the panelled floor of the bridge. The escort squadron moved into formation on the viewscreens, followed by the *Waning Moon* and the *Boundless*.

Whatever was out there, they would find out soon enough.

'THERE IS AN energy trail here. It's degraded but discernible,' said Principal Navigator Orcadus's voice from his inner sanctum on the *Wrathful*.

The Imperial ship and her fleet had reached the region of real space as indicated by the co-ordinates provided by Captain Cestus, the supposed site of the destruction of the *Fist of Macragge*, in short order. They found no sign of the Ultramarine vessel. There was merely a faint energy trace that matched the *Fist of Macragge*'s signature. Unlike battles on land, where evidence of a fight could be seen clearly and obviously, conflicts in space were not so easily identifiable. Wrecks drifted, ships could be caught and destroyed in black holes, space debris drawn into the gravity well of a passing moon or small planet, even solar wind could scatter the final proof of a battle ever having taken place. So it was that Kaminska had instructed her Navigator to search for whatever energy traces remained behind, those last vestiges of plasma engine discharge that lingered in spite of all other evidence dissipating due to the ravages of space.

'By Saturn, the output must have been massive,' Orcadus continued with rare emotion. 'Whatever ship left this wake is gargantuan, admiral.'

'It is possible to follow it then?' Kaminska asked, swivelling in her command throne to regard Captain Cestus standing silently alongside her.

Orcadus's reply was succinct.

'Yes, admiral.'

'Do it,' Cestus told Kaminska grimly, his expression far away.

Kaminska scowled at what she perceived as arrogance, and returned to her original position.

'Then do so. Set radar array to full power, Mister Orcadus. Take us onward.'

'BROTHERHOOD,' SAID ZADKIEL, 'is power.'

Surrounded by novices in the sepulchral gloom of the cathedra, he loomed high above the assembly within a raised pulpit of black steel.

'It is at the core of all authority in the known galaxy, and the source of humanity's dominion. This is the Word of Lorgar, as it is written.'

'As it is written,' echoed the novices.

Over fifty Word Bearers had gathered for the seminary and knelt in supplication before their lord, wearing grey initiate robes over their crimson armour. The cathedral's ceiling soared on stone-clad struts overhead, adding acoustic power to Zadkiel's oratory, and the air was as still and cold as a vault. The floor, tiled with stone pages cut with passages from the Word, emphasised that this was a place of worship. It was the very thing that the Emperor had forbidden in his Legions. Idolatry and zealous faith had no place in the Master of Mankind's new age of enlightenment, but here, in this place, and in the hearts of all Lorgar's children, faith would be honed into a weapon.

One of the initiates stood among the congregation, indicating his desire to respond.

'Speak,' said Zadkiel, quelling his annoyance at the impromptu interruption.

'Brother can turn on brother,' said the novice, 'and thus become weakened. Where, then, is such power?'

In the half-light, Zadkiel recognised Brother Ultis, a zealous youth with ambitious temperament.

'That is the source of its true power, novice, for there is no greater rivalry than that which exists between siblings. Only then will one seek to undo the works of the other with such vehemence, giving every ounce of his being to claim victory,' Zadkiel said, arrogantly, enjoying the feeling of superiority.

'Upon gaining mastery over his kin, that brother will have forged a mighty army so as to overthrow him. He will have plumbed deep of his core and unleashed his hate, for in no other way can such a victory be achieved.'

'So you speak of hate,' said Ultis, 'and not brother-hood at all.'

Zadkiel smiled thinly to conceal his impatience.

'They are two wings on the same eagle, equal ele-ments of an identical source,' Zadkiel explained. 'We are at war with our brothers, make no mistake of that. In his short-sightedness, the Emperor has brought us to this inexorable fate.

'With our hate, our devotion to the credos of our pri-march, the all-powerful Lorgar, we will achieve our victory.'

'But the Emperor holds Terra, and in that surely there is strength,' Ultis countered, forgetting himself.

'The Emperor is brother to no one!' cried Zadkiel, stepping forward as his words crushed Ultis's challenge easily.

Silence persisted for a moment, Ultis shrinking back before his master as he was being chastened. None in the cathedral dared speak. All were cowed by Zadkiel's obvious power.

'He lurks in his dungeons on Terra,' Zadkiel contin-ued with greater zeal, but now addressing the entire congregation. 'The eaxectors and bureaucrats, the flock of Malcador, who run Terra's regency, they shy away from all ties of brotherhood. They sit on a pedestal, above reproach, above their brothers, above even our noble Warmaster!'

The crowd roared in ascent, Ultis among them, kneel-ing once more.

'Is that brotherhood?'

The novices roared again, gauntleted fists pounding the breast plates of their armour to emphasise their fervour.

'These regents create a stale, meaningless world where all passion is dead and devotion is regarded as heresy!' Zadkiel spat the words, and was suddenly aware of a presence in the shadows behind him.

One of the *Furious Abyss*'s crew, Helms-mate Sarkorov, a man with delicate data-probes instead of fingers, was patiently awaiting Zadkiel's notice.

'My apologies, lord,' he said, once he had crossed the few metres between them, 'but Navigator Esthemya has discovered a fleet of pursuing vectors in our wake.'

'What fleet?'

'Two cruisers, an escort squadron and an Astartes strike vessel.'

'I see.' Zadkiel turned back to the congregation. 'Novices, you are dismissed,' he said without ceremony.

The assembled Word Bearers departed in silence into the shadows around the edge of the cathedral, heading back to their cells to ruminate on the Word.

'They are gaining ground, my lord,' said Sarkorov once they were alone. 'We are powerful, but these ships are smaller and outmatch us for speed.'

'Then they will reach us before we arrive at the Tertiary Core Transit.' It was a statement, not a question.

'They will, my lord. Should I instruct the magos to force the engines to maximum power? It is possible we could make warp before we are intercepted.'

'No,' said Zadkiel, after some thought. 'Maintain course and keep me updated as to the fleet's progress.'

'Yes, sire,' replied Sarkorov, saluting and then turning sharply to return to the bridge.

'My Lord Zadkiel,' said a voice from the gloom. It was Ultis, concealed by the shadows, but now stepping into the light at the centre of the cathedra.

'Novice,' said Zadkiel, 'why have you not returned to your cell?'

'I would speak with you, master, of the lessons imparted.'

'Then illuminate me, novice.' There was the slightest trace of amusement in Zadkiel's tone.

'The brothers of whom you spoke, you were referring to the primarchs,' Ultis ventured.

'Go on.'

'Our current course will bring us into conflict with the Emperor. To the unenlightened observer, it would appear that the Emperor rules the galaxy and the throne of Terra cannot be usurped.'

'What of the enlightened, novice, what do they see?'

'That the Emperor's power is wielded through his primarchs,' Ultis said with growing conviction, 'and by dividing them, the power of which you spoke is realised.'

Zadkiel's silence bade Ultis to continue.

'It is how Terra can be defeated, when Lorgar's brothers join with him, when we bring war to those who will inevitably side with the Emperor. We will yoke our hatred and use it as a weapon, one that will not be denied!'

Zadkiel nodded sagely, suppressing a prickle of annoyance at this precocious, yet insightful, youth. Ultis, however, had overreached himself. Zadkiel saw the naked ambition in his eyes, the flame within that threatened to devour Zadkiel's own.

'I merely seek to understand the Word,' Ultis added, exhaling his fervour.

'And you shall, Ultis,' Zadkiel replied, a plan forming in his mind. 'You will be an important instrument in the breaking of Guilliman.'

'I would be honoured, lord,' said Ultis, bowing his head.

'Truly blind men like Guilliman are few,' Zadkiel counselled. 'He believes religion and devotion to be a corrupting force, something to be abhorred and not embraced as we followers of the Word do. His pragmatic retardation is his greatest weakness and in his dogmatic ignorance we shall strike at the heart of his favoured Legion.'

Zadkiel spread his arms wide to encompass the cathedral, its high vaults and fluted columns, its pages of the Word, its altar and pulpit. 'One day, Ultis, the whole galaxy will look like this.'

Ultis bowed once more.

'Now, return to your cell and think on these lessons further.'

'Yes, my lord.'

Zadkiel watched the novice go. A great passage in the sermon of the Word was unfolding and Ultis would play his part. Zadkiel turned back to the pulpit, behind which was a simple altar. Zadkiel lit a candle there for the soul of Roboute Guilliman. Blind he might be, but he was a brother of sorts, and it was only right that his future death be commemorated.

ABOARD THE WRATHFUL, on one of the ship's training decks, two World Eaters clashed furiously in a duelling pit. It was one of several arenas in a much wider gymnasium that was replete with dummies, weights and training mats. Weapon ranks lined the walls. The Astartes had brought their own stocks of training weapons with them, and sword-breakers, short-blades, bludgeons and spears were all in evidence. It appeared that the concept of simple training was anathema to the duelling sons of Angron. Amidst the storm of blades and unbridled blood-lust the World Eaters fought as if to the death.

Armed with unfettered chainaxes and stripped to the waist, wearing crimson training breeches and black boots, their muscled bodies revealed gruesome welts and long, jagged scars.

With a roar, they broke off for a moment, and began circling each other in the sunken chamber of the pit. White marble showed up dark splashes from where the gladiators had wounded each other early on in the contest. A narrow drain at the centre of the pit was already clogging with blood.

'Such anger,' Antiges commented, overlooking the contest from a seated position at the back of the auditorium before which it was staged.

'They are Angron's progeny,' said Cestus, alongside him, 'it is their way to be wrathful. Properly employed, their wrath is a useful tool.'

'Yes, but their reputation is a dire one, as is their lord's,' replied Antiges, his expression stern. 'I for one do not feel at ease with their presence on this ship.'

'I have to concur with my brother, Captain Cestus,' added Thestor, who was watching the show alongside Antiges. The burly Astartes was the biggest of the honour guard. Unsurprisingly, his bulk went well with his role of heavy weapons specialist. The rest of the honour guard were nearby, except for Saphrax, watching the ferocious display with mixed interest and disdain. Thestor echoed the thoughts of all his brothers when he next spoke.

'Was it necessary to bring them with us at all?' he asked, his gaze shifting back from his captain to watch the fight. 'This is the business of the Ultramarines. What has it got to do with our Legion brothers?'

'Thestor, do not be so narrow-minded as to think we do not need their aid,' Cestus chastened the heavy-set Astartes, who glanced over at his captain. 'We are a brotherhood: all of us. Though we each have our differences, the Emperor has seen fit for us to conquer the galaxy in his name together. The moment we seek our own personal glories, when we abandon solidarity for pride, is the moment when brotherhood will be shattered.'

Thestor regarded the floor when his captain had finished, shamed by his selfish remarks.

'You may take your leave, Thestor,' said Cestus. It wasn't a request.

The big Astartes got to his feet and left the training arena.

'I agree with you, Cestus, of course I do,' said Antiges, once Thestor had gone, 'but they are like savages.'

'Are they, Antiges?' Cestus challenged. 'Are Brynngar and the wolves of Russ not savages, too? Do you hold them in such disregard also?'

'Of course not,' Antiges replied. 'I have fought with the Space Wolves and know of their courage and honour. They are savages in their own way, yes, but the difference is that they are possessed of a noble spirit. These sons of Angron are blood-letters, pure and simple. They kill for the simple joy of it.'

'We are all warriors,' Cestus told him. 'Each of us kills in the Emperor's name.'

'Not like them we don't.'

'They are Astartes,' Cestus said, biting out his words, and turning on his battle-brother. 'I will hear no more of this. You forget your place, Antiges.'

'I apologise, captain. I spoke out of turn,' Antiges replied after a moment of stunned silence. 'I only meant to say that I do not approve of their methods or their deeds.' At that, the Ultramarine turned back to watch the battle.

Cestus followed his battle-brother's gaze. The Ultramarine captain did not know either of the World Eaters in the duelling pit. He knew precious little of their leader, Skraal. This was ritual combat. No slight, no besmirching of honour had occurred to bring it about. Yet it was bladed and deadly.

'I do not, either,' Cestus admitted, watching as one of the combatants nearly lost his arm to a wild swing of his opponent's chainaxe.

The Ultramarine had heard stories from his fellow Legionnaires about the so called 'cleansing' of Ariggata, one of the World Eaters' more infamous battle actions. The Legion's assault on the citadel there had reputably left a charnel house in its wake. Cestus knew full well that Guilliman still sought a reckoning with his brother primarch, Angron, concerning the dire events of that mission, but this was no time for recrimination. Necessity had forced Cestus's hand, and whether he liked it or not, this is what he had been dealt.

Skraal led twenty World Eaters on the *Wrathful* and Cestus was determined to make the best use of them. Brynngar had brought the same number of Blood Claws, and while they were raucous and pugnacious, especially when forced into idleness in the confines of the ship, they did not harbour the same homicidal bent as the bloody sons of Angron. Mhotep was the only Astartes not aboard the *Wrathful*. He had his own ship, the *Waning Moon*, but no squads of Thousand Sons, just cohorts of naval arms-men at his command.

Barely fifty Astartes and the vessels of their makeshift fleet, Cestus hoped it would be enough for whatever was in store.

'What troubles you, brother?' asked Antiges, their brief altercation swiftly forgotten. The Ultramarine finally turned his back on the battling World Eaters, deciding he had seen enough.

'The message at Coralis dock sits heavily on me,' Cestus confessed. 'The clenched fist, crested by a laurel crown represents Legion... our Legion. The golden book – I don't know what that means, but I saw something else.'

'In the reactor flare,' Antiges realised. 'I had thought I was hearing things when you asked us if we'd seen anything.'

'You were not, and yes, I saw it in the reactor flare, so fleeting and indistinct that at first I believed it was my imagination, that my mind was articulating what my heart longed for.'

'What did you see?'

Cestus looked Antiges directly in the eyes.

'I saw Macragge.'

Antiges was nonplussed. 'I don't–'

'I saw Macragge and I felt despair, Antiges, as if it presaged something terrible.'

'Signs and visions are the province of witchery, brother-captain,' Antiges counselled warily. 'We both know the edicts of Nikea.'

'Brothers,' a voice broke in before Cestus could respond. It was Saphrax, come from the bridge where Cestus had instructed he maintain a watch on proceedings.

Both Saphrax's fellow Ultramarines turned to him expectantly.

'We have made visual contact with the ship from the site of the *Fist*'s destruction.'

* * *

'THAT IS A Legion ship, captain. You are not suggesting that a vessel of the Imperium fired upon one of its own?' Admiral Kaminska warned the Astartes.

Following Saphrax's report, Cestus and Antiges had made for the bridge at once. What they saw in the viewscreen when they got there had stunned them both.

The vessel they tracked in the void was of Mechanicum design and clearly made for the Legion. It was bedecked in the iconography of the Word Bearers.

It was the largest ship that Cestus had ever seen. Even at a considerable distance it was massive, easily three times the size of the *Wrathful*, and would have dwarfed an Emperor-class battleship. It bore an impressive array of weapons; tech-adepts aboard the *Wrathful* had suggested port and starboard broadside laser batteries and multiple torpedo tubes to the prow and stern. It was the monolithic statue towering at the vessel's prow, however, that gave Cestus the most concern: a gigantic golden book, the echo of the fragmented image in the astropathic message on Vangelis.

'We're at extreme strike range,' said Captain Commander Vorlov. 'What are your orders, admiral?'

'Hold them back,' said Cestus, deliberately interrupting Kaminska. 'They are our Legion brothers. I am certain they will be able to account for themselves. They may have information regarding the *Fist of Macragge*.'

Vorlov was a paunchy man with jowls that wobbled independently of the rest of his body. He had a gnarled red nose that spoke of long nights drinking to keep away the cold of space, and dressed in the heavy furs typical of his Saturnine heritage. His presence filled the viewscreen through which he was communicating with the bridge of the *Wrathful*. 'Yes, my lord,' he said.

'No point rattling the sword without reason,' Cestus muttered to Antiges, who nodded his assent. 'Hang back and keep them within range, but do not approach. Admiral Kaminska, bring the *Wrathful* in at the lead. Keep the *Waning Moon* and the escort fleet in our wake.'

'As you wish, my lord,' she said, swallowing her annoyance and her pride. 'Relaying orders now.'

The tension around the bridge was palpable. Brynngar, having joined them a moment before, growled beneath his breath.

'What is your plan, Cestus?' he asked, eyes locked on the viewscreen and the mighty vessel visible beyond it.

'We draw in close enough to hail them and demand to know their business.'

'On Fenris, when stalking the horned orca, I would swim the icy depths of the ocean taking care to stay in the beast's wake,' Brynngar said with intensity. 'Once I drew close enough I would slip my baleen spear from my leg and launch it into the orca's unprotected flank. Then I would swim, long and hard, to reach the beast before it could turn and impale me on its horn. Within its thrashing swell I would seize upon it and with my blade pare its flesh and gut its innards. For the orca is a mighty beast, and this was the only way to be sure of its demise.'

'We will hail them,' Cestus affirmed, noting the savagery that played across Brynngar's features with unease. 'I won't commit us to a fight over nothing.'

'Admiral,' the Ultramarine added, turning to Kaminska.

'Helms-mate Kant, open up a channel to the vessel at once,' she said.

Kant did as ordered and indicated his readiness to his commander.

Kaminska nodded to Cestus.

'This is Captain Cestus of the Ultramarines Seventh Chapter. In the name of the Emperor of Mankind, I am ordering you to state your designation and business in this subsector.'

Static-fringed silence was the only reply.

'I repeat: this is Captain Cestus of the Ultramarines Seventh Chapter. Respond,' he barked into the bridge vox.

More silence.

'Why do they not answer?' asked Antiges, his fists tightly clenched. 'They are Legionaries, like us. Since when did the sons of Lorgar fail to acknowledge the Ultramarines?'

'I don't know. Perhaps their long-range vox is out.' Cestus was reaching for answers, trying to deny what he had known in his heart ever since Vangelis, that something was wrong, terribly, terribly wrong.

'Signal one of the frigates to make approach,' Cestus ordered after a brief silence, eyes fixed on the viewscreen like every other soul on the bridge. 'I don't want to come in with our cruisers,' he reasoned. 'It might be perceived as a threat.'

Kaminska relayed the order in curt fashion and the *Fearless* closed on the unknown vessel.

'I shall follow them in,' said Mhotep from a second viewscreen on the bridge. 'I have half a regiment of Prospero Spireguard standing by to board.'

'Very well, captain, but keep your distance,' Cestus warned.

'As you wish.' The viewscreen went blank as Mhotep took active command of the *Waning Moon*.

A tactical array abruptly activated, depicting the closing vessels that were virtually lost from sight in the viewport. The Word Bearers ship was a red icon on the display surrounded by sensor readings of the approaching frigates, little more than green blips in its presence.

'This reeks,' snarled Brynngar, who had begun prowling the bridge with impatience, 'and my nose never lies.'

Cestus kept his eyes on the tactical array.

Macragge. The image of his Macragge, seen as part of the astropathic warning in the reactor core, came to mind once more. How were the fates of this vessel and his home world entwined?

The Word Bearers were his brothers; surely they had nothing to do with the destruction of the *Fist of Macragge*? Such a thing was unconscionable.

Cestus would have his answers soon enough.

The *Fearless* had reached its destination.

FIVE

A line is drawn/Silver Three down/Open book

'YOUR ORDERS, CAPTAIN?' came the vox from the ordnance deck.

Zadkiel sat back on his throne. The feeling of power was intoxicating. The battleship was his to command, like an extension of his body, as if the torpedo tubes and gun turrets were his hands. He could simply spread his fingers and will destruction on the enemy.

'Hold,' said Zadkiel.

The central viewscreen showed the closing vessels: a frigate with a strike cruiser in its wake. The frigate did not interest the Word Bearer captain, but the cruiser was an entirely different prospect: fast, well-armed and designed for precision attacks and boarding actions. It was painted in the livery of the Thousand Sons.

'Magnus's brood,' said Zadkiel, idly. Astride his command throne, he glanced at a supplementary screen that depicted a tactical readout of the ship. The *Furious Abyss*'s archive had identified it as the *Waning Moon*. It had many battle honours, and had followed the Thousand Sons Legion across half the galaxy prosecuting the Great Crusade. 'I have always admired their imagination.'

Assault-Captain Baelanos was standing behind the command throne.

'They're within range, sire.'

'There is no hurry, captain,' said Zadkiel. 'We should savour this moment.' Additional readings flicked up on the viewscreen. The *Waning Moon* was showing lifesigns equivalent to a full regiment of troops gathering at the boarding muster points.

'Helms-mate Sarkorov, open up a clandestine channel to the *Waning Moon*,' Zadkiel ordered.

'At once, my lord,' came the reply from deep inside the dark city of the bridge.

After a moment, Sarkorov added.

'Channel is secure.'

'On screen.'

The central image was replaced with a view of the *Waning Moon*'s gilded bridge. The Astartes in the command throne, which was massively ornate and inset with numerous jewels and engraved runes, looked up in mild surprise. He had light brown skin and hooded eyes, with a face that spoke of discipline and resolve.

'This is Captain Zadkiel, addressing you from the *Furious Abyss*. Am I speaking to the captain of the *Waning Moon*?' asked Zadkiel.

'You are. I am Captain Mhotep of the Thousand Sons. Why have you not responded to our hails?'

'No, captain, I demand to know what this display of force means,' Zadkiel said, unwilling to be interrogated by his brother Astartes. 'You have no authority here. Disengage at once.'

'I repeat, why have you not responded to our hails and what do you know of the *Fist of Macragge* and its fate?' Mhotep was relentless and would not be cowed.

'I do not appreciate your tone, brother. I know nothing of the vessel you speak of,' Zadkiel replied. 'Now, disengage.'

'I do not believe you, brother,' said the Thousand Son with certainty.

Zadkiel smiled mirthlessly.

'Then I shall give you the truth. Great deeds are unfolding, Captain Mhotep. Lines will be drawn. Flame and retribution is coming, and those who are on the wrong side of that line will be burned to ash.' Zadkiel paused for a moment, allowing his words to sink in.

Mhotep remained impassive. The Thousand Sons were quite the experts at concealing their true emotions.

'We are on a secure channel, Captain Mhotep, and the Legion of the Word have ever been supporters of your lord Magnus. The events of Nikea must rankle.' That got a reaction, near imperceptible, but it was there.

'What are you suggesting, Word Bearer?'

Hostility now, the icy reserve was thawing at the mention of what many in the Legion regarded as Magnus's trial and that what happened at Nikea was performed by a council in name only.

'Lorgar and Magnus are brothers. So are we. What side of the line will you stand on, Mhotep?'

The retort was curt. The Thousand Son's face was set like stone.

'Prepare to be boarded,' he said.

'As you wish,' replied the Word Bearer.

The vox link to the *Waning Moon* was cut.

'Master Malforian,' said Zadkiel, levelly.

The ordnance deck flashed up on the viewscreen, a deep metal canyon beneath the prow crowded with sweating ratings hauling massive torpedoes.

'My lord.'

'Fire.'

A spread of torpedoes flew from the *Furious Abyss* towards the *Waning Moon*, which had positioned itself before the massive ship's prow. Starboard, a bank of laser batteries lit up at once, and beams of crimson light stabbed into the void. They struck the *Fearless* and the frigate was broken apart in a bright and silent flurry of blossoming explosions.

'THRONE OF TERRA!' Cestus could not believe what he was seeing through the *Wrathful*'s viewscreen. Powerless, and benumbed, he watched the *Fearless* fragment like scrap as a firestorm ravaged it, hungrily devouring the oxygen on board and turning it into a raging furnace. It was over in seconds, and after the conflagration had died all that remained was a blackened ruin. Then the torpedoes hit the *Waning Moon*.

'SHARKS IN THE void!' cried Helms-mate Ramket from the sensorium on the bridge of the *Waning Moon*. The crew were all at battle stations, carefully monitoring the actions of the Word Bearer ship. The lights in the elliptical chamber were dimmed as was protocol for combat situation, and the tiny blips that represented the ordnance launched by the *Furious Abyss* glowed malevolently on one of the bridge's tactical display slates.

'Evasive manoeuvres. Turrets to full! Withdraw boarding parties to damage control stations!' Mhotep scowled and gripped the lip of the command console in front of him. Shields were useless against torpedoes; he had to hope their hull armour could bear the brunt of the *Furious Abyss*'s opening salvo.

'At your command, my lord,' came Ramket's reply.

Warning runes flashed on multiple screens at once, presaging the missile impacts. Mhotep turned again to his helms-mate.

'Open a channel to the *Wrathful*,' he ordered as the first of the torpedoes hit, sending damage klaxons screaming as a massive shudder ran through the bridge.

'Mhotep, what's happening out there?' asked Cestus over the ship-to-ship vox array.

'The *Fearless* is gone. We are taking fire and attempting to evade. The Word Bearers have turned on their own, Cestus.'

A burst of crackling static held in the air for the moment combining with the din of relayed orders and cogitator warnings.

When he finally spoke, the Ultramarine's voice was grim.

'Engage and destroy.'

'Understood.'

THE BRIDGE OF the *Wrathful* moved to battle stations, Kaminska barking rapid orders to her subordinates with well-drilled precision and calm. The professionalism of the Saturnine Fleet's officer class was evident as the weapons were brought to bear and shields focused prow-ward.

'How shall we respond, lord Astartes?' she asked, once they were at a state of readiness.

Cestus fought a cold knot of disbelief building in the pit of his stomach as he watched the spread of blips on the tactical display move into attack positions.

The Word Bearers have turned on their own.

Mhotep's words were like a hammer blow.

His words, the words that Cestus had spoken earlier on the training deck to Thestor and Antiges, of brother-hood and the solidarity of the Legions, suddenly turned to ash in his mouth. He had admonished his brothers for even voicing mild dissent against a fellow Legion-naire, and now, here they were embattled against them. No, they were not World Eaters. They were not the mur-derous, blood-letters that Antiges had described. They were the devout servants of the Emperor. Ostensibly they were his most vehement and staunchest support-ers.

How far did this treachery go? Was it confined merely to this ship, or did it permeate the entire Legion? Surely, with the vessel crafted by the Mechanicum it had the sanction of Mars. Could they be aware of the Word Bearers' defection? Such a thing could not be counte-nanced. With these questions running through his mind like a fever, Cestus could not believe what was happening. It did not feel real. From disbelief, anger and a desire for retribution was born.

'Break that ship in two,' Cestus said, full of righteous conviction. He could feel the ripples of shock and dis-belief passing through the non-Astartes as the full horror of what they had witnessed sank in. He would show them that the true servants of the Emperor did not tolerate traitors and any act of heresy would be sum-marily dealt with. Cestus's feelings and the ramifications of what had transpired would have to wait and be rationalised later. 'Relay astropathic messages to Macragge and Terra at once,' the Ultramarine added. 'The sons of Lorgar will be held to account for this. Admiral Kaminska, you have the helm.'

'As you wish, my lord.' Kaminska said. Trying her best to maintain her cold composure in the face of such developments, she swivelled the command throne as the screens around her shifted to show every angle around the ship. 'Captain Vorlov, are you with me?'

'Say the word, admiral.' Vorlov's enthusiasm was obvious, despite the static flickering through the fleet's vox array.

'Take the lead behind the *Waning Moon*. If they stay on the Astartes ship, swing up in front of them. Give them a bloody good broadside up the nose, and scramble attack craft. Keep their gunners busy. I'll send what's left of our escorts with you. In the name of Emperor.'

'At your command, admiral,' replied Vorlov with relish. 'Main engines to full, all crew to battle stations. Watch my stern, admiral, and the *Boundless* will pick this swine apart! In the name of Emperor.'

'Mister Castellan,' Kaminska barked, terminating the vox link with the *Boundless*. The *Wrathful*'s Master of Ordnance appeared on screen, toiling ratings just visible behind him on the gun decks.

'A lance salvo to their dorsal turret arrays and engines, if you please,' said Kaminska. 'Load prow plasma torpedoes, but hold in reserve, I want something up our sleeve.'

'At your command, admiral,' came the clipped response from Master of Ordnance Castellan, who snapped a curt salute before the screen blanked.

CESTUS WATCHED AS the organised chaos of battle stations unfolded. Every crewman on the bridge had his own role to play, relaying orders, monitoring sensorium and viewscreens, or making minute adjustments to the ship's course. One of the tables on the bridge unfolded into a stellar map where holographic simulacra were moved around to represent the relative positions of the ships in the fleet.

'Traitorous whoresons,' snarled Brynngar, 'it'll be Lorgar's head for this.'

Cestus could see the hairs on the back of the Space Wolf's neck rise. In this fell mood and with the dimmed battle stations gloom, he took on a feral aspect.

'Scuttle her and I'll lead the sons of Russ aboard,' he growled darkly. 'Let the wolves of Fenris gut her and I'll tear out the beating heart myself.'

Brynngar hawked and spat a gobbet of phlegm onto the deck as if what was transpiring in the void had left a bitter taste. There were a few raised eyebrows, but the Wolf Guard paid them no heed.

Cestus's reply was terse. 'You'll get your chance.'

Brynngar roared, baring his fangs.

'I can no longer sit idle,' he snapped savagely, turning on his heel. 'The warriors of Russ will make ready at the boarding torpedoes. Do not make us wait long.'

Cestus couldn't be certain if the last part was a request or a threat, but he was, for once, glad of the Wolf Guard's departure. His mood, since they'd hit the void and encountered the Word Bearers had grown increasingly erratic and belligerent. The Ultramarine sensed that the wolves of Russ did not relish such encounters. The fact that Brynngar was so eager to spill the blood of fellow Astartes only caused Cestus greater discomfort.

At war with our Legion brothers, the very idea scarcely seemed possible, yet it was happening.

Cestus watched the space battle unfold with curious detachment and felt his sense of foreboding grow.

* * *

THE WANING MOON had burned its retro engines to kill its speed, and fired all thrusters on its underside to twist upwards and present its armoured flank to a second torpedo volley shimmering towards it.

The first torpedoes missed high, spiralling past the ship to be lost in the void.

A handful detonated early, riddled with massive-calibre fragmentation shells from the defence turrets mounted along the flank of the *Waning Moon*.

Several found their mark just below the stern. Another streaked in with violent force, and then two more amidships. Useless energy shields flared black over the impact points as hull segments spun away from the ship, the torpedoes gouging their way through the outer armour.

'Damage report!' shouted Mhotep above the din of the bridge.

'Negligible, sire,' Officer Ammon answered from the engineering helm.

'What?'

'Minimal hull fractures, my Lord Mhotep.'

'Sensorium definitely read four impacts,' confirmed Helms-mate Ramket watching over the readouts.

Embedded deep in the hull of the *Waning Moon*, the outer casing of each torpedo split with a super-heated incendiary and six smaller missiles drilled out from their parent casing. They were ringed with metallic teeth and bored through the superstructure of the strike cruiser as they spun. Drilling through the last vestiges of hull armour, the missiles emerged into the belly of the vessel and detonated with a powerful explosive charge. With a deafening *thoom-woosh* of concussive heat pressure, the gun decks were ruined. Ratings and indentured workers died in droves, burned by the intense conflagration. Heaps of shells exploded in the firestorm, throwing lashes of flame and chunks of spiralling shrapnel through the decks. Master Gunner Kytan was decapitated in the initial barrage, and dozens of gunnery crew met a similar fate as they scrambled for cover as the gun-decks became little more than an abattoir of charred corpses and hellish screaming.

THE WANING MOON shuddered as explosions tore through its insides. A destructive chain reaction boiled through the upper decks and into crew quarters. Sternwards, detonations ripped into engineering sections, normally well shielded from direct hits, and ripped plasma conduits free to spew superheated fluid through access tunnels and coolant ducts.

Damage control crews, waiting at their muster points to douse fires and seal breaches, were torn asunder by the resultant carnage from amidships. Orderlies at triage posts barely had time to register the pandemonium on the gun decks before the blunt bullet of a warhead thundered through into the medicae deck and annihilated them in a flash of light and terror.

Chains of explosions ripped huge chunks out of the *Waning Moon*'s insides. Like massive charred bite marks, whole sections were reduced to smouldering metal and hundreds of crewmen were lost to the cold of the void as the vessel's structural integrity broke down.

'REPORT THAT!' ORDERED Mhotep, clinging to his command throne on the bridge as sections of the ship collapsed around him, revealing bare metal and sparking circuitry. The lights around the bridge were stuttered intermittently as the *Waning* registered power loss and damage across all decks. Mhotep's crew were doing their best to marshal some semblance of order, but the attack had been swift and far-reaching.

'Massive internal and secondary explosions,' replied Officer Ammon, struggling to keep pace with the warning runes dancing madly over the engineering helm, and snapping off further reports. 'Plasma venting from reactor seven, gun crews non-responsive and medicae has taken severe damage.'

'Tertiary shielding is breached,' said Mhotep as the ship-to-ship vox crackled into life.

'Mhotep, report your status at once! This is Captain Cestus.' The impacts had shaken the vox array and the Ultramarine's voice was distorted with static.

'We are wounded, captain,' said Mhotep grimly. 'Some kind of Mechanicum tech that I have never seen before burned our insides.'

'Our lances are firing,' Cestus informed him. 'Can you stay engaged?'

'Aye, son of Macragge, we're not done yet.'

A further crackle of static and the vox went dead.

The bridge of the *Waning Moon* was alive with transmissions from the rest of the ship: some calm, reporting peripheral damage to minor systems; others frantic, from plasma reactor seven and the gun decks, and there were those that were unintelligible through raging fire and screaming: the last words of men and women dying agonising deaths.

'Be advised, captain, they are coming about.' Principal Navigator Cronos was eerily calm as his voice came through the internal vox array. Mhotep scrutinised the tactical holo-display above the command console. The *Furious Abyss* was changing course. It was suffering lance impacts from the *Wrathful* and was turning to present its heavily armoured prow to the aggressors.

'What folly from this Bearer of his Word,' Mhotep intoned. 'He thinks we will flee like the jackal, but his only victory is in raising the ire of Prospero! Mister Cronos, bring us across his bow. Gun decks port and starboard, prepare for a rolling broadside!'

THE WANING MOON rotated grandly, as if standing on end in front of the *Furious Abyss*. The Word Bearer vessel had not reacted, and its blunt prow faced the damaged strike cruiser.

Deep scores, like illegible signatures, were seared into the prow armour of the traitors' ship by the *Wrathful*'s laser batteries. An insane crosshatch of crimson lance beams erupted between the two vessels with pyrotechnic intensity as they traded blows, silent shield flares indicating absorbed impacts.

Errant bursts glittered past the *Waning Moon* as it opened up its gun ports and the snouts of massive ship-to-ship cannon emerged. Behind them, sweat-drenched ratings toiled to load the enormous guns and avenge their dead. They chanted in gun-cant to keep their rhythm strong, one refrain for hauling shells out of the hoppers behind them, another for ramming it home, and yet another for hauling the breech closed.

The signal to fire reached them from the bridge. The rating gang leaders brought hammers down on firing pins and inside the ship, thunder screamed through the decks.

Outside, jets of propellant and debris leapt the gap between the two ships. A split second later the shells impacted, explosive charges blasting deep craters into the enemy vessel.

* * *

THE BRIDGE OF the *Furious Abyss* stayed calm.

Zadkiel was pleased. His ship, the city over which he ruled, was not governed by panic.

'My lord, should we retaliate?' asked Helms-mate Sarkorov.

'For now, we wait,' said Zadkiel, content to absorb the punishment as he sat back on the command throne watching images of the *Waning Moon*'s assault on the viewscreens above him. 'There is nothing they can do to us.'

'You would have us sit here and take this?' snarled Reskiel at his master's side.

'We will prevail,' said Zadkiel, unperturbed.

Dozens of new contacts flared on the viewscreens, streaking from the launch bays of a ship identified as the *Boundless*.

'Assault boats, sire,' Sarkorov informed him, monitoring the same feed. 'Escorts are closing.'

Zadkiel pored over the hololithic display.

'They intend to attack from all angles and confuse us, and while we weather this storm, their assault boats and escorts will pick us apart.' Zadkiel provided the curt tactical analysis coldly, his face aglow in the display.

'What is our response?' asked Reskiel.

'We wait.'

'That's it?'

'We wait,' repeated Zadkiel, his voice like iron. 'Trust in the Word.'

Reskiel stood back, watching the fire hammering in from the *Waning Moon*, and listening to the dull thuds of explosions from within the *Furious*'s prow.

THE ATTACK CRAFT wing of the *Boundless* swept in tight formation through the veil of debris building up from the damage to the two ships ahead of them. The *Waning Moon* and the *Furious Abyss* were locked in the Spiral Dance: the long, painful embrace that saw one ship circle another pumping broadsides into the enemy as it spun. Like everything else in space the Spiral Dance had its own mythology, and to a lifelong pilot of the Saturnine Fleet it meant inevitable doom and the spite of one ship lashing out at the enemy in its death throes. It was desperation and tragedy, like a dying romance or a last stand against vast odds.

The fighters, ten-man craft loaded with short-range rockets and cannon, streaked past the *Waning Moon*, the pilots saluting their fellow ship as custom dictated. They locked on to the *Furious Abyss*, the squadron leaders marking out targets on the immense dark red hull already pocked with lance scars and broadside craters from the battering the *Wrathful* had given it. Shield housings, sensor clusters and exhaust vents all lit up on the tactical display in a backwash of emerald light. Targeting cogitators locked on and burned red.

Silver Three, flown by Pilot Second-Class Carnagan Thaal, matched assigned approach vectors and built to full attack run speed. Through the shallow forward viewscreen, Thaal could see the *Furious Abyss* crisscrossed by laser battery barrage, its prow a flickering mass of smouldering metal.

He ordered his weapons officers to lock on to their target, a stretch of gun turrets along the *Furious*'s dorsal spine. The port guns obeyed, the lascannon mounts swivelling into position.

The starboard guns did not move.

Pilot Thaal repeated his order through the ship's vox. His co-pilot, Rugel, checked the array, but found nothing amiss.

'Rugel, go down to the armaments deck and align those guns,' Thaal ordered, deciding there was enough time before they hit their final approach vector.

The co-pilot nodded and tore out the wires attaching him to his seat and the console in front of him, and swung around in his chair.

'Scell, what are you doing?' Thaal heard his co-pilot ask and turned to get a good look at what was going on.

He started when he saw Weapons Officer Carina Scell standing there with her autopistol in her hand. Thaal was about to tell her to get back to her post and get the damn cannons locked on when Scell shot him in the face.

She took Rugel in the chest, stepping forward to deliver the shot point-blank. Bleeding badly, the co-pilot scrabbled to get his sidearm out of its holster.

'It is written,' Scell said, and shot him twice more in the head.

Silver Three continued on its attack vector. Scell headed below decks to finish her work.

'SILVER THREE'S DOWN,' said Officer Artemis on the fighter control deck of the *Boundless*. The deck ran almost a third of the length of the *Boundless* to accommodate the numerous tactical consoles.

Captain Vorlov, his face awash in the reflected ochre glow of datascreens, paid it little heed as he prowled the ranks of fighter controllers. Attack craft were always lost. It was the way of the void.

Vorlov continued his tour, preferring to witness first-hand the actions of his fighters rather than make do with the fragmented reports filtering through to the bridge. The *Boundless* was a dedicated carrier for attack craft and his duties were here, listening to the fates of his fighter wings. His helms-mate was perfectly capable of keeping the ship running in his absence.

'Any defensive fire?' asked Vorlov of the nearest control overseer.

'None yet,' said the overseer, whose shaved scalp was festooned with wires feeding information from each controller into her brain.

'But we're in range of their countermeasures,' said Vorlov, a thought occurring to him. 'You! What took down Silver Three?'

The controller looked up from his screen. 'Unknown. The pilot went off my screen. Possible crew casualties.'

'Non-standard transmissions from Gold Nine,' said another controller hunched over his screen. He held one of his earphones tight against his head and winced as he tried to hear more clearly. 'Some kind of commotion aboard ship, sire. They're not responding to protocols.'

'Bring them in. The rest of you, report any further anomalies!' Vorlov harrumphed in annoyance and leaned forward on his cane. The Saturnine Fleet had the best small craft pilots this side of the galactic centre. They didn't just flake out during a firefight.

'Gold Nine is lost, captain,' reported the controller. 'I detected small-arms fire in the cockpit.'

'Get me word on what the hell's going on or I'll have your commission,' barked Vorlov at the overseer.

'Yes, captain.'

'Fragmented reports are coming in from Silver Prime,' interrupted yet another controller. 'They say they've lost control of the engine crew.'

'Get all this on air!' shouted Vorlov. The overseer fiddled with a couple of settings and cockpit transmissions crackled through the deck's vox-caster.

'…gone insane! He's barricaded himself in the aft quarters. Esau's dead and he's venting the bloody air. I'm pulling out from attack vectors and going down there to shoot him.'

'I am the light that shines always. I am the lord of the dawn. I am the beginning and the end. I am the Word.'

'Agh, I'm… I'm bleeding out… Heral's dead, but I'm not going to make it.'

'Gold Twelve just opened fire on us! We're hit aftwards, pulling back and venting engine three.'

Vorlov was assailed by the desperate voices and distorted screams, dozens of them, all from experienced assault pilots, all tinged with fear or disbelief, or pain. Reports of colleagues sabotaging engines or murdering crew, ranting paranoia and delusion spewed forth from the vox. Vorlov couldn't believe what he was hearing. His wings were in total disarray and the glorious attack run he had envisaged had failed utterly without the enemy firing off a shot. He had never even read about such a thing in the histories of the Saturnine Fleet.

'It's as if they're going mad, captain,' said the overseer, struggling to keep her voice level, 'every one of them.'

'Abort!' shouted Vorlov. 'All wings! Abort attack run and return to the *Boundless*!'

'WE ARE SUCCESSFUL, lord,' the sibilant voice of Chaplain Ikthalon said through the vox array. 'The supplicants have effectively neutralised their fighter assault.'

'You are to be commended, chaplain. Ours is a divine purpose and you have ensured your name will be remembered in the scriptures of Lorgar,' Zadkiel replied coldly from the command throne, before turning to address Helms-mate Sarkorov.

'Let the escort craft close and then open the book.'

'Yes, my lord.' Sarkorov relayed the order at once.

Zadkiel watched a close-up of the sector of space through which the *Boundless*'s attack wings were flying. Fighters were already tumbling, glittering short-lived explosions as their colleagues shot them down. Others were spiralling off-course. The pathetic assault was in ruins.

'Behold,' Zadkiel said to his second standing alongside him, 'the power of the Word, Reskiel.'

'It is indeed humbling,' Reskiel replied, bowing deeply to his lord.

Zadkiel found the obvious toadying distasteful. Even so, this was a great moment, and he allowed himself to bask in it before returning to the vox.

'Ikthalon, how many supplicants did we lose?'

'Three, Lord Zadkiel,' the chaplain replied. 'The weakest.'

'Keep me appraised.'

'As you wish.' Ikthalon said, and terminated the link.

Zadkiel ignored the impudence and sat back in his command throne to watch the damage control reports flicker by. The prow was mangled, chewed up by the *Waning Moon*'s broadsides and torn by the lances of the *Wrathful*, but the prow was merely armour plating and empty space. It didn't matter. It could soak up everything they could throw at it for hours before the shells penetrated live decks. Even then, only Legion menials would perish, the unaugmented humans pledged to die for Lorgar.

'This is the *Fireblade*,' came the transmission intercepted by the *Furious Abyss*'s advanced sensorium from one of the approaching escort ships. 'We've got a clear run. Lances to full.'

'On your tail, *Fireblade*,' came the reply from a second frigate.

'Master Malforian, bring turrets to bear and reload ordnance,' said Zadkiel. He followed the blips of the escorts as they negotiated the graveyard of fighter craft, intent on helping the *Waning Moon* finish off the *Furious*.

Zadkiel allowed himself a thin smile.

'THE FIGHTERS ARE lost,' said Vorlov. His face was ruddy with frustration as it glowered out of the viewscreen on the bridge of the *Wrathful*.

Almost to a man, the crewmen of the ship were watching Captain Vorlov's report of the total failure of the attack run.

'What, all of them?' asked Admiral Kaminska.

'Twenty per cent are en route back to the *Boundless*,' said Vorlov. 'The rest are gone. Our crews turned on each other.'

'You think this was a psychic attack, captain?' asked Cestus, suddenly glad that Brynngar was off the bridge.

'Yes, lord, I do,' Vorlov breathed, fear edging his voice.

This was a worrying development. All the Legions knew full well what had been decided on Nikea, and the censure imposed by the Emperor on dabbling in the infernal powers of the warp and the use of sorcery. The Ultramarine turned to Admiral Kaminska.

'What of our remaining escorts?'

'Captain Ulargo on the *Fireblade* is leading them in,' she replied. 'No problems so far.'

Cestus nodded, processing everything unfolding on the bridge.

'Maintain lance barrage from the *Wrathful* and the *Waning Moon*. Captain Vorlov, add the *Boundless*'s from distance and let the escorts engage. No ship, however massive, can withstand such a concentrated assault.'

'At your command, my lord,' Vorlov returned.

Cestus turned to regard Kaminska, seething at her command throne.

'As you wish, captain,' she responded coolly.

THE FIREBLADE STITCHED the first volleys of lance fire down against the upper hull of the *Furious Abyss*. It had nothing like the firepower of the fleet's cruisers, but up close it could pick its targets, and each lance fired independently to blast off hull plates and shear turrets from their emplacements with fat bursts. Defensive guns retaliated in kind and shots blistered against the *Fireblade*'s shields, some making it through to the escort's dark green hull. The *Fireblade* twisted out of arcs of fire and sent a chain of incendiaries hammering down into the dorsal turret arrays. Silent explosions blossomed and were swallowed by the void, leaving glittering sprays of wreckage like silver fountains.

The *Fireblade*'s hull was resplendent with kill markings and battle honours. It had done this many times before. It was small, but it was agile and packed a harder punch than its size suggested. Behind it was the *Ferox*, its younger sister ship, using the heat signatures of the *Fireblade*'s strikes to throw bombs and las-blasts through the tears opened up in the upper hull.

The *Fireblade* finished its first run and corkscrewed up over the *Furious*'s engine housings, letting the heat wash of the battleship's engines lend a hand in catapulting it void-wards before it lined up for another pass.

Below the two escorts, the last of the squadron, now just the *Ferocious* with the dramatic and sudden demise of the *Fearless*, was making its run along the underside of the massive vessel, pouring destruction into the ventral turrets. All three remaining escorts came under fierce fire, but their shields and hull armour held, their speed too great to allow a significant number of defensive turrets to bear at once and combine their efforts.

Captain Ulargo, at the helm of the *Fireblade*, commented to his fellow escort captains that the Word Bearers appeared to want to die.

ANOTHER BROADSIDE THUNDERED from the *Waning Moon* as the strike cruiser turned elegantly, keeping level with the *Furious Abyss*'s prow. The void was sucking fire out of the prow, so it looked like the head of a fire-breathing monster made of smouldering metal.

The enormous book that served as the ship's figurehead was intact. Slowly, silently, the metal book cracked open and folded outwards.

The massive bore of a gun emerged from behind it.

The end of the barrel glowed red as reactors towards the rear of the ship opened up plasma conduits to the prow and the weapon's capacitors filled. Licks of blue flame ran over the ruined prow, ignited by the sheer force of the building energy.

The prow cannon fired. A white beam leapt from the *Furious Abyss*. At the same time thrusters kicked in, rotating the *Furious* a couple of degrees so that the short-lived beam played across the void in front of it.

It struck the *Waning Moon* just fore of the engines. Vaporised metal formed a billowing white cloud, like steam, condensing into a silver shower of re-solidified matter. Secondary explosions led the beam as it scored across the strike cruiser's hull, until finally it was lost in the shower of debris and vapour as its energy expended and the glowing barrel began to cool down in the vacuum.

Further explosions rippled across the *Waning Moon* in the wake of the crippling barrage, and the rear third of the strike cruiser was sheared clean off.

SIX

The void/Squadron disengage/A way with words

THE PACE OF space battles was glacially slow. Even when seen through viewscreens it was carried out at extreme ranges, with laser battery salvoes taking seconds to crawl across the blackness.

The battle had been raging for over an hour when the cannon on the prow of the *Furious Abyss* fired its maiden shot. The broadside from the *Waning Moon* had crossed a gulf of several hundred kilometres before impacting on the enemy ship's prow and that had been point-blank by the standards of ship-to-ship warfare. The *Boundless*'s fighter wings had flown distances that would have taken them across continents on a planet's surface.

When something happened quickly, it was a sudden, jarring occurrence that threw everything else out of kilter. The slow ballet of a ship battle was broken by the discordant note of a rapid development, and all plans had to be re-founded in its wake. An event that could not be reacted to, that was over too quickly to change course or target, was a nightmare that many ship captains struggled to cope with.

It was unfortunate for the captains of the Imperial fleet, then, that the death of the *Waning Moon* happened very quickly indeed.

'BY TITAN'S VALLEYS,' gasped Admiral Kaminska on the bridge of the *Wrathful*. 'What was that?'

The instruments on the bridge suddenly lit up as one as an intense flare of light filled the forward viewscreen.

'Massive energy reading,' came the confused reply from Helmsmistress Venkmyer. 'Energy sensorium's blind.'

'Did the *Waning Moon* just go plasma-critical?'

'There were no damage control signs that suggested major engine damage. They'd got the reactor-seven leak locked down. Maybe a weapons discharge?'

'What weapon could do that?'

'A plasma lance,' replied Cestus.

Kaminska turned to face the Ultramarine, whose grim expression betrayed his emotions.

'I did not know such a device had been wrought and fitted,' he added.

The admiral's initial shock turned to stern pragmatism.

'My lord, if I am to risk my ship and the souls onboard, I would have you tell me what we are up against,' she said, with no little consternation.

'I have little idea,' Cestus confessed, staring into the viewscreen, analysing and appraising tactical protocols in nanoseconds as he considered Kaminska's question. 'The Astartes are not privy to the secret works of the Mechanicum, admiral.' The Ultramarine sensed the challenge from Kaminska, her growing discontent, and was determined to crush it. 'Suffice to say that the plasma lance was developed as a direct fire close-range weapon for ship-to-ship combat. In any event, it matters not. Your orders are simple,' said Cestus, turning his steely gaze upon Admiral Kaminska in an attempt to cow her veiled truculence. 'We are to destroy that ship.'

'They are Astartes aboard that ship, Cestus, our battle-brothers,' Antiges said quietly. Until now, the fellow Ultramarine had been content to maintain his silence and keep his own council, but events were unfolding upon the bridge of the *Wrathful* and out in the wide, cold reaches of real space that he could not ignore.

'I am aware of that, Antiges.'

'But captain, to condemn them to–'

'My hand is forced,' Cestus snarled, suddenly turning on Antiges. 'Know your place, battle-brother! I am still your commanding officer.'

'Of course, my captain.' Antiges bowed slightly and averted his gaze from his fellow Ultramarine. 'I would request to leave the bridge to inform Saphrax and the rest of the squad to prepare for a potential boarding action.'

Cestus's face was set like stone.

Antiges met it with a steely gaze of his own.

'Granted.' His captain's curt response was icy.

Antiges saluted, turned on his heel and left the bridge.

Kaminska said nothing, only listened to what Cestus ordered next.

'Raise Mhotep at once.'

The admiral turned to regard her helms-mate monitoring communications with the *Waning Moon*.

'We cannot, sire,' Kant replied. 'The *Waning Moon*'s vox array is not operational.'

Kaminska swore beneath her breath, turning to the tactical display in the hope that a solution would present itself. All she saw was the massive enemy ship manoeuvring for a fresh assault against the *Boundless*.

'Captain Vorlov,' she barked into the vox, 'this is the *Wrathful*. She's heading for you next. Get out of there.'

There was a crackle of static and Vorlov's voice replied, 'What is this monster you have us hunting, Kaminska?'

There was a slight pause, and suddenly Kaminska looked very old as if the many juvenat treatments she'd undertaken to grant her such longevity had been stripped away.

'I don't know.'

'I never thought I'd hear you at a loss for words,' said Vorlov. 'I'm breaking off and hitting warp distance. I suggest you do the same.'

Kaminska looked at Cestus. 'Do we run?'

'No,' said Cestus. His jaw was set as he watched the debris from the *Waning Moon* rain in all directions as the ship's hull split in two.

'That's what I thought. Helmsmistress Venkmyer, relay orders to engineering to make ready for full evasive.'

THE BRIDGE OF the *Waning Moon* was in ruins. Massive feedback had ripped through every helm. Crewmen had died as torrents of energy had hammered through their scalp sockets and into their brains. Others were burning in the wreckage of exploded cogitators. Some of them had got out, but there was little indication that anywhere on the ship was better off. There was smoke everywhere, and all sound was swamped by the agonising din of screaming metal from the rear of the ship. The ship's spine was broken and it could no longer support its own structure. The *Waning Moon's* movement was enough to force it apart with inertia.

The blast doors had buckled under the extreme damage inflicted upon the stricken vessel and would not open. Mhotep had drawn his scimitar and cut through them with ease, forcing his way out of the bridge.

Engineering was gone, simply gone. The last surviving readouts on the bridge had been tracking the engines as they spun away below the ship, ribbons of burning plasma and charred bodies spilling from the ship's wounds like intestines.

No order had been given to abandon ship. Mhotep hadn't needed to give it.

'Captain, power is falling all across the ship,' shouted Helms-mate Ramket, his voice warring against the din of internal explosions somewhere below decks.

'We are beyond saving, helms-mate. Head for the starboard saviour pods immediately,' Mhotep replied, noting the savage gash across Ramket's forehead where he'd been struck by falling ship debris.

Ramket saluted and was about to turn and do as ordered when a sheet of fire rippled down the corridor, channelled through the *Waning Moon's* remaining oxygen. It flowed over Mhotep in a coruscating wave, spilling against his armour as it was repelled. Warning runes within his helmet lens display flashed intense heat readings. Ramket had no such protection, and his scream died in his burning mouth as the skin was seared from his body. Smothered by fire, as if drowning, Ramket thundered against the deck in a heap of charred bone and flaming meat.

Mhotep forced his way through the closest access portal and hauled it shut against the blaze. The fire had caught on the seals of his armour and he patted them out with his gauntleted palm. He had emerged from the conflagration into one of the ship's triage stations, where the wounded had been brought from the torpedo strikes on the gun decks. The injured were still lying in beds hooked up to respirators and life support cogitators. The orderlies were gone; ship regulations made no provision for bringing invalids along when abandoning ship.

They had given their lives to the Thousand Sons. They had known that they would die in service, one way or another. Mhotep ignored the dead and pressed on.

Beyond the triage station were crew quarters. Men and women were running everywhere. Normally, they would know exactly where to head in the event of an abandon ship, but the *Waning Moon's* structure was coming apart and the closest saviour pods were wrecked. Some were already dead, crushed by chunks of torn metal crashing through the ceiling or thrown into fiery rents in the deck plates. In spite of the confusion, they stood aside instinctively to allow Mhotep clear passage. As an Astartes and their lord, his life was worth more than any of theirs.

'Starboard saviour pods are still operational, captain,' said one petty officer. Mhotep remembered his name as Lothek. He was just one of the many thousands of souls about to burn in the void.

Mhotep nodded an acknowledgement to the man. The Thousand Son's own armour was still smouldering and he could feel points of hot pain at the elbow and knee joints, but he ignored them.

Abruptly, the crew quarters split in two, one side hauled sharply upwards in a scream of twisting metal. Lothek went with it, smashed up into the ceiling and turned to a grisly red paste before his mouth had even formed a terrified scream.

A huge section of the *Waning Moon's* structure had collapsed and given way. Its inertia ripped it out of the ship's belly and air shrieked from the widening gaps. Mhotep was staggered by the unexpected rupture and grabbed the frame of a door as air howled past him. He saw crewmen wrenched off their feet and dashed against torn deck plating that bent outwards like jagged, broken teeth. The tangled mass before him gave way and tumbled off into the void, over a dozen souls screaming silently as they went with it. Their eyes widened in panic even as they iced over. They gasped out breaths, or held them too long, and ruptured their lungs, spewing out ragged plumes of blood. Hitting space, their bodies froze in spasm, limbs held at awkward angles as they drifted away into the star-pocked darkness. The scene was bizarrely tranquil as Mhotep regarded it, the swathe of black-clad nothing silent and endless where distant constellations glittered dully and the faded luminescence of far off suns left a lambent glow in the false night.

Gravity gave way as the structure was violated.

Mhotep held on, armoured fingers making indentations in the metal, as the last gales of atmosphere hammered past. A corpse rolled and bumped against his armour, on its way to the void. It was Officer Ammon, his eyes red with burst veins.

They were dead: thousands all dead.

Mhotep felt some grim pride, knowing that, had they seen it would end this way, the crew would all still have given their lives to Magnus and the Thousand Sons. With no time for reverie, the Astartes pulled himself along the wall, finding handholds among shattered mosaics. With the air gone, the only sound was the groaning of the ship as it came apart, rumbling through its structure and up through the gauntlets of Mhotep's armour. His armour was proof against the vacuum, but he could only survive for a limited time.

The same was not true of anyone else aboard ship.

Mhotep passed through the crew quarters. In the wake of its demise, the *Waning Moon* had become an eerily silent tomb of metal. As power relays failed, lights flashed intermittently, the illumination on some decks made only by crackling sparks. Gobbets of blood broke against Mhotep's armour as he moved, and icy corpses bobbed with the dead gravity as if carried by an invisible ocean. The Astartes shoved tangled bodies aside, faces locked in frozen grimaces, as he fought his way to a pair of blast doors and opened them. The air was gone beyond them, too, and more crewmen floated in the corridor leading down to the saviour pod deck. One of them grasped at Mhotep's arm as the Astartes went past him. It was a crewman who had emptied his lungs as the air boomed out and had, thus, managed to stay conscious. His eyes goggled madly. Mhotep swept him aside and carried on.

The starboard saviour pods were not far away, but the Thousand Son had to take a short detour first. Passing through a final corridor, he reached the reinforced blast door of his sanctum. Incredibly, the chamber still retained power, operating on a heavily protected, separate system from the rest of the ship. Mhotep inputted the runic access protocol and the door slid open. The oxygen that remained in the airtight sanctum started to pour out. Mhotep stepped over the threshold quickly and the door sealed shut behind him with a hiss of escaping pressure.

Ignoring the damage done to the precious artefacts within the room, Mhotep went straight to the extant sarcophagus at the back of the sanctum. Opening it with controlled urgency, he retrieved the short wand-stave from inside it and secured the item in a compartment in his armour. When Mhotep turned, about to head for the saviour pods, he saw a figure crushed beneath a fallen cry-glass cabinet. Shards of glass speared the figure's robed body, and vital fluids trickled from its bloodless lips.

'Sire?' gasped Kalamar, using what little oxygen remained in the chamber.

Mhotep went to the ageing serf and knelt beside him.

'For the glory of Magnus,' Kalamar breathed when his lord was close.

Mhotep nodded.

'You have served your master and this vessel well, old friend,' the Astartes intoned and stood up again, 'but your tenure is at an end.'

'Spare my suffering, lord.'

'I will,' Mhotep replied, mustering what little compassion existed in his cold methodical nature and, drawing his bolt pistol, he shot Kalamar through the head.

THE SAVIOUR POD deck was situated next to the hull, a hemispherical chamber with six pods half-sunk into the floor. Two had been launched and another was damaged beyond repair, speared through by a shaft of steel fallen from the ceiling.

Mhotep pulled himself down into one of the remaining pods. Contrary to naval tradition, he would not be going down with his ship. In his chambers, just prior to docking at Vangelis, he had seen a vision of himself standing upon the deck of the *Wrathful*. This was his destiny. The hand of fate would draw him here for some, as of yet, unknown purpose.

Mhotep engaged the icon that would seal the saviour pod. It closed around him. There was room for three more crew, but no one was alive to fill it. He hit the launch panel and explosive bolts threw the pod clear of the ship.

He watched the *Waning Moon* turning above him as the pod spiralled away. The aft section had burned out and was just a black flaking husk, disappearing against the void. The main section of the ship was tearing itself apart. The fires were mostly out, starved of fuel and oxygen, and the *Waning Moon* was a skeleton collapsing into its component bones.

In the distance, thousands of sparks burst around the *Furious Abyss,* as if it were at the heart of a vast pyrotechnic display.

Mhotep was as disciplined as any Thousand Son, and Magnus made the conditioning of his Legion's minds the most important part of their training. He could subsume himself into the collective mindset of his battle-brothers, and as such was rarely troubled by emotions that did not serve any immediate purpose.

He was disturbed. He very much wanted to exact the hatred he felt on the *Furious Abyss*. He wanted to tear it apart with his bare hands.

Perhaps, Mhotep told himself, if he was patient, he would find a way to do that.

THE FIGHTERS HAD come from nowhere.

With the violent death of the *Waning Moon,* the remaining escort ships, the *Ferox* and the *Fireblade,* were locked in a deadly duel with the massive enemy vessel. Even with the *Boundless* in support and the *Wrathful* inbound they would not last long against the Word Bearer battleship. The frigates would have to use their superior speed to endure while aid arrived. That advantage was summarily robbed with the appearance of crimson-winged fighter squadrons issuing from the belly of the *Furious Abyss* in an angry swarm.

It was impossible for such a ship, even one of its impressive size, to harbour fighter decks and the weapons system that had destroyed the *Waning Moon*. This fact had informed every scenario the escort squadron's captains had developed for any reaction to their attack runs. The *Furious Abyss*, however, was no ordinary ship.

The destruction of the *Waning Moon*, appalling as it was, had at least given the escort ships the certainty that the Word Bearers would not have the resources for attack craft. That was before the launch bays had opened like steel gills down the flanks of the battleship, and twinkling blood-slick darts had shot out on columns of exhaust.

Captain Ulargo stood in a corona of light on the bridge of the *Fireblade*. The rest of the bridge was drenched in darkness with only the grainy diodes of control consoles punctuating the gloom. Arms behind him, surrounded by the hololithic tactical display and with vox crackling, the terrible choreography of war played out with sickening inevitability.

'*Ferox* engaged!' came the alert from Captain Lo Thulaga. 'Multiple hostiles! Fast attack craft, registering impacts. Shutting down reactor two.'

'Shield your engines, for Terra's sake!' snapped Captain Ulargo, watching the grim display from the viewport.

'What do you think I'm doing?' retorted Lo Thulaga. 'I have fighters port, aft and abeam. They're bloody everywhere.'

The *Ferox* spiralled away from its attack run on the underside, pursued by a cloud of vindictive fighters. Tiny explosions stitched over the hindquarters of the escort ship, ripping sprays of black debris from the engine housings. Turrets stammered back fire from the belly and sides of the *Ferox*, but for every fighter reduced to a bloom of plasma residue there were two more pouring fire into it.

It was like a predator under attack from a swarm of stinging insects. The *Ferox* was far larger than any of the fighters, which were shaped like inverted Vs with their stabiliser wings swept forwards. Individually its turrets could have tracked and vaporised any of the enemy before they got in range, but there were over fifty of them.

'I cannot shake them,' snarled Captain Vorgas on the *Ferocious*, his voice ragged through the vox.

'They're bloody killing us!' yelled Lo Thulaga, whose voice was distorted by the secondary explosions coming from the escort's engines.

Ulargo wore a disgusted expression. In his entire career, he had never backed down from a fight. He hailed from the militaristic world of Argonan in Segmentum Tempestus, and it was not in his nature to capitulate. Clenching his fists, he bawled the order.

'Squadron disengage!'

Fireblade pulled away from the *Furious Abyss*, followed by the *Ferocious*. The *Ferox* tried to pull clear, but the enemy fighters hounded it, darting into the wake of the escort's engines, risking destruction to fly in blind and hammer laser fire into its engineering decks.

One of the reactors on the embattled frigate melted down, its whole rear half flooding with plasma. The forward compartments were sealed off quickly enough to save the crew, but the ship was dead in the void, only its momentum keeping it falling ponderously away from the upper hull of the *Furious Abyss*. The fighters circled it, flying in wide arcs around the dead ship and punishing it with incessant fire. Crew decks were breached and vented. Saviour pods began to launch as Lo Thulaga gave the order to abandon ship.

The *Furious Abyss* wasted no time sending fighters to assassinate the saviour pods as they fled the stricken *Ferox*.

The *Ferocious* pulled a dramatic hard turn, ducking back towards the enemy battleship to fox the fighters lining up for their attack runs. It strayed into the arcs of the *Furious Abyss*'s ventral turrets, and a couple of lucky shots blew plumes of vented atmosphere out of its upper hull. The fighters closed and targeted the breach, volleys of las-fire boring molten fingers into the frigate. Somewhere amidst the bedlam the bridge was breached and the command crew died, incinerated by sprays of molten metal or frozen and suffocated as the void forced its way in.

The remaining turrets on the *Furious Abyss* targeted the fleeing *Fireblade*, the last vessel of the escort. Most of the battleship's attention was away from the frigate, representing as it did a mere annoyance. Its vengeful ire was focused squarely on the *Boundless*.

'THE FEROX AND the *Ferocious* are gone,' Kaminska stated flatly, watching the blips on the tactical display blink out. 'How on Titan can that thing support those fighter wings?'

'The same way it has a functioning plasma lance,' said Cestus, grimly. 'The Mechanicum know more about what they're doing than they are letting on, and are ignoring Imperial sanctions.'

'In the name of Terra, what is happening?' Kaminska asked, seeing the enemy battleship turn its cross hairs on the *Boundless*.

For the first time, the Ultramarine thought he could detect a hint of fear in the admiral's voice.

'We cannot win this fight, not like this,' he said. 'Bring the *Boundless* in, we need to regroup.'

Kaminska cast her eye over the tactical display. Her voice was choked. 'It's too late for that.'

'Damnation!' Cestus smashed his fist hard against a rail on the bridge and it buckled. After a moment, he said, 'Contact your astropath, and find out what is keeping that message. I must warn my lord Guilliman at once.'

Kaminska raised the astropathic sanctum on the ship-to-ship vox, even as Helmsmistress Venkmyer relayed disengagement protocols to engineering.

Chief Astropath Korbad Heth's deep voice was heard on the bridge.

'All our efforts to contact Terra or the Ultramarines have failed,' he revealed matter-of-factly.

'By order of the Emperor's Astartes, keep trying and you will prevail,' said Cestus.

'My lord,' Heth began, unmoved by the Ultramarine's threatening tone. 'The matter is more fundamental than you appreciate. When I say our efforts have failed, I mean utterly. The Astronomican is gone.'

'Gone? That's impossible. How can it be gone?'

'I know not, my lord. We are detecting warp storms that could be interfering. I will redouble our endeavours, but I fear they will be in vain.' The vox went dead and Heth was gone again.

Antiges's return to the bridge broke the silence.

'We must return to Terra, Cestus. The Emperor must be warned.'

'What of Calth and Macragge? Our Legion is there, and our primarch; they are in imminent danger and the ones who must be warned. I do not doubt the strength of our battle-brothers and the fleet above Macragge is formidable, as are its ground defences, but there is something about this ship... What if it is merely the harbinger of something much worse, something that can be a very real threat to Guilliman?'

'Our primarch has ever taught us to exercise pragmatism in the face of adversity,' Antiges reasoned, stepping forward. 'Upon our return, we could send a message to the Legion.'

'A message that would never reach them, Antiges,' Cestus replied with anger. 'No, we are the Legion's last hope.'

'You are letting your emotion and your arrogance cloud your judgement, brother-captain,' said Antiges, drawing in close.

'Your loyalty deserts you, brother.'

Antiges bristled at the slight, but kept his composure. 'What good is it if we sacrifice ourselves on the altar of loyalty?' he urged. 'This way, we at least stand a chance of saving our brothers.'

'No,' said Cestus with finality. 'We would only condemn them to death. Courage and honour, Antiges.'

Cestus's fellow Ultramarine saw the vehemence in his eyes, remembering his conviction that he knew some terrible peril was creeping towards Macragge and the Legion. His brother-captain had been right thus far, and suddenly Antiges felt shamed that his dogged pragmatism had so blinded him to that truth.

'Courage and honour,' he replied and clapped his hand upon Cestus's shoulder in an apologetic gesture.

'So, we follow them into the warp,' Kaminska interrupted, assuming that the matter was settled. 'We feign flight and get on the ship's tail as soon as it readies to go into the Tertiary Core Transit,' she added.

Cestus was about to give his assent when Helms-mate Kant delivered a report from the sensorium.

'Impacts on the *Boundless*.'

THE BOUNDLESS TOOK longer to die than the *Waning Moon*.

Another volley of torpedoes sailed out from the *Furious Abyss*, this time in a tight corkscrew like a pack of predators arrowing in on the prey instead of spread out in a fan.

High explosives tipped the torpedo formation. They penetrated shields and used up the first volleys of turret fire from the *Boundless*.

The main body of the torpedoes were the same kind of bore-header cluster munitions that had ripped into the *Waning Moon*. A few magnetic pulse torpedoes were part of the volley, too. They ripped through the sensors of the *Boundless* and blinded it. There was no longer any need to conceal the full arsenal of the *Furious Abyss*.

Cluster explosions, like flowers of fire, blossomed down one flank of the *Boundless*. Shock waves rippled through the fighter bays, throwing attack craft aside like boats on a wave. Refuelling tanks exploded, their blooms lost in the torrents of flame that followed the first impacts. Fighter crews that had survived the madness of the attack runs were rewarded by being shredded by shrapnel or drowned in fire. The flank of the *Boundless* was chewed away as if it were ageing and decaying at an impossible rate, holes opening up and metal blackening and twisting to finally flake away like desiccated flesh.

The final torpedo wave had single warheads that forced enormous bullets of exotic metals at impossible speeds. They shot like lances from their housings, shrieking right through the *Boundless* and emerging from the other side, sowing secondary explosions of ignited fuel and vented oxygen, transfixing the carrier like spears of light.

Finally, the *Furious Abyss* took up position at medium range from the Imperial ship. It paused, as if observing the wracked vessel, sizing up the quarry one last time before the kill.

The plasma lance emerged, the energy building up and the barrel glowing. The surviving crew of the *Boundless* knew what was coming, but all their control systems were shot through. A few thrusters sputtered into life as the *Boundless* tried desperately to limp away from its would-be executioner, but the carrier was too big and badly wounded.

The plasma lance fired. It hit the *Boundless* amidships, at enough of an angle to rip through to the plasma reactors. The entire vessel glowed, the heat of the fusing plasma conducted through its structure and hull.

Then the plasma overspilled and, spitted like prey on the solid beam of the plasma lance's light, the *Boundless* exploded.

FROM HIS IMPERIOUS position on the bridge of the *Furious Abyss*, Zadkiel watched the burning wreck of the enemy cruiser flicker into lifeless darkness.

'Glory to Lorgar,' said Reskiel, who was standing behind him.

'So it is written,' Zadkiel replied.

'Two vessels remain, my lord,' added his second, obsequiously.

Zadkiel observed the tactical display. The remaining cruiser was intact, and the final escort being pursued by the *Furious Abyss*'s fighter wings would probably also escape.

'By the time they get to Terra, it will be too late for any warning,' Zadkiel said confidently. 'The warp is with us. We risk far more tarrying here to hunt them down.'

'I will instruct Navigator Esthemya that we are to enter the warp.'

'Do so immediately,' confirmed Zadkiel, his mind on the transpiring events and their impending foray into the empyrean.

Reskiel nodded and activated the ship's vox-casters, transmitting Zadkiel's relayed orders into the engine rooms and ordnance decks. 'All crew, make ready for warp entry.'

'Reskiel, have Master Malforian load the psionic charges,' Zadkiel said as an afterthought. 'Once we are in the warp, you will have the bridge. I will be inspecting the supplicants in the lower decks. Ensure Novice Ultis attends.'

'As you wish, my lord,' said Reskiel, bowing deeply. 'And if the Ultramarines try to follow?'

'Commend their souls to the warp,' Zadkiel replied coldly.

THE WRATHFUL WENT dark, to simulate the diversion of its power to the engines for escape. The entire bridge was drenched in shadow. The crew was stunned into sudden silence and, for a fraction of a second, stillness, as they struggled to comprehend what they had witnessed.

Kaminska was as quiet as the ship. She gripped the arms of her command throne tightly. Vorlov had been her friend.

'A saviour pod jettisoned from the *Waning Moon* before its destruction, admiral,' announced Helms-mate Venkmyer at the sensorium helm, breaking the silence.

'Can you tell who is on board?' asked Cestus, along-side the admiral, watching impotently as the Word Bearer vessel grew farther and farther away as the *Wrathful* made its mock retreat.

'Lord Mhotep, sire,' Venkmyer replied. 'He's on his way to us. I've instructed crews to be ready to retrieve him when he docks.'

'Antiges, have Laeradis join the dock crews. Mhotep might be injured and in need of an apothecary.'

'At once, brother-captain.'

Antiges turned and was about to head off again when Cestus added, 'Disband the boarding parties and return to the bridge. Instruct Brynngar to do the same on my authority. Bring Saphrax and the Legion captains with you.'

The other Ultramarine nodded and went to his duties.

SAPHRAX ARRIVED ON the bridge with Antiges as ordered. Brynngar and Skraal joined them, feral belligerence and unfettered wrath increasing the already knife-edge tension.

With this many Astartes present, the bridge of the *Wrathful* felt very small. Saphrax wore his ceremonial honour guard armour, the gold of his armour plates glinting dully. Skraal, on the other hand, made do with little in the way of decoration. Cestus could not help noticing the kill-tallies on his chainaxe, bolt pistol and armour plates: a testament to violence. Killing was a matter of pride for the World Eaters and Skraal had several names etched on his shoulder pad, around the stylised devoured planet symbol of his Legion.

'Battle-brothers, fellow captains,' Cestus began as the Astartes present took position around the dead tactical display table. 'We are to enter the empyrean and give chase to the Word Bearers. Our Navigators have discerned that they are on course for a stable warp route. Following them won't be a problem.'

'Though, facing them will,' said Saphrax, ever the voice of reason. 'That ship destroyed two cruisers and the same in frigates. What is your plan for overcoming such odds?' It wasn't an objection. Saphrax was not given to questioning the decisions of his superiors. In his mind, the hierarchy of command was absolute, and much like the Ultramarine's posture, it would brook no bending.

'If we go back to Terra,' said Cestus, 'we could try to raise the alarm. If the warp quietened then we could get a message to Macragge and forewarn the Legion.' Cestus knew there was no conviction in his words as he spoke them.

'You have already decided against that course, haven't you, lad,' said venerable Brynngar.

'I have.'

The old wolf smiled, revealing his razor-sharp incisors. There was something stoic and powerful in the steel grey of his mane-like hair and beard, implacability in the creamy orb of his ruined eye and the ragged scars of previous battles. But for all the war-like trappings, the obvious martial prowess and savagery, there was wisdom, too.

'When the sons of Russ march to war, they do not cease until battle is done,' he said with the utmost conviction. 'We will chase those curs into the eye of the warp if necessary and feast upon their traitorous hearts.'

'The World Eaters do not flee when an enemy turns on them,' offered Skraal with blood lust in his eyes. 'We hunt them down and kill them. It's the way of the Legion.'

Cestus nodded, appraising the brave warriors before him with great respect.

'Make no mistake about this: we are at war,' the Ultramarine warned them, finally. 'We are at war with our brothers, and we must prosecute this fight with all the strength and conviction that we would bring against any foe of mankind. We do this in the name of the Emperor.'

'In the name of the Emperor,' growled Skraal.

'Aye, for the Throne,' Brynngar agreed.

Cestus bowed deeply.

'Your fealty does me great honour. Prepare your battle-brothers for what is ahead. I will convene a council of war upon Captain Mhotep's return to the *Wrathful*.'

Cestus noticed the snarl upon Brynngar's face at the last remark, but it faded quickly as the Astartes took their leave and returned to their warriors.

'Admiral Kaminska,' said the Ultramarine, once the other Legionaries were gone.

Kaminska looked up at him. Dark rings had sunk around her eyes. 'I shall have to prepare Navigator Orcadus. We can follow once the enemy is clear.' She thumbed a vox-stud on the arm of her command throne. 'Captain Ulargo, report.'

'We've got mostly superficial damage; one serious deck leak,' replied Ulargo on the *Fireblade*.

'Make your ship ready. We're following them,' Kaminska told him.

'Into the Abyss?'

'Yes. Do you have any objections?'

'Is this Captain Cestus's order?'

'It is,' she said.

'Then we'll be in your wake,' said Ulargo. 'For the record, I do not believe a warp pursuit is the most suitable course of action in our current situation.'

'Noted,' said Kaminska. 'Form up to follow us in.'

'Yes, admiral,' Ulargo replied.

As the vox went dead, Kaminska sagged in her command throne as if the battle and the comrades she had lost were weighing down on her.

'Admiral,' said Cestus, noting her discomfort, 'are you still able to prosecute this mission?'

Kaminska whirled on the Ultramarine, her expression fierce and the rod at her back once more.

'I may not have the legendary endurance of the Astartes, but I will see this through to the end, captain, for good or ill.'

'You have my utmost faith, then,' Cestus replied.

The voice of Helms-mate Venkmyer at the sensorium helm helped to ease the tension.

'Captain Mhotep's saviour pod is locked on,' she said, 'and the *Fireblade* has picked up additional survivors from the *Waning Moon*.'

'What of the *Boundless*?' asked Kaminska.

'I'm sorry, admiral. There were none.'

Kaminska watched the tactical display on the screen above her as the *Furious Abyss*'s blip shivered and disappeared, leaving behind a trace of exotic particles.

'Take us into that jump point and engage the warp engines,' she ordered wearily, Venkmyer relaying them to the relevant parties aboard ship.

'Captain Mhotep is secured, admiral,' Venkmyer said afterwards.

'Take us in.'

ABOARD THE FURIOUS *Abyss*, the supplicants' quarters were dark and infernally hot. The air was so heavy with chemicals that anyone other than an Astartes would have needed a respirator to survive.

The supplicants, sixteen of them in all, knelt by the walls of the darkened rooms. Their heads were bowed over their chests, but the shadows and darkness could not hide their swollen craniums and the way their features had atrophied as their skulls deformed to contain their grotesque brains. Thick tubes snaked down their noses and throats, hooking them to life support units mounted on the walls above. Wires ran from probes in their skulls. They were dressed neatly in the livery of the Word Bearers, for even in their comatose states they were servants of the Word just like the rest of the crew.

Three of the supplicants were dead. Their efforts in psychically assaulting the Imperial fighter squadrons had taxed them to destruction. The skull of one had ruptured, spilling rust-grey cortex over his chest and stomach. Another had apparently caught fire, and his blackened flesh still smouldered. The last was slumped at the back of the quarters, lolling over to one side.

Zadkiel entered the chamber. The sound of his footsteps and those of one other broke the hum of the life support systems.

'This is the first time you have seen the supplicants, isn't it?' said Zadkiel.

'Yes, my lord,' said Ultis, though his answer was not necessary.

Zadkiel turned to the novice. 'Tell me, Ultis, what is your impression of them?'

'I have none,' the novice answered coldly. 'They are loyal servants of Lorgar, as are we all. They sacrifice themselves in a holy cause to further his glory and the glory of the Word.'

Zadkiel smiled at the phlegmatic response. Such zeal, such unremitting fervour; this Ultis wore ambition like a medal of honour emblazoned upon his chest. It meant he was dangerous.

'Justly spoken,' offered Zadkiel. 'Was it a worthy sacrifice?' he added, probing the depths of the novice's desire for advancement without him even knowing.

'No one ever served the Word without understanding that they would eventually give the Word their life,' Ultis responded carefully.

He is aware that I am testing him. He is more dangerous than I thought.

'Very true,' Zadkiel said out loud. 'Still, some would think this sight distasteful.'

'Then some do not deserve to serve.'

'You always answer with such conviction, Ultis,' said Zadkiel. 'Are you so sure in your beliefs?'

Ultis turned to regard his lord directly. Neither of the Astartes wore a helmet, and their gazes locked in unspoken challenge.

'I have faith in the Word. It is such that I need not hesitate; I need only speak and act.'

Zadkiel held the novice's vehement gaze for a moment longer before he broke away willingly and knelt down by the third dead supplicant. The Word Bearer tipped its head upwards to reveal burned out eyes.

'This is conviction, Ultis. This is adherence to the creed of Lorgar,' Zadkiel told him.

'Lorgar's Word is powerful,' Ultis affirmed. 'None of his servants would ever forsake it.'

'Perhaps, but think upon it. Many of our Legion have a seductive way with words. We are passionate about our lord primarch and his teachings. We are most talented in spreading that to others. Could it not be said that this blinds lesser men? That to blind them with such passion, and have them do our bidding, is no different to slavery?'

'Even if it could be said,' replied Ultis carefully, 'it does not follow that we would be in the wrong. Perhaps some are more use to the galaxy as slaves than as free men, doing as their base instincts tell them.'

'Were these men suited to being slaves?' asked Zadkiel, indicating the supplicants.

'Yes,' said Ultis. 'Psykers are dangerous when left to their own devices. The Word gave them another purpose.'

'Then you would enslave others to do Lorgar's will?'

Ultis thought about this. The novice was no fool, and would be well aware that Zadkiel was evaluating his every word, but failing to answer at all would be by far the most damning result.

'It is better,' said Ultis, 'that lesser men like this lose their freedom than that the Word remains unspoken. Even if what we do is slavery, even if our passion is like a chain that holds them down, these are small prices to pay to see Lorgar's Word enacted.'

Zadkiel stood up. 'These supplicants will require some time to recover. Their psychic exertions have drained them. It is good that the weaker were winnowed out, at least. The warp will not be kind to them.

You show remarkable tolerance, Novice Ultis. Many Astartes, even those of our Legion, would balk at the use of these supplicants.'

'Those are the lengths to which we must go,' said Ultis, 'to fulfil the Word.'

Yes, very ambitious, Zadkiel decided.

'How far would you go, Brother Ultis?'

'To the very end.'

Driven, too.

Zadkiel smiled thinly.

Dangerous.

'Then, there is little left to teach you,' said the Word Bearer captain.

The vox-emitter in Zadkiel's gorget chirped. 'Master Malforian has indicated that he is ready,' said Helmsmate Sarkorov.

Delegating already, are we Reskiel? thought Zadkiel, seeing rivals and potential usurpers in every exchange, every obsequious nod.

'Deploy at once,' said Zadkiel.

'Yes, sire.'

'They pursue us still?' asked Ultis.

'It was to be expected,' Zadkiel replied. 'Doubtless, some sense of duty compels them. They will soon learn the folly of that emotion.'

'Pray enlighten me, my lord.'

Zadkiel considered the novice as he bowed before him.

'Join me on the bridge, Brother Ultis,' he said, 'and merely watch.'

THE WARP WAS madness made real. It was another dimension where the rules of reality did not apply. The human mind was not evolved to comprehend it, for it had no rules or boundaries to define it. It was infinite, and infinitely varied. Only a Navigator, a highly specialised form of stable mutant, could look upon it and not go insane. Only he could allow a ship to travel the stable channels of the warp, fleeting as they were, and emerge through the other side. To traverse an unstable warp route, even with a Navigator's guidance, would put a vessel at the capricious mercy of the empyrean tides.

The *Furious Abyss* had plunged into this sea. It was kept intact by a sheath of overlapping Geller fields, without which it would disintegrate as its component atoms ran out of reasons to stay neatly arranged in its metals.

From the ordnance bay, wrapped in its own complement of fields, emerged a large psionic mine, spinning rapidly as it tumbled away from the Word Bearers' ship. Though not visible on the outside, within the mine's inner core was a coterie of screaming psykers, insane with a poisonous vapour that had been pumped into the chamber and then hermetically sealed. Their combined death cry would send psionic ripples through the empyrean. With a flash of light, which bled away into emotion as it was absorbed into the warp, the mine and all its raving cargo detonated.

The warp quaked. Love and hate boiled and ran together like paint, the agony of billions of years breaking and shifting like spring ice. Mountains of hope crumbled, and oceans of lust drained into the nothingness of misery.

With a sound like every scream ever uttered, the Tertiary Core Transit collapsed.

SEVEN

Ghosts in the warp/Hellbound/Legacy of Magnus

'Ulargo!' shouted Kaminska. 'You're breaking up. I can barely hear you. Keep the fields up and get into our wake!'

The *Wrathful*, with the *Fireblade* in tow, had entered the infinite that was the warp. Interference from the rolling shadow sea had rendered vox traffic all but dead as the last vestiges of realspace fell away. The final transmissions from the escort ship were fraught with panic and desperation as the *Fireblade* encountered unknown difficulties during transit.

Ulargo's voice was heavily distorted as he relayed a fragmentary message, the words dissolving into crackling non sequiturs. Strange waves of static flowed through the *Wrathful's* bridge speakers, the short distance between it and the *Fireblade* filling up with the impossible geometries of the warp.

Entering the warp through a stable route, even guided by a Navigator, was dangerous. To do so once that route had collapsed and without the beacon of the Astronomican was nigh-on suicidal.

Admiral Kaminska swore beneath her breath, smashing her fist against the arm of her command throne in frustration.

'The link is severed,' she muttered darkly.

'We'll get no further contact with the *Fireblade* until we leave warpspace, admiral,' said Venkmyer.

Kaminska and her crew were alone on the bridge. Captain Cestus and the other Astartes had convened in one of the vessel's many conference rooms to receive Captain Mhotep, find out what he knew and formulate some kind of plan.

The mood was subdued because of the warp transit, and the unknown fate of the *Fireblade* had not alleviated the grim demeanour that pervaded on the bridge.

'I know, helmsmistress,' Kaminska answered with resignation.

The *Wrathful* shuddered. Warning lights flickered up and down the bridge, and in the decks beyond klaxons sounded.

'We're on full collision drill,' Helms-mate Kant informed them.

'Good,' said the admiral. 'Keep us there.'

The whole bridge heaved sideways, scattering navigational instruments and tactical manuals. Kant grabbed the edge of a map table to keep his footing with the sudden warp turbulence.

'At your command,' he replied.

Kaminska sat back in her command throne, exhausted. She had finally come up against a problem she couldn't solve with tactical acumen and audacity. The Astartes captain of the Ultramarines had put her in this situation, and for all her loyalty to the Imperium and the greater glory of mankind, she resented him for it. Lo Thulaga, Vargas, Abrax Vann of the *Fearless* and now Ulargo, all gone. Vorlov, of the *Boundless*, had been her friend and he too had fallen ignominiously in pursuit of an unbeatable foe at the behest of a reckless angel of the Emperor.

Now, in the thrall of the warp and impotent as she was, trusting to her Navigator to guide them out safely, Kaminska's anger was only magnified.

'Helms-mate, get me Officer Huntsman of the Watch,' she ordered with forced resolve.

'Admiral,' said Huntsman's voice over the vox array after a few moments.

'Assemble your best men and have them patrol decks. I don't want any surprises or unforeseen accidents during transit,' she replied. 'Any signs, any at all, and you know what to do.'

'I shall prosecute my duty with due and lethal diligence, admiral,' Huntsman responded.

HUNTSMAN KILLED THE vox link and turned to the three armsmen waiting patiently for him in the upper deck barracks. They were equipped with pistols and shock mauls and light flak jackets. The four men stood in a small group, their features cast with deep shadows from the low-level lighting that persisted whilst the *Wrathful* was in warp transit. The rest of the barrack room, all gunmetal with stark walls and bunks, was empty.

'Four teams, decks three through eighteen,' said Huntsman with curt and level-headed precision. 'I want regular reports from the below decks overseers, every half hour.'

The three armsmen nodded and left to gather the enforcers.

As Officer of the Watch, it was Huntsman's job to ensure that order and discipline were maintained aboard ship. He was brutal in that duty, an unshakeable enforcer who suffered no insubordination. He had killed many men in pursuit of his duty and felt no remorse for it.

Warp psychosis could affect any man, and even Huntsman, though possessed of a stronger will than most, felt its presence, even through the shielding of the Geller fields surrounding the ship that acted as a barrier against the empyrean. He had seen many suffering from the malady, and it took many forms. Both physical and mental abnormalities could present themselves: hair loss, babbling, catatonia, even homicidal dementia, were common. Huntsman had the cure for each and every one of them sitting snugly in his hip holster.

Wiping a hand across his closely-cropped hair, Huntsman checked the load in his sidearm and patiently awaited the return of his men.

CESTUS, ANTIGES AND the other Astartes captains sat around a lacquered hexagonal table in one of the *Wrathful*'s conference rooms. Wood panelling decorated the room and gave it false warmth, despite its obvious militaristic austerity. Plaques hung on the walls describing the deeds of the many great commanders, captains and admirals that had served in the Saturnine fleet. Kaminska's was amongst them. Her roll of honour was long and distinguished.

There were several artefacts too: crossed cutlasses, an antique pistol and other traditional oceanic trappings. Presiding over all was an icon that spoke of the new age. The Imperial eagle was the symbol of the Emperor's War of Unification and a symbol of the union between Mars and Terra. It was a stark reminder of all they were fighting for and the fragility inherent within it.

'As soon as we leave warp we get into their wake and launch boarding torpedoes at their blind side. Let the fury of the wolf gut this prey from within!' snarled Brynngar. The Wolf Guard, unlike the rest of them, was on his feet and had taken to pacing the room.

'They would shoot our torpedoes down before they even breached their shields,' countered Mhotep. The Thousand Son had been given the all-clear by Apothecary Laeradis after his ship had been destroyed and was keen to attend the council. 'And should they not,' he added, before the Wolf Guard could protest, 'we do not know what kind of armour they have or what forces are onboard. No, we must be patient and wait until the *Furious Abyss* is vulnerable.'

The debate as to how to stop the Word Bearers had been raging for over an hour. In that time, Mhotep had revealed what little he knew: the name of the vessel and its admiral, the weapon systems that had crippled his vessel and the heresy embraced by the Word Bearers. He neglected to speak of Zadkiel's offer of alliance, leaving that to his own counsel. Despite the heated arguments, little had been agreed upon, other than that they were committed to their current course of action and that an all-out assault upon the *Furious Abyss* was tantamount to suicide.

'Bah! Typical of the sons of Magnus to advise caution in the face of action,' bellowed the Space Wolf, his feelings for the Thousand Son as direct and pointed as his demeanour.

'I agree with the wolf,' said Skraal. 'I cannot abide waiting in the dark. If we are to sacrifice our lives to ensure the destruction of our enemies then so be it.'

'Aye!' Brynngar agreed, making the most of the support. 'Any other course smacks of cowardice.'

Mhotep bristled at the slight and looked unshakeably into the feral grin that had crept across the Space Wolf's savage features, but he would not be goaded.

'This gets us nowhere,' Cestus broke in. 'We know for certain that the Astartes aboard that ship have turned traitor. What that means for the rest of the seventeenth Legion, I do not know. Certainly, the Mechanicum built the vessel and that raises further questions about the nature of its construction. The fact it was kept secret suggests complicity on their part, at least to some degree.'

Cestus allowed a moment's pause before he spoke.

'Something is deeply wrong. It is my belief that the Word Bearers are allied against my Legion, and, in so doing, against the Emperor too. They have supporters in the Mechanicum. How else could such a vessel have been made yet none of us have known of it?'

At that remark the Astartes were united in a common purpose. What the Word Bearers had committed was an outright act of war, but it smacked of something more. Though they had their differences, the sons of the Emperor were all siblings after a fashion. They would fight and die together against a common enemy. The Word Bearers were now just such a foe.

'What then are we to do?' Brynngar asked at last, his choleric mood abating, even though he cast a baleful glance at the Thousand Son sitting opposite.

Cestus caught the path of the Space Wolf's gaze, but ignored it for the moment.

'We must find a way to disable the ship. Attack it when it is vulnerable,' the Ultramarines captain told them. 'For we are at least agreed that our enemy is our brother no longer. They shall be destroyed for this treachery, but not before I find out how deep it goes. The Warmaster must know of the enemies arrayed against him. So, for now, we follow the ship and await our opening.'

'Still sounds like cowardice to me,' grumbled Brynngar, taking his seat at last and slouching back in it.

Cestus got to his feet quickly, fixing the Space Wolf with a steely gaze.

'Do not dishonour me or your Legion further,' he warned.

The Wolf Guard matched the Ultramarine's hard stare, but nodded, grumbling his assent beneath his breath.

Mhotep remained silent throughout the exchange, as ever careful to mask his thoughts.

Cestus sat back down, regarding the animosity of his brother Astartes sternly. The Great Crusade had united the Legions in common purpose. Many were the times that he had fought alongside both the sons of Russ and Magnus. Yes, the primarchs each had their differences, and this was passed down to their Legions, and though they bickered like brothers, they were as one. He could not believe that the foundation of their bonds, and the bonds between all of the Legions, were so fragile that by merely putting them in a room together outright war would be declared. What the Word Bearers had done was an aberration. It was the exception, not the rule.

The walls of the conference chamber shook violently, interrupting Cestus's thoughts.

Brynngar sniffed at the air.

'The stink of the warp is thick,' he snarled, with a glance at Mhotep despite himself.

Another tremor struck the room, threatening to tip the Astartes off their feet. Warning klaxons howled in the corridors beyond and the decks below.

Mhotep gazed into the reflective sheen of the conference table, before looking up at Cestus. 'Our passage through the empyrean has been compromised,' he told him.

The Ultramarine returned the Thousand Son's gaze.

'Antiges,' he said, his eyes still upon Mhotep, 'accompany me to the bridge.'

Cestus turned to address the gathering.

'This isn't over. We reconvene once we have left warp-space.'

Muttered agreement answered him, and Cestus and Antiges left for the bridge.

'I TAKE IT you have come to find out why our transit isn't exactly smooth, my lord,' said Admiral Kaminska, who was standing next to her command throne. She had been appraising tactical data garnered from the disastrous battle against the enemy ship and was in close conversation with Venkmyer, her helmsmistress, when Cestus arrived on the bridge. Alongside the strategic display was the sudden fluctuation in the external warp readings.

'Your instincts are correct, admiral,' Cestus replied. Despite their shared experience fighting the *Furious Abyss* and the obvious validation of his mission, Kaminska's demeanour towards the Ultramarine was still icy. Cestus had hoped it would have thawed slightly in the cauldron of battle, but he had effectively taken her ship, despite her experience and her knowledge. Though Cestus was a fleet commander and his naval tactical acumen was superior to Kaminska's, given that he was an Astartes, he had trampled on her command as if it was nothing. It did not sit well with him, but needs must in the situation they were in. Macragge, maybe more besides, was at stake. Cestus could feel it, and that burden must rest squarely on his shoulders. That meant taking command of the mission. If it also meant that he had to put a vaunted Imperial admiral's nose out of joint then so be it.

'I am about to visit my chief Navigator for an explanation, if you would like to accompany me.' Kaminska's attempt at being cordial was forced as she left the command dais.

Both Cestus and Antiges were about to follow when she added.

'The Navigator sanctum is small, captain. There will only be room for one of you.'

Cestus turned to Antiges, who nodded his understanding and took up a ready position at the bridge.

IN THE CLOSE confines of the Navigator sanctum, Cestus felt the bulk of his power armour as never before. The tiny isolation chamber above the bridge, where Orcadus and his lesser cohorts dwelt whilst in warp transit, was bereft of the ornamentation ubiquitous in the rest of the ship. Bare walls and grey gunmetal austerity housed a trio of translucent blister-like pods in which the Navigators achieved communion with the Astronomican and traversed the capricious ebbs and flows of warpspace.

Kaminska who was looking less dignified than usual in the cramped space next to the Astartes, addressed her chief Navigator.

'Orcadus.'

There was a moment's pause and then a hooded and wizened face appeared in the central blister, blurred through the translucent surface. There was the suggestion of wires and circuitry hanging down from some unseen cogitator in the domed ceiling of the pod.

'What has happened?' asked Kaminska.

With a hiss of hydraulics, the central blister broke apart like petals on a rose and Orcadus emerged through a gaseous cloud of vapour, rising as if from a pit.

'Greetings, admiral,' said Orcadus, his voice low and rasping outside of the blister, as if he were struggling to speak. The Navigator's skin was a sweaty grey and he wheezed as he breathed. 'When I was preparing to enter the warp and traverse the Tertiary Coreward Transit as instructed, the empyrean ocean swirled and split.'

'Make your explanations brief please, Navigator, I am needed at the bridge,' Kaminska prompted.

Cestus was gladdened to see that her ire was not reserved for Astartes hijacking her ship.

Though much of Orcadus's face was concealed by his hood, Cestus could see a tic of consternation on his lip. All Navigators possessed a third eye, and it was this tolerated mutation that allowed them to plot a course through the warp. To look into that eye would drive a normal man insane.

'The Tertiary Coreward Transit is down,' he explained simply. 'I had detected a worsening of the abyssal integrity, prior to the collapse, but we were already too far engaged in the warp to turn back,' he said.

'How is this possible?' Cestus asked. 'How did the enemy collapse the route?'

Orcadus's attention fell on the Astartes for the first time during the exchange. If he thought anything of the Ultramarine's presence in his sanctum, he did not show it.

'They deployed some kind of psionic mine,' Orcadus replied. 'The effect would have been felt by our astropaths. As of now, we are sailing the naked abyss,' he stated, switching his attention back to Kaminska. 'What are your orders, admiral?'

Kaminska could not keep the shock from her face. To be effectively cut adrift in the warp was a death sentence, one that she was powerless to do anything about.

'We follow the enemy vessel and stay in its wake as best we can,' said Cestus, cutting in. 'They are bound for Macragge.'

'From Segmentum Solar to Ultramar, outside stable routes?'

'Yes.'

'The chances of success would be minimal, my lord,' Orcadus warned without emotion.

'Even so, that is our course,' Cestus told him.

Orcadus considered for a moment before replying.

'I can use their vessel as a point of reference, like a beacon, and follow it, but I cannot speak for the warp. If the abyss sees fit to devour us or make us its prey then the matter is out of my hands.'

'Very well, chief Navigator, you may return to your duties,' Cestus told him.

Orcadus bowed almost imperceptibly and, just before retreating back to his station, said, 'There are things abroad in the empyrean, the native creatures of the abyss. A shoal of them follows the enemy ship. The warp around it is in tumult, as it has been in the abyss these last several months. It does not bode well.'

At that Orcadus took his leave, swallowed up into the blister once more.

Cestus made no remark. In his experiences as a fleet commander, he was all too aware of the creatures that lurked in the warp. He did not know their nature, but he had seen their forms before and knew they were dangerous. He did not doubt that Kaminska knew of them, too.

With a shared looked of understanding, Cestus and Kaminska left the sanctum and headed back down through a sub-deck tunnel that led to the bridge. They had been walking for several minutes before the Ultramarine broke the charged silence.

'Your attitude towards me and this mission has been noted, admiral.'

Kaminska breathed deep as if trying to master her emotions and then turned.

'You took my ship and usurped my command, how would you feel?' she snapped.

'You serve the Emperor, admiral,' Cestus told her in a warning tone. 'You'd do well to remember that.'

'I am no traitor, Captain Cestus,' she replied angrily, standing her ground against the massive Astartes despite his obvious bulk and superior height. 'I am a loyal servant of the Imperium, but you have ridden roughshod over my authority and my ship for a chase into shadows and probable death. I will lay my life on the altar of victory if I must, but I will not do so meaninglessly and without consideration.'

Cestus's face was an unreadable mask as he considered the admiral's words.

'You are right, admiral. You have shown nothing but courage and honour throughout this endeavour and I have repaid it with ignorance and scorn. This is not fitting behaviour for a member of the Legion and I offer my humble apology.'

Kaminska was taken aback, her expression sketched into a defiant response. At last, her face softened and she exhaled her anger instead.

'Thank you, my lord,' she said quietly.

Cestus bowed slowly to acknowledge the admiral's gratitude.

'I shall meet you on the bridge,' said the Astartes and departed.

When Cestus was gone, Kaminska realised that she was shaking. The vox array crackling into life got her attention.

'Admiral?' said Helmsmistress Venkmyer's voice through the conduit wall unit.

'Speak,' Kaminska answered after a moment as she mustered her composure.

'We've made contact with the *Fireblade*.'

AFT DECKS THREE through six of the *Wrathful* were clear. Most of the non-essential crew were locked down in isolation cells for their own protection. For Huntsman and his small band of three armsmen, it was like patrolling the halls of a ghost ship.

'Squad Barbarus, report.' Huntsman's voice broke the grave-like silence as he strafed a handheld lume-lamp back and forth across the corridor. Shadows recoiled from the grainy blade of light, throwing archways and alcoves into sharp relief.

Huntsman could feel the tension of his men, drawn up in 'V' formation behind him as the radio-silence from the vox-bead in the officer's ear persisted.

'Squad Barbarus,' he repeated, adjusting his grip on the service pistol outstretched in his hand next to the lume-lamp by way of nervous reflex.

Huntsman was about to send two of his armsmen in search of the errant squad when the vox crackled.

'Squad Barb… report… experiencing interfer… all clear.' The clipped reply was fraught with static, but Huntsman was satisfied.

The Officer of the Watch was breathing a sigh of relief when a figure darted across a T-junction ahead, picked out briefly in the light beam.

'Who goes there?' he asked sternly. 'Identify yourself at once!'

Huntsman moved to the T-junction quickly, but with measured caution, using battle-sign to order his arms-men to fan out behind him and cover his flanks.

Reaching the end of the corridor, Huntsman looked left, strafing the light beam quickly.

'Sir, I've got him. This way,' said one of the armsmen, checking down the opposite channel.

Huntsman turned, in time to see the same figure disappearing down another corridor. He could swear he was wearing deck crew fatigues, but they weren't the colours for the *Wrathful*.

'This area is locked down,' barked Huntsman, heart racing. 'This is your final warning. Make yourself known at once.'

Silence mocked him.

'Weapons ready,' Huntsman hissed and stalked off down the corridor, armsmen in tow.

AFTER THE DISASTROUS war council in the conference room, Mhotep had taken his leave of the other Astartes and retired to one of the *Wrathful*'s isolation cells, intending to meditate for the remainder of their transit through the warp. In truth, the confrontation with the Space Wolf had vexed him, more-so his loss of control in the face of Brynngar's berating, and he sought the solitude of his own company to gather his resolve.

Mhotep reached down to the compartment in his armour that contained the wand-stave rescued from the *Waning Moon*. Seeing that the item was intact, he muttered an oath to his primarch. Sitting upon a bench in the cell, the only furnishing in an otherwise Spartan room, Mhotep regarded the wand-stave. In particular, he scrutinised a silvered speculum at the item's tip and stared into its depths.

Focusing his thoughts, Mhotep slipped into a meditative trance as he considered the events unfolding, drawing on the mental acumen for which his Legion was famed.

An anomalous flicker, something inconsistent and intangible, flashed into existence abruptly and was gone.

The Geller field, Mhotep realised. It was the soft caress of the unfettered warp that he had felt, so brief, so infinitesimal that only one of Magnus's progeny, one with their honed psychic awareness, could have detected it.

And something else… Though this, for now at least, slipped beyond Mhotep's mental grasp like tendrils of smoke through his fingers.

The Thousand Son broke off the trance at once and returned the wand-stave to its compartment in his armour. Donning his helmet, he headed for the *Wrathful*'s primary dock.

CAPTAIN ULARGO SAT strapped into his command throne as the warp breached the blast doors at the back of the *Fireblade*'s bridge. All around him was chaos as the hapless crew screamed and thrashed in terror as their minds were unravelled by the warp. Some were already dead, killed by flying debris or simply torn apart as the warp vented its wrath upon them. Ulargo's calm in the face of certain disaster, with chunks of metal hull tearing away into nothing as his bridge was disassembled, was unnerving. The entire chamber was cast in an eldritch light and strange riotous winds buffeted crew and captain alike.

'It goes on... it goes on forever,' he said, his voice caught halfway between wonderment and fear. 'I can see my father, and my brothers. I can hear them... calling me.'

They had entered the empyrean in the *Wrathful*'s wake in accordance with Admiral Kaminska's orders, but upon the collapse of the Tertiary Coreward Transit, their Gellar fields had suffered catastrophic failure, leaving them undefended against the raw emotions of warp space.

It had already changed the place. The bridge shimmered with the skies of Io and the canyons of Mimas, the places where Ulargo had grown up and trained as a pilot in the Saturnine Fleet. The corpses of the navigation crew, slumped over the sextant array, had sprouted into Ganymedian mangrove trees, twisted roots looping through the steel floor of the bridge that in turn was seething with river grass. Waterfalls ghosted over reality, shoals of fish leaping through the shattered viewport. Ulargo wanted very much to be there, back in the places that lived on only in his memory, back when he had been a boy and the universe had felt so infinite and full of wonders.

He held out his hands and felt them brush against the reeds that grew by the River Scamandros on Io. Reptilian birds wheeled in a sky that he could somehow see beyond the torn ceiling of the bridge, as if the torn metal and loops of severed cabling were in another dimension and the reality in his head was bleeding through.

He stepped forwards. The rest of the crew were dead, but that did not mean anything any more. They were ghosts, too.

The stuff of the warp seethed through the blast doors and caught Ulargo up in a swirl of raw emotions. He filled up with regret, then fear, then love, each feeling so powerful that he was just a conduit for them, a hollow man to be buffeted by the warp: the way his father's eyes lit up with pride when he received his first commission. The grief in his mother's eyes, for she knew so many who had lost sons to the void. The fury of space, the ravenous vacuum, the thirsting void, that he always knew one day would devour him. In the warp they were ideas made as real as the mountains of Enceladus.

The side of the bridge gave away. The air boomed out and flung the corpses of the bridge crew out with it. One of the bodies was not yet dead, and in the back of his mind, Ulargo recognised that another human being was dying.

Then he saw the warp beyond the *Fireblade*.

Titanic masses of emotion went on forever, seen not with his eyes, but with his mind: rolling incandescent mountains of Passion, an ocean of grief, leading down to infinity through caves of misery, dripping with the poison of anger.

Hatred was a distant sky, heaving down onto the warp, smothering. Love was a sun. The winds that stripped away the hull of the *Fireblade* were fingers of malice.

It was wondrous. Ulargo was filled with the sight of it; no, not the sight, but the sheer experience, for the warp was not composed of light, but of emotion, and to experience it was to let it speak to the most fundamental parts of his soul.

The sky of hatred split apart and a yawning mouth opened up above Ulargo's soul. Teeth of wrath framed the maw. Beyond it was a black mass, seething like a pit of vermin. It was terror.

Mouths were opening up everywhere. Mindless things, like sharks made of malicious glee, slid between the thunderheads of passion. They snatched at the soul-specks of the *Fireblade*'s crew, teeth like knives through what remained of their minds.

Even love was turning on them, filling them in their last moments of existence with a horrendous longing for all the things they would never have, and appalling, consuming grief for everything they once had, but would never see again.

The maw bore down on Ulargo. Teeth closed in on him, an appalling coldness sheared through him and he knew that it was the purity of death.

The boiling mass seethed. The last vestiges of his physical self recoiled as worms forced themselves into a nose and mouth that no longer existed.

The warp turned dark, and Ulargo drowned in fear.

ADMIRAL KAMINSKA REACHED the bridge to find an ashen-faced crew before her. Cestus had just arrived, his countenance stern and pensive as the distress signal emanating from the *Fireblade* repeated on the ship-to-ship vox.

'This… Ulargo… Fireblade… damaged in transit… request dock… repairs…'

'Impossible,' said Kaminska, feeling all colour drain from her face as she heard the voice of a man she thought was dead. 'Vox traffic is rendered null whilst in warp transit.'

'Admiral, the *Fireblade* claims to be abeam to our port side,' offered Helms-mate Kant as he monitored further communications.

Kaminska looked instinctively over to the viewport and, despite the shimmering interference caused by the

Geller field, she could see Ulargo's ship, a little battered by the initial sortie against the *Furious Abyss*, but otherwise fine.

Common sense warred with the emotions of her heart. Ulargo was a comrade in arms. Kaminska had thought him lost and now she had an opportunity to save him.

'Guide them in to make dock at once.'

HUNTSMAN HAD CHASED the elusive figure to a dead end in the complex of corridors aboard Aft Deck Three of the *Wrathful*. Doors punctuated the apparently endless passageways that led into more barrack rooms and occasionally isolation cells.

As he approached slowly, drawing the lume-lamp across the figure's body, he noticed that his quarry faced the wall. He also saw the fatigues it was wearing more clearly. It was the deck uniform of the *Fireblade*.

'Halt,' he ordered the figure sternly, with a quick glance behind to ensure that his armsmen were still in support.

From the back, he judged the figure to be male, but a scraggly wretch to be sure with unkempt hair like wire and a stench that suggested he hadn't washed in many days.

Huntsman activated the vox-bead.

'Bridge, this is Officer Huntsman. I have detained a male deck crew in Aft-Three,' he said. 'He appears to be wearing a *Fireblade* uniform.'

Helms-mate Kant's response came through crackling static.

'Repeat. Did you say the *Fireblade*?'

'Affirmative – a deck hand from the *Fireblade*,' Huntsman replied, edging closer.

'That's impossible. The *Fireblade* has only just docked with us.'

Huntsman felt a cold chill run down his marrow as the figure turned.

Somehow, the light from the lume-lamp wasn't able to illuminate a belt of shadow across the top of the figure's head and eyes, but Huntsman saw its mouth well enough. The deck hand made a wide, gash-like smile with rotten lips caked in dry blood.

'In the name of Terra,' Huntsman breathed as the figure's jaw distended impossibly wide and revealed dozens of needle-like teeth. Fingers lengthened into talons, nails drenched in blood and razor-sharp. Eyes flashed red in the darkness, like orbs of hate. Huntsman fired.

ON THE BRIDGE, rending screams and scattered gunfire emitted from the vox followed by an almighty static discharge that ended in total silence.

'Raise the Officer of the Watch at once!' Kaminska ordered.

Kant worked at the array, but looked up after a few minutes.

'There is no response, admiral.'

Kaminska snarled, hammered an icon on her command throne and opened another channel.

'Primary dock, respond. This is Admiral Kaminska. Disengage from the *Fireblade* at once,' she said, shouting the orders.

Nothing. Communications were dead.

A warning klaxon sounded on the bridge. Seconds later, the *Wrathful* shook with external hull detonations.

'Admiral,' cried Helmsmistress Venkmyer, 'I'm reading armour damage to the port side, upper decks. How is that even possible?'

'The *Fireblade* is firing its dorsal turrets,' she answered grimly.

'It seems Ulargo's ship survived after all,' said Cestus, donning his battle helm, Antiges following his lead, 'only not in the way we had hoped.

'All Astartes,' he barked into his helmet vox, mercifully unaffected by the radio blackout, 'convene on Aft-Three, Primary Dock, immediately.'

A LONG, LOW scream keened through the *Wrathful*, vibrating through the hull, then another and another until a chorus of them was shrieking through the ship. It sounded like the death screams of hundreds of terrified men.

Mhotep lowered his smoking boltgun once he had dispatched the creature back to the ether. He had arrived too late to save the Officer of the Watch and his arms-men who lay eviscerated on the floor and part way up the blood-slicked walls.

The thing had been warp spawn, that much was apparent, wearing a shadow form of one of the *Fireblade*'s crew rather than inhabiting a body directly. The momentary breach in the *Wrathful*'s Geller field had allowed it aboard ship. Mhotep's instincts told him that it was just a harbinger, and he headed off quickly to the Primary Dock.

Crewmen were hurrying down the *Wrathful*'s corridors, and they struggled to get past the bulky armoured Astartes as he fought to gain the Primary Dock. The engine sections started just stern-wards of the shuttle decks and the ship was getting up to full evasion power.

Shouldering past the frantic crew, Mhotep saw another figure impeding his progress, but one of flesh and blood, standing rock-like in grey power armour.

'Brynngar,' said the Thousand Son levelly at the Space Wolf who had just emerged from an adjacent corridor.

The World Eater, Skraal, with two of his Legion brothers appeared suddenly alongside him from the opposite corridor. Standing at the intersection of the crossroads, a strange sense of impasse existed for a moment before the Wolf Guard snarled and turned away, heading for the Primary Dock.

THE FIVE ASTARTES emerged into chaos.

Men and women of the *Wrathful* fled in all directions, screaming and shouting. Some brandished weapons, others sought higher ground only to be torn down and butchered. Blood swilled like a slick on the dock as the attendant deck crews of the *Wrathful* were torn apart by fell apparitions dressed in the garb of the *Fireblade*. The crew of the lost escort ship had changed. Their mouths were long and wide as if fixed in a perpetual sadistic grin. Needle-like fangs filled their distended maws like those of the long-extinct Terran shark, while long, barbed fingers curled like claws tearing at skin, flesh and bone.

They fell upon the human deck crews with reckless abandon and were devouring them, the bloodied rotten faces of the gruesome predators alive with glee.

'In the name of Russ,' Brynngar breathed as he saw the docking ports that joined the two ships disgorge numberless hordes of twisted *Fireblade* crew.

'They are warp spawn!' Mhotep told them, drawing his scimitar, 'wearing the bodies of our allies, whose souls are now hell-bound, lost to the empyrean. Destroy them.'

Brynngar threw his head back and roared, the sound eerie and resonant from within the confines of his battle helm. With Felltooth in one hand and bolt pistol in the other, he charged into the fray.

Skraal and the World Eaters followed, brandishing chainaxes and bellowing the name of Angron.

A TRIO OF vampire-like warp spawn fell under the withering report of Mhotep's bolter as he trudged across the Primary Dock and through the visceral mire sloshing at his feet. The copper stink assailing his nostrils would have overpowered a normal man, but the Thousand Son crushed the sensation and closed with the enemy.

Barks of bolter fire were tinny and echoing through his helmet as he cut down an advancing warp spawn, parting its sternum and decapitating it with the return swing. The hordes were everywhere and soon surrounded him. The muzzle-flare from his weapon illuminated the grim destruction he wrought with flashing intermittence, the keening wail of his scimitar a high-pitched chorus to the din of explosive fire.

He felt something trying to push at the edges of his mind, testing his psychic defences with tentative mental probing. Slogging through the despicable horde, he was drawn closer to the source of it, even as it was drawn to him, and he felt the pressure on his sanity increase.

BRYNNGAR SHRUGGED OFF a creature clinging to his arm and smashed it with Felltooth, the rune axe cutting through wasted bone like air. He thrust his bolt pistol into another and used the warp spawn's momentum to lift it from the ground. Triggering the weapon, he blasted the creature apart in a shower of bone and viscera. Then the Space Wolf lunged and butted a third, almost dissolving its rotted cranium against his battle helm. Gore and brain matter spoiled his vision, and

Brynngar wiped his helmet visor clean with the back of his gauntleted hand.

With the destruction of the physical body, the warp spawn appeared to lose their hold on the material plane and dissipated. They were easy meat. Brynngar had fought far hardier foes, but in such swarms they were starting to tax him. Even his gene-enhanced musculature burned after the solid fighting. For every three the Wolf Guard slew, another six took their place, pouring like rancid ants from the docking portals.

Brynngar realised to his dismay, hacking down another spawn, that gradually he was being pushed back.

He caught sight of Skraal through the melee. The World Eater was similarly pressed, though a bloody mist surrounded him from the churning punishment wreaked by his chainaxe. He could not see Skraal's fellow Legionaries; Brynngar assumed they had been swallowed by the horde.

A sudden tearing of metal, mangled with the sound of tortured souls, rent the air, and Brynngar felt the deck lurch from under him as it seemed to twist in on itself.

The integrity fields, which kept the dock pressurised when the dock ports were open, flickered once, but held. The physical structure did not. A huge chunk ripped out of the deck as if bitten by unseen jaws, three decks high. Debris was tumbling out into the ether. Brynngar looked away, for to do otherwise would be to comprehend the naked warp and embrace madness.

Something stirred beyond the breach, out in the infinite. Brynngar felt it as the hackles rose on the back of his neck and the feral nature of his Legion became suddenly emboldened. For a brief moment, the Space Wolf wanted to tear off his helmet and gauntlets and gorge himself on flesh like a beast of the wild. He backed away of his own volition, realising that something primal and terrible was with them on the dock.

MHOTEP HAD FORCED his way to the docking portals, through a swathe of warp spawn. His armour was dented and scratched from their ether claws and his body heaved with exhaustion. It was not physical prowess that would save them here, but the discipline of the mind that needed to hold fast.

Mhotep had felt the presence, too, and standing before the docking portal he beheld it in his mind's eye. It was dark and seething: a pure predator.

'It has seen me,' he said calmly into his helmet vox, the warp spawn hordes recoiling suddenly from the Thousand Son, regarding him in the same way a Prosperine spirehawk regards its prey. 'I cannot hide from it now.'

BRYNNGAR WAS ALMOST back to back with Skraal, the two Astartes having been fought back to the blast doors, when he heard Mhotep through his vox.

'Seen what?' snarled the Space Wolf, gutting another warp spawn as Skraal cleaved the arm from another.

'You cannot prevail here,' the voice of Mhotep came again. 'Get out and seal the doors. I will remain and activate the dock's auto-destruct sequence.'

Many vessels of the Imperial Fleet came with such precautionary measures built in to their design by the Mechanicum. They were meant as weapons of last resort, should a ship be overrun and in danger of capture. If a ship could not be defended or retaken from an enemy then it would be denied to them utterly, although in this case, Mhotep's sacrifice would not destroy the ship, only vanquish the foes that were besieging it.

'Do so now!' urged the Thousand Son.

Brynngar had lost sight of him, though his view was curtailed as he forced himself to look away from the tear into the naked warp beyond. Although it rankled, the Space Wolf knew when he was chasing a lost cause.

'Come on,' he snarled to Skraal who hacked and hewed with berserk fury, 'we are leaving.'

'The sons of Angron do not flee the enemy,' he raged in response.

'Even so,' Brynngar said, smashing a warp spawn aside. Ducking a blood-maddened sweep of Skraal's chainaxe, he punched the World Eater hard in the chest with the flat of his hand. The stunned Astartes was lifted off his feet and sent sprawling through the open blast doors. Brynngar trudged after Skraal's prone form, carving a path through the horde with Felltooth.

A few of the warp spawn had found their way through to the other side of the blast doors that led from the Primary Dock. Brynngar was about to hunt them down when a barrage of bolter fire scythed through them like wheat.

Inside his battle helm, the Space Wolf grinned as he saw the battered forms of the Ultramarines.

'Down!' cried Cestus who was leading the group, and Brynngar hit the deck as a fusillade of fire erupted overhead.

Arching his neck, the Space Wolf saw the smoking bodies of more warp spawn fall into a heap at the dock threshold. Swinging out a hand, he thumped the portal icon and the blast doors slid shut with a hydraulic pressure-hiss.

'We must seal the doors,' he snarled, rolling on his back as Antiges, Morar and Lexinal charged past him to guard the portal.

STRIPPING AWAY THE verisimilitude of the warp spawn crew, Mhotep saw that they were not separate entities at all. They were the extension of a single conjoined conscious, raw emotion given form. Tentacles snaked from three gaping maws lined with cruel teeth that had once been the docking portals, and flesh sacks like finger puppets danced along them.

As he stepped forward, he brandished his scimitar, a power sword engraved with hieroglyphics: the old tongue of Prospero. Mhotep was acutely aware of the blast doors shutting behind him, though the sound was far off, as if listened to in a separate dimension from the one he currently inhabited. Realising he was alone, the Thousand Son tapped into the innate power of his Legion, the psychic mutation common to all sons and daughters of Prospero that had earned Magnus the condemnation of Nikea. Mhotep's power, like that of all the Astartes of his Legion, was honed to a rapier-like point and when properly channelled could be deadly. The nay-sayers of Nikea had been right to fear it.

Mhotep stowed his bolter, for it would not avail him here, and drew forth the wand-stave. Inputting a rune sequence, played out in the jewels along its short haft, the item extended into the length of a staff. Holding the weapon up to his helmet lens, Mhotep peered through the speculum at the tip. The tiny, silvered mirror became transparent and, through it, the Thousand Son saw the entity for what it was.

The warp had been cruel. It had taken the ship and its crew and transfigured it into something wretched and debased. Tiny black eyes rolled in the armoured carapace and the bodies of its crew writhed all over the surface of the ship, trapped within a translucent membrane that sheathed it like living tissue. They were deformed, fused together with their tortured expressions stretched out as if melted. These were the souls of the *Fireblade*'s crew and they were lost to the warp forever.

The portion of the escort ship that had penetrated the cargo hold eked from the belly of the ship like an umbilical cord, the tentacle strings spilling from the maws at the end of them revealed to be tongues. The sound that emanated from them was appalling. The warp screamed from the *Fireblade*'s throat, a screeching gale that threatened to knock Mhotep off his feet. He stayed upright, however, and found what he was looking for in the partly insubstantial hull of the former Imperial ship.

The Thousand Son intoned words of power and an ellipsis of light burned into the deck plate. The Prosperine hieroglyphics on his staff flared bright vermillion. Spinning the staff around, Mhotep drove the scimitar into it pommel first and it became a spear.

'Back to the deeps!' bellowed the son of Magnus, his aim fixed upon the warp-entity's tainted core. 'There will be no feasting here for you, dead thing! By the Silver Towers and the Ever-Burning Eye, begone!'

Mhotep flung the spear just as the tentacles closed on him, a burning trail of crimson light following its psychic trajectory. It struck the *Fireblade* in the heart of its central maw and a great explosion of light detonated within. Spectral blood fountained and the reaching tentacles withered and burned.

The illumination built, blazing out of the maw and Mhotep was forced to look away from its brilliance. The scent of acrid smoke filled his nostrils, penetrating his helmet filters, and raging flames engulfed his senses together with the primordial scream of something dying in the fathomless ether.

IN THE CORRIDOR beyond the Primary Dock, ceiling plates fell like rain as the walls of the *Wrathful* shuddered with fury. Cestus and Antiges fought to get to the doors as the tremors hit. The rippling shock waves were coming from the Primary Dock.

Staying on his feet, Cestus drew his power sword and was about to beckon forward a group of engineers, who were lingering behind them, to fuse the blast doors when the horrific din emanating from within stopped. Smoke and faint, white light issued through the cracks.

All was quiet and still for a moment.

'Where is Mhotep?' the Ultramarine asked, sheathing the blade. He'd been monitoring the helmet vox transmissions and knew that the Thousand Son had been at the Primary Dock. During the warp phenomenon, battles had erupted all across the *Wrathful*, and the secondary and tertiary docks had also come under attack. Reports were flickering past on Cestus's helmet vox that the warp spawn had abated abruptly for reasons unknown, dissolving back into the ether.

Skraal was still out of it on the deck, babbling in enraged delirium, so Cestus turned to Brynngar for his answer.

'He made a noble sacrifice,' intoned the Space Wolf, as he got to his feet.

'That almost sounds like respect,' Cestus said, his voice tinged with bitterness.

'It is,' growled Brynngar. 'He gave his life for this ship and in so doing saved us all. For that he will have the eternal gratitude of Russ. I am not so proud to admit that I misjudged him.'

Whining servos and the hiss of released pressure made the Space Wolf turn with bolt pistol raised as the blast doors ground open. Cestus and the other Astartes joined him with weapons levelled at the flickering dark beyond.

Mhotep emerged from the scorched ruin of the Primary Dock, staggering, but very much alive. Tendrils of smoke rose from his pitted armour and he was drenched in viscous, translucent gore. In spite of his appearance and obvious injuries, he still retained his bearing, that nobility and arrogance so typical of Prospero's sons.

'It is not possible,' Brynngar breathed, taking a step back as if Mhotep were some apparition from the fireside sages of Fenris. 'None could have survived in such a conflagration.'

Cestus lowered his bolter cautiously and then his hand in a gesture for the other Ultramarines to do the same.

'We thought you were dead.'

Mhotep unclasped and removed his helmet, breathing deep of the recycled air. His eyes were black orbs and a riot of purple veins wreathed his face, but was slowly disappearing beneath his skin.

'As... did... I,' gasped the Thousand Son, helmet clattering to the deck as it fell from nerveless fingers.

Cestus caught his fellow Astartes as he lurched forward and bore him down to the floor, half-cradled in his arms.

'Summon Laeradis at once,' he told Antiges, who was stunned for a moment before he came to his senses and went off to find the Ultramarine apothecary.

'He lives, yet,' Cestus added, noting Mhotep's fevered breathing.

'Aye,' Brynngar muttered darkly, having overcome his superstition, 'and there is but one way that could be so…' The Space Wolf's lip curled up in profound distaste. '…Sorcery.'

EIGHT

Nikea/Advantage/Bakka Triumveron

IN HIS PRIVATE quarters, Zadkiel regarded the pict screen on the console before him with interest. The room was drenched in sepulchral light, the suggestion of idols and craven icons visible at the edge of the shadows. Zadkiel's face was bathed in cold, stark light from the pict screen, making him appear gaunt and almost lifeless.

Battle scenarios were displayed on the surface of the screen. An astral body, the size of a moon, exploded moments after being struck by a missile payload. Debris spread outward in a wide field, showering a nearby planet with burning meteors. An icon in the scenario represented a ship, the *Furious Abyss*, as it moved through the debris field. Trajectory markers with distances indicated alongside were displayed, originating at the ship icon and terminating at the planet's surface. The image paused momentarily and then cycled back to the beginning again.

Zadkiel switched his attention to a vertical row of three supplementary screens attached to the main pict screen. The uppermost one was full of streaming data that bore the Mechanicum seal. Calculations concerning armour tolerances, projected orbital weapon strengths and extrapolated endurance times based upon the first statistic versus the other scrolled by. Angles, probable firepower intensities and shield indexes were all considered in exacting detail. The middle screen contained four stage-by-stage picts showing the effects of a particular viral strain upon human beings. A time code at the bottom right corner of the final pict displayed 00:01:30.

The final screen displayed projected casualty rates: Macragge orbital defences – 49%; Macragge orbital fleet – 75%; Macragge population – 93%. Kor Phaeron and the rest of the Word Bearers' fleet would account for the rest. Zadkiel smiled; with a single blow they would all but wipe out the Ultramarines' home world and the Legion with it.

'I SAW IT myself, with this very eye,' snarled Brynngar, pointing to the non-cloudy orb. 'The Kolobite drone king did not blind me so much that I cannot see what is before my face.'

Brynngar had joined Cestus, Skraal and Antiges in a waiting room outside of the medi-bay where Laeradis ministered to Mhotep after his collapse. The Wolf Guard stalked back and forth across the small, sanitised chamber, which was all white tile and stark lighting, impatiently awaiting the Thousand Son's return.

'No man, not even an Astartes, could have faced those hordes and lived,' offered Skraal, 'although I would have gladly laid down my life to dispatch them to the hell of the warp.' The World Eater was raging as he spoke, blood fever clouding his vision as the endless need for violence and slaughter nagged at him. He had confessed earlier that he remembered little of the fight, engaged as he was in a haze of fury, only waking in the access corridor to the primary dock. Brynngar had deliberately chosen not to enlighten him, deciding that he didn't want to risk the World Eater's wrath.

'Aye, and I can think of no other way that such a deed could have been done,' said Brynngar, coming to rest at last.

'You speak of witchcraft, Space Wolf,' said Antiges with a dark glance at Cestus.

The Ultramarines captain had remained silent throughout. If what Brynngar said was true then it had dire ramifications. What was beyond doubt was that Mhotep's actions had saved the *Wrathful* from certain doom, but the edicts of the Emperor, laid down at Nikea, were strict and without flexibility. Such things could not be ignored, to do so would damn them as surely as the Word Bearers. Cestus would not embrace that fate, however rational it might seem.

'We do not know for certain that Mhotep employed such methods and devices, only that he lived where perhaps he should not have,' he said.

'Is that not proof enough?' Brynngar cried. 'The acts of Zadkiel, of this treacherous vermin is one thing, but to have a heretic aboard ship is quite another. Let me wring the truth out of him, I'll–'

'You will do what, brother?' asked Mhotep, standing in the open archway of the waiting room. Like the other Astartes, he wasn't wearing his helmet, but he was also stripped out of his power amour and clad in robes.

Apothecary Laeradis, together with another of the honour guard, Amryx, there by way of additional security, was visible behind him. The Apothecary was collecting his various apparatus as stooped Legion serfs scurried around him gathering up Mhotep's discarded armour.

Brynngar stared at the Thousand Son, fists clenched, his face reddening as he bared his fangs.

'Laeradis?' asked Cestus, stepping in front of the Space Wolf in order to diffuse the tension.

The Apothecary had just emerged into the room. Amyrx was standing silently next to him.

'No lasting injuries that his metabolism cannot cure,' Laeradis reported.

'Good,' Cestus replied. 'Rejoin your battle-brothers in the barracks.'

'My captain,' said the Apothecary, and gratefully left the charged atmosphere of the waiting room with Amryx, obsequious Legion serfs in tow.

'What happened at the dock?' asked Skraal, weighing in on Brynngar's behalf. 'I lost two Legion brothers to that fight, how were you able to survive?'

The two World Eaters had been discovered later, recovered by blind servitors before the dock was locked down permanently and bulk heads put in place. The unfortunate Astartes had been transfixed by the blade claws of the warp spawn and died gurgling blood. Their scorched remains rested in one of the *Wrathful*'s mausoleums, awaiting proper ceremony.

'When I reached the auto-destruct console I found that the protocols were off-line,' Mhotep explained, his face unreadable. 'Favour smiled on me though as during the battle, a fuel line linked to one of the docking ports had come loose from its housing and I was able to ignite it. I fought my way to a place where I was shielded from the blast and the resultant conflagration destroyed the entities with purging fire.'

'Your silver tongue is fat with lies,' Brynngar accused him, stepping forward. 'The air is thick with the stink of them.'

Mhotep turned his stony gaze on the Space Wolf.

'I can assure you, Son of Russ, whatever odour you are detecting is not emanating from me. Perhaps you should seek your answer nearer to your own bedraggled self.'

Brynngar roared and launched himself at the Thousand Son, bearing him to the ground with his massive bulk.

'Drink it in, witch,' snarled the Wolf Guard, intent on forcing Mhotep's head into the tiled floor. A splash of spittle landed on the Thousand Son's grimacing face as he thrashed against the Space Wolf's superior strength.

Cestus, using all of his weight, smashed into Brynngar's side to dislodge him. The Wolf roared again as he was toppled from the Thousand Son.

Skraal was about to wade in, but Antiges blocked his path, the Ultramarine's hand resting meaningfully on the pommel of his short-blade.

'Stand fast, brother,' he warned.

Skraal's hand wavered near his chainaxe, but he snorted in mild contempt, and in the end relented. This was not the fight he wanted.

Brynngar rolled from Cestus's body charge and swung to his feet. The Ultramarines captain was quick to interpose himself between Space Wolf and Thousand Son, his posture low in a readied battle stance.

'Stand aside, Cestus,' Brynngar growled.

Cestus did not move, but instead kept his gaze locked with the Space Wolf.

'Do so, now,' Brynngar warned him again, his tone low and dangerous.

'This is not the way of the Astartes,' Cestus said, his voice calm and level in response.

Behind the Ultramarine, Mhotep got to his feet, a little shaken, but otherwise defiant in the face of his aggressor.

'No: it is not the way of Guilliman's Legion, you mean,' answered Brynngar.

'Even so, I am in charge of this ship and this mission,' Cestus asserted, 'and if you have issue with my commands, then you will take them up with me.'

'He defies the Emperor's decree and yet you defend him!' Brynngar raged and took a step forward. He stopped when he realised that the Ultramarine's short-blade was at his throat.

'If Mhotep is to answer charges then he will do so at my behest and in a proper trial,' Cestus told him, the blade in his hand steady. 'The feral laws of Fenris are not recognised on this ship, battle-brother.'

Brynngar growled again as if weighing up his options. In the end, he backed down.

'You are no brother of mine,' he snarled, and stalked from the chamber.

Skraal followed him, a thin smile on his lips.

'That went well,' said Antiges, sighing with relief. He had not been relishing the idea of facing one of Angron's Legion, nor had he a desire to see Brynngar go toe-to-toe with his brother-captain.

'Sarcasm does not become you, Antiges,' said Cestus darkly. Brynngar was his friend. They had fought together in countless campaigns. He owed the old wolf his life, and more than once, Antiges too had a similar debt to the Wolf Guard. Cestus had defied him, however, and in so doing had besmirched his honour. Yet, how could he not give Mhotep the benefit of the doubt, without proof of his supposed actions? Cestus admitted to himself that his experience in the reactor chamber at Vangelis, the vision of Macragge he had witnessed, might be affecting his decisions.

'I am grateful to you, Cestus,' said Mhotep, smoothing out his robes after the Space Wolf's rough treatment.

'Don't be,' the Ultramarine snapped, in part angry at himself for his self doubt. His gaze was cold and unforgiving as it turned on the Thousand Son. 'This is not over, nor am I satisfied with your explanation for what happened at the dock. You will be remanded to your quarters until we leave the warp and I have time to decide what is to be done.

'Antiges,' Cestus added, 'have Admiral Kaminska send the new Officer of the Watch and a squad of armsmen to escort Captain Mhotep to his cell.'

Antiges nodded briskly and went off towards the bridge.

'I could overwhelm a mere band of armsmen and defy this order,' Mhotep said, matching the Ultramarine's steely gaze.

'Yes, you could,' said Cestus, 'but you will not.'

'LET IT NOT be said,' uttered Zadkiel, 'that the warp is without imagination.'

Before Admiral Zadkiel, who, having left his private quarters, was in the *Furious Abyss*'s cathedra, stood rank upon rank of Word Bearers. Their presence in the vaulted chamber was an echo of what had faced him at the vessel's inaugural launch at Thule. It was a sight that filled Zadkiel with a sense of power.

The warriors represented the Seventh Company of the Quillborn Chapter, one of those that made up the greater Word Bearers Legion. Every Chapter had its own traditions and its own role within Lorgar's Word. The Quillborn were so named because their traditions emphasised their birth, created in the laboratories and apothecarions of Colchis. They were written into existence, born as syllables of the Word. A dedicated naval formation, the Quillborn were true marines, fighting ship-to-ship, completely at home battling through the cramped structure of a starship. At their head was Assault-Captain Baelanos, the acting captain of the company, although Zadkiel was their overlord.

'The ghost of one of their vessels has waylaid them,' continued Zadkiel with rising oratory. 'It was promised that in the warp we would find our allies. The fate of our pursuers aboard the *Wrathful* has shown that promise to have been kept.'

Baelanos stepped forwards. 'Who will hear the Word?' he bellowed.

As one, a hundred Word Bearers raised their guns and chanted in salute.

'They will be harrying us from here to Macragge,' said the assault-captain, his belligerence a contrast to Zadkiel's authoritative confidence, 'and they will die for it! Perhaps the warp will send them to us in the end, so we can show them how we deal with the blind in real space!'

The Word Bearers cheered. Zadkiel saw Ultis among them, and felt a pang of agitation at his presence in the throng.

His fate is written, Zadkiel thought.

'The warp is yet a strange place to us,' said Zadkiel. 'Though it holds nothing for us to fear, for Lorgar knows it better than any mind ever has, you will be assailed by mysteries. You might dream that which your mind has hidden from you. Perhaps you will even see them, as clear as day. These are the ways of the warp. Remember in all things the Word of Lorgar, and it will lead you back to sanity. Lose sight of the Word, and your mind will be carried away on currents from which it might never return. Make no mistake, the warp is dangerous. It is the Word, and the Word alone, that lets us navigate its waters.

'Soon we must make dock. The earlier battle took more of a toll than we thought. The way-station at Bakka Triumveron is our next destination.'

Zadkiel did not tell them that his over-confidence had resulted in the damage to the ship that meant they were forced into a detour. A lucky hit from the *Waning Moon*'s lances had cut off the engineering teams from the *Furious Abyss*'s stores of fuel oil as well as rupturing the primary coolant line. Without regular supply, they could not function, and so it was imperative that the damage be cleared in order to allow the crews access. That could only be done whilst at dock.

'Shortly after that, we shall be at Macragge,' Zadkiel continued. 'Then our chapter of the Word will be completed. To your duties, Word Bearers. You are dismissed.'

The Word Bearers filed out of the cathedra, many of them heading to reclusium cells.

Baelanos approached the pulpit where Zadkiel was standing. 'We won't have long at Bakka,' he said. 'What are your orders to the astropathic choir?'

'I need to make contact with my lord Kor Phaeron,' said Zadkiel, 'and apprise him of our progress.'

'What of Wsoric?' asked Baelanos, a momentary tremor evident in his outward resolve at mention of the name.

'He stirs,' replied Zadkiel. 'We have only to cement our pact with the empyrean with blood, and then he will act.'

'The lap dogs of the Emperor are ever tenacious, my lord.'

'Then we shall cast them off,' Zadkiel told him, 'but for now, we wait. Asking too many favours of the empyrean may not behove us well.'

'As you wish, my lord,' said Baelanos, bowing slightly, but his reluctance was obvious.

'Trust me to fulfil my duties to the Word, Baelanos, as I trust you,' said Zadkiel.

'Yes, admiral,' replied the assault-captain. Baelanos saluted and headed for the engine decks.

Zadkiel remained in the cathedra, for a moment, deep in thought. It was so easy to lose sight of the Word, to become wrapped up in power. It would have been simple for him to forget what he was and where his place was in the galaxy.

That was why Lorgar had chosen him for this mission. There was no more dedicated servant of the Word, save for Lorgar.

Zadkiel knelt before the altar, murmured a few words of prayer, and headed back up towards the bridge.

'CAPTAIN CESTUS?' SAID Kaminska's voice over the Ultramarine's helmet vox. The engine servitors of the *Wrathful* had managed to bring on-ship communications back on line.

'Speaking,' he replied, more irritably than he'd intended. The confrontation with Brynngar in the medi-bay waiting room was weighing on his mind, that and whatever Mhotep was hiding from them behind that veneer of indifference.

'Meet me on the bridge at once.'

Cestus sighed deeply at the admiral's curt response. He had intended to patrol the lower aft decks with Antiges. In the wake of the officer of the watch's death, together with all of his most experienced armsmen, the ship was short-handed. The Astartes captain had taken it upon himself to make up the shortfall and ensure that no other unforeseen difficulties arose for whatever time remained of their warp passage.

Given Admiral Kaminska's tone, the patrol would have to wait, so Cestus and Antiges headed for the bridge.

KAMINSKA KEPT A lean bridge when not in combat. Crewmen at the sensorium, navigation and engineering helms were all that were present. The admiral was standing at a table illuminated by a hololithic star map. She looked ragged as he approached her, with dark rings around her eyes and a greyish pallor to her complexion.

Cestus couldn't help think how long it had been since she had slept. An Astartes could go for several days without, but Kaminska was merely human. He wondered how long she could keep going.

'My lord,' she said, acknowledging the giant Astartes.

'Admiral. What is it you wish to bring to my attention?'

Kaminska indicated the star map in front of her. It showed the sector of the galaxy around the dense galactic core. The core was impassable, and so much of the map was taken up with a blank void. Notations and calculations were scrawled in the margins. Beside the map was a printout from one of the sensorium pict screens. It was a close-up of the *Furious Abyss*'s hull.

'See this?' said Kaminska, indicating a white plume issuing from the side of the Word Bearers ship. The grainy resolution made it look like gas was being vented.

'They have an air leak?'

'Better than that,' said Kaminska. 'It's damage to the coolant lines. If they push the engines, the plasma reactors will burn up, and, pursued by *this* ship, if they want to stay ahead of us, they'll have to push the engines.'

Cestus smiled grimly at the sudden turn in fortune. It was small recompense for all they'd lost.

'So the *Furious Abyss* will have to make dock to effect repairs,' the Ultramarine guessed.

'Yes. They'll also be reloading ordnance and using the time to service their fighters after the battle outside the Tertiary Coreward Transit.'

'Show me the location, admiral,' said Cestus, assuming that Kaminska had already planned their strategy in part.

Kaminska laid her finger on the hololithic display in triumph. 'Outside the Solar System there aren't many orbital docks that can support a ship that size.'

The Bakka system was already circled on the map.

'Bakka,' said Cestus. 'My Legion mustered there for the Karanthas Crusade. It's the Imperial Army's staging post for half the galactic south.'

'It has the only docks between the galactic core and Macragge that could handle the *Furious Abyss*,' Kaminska told him. 'I'd bet my commission that this is where they'll head.'

Cestus thought for a moment. A plan was forming.

'How long before we break warp?'

'Several hours yet, but delay or not, we can't beat the *Furious Abyss* in a straight fight.'

'Tell me this, admiral,' Cestus said, looking into Kaminska's eyes. 'When is a ship most vulnerable?'

Kaminska smiled despite her weariness.

'When she's at anchor.'

Cestus nodded. Turning away from the admiral, he raised the other Astartes captains on the vox array and told them to meet him in the conference room immediately.

'WHAT NEWS HAVE you, Brother Zadkiel?' mouthed the supplicant.

Somehow, the creature's lolling mouth formed the words in such a way that Kor Phaeron's short temper and self-confidence were perfectly enunciated.

'We are on our way, my lord,' said Zadkiel, bowing.

Kor Phaeron was one of the arch commanders of the Legion, foremost in Lorgar's reckoning. He was the primarch's greatest champion and it was he, this ancient warrior of countless battles, that would command the forces to attack Calth where Guilliman mustered and destroy the Ultramarines utterly. It was a singular honour to be in Kor Phaeron's presence, albeit across the infinity of warp space, and Zadkiel was at once humbled by the experience. It was not an emotion he had great affinity with.

The supplicant chamber of the *Furious Abyss* was bathed in darkness, but the presence of the astropathic choir behind the supplicant was powerful enough to remove the need for light. The choir consisted of eight astropaths, but the *Furious*'s astral cohort differed from those on any Imperial ship. The fact that there were eight of them suggested their instability. The *Furious Abyss's* route through the warp, and the forces brought to bear on it, eroded the mind of an astropath with dismaying speed, and while such creatures were all blind, they did not have the heavy ribbed cables running from each eye socket attaching them to the macabre contraption clamped around the supplicant's swollen cranium.

'How goes your progress?' asked the mighty champion of the Word Bearers.

'Half a day longer in the warp, until we reach the fringes of the galactic core. We must make vital repairs at Bakka, before heading onwards to Macragge.'

'I recall no such deviation in the mission plan, Zadkiel.' Despite the fact that Kor Phaeron was doubtless aboard the Word Bearers battle-barge the *Infidus Imperator*, in deep communion with its own astropathic choir and speaking through a flesh puppet, his tone and manner were still dangerous.

'During a brief sortie with a fleet of Imperial ships we sustained minor damage that could not be ignored, my lord,' Zadkiel explained more hurriedly than he liked.

'A military action?' Kor Phaeron's disdain was clear. 'Did any survive?'

'A single cruiser pursues us yet through the warp, liege.'

'So they do not seek to raise a warning back on Terra,' mused the arch champion, his considered tone at odds with the slack-jawed, drooling visage of the supplicant. 'A pity. I suspect Sor Talgron is itching in his traitor's shackles.'

'I trust that Brother Talgron would have acquitted himself with distinction, Kor Phaeron.'

In the eyes of Zadkiel, Sor Talgron's mission was not a desirable one. The lord commander was to remain in the Solar System, his four companies ostensibly guarding Terra, in order to maintain the pretence that Lorgar still sided with the Emperor when in fact, he had been instrumental in the Warmaster's defection.

'It matters not, my lord. The prospect of word reaching Terra should not concern us. The warp's disquiet would prevent any warning getting to Macragge.'

'I disagree.' The supplicant sneered in an echo of Kor Phaeron's idiosyncratic expression. 'Any deviation from the plan as written holds the potential for disaster. The entire Word could go disobeyed!'

'We will be a few hours at Bakka at the most, exalted lord,' said Zadkiel plaintively, wary of his master's wrath. 'Then we will be on our way. If our pursuer catches up with us, she will be destroyed as her sister ships were. In any case we will not be late; our passage through the warp was swift. But what of you, my lord?'

'We've joined up with the other elements of the Legion and all is proceeding as written.'

'Calth has no hope.'

'None, my brother.'

The supplicant lolled back, drooling blood as the connection was broken. The astropathic choir sank into silence, only their ragged breathing suggesting the great effort required to maintain the link across the immaterium.

Zadkiel regarded the dead supplicant with detached interest. It was interesting to him to see how easily their physical forms could be destroyed when their minds were so strong. He considered that he would like to test that theory.

'All is well, my lord?' asked Ultis. The novice was standing behind Zadkiel.

'All is well, novice,' said Zadkiel. 'You will join Baelanos at Bakka, Ultis. Take the Scholar Coven. They will know to obey you.'

Ultis saluted. 'It will be an honour, admiral.'

'One you have earned, novice. Now, be about your duties.'

'Yes, my lord.'

Ultis turned smartly and headed for the cell deck where the Scholar Coven would be undergoing their scheduled meditation-doctrine training.

Zadkiel watched him go and smiled darkly. Such potential, such relentless ambition; the upstart would soon learn the folly of overreaching.

Soon, Zadkiel told himself, forcing down a thrill of excitement. *Soon, Guilliman will burn and Lorgar will rule the stars.*

Zadkiel could feel that time approaching. That age was in its infancy, but it only needed time to come about. Zadkiel knew this as surely as he had ever known anything, because it was written.

THE WRATHFUL BROKE out of the warp, almost gasping in relief as it slid back into real space.

The vessel's hull was torn and scorched, and chunks of its engine cowlings were ripped out. The winds of the warp had carved strange patterns into its armour plate around the prow and all over the underside. Claws had raked deep gouges all over the upper hull and torn turrets from their mountings.

Sitting in her command throne, Admiral Kaminska looked out of the viewport and saw that the *Wrathful* had not emerged alone.

Leprous and wretched with its pitted, rusting hull and disease-ridden ports, the *Fireblade* limped into existence alongside them.

It was a ship of the damned, the thousands of souls aboard condemned to endless, torturous oblivion.

Such a thing could not be allowed to endure.

Kaminska gave the order to train laser batteries on the decrepit vessel. There was a few seconds' pause when the *Wrathful* unleashed a blistering salvo of fire. Without operational shields, the *Fireblade* crumpled under the onslaught. A few seconds more and all that remained of the blighted escort ship was a scorched wreck and space debris.

It was a duty that gave Kaminska no pleasure, but necessary all the same, much like the expulsion of their own dead. It was bad luck to keep the deceased on board, not to mention unhygienic. Bodies were never returned to their home port in the Saturnine Fleet. What the void killed, it kept.

The tiny gleaming sparks that fell away from the *Wrathful* were corpses enclosed in body bags, reflecting the light of the star Bakka that burned in a magnesium spark a few light hours away. Much closer was Bakka Triumveron, a titanic gas cloud far bigger than the Solar System's Jupiter, bright yellow streaked with violet and ringed with scores of shimmering bands of ice and rock. Bakka was a mystery, its gaseous form far too stormy and strange to admit any craft, while its rings were death-traps many times more lethal than the rings of Saturn. Bakka's outlying moons, however, were habitable, each one almost the size of Terra and all of them heavily populated. Rogelin, Sanctuary, Half Hope, Grey Harbour: these hive cities were just fledglings compared to the teeming pinnacles of the Solar System, but they were still home to billions of Imperial citizens. The Bakka system was one of the most populated in the segmentum, certainly the largest concentration of human life this close to the galactic core.

Bakka Triumveron's fourteenth moon had no cities, but instead was enclosed within a thin black spider web that looked like some planetary disease. It was, in fact, the underlying structure of its orbital docks, held over the moon so that they could benefit from its enormous stores of geothermal energy. The moon was uninhabited, thanks to its relentlessly shifting tectonic plates and accompanying cataclysms, but the dockyards above Triumveron 14 were some of the main reasons why Bakka was populated at all.

THREE ASSAULT-BOATS HEADED out from the launch bays of the *Wrathful*. They approached the farthest docking spike of Bakka Triumveron 14 and did so with stealth and subterfuge. It was imperative that they not be discovered by the enemy. It also meant that the troops on board would have a long trek to the *Furious Abyss*.

Three assault-boats; three discreet combat formations. Skraal joined his Legion warriors in one. Their mode of approach was a central avenue between overlooking docking towers, decks sprawling out from jutting bartizans, and the World Eaters and their captain were to take the lead. Two flanks branched out from the central avenue and these channels would be taken by the Blood Claws, led by Brynngar in spite of the Space Wolf's earlier altercation with Cestus, and a second group of World Eaters led by the only Ultramarine in the raiding party.

Antiges sat bolt upright in the flight couch of the gloom-drenched troop hold of an assault-boat as they made their way closer to the gaseous expanse that was Bakka Triumveron and the moon that would support their embarkation. He was the only Ultramarine aboard the assault-boat, accompanied, as he was, by two combat-squads of Skraal's remaining World Eaters. To Antiges's mind they were brutal warriors, festooned with the trophies of war, crude kill-markings like badges of honour carved into their armour. Each and every one was possessed of a murderous mien, a faint echo of their primarch's battle rage.

Dimly, as if the infinite expanse of black space that existed between them had smothered it, Antiges recalled his last conversation with his captain.

'STAND ASIDE, ANTIGES,' Cestus barked, bedecked in a stripped down version of his honour guard regalia and battle-ready with short-blade, power sword and bolter.

Adjusting to the half-light of the assembly deck, Cestus saw that his battle-brother was similarly attired.

'I have told you before, Antiges. The sons of Guilliman will remain aboard ship in case anything goes wrong. I shall accompany the mission as its leader to ensure that it goes to plan.'

Cestus had gone over the plan several times since it was first broached in the conference room to the rest of the Astartes captains. If they were to make the most of the *Furious Abyss*'s current disposition, they would need to act in subterfuge and in secret. Even with that caveat in mind, the strike would need to be brutal and at close-quarters. The World Eaters and the Space Wolves had no equals in that regard, save for the sons of Sanguinius, but the Angels were far off in another part of the galaxy. These were the tools at their disposal; they had but to unleash them.

The assault force was to infiltrate Bakka Triumveron 14, where the Word Bearers had made dock, in three teams in a classic feint and strike manoeuvre in order that they get close enough to scupper the ship at close-range. Incendiary charges: krak and melta bombs, were to be carried as standard. It was a faint hope, but it was hope none the less and all had embraced it. Even Brynngar, his demeanour sullen and belligerent, had acceded to the plan, doubtless eager to vent his wrath much like his brother captain, Skraal.

'With respect, brother-captain,' said Antiges levelly, purposefully standing his ground. 'You shall not.'

Cestus's face creased in consternation.

'I did not expect disobedience from you, Antiges.'

'It is not disobedience, sire. Rather, it is sense.' Antiges still did not move. His expression brooked no argument.

'Very well,' said Cestus, letting his battle-brother have this indulgence before he rebuked him for his insolence. 'Explain yourself.'

Antiges's face softened, a trace of pleading behind his eyes.

'Allow me to lead the strike,' he said. 'This mission is too dangerous and our plight too great to risk your life, my captain. Without you, there is no mission. Even now, we hold to our cause by a mere thread. Were you to be lost, then so too would be Macragge. You know this to be true.'

Antiges stepped forward, allowing the light to fall on his face and armour. The effect was not unlike a bodily halo. 'I entreat you, liege, let me do this service. I shall not fail you.'

At first, Cestus had thought to deny him, but he knew his brother Ultramarine was right. Cestus was acutely aware of the other combat squads mustering on the deck behind him, readying to take to the assault-boats.

'It would do me great honour to have you, Brother Antiges, as my representative,' he said and clapped Antiges on the shoulder.

'My lord,' the fellow Ultramarine intoned and bowed to his knee.

'No, Antiges,' said Cestus, grasping his battle-brother's shoulder to stop him mid-genuflect. 'We are equals and such deference is not necessary.'

Antiges rose and nodded instead.

'Courage and honour, my brother,' said Cestus.

'Courage and honour,' Antiges replied and turned to walk away towards the assault-boats.

THE WORDS WERE distant now, and Antiges crushed whatever sentiment they held as he intoned the oaths of battle.

The World Eaters were similarly engaged, their lips moving in entreaty to their weapons and armaments that they should not fail them, and rather that they be covered in glory and speak with righteous anger.

The warriors of the XII Legion were well-armed with chainaxes and storm shields. They bore side arms too, but Antiges suspected that they were rarely drawn. World Eaters fought up close, in face-to-face melee, where the force of a charge and the shock of their ferocity counted the most.

Antiges steeled himself and mouthed the name of Roboute Guilliman as the assault-boat screamed towards its destination.

THE DOCK-MASTER HAD demanded to know why prior notification had not been given for the arrival of such an enormous ship. His obstinate and imperious attitude had faltered and withered upon the arrival of the Astartes on his deck.

Once Ultis had gained entry to the observation balcony, he had had the dock master put his deck crews to work to receive the *Furious Abyss*. Violence, at this point, was unnecessary. To the menials and underlings of Bakka Triumveron 14, they were still Astartes and as such their word carried the authority of the Emperor. No man of the Imperium would dare brook that.

From the observation balcony overlooking the battleship dock, Ultis could see the automated coolant tanks picking their way through the docking clamps and other dockside detritus towards the towering shape of the *Furious Abyss*. The dock was a hive of activity, tracked-servitors and human indentured workers bustling back and forth on loaders, carrying massive fuel drums and swathes of heavy piping. The frenetic scene, fraught with activity, was as a mustering of ants before the towering hive that was the Word Bearers ship.

It was the first time Ultis had been able to truly appreciate the vessel's gigantic size. Like a city of crenellated towers, arching spires and fanged fortress-like decks, it dwarfed the puny dock, easily clearing the highest antennae and cranes. The book, resplendent upon the *Furious*'s prow easily eclipsed the observation building in which Ultis was standing.

'We are in control,' Ultis voxed privately through his helmet array, the dock master busied at his consoles with the massive ship's sudden arrival.

'Good,' said Zadkiel, back on the ship. 'Did you encounter any resistance?'

'They accept the authority of the Astartes like the dutiful and deluded lapdogs they are, my lord,' Ultis replied, looking around at the Scholar Coven.

These warriors had been assembled from the Word Bearers under Zadkiel's command who showed the greatest adherence to Lorgar's Word. They were all more recent recruits to the Legion, all from Colchis and all dedicated scholars of Lorgar's writings. They were motivated not by the glory of the Great Crusade, but by the ideology of the Word Bearers. Zadkiel greatly valued such followers since they could be counted on to support the Legion's latest endeavours, which would be sure to bring the Word Bearers into conflict with elements of the Imperium before long. Ultis looked over at the man he would soon kill, once preparations were fully underway, and reasoned that the conflicts were already beginning to come about.

The fact meant absolutely nothing to him. Ultis had no loyalty save to the Word. There was nothing in the galaxy in that moment, other than that which was written.

The novice smiled.

This day, his destiny would be etched in the Word for all time.

NINE

Infiltration/Ambush/Sons of Angron

THE ASSAULT-BOATS DOCKED quickly and without incident, the pilot having avoided radar and long-range scans to insert the Astartes squads outside the main thoroughfares of Bakka Triumveron 14.

Antiges, clad in the blue and gold of his Legion's honour guard, was first out of the assault-boat, speeding from the embarkation ramp. Chainsword held low at his hip and adopting a crouching stance, he moved stealthily across an open plaza of steel plates, flanked by towering cranes and disused craft in for non-urgent repairs. The few servitors meandering back and forth on tracks and slaved to an aerial rail system ignored the Astartes. Working through pre-assigned protocols as dictated by their command wafers, they were not even aware of their presence.

Close behind the Ultramarine, one of the World Eaters, Hargrath, gave the servitors a wary glance as he piled through the open channel with his battle-brothers.

'Pay them no heed,' Antiges hissed, looking back to check on his charges.

Hargrath nodded and continued on his way towards the massive crimson horizon ahead, visible across the entire length of the shipyard: the *Furious Abyss*, the largest vessel any of them had ever seen.

'Keep in cover,' said Antiges as the plaza gave way to a maze-like refuelling and maintenance bay full of passing loaders and stacks of drums. The Ultramarine was careful to keep his squad out of the view of the labouring indentured workers and other menials busying themselves at the dock. They clung to the shadows, using them like a second skin.

Once they had reached their destination, their targets would be the engines and ordnance ports. The Ultramarine checked a bandoleer of krak grenades at his hip. There was a cluster of melta bombs flanking it on the opposite side and as the *Furious Abyss* drew closer, he hoped it would be enough.

BRYNNGAR WAS FESTOONED with trophies and fetishes: wolf's teeth and claws, and a necklace of uncut gemstones, polished pebbles carved with runes. If he were to go to war at last against his brother Astartes then he would do so in his full regalia. Let them witness the majesty and savage power of the Sons of Russ in their most feral aspect before they were torn asunder for their treachery.

The Wolf Guard was focused on the battle ahead, crushing all thoughts of his altercation with Cestus to the back of his mind for now. There would be time for a reckoning later. It was only a pity that the Ultramarine had eschewed the mission in favour of overall command aboard the *Wrathful*. Brynngar wanted to think him cowardly, but he had fought alongside the son of Guilliman many times and knew this not to be the case. It was probably a display of the XIII Legion's much vaunted tactical acumen.

The Space Wolves' aspect of attack was a narrow cordon riddled with junked carriers used for spare parts. It was more like an open warehouse with machine carcasses piled high and banded tightly together to prevent them toppling when stacked. Servitors slaved to loaders hummed back and forth amongst the towers of rusted metal like bees harvesting a nest. If they cared about the Space Wolf captain and his Blood Claws, tooled up with broad-bladed axes and bolt pistols, and weaving crisscross fashion through their domain, they did not show it.

Brynngar knew that he would spill blood this day, and it would be the blood of his erstwhile brothers. This was no fight against mere heathen men, misguided in their beliefs, nor was it foul xenos breeds ever intent on corralling the human galaxy to their yoke. No, this was Astartes against Astartes. It was unprecedented. Thinking of the devastation the Word Bearers had already wrought, the Space Wolf took a better grip of Felltooth and vowed to make the traitors pay for their transgressions.

'THEY ARE MAKING their final approach towards the dock,' said Kaminska poring over the hololithic tactical display in front of her command throne. Having been preparing the other Ultramarines for potential combat and distributing them around the ship accordingly, Cestus had returned to the bridge and joined the admiral at the tactical display table.

Hazy runes moved over a top-down green-rimed blueprint of Bakka Triumveron 14, indicating the progress of the three attack waves heading for the immense swathe of bulky red that represented the *Furious Abyss*. The ship's magos, Agantese, had tapped into one of the satellite feeds of the orbital moon and was using it to re-route images to the *Wrathful*'s tactical network. It had a short delay, but was an otherwise excellent way to keep track of their forces on the ground. Even so, Cestus felt impotent, directing the action from the relative safety of real space where the cruiser lingered to stay out of radar and sensorium range.

'Antiges, report,' he barked into the ship's vox, synced with his fellow Ultramarine's boosted helmet array.

'Assault protocol alpha proceeding as planned, captain,' Antiges's voice said after a few seconds delay. The reply was fraught with static. Even with the boosted array rigged by the *Wrathful*'s engineers, the gulf of real space between them impinged greatly.

'We will be making our initial insertion onto the dock in T-minus three minutes.'

'Well enough, Brother Antiges. Keep me appraised. If you meet any resistance, you have your orders,' said Cestus.

'I shall prosecute my duties with all the fury of the Legion, my lord.'

The vox cut out.

Cestus sighed deeply. To think it had come to this. This was no foray into the jaws of alien overlords or the misguided worshippers of the arcane, not this time. It was brother versus brother. Cestus could barely bring himself to think on it. Fighting across the gulf of real space was one thing, but to be face-to-face with those who had betrayed the Emperor, those who had killed warriors they once called friend and comrade in cold blood, was indeed harrowing. It felt like an end of things, and the sense of it caught in the Ultramarine's throat.

'Admiral Kaminska,' said Cestus after the momentary silence, 'you have risked much in the pursuit of this mission. You have done, and continue to do, me great honour with your sterling service to our cause.'

Kaminska was clearly taken aback and failed to hide her shock from the Ultramarine completely.

'I thank you, lord Astartes,' she said, bowing slightly, 'but if I am honest, I would have chosen to undertake this duty, although perhaps of my own volition,' she added candidly.

Cestus's gaze was mildly questioning.

'I am the last of a dying breed,' she confessed, her shoulders sagging and not from physical fatigue. 'The Saturnine Fleet is to be decommissioned.'

'Is that so?'

'Yes, captain. It doesn't do to have such an anachronism on the rostrum of the new Imperium. All those gentlemen in their powdered wigs talking about good breeding, it hardly speaks of efficiency and impartiality. Our ships are to be refitted for a new Imperial Navy. I'm a part of the last generation. I suppose I should be glad that at least Vorlov didn't see it.

'You see, captain, this is really my last hurrah, the last great journey of the *Wrathful* as I know it.'

Cestus smiled mirthlessly. His eyes were cold orbs, tinged with a deep sense of burden and regret.

'It might be for us all, admiral.'

SKRAAL'S ASSAULT FORCE sped down the central channel of the dock, a loading bay for fuel and munitions tankers, with reckless abandon. The berserker fury was building within the World Eater captain and he knew his battle-brothers were experiencing the same rush. They were the sons of Angron and like their lord they were implanted with an echo of the neural technology that had unlocked the primarch's violent potential. At the cusp of battle, the Astartes warriors could tap into that font of boiling range and use it like an edged blade to cut their enemies down. After several bloody incidents, the Emperor had censured the further use of implants in the false belief that they made the World Eaters unstable killing machines.

Angron, in his wisdom, had eschewed the edict of the Emperor of Mankind and had continued in spite of it. They were killing machines, Skraal felt it in his burning blood and in the core of his marrow, but then what greater accolade was there for the eternal warriors of the Astartes?

Though the orders of the Ultramarine, Antiges, had forbidden it, Skraal encouraged his warriors to kill as they converged on the *Furious Abyss*. A spate of bloodletting would sharpen the senses for the battle to come. The only directive: leave none alive to tell or warn others of their approach. The World Eaters pursued this duty with brutal efficiency and a trail of menial corpses littered the ground between the assault-boat insertion point and their current position.

Such reckless slaying had not, however, gone unnoticed.

'MY LORD,' HISSED Ultis into the vox array of the observation platform.

Zadkiel's voice responded from the *Furious*.

'It seems we are not alone,' Ultis concluded.

The novice in command of the Scholar Coven consulted a holo-map of the entire dockyard. His gauntleted finger was pressed against a flashing diode near one of the many refuelling conduits.

'Where is that?' he demanded of the dock-master, still engrossed in the refit and refuel of the vast starship.

'Tanker Yard Epsilon IV, my lord,' said the dock-master, who looked closer when he saw the flashing red diode. 'An emergency alarm.' The dock-master moved to another part of the console and brought up a viewscreen. Warriors in blue and white power armour were visible in the grainy resolution surging through the tanker yard. Prone forms, dressed in worker fatigues, slumped in their wake surrounded by dark pools.

'By Terra,' said the dock-master, turning to face Ultis, 'they are Astartes.'

The novice faced the dock-master and shot the man through the face point-blank with his bolt pistol. After his head exploded in a shower of viscera and bone-riddled gore, his streaming carcass slid to the deck.

The rest of the dock crew on the observation platform had failed to react before the rest of the Scholar Coven had taken Ultis's lead and shot them, too.

'The Astartes have tracked us here and move in on the *Furious Abyss* as we speak,' said Ultis down the vox. 'I have eliminated all platform personnel to prevent any interference.'

'Very well, Brother Ultis. You have your orders,' said Zadkiel's voice through the array.

Ultis looked down through the building's windows to the expanse of the docking stage. Baelanos's assault squad was standing guard there.

'I shall show them what fates are written for them,' said Ultis, drawing his sword.

'Educate them,' replied Zadkiel.

THE BATTLESHIP DOCK looked like a tangled web of metal as Skraal and his warriors forged onward. Beyond that the massive *Furious Abyss* loomed like a slumbering predator in repose.

The stink of blood from the previous slaughter was heady through the World Eater captain's nose grille as he raced towards the end of the channel and the open dock beyond. The cordon tightened ahead and the Legionaries were forced together as they rifled through it. Just as Skraal was feeling confident that they had not been discovered, a group of Word Bearers in crimson ceramite emerged before them to block their path.

Bolter fire wreathed the opening, lighting up the half-dark of the channel with four-pronged muzzle flares. Kellock, the warrior next to Skraal, took a full burst in the chest that tore open his armour and left him oozing blood. Kellock crumpled and fell, both his primary and secondary hearts punctured.

The combat squads were pinned on either side by fuel drums, stacked against bulky warehouse structures. Fleeing menials and mindless servitors, alerted by the commotion, wandered into their path and were cut down with chainblades or battered by shields as the World Eaters sought to close with the foe and wrest the advantage back. One of the drums was struck by an errant bolter round and exploded in a bright bloom of yellow-white fury. A fiery plume spilled into the air, like ink in water, and a wrecked servitor was cast like a broken doll at the edge of its blossoming blast wave. Three World Eaters were shredded by the concussive force of the explosion and smashed aside into the metallic siding of a warehouse unit. The siding didn't yield to the sudden impact of massed flesh and ceramite, and the two warriors were crushed.

Skraal felt the heat of the explosion against his face even through his helmet as the warning sensors went crazy. He staggered, but kept his footing and yelled the order to charge.

ANTIGES WAS STALKING through the refuelling bay when he heard the explosion from across the dock and saw fire and smoke billowing into the air. They were close. The *Furious Abyss*, a dense dark wall, filled the Ultramarine's sights.

'Antiges, report,' Cestus's voice said through the helmet vox, the tactical display obviously registering the sudden influx of heat.

'An explosion in the central channel. I fear we are discovered, brother-captain.'

'Get over there, unite your forces and push on through to the *Furious*.'

'As you command, captain,' he replied and ordered his combat squads through a maze of piping that connected to the central channel where he knew Skraal and his insertion team were placed. As they moved, Antiges at the lead, a shadow fell across the Ultramarine, cast by the vast observation platform overlooking the dock above.

Out of instinct, he looked up and saw the line of crimson armoured warriors bearing down on them with bolter and plasma gun.

Death rained down in a hail of venting promethium and spent electrum. Antiges rolled out of its way into the shadow of the docking clamp. Hargrath was distracted and a fraction slower. He paid for his laxity when a bolt of searing plasma blasted a hole in his torso, cooking the World Eater in his armour. He fell with a resounding clang, the wound cauterised before he hit the ground. Several of his brothers heaved his body towards them, but to act as improvised cover, rather than out of any sense of reverence for their dead comrade.

Antiges replied with barking retorts of his bolt pistol, half-glimpsing the target above between bursts of chipped plascrete and metal as the docking clamp was chewed up around him.

The rest of the World Eaters followed his lead, stowing storm shields and drawing bolt pistols, their weapons adding to the return fire.

Menials, put to flight at the start of the attack, and spilling into the rapidly erupting war zone were ripped apart in the crossfire. The roar of gunfire and the shriek of shrapnel mangled together with their screams.

Antiges pressed up against the closest docking clamp and looked around it, gauging the terrain leading the rest of the way to the *Furious Abyss*. The docks formed a landscape of narrow fire lanes between clamps and fuel tanks. Above was the observation platform, strung on metal struts, and beyond that rings of steel holding fuelling gantries, defence turrets and bouquets of sensor spines.

Antiges slammed himself back against the steel of the docking clamp as bolter fire continued to pin them.

'Captain, we are ambushed!' he yelled into the vox, in an attempt to overcome the din. Despite his volume, the Ultramarine's tone was calm as he cycled through a number of potential battle protocols learned by rote during his training.

There was a moment's pause as the message went through and his captain assessed the options open to him.

'Relief is incoming,' came the clipped reply. 'Be ready.'

AFTER A SECOND bout of return fire, a chain of small explosions erupted across the observation platform, showering frag.

Beyond the destruction and across the dockyard, embarkation ports were opening in the side of the *Furious Abyss*.

Antiges was on his feet and bellowing orders before the resulting smoke had cleared.

'Don't give them time! Hit them! Hit them now!'

The Astartes broke cover and charged, leaving the dead in their wake.

Two hundred robed cohorts in the crimson of the Word Bearers emerged from the *Furious Abyss*, and charged right back.

'Open fire!' shouted Antiges. The Ultramarine felt the immediate pressure wave of discharged bolt pistols behind him as the World Eaters obeyed.

The effect was brutal. Lines of the crudely armoured Word Bearer lackeys fell beneath the onslaught. Bodies pitched into their comrades, jerked and spun as the munitions struck. Blood sprayed in directions too numerous to count and the corpses mounted like a bank of fleshy sandbags, tripping those following. There was only time for a single volley, and the disciplined Astartes holstered pistols before closing with the first of the *Furious's* cannon fodder.

A brutish cohort, scarred and tarnished like an engine ganger, came at Antiges with an axe blade. The Ultramarine met the ganger's roar with the screech of his chainsword, plunging it into the man's chest. The cohort fell, wrenching the weapon from Antiges's hand. The Astartes didn't pause and threw the wretch aside with such force that the corpse spun in the air before crashing into its debased brethren. The Ultramarine drew his short-blade, duelling shield already in hand and cut down a second assailant with a low, arcing sweep.

Rorgath, a World Eater sergeant, came alongside Antiges and forged into the melee with brutal abandon. Limbs fell like rain as he churned through his enemies, his face a grisly mask of wrath without his helmet.

Out of the corner of his eye, Antiges saw another of Rorgath's kin decapitate a cohort officer trying to ram home the charge and extol his warriors to greater fervour. Others disappeared in clouds of red mist and the dreadful din of chainaxes rending bone. Yet, despite the relentless carnage wreaked upon them, the lowly cohorts refused to break, and the killing ground became mired in blood.

'They're fanatics,' grumbled Rorgath, burying his blade in the face on an oncoming cohort.

'Drive them back,' snarled Antiges through gritted teeth, smashing an enemy with the blunt force of his duelling shield. About to redouble his efforts, the Ultramarine fell back, as two or three bodies flew at him. In the madness, he dropped his short-blade, but as he foraged for it in the sea of pressing bodies, he found the hilt of his chainsword. Tearing the weapon loose, Antiges cut a path through bone and flesh to free himself. Hands were grabbing at him to drag the Astartes down, and even as he tried to emerge, bullets rang off his armour. One of the World Eaters yelled in anger and pain. The *Furious Abyss* disappeared from view as more enemy crewmen threw themselves forward.

This was not how men fought. Very few xenos were content to simply die, even when there was something to be gained by it. That was why the Astartes were such lethal warriors; they were the ultimate weapon against any enemy tainted by natural cowardice, since a Space Marine could control and banish his own fear. The Word Bearers had created another kind of enemy, one that even Space Marines could not break.

'Damn you,' hissed Antiges as he threw another man off him, and was sprayed by a shower of blood as Rorgath disembowelled yet another. 'Now we have to kill them all.'

Driving on, pain burst against Antiges's side as a blade or a bullet found its way through his armour. He staggered and it gave the enemy the opening they needed. A sudden flurry of cohorts sprang on the stricken Astartes. Then the weight of the attacks was dragging him down, their death-cries and the smell of their sundered bodies filling his senses.

BRYNNGAR HEFTED HIS last belt of frag grenades at the observation platform. A cluster of explosions rippled over the pitted surface, hewing off chunks of ferrocrete and scorching metal. The assault had achieved its desired effect, forcing the ambushers above Antiges's position back for a few moments, who were unseen from the channel the Space Wolf and his Blood Claws charged down, and switching their attention.

Fire erupted again from the platform before the last of the grenades had even detonated, but this time their focus was upon the Wolf Guard and his squad. Brynngar's highly attuned animal senses picked up on the stink of cordite and blood, and the sporadic clatter of weapon's fire, and he assumed that his brother Ultramarine was otherwise occupied, hence their popularity.

Rujveld slid into cover beside his venerable leader as he appraised the disposition of the ambushers strafing them. Fire streaked down from the observation gallery and prevented them joining the fight beyond.

'They knew we were coming,' Brynngar growled to the stony-faced Blood Claw.

'What are your orders, Wolf Guard?'

Brynngar turned his feral gaze onto his pack brother.

'We bring them down,' he grinned, displaying his fangs. 'Yorl, Borund,' bellowed the Space Wolf captain, and two of his charges abandoned their ready positions to approach their leader.

'Melta bombs,' snarled Brynngar. 'One of those struts.' He pointed to the source of the platform's elevation.

Yorl and Borund nodded as one, priming their melta charges before heading across a gauntlet of open ground that led to the structure. Withering fire struck the first Blood Claw before he ventured more than a few feet, the impacts kicking him off his feet and spinning him around before he fell in a bloody heap.

Borund had greater fortune, a feral war cry on his lips as he reached the base of the platform. Clamping the charge onto one of the struts, he took a hit in the shoulder. Another struck him across the torso as Word Bearers positioned neared the building's base realised what he was doing. Borund pressed the detonator before they could stop him. He roared in savage defiance as the melta bomb exploded, vaporising him in a flare of super-heated chemicals.

The platform held.

Brynngar was about to head into the gauntlet to finish the job when a second explosion erupted after the first. The Space Wolf captain turned away from the sudden blast, an actinic stench prickling his nostrils when he looked back. The sound of wrenching metal followed and the observation platform finally collapsed, kicking up clouds of dust and ferrocrete. The structure was robust and Astartes could withstand worse. There would be survivors.

Unconcerned where the secondary blast had come from, Brynngar got to his feet and howled in triumph. Running across the open to the ruined mass of crumpled metal and broken ferrocrete, he swung his rune axe in preparation for battle, knowing that his Blood Claws were right behind him.

ABOARD THE WRATHFUL, Cestus wore a pained expression as he reviewed the tactical display. Frantic vox chatter was coming in over the ship's array, but it was indistinct and impossible to discern.

The three icons, representing the relative positions of his assault teams had stalled. A silver icon, indicating the Space Wolves and Brynngar's warriors, was moving slowly towards an area obscured by a sudden belt of smoke and bright light, hazing the readout. Judging from the schematic, this was the observation platform.

Cestus assumed that the attack had been successful.

Elsewhere in a flanking channel close by, an azure icon represented Antiges and was shown embroiled in a brutal close-quarters fight against massed enemies. The dark slab of crimson that was the *Furious Abyss* was not far beyond the melee, but it didn't appear as if the

Ultramarine was making progress. All Cestus's subsequent attempts to raise Antiges on the vox had thus far failed. A third icon, depicted in stark white, converged on Antiges's position.

To Cestus's dismay, they were not alone.

TEN

Into the belly of the beast/Sacrifice/My future is written

THE SCREAM OF chainaxes brought Antiges to his senses. The whine of their spinning teeth turned to a crunching drone as they bit into flesh and bone.

Antiges saw white armour trimmed with blue, sprayed liberally with crimson and the Legion markings of a captain.

Skraal dragged the Ultramarine out of the mess of bodies. The *Furious*'s crewmen were being bludgeoned to the ground or thrown through the air, the World Eaters squad painting every surface with crescents of gore. Antiges took a moment to set himself, such was the impact of the second charge from Skraal's World Eaters.

The captain of the XII Legion was butchering a man on the floor.

Such reckless murderous enthusiasm was alien to the Ultramarines and Antiges fought the urge to put a stop to it. The battlefield was no place for recrimination.

Instead, the Ultramarine looked across the dock, a brief lull in the fighting provided by the sudden appearance of Skraal's forces allowing him to take stock. A clutter of crimson-armoured corpses lay at the end of the central channel, victims of the World Eaters' ferocity. He also saw Brynngar leading his Blood Claws, tangled up in a short-range firestorm with a squad of Word Bearers emerging from the ruin of the collapsed observation platform. The fighting was fierce and it didn't look like the sons of Russ would be able to bolster them.

Skraal heaved a dying man off the floor and cut him in two at the waist with a slash of his chainaxe. It got Antiges's attention.

'Captain,' cried the Ultramarine, seeing a break in the cohort's ranks for the first time, 'drive on to the ship, now!'

Skraal looked back at him. For a split second there was nothing in the World Eater's face but hatred, nothing to suggest that he saw Antiges as anything but another enemy.

The moment passed and the eyes that looked at the Ultramarine belonged to Skraal again. The World Eater picked up his shield from the ground, discarded in his lust for carnage, shook his head to get the worst of the blood out of his eyes, and called to his squad to follow.

'Form up on me, and keep moving!' shouted Antiges, pointing towards the *Furious Abyss* with his chainsword.

A WORD BEARER stumbled out of the wreckage of the platform, strafing wildly with his bolter. Brynngar stepped out of the kill-zone and beheaded the Astartes with a sweep of Felltooth. A second followed and the Space Wolf leapt forward, burying the blade in the Legionary's cranium. A third was dragged from the collapsed building, half-dazed, by Rujveld who executed him with a burst from his bolt pistol.

After the initial slaughter, though, the Word Bearers managed to put up more of a fight. Wreathed in super-heated plasma, Elfyarl fell screaming and Vorik was dismembered by a fusillade of bolter fire.

Brynngar snarled at the losses, whipping another Word Bearer off his feet at the edge of the ruins before lunging down to tear out his throat with his teeth. Howling in fury, the Wolf Guard was about to press on when whickering bolter fire churned up the ferrocrete debris around him. Reeling against the sudden assault, the venerable wolf could only watch as a line of blood stitched up Svornfeld's cuirass. He spun and fell in a lifeless heap.

A second squad of Word Bearers advanced on them, unseen from the original route of attack.

Brynngar unhitched his bolter in the face of this new threat and blew the faceplate off one Word Bearer's helmet and smashed a chunk from the shoulder pad of another as they came on.

'Into them!' he raged, weapon blazing as he charged the enemy.

The howling reply of his remaining Blood Claws was a feral chorus to the brutal bolter din.

ANTIGES THRUST HIS chainsword through the Word Bearer's chest.

As they'd closed on the *Furious Abyss*, the cohorts a bloody mess in their wake, another line of defenders had emerged: fellow Astartes, their erstwhile brothers the Word Bearers. Decked in crimson armour replete with debased scratchings and ragged scrolls of parchment, they were a dark shadow of the proud warriors Antiges remembered.

The Word Bearer jerked as he tried to wrench himself free of the churning blade that impaled him, but then it passed through his spine and all he could do was vomit a plume of blood.

Suddenly, it was real.

These Word Bearers, Astartes and brothers to all Space Marines, were the enemy. Antiges realised in that moment that he hadn't really believed it before. There was no time to consider it further as a second Word Bearer came at him with a power maul. Antiges caught the weapon just before it cleaved through his face, and rammed his knee into the Astartes's stomach, but his enemy stayed locked with him. Behind the lenses of the Word Bearer's helmet the Ultramarine could just see an eye narrowed in anger. There was no brotherhood there.

In a sudden fury of churning steel and wrath, Skraal tore the Word Bearer off Antiges and ripped him apart with his chainaxe. Finishing the grisly work quickly, the World Eater glanced back at his battle-brother.

'Too intense for you, Ultramarine?'

A WORD BEARER's elbow caught Brynngar in the side of the head and the Space Wolf fell back. Rolling out of a second attack, he switched to his bolter and, one-handed, unloaded the magazine into his assailant's stomach. The Word Bearer had life in him yet, though, and Rujveld stalked forward, drawing a knife from a scabbard at his waist. He jammed the point through the gap in the wounded traitor's gorget.

Brynngar grunted thanks to the Blood Claw and moved on into the Word Bearer squad that had set upon them. Combined with the survivors from the platform's destruction, the Space Wolves were hard-pressed. The Wolf Guard was determined to lead by example, however, and scythed through crimson ceramite, the bloody Felltooth clutched in his grasp.

Cutting down an enemy Astartes with a swift diagonal slice across the neck and chest, Brynngar kicked the Word Bearer aside to face a new opponent. Suddenly, the tempo of the battle changed. The fury and ferocity exploding around him dulled and slowed as he stood eye-to-eye with a fellow captain. This was clearly their leader, clearly a veteran if the ruin and subsequent reconstruction of his face was any measure. A two-handed power sword swung freely in his fists, which he wielded like a mace. A trio of Blood Claws lay at the warrior's feet. They had died on that sword, their bodies split in two and spilling organs over the floor of the dock.

'Now face me,' snarled the Wolf Guard and hefted Felltooth in a feral challenge.

The Word Bearer captain drove at the Space Wolf using his body like a battering ram, the blade as its tip. The charge was fast, so fast that Brynngar didn't get out of the way in time and took a glancing blow against his pauldron. White fire surged into his shoulder, but the Wolf Guard mastered the pain quickly and turned with the attack, using its momentum and raking Felltooth down his opponent's back.

The Word Bearer roared and spun on his heel, driving the two-handed blade at him like a spear at first to pitch the Space Wolf off balance and then as a club to bludgeon him to death. A wild swipe slapped the flat edge of the weapon against Brynngar's outstretched arm. His bolter fell from nerveless fingers as the blow struck a muscle cluster, numbed even through his power armour.

Brynngar smashed the brutal sword aside as it came for another slash, and used his forward momentum to get inside his attacker's reach. Pressing a rune on Felltooth's hilt, a long spike slid from the tip of the axe. Brynngar roared in savage exultation as he plunged it deep into one of the Word Bearer's biceps and twisted. The Word Bearer's arm was torn open revealing wet muscle and gore. No pain registered on his face as he leapt towards Brynngar in an attempt to throw him off-balance and bring his sword to bear again.

Using his opponent's momentum, Brynngar lifted the Word Bearer off his feet and smashed him to the ground. He yanked the dazed enemy captain up again, gripping his gorget, and seized his head by the chin. Emitting a terrible roar that flung blood and spittle into his enemy's face, Brynngar rammed the spike of Felltooth through his throat.

The Word Bearer's good eye bulged out as it fought the wracking pain of his imminent death. He coughed up blood, and it sheeted down the front of his armour, covering it with a new wet shade of crimson.

Brynngar spat in his face and let the Word Bearer fall.

Bolter shells blistered the ground around him as yet more Word Bearers converged on them. Brynngar and what was left of his Blood Claws returned fire and sought cover even as they fell back. The attack was short-lived, the Astartes merely dragging away the body of their fallen captain before retreating too.

Indiscriminate and sporadic gunfire kept the Space Wolves at bay as the remaining Word Bearers fell back. Crouching behind the ruin of a disused fuel tanker Brynngar snatched a glance across the battlefield. Skraal and Antiges were advancing towards the *Furious Abyss* with a small combat squad of World Eaters, scattering crewmen from the battleship as they went.

Brynngar envied them. Even before the plasma drives of the Word Bearers' mighty battleship started to power up, he knew that the enemy was leaving. The pinning fire from their retreating assailants was gradually diminishing, and all across the dockyard, enemy Astartes were heading back to embarkation ports in the hull of the vast vessel.

Like the orca, I would've gutted that beast inside out, he thought with dark regret and cried out his lament. Blood flecked from his beard and hair as he threw back his head and the long, hollow note tore from his throat. Taking up the call, his Blood Claws arched their necks back as one and joined the chorus howl.

GUNFIRE SPATTERED DOWN at the Astartes, ricocheting off metal and kicking out sparks.

Together with the Ultramarine, Antiges, and three of his battle-brothers, the World Eater captain had gained the *Furious Abyss*, entering into the belly of the ship through one of the embarkation ports and heading down. Their progress had been arrested inevitably when the onboard patrols had caught up with them at the intersection of a coolant pipe. The fire was coming from one end of the corridor, distant, shadowy figures tramping urgently down the wide, curved diameter of the pipe. Metal instrumentation provided some cover, but the Astartes were as good as dead if they didn't move on quickly.

Skraal took part of the fusillade on his storm shield, casings striking the grating at his feet like brass rain: bolter fire.

Shadows danced against the muzzle flashes. Huge armoured bodies, helmets and shoulder pads: Astartes. Word Bearers.

One of Skraal's warriors, Orlak, cut through a hatch in the ceiling with his chainaxe. The slab of metal clanged down and he hauled himself up swiftly. Rorgath stood point as the Legionaries made their way further inwards. Having lost both his weapons in the brutal melee outside the ship, he slammed the bolter he had scavenged into rapid fire and hosed the conduit, punching ragged holes into the metal. The other World Eaters lent the fire of their bolt pistols, keeping their enemies at bay.

Half the World Eaters were through the hatch before the Word Bearers returned fire. Only Skraal and Antiges remained, the Ultramarine taking over from Rorgath as he unclipped a brace of frag grenades from his belt and rolled them down the conduit. Skraal leapt up the hatch as return bolter fire blazed past him. Antiges followed, the World Eater captain hauling the Ultramarine up as the first of the explosions ripped down the conduit, shredding plating and buying time.

'MOUNTAINS OF MACRAGGE,' breathed Antiges.

The engine room of the *Furious Abyss* was like a cathedral to machinery. It was vast. The criss-crossing ribs of a vaulted ceiling reached through the gloom. The immense hulks of the cylindrical exhaust chambers were decorated with steel ribbing and iron scrollwork, and inscribed with High Gothic text running along their whole length. Multiple levels were delineated by gantries and lattice-like overhead walkways. Word Bearers' banners hung from the web of iron above them, bearing the symbols of the Legion's Chapters: a quill with a drop of blood at its nib, an open hand with an eye in the palm, a burning book, and a sceptre crowned with a skull. The metallic throb of the engines was like the ship's own monstrous heartbeat.

The conduit in the labyrinthine ship had led the Astartes to this place and though the sounds of pursuit were distant and hollow, the enemy would not be far behind.

'Find something to destroy,' said Skraal. 'Get to the reactors if you can.'

Antiges tried to take in the vastness of the engine room. Even with the munitions they had at their disposal and the fact that they were Astartes, they would still have a hard time doing anything that could cripple the *Furious Abyss*.

'No,' said Antiges, 'we drive onwards. Look for ordnance or cogitators. We can't sabotage this vessel attacking blindly.'

Skraal looked back at his squad. The last of them was being dragged up through the hatch. The coolant pipe they had entered through was one of many forming a tangle of pipes and junctions around the exhaust chambers. Between the pipes was darkness and there was no telling how far down it went.

'We might not find our–'

'We're not getting back out,' snapped Antiges.

Skraal nodded. 'Forwards, then.'

Antiges led the Astartes up onto the nearest walkway, above the exhaust chambers. The immense shapes of generatoria loomed towards the ship's stern, connected to the even larger plasma reactors somewhere below. Ahead of them, the walkway wound into a dark steel valley between enormous pounding pistons. Shapes were gathering on a walkway above them, hidden by the solid metal of a control deck. It seemed that the engineering menials had been ordered out of the chamber, which meant that the Word Bearers planned to stop them here.

'Cover!' shouted Skraal, but there was little to be had when the bolter fire from the Word Bearers hammered down at them. Rorgath returned fire with his scavenged bolter, but there was little the others could do with pistols and close combat weapons. One of Skraal's battle-brothers was hit square in the chest and knocked over a guardrail. He fell onto the engine block below and was pounded flat by a piston hammering down on him. Orlak's arm disappeared in a spray of blood and he fell to the walkway. Antiges hoisted him bodily to his feet and dragged him along as more gunfire streaked from above.

'Break for it!' Skraal bellowed, seeing a lull in the fusillade hammering them. Then he was on his feet and running for the cover at the far end of the engine block, where the walkway led up into a great wall of galleries and machinery. Even hurried by Antiges, Orlak lingered behind and was speared through the back by storm bolter rounds. Smoke poured from the backpack of his armour, mixed with a spray of blood.

Orlak: Skraal had led him through a dozen battlefields. He was a brother, as they all were.

The World Eater captain took that grief and locked it away beneath his consciousness, where it mixed with the pool of rage that he would call on again when the time was right.

Skraal reached cover. The *Furious Abyss* closed around him. He was in an equipment room, the walls covered in racks of hydraulic drills, wrenches and hammers. Human deck-crews fled in wild panic as the World Eaters burst in, followed by Antiges. There were just three left. It was hardly the raiding force they needed to bring the vast ship to heel.

Skraal noticed something inscribed on the ceiling of the chamber.

BATTLE FOR THE ABYSS

BUILD THE WORD OF LORGAR FROM THIS STEEL
LIVE AS IT IS WRITTEN

'Move! Move! They're heading down after us!' bellowed Antiges, demanding his attention.

'We need to hold them up. No way we can dodge bolter fire and wreck the ship at the same time,' said Skraal, slamming the portal shut behind them and using a stolen wrench to wedge it.

'Three squads at least,' Antiges replied, his breathing heavy, but measured. 'No way we can beat them.'

'I'll slow them,' said Rorgath, planting his feet and checking the clip in his bolter.

Antiges regarded the World Eater. The white and blue of his armour was already scored by bullet wounds and scorched by plasma burns.

'Your sacrifice will be remembered,' said Antiges, reverently.

No such sentiment was evident from the World Eater's captain, who tossed Rorgath his bolt pistol.

'Give them no quarter,' he snarled, turning abruptly to lead what was left of the raiding party through the tangle of anterooms and corridors. The shouts of pursuers relaying their position followed them like hollow, ghost whispers, and the thud of armoured feet on the floor was dull and resonant in their wake.

Together, Antiges and Skraal moved swiftly across the hinterlands of the engine room and through a doorway in the bulkhead. Not long before they had left the chamber, the fierce bark of bolter fire erupted behind them.

It didn't last long and deathly silence reigned for a moment before their relentless pursuers could be heard once more. Mangled with a cacophony of voices emitted from the ship's vox array, it became obvious that a widespread search had begun. The *Furious*'s warriors were converging on the Astartes. They were getting closer every second.

Passing through an empty storage chamber, Skraal kicked open a door to reveal another corridor. The atmosphere was close and hot, the walls lined with burning torches. The sight was incongruous amongst the decks and trappings of a spaceship, but it also led downwards and prow-wards, in the direction where the Astartes guessed the primary ordnance deck would be.

'What did they build in here?' hissed Antiges, giving voice to his thoughts as they moved down the corridor. The Ultramarine got his answer as he emerged from the far end of the tunnel.

A vast plaza stretched out in front of them. Walls lined with baroque statues of deep red steel rose up into a domed ceiling. The vault at the apex of the massive chamber was hazy with incense and supported by dramatic false columns. Prayers were inscribed on the flagstone floor. An altar and pulpit stood at the far end of a central aisle. There was only one word to describe it: a cathedral. In the supposed age of enlightenment, when all superstition and religion was to be expunged from the galaxy to be replaced by science and understanding, all that the Emperor had decreed was dishonoured by the chamber's very existence.

Antiges found that it left a bitter taste in his mouth and was ready to tear down the effigies and rend this temple of false idolatry to the ground with his bare hands, when a voice echoed out of the surrounding gloom.

'There is no escape.'

The Ultramarine saw Skraal throw himself against a pillar. Antiges swiftly adopted a crouching position, bolt pistol outstretched in a two-handed grip, scanning the darkness. He could just make out the crimson armour at the far end of the cathedral. The speaker, his tone eerily calm and cultured, was sheltering behind the altar. The Word Bearer was not alone.

Booted feet clacking against the stone floor behind the Astartes confirmed the threat. Antiges and the World Eater were covered from both sides of the chamber.

'I am Sergeant-Commander Reskiel of the Word Bearers,' said the speaker, identifying himself. 'Throw down your arms and surrender at once,' he warned, all the culture evaporating.

'After you fired on us and slew our brothers!' Skraal raged.

'This need not end in further bloodshed,' Reskiel added.

Antiges felt the enemy converging on them, heard the faint scrape of ceramite against stone as they closed.

'What is this place, Word Bearer?' asked the Ultramarine, panning his sights first across the pulpit and then further out until he had swept the gloom around them. 'Such religiosity is not condoned by the Emperor. You openly defy his will. Have you reverted to primitive debasement and superstition?' he asked, trying to goad them, trying to find time to devise a plan, expose a weakness. 'Is all Colchis like this now?'

'There is nothing primitive about the vision of our primarch or his home world,' said Reskiel levelly, clearly wise to the Ultramarine's stratagem. Stepping out from behind the altar, the sergeant-commander allowed the diffuse torchlight to bath him in its glow.

He was young, but highly decorated judging by the honour studs and medals on his crimson armour. The trappings of heroism and glory warred with strips of parchment and leaves of tattered vellum scripted in wretched verse.

A squad of Word Bearers emerged into the cathedral behind him, their bolters trained on the shadows where Antiges and Skraal were in cover.

'Show yourselves, and let us speak brother to brother,' said Reskiel, allowing his guardians to move in front of him.

'You are no brother of mine!' shouted Skraal.

'Get ready,' Antiges hissed to his ally as Reskiel raised a hand. The Ultramarine knew, with an ingrained warrior instinct, that he was about to give the order to open fire. He trained his bolt pistol on a cluster of Word Bearers at the front of the advancing guards.

Skraal roared, surging out of cover and throwing his chainaxe. He thumbed the activation stud as it left his hand and the weapon shrieked through the air. With a scream of ceramite on metal, the axe bypassed the guards and sliced clean through Reskiel's wrist, embedding itself in the altar. Shield upraised, a war cry on his lips, the World Eater charged.

Antiges cursed the son of Angron's impetuous battle lust and triggered the bolt pistol, running forward as the muzzle flare gave away his position. Bolt rounds hammered into the approaching Word Bearers and three of the warriors collapsed in a heap against the fury.

Bedlam filled the cathedral. Skraal covered the distance between him and his enemy so fast that none of the opening bolter shots hit him.

Antiges followed, acutely aware that he had foes behind as well as in front. An errant shot clipped his pauldron, another chipped his knee guard and he staggered briefly but kept on into the maelstrom, the name of Guilliman in his furious heart.

'This is sacred ground!' wailed Reskiel, clutching the stump of his arm as blood spurted freely from it. Skraal battered the Word Bearers in his path aside and when he reached the sergeant-commander, backhanded him across the face with his shield by way of a reply, and wrenched his chainaxe from the altar. He spun and slammed the head of the axe into the head of a red-armoured warrior charging behind him. The Word Bearer was thrown off his feet and skidded along the floor on his back, his face a red ruin of bone and shattered ceramite.

The ambushers from behind the two Astartes fell into the fray.

Skraal fought as if possessed by the spirit of Angron, slaying left and right as a terrible bloody rage overtook him. He embraced the cauldron of fury within and used it to kill, to ignore pain. Word Bearers fell horribly before his onslaught, so fierce that those surrounding the assault gave ground and retreated to the cathedral door. The one who called himself Reskiel was dragged out by one of his battle-brothers, the blood clotting on the stump of his wrist as he screamed his choler.

Bolter fire was hammering away towards the rear of the cathedral. Antiges could hear it echoing loudly inside his helmet as Skraal turned from the carnage he was wreaking to look at him.

A line of pain sketched its way down the Ultramarine's back and he realised he'd been hit. This time the shot pierced his armour. Something warm welled in his chest and Antiges looked down to see a wet ragged hole. As his mind suddenly made the connection to what his body already knew, he slumped against a pillar, spitting blood. Lungs heaving, he tried to force his augmented body back into action and cranked another magazine into his bolt pistol. One hand clamped over the wound, the other triggering the bolter, Antiges resolved to go down fighting. In the distance, vision fogging, a shadow fell.

White spikes of pain were flashing before his eyes as he turned to look back at Skraal amidst the bloodbath at the altar.

'Go,' gasped Antiges.

The World Eater paused for a second, about to run back in and rescue the Ultramarine. A thrown grenade exploded near the pillar and Antiges's world ended in a billow of smoke and shrapnel.

SKRAAL DIDN'T WAIT to see if the Ultramarine had survived. One way or another, Antiges was lost. Instead, he ran from the cathedral, storm shield warding off the worst of the bolter fire hammering across the cathedral towards him.

As he fled into the endless darkness, the shifting of the vessel's hull echoing as if venting its displeasure, a thought forced its way into his mind in spite of the battle rage.

He was alone.

ZADKIEL WATCHED THE battle unfolding through the docking picters mounted along the hull of the *Furious Abyss.*

Baelanos had fallen, yet his inert body had been recovered and lay in the laboratorium of Magos Gureod.

He would serve the Word, yet.

Baelanos's dedication to the Word was that of a soldier to his commander, and he had never appreciated the more intellectual implications of Lorgar's beliefs. Nevertheless, he was a loyal and useful asset. Zadkiel would not throw him away cheaply.

Ultis was doubtless buried beneath the rubble of Bakka Triumveron 14. In that, Baelanos had served Zadkiel too. It was another thorn removed from his side, the potential usurper despatched.

Yes, for that deed you will receive eternal service to the Legion.

'We're breached.' Sergeant-Commander Reskiel's voice came through on the vox, down where the engines met the main body of the battleship.

'How many?'

'Only one remains, my lord,' Reskiel replied. 'They made it in through the coolant venting ports, open for the re-supplying.'

'Hunt him down with my blessing, sergeant-commander,' Zadkiel ordered, 'but be aware that you will be making your pursuit under take-off conditions.'

Another thorn, thought Zadkiel.

'Sire, there are still warriors of the Legion fighting on the dock,' countered Reskiel at the news of their imminent departure.

'We cannot tarry. Every moment we stay to fight is another moment for the *Wrathful* to reach strike range or for our stowaway to damage something that cannot be replaced, not to mention the fact that the dockyard's defences might be brought to bear. Sacrifice, Reskiel, is a lesson worth learning. Now, find the interloper and end this annoyance.'

'At your command, admiral. I'm heading into the coolant systems now.'

Zadkiel cut the vox and observed the viewscreens above his command throne. A tactical map showed the *Furious Abyss* and the complex structure of the orbital docks around it. Crimson icons represented the Word Bearer forces still fighting and dying for their cause.

Zadkiel reached back for the vox and gave the order to take off.

ULTIS WATCHED FROM the rubble of the collapsed observation platform as the *Furious Abyss* begin to rise.

The engines of the battleship threw burning winds across the dockyards. Docking clamps and supply hangars melted to slag. Gantries burned and fuel tankers exploded, blossoms of blue-white thrown up amidst the firestorm. Fiery gales whipped around the open metal plaza, cooking cohorts and Astartes alike in the burgeoning conflagration surging across Bakka Triumveron 14. Scalding winds singed his face, even shielded by the wrecked chunks of ferrocrete. He saw the crimson paint on his armour blistering in the backwash of intense heat.

The maelstrom engulfed the bodies fighting outside it and they became as shadows and ash before it, as if frozen in time, eternally at war.

This was not the future he had envisaged for himself as he watched the *Furious Abyss* rise higher from the deck with a blast from its ventral thrusters.

He had been betrayed: not by the Word, but by another on board ship.

A shadow eclipsed the stricken Word Bearer, prone in the rubble.

'Your friends desert you, traitor whelp,' said a voice from above, old and gnarled.

Ultis craned his neck around to see, vision hazing in and out of focus, dimly aware of the blood that he had lost.

A massive Astartes in the armour of Leman Russ's Legion reared over him like a slab of unyielding steel. Bedecked in trophies, pelts and tooth fetishes, he was every inch the savage that Ultis believed the Space Wolves to be.

'I serve the Word,' he said defiantly through blood-caked lips.

The Space Wolf shook the blood out of his straggly hair and grinned to display his fangs.

'The Word be damned,' he snarled.

The Space Wolf's gauntleted fist was the last thing Ultis saw before all sense fled and his world went black.

ELEVEN

Survivors/Aftermath/I will break him

Buoyed upon hot currents of air vented by the *Furious Abyss*, what was left of the assault boats carrying the Astartes strike force made their escape from Bakka Triumveron 14 and back to the *Wrathful* held in orbit around the moon.

Cestus was waiting for the atmospheric craft in the tertiary docking bay when a single vessel touched down. Its outer hull shielding was badly scorched and its engines were all but burned out as it *thunked* to an unwieldy stop on the metal deck.

One assault boat, thought the Ultramarine captain, waiting with Saphrax and Laeradis, the apothecary ready with his narthecium injector. How many casualties did we sustain?

Engineering deck-hands hurried back and forth, hosing down the superheated aspects of the boat with coolant foam, and brandishing tools to affect immediate repairs. One of the officers stood at a distance with a data-slate, already compiling an initial damage report.

Cestus was oblivious to them all, his gaze fixed on the embarkation ramp as it ground open slowly with a hiss of venting pressure. Brynngar and his Blood Claws stepped out of the compartment.

The Ultramarine greeted him cordially enough.

'Well met, son of Russ.'

Brynngar grunted a response, his demeanour still hostile, and turned to one of his charges.

'Rujveld, bring him out.'

One of the Blood Claws, a youth with bright orange hair worked into a mohawk and a short beard festooned with wolf fetishes, nodded and went back into the crew compartment. When he returned, he was not alone. A pale-faced warrior was with him, his hands and forearms encased by restraints linked by an adamantium cord, his face fraught with cuts, and a massive purple-black bruise over one eye the size of Brynngar's fist. Bent-backed and obviously weak, he had a defiant air about him still. He wore the armour of the XV Legion: the armour of the Word Bearers.

'We have ourselves a prisoner,' Brynngar snarled, stalking past the trio of Ultramarines without explanation, his Blood Claws with their prize in tow.

'Find me an isolation cell,' Cestus overheard the Wolf Guard say to one of his battle-brothers. 'I intend to find out what he knows.'

Cestus kept his eyes forward for a moment, striving to master his anger.

'My lord?' ventured Saphrax, the banner bearer clearly noticing his captain's distemper.

'Son of Russ,' Cestus said levelly, knowing he would be heard.

The sound of the departing Space Wolves echoing down the deck was the only reply.

'Son of Russ,' he bellowed this time and turned, his expression set as if in stone.

Brynngar had almost reached the deck portal when he stopped.

'I would have your report, brother,' said Cestus, calmly, 'and I would have it now.'

The Wolf Guard turned slowly, his massive bulk forcing the Blood Claws close by to step aside. Anger and belligerence were etched on his face as plain as the Legion symbols on his armour.

'The assault failed,' he growled. 'The *Furious Abyss* is still intact. There, you have my report.'

Cestus fought to keep his voice steady and devoid of emotion.

'What of Antiges and Skraal?'

Brynngar was breathing hard, his anger boiling, but at the mention of the two captains, particularly Antiges, his expression softened for a moment.

'We were the only survivors,' he replied quietly and continued on through the deck portal to the passageways beyond that would lead eventually to the isolation chambers.

Cestus stood for a moment, allowing it to sink in. Antiges had been his battle-brother for almost twenty years. They had fought together on countless occasions. They had brought the light of the Emperor to countless worlds in the darkest reaches of the known galaxy.

'What are your orders, my captain?' asked Saphrax, ever the pragmatist.

Cestus crushed his grief quickly. It would serve no purpose here.

'Get Admiral Kaminska. Tell her we are to continue pursuit of the *Furious Abyss* at once, with all speed.'

'At your command, my lord.' Saphrax snapped a strong salute and left the dock, heading for the bridge.

Cestus's plan had failed, catastrophically. More than sixty per cent casualties were unacceptable. It left only the Ultramarines honour guard, still stationed aboard ship by way of contingency, and Brynngar's Blood Claws. The Space Wolf's continued defiance was developing into open hostility. Something was building. Even without the animal instincts of the sons of Russ, Cestus could feel it. He wondered how long it would be before the inevitable storm broke.

Here they were, at war with their fellow Legions. Guilliman only knew how deep the treachery went, how many more Legions had turned against the Emperor. If anything, the loyal Legions needed desperately to draw together, not to fight internecine conflicts between themselves in the name of petty disagreements. When the final reckoning came, where would Brynngar and his Legion sit? Guilliman and his Ultramarines were dogmatic in their fealty to the Emperor; could the same be said of Russ?

Cestus left such dark thoughts behind for now, knowing it would not aid him or their mission to dwell on them. Instead, his mind turned briefly to Antiges. In all likelihood, he was dead. His brother, his closest friend slain in what had been a fool's cause. Cestus cursed himself for allowing Antiges to take his place. Saphrax was an able adjutant, his dedication to the teachings of Guilliman was unshakeable, but he was not the confidant that Antiges had been.

Cestus clenched his fist.

This deed will not go unavenged.

'Laeradis, with me,' said the Ultramarine captain, marching off in the direction that Brynngar had taken.

The Apothecary fell into lockstep behind him.

'Where are we going, captain?'

'I want to know what happened on Bakka Triumveron and I want to find out what our Word Bearer knows about his Legion's ship and their mission to Macragge.'

BY THE TIME Cestus and Laeradis reached the isolation cells, Brynngar was already inside, the door sealed with Rujveld standing guard.

The isolation cells were located in the lower decks, where the heat and sweat of the engines could be heard and felt palpably. Toiling ratings below sang gritty naval chants to aid them in their work and the resonant din carried through the metal. It was a muffled chorus down the gloom-drenched passages that Cestus and Laeradis had travelled to reach this point.

'Step aside, Blood Claw,' ordered Cestus without pre-amble.

At first it looked as if Rujveld would disobey the Ultramarine, but Cestus was a captain, albeit from a different Legion, and that position commanded respect. The Blood Claw lowered his gaze, indicating his obedience, and gave ground.

Cestus thumbed the door release icon as he stood before the cell portal. The bare metal panel slid aside, two thins jets of vapour escaping as it did so.

A darkened chamber beckoned, barely illuminated in the half-light of lume-globes set to low-emit. A bulky shape stood within, with two shrivelled, robed forms to either side. Brynngar had stripped out of his armour, aided by two attendant Legion serfs. The menials kept their heads low and their tongues still. The Wolf Guard was naked from the waist up, wearing only simple grey battle fatigues. His torso was covered in old wounds, scars and faded pinkish welts creating a patchwork history of pain and battle.

Standing without his armour, his immense musculature obvious and intimidating, and with the great mass of his hair hanging down, Brynngar reminded the Ultramarine of a barbarian of ancient Terra, the kind that he had seen rendered in frescos in some of the great antiquitariums.

The Wolf Guard turned at the interruption, the shadow of another figure strapped down in a metal restraint frame partly visible for a moment before the Space Wolf's bulk took up the space again.

'What do you want, Cestus? I'm sure you can see that I'm busy.' Brynngar's knuckles were hard and white as he clenched his fists.

As he had stormed from the tertiary dock after the Space Wolf and his battle-brothers, Cestus had thought to intervene, the idea of torturing a fellow Legion brother abhorrent to him. Now, standing at the threshold of the isolation chamber, he realised just how desperate their plight had become and that victory might call for compromise.

Just how far this compromise would go and where it would eventually lead, Cestus did not care to think. It was what it was. They were on this course now and the Word Bearers were enemies like any other. They had not hesitated when they destroyed the *Waning Moon*, nor had they paused to consider their actions during the slaughter on Bakka Triumveron 14.

'I would speak to you again, Brynngar,' the Ultramarine captain said, 'once this is over. I would know the details of what happened on Bakka.'

'Aye, lad.' The Space Wolf nodded, a glimmer of their old rapport returning briefly to his features.

Cestus glimpsed the prone form of their prisoner as Brynngar turned back to his 'work'.

'Do only what is necessary,' the Ultramarine warned, 'and do it quickly. I am leaving Laeradis here to… assist you if he can.'

The Apothecary shifted uncomfortably beside Cestus, whether at the thought of partaking in torture or the prospect of being left alone with Brynngar, the Ultramarines captain did not know.

Brynngar looked over his shoulder just as Cestus was leaving.

'I will break him,' he said with a predatory gleam in his eye.

'WE HID BEHIND Bakka Triumveron to keep the *Furious Abyss* from sending torpedoes after us. We're heading on course for a warp jump vector as we speak.'

Kaminska was, as ever, on station at her command throne on the bridge. Saphrax was there, also, straight backed and dour as ever. Cestus had headed there alone after leaving Laeradis with Brynngar in the isolation chamber. In the scant reports he'd received from the admiral regarding information gleaned from the assault boat pilot, Cestus had learned a little more of what had happened at Bakka. They'd lost the other two assault boats during the extraction, swallowed up by the fire of the *Furious*'s engines that had turned much of Bakka Triumveron 14 into a smoking wasteland of charred and twisted metal. The tactical readouts aboard ship had disclosed precious little, save that it was chaotic and not to plan. One of Guilliman's edicts of wisdom was that any plan, however meticulously devised, seldom survives contact with the enemy. The primarch spoke, of course, of the need for flexibility and adaptation when at war. Cestus thought he should have heeded those words more closely. It appeared, also, that the Word Bearers had been forewarned of the Astartes' attack, a fact that he resolved to discover the root of. He considered briefly the possibility of a traitor in their ranks aboard the *Wrathful*, but dismissed the thought quickly, partly because to countenance such a thing would breed only suspicion and paranoia, and also because to do so would implicate the Astartes captains or Kaminska.

'What of our prisoner, Captain Cestus?' asked Kaminska, after consulting the battery of viewscreens in front of her, satisfied that all necessary preparations were underway for pursuit.

'He is resting uncomfortably with Brynngar,' the Ultramarine replied, his gaze locked on the prow-facing viewport.

'You believe he knows something about the ship that we can use to our advantage?'

Cestus's response was taciturn as he thought grimly of the road ahead and of their options dwindling like parchment before a flame.

'Let us hope so.'

Kaminska allowed a moment's pause, before she spoke again.

'I am sorry about Antiges. I know he was your friend.'

Cestus turned to face her.

'He was my brother.'

Kaminska's vox-bead chirped, interrupting the sentiment of the moment.

'We have reached the jump point, captain' she said. 'If we hit the warp now, Orcadus has a chance of finding the *Furious Abyss* again.'

'Engage the warp drives,' said Cestus.

Kaminska gave the order and after a few minutes the *Wrathful* shuddered as the integrity fields leapt up around it, ready for its re-entry into the warp.

ZADKIEL PRAYED TO the bodies in front of him.

The Word Bearer was situated in one of the many chapels within the lower decks of the *Furious Abyss*. It was a modest, relatively unadorned chamber with a simple shrine etched with the scriptures of Lorgar and lit by votive candles set in baroque-looking candelabras. The room, besides being the ship's morgue, also offered solace and the opportunity to consider the divinity of the primarch's Word, of his teachings and the power of faith and the warp.

Prayer was a complicated matter. On the crude, fleshly level it was just a stream of words spoken by a man. It was little wonder that Imperial conquerors, without an understanding of what faith truly was, saw the prayers of primitive people and discarded them as dangerous superstition and a barrier to genuine enlightenment. They saw the holy books and sacred places, and ascribed them not to faith or a higher understanding but to stupidity, blindness, and an adherence to divisive, irrelevant traditions. They taught an Imperial Truth in the place of those simple religions and wiped out any evidence that faith had once been a reality to those worlds. Sometimes that erasure was done with flames and bullets. More often it was done with iterators, brilliant diplomats and philosophers, who could re-educate whole populations.

Zadkiel's belief, the root of his vainglorious conviction, was that the Throne of Terra would be toppled, not by the strength of arms wielded by the Warmaster, nor even by the denizens of the warp, but by faith. Simple and indissoluble, the purity of it would burn through the Imperium like a holy spear, setting the non-believers and their effigies of science and empirical delusion alight.

Zadkiel shifted slightly in his kneeling position, abruptly aware that another presence was in the chapel-morgue with him.

'Speak,' he uttered calmly, eyes closed.

'My lord it is I, Reskiel,' the sergeant-commander announced.

Zadkiel could hear the creak of his armour as he bowed, in spite of the fact that he could not see him.

'I would know the fate of Captain Baelanos, sire,' Reskiel continued after a moment's pause. 'Was he recovered?'

Doubtless, the ambitious cur sought to supplant the stricken assault-captain in Zadkiel's command hierarchy, or manoeuvre for greater power and influence in the fleet. This did not trouble the Word Bearer admiral. Reskiel was easy to manipulate. His ambition far outweighed his ability, a fact that was easy to exploit and control. Unlike Ultis, whose youthful idealism and fearlessness threatened him, Zadkiel was sanguine about Reskiel's prospects for advancement.

'Though mortally injured, the good captain was indeed recovered,' Zadkiel told him. 'His body has gone into its fugue state in order to heal.' Zadkiel turned at that remark, looking the sergeant-commander in the eye. 'Baelanos will be incapacitated for some time, captain. This only strengthens your position in my command.'

'My lord, I don't mean to imply–'

'No, of course not Reskiel,' Zadkiel interjected with a mirthless smile, 'but you have suffered for our cause and such sacrifice will not go unrewarded. You will assume Baelanos's duties.'

Reskiel nodded. The World Eater had shattered the bones down one side of his skull and his face had been reinforced with a metal web bolted to his cheek and jaw.

'We have lost many brothers this day,' he said, indicating the Astartes corpses laid out before his lord.

'They are not lost,' said Zadkiel. Each of the slain Word Bearers was set upon a mortuary slab, ready for their armour to be removed and their gene-seed recovered. One of them lay with his eyes staring blankly at the ceiling. Zadkiel closed them reverently. 'Only if the Word had no place for them would they be lost.'

'What of Ultis?'

Zadkiel surveyed the array of the dead. 'He fell at Bakka,' he lied, 'and the Scholar Coven with him.'

Reskiel clenched his teeth in anger. 'Damn them.'

'We will not damn anyone, Reskiel,' said Zadkiel sharply, 'nor even will Lorgar. The Emperor's gun-dogs will damn themselves.'

'We should turn about and blast them out of real space.'

'You, sergeant-commander, are in no place to say what this ship should and should not do. In the presence of these loyal brothers, do not debase yourself by forgetting your purpose.' Zadkiel did not have to raise his voice to convey his displeasure.

'Please forgive me, admiral. I have... I have lost brothers.'

'We have all lost something. It was written that we would lose much before we are victorious. We should not expect anything else. We will not engage the *Wrathful* in a fight because to do so would use up time that we no longer have to spare, and our mission depends on its timing. Kor Phaeron will not be late, so neither will we. Besides, we have other options when dealing with the *Wrathful*.'

'You mean Wsoric?'

Zadkiel clenched his fist in a moment of unsuppressed emotion. 'It is not appropriate for his name to be spoken here. Make the cathedral ready to receive him.'

'Of course,' said Reskiel. 'And the surviving Astartes?'

'Hunt him down and kill him,' said Zadkiel.

Reskiel saluted and walked out of the chapel-mortuary.

Certain that the sergeant-commander was gone, Zadkiel gestured to the shadows from which a clandestine guest emerged.

Magos Gureod shuffled into the light of the votive candles slowly, mechadendrites clicking like insectoid claws.

'You have received Baelanos?' the admiral asked.

The magos nodded.

'All is prepared, my lord.'

'Then begin his rebirth at once.'

Gureod bowed and left the chamber.

Now truly alone, Zadkiel looked back at the bodies lying arranged in front of him. In another chamber, together with the many crew of the *Furious* who had died, were the enemy Astartes, slain in the engine room and the cathedral. They would not receive benediction. They would have refused such an honour even if it could be given, because they did not understand what prayer and faith meant. They would never be given their place in the Word. They had forsaken it.

Those Astartes, the declared enemies of Lorgar, were the ones who were truly lost.

AN HOUR AFTER the *Wrathful* had entered the warp, Cestus went to the isolation chambers. Upon his arrival, he found Rujveld still dutifully in his position. This time, though, the Blood Claw stepped aside without being ordered and offered no resistance, it being ostensibly clear that the Ultramarine would brook none.

The gloom of the isolation, cum interrogation, chamber was as Cestus remembered it, although now, the air was redolent of copper and sweat.

'What progress have you made?' the Ultramarine captain asked of Laeradis, who stood at the edge of the room. The apothecary's face was ashen as he faced his brother-captain and saluted.

'None,' he hissed.

'Nothing?' asked Cestus, nonplussed. 'He hasn't yielded any information whatsoever?'

'No, my lord.'

'Brynngar–'

'Your Apothecary has the strength of it,' grumbled the Space Wolf, his back to Cestus, body heaving up and down with the obvious effort of his interrogations. When he turned, Brynngar's face was haggard and his beard and much of his torso were flecked with blood. His meaty fists were angry and raw.

'Is he alive?' Cestus asked, concern creeping into his voice, not at the fate of their prisoner but at the prospect that they might have lost their one and only piece of leverage.

'He lives,' Brynngar answered, 'but, by the oceans of Fenris, he is tight-lipped. He has not even spoken his name.'

Cestus felt his spirit falter for a moment. Time was running out. How many more warp jumps until they reached Macragge? How many more opportunities would they get to stop the Word Bearers? It was irrational to even comprehend that one ship, even one such as the *Furious Abyss*, could possibly threaten Macragge and the Legion. Surely, even the mere presence of the orbital fleet above the Ultramarines' home world would be enough to stop it, let alone Guilliman and the Legion mustering at nearby Calth. Something else was happening, however, events that, as of yet, Cestus had no knowledge of. The *Furious Abyss* was a piece of a larger plan, he could sense it, and one that posed a very real danger. They needed to break this Word Bearer, and quickly, find out what he knew and a way to stop the ship and its inexorable course.

Brynngar was possibly the most physically intimidating Astartes he had ever known, aside from the glory and majesty of the noble primarch. If he, with all his bulk and feral savagery, could not break the traitor then who could?

'There is but one avenue left open to us,' said Cestus, the answer suddenly clear, even though it was an answer muddied with the utmost compromise.

Brynngar held Cestus's gaze, his eyes narrowed as he fought to discern the Ultramarine's meaning.

'Speak then,' he said.

'We release Mhotep,' Cestus answered simply.

Brynngar roared his dissent.

MHOTEP SAT IN quiet contemplation in the quarters made ready for him aboard the *Wrathful*. As ordered, he had not left the relatively spartan chamber since his incarceration after he had vanquished the *Fireblade*. He sat, naked of his armour, in robes afforded to him by attendant Legion serfs, long since departed, in deep meditation. His gaze was fixed upon the reflective surface of the room's single viewport, poring into the unfathomable depths of psychic space and communion.

When the door to his cell slid open, Mhotep was not surprised. He had followed the strands of fate, witnessed and understood the web of possibility that brought him to this point, this meeting.

'Captain Cestus,' muttered the Thousand Son with an air of prescience from beneath a cowl of vermillion.

'Mhotep,' Cestus replied, taken a little aback by the Thousand Son's demeanour. The Ultramarine wasn't alone; he had brought Excelinor, Amryx and Laeradis with him.

'The assault at Bakka Triumveron failed, didn't it?' said the Thousand Son.

'The enemy obviously had prior warning of our intentions. It is part of the reason I came here to meet with you.'

'You believe that I can provide an answer to this conundrum?'

'Yes, I do,' Cestus replied.

'It is simple,' said Mhotep. 'The Word Bearers have made a pact with the denizens of the warp. They forewarned them of your attack.'

'There is sentience in the empyrean?' the Ultramarine asked in disbelief. 'How is it we do not know this? Are the primarchs privy to this? Is the Emperor?'

'That I do not know. All I can tell you is that the warp is beyond the comprehension of you or I, and things exist in its fathomless depths that are older than time as we know it.'

Mhotep paused for a moment as if in sudden contemplation.

'Do you see them, son of Guilliman?' he asked, still locked in his meditative posture. 'Quite beautiful.'

Cestus followed the Thousand Son's gaze to the viewport and saw nothing but the haze of the integrity fields and the bizarre and undulating landscape of the warp.

'Don't make me regret what I am about to do, Mhotep,' he warned, glad of his battle-brothers' presence behind him. The Ultramarine captain had already dismissed the armsmen guarding the door, an order they responded to with no shortage of relief. It was a moot gesture, really; Mhotep could have left at any time, irrespective of their presence. The fact that he had not somewhat mitigated what Cestus was about to say.

That was, before Mhotep pre-empted him.

'I am to be released.' It wasn't a question.

'Yes,' said Cestus, carefully. 'We have a prisoner aboard and precious little time to find out what he knows.'

'I take it conventional methods have already failed?'

'Yes.'

'Small wonder,' said Mhotep. 'Of all the children of the Emperor, the seventeenth Legion are the most fervent and impassioned. Mere torture would not prevail against such ardent fanaticism and zealotry.'

'We require a different tack, one which I do not relish undertaking, but which I am compelled to employ.'

Mhotep stood, setting back his hood and turning to face Cestus.

'Ultramarine, there is no need to convey your reluctance to me. I am sure the account of this day, if such records ever come to pass given our current predicament, will state that you acted under the most profound duress,' he said smoothly, the trace of a smile appearing on his lips before it was lost in the mask of indifference.

'I do not know what powers you possess, brother,' said Cestus. 'I had thought to make you stand trial and answer that question for me. It seems, however, that events have overtaken us.'

'Indeed,' answered Mhotep. 'I am as moved by my duty as you are, Ultramarine. If I am freed then I will fight as hard as any and pledge my strength to the cause.'

Cestus nodded. His stern expression gave away the warring emotions within him, the abhorrence of flouting the Emperor's decree matched against the needs of the situation.

'Gather your armour,' he ordered. 'Brothers Excelinor and Amryx will accompany you to the isolation cell.' Cestus about turned and was walking away with Laeradis when Mhotep spoke again.

'What of the son of Russ? What does he make of my emancipation?'

The bellowing and violent protests of Brynngar were still ringing in the Ultramarine's ears.

'Let me worry about that.'

CESTUS AND LAERADIS were waiting when Mhotep, with Excelinor and Amryx in tow, reached them at the isolation cell. Brynngar and Rujveld had already stormed off in the wake of the Space Wolf captain's explosive discontent.

Cestus nodded to his battle-brothers as they approached. The two Ultramarines reciprocated the gesture and fell in beside their captain.

'The prisoner is within,' the Ultramarine captain told Mhotep, who had reached the door and stood before it calmly. 'Will you require Laeradis's assistance?' he added.

'You can have your chirurgeon go back to his quarters,' replied the Thousand Son, his gaze fixed upon the sealed portal as if he could see through it.

Cestus nodded to his Apothecary, indicating that his duty was done.

If Laeradis thought anything of the slight that Mhotep had delivered, he did not show it. Instead, he snapped a sharp salute to his captain and left for his quarters as directed.

Mhotep thumbed the activation icon and the portal slid open, showing the darkened cell.

'Once it begins,' he said, 'do not enter.' Mhotep turned to face the Ultramarine. 'No matter what you hear or see, do not enter,' he warned, and all trace of superiority vanished from his face.

'We will be outside,' Cestus replied, Excelinor and Amryx grim-faced behind their captain, 'and watching everything you do, Thousand Son.' The Ultramarine captain indicated a viewport that allowed observation into the isolation cell. 'I see anything I don't like and you'll be dead before you can utter another word.'

'Of course,' said Mhotep, unperturbed as he entered the chamber, the door sliding shut in his wake.

MHOTEP STEPPED CAREFULLY into the gloom, surveying his immediate surroundings as he went. Dark splashes littered the floor and walls; even the ceiling was not devoid of the evidence of torture. A suit of armour had been thrown into one corner, together with the body-glove that went beneath it. This was not considered disrobing by a coterie of acolytes. No, this was frenzied: an attempt to get to the soft meat of the flesh and exact pain and profound suffering. Mhotep's expression hardened at such barbarism. Implements, crude and brutish to the Thousand Son's eyes, lay discarded on a silver tray, also speckled in blood. Some of the devices even bore traces of meat, doubtless rent from the unfortunate subject when his tongue failed to loosen under the fists of the Space Wolf. The chirurgeon's methods, then, had been equally ineffective.

'You are quite tenacious,' Mhotep said. There was a trace of menace in his calm inflection as he approached the metal cruciform frame to which the prisoner was affixed. The Thousand Son ignored the rapacious bruising, the cuts, gouges and tears that afflicted the subject's battered body. Instead, he focused on the eyes. They were still defiant, albeit slightly groggy from the beatings the prisoner had been given.

'What compromise you force us to endure,' he whispered to himself, drawing close so that their faces almost touched. 'Tell me, what secrets do you possess?'

The response came stuttering through blood-caked lips.

'I... serve... only... the... Word.'

Mhotep reached for the scarab earring and removed it. He manipulated the small object with his thumb and forefinger, and placed it upon his forehead, where it stayed affixed in the shape of a gold eye, the symbol of Magnus.

'Do not think,' he warned, placing his fingers against the prisoner's skull and pressing hard, 'that you can hide from me.'

When Mhotep's fingers penetrated the flesh, the screaming began.

TWELVE

Sirens/Screams and silence/Here be monsters

CESTUS'S TEETH CLENCHED at the horrific noises emanating from within the isolation chamber. Excelinor and Amryx followed their captain's example, stoically bearing the sounds of psychic torture, secretly glad that they were not the subject of Mhotep's attentions.

Through the viewport, the isolation cell was shrouded in shadow. Cestus could see Mhotep from the back only. The Thousand Son moved almost imperceptibly as he stood before the prisoner who, by contrast, spasmed intermittently as his mind was ransacked.

On several occasions, when the screaming was at its height, Cestus had wanted to go in and end it, abhorred at the mental damage being inflicted on what was once a brother Astartes, but he had stopped himself every time, even warning off Excelinor and Amryx from taking action. Instead, the two battle-brothers had turned away from the viewport, leaving

Cestus alone to observe the imagined horrors of the Word Bearer's torture.

Twice already, he had angrily ordered worried arms-men away, after they had come to investigate the sound, fearing another warp attack as they patrolled the decks.

As the shipboard vox crackled, issuing a warning, obliquely, they were right.

'Captain Cestus, come to the bridge at once. We are under attack!'

LOATHE AS HE was to leave Mhotep, albeit with Excelinor and Amryx, Cestus had little choice but to do as bidden. He reached the bridge quickly and Saphrax quickly apprised him of the situation.

The alert had come when several unknown projectiles had been expelled from the vicinity of the *Furious Abyss*, and were snaking across the warp towards the *Wrathful*. At first it was believed that the missiles were in fact tor-pedoes launched in a punitive attempt to dissuade pursuit. That assumption was crushed in the moment when Admiral Kaminska's helmsmistress, Venkmyer, had identified their erratic trajectory and the truth had been revealed.

'Sirens,' Kaminska breathed, looking up at the tactical display before her that showed the inexorable advance of the creatures. A dark atmosphere seemed to pervade the bridge, and the admiral looked uncomfortable because of it. Her uniform was in slight disarray – she had clearly been roused from quarters when the alert had come in – and only added to her apparent sense of unease. 'I had thought such things were void-born myths.'

'They are the denizens of the empyrean,' Cestus told her, the disquieting mood affecting him less acutely.

Something was awry. The Ultramarine captain put it down to the sudden appearance of the warp beasts. 'Can we avoid them, admiral?'

Kaminska's face was grave as she considered the path of the warp creatures on the tactical display in front of her command throne.

'Admiral,' Cestus said sternly, snapping Kaminska free of the dark mood that had suddenly ensnared her.

'Yes, captain?' she gasped, face pale and unsteady in her command throne.

'Can Orcadus find a way around these creatures?'

Kaminska shook her head. 'We are on a collision course.'

Cestus turned to Saphrax.

'Ready the honour guard and have them gather on the assembly deck at once; Amryx and Excelinor, too.' He didn't want to leave Mhotep alone, but the warp creatures threatened the safety of the ship and he would need all of his battle-brothers to defend it. On balance, it was a risk worth taking.

'Captain,' said Kaminska as the Ultramarine was leaving.

Cestus turned and looked at her, noticing that Helmsmistress Venkmyer had moved to her aid. Kaminska warned off her second-in-command with a glance.

'What is it, admiral?' Cestus asked.

'If these creatures are indeed native to the warp, how are we to stop them?'

'I don't know,' answered the Astartes and then left the bridge.

QUITE WHAT THE warp looked like was a question that could never be answered. The human mind was not designed to comprehend it, which was why only specialised mutants like Orcadus could look upon it, and even then with a third eye that did not truly perceive it, merely filtering out the parts that would otherwise drive him mad.

Certainly, there was something ophidian or shark-like about the creatures that closed in on the *Wrathful*. In truth, they neither intercepted nor followed it, but stalked it from all directions at once, creeping up from the past and gliding in from the future to converge on the point of fragile space-time that held the *Wrathful* in its bubble.

They had eyes, lots of eyes. Their bodies were writhing strings of non-matter, which could take on any shape, because they had no true form to begin with, but there were always eyes. They had wings, too, which were also claws and fangs, and masses of pendulous blubber to keep them warm against the nuclear cold of the warp's storms. They burned and shimmered with acid, and shed daggers of ice from their scales. They had been born in the abyss, and had never been forced by the tyranny of reality into one form. To stay the same from one moment to the next would have been as alien to them as the warp was to a human mind.

Lamprey mouths opened up. The predators made themselves coterminous with the *Wrathful*, forcing themselves into unfamiliar frames of logic to avoid annihilation by the protective energy fields that surrounded the ship.

The minds inside were brimming with the potential for madness, delicious insanity to be suckled upon. The predators fed normally on scraps: moments of emotion or agony, powerful enough to bloom in the warp and be consumed. Here there were lifetimes worth of sensation to be drained, enough for any one of the wraiths to become bloated and terrible, a whale drifting through the abyss big enough to feed upon its own kind.

Thousands of bright lights flickered in the ship, each one both a potential feast, and a gateway for the non-physical predators.

One of them found an unprotected mind and, easing itself painfully into the rules of reality, forced its way in.

The screams were the first signs that anything was wrong on the lance deck.

The lances, immense laser cannon hooked up to the plasma reactors in the ship's stern, had been silent since the duel with the *Furious Abyss* outside the Solar System. The gun gangs still tended to them, because lasers were temperamental, especially when they had to funnel the titanic levels of power that could surge through a laser lance, and the gun gangs were constantly busy hammering out imperfections in focusing lenses and cleaning the laser conduits, which could misfire if any blemish refracted too much power in the wrong direction.

One ganger fell from his perch high up on the inner hull, where he had been aligning one of the huge mirrors. He hit the ground with a wet crump that told the gang chief that he was most certainly dead. It was a sound he had heard many times before.

The gang chief was in no hurry to see what had become of the fallen ganger. Deaths meant hassle. The gang would be one short, so someone would have to be drafted from somewhere else on the ship and the *Wrathful* had lost plenty of men already, and they were in the abyss.

For a man to die in the abyss was bad luck. Some said if you died in the warp you never got out, and even with the suppression of religions in the fleet you couldn't stop a void-born superstition like that.

The dead man, however, was not dead. When the gang chief reached the body he saw it mewling like a drowning animal, writhing around on its back with its wrists and ankles shaking as if it was trying to right itself.

The gang chief expressed displeasure that the man was still alive, since he would undoubtedly die soon and carting him off to the sick bay was another inconvenience the gun crews didn't need.

The dying man's body distended with the cracking of ribs. One side of his body split off from the other, organs separating as his pelvis split. His sternum snapped free and false ribs pinged against the laser housing beside him. His body rippled up from the floor into a writhing, pulsing arch of flesh and bone, drizzling blood onto the gunmetal deck. The crewman's head lolled to one side, its jaw wrenched at an angle, its eyes still open.

The space within the arch twisted and went dark. The predator forced its way through, spilling out onto the floor like the contents of a split belly, feeling blindly, eyes blinking as they evolved to absorb light.

Then the screaming started.

IT WAS CARNAGE in the lance decks, absolute carnage.

The warning icons had blazed through the ship, coupled with frantic vox chatter about monsters and the dead coming back to life, before it cut off ominously. Reconnoitring with his battle-brothers on the assembly deck, Cestus had led the honour guard, fully armed, to the lance decks and there they stood to bear witness to the horror.

The Ultramarine captain wondered, for a moment, whether he had been wrong all along, whether the Imperial Truth itself was wrong, and that the hells of those primitive faiths really did exist to be given form in the lance decks. He dismissed his doubts as heretical, crushing them beneath his iron-hard resolve and his loyalty to Roboute Guilliman. Even still, what he saw warred with what he desperately tried to believe. Bodies were painted across the walls in ragged smears of skin and muscle. The faces of the gang ratings were ripped open in expressions of horror, and stared out from heaps of torn limbs. Flesh and viscera were draped across high girders ahead, or over the massive workings of the lances themselves. The focusing mirrors and lenses were sprayed with blood. The living writhed in a single mass, smearing themselves with gore and sinking their teeth into one another.

Spectral threads of glowing black wrapped around the spines of the bleeding revellers. The threads led up to the ceiling of the lance deck where a titanic mass of darkness squatted, a seething thing of eyes and mouths gibbering and chuckling as it manipulated the lance deck's crew into further depths of suffering.

Cestus was an Astartes. He had seen extraordinary, horrible things: amorphous aliens that consumed their own to be ready for battle; insect-things that broke up into swarms of seething, biting horrors; whole worlds infected or dying, whole stars boiling away in the death throes of a species, but he had never seen anything like this.

'Weapons free,' he raged.

A brutal chorus of bolter fire rang out to his order, puncturing the mass of flesh and exploding it from within. Thestor swung his heavy bolter around and added his own punishing shots to the salvo.

Terrible screeching filled the tight space and resonated in his battle helm, auditory-limiters struggling to modulate the horrible keening of the damned ratings.

The dangling threads held by the warp creature began to sever one by one as the munitions of the Astartes struck and detonated with fury. It snarled its displeasure, revealing row upon row of fine needle-like fangs and a slathering spectral tongue that appeared to taste their essence. Like a lightning strike, the tongue lashed out and speared Thestor through his cuirass. He bellowed in pain, heavy bolter fire flaring as he triggered the weapon in his death throes. The honour guard scattered as the errant shells strafed the deck, and Thestor shook and went into spasm as he was lifted into the air, impaled on the warp spawn's tongue.

'Burn it!' cried Cestus in desperation. 'Burn it all!'

Morar stepped forward with his flamer and doused the tunnel in roaring, white-hot promethium. Thestor and the creature's transfixing tongue were immolated in cleansing fire. The warp spawn reeled, shrieking in anger as it recoiled from the attack. Morar swept the cone of intense heat downward, cooking the conjoined mass of the dead ratings.

As the warp spawn gave ground, Cestus noticed patches of ichorous fluid spattering the deck in its wake.

If it can bleed, he thought, we can kill it.

'Advance on me,' cried the Ultramarine captain. 'Courage and honour!'

'Courage and honour!' his battle-brothers bellowed in reply.

BROODING IN THE temporary barrack room afforded to the Space Wolves onboard the *Wrathful*, Brynngar had heard the alert screaming through the ship and had mustered his warriors.

Tracking the commotion to the lower lance decks, he and his Blood Claws were unprepared for the sight that greeted them as they descended into the gloom. It was a charnel house. Flayed flesh lined the walls and blood slicked the floor. Bones, still red with gore, lay discarded in mangled piles. Screams were etched upon the visages of skulls, locked in their last moments of agony.

The bloody massacre was not, however, what gave the Space Wolf captain pause. It was the nightmare creature, tearing at chunks of flesh with its teeth. At their approach, the beast, a luminous, shark-like horror, turned, its lipless maw smeared with blood, its swollen belly engorged.

'Here be monsters,' Brynngar breathed and felt a quail of something unfamiliar, an alien emotion, trickle down his spine.

He found his courage quickly, baring his fangs as he howled.

The Space Wolves launched at the creature, blades drawn.

MHOTEP STAGGERED FROM the isolation chamber, not surprised to see that he was alone. He had broken the traitor, though it had not been easy. He felt the sweat of his exertions beneath his helmet and was breathing heavily as he stepped into the adjoining corridor. Of the subject known as Ultis, for he had given his name before the end, there was precious little left. A drooling cage of flesh and bone were all that remained. His conditioned defences, ingrained by years of fanatical indoctrination, had been tough to break, but as a result, when they had fallen, they had fallen hard. Only a shell remained, a gibbering wreck incapable of further defiance, incapable of anything.

Exhausted as he was, Mhotep groaned when he detected the rogue presence onboard the ship. Mustering what reserves of strength he had left, he made for the lance decks.

MORAR WAS DEAD. His bifurcated body lay in two halves across the deck. Amyrx was badly wounded, but alive. He slumped against an upright, beneath a metal arch, a chunk of flesh ripped from his torso.

A dark mass was boiling down the corridor behind Cestus, even as the honour guard faced off against the first warp predator, torrents of semi-liquid flesh bursting through doorways in a flood. Eyes formed in the mass, focusing on the Astartes.

The Ultramarine swivelled his body around, barking a warning before his bolter blazed, the muzzle flare lighting up the dark around him. A long tongue of dark muscle thrashed blindly past him from the creature's gaping mouth, and Cestus threw himself out of its path. Laeradis, desperately ministering to the wounded Amyrx, was not so lucky. The membrane lashed around him, sending spines of pain throughout his body. The Apothecary screamed as the flesh suddenly dried and split open, fist-sized seeds spilling from the fibrous interior.

The seeds burst into life, tiny buzzing wings shearing through the shells and long sharp mandibles splintering out. Laeradis was eviscerated in the storm in a bloody haze of bone, flesh and armour.

Cestus cried out and swung his bolt pistol back around. He picked off the insectoid creatures with precise shots as they buzzed towards him, letting out his breath to steady his aim. He caught the last with his free hand. Cestus mashed it into the wall before it could chew through the ceramite of his gauntlet.

With the two warp creatures on either side, the Ultramarines were being crushed into a tight circle.

Even as he continued to pummel the second warp fiend with bolt pistol fire, he heard Saphrax bellow the name of Roboute Guilliman, punctuated by the retort of his weapon. The burning flare of expelled plasma lit the side of his face, and the Ultramarine captain knew that their other special weapon bearer, Pytaron, was still with them. Muzzle flashes blazing, Lexinal and Excelinor continued to fire their bolters, war cries on their lips.

The chorus of battle raged as the warp predators closed, weaving and twisting impossibly from the worst of the Ultramarines' fusillade, shrieking and screeching whenever they were struck and forced back.

Cestus checked the ammo-reader on his bolt pistol. His remaining rounds wouldn't last long. Divided as they were, he and his battle-brothers would be unable to destroy either creature like this. With little recourse left, he made his decision.

'All guns with me!' he cried. 'In the name of Guilliman, concentrate fire.'

With no hesitation, the Ultramarines turned their combined fire onto one of the warp creatures. Not expecting the sudden storm, the beast was caught unawares. Desperately trying to weave and jink out of harm's way, it was struck by a barrage of bolter rounds. Super-heated plasma scorched its flank and a precise salvo from Cestus struck it in the eye. A keening wail emanated from the dread creature as it shuddered out of existence, expelled from the bubble of real space within the *Wrathful*. However, the victory proved costly, as the second creature surged, unhindered, to the Ultramarines' position, suddenly buoyed by the presence of three more of its kin.

Cestus and his battle-brothers turned as one, defiant war cries on their lips as they prepared to sell their lives dearly.

The rending of flesh as their bodies were torn asunder, the stench of blood and the sound of shredding bone failed to materialise.

Poised with jaws outstretched, ready to devour the Astartes, the warp creatures were assailed by a blazing crimson light that bathed the corridor in an incandescent lustre. The beasts recoiled and shrank before him, snapping ineffectually at the air as the building aura seared them.

'Warp spawned filth!' spat a voice behind Cestus, echoing with power. 'Flee back into the abyss and leave this plane of existence.'

Shielding his eyes against the brilliance of the light, Cestus saw Mhotep striding towards them, a cerulean nimbus of psychic energy coursing over his armoured body. He held a golden spear in his outstretched hand.

'Down, now!' he cried and the Ultramarines hit the floor with a crash of ceramite.

The spear arced over their heads like a divine bolt of lightning and pierced the first warp beast, tearing through its slithering flank and slathering the deck with dark grey, spilling gore.

Its death cry reverberated in the confines of the vaulted tunnel, the metal uprights screaming before it. Then it was gone, leaving an actinic stench in its wake.

The kindred beasts came at him, enduring the furious energy that the Thousand Son had unleashed, but were driven back as Cestus and his honour guard crouched on their knees and delivered a punishing salvo.

'Blind them,' Mhotep cried, plucking his spear from the air as it returned to him as if magnetised to his gauntlet.

The Ultramarines obeyed, aiming for the hideous black orbs that served the shark-like predators as eyes. More screeching filled the corridor as the shots found their marks, rupturing the glassy orbs. Mhotep cast his spear again and another of the creatures was thrust back into the immaterium.

The last predator turned in on itself and re-formed. It grew fresh eyes, dripping with glowing ichor. It extruded a frill of tendrils from what Cestus assumed was its head end, and they became tough jointed limbs tipped with claws. Snakelike tongues whipped from its mouth.

A hail of fire struck it and it was blasted into a gory mess upon the deck.

Curious, ringing silence filled the void where the eruption of bolters and the bark of shouting had been. Red-tinged gloom from the emergency lights drifted back into focus after the monochromatic battle flare of muzzle flashes and psychic conflagration.

Cestus surveyed his battle-brothers. Amyrx lay still against the upright, injured but alive. The service of Laeradis and Morar, though, had ended, their final moments awash with blood and pain. The rest had survived. A weary nod from Saphrax confirmed it.

Breathing hard, a strange, subdued exultance at their victory sweeping over him, Cestus looked back around at Mhotep.

The Thousand Son staggered, the crimson light extinguished.

'They are gone,' he breathed and fell hard onto the deck.

THIRTEEN

Legacy of Lorgar/Proposition/Honour duel

As Skraal delved deeper into the *Furious Abyss*, the world around him got stranger. The ship was the size of a city, and just like a city it had its hidden corners and curiosities, its beautiful clean-cut vistas and its dismal bordellos of decay.

Though supposedly newly fashioned, the vessel felt very old. Its concomitant parts had spent so many decades being built and rendered in the forges of Mars that they had acquired a history of their own before the battleship was ever finished, let alone launched. It had a presence, too, a kind of impalpable sentience that exuded from its steel walls and clung to its corridors and conduits like gossamer threads of being.

Skraal passed under a support beam, his chainaxe held out warily in front of him, and saw the signature of a Mechanicum shipwright inscribed in binary. The passageway of steel looked like an avenue in a wealthy spire-top, the low ceiling supported by caryatids and columns; a nest of shanties, perhaps the lodgings of the menials, who had once laboured to build the ship, their ramshackle homes abandoned between two generatorium housings: the vessel was intricate and immense. The World Eater saw chambers he could only assume were for worship, with altars and rows of prayer books etched in the Word of Lorgar. A temple, half wrought in stone and symbiotically merged with deep red steel, was housed in a massive false amphitheatre, its columned front and carved pediment providing a medieval milieu. The wide threshold was lit by braziers of violet fire. Skraal thought he had seen something moving inside and took care to avoid it.

The World Eater had no time for distractions. The denizens of the *Furious Abyss* hunted him, and even in a ship as vast as it, the chase would not last indefinitely. Melta bombs and belts of krak grenades clanked against his armour as he moved, reminding him of their presence and the urgency with which he needed to put them to some use.

In a fleeting moment, when Skraal had paused to try and get some kind of bearing, he thought of Antiges.

The Ultramarines believed themselves to be philosophers, or kings, or members of the galaxy's rightful ruling class. They did not appreciate the purity of purpose that could only be found in the crucible of war as did Skraal's Legion. They were most concerned with forging their own empire around Macragge. Antiges had demonstrated his warrior spirit, though, fighting and dying in the cauldron of war, driven by simple duty.

Skraal mourned his passing with a moment of silence, honouring his valourous deeds, and, in that moment, he made a promise of revenge.

A great set of double doors carved from lacquered black wood blocked the World Eater's path. Skraal could not turn back from the barrier, incongruous like so much of what he had witnessed on the *Furious Abyss*. Instead, he pushed the door open. There was light inside, but still the silence persisted, so, he entered into what was a long, low chamber. Beyond it was a gallery full of artefacts. Tapestries lined the walls, displaying the victories and history of the Word Bearers. He saw a comet crashing down to their native earth of Colchis and a golden child emerging from the conflagration left from its impact. He saw temples, their spires lost in a swathe of red cloud, and lines of pilgrims trailing off into infinity. It was a world stained with tragedy, the gilded palaces and cathedrals tarnished, and every statue of past religious dynasts missing an arm or an eye. In the middle of this fallen world, like a single point of hope, was the smouldering crater of their saviour's arrival.

The ceiling was a single endless fresco depicting Lorgar's conquest of Colchis. Here it was a corrupt place cleansed by the primarch, whose image shone with the light of reason and command as robed prophets and priests prostrated themselves before him. Armies laid down their arms and crowds cheered in adulation. At the far end of the museum the story ended with Colchis restored and Lorgar a scholar-hero writing down his history and philosophy. This epilogue ended with a truth that Skraal knew, the Emperor coming to the world to find Lorgar, just as he had come to the World Eaters' forgotten home world to install Angron as the Legion's primarch.

The paintings, frescoes and tapestries gave way to trophies displayed on plinths and suspended from the vaulted ceiling. Skraal ignored them and pressed on.

'You look upon the soul of our Legion, brother,' boomed a voice suddenly through the vox-casters in the gallery.

Skraal backed up against the wall, which was painted with an image of Lorgar debating with a host of wizened old men in a Colchian amphitheatre.

'I am Admiral Zadkiel of the Word Bearers,' said the voice, when the World Eater answered with silence. 'You are aboard my ship.'

'Traitor whoreson, does your entire Legion cower behind words?' Skraal snapped, unable to contain his anger.

'Such a curious term, World Eater,' the voice of Zadkiel replied, ignoring the slight. 'You dub us traitors, and yet we have never been anything but loyal to our primarch.'

'Then your lord is also a traitor,' Skraal growled in return, hunting the shadows for any sign of movement, any hint that he was being stalked.

'Your own lord, Angron, calls him brother. How then can Lorgar be regarded as a traitor?'

Skraal cast his gaze around, trying to locate the picter observing him or the vox-caster broadcasting Zadkiel's voice. 'Then he has betrayed my primarch and in turn his Legion.'

'Angron was a slave,' said Zadkiel. 'The very fact shames him. He despises what he was, and what other men made of him. It is from this that his anger, that the anger of all the World Eaters stems.'

Certain that there was no one else in there with him, Skraal started moving cautiously through the gallery, looking for some way out other than the double doors at either end. He would not be swayed by Zadkiel's words, and focused instead on the hot line of rage building inside him, using it to galvanise himself.

'I saw the echo of that anger at Bakka Triumveron,' said Zadkiel. 'It was enacted against the menials that drowned in their own blood at the hands of you and your brothers.'

Skraal paused. He had thought no one knew of the slaughter he had perpetrated at the dock.

'Angron sought to bring his brothers closer to him in that aspect, did he not?' Zadkiel was relentless, his words like silken blades penetrating the World Eater's defences. 'It was the Emperor's censure that forbade it, the very being that holds you and your slave primarch in his thrall. For what is Angron if not a slave? What accolades has he won that the Angel or Guilliman have not? What reward has Angron been given that can equal the empire of Ultramar or the stewardship of the Imperial Palace granted to Dorn? Nothing. He fights for nothing save by the command of another. What can such a man claim to be, other than a slave?'

'We are not slaves! We will never be slaves!' Skraal cried in anger and carved his chainaxe through one of the museum's stone pillars.

'It is the truth,' Zadkiel persisted, 'but you are not alone, brother; yours is not the only Legion to have been thus forsaken,' he continued. 'We Word Bearers worshipped him, worshipped the Emperor as... a... god! But he mocked our divinity with reproach and reprimand, just as he mocks you.'

Skraal ignored him. His faith in his Legion and his primarch would not easily be undone. This Word Bearer's rhetoric meant nothing. Duty and rage: these were the things he focused on as he sought to escape from the chamber.

'Look before you, World Eater,' Zadkiel began again. 'There you will find what you seek.'

Despite himself, Skraal looked.

There, within an ornate glass cabinet, forged of obsidian and brass and once wielded by Angron's hand, was a chainaxe. Decked with teeth of glinting black stone, its haft wrapped in the skin of some monstrous lizard, he knew it instinctively to be Brazentooth, the former blade of his primarch.

The weapon, magnificent in its simple brutality, had taken the head of the queen of the Scandrane xenos, and cleaved through a horde of greenskins following the Arch-Vandal of Pasiphae. A feral world teeming with tribal psychopaths had rebelled against the Imperial Truth, and at the mere sight of Brazentooth in Angron's hand they had given up their revolt and kneeled to the World Eaters. Until the forging of Gorefather and Gorechild, the twin axes Angron now wielded, Brazentooth had been as much a symbol of Angron's relentlessness and independence as it was a mere weapon.

'Gifted unto Lorgar, it symbolises our alliance,' Zadkiel told him. 'Angron pledged himself to our cause, and with him all the World Eaters.'

Skraal regarded the chainaxe. Thick veins stuck out on his forehead, beneath his skull-helmet, exacerbated by the heat of his impotent wrath.

'It is written, World Eater, that you and all your brothers will join with us when the fate of the galaxy is decided. The Emperor is lost. He is ignorant of the *true* power of the universe. We will embrace it.'

'Word Bearer,' Skraal said, his lip curled derisively, 'you talk too much.'

The World Eater shattered the cabinet with a blow from his fist and seized Brazentooth. Without pause, he squeezed the tongue of brass in the chainaxe's haft, and the teeth whirred hungrily. The weapon was far too heavy and unbalanced for Skraal to wield; it would have taken Angron's own magnificent strength to use it. It was all he could do to keep the bucking chainblade level as he put his body weight behind it and hurled it into the nearest wall.

Brazentooth ripped into a fresco depicting Lorgar as an educator of the benighted, thousands of ignorant souls bathing in the halo of enlightenment that surrounded him. The image was shredded and the weapon, free of Skraal's hands, bored its way through, casting sparks as it chewed up the metal beneath.

'You're doomed, Zadkiel!' bellowed Skraal over the screech of the chainblade. 'The Emperor will learn of your treachery! He'll send your brothers to bring you back in chains! He'll send the Warmaster!'

The World Eater hurled himself through the ragged tear in the museum wall and fell through into a tangled dark mess of cabling and metal beyond.

Zadkiel's laughter tumbled after him from the vox-caster.

ZADKIEL SWITCHED OFF the pict screens adorning the small security console at the rear of the temple. 'Tell me, chaplain, is everything prepared?'

Ikthalon, decked in his full regalia including vestments of deep crimson, nodded and gestured towards a circle, drawn from a paste mixed from Colchian soil and the blood that had been drained from the body of the Ultramarine, Antiges.

The Astartes inert body lay at its nexus, his cuirass removed and his chest levered open to reveal the congealed vermillion mass of his organs. Symbols had been scratched on the floor around him, using his blood. His helmet had been removed, too, and his head lolled back, glassy-eyed, its mouth open as if in awe of the ritual he would facilitate in death.

'It is ready, as you ordered,' uttered Ikthalon, the chaplain's tone approaching relish.

Zadkiel smiled thinly and then looked up at the sound of shuffling feet. An old, bent figure ascended the steps at the temple entrance and the candles on the floor flickered against its cowl and robe as it entered between the pillars.

'Astropath Kyrszan,' said Zadkiel.

The astropath pulled back his hood, revealing hollow sockets in place of his eyes as inflicted by the soul-binding.

'I am at your service,' he hissed through cracked lips.

'You know your role in this?'

'I have studied it well, my lord,' Kyrszan replied, leaning heavily on a gnarled cane of dark wood as he shuffled towards Antiges's corpse.

Kyrszan knelt down and held his hands over the body. The astropath smirked as he felt the last wreaths of heat bleeding from it. 'An Astartes,' he muttered.

'Indeed,' added Ikthalon. 'You'll find his scalp has been removed.'

'Then we can begin.'

'I will require what is left after this is done,' added Ikthalon.

'Don't worry, chaplain,' said Zadkiel. 'You'll have his body for your surgery. 'Kyrszan,' he added, switching his gaze to the astropath, 'you may proceed.'

Zadkiel threw a book in front of him. Kyrszan felt its edges, ran his fingers over its binding, the ancient vellum of its pages and breathed deep of its musk, redolent with power. His spidery digits, so sensitive from a lifetime of blindness, scurried across the ink and read with ease. The script was distinctive and known to him.

'What… what secrets,' he whispered in awe. 'This is written by your hand, admiral. What was it that dictated this to you?'

'His name,' said Zadkiel, 'is Wsoric and we are about to honour the pact he has made with us.'

IN THE HOURS that followed, the warp was angry. It was wounded. It bled half-formed emotions, like something undigested: hatred that was too unfocused to be pure, love without an object, obsession over nothing and gouts of oblivion without form.

It quaked. It thrashed as if being forced into something unwilling, or trying to hold on to something dear to it. The *Wrathful* was thrown around on the towering waves that billowed up through the layers of reality and threatened to snap the spindly anchor-line of reason that kept the ship intact.

The quake subsided. The predators that had homed in on the disturbance scented the corpses of their fellow warp-sharks in the *Wrathful*, and hastily slunk back into the abyss. The *Wrathful* continued on its way, following eddies left by the wake of the *Furious Abyss*.

'HAS THERE BEEN any change?' asked Cestus as he approached Saphrax.

The banner bearer stood outside the medical bay, looking in at the prone form of Mhotep, laid as if slumbering, on a slab of metal.

'None, sire. He has not stirred since he fell after the battle.'

The Ultramarine captain had recently been tended to by the *Wrathful*'s medical staff, an injury sustained to his arm that he had not realised he had suffered making its presence felt as he'd gone to Mhotep's aid. In the absence of the dead Laeradis, the treatment was rudimentary but satisfactory. The bodies, what was left of them, of the Astartes, two of the Blood Claws included, had been taken to the ship's morgue.

Cestus's mind still reeled at what he'd witnessed on the lance decks and the powers that the Thousand Son had unleashed. Truly, there was no doubt as to his practising psychics. That in itself left an altogether different and yet more pressing question: Brynngar.

The Wolf Guard had also been down in the lance decks, though Cestus was not aware of it until the battle was over, and had banished three of the warp spawn with his Blood Claws. The artifice of the Fenrisian rune priests, in their fashioning of Felltooth, was to thank for it. For once, reunited at the centre of the deck, Brynngar had curtly disclosed how the creatures parted easily before the blade and fled from the Space Wolves' fury. The Ultramarine believed that some of the account was embellished, so that it might become worthy of a saga, but he did not doubt the veracity at the heart of Brynngar's words.

It mattered not. Whatever the Wolf Guard intended to do about Mhotep and, indeed, Cestus, he would do regardless. Right now, the Ultramarine captain had greater concerns, namely, that the traitor had been broken, for Saphrax had discovered his shattered body in the isolation chamber, but that whatever secrets he had divulged were denied to them while Mhotep was incapacitated. It felt like a cruel irony.

'Do you know what we do with witches on Fenris, Ultramarine?'

Cestus turned at the voice and saw Brynngar standing behind him, glowering through the glass at Mhotep.

'We cut the tendons in their arms and legs. Then we throw them in the sea to the mercy of Mother Fenris.'

Cestus moved into the Space Wolf's path.

'This is not Fenris, brother.'

Brynngar smiled, mirthlessly, as if at some faded remembrance.

'No, it is not,' he said, locking his gaze with Cestus. 'You give your sanction to this warp-dabbler, and in so doing have twice besmirched my honour. I will not let his presence stand on this ship, nor will I let these deeds go unreckoned.'

The Space Wolf tore a charm hanging from his cuirass and tossed it at the Ultramarine's feet.

Cestus looked up and matched the Wolf Guard's gaze.

'Challenge accepted,' he said.

BRYNNGAR WAITED IN the duelling pit in the lower decks of the *Wrathful*. The old wolf was stripped down to the waist, wearing grey training breeches and charcoal-coloured boots, and flexed his muscles and rotated his shoulders as he prepared for his opponent.

Arrayed around the training arena, commonly used for the armsmen to practise unarmed combat routines, were what was left of the Astartes: the Ultramarine honour guard, barring Amryx, who was still recovering from his injuries, and a handful of Blood Claws. Admiral Kaminska, as the captain of the ship, was the only non-Astartes allowed to attend. She had forbidden any other of the crew from watching the duel. The realisation that the Astartes in the fleet were turning on one another was a sign of the worst kind, and she had no desire to discover its effects upon morale if witnessed by them first hand.

She watched as Cestus stepped into the arena, descending a set of metal steps that retracted into the wall once he was within the duelling pit. The Ultramarine was similarly attired to Brynngar, though his training breeches were blue to match the colour of his Legion.

At the appearance of his opponent, Brynngar swung the chainsword in his grasp eagerly.

The assembled Astartes were eerily silent; even the normally pugnacious Blood Claws held their tongues and merely watched.

'This is madness,' Kaminska hissed, biting back her anger.

'No, admiral,' said Saphrax, who towered alongside her, 'it is resolution.'

The Ultramarine banner bearer stepped forward. As the next highest ranking Astartes, it was his duty to announce the duel and state the rules.

'This honour-duel is between Lysimachus Cestus of the Ultramarines Legion and Brynngar Sturmdreng of the Space Wolves Legion,' Saphrax bellowed clearly like a clarion call. 'The weapon is chainswords and the duel is to blood from the torso or incapacitation. Limb or eye loss counts as thus, as does a cut to the front of the throat. No armour; no fire arms.'

Saphrax took a brief hiatus to ensure that both Astartes were ready. He saw his brother-captain testing the weight of his chainsword and adjusting his grip. Brynngar made no further preparation and was straining at the leash.

'The stakes are the fate of Captain Mhotep of the Thousand Sons Legion. To arms!'

The Astartes saluted each other and levelled their chainswords in their respective fighting stances:

Brynngar two-handed and slightly off-centre, Cestus low and pointed towards the ground.

'Begin!'

BRYNNGAR LAUNCHED HIMSELF at Cestus with a roar, channelling his anger into a shoulder barge. Cestus twisted on his heel to avoid the charge, but was still a little sluggish from the earlier battle and caught the blow down his side. A mass of pain numbed his body, resonating through his bones and skull, but the Ultramarine kept his feet.

Blows fell like hammers against Cestus's defensive stance, his chainblade screeching as it bit against Bryn-ngar's weapon. Teeth were stripped away and sparks flew violently from the impact. Two-handed, the Ultra-marine held him, but was forced down to one knee as the Space Wolf used his superior bulk against him.

'We are not in the muster hall, now,' he snarled. 'I shall give no quarter.'

'I will ask for none,' Cestus bit back and twisted out of the blade lock, using Brynngar's momentum to overbal-ance the Space Wolf.

The Ultramarine moved in quickly to exploit the advan-tage with a low thrust, intending to graze Brynngar's torso, draw blood and end the duel. The old wolf was canny, though, and parried the blow with a flick of his sword, before leaning in with another shoulder charge. It lacked the sudden impetuous and fury of the first, but jolted Ces-tus's body all the same. The Ultramarine staggered and Brynngar swept his weapon downward in a brutal arc that would have removed Cestus's head from his shoulders. Instead he rolled and the blade teeth carved into the metal floor of the duelling pit, disturbing the streaks of old blood left by the World Eater's earlier contest.

Cestus came out of the roll and was on his feet. There was a little distance between the two Astartes gladiators, and they circled each other warily, assessing strength and searching for an opening.

Brynngar didn't wait long and, howling, hurled his body at the Ultramarine, chainsword swinging.

Cestus met it with his blade and the two weapons came apart with the force of the blow, chain teeth spitting from their respective housings.

Brynngar cast the ruined chainsword haft aside and powered a savage uppercut into Cestus's chin that nearly shattered the Ultramarine's jaw. A second punch fell like a piston and smashed into his ear. A third lifted him off his feet, hammering into the Ultramarine's gut. The sound of Brynngar's grunting aggression became dull and distant as if Cestus was submerged below water, as he fought to get his bearings.

He was dimly aware of falling and had the vague sense of grasping something in his hand as he hit the hard metal floor of the duelling pit.

Abruptly, Cestus found it hard to breath and realised suddenly that Brynngar was choking him. Strangely, the Ultramarine thought he heard weeping. With a blink, he snapped back into lucidity and smashed his fists down hard against Brynngar's forearms, whilst landing a kick into his sternum. It was enough for the Space Wolf to loosen his grip. Cestus head-butted him in the nose and a stream of blood and mucus flowed freely after the impact.

Feeling the ground beneath him again, Cestus ducked a wild swing and lashed out beneath Brynngar's reach. The Ultramarine wasn't quick enough to avoid a back-hand swipe and took it in the side of the face. He was reeling again, dark spots forming before his eyes, hinting that he was about to black out.

'Yield,' he breathed, sinking to his knees, his voice groggy as he pointed to the Space Wolf's torso with the chainsword tooth clutched in his outstretched hand.

Brynngar paused, fists clenched, his breathing ragged and looked down to where Cestus was pointing.

A line of crimson was drawn across the Space Wolf's stomach from the tiny diagonal blade in his opponent's grip.

'Blood from the torso,' Saphrax announced with thinly veiled relief. 'Cestus wins.'

FOURTEEN

Hunted/A single blow/We are all alone

TIME HAS LITTLE meaning in the warp. Weeks become days, days become hours and hours become minutes. Time is fluid. It can expand and contract, invert and even cease in those fathomless depths of infinite nothing; endless everything.

Leaving the gallery and Zadkiel's echoing laughter behind him, Skraal had fled into the pitch dark.

Crouching in the blackness with naught but the groans of the *Furious Abyss* for company it felt like the passage of years, and yet it could have been no more than weeks or as little as an hour. Heaving, shifting, baying, venting, the vessel was like some primordial beast as it ploughed the empyrean tides. Sentience exuded from every surface: the moisture of the metal, the blood, oil and soot in the air. Heat from generatoria became breath, fire from blast furnaces anger and hate, the creak of the hull, dull moans of pleasure and annoyance. Perhaps this awareness had always existed and lacked only form to give it tangibility. Perhaps the skeleton the adepts of Mars had forged provided merely a shell for an already sentient host.

The World Eater decided that his thoughts heralded the onset of madness at being hunted for so long, the thin talons of paranoia pricking his skull and infecting his mind with visions.

After his discovery in the gallery, he had gone to ground, questing downwards through the inner circuitry and workings of the *Furious Abyss* in some kind of attempt at preservation. It was not cowardice that drove him, such a thing was anathema to the Astartes: a World Eater was incapable of the emotion. Fear simply did not have meaning for them. No, it was out of a desire to regroup, to plan, to achieve some petty measure of destruction that might not at least escape notice, that meant something. Into the heat and fire he'd passed arches of steel, vast throbbing engines and forests of cables so thick that he'd needed to cut them down with his chainaxe. It was in this manufactured hell that he'd found refuge.

Bones lay on the lower decks, pounded to dust by pistons, though some were intact. They were the forgotten dead of the *Furious*'s birth, sucked into machinery or simply lost and left to starve or die of thirst in the ship's labyrinthine depths.

During his flight into this cauldron, Skraal had seen things. The dark had played with him, the heat, too, and the endless industrial din. Glowing eyes would watch the World Eater, only to then melt away into the walls. A landscape had opened up before him, its edges picked out in darkness: a vast land of bloody ribs and palaces of bone, with mountains of gristle and labyrinths carved down into plains of rippling muscle. Humanoid shapes danced in rivers of blood as the whole world swelled and fell with an ancient breath.

Then it was gone, replaced by the darkness, and so he had driven on.

Here in the searing depths, he'd found some respite.

It could have been days that he'd lingered in meditative solitude, listening to the pitch and pull of the vessel, marshalling his thoughts and his resolve so as not to give in to insanity. Way down in the stygian gloom, Skraal couldn't hear the vox traffic, didn't sense the patrols at his heels and so didn't know if he was still hunted.

Sheltering in a crawl space large enough to accommodate his power-armoured frame, within a cluster of pipes and cables, the World Eater snapped abruptly to his senses. Disengaging the cataleptic node that allowed him to maintain a form of active sleep, Skraal became aware of a shadow looming in the conduit ahead. He was not alone.

The passing of menials was not uncommon, but infrequent. Skraal had listened to their pathetic mewlings as they serviced and maintained the ship, with disgust. Such wretches! It had taken all of his resolve not to spring out of his hiding place and butcher them all like the cattle they were, but then the alarm would have been raised and the hunt begun anew. He needed to think, to devise his next move. Not gifted with the tactical acumen of the sons of Guilliman or Dorn, Skraal was a pure instrument of war, brutal and effective. Yet now he needed a stratagem and for that he required time. Survival first, then sabotage; it was his mantra.

That doctrine dissolved into the ether with the shadow. No menial this, it did not mewl or bay or weep, it was silent. It was something else, massive footfalls resonating against metal with every step, and it was seeking him. Skraal extracted himself from the crawl space and bled away into the darkness, eyes on the growing gloom he left behind him, and went onwards into the *Furious Abyss*.

'THEY TAIL us ever doggedly, my lord,' uttered Reskiel as he considered the reports of Navigator Esthemya clutched in his gauntlet.

Zadkiel appeared sanguine to the fact that the *Wrathful* continued to follow them into the warp as he regarded the scrawlings on the cell wall of one of the ship's astropathic choir.

It was a spartan chamber with little to distinguish it. A narrow cot served as a bed, a simple lectern as a place to scribe. Function was paramount here.

'Wsoric is with us,' he said, emboldened enough in the surety that they had sealed their pact with the ancient creature to speak his name, 'and once he reveals his presence, the pawns of the False Emperor will learn the folly of their pursuit. The horrors endured thus far will be as nothing compared to the torture he will visit upon them.'

'Yes, my lord,' Reskiel said humbly.

'We are destined to achieve our mission, Reskiel,' Zadkiel went on, 'just as this one was destined to die for it.' The admiral turned the corpse of a dead astropath over. It was lying in the middle of the cell in a pool of its own blood. The face was female, but twisted into a rictus of fear and pain so pronounced that it was hard to tell. Black, empty orbs stared out from crater-like sockets.

Communications were difficult even for those who claimed the warp as an ally, and the messages of the

Furious's astropathic choir were proving ever more unreliable and difficult to discern. Zadkiel had some skill at divination, however, and carefully deconstructed nuances of meaning, subtle vagaries of sense and context in the symbolic renderings of the dead astropath.

'Anything?' asked Reskiel.

'Perhaps,' said Zadkiel, sensing the desperate cadence in the sergeant-commander's voice. 'Once we reach the Macragge system we will have no further need of them,' he added. 'You need not fear us floundering blind in the immaterium, Reskiel.'

'I fear nothing, lord,' Reskiel affirmed, standing straight, his expression stern.

'Of course not,' Zadkiel replied smoothly, 'except, perhaps, our intruder. Do the sons of Angron hold an inner dread for you sergeant-commander? Do you recall all too readily the sting of our erstwhile brother's wrath?'

Reskiel raised his gauntlet to the crude repairs of his face and cheekbone almost subconsciously, but then retracted it as if suddenly scalded.

'Is that the reason that our interloper still roams free aboard this ship?' Zadkiel pressed.

'He is contained,' Reskiel snarled. 'Should he surface then I will know, and mount his head upon a spike myself!'

Zadkiel traced a shape out of the dense scribblings on the wall, deliberately ignoring the sergeant-commander's impassioned outburst.

'Here,' he hissed, finding the meaning he sought at last.

The astropath had written the message in her vital fluids, the parchment pages of her symbol log overloaded with further crimson data and strewn about the cell floor like bloodied leaves.

'The crown is Colchis,' said Zadkiel, indicating a smeared icon. 'These ancillary marks indicate that this dictate comes from a lord of the Legion,' he added, a sweep of his gauntleted hand encompassing a range of symbols that Reskiel could not fathom.

Astropaths rarely had the luxury of communicating by words or phrases. Instead, they had an extensive catalogue of symbols, which were a lot easier to transmit psychically. Each symbol had a meaning, which became increasingly complex the more symbols were added. The Word Bearers fleet had their own code, in which the crown was modelled after the Crown of Colchis and represented both the Legion's home world and the leadership of the Legion.

'Two eyes, one blinded,' continued Zadkiel. 'That is Kor Phaeron's Chapter.'

'He asks something of us?' asked Reskiel.

Zadkiel picked out another symbol from the miasma, most of which was eidetic doggerel coming out in a rush of mindless images and non-sequitous ravings, a coiled snake: the abstract geometrical code for the Calth system.

'His scouts have confirmed that the Ultramarines are mustering at Calth,' Zadkiel answered, 'all of them. There are but a few token honour guards not present.'

'Then we will strike them out with a single blow,' stated the sergeant-commander confidently.

'As it is written, my brother,' Zadkiel replied, looking up from the scrawlings and offering a mirthless smile. He finished examining the astropath's message and brushed the flakes of dried blood from his gauntlets.

'All is in readiness,' he said to himself, imaging the glory of their triumph and the plaudits he, Zadkiel, would garner. 'Thy Word be done.'

* * *

CESTUS FILLED HIS time with training regimens and
meditation, in part to occupy his mind whilst the
Wrathful traversed the warp, but also to recondition
his body after the brutal duel with Brynngar.

Something had possessed the Space Wolf during
the fight, Cestus had felt it in every blow and heard it
in the Wolf Guard's battle cries. It was not a change in
the sense that the warp predators took on the form of
the *Fireblade*'s crew. No, it was something less
ephemeral and more intrinsic than that, as if a part of
the gene-code that made up the zygotic structure of
Leman Russ's Legion had been exposed somehow
and allowed free rein.

Base savagery, that was how Cestus thought of it, an
animalistic predilection let slip only in the face of the
Space Wolves' foes. Was the warp the cause of this loosening of resolve? Cestus felt its presence constantly. It
was clear that the crew did also, though they appeared
to be more acutely afflicted. Armsmen patrols had doubled over the passing weeks. Rotations of those patrols
had also increased and prolonged exposure to the warp
even whilst in the protective bubble of the *Wrathful*'s
integrity fields took its toll.

There had been seventeen warp-related deaths after
the attack on the lance decks, the entirety of which had
been fusion-sealed in the wake of the horrors perpetrated there. Damage sustained whilst in battle against
the Word Bearers' ship had rendered the weapon systems inoperable in any case, and no one on the *Wrathful*
had any desire to tread those bloody halls again. Sui-
cides and apparent accidents were common, one rating
was even murdered, the perpetrator still at large, as the
products of warp-induced psychosis made their presence felt.

Of the *Furious Abyss*, there had been little sign. It continued to plough through the empyrean, content to let the *Wrathful* follow. Cestus didn't like the calm; trouble invariably followed it.

A stinging blow caught the Ultramarine captain on the side of the temple and he grimaced in pain.

'You seem preoccupied, my lord,' said Saphrax, standing opposite him in a fighting posture. He twirled the duelling staff in his hands with expert precision as he circled his captain.

The two Astartes faced each other in one of the vessel's gymnasia, wearing breeches and loose-fitting vests as they conducted the daily ritual of their training katas. Routine dictated the duelling staff as the weapon of choice for this session.

Cestus's body was already bruised and numb from a dozen or more precise blows landed by his banner bearer. Saphrax was right; his mind was elsewhere, still in the duelling pit facing off against Brynngar.

'Perhaps, we should switch to the rudius?' Saphrax offered, indicating a pair of short wooden swords clutched by a weapons servitor, two amongst many training weapons held by the creature's rack-like frontal carapace.

Cestus shook his head, giving the battle-sign that he had had enough.

'That will suffice for today,' he said, lowering the staff and reaching for a towel offered by a Legion serf to wipe down his naked arms and neck.

'I don't like this, Saphrax,' he confessed, handing the duelling weapon back to the servitor as it approached.

'The training schema was not satisfactory?' the banner bearer asked, unlike Antiges, unable to penetrate the deeper meaning of his captain's words.

'No, my brother. It is this quietude that vexes me. We have seen little in the way of deterrent from the *Furious Abyss* for almost two weeks, or at least as close to two weeks as I can fathom in this wretched empyrean.'

'Is that not a boon rather than a cause of vexation?' Saphrax asked, commencing a series of stretching exercises to loosen his muscles after the bout.

'No, I do not think so. Macragge draws ever closer and yet we seem ever further from finding a way to stop the Word Bearers. We do not even know of their plan, damn Mhotep in his coma state.' Cestus stopped what he was doing and looked Saphrax in the eye. 'I am losing hope, brother. Part of me believes the reason they have ceased in their attempts to destroy us is because they do not need to, that we no longer pose a significant threat to their mission, if we ever did.'

'Put your belief in the strength of the Emperor, captain. Trust in that and we shall prevail,' said the banner bearer vehemently.

Cestus sighed deeply, feeling a great weight upon his shoulders.

'You are right,' said the Ultramarine captain. Saphrax might not possess the instinct and empathy of Antiges, but his dour pragmatism was an unshakeable rock in a sea of doubt. 'Thank you, Saphrax,' he added, clapping his hand on the banner bearer's shoulder while nodded in response.

Cestus wrenched off the vest, sodden with his sweat, and donned a set of robes as he padded across the gymnasium to the antechamber, where Legion serf armourers awaited him.

'If you do not need me further, captain, I shall continue my daily regimen in your absence,' said the banner bearer.

'Very well, Saphrax,' Cestus replied, his thoughts still clouded. 'There is someone else I need to see,' he added in a murmur to himself.

BRYNNGAR SLUMPED FORLORNLY onto his rump in the quarters set aside for him by Admiral Kaminska. He was alone, surrounded by a host of empty ale barrels, his Blood Claws isolated to the barracks, and belched raucously. He had come here after losing the honour duel, speaking to no one and entertaining no remarks, however placatory, from his fellow Space Wolves. The old wolf's demeanour made it clear that he wished to be alone. Not everyone got the message.

Brynngar looked up from his dour brooding when he saw Cestus enter the gloomy chamber.

'Wulfsmeade is all gone,' he slurred, impossibly drunk despite the co-action of the Space Wolf's preomnor and oolitic kidney. The beverage, native to Fenris, was brewed with the very purpose of granting intoxication that overrode even the processes of the Astartes' gene-enhanced physiognomy, albeit temporarily.

'You keep it, my friend,' Cestus replied with mock geniality, despite his apprehension.

Brynngar grunted, kicking over his empty tankard as he got up. The old wolf was stripped out of his armour and wore an amalgam of furs and coarse, grey robes. Charms and runic talismans clattered over his hirsute chest, the nick from the chain tooth still visible, though all but healed.

'You seem well recovered, Ultramarine,' grumbled the Wolf Guard, irascibly. Brynngar's belligerence had not dimmed with the passage of hours in the warp.

In truth, Cestus still felt the ache in his jaw and stomach in spite of the larraman cells in his body speeding up the healing process exponentially. The Ultramarine merely nodded, unwilling to disclose his discomfort.

'Now it is done,' he said. 'You are an honourable warrior, Brynngar. What's more, you are my friend. I know you will abide by the outcome of the duel.'

The Space Wolf fixed his good eye on him, pausing as he hunted around for more ale to quaff. He snarled, and for a moment Cestus thought he might instigate another fight, but then relaxed and let out a rasping sigh.

'Aye, I'll abide by it, but I warn you, Lysimachus Cestus, I will hold no truck with warp-dabblers. Keep him away from me or I will visit my blade upon his sorcerer's tongue,' he promised, drawing closer, the rustle of his beard hair the only clue that the Space Wolf's lips were actually moving. 'If you stand in my way again, it will be no honour duel that decides his fate.'

Cestus paused for a moment, matching Brynngar's intensity with a stern expression.

'Very well,' the Ultramarine replied, and then added, 'I need you in this fight, Brynngar. I need the strength of your arm and the steel of your courage.'

The old wolf sniffed in mild contempt.

'But not my counsel, eh?'

Cestus was about to counter when Brynngar continued.

'You'll have my arm, and my courage, right enough,' he said, waving Cestus away with his clawed hand. 'Leave me, now. I'm sure there's more to drink in here somewhere.'

Cestus breathed in hard and turned away. Yes, Brynngar remained in the fight, the Ultramarine had gained that much, but he had lost something much more potent: a friend.

* * *

CESTUS DID NOT have much time to lament the ending of Brynngar's friendship as he made for the bridge. Down one of the *Wrathful's* access corridors, he received a vox transmission that crackled in the receiver node on his gorget.

'Captain Cestus,' said Admiral Kaminska's voice.

'Speak admiral, this is Cestus.'

'You are required at the isolation chambers at once,' she said.

'For what reason, admiral?' Cestus replied, betraying his annoyance at the admiral's brevity.

'Lord Mhotep is awake.'

ONCE CESTUS HAD left, Brynngar found a last barrel of Wulfsmeade and guzzled it down, foam and liquid lapping at his beard. He cared little for the revival of the Thousand Son and slumped back into melancholy, their passage through the warp affecting him more than he would admit.

A haze overtook his vision and he could smell the scent of the cold and hear the lap of Fenrisian oceans.

Brynngar wiped his eyes with the back of his hand and remembered standing atop a jagged glacier with nought but a flint knife and a loincloth to cover his dignity.

This was not a punishment, he recalled, recognising the place from his past, it was a reward. Only the toughest Fenrisian youths were considered for the test. It was called the Blooding, but so rarely did a Space Wolf speak of it that it barely needed a name at all.

Faced with the bleak white nightmare of the Fenrisian winter, Brynngar had found the bone of a long-dead ice predator and had fixed his knife to it to make a spear.

He had stalked patiently, following the short-lived tracks of the prey-beast across the ice and tundra.

When he had killed it, it had put up a mighty fight, because even the most docile of Fenrisian creatures were angry monsters. After consuming its flesh, he had skinned it, and worn the skin as a cloak as if part of the beast's essence lived on within him. Without its fur and flesh, he would have died during the first night. He had then sharpened its bones into more blades, in case he lost his knife. He wove a line from its tendons and made a hook from a tiny bone in its inner ear, using it to pull fish from the sea. He split its jawbone in two and carried it as a club.

Brynngar trekked his way back towards the Fang, using faint glimpses of the winter sun to show him the way as he descended the glacier. Upon a rugged place of razor shards, the ice collapsed to pitch him into a sickle-tooth den. He fought his way free of the scaly predators with his jawbone club. Onwards he pressed, and a frost lynx ambushed him, but he wrestled the writhing feline to the ground and bit out its throat, saturating himself in gore. The journey was long. He had killed a skyblade hawk with a thrown bone knife. He had scaled mountains.

When, finally, he saw the gates of the Fang ahead, Brynngar understood the lesson that the Blooding was supposed to teach him. It was not about survival, or fighting, or even the determination required of an Astartes. Any prospective Space Wolf who made it to the Blooding had already shown that he had those skills and qualities. The Blooding's message was far harder to learn.

'We are all alone,' Brynngar muttered, having drained the last of the Wulfsmeade.

Briefly, his mind wandered back to the Blooding. He remembered that an enormous, shaggy, black wolf had appeared on a crag overlooking the path he was to take. It had watched him for a long time, and he had known that it was a wulfen: the half-mythical predators said to be born from the earth of Fenris to winnow out the weak. The wulfen had not approached him, but Brynngar had felt its eyes watching him for days on end. He wondered if the creature's gaze had ever left him.

The same wulfen was now sitting before him, regarding Brynngar with its black eyes. The Wolf Guard returned its gaze and saw his face mirrored in the beast's pupils.

'You're alone,' he said. 'We're pack animals all of us, but that's just... that's just on the surface. We cling to the pack because if we did not there would be no Legion. We are alone, all of us. There might as well be no one else on this bloody ship.'

The Wulfen did not reply.

'Just you and me,' said Brynngar, huskily.

The Wulfen shook itself, like a dog drying its fur. It growled powerfully and stood up on all fours. It was the size of a horse, its head level with the Space Wolf's.

The Wulfen bowed down and picked something up off the floor with its jaws. With a flick of its head he threw it at Brynngar's feet.

It was a bolt pistol. The grip was plated with shards of the bone knife that Brynngar had been carrying when he arrived at the Fang after his Blooding. His fishhook hung from the butt of the gun on a thong made from animal tendon. Skyblade talons and frost lynx teeth decorated the body of the weapon in an intricate mosaic depicting a black wolf against the whiteness of a Fenrisian winter.

'Ah,' said the Wolf Guard, picking the weapon up, 'that's where it got to.'

FATE WAS A lattice of interconnecting strands of potential realities and possible futures. Eventualities flowed in bifurcating lines and paradoxes. Destiny was unfixed, existing purely as a series of outcomes, and even the most infinitesimal action had consequence and resonance.

Mhotep regarded the myriad strands of fate in his mind. Focusing on the silence and solace of the isolation chamber, visions sprang unbidden to his mind. Glorious mountains of power rose up before him. Galaxies boiled away in the distance, points of burning light on an endless silver sky. Infinite layers of reality fell, each one teeming with life. Mhotep's concepts of history and humanity saw endless cities springing up like grass and withering away again to be replaced by spires greater than those on Prospero. Mhotep's memories flared up against the sky and became whole worlds.

Subsumed completely within the meditative trance state, he saw the magnificence of the Emperor's Palace, its golden walls resplendent against the Terran sun. He saw the finery and gilded glory torn down, artistry and mosaic replaced by gunmetal steel. The palace became a fortress, cannons like black fingers pointing towards an enemy burning from the sky above. Driven earth and waves of blood tarnished its glory. Brother fought brother in their Legions and changeling beasts loped out of the dark at the behest of fell masters.

War machines soared, their titanic presence blotting out the smoke-scarred sun. Thunder boomed and lightning split the blood-drenched sky as their weapons spoke. Laughter peeled across the heavens and the

Emperor of Mankind looked skyward where shadows blackened the crimson horizon. Light, so bright that it burned Mhotep's irises, flared like the luminance of an exploding star. When he looked back, the battlefield was gone, the Emperor was gone. There was only the isolation chamber and the escaping resonance of purpose drifting out of Mhotep's consciousness.

'Greetings Cestus,' he said, noting the Ultramarine's presence in the room as he shrouded the disorientation and discomfort he felt after leaving the fate-trance.

'It is good to have you back with us, brother,' said Cestus, who had lingered at the threshold, but now stepped fully into the chamber to stand in front of his fellow Astartes.

Mhotep turned to face the Ultramarine and gave a shallow bow.

'I see you still do not see fit to offer better accommodations.'

Prior to the Thousand Son's revival, Cestus had ordered that as soon as he awoke and his vital signs were confirmed, Mhotep should be taken at once to the isolation chamber. There existed no doubt of his abilities. It meant that he had defied the edicts of Nikea, and it meant that he had a connection to the warp. Whether it was one he could exploit or would need to sever, Cestus did not yet know.

'You come to learn of what I gleaned from Brother Ultis,' Mhotep stated, content to guide the conversation.

The Ultramarine found his prescience unnerving.

'Don't worry, Cestus, I am not probing your mind,' added the Thousand Son, sensing his fellow Astartes' unease. 'What other possible reason could there be for you to have been summoned to my presence so urgently?'

'Ultis: that is his name?'

'Indeed,' Mhotep answered, parting the robes he wore to sit upon the bunk in the chamber. The Astartes armour had been removed during his time in the medibay. There it lay still, with the rest of the Thousand Son's accoutrements. Cestus noted, however, that Mhotep still wore the scarab earring, glinting in the depths of his cowl from the ambient light in the room, and remained hooded throughout the exchange.

'What else did you learn? What do the Word Bearers plan to do?'

'Formaska is where it begins,' Mhotep answered simply.

Cestus made an incredulous face.

'The second moon of Macragge. It's a barren rock. There is nothing there.'

'On the contrary, Ultramarine,' countered Mhotep, lowering his head. 'Everything is on Formaska.'

'I don't understand,' said Cestus.

Mhotep lifted his head. His eyes were alight with crimson flame. 'Then let me show you,' he said as Cestus recoiled, lunging forward to thrust his open palm against the Ultramarine's head.

FIFTEEN

Desecration/Communion/Visions of death

SKRAAL SURGED THROUGH the dark and the heat, rising now, exploiting conduits and pipes and using any means he could to secrete his ascent up the decks of the *Furious Abyss*. Finally he arrived, incredulously, at the place where weeks before he had fled, leaving Antiges to his death. He had returned to the temple.

Skraal found that Antiges remained, too.

Dismembered in his armour, the dark blue of the ceramite almost hidden by the red sheen of blood, the World Eater could only tell it was Antiges by his Chapter symbols. Little more than a collection of body parts existed now. What lay before him on a pall, attended by silent acolytes could barely be considered a corpse. Antiges's head was missing.

Skraal had heard of the inhabitants of feral worlds who dismembered their foes or sacrificed humans to their heathen gods. The World Eaters had their own warrior traditions, most of them bloody, but nothing to compare to the religious mutilation he had seen among the savages. To see Astartes, especially the self-righteously sophisticated Word Bearers, doing thus, shocked Skraal as much as the moment that the *Furious Abyss* had turned on the Imperial fleet.

The galaxy was changing very quickly. The words of Zadkiel, spoken so many days ago in the gallery, echoed back at him.

The World Eater shrank deeper into the shadows as he saw Astartes entering the chamber. One, the warrior he had fought earlier in the temple during his escape, he recognised. It was not with a little satisfaction that he saw the metal artifice attached to the Word Bearer's face where Skraal had broken his jaw and shattered his cheekbone.

A darkly-armoured chaplain accompanied the warrior, Reskiel. One of the demagogues of the Legion, the chaplain wore a skull-faced battle helm with conjoined rebreather apparatus worked into the gorget and carried a crozius, the icon of his office.

Silently, Reskiel gave the acolytes orders. As if understanding on some instinctive level, they bowed curtly and proceeded to lift what was left of Antiges on a steel pall. Together, they raised him up onto their shoulders and, led by the chaplain, left the room.

Reskiel lingered in their wake, probing the shadows and, for a brief moment, Skraal thought he was discovered, but the Word Bearer turned eventually and followed the macabre procession.

Loosening the grip on his chainaxe, the World Eater went after them.

Tailing the enemy at a discrete distance, Skraal was led down a pathway lined with statues that flowed towards what he assumed was the prow of the ship. He had previously steered clear of the vessel's forward sections, preferring to hide himself in the industrial tangle of the stern-ward engine decks, but a greater understanding of his enemy was worth the risk. Continuing his pursuit, the World Eater found himself in darkness, lit only by candles mounted in alcoves.

Watching intently, Skraal witnessed the pallbearers saying a prayer at a set of blast doors – the exact words were indiscernible, but their reverence was obvious – before continuing into a dim chamber beyond.

Using the shadows like a concealing cloak, Skraal moved into the room. As he got further inside, he realised that it was an anatomy theatre. A surgeon's slab dominated the centre of the room, surrounded by circular tiers of seating, though they were not occupied. Whatever ritual or experiment was to be performed here was a clandestine one.

The chaplain, the vestments he wore across his armour fringed with black trim, beckoned the acolytes forward.

The debased creatures, hunch-backed and robed, slunk to the table as one. Sibilant emanations pierced the silence softly as they took the disparate sections of Antiges's corpse and laid them out on the slab. Obscene and profane, the gorge in Skraal's throat rose and his anger swelled at the sight of the act. Taken apart like that: it was as if Antiges was no more than a machine to be stripped down or meat cleaved at the butcher's block.

Coldness smothered the anger and bile within Skraal, as if his blood had been drained away and replaced with ice. It was as if a film of dirt overlaid him, and choked him all at once.

Skraal had done terrible things. At the Sack of Scholamgrad and the burning of the Ethellion Fleet, innocents had died. Even at Bakka Triumveron, he had killed in cold blood for the sake of slaking his thirst for carnage, but this was different. It was calculated and precise, the systematic and ritual dismemberment of another Astartes so invasive, so fundamentally destructive that his essence was forever lost. There would be no honours for him, no clean death on the field of battle as it should be for all warriors; there was dignity in that. No, this was an aberration, soulless and terrible. To think of a fellow Astartes being so shamed and by one of his battle-brothers... it took all of Skraal's resolve not to wade in and kill them all for such defilement.

Stepping forward, the chaplain approached the table, the acolytes retreating obsequiously as he picked up one of Antiges's arms to inspect it.

'There is no head?' he asked, setting the limb back down as he turned to his fellow Word Bearer.

'Wsoric required it,' replied Reskiel.

'I see, and now our omniscient lord would have us yoke this body for further favours of the warp.' There was an almost contemptuous tone to the chaplain's words.

'You speak out of turn, Ikthalon,' Reskiel snapped. 'You would do well to remember who is master aboard this ship.'

'Be still, sycophant.' The chaplain, Ikthalon, fashioned his retort into a snarl. 'Your allegiance is well known to all, as is your ambition.'

Reskiel moved to respond, but was cut off.

'Hold your tongue! Think on the fate of those left at Bakka Triumveron. Think of Ultis before you speak of whom is master. In this place,' he said, spreading his arms to encompass the macabre surgery, 'you supplicate

yourself to me. Zadkiel's wizened astropath has had his
turn and sealed the pact with Wsoric, now I will divine
what I can from what remains. Speak no further. I have
need to concentrate, and you try my patience, Reskiel.'

The other Word Bearer, cowed by the tirade, retreated
back into the shadows to let the chaplain work.

Skraal kept watching with abhorred satisfaction, but
was intrigued by the obvious dissension within the
Word Bearers' ranks.

'Warrior's hands,' said Ikthalon, gauntleted fingers
tracing Antiges's palm as he resumed his morbid examination, 'strong and instinctive, but I will need more.'
The chaplain gestured at the former Ultramarine's torso.
'Open it.'

One of the acolytes took a las-cutter from beneath the
slab and sheared through the front of Antiges's breastplate. The gilded decoration split off from the ceramite
and clattered to the floor. The Word Bearers ignored it.
Once the acolyte with the cutter retreated, Ikthalon
inserted his fingers into the cut. With a grunt of effort,
he forced the Ultramarine's chest open.

The complex mass of an Astartes's organs was
exposed. Skraal could make out the two hearts and
third lung, together with the reverse of the bony breastplate that fused from every Astartes's ribs.

The chaplain dug a hand into the gory dark and
extracted an organ. It looked like the oolitic kidney, or
perhaps the omophagaea. Ikthalon regarded it coolly,
putting the organ down and yanking out a handful of
entrails. He cast them across the slab, and stood for a
long time peering into the loops of tissue and sprays of
blood.

'Macragge suspects nothing,' he hissed, discerning
meaning from the act. Running a finger through the

bloody miasma, he added. 'Here, that's our route. It lies open to us.'

'What of Calth?' Reskiel asked from the darkness.

'That is unclear,' Ikthalon replied. 'Kor Phaeron has no obstacles, save any he makes for himself.' The chaplain peered into Antiges's open chest again. 'There is veining on the third lung. Guilliman is represented there as just a man. Not a primarch, just a man ignorant of his fate.' Ikthalon's voice dripped with malice.

The chaplain looked further, his gaze lingering for a moment on one of Antiges's hearts before his head snapped up quickly.

'We are not alone,' he snarled.

Reskiel's bolter swung up in readiness and he barked into the transponder in his gorget.

'In the anatomy theatre, now!'

A troop of four Word Bearers barged into the room, weapons drawn.

'Spread out,' Reskiel bellowed. 'Find him!'

Skraal backed out of the chamber. He forged back the way he had come and split off from the candlelit path, kicking open a maintenance hatch and dropping into a tangle of wiring and circuitry. He stormed ahead, relying on the ship to hide him for a little longer. He wanted to feel rage, and be comforted by it, but he couldn't reach it. He felt numb.

VISIONS RACED INTO Cestus's mind as he felt all of tangible reality fall away around him. At once, he was suspended in the depths of real space. Formaska rolled beneath, its laborious orbit somehow visible. Silvered torpedoes struck suddenly against its surface at strategic points across the moon. Miniature detonations were discernible as a slow shockwave resonated over it in ripples of destructive force. Cestus saw tiny fractures in the outer crust, magnifying with each passing second into massive fissures that yawned like jagged mouths. Formaska glowed and pulsed as if it were a throbbing heart giving out its last, inexorable beat. The moon exploded.

Debris cascaded outwards in shuddering waves, miniscule asteroids burning up in the atmosphere of nearby Macragge. A fleet suspended in the planet's upper atmosphere was destroyed. Impossibly, Cestus heard the screams of his home world's inhabitants below as the detritus of Formaska's death rained upon them in super-heated waves of rock.

Something moved in the debris field, shielded from the thundering defence lasers of Macragge's surface. Getting ever closer, the dark shape breached the planet's atmosphere. The vision shifted to the industrial hive of the cities. A cloud of gas boiled along the streets, engulfing the screaming populous.

The image changed again, depicting other ships, great vessels of the Crusade, held in orbit at Calth hit by an errant meteor storm. Cestus watched in horror as they broke up against the onslaught, the stylised 'U' of his Legion immolated in flame. The meteor shower struck Calth, forcing its way through the planet's atmosphere to where his battle-brothers mustered below. Cestus roared in anguish, furious at his impotence, screaming a desperate warning that his brothers and his primarch would never hear.

The scene changed once more as the void of real space became metal. As if propelled at subsonic speed, Cestus flew through the tunnels and chambers of a ship. Through conducts, across heaving generators, beyond the fire of immense plasma-driven engines, he came at last to an ordnance deck. There, sitting innocuously amongst the other munitions, was a lethal payload. Though he could not explain how, he knew it at once to be a viral torpedo and the effective death warrant of Macragge.

World killer.

The words resolved themselves in the Ultramarine's mind, taunting him, goading him.

Cestus railed against the sense of doom, the fathomless despair they evoked. He bellowed loud and hard, the only name he could think of to repel it.

'Guilliman!'

Cestus was back in the isolation chamber. He saw Mhotep sitting across from him. The Thousand Son's face was haggard and covered in a sheen of sweat.

Cestus staggered backwards as recall returned, wrenching his bolt pistol from its holster with difficultly and pointing it waveringly at Mhotep.

'What did you do to me,' he hissed, shaking his head in an effort to banish the lingering images and sensations.

'I showed you the truth,' Mhotep gasped, breathing raggedly as he propped himself up against the wall of the cell, 'by sharing my memories, the memories of Ultis, with you. It is no different to the omophagea, though the absorption of memory is conducted psychically and not biologically,' he pleaded.

Cestus kept his aim on the Thousand Son.

'Was it real?' he asked. 'What I witnessed, was it real?' he demanded, stowing the bolt pistol in favour of grabbing Mhotep by the throat.

'Yes,' the Thousand Son spat through choking breaths.

Cestus held him there for a moment longer, thinking that he might crush the life out of the fellow Astartes.

Exhaling deeply, Cestus let Mhotep go. The Thousand Son doubled over coughing as he gasped for breath and rubbed his throat.

'They do not plan to attack Calth, or destroy Macragge. They want to conquer them both and bring the Legion to heel or vanquish it if it does not yield,' said Cestus, his thoughts and fears coming out in a flood.

Mhotep looked up at the frantic Ultramarine, and nodded.

'And the destruction of Formaska is where it will begin.'

'The ship,' Cestus ventured, beginning to calm down. 'That was the *Furious Abyss*, wasn't it? And the viral payload is the method of extermination for the people of Macragge.'

'You have seen what I saw, and what Ultis knew,' Mhotep confirmed, regaining his composure and sitting up.

Cestus's gaze was distant as he struggled to process everything he'd learned, together with resisting the urge to vomit against the invasive psychic experience. He looked back at Mhotep, a suspicious cast to his eyes and face.

'Why are you here, Mhotep? I mean, why are you really here?'

The Thousand Son gazed back for a moment and then withdrew his hood and sighed deeply.

'I have seen the lines of fate, Ultramarine. I knew long before we made contact with the *Furious Abyss*, back when we were on Vangelis, that my destiny lay with this ship, that this mission, *your* mission, was important.

'My Legion is cursed with psychic mutation, but my lord Magnus taught us to harness it, to commune with

the warp and fashion that communion into true power.'
Mhotep ignored the growing revulsion in Cestus's face
as he spoke of the empyrean, and went on. 'Nikea was
no council, Ultramarine. It was a trial, not only of my
lord Magnus but of the entire Thousand Sons Legion.
The Emperor's edict wounded him, like a father's disapproval and chastisement would wound any child.

'What I told you at Vangelis, that I sought to improve
the reputation of my Legion, in the eyes of the sons of
Guilliman if no other, was in part true. I desire only to
open your eyes to the potential of the psychic and how
it is a boon, a ready weapon to use against our enemies.'

Cestus's expression was stern in the face of Mhotep's
impassioned arguments.

'You saved us all in the lance deck,' said the Ultramarine. 'You probably did the same when we fought what
became of the *Fireblade*. But, your ambition overreaches
you, Mhotep. I have stayed Brynngar's hand, but from
this point on you will remain here in isolation. If we are
successful and can reach Macragge or some other Imperial stronghold, you will face trial and there, your fate
will be decided.'

Cestus got to his feet and turned. As he was about to
leave the room, he paused.

'If you ever invade my mind like that again, I will execute you myself,' he added and left, the cell door sliding
shut behind him.

'How narrow your mind is,' Mhotep hissed, focusing
at once on the reflective sheen of the cell wall. 'How
ignorant you are of what is to come.'

SIXTEEN

Fleet/Kor Phaeron/A storm breaks

'THAT,' SAID ORCADUS, 'is Macragge.'

The Navigator had received instructions from his admiral that whilst they were still in the warp he should make regular reports of their progress. The appearance of the Ultramarines' home world, albeit through the misted lens of the empyrean, was worthy of note and so he had summoned her.

The observation blister was a chamber on the same deck of the *Wrathful* as the bridge and within walking distance. The room was usually reserved for formal gatherings, when officers came together to formalise some business within the Saturnine Fleet. Its grand transparent dome afforded a view of space that lent gravitas to the matters at hand. In the warp, of course, it was strictly off-limits and its eye was kept permanently closed.

The eye was open, but the dome was masked with heavy filters that kept all but the most mundane wavelengths of light out of the blister.

Admiral Kaminska faced away from the Navigator and actually followed Orcadus's gaze through a mirror screen that offered a hazy representation of what he was seeing. To look at the warp, even filtered as it was, would be incredibly dangerous for her.

'If you could see it as I can,' Orcadus hissed, allowing a reverent tone to colour his voice. 'What wonders there are out in the void. There is beauty in the galaxy, for those who can but see it.'

'I'm happy staying blind,' said Kaminska. The view through the filters and reflected by the mirror screen was heavily distorted, but she could make out a crescent-shaped mass of light hanging over the ship. Though she had no frame of reference, she had an impression of enormous distance.

'Macragge,' muttered Orcadus. 'See how it glows, the brightest constellation in this depth of the abyss? All those hard-working souls toiling at its surface; their combined life-spark is refulgent to my eyes. Ultramar is the most heavily populated system in the whole segmentum and the minds of its citizens are bright and full of hope. That is what I mean by beauty. It is a beacon, one that shines amidst the malice and bleakness of the empyrean tide.'

Kaminska continued to regard the dim mirror image of the warp through the minute aperture offered by the filters. Old space-farers' tales were full of the effects the naked warp could have on a human mind. Madness was the most merciful fate, they said: mutation, excruciating spontaneous cancers and even possession by some malfeasant presence all featured prominently. Kaminska felt a flicker of vulnerability, and was glad that only the Navigator was there with her.

'Is this why you summoned me?' she asked, having little time or inclination for a philosophical debate concerning the immaterium. Her mind was on other matters, namely the sudden revival of Mhotep and Cestus's meeting with the Thousand Son. She hoped it would yield some good news.

'No,' Orcadus answered simply, puncturing the admiral's introspection, and pointing to a different region of the warp. It was a dim mass of glowing bluffs, like the top of endless cliffs reaching down into blackness. Above the cliffs was a streak of red.

'I am not well-versed in reading the empyrean tides, Navigator,' she snapped, weary of Orcadus's eccentricities, which were ubiquitous amongst all the great Navigator houses. 'What am I looking at?'

'Formations like these cliffs are common enough in the abyss,' he explained, oblivious to Kaminska's impatience. 'I am steering us well clear of them, and I am certain that our quarry has taken the same route. The formation above them, however, is rather more troubling.'

'Another world, perhaps?' ventured Kaminska. 'There's plenty of new settlement out here near the fringe.'

'I suspected that, but it is not a planet. I believe it is another ship.'

'A second vessel?'

'No. I think it is a fleet.'

'Are they following us?' asked Kaminska, a knot of dread building in her stomach.

'I cannot tell. Distance is relative down here,' the Navigator admitted.

'Could it be the Ultramarines? Their Legion was heading for Calth.'

'It is possible. Calth could be its destination, I suppose.'

'If not, then what is the alternative, Navigator?' Kaminska didn't like where this was going as the knot in her stomach became a fist.

'It could be another Legion fleet,' said Orcadus, leaving the implication hanging.

'You mean more Word Bearers.'

'Yes,' the Navigator confirmed after a moment's pause.

LORD KOR PHAERON of the Word Bearers scowled. 'He's behind schedule,' he said. Aboard the *Infidus Imperator* he and his warriors made their inexorable course towards Ultramar, the great flagship leading the dread fleet of battleships, cruisers, escorts and frigates towards their destiny.

The arch commander of the Legion, favoured of Lorgar, was immense in his panoply of war. Seated upon a throne of black iron, he towered like an all-powerful tyrant, the surveyor of all his deadly works. Votive chains, festooned with tiny silver skulls, and icons of dedication, arched from his shoulder pads to his cuirass. A spiked halo of iron arced across his mighty shoulders, fixed to his armoured backpack. The stout metal gorget fixed around his neck was forged into a high and imperious collar that bore the symbol of the Legion. The tenets of it were etched ostensibly across every surface of Kor Phaeron's armour in the epistles of Lorgar. Parchments unfurled like ragged, script-ridden pennants from studded pauldrons; seals and scraps of vellum covered his leg greaves like patchwork.

In the eyes of the arch-commander there burned a relentless fervour that flowed outwards and ignited the room. It was almost as if any who fell beneath his glowering gaze would be immolated in righteous fire should they be found wanting. His voice was dominance and zeal, his Word the dictate of the primarch. This would be his finest hour, as it was written.

Six Chapter Masters of the Word Bearers stood behind Kor Phaeron, each resplendent in their respective panoplies. They still managed to fill the immense council chamber of the *Infidus Imperator* with their presence. Above them curved a great domed roof hung with smoking censers. The floor was a giant viewscreen, showing a stellar map of the space surrounding Ultramar.

'Our most recent reports indicate that Zadkiel was being followed,' said Faerskarel, Master of the Chapter of the Opening Eye. 'It is possible that he is just showing caution.'

'He has the *Furious Abyss*!' roared Kor Phaeron. 'He should have been able to see off anything that stood in his way. Zadkiel had better know the consequences for us all if we fail.'

Deinos, Master of the Burning Hand Chapter, stepped forwards. 'Lorgar shows Admiral Zadkiel all honour,' he said. In keeping with the name of his Chapter, Deinos's gauntlets were permanently wreathed in flames from gas jets built into his vambraces. 'It was written that we will succeed.'

'Not,' said Kor Phaeron, measuredly, 'that we will do so without great loss. Calth will fall and the Ultramarines with it, that is already decided, but there is plenty of scope for our Legion to lose a great many brothers, and we certainly shall if Zadkiel cannot fulfil his mission.'

'My lord, surely Zadkiel makes his own fate? We should be minded only with the progress of our own fleet.' It was Rukis, the Master of the Crimson Mask Chapter, who spoke. The faceplate of his helmet was wrought to resemble a fearsome red-skinned snarling creature.

'I will not allow our brother to fail us,' hissed Kor Phaeron, intent on the stellar map and the alleged progress of the *Furious Abyss*. 'I had not wanted to use my hand in this matter, but it seems that circumstances allow no other recourse. Much is written of Zadkiel's success and its bearing upon our own. To prosecute the war on Calth, we must risk nothing. Is that understood?'

The Chapter Masters' silence constituted their agreement. Skolinthos, Master of the Ebony Serpent Chapter, broke the quietude once his assent and that of his brothers was clear. Skolinthos's oesophagus had been crushed in the early years of the Great Crusade when it was the Emperor whom the Word Bearers vaunted above all others. His voice crackled sibilantly through a vocal synthesiser on his chest, the honorific of his Chapter somehow perversely apt given his affliction. 'Then how might we assist the admiral?'

'There are still words newly written,' said Kor Phaeron, 'that you do not know of. They concern the warp through which we travel. We can reach Zadkiel even though the *Furious Abyss* lies many days ahead of us. Master Tenaebron?'

Chapter Master Tenaebron bowed in supplication behind his lord. The Chapter of the Void was probably the least respected among the Word Bearers Legion for it was by far the smallest, with less than seven hundred Astartes. There was little glory in its history, used moreover as a reserve force that enacted its missions behind the front line. This grim, dishonourable purpose fell to the Void and Tenaebron, their master, did not complain, for he knew that his Chapter's true role was to create and test new weapons and tactics for the rest of the Legion. It had not gone unnoticed that Lorgar's most recent orders to Tenaebron had concerned the exploitation of the Word Bearers' psychic resources.

'I trust you will require the use of the supplicants?' said Tenaebron.

'How many remain?' asked Kor Phaeron, votive chains jangling as he shifted in his throne.

'One hundred and thirty, my lord,' Tenaebron replied. 'Seventy here on the *Infidus*, thirty on the *Carnomancer* and the remainder are spread throughout the fleet. I have ensured they are kept in a state of readiness; they can be awakened within the hour.'

'Get them ready,' Kor Phaeron ordered. 'How many can we afford to lose?'

'More than half would compromise the masking of the Calth assault,' Tenaebron answered humbly.

'Then be prepared to lose them.'

'Understood, my lord. What will you have them do?'

Kor Phaeron cracked his knuckles in annoyance. There could be no doubt that he had hoped everything would go more smoothly than this. Zadkiel's mission was supposedly easy. The assault on Calth would be far more complex, with much more to go wrong. If Zadkiel could not fulfil his written role, then the problems at Calth would be magnified greatly.

'Give me a storm,' said the arch-commander, darkly.

TENAEBRON LED KOR Phaeron down into the supplicant chambers of the *Infidis Imperator*. The arch-commander had since dismissed the other masters to their respective duties, ignoring their obvious surprise at his bold stratagem. The *Infidis Imperator* was a great and mighty flagship that almost rivalled the immensity of the *Furious Abyss*. It took some time to traverse the proving grounds and ritual chambers, the ranks of Word Bearers honing their battle-skills with bolter and blade in the arenas. Down here, upon every surface, the Word was ubiquitous. Sentences inscribed on bulkheads and support ribs, tomes penned by Lorgar on pulpits overlooking halls and seminary chapels, libraries of lore, the vessel was drenched in the primarch's wisdom and zealotry.

The ship had once been known as the *Raptorous Rex*, a vessel devoted to the Emperor, who had plucked Lorgar from Colchis and placed the Word Bearers at his command. It was a temple to another, more willing and appreciative idol now, the False Emperor of Mankind having been stricken from its corridors.

Tenaebron reached the narrow, high chamber, like a steel canyon, where the supplicants resided. Held in glass blisters on the walls, each served by a bulky life support system feeding oxygen and nutrients, the supplicants slumbered. Curled up and naked, twitching with the force of the power held in their swollen, lacerated craniums it looked like they were dreaming. Their eyes and mouths had grown shut. Some had no facial features at all, their bodies abandoning the need to breathe, eat or experience externally.

A trio of Word Bearers Librarians saluted their Chapter Master as Tenaebron examined the vital-signs on a pict screen, slaved to the individual life supports, in the centre of the room. The Librarians bowed deeply as Kor Phaeron walked in, and genuflected silently before him.

'Rise,' he intoned, and the Librarians obeyed. 'Is everything in preparation?' he asked, directing the question at the Chapter Master.

Tenaebron consulted the data on the pict screen, turned to his lord and nodded. 'Marshal the storm,' he growled. 'Let them be broken by its wrath.'

The Chapter Master nodded again, and proceeded to order his Librarians to activate the cogitators hooked up to the supplicants' blisters. Kor Phaeron left Tenaebron to his duties without further word.

Up on the walls the supplicants stirred, as if the dream had become a nightmare.

ZADKIEL ARRIVED ON the bridge as the storm broke.

The vista below him was bathed in strobing hazard lights as if lashed by lightning. Complicated symbolic maps of the warp shone on the three main viewscreens and indicated that it was in violent flux. Bridge crew, Helmsmaster Sarkorov barking orders at them, bent over their picters, faces picked out in the green glow of reams of scrolling data.

'The warp rebels!' hissed Zadkiel.

'Perhaps not,' muttered Ikthalon. The chaplain, having left Reskiel to his pursuit of their stowaway, had been summoned to the bridge and stood alongside the command throne. 'The supplicants were recently animated. It was probably a foreshadowing of the empyrean's current state of turmoil. I believe that a higher purpose is at work. Confidence, it seems, in our ability to prosecute this mission, is waning.' Ikthalon was careful to keep the barb well-hidden, but the implication at Zadkiel's ineptitude was still there.

The admiral ignored it. The warp storm, and its origin, was of greater concern to him at that moment

'Kor Phaeron?' he wondered.

'I can think of no other, save our arch lord, who would intercede on our behalf.'

Zadkiel sneered as another thought occurred to him.

'It is Tenaebron, no doubt, trying to claim for the Chapter of the Void that which belongs to the Quill.'

'He is ever ambitious,' Ikthalon agreed, keeping his voice level.

Zadkiel assumed his position on the command throne.

'It would be rude,' Zadkiel sneered, 'to deny Tenaebron his sliver of victory. It will be eclipsed utterly by our own. Helmsmaster Sarkorov,' he snapped, 'press on for Macragge. Let the warp take the *Wrathful*.'

CESTUS WAS THROWN against the wall as the *Wrathful* shuddered violently. He was heading back to the bridge in order to convene with Kaminska and the remaining Astartes when the storm wave hit. Debris was flung throughout the corridors, medi-bays were in disarray as desperate orderlies fought to hang on to the wounded, armsmen were smashed against bulkheads and ratings fell to their deaths as the *Wrathful* pitched and yawed. A terrible metallic moaning came from the engine sections as the ship fought to right itself. Cestus could feel the structure flexing and straining through the floor, as if the vessel was on the verge of snapping in two under the strain.

The Ultramarine made his way through the mayhem until he reached the bridge, blast doors opening to allow him access. The crew clung to their posts, Helmsmistress Venkmyer issuing frantic orders set against the unearthly calm of servitors running through their emergency protocols. Drenched in crimson gloom from vermillion alert status, the bridge looked bloody in the half-light.

'Navigator Orcadus, report!' snapped Kaminska, gripping the sides of her command position as the shaking *Wrathful* threatened to dethrone her.

'A storm,' Orcadus's voice said over the bridge vox-caster, the Navigator sounding strained, 'came out of nowhere.'

'Evade it,' ordered Kaminska.

'Admiral, we are already in it!' replied the Navigator.

'Damage control to your posts!' bellowed Kaminska. 'Close off the reactor sections and clear the gun decks.'

Cestus reached the admiral. 'This is the Word Bearers' doing,' he shouted against the din of warning sirens and frantic reports from the crew. Another wave slammed into the *Wrathful*. Bursting pipes vented vapour and gas. Crewmen were thrown off their feet. A viewscreen was sheared off its moorings and fell in a shower of sparks and shattered glass, landing in the middle of the bridge.

'Orcadus, can we ride it out?' asked Kaminska, her eyes on the Ultramarine.

'I see no end to it, admiral.'

'Captain Cestus?' she asked of the Astartes.

'If we drift here and ride it out, the *Furious Abyss* escapes,' Cestus confirmed. 'There is no choice left to us but to drive through it.'

Kaminska nodded grimly. If they failed it would mean the destruction of the ship and the deaths of over ten thousand crew. Her order would condemn them all to their fates.

'Engage the engines to full power!' she ordered. 'Let's break this storm's back!' she snarled with fire in her eyes. 'We'll teach the warp to fear us!'

* * *

FROM WITHIN THE confines of the isolation cell, Mhotep could hear the anarchy outside. He ignored it, poring over the reflective sheen of the polished gunmetal walls instead. A window of fate opened up to him as he channelled his powers. Panic reigned on the *Wrathful*. He saw fire, men and women burning, thousands sacrificed upon the altar of hopeful victory. They became ghosts in his mind's eye, their penitent souls devoured hungrily by the warp and scattered into atoms until only residue remained.

Death awaited on this ship: his death. The certainty of that fact instilled calm in him rather than fear. His place amongst the myriad strands of fate was fixed.

The vista changed and Mhotep's mind ranged beyond the *Wrathful* and into the churning abyss. The *Furious Abyss* loomed through the haze of resolution as a new scene presented itself. The vessel was immense, like a city laid on its side and falling towards the *Wrathful*. Thousands of gun ports opened up like mouths, the primed, glowing barrels of magna-lasers and cannon like tongues ready to roar. The *Furious Abyss* was utterly hideous, a monstrosity of dark crimson steel, and yet the beauty of its majesty overcame any aesthetic offence.

Mhotep drifted further across the gulf, through ersatz reality. As his mind expanded, he could taste the warp, the endless flavours, sounds and sensations of the abyss, calling to him. Probing tendrils pricked at his sanity and the Thousand Son attempted to disengage. He couldn't, and panic rushed into him like a flood. Mhotep mastered it quickly, recognising at once that he was in peril. The warp had seen him and it sought to drive his mind asunder.

It showed him visions of destruction, the spires of Prospero aflame and his Legion cast into the warp. In another vista, he knelt before a throne of black iron in supplication before the icon of the Word Bearers. Screams filled his ears, together with the howling of wolves.

Mhotep clawed back some semblance of control. He fashioned the image of a cyclopean eye in his mind. It glowed with scarlet radiance, and, as if following a beacon to safe harbour, Mhotep used it to guide himself away from the clutches of the empyrean. He emerged at last, drained of all will, of all strength and collapsed to the floor of the cell. The metal was cool against his cheek. Though hard and unyielding, it was the most invigorating salve he had ever felt. He had resisted, though the lines of fate had been laid open to him. Mhotep knew, as he slipped into unconsciousness, what the visions had been about. It was not a lure into madness; it was something far more sinister and invasive. It was temptation.

'THEY ARE LOST,' said Zadkiel, smiling with malice. He looked up at the centre viewscreen, showing little emotion as alarming numbers scrolled past the symbol representing the *Wrathful*. He looked more thoughtful than triumphant. 'Do we have any readings from their engines? Are they still void-worthy?'

'No readings,' Sarkorov replied. 'The storm is too strong.'

'I have seen enough,' Zadkiel said, his response was curt. 'Continue at all speed.'

'You won't wait until we are certain of the *Wrathful*'s destruction?' counselled Ikthalon, a sliver of doubt evident in his voice at Zadkiel's order.

'No, I will not,' answered the admiral. 'Our mission is to reach Macragge in time for Kor Phaeron's assault. I cannot tarry here in order to make certain of what is inevitable. We need to be out of this region and back on our way. Return to your chambers, chaplain. Have the supplicants watch for the *Wrathful*'s death throes. Even in a warp storm such as this, that many deaths should make some ripple.'

'As you wish, my lord.' Ikthalon bowed and left the bridge.

The *Furious Abyss* resumed its former heading in short order. Kor Phaeron's plan had worked in so far as they were undamaged by the storm. Whether it had also put paid to the *Wrathful* did not concern the admiral.

A petty creature might have been angry at his lord's meddling, but Zadkiel was sanguine. Let lesser minds worry on such things. The Word would play out as written. Nothing else mattered.

SEVENTEEN

Strategy/Out of the warp/Formaska in sight

CESTUS TURNED HIS head away as the warp glared against the *Wrathful*'s port side.

The force of it shone through the metal of the ship's hull, as if the *Wrathful* was made of paper, transparent against the light of the abyss. Cestus heard screams and laughter as men's minds were stripped away by it. He threw himself against the housing of a torpedo tube entrance, willing himself not to look. Saphrax and Brother Excelinor were beside him and they too averted their gaze.

Cestus had left the bridge almost as soon as he'd arrived. He'd gathered his fellow Ultramarines to patrol the corridors, knowing full well what awaited them and the crew of the *Wrathful*. Two teams of what was left of the honour guard and Brynngar's wolves moved through the decks and corridors in an effort to steel resolve, and snuff out manifesting psychosis wherever they found it.

Cestus hoped the presence of the Astartes would be enough. The need for them to be the Angels of the Emperor was greater than any other.

'It is as if the warp is at their very beck and call,' bellowed Excelinor, his voice tinny through his Corvus-pattern nose cone.

Cestus did not reply, for he knew of the terrible truth of his battle-brother's words. Moving defiantly down the corridor, the infernal light of the empyrean was scarlet through his eyelids. Silhouettes of bodies fell in the blazing vista; men and women fell to their knees, weeping and screaming; a gunshot rang out as an officer turned his sidearm on himself. The sound of a female voice was contiguous with it, reciting paragraphs from the Saturnine Fleet's rules and regulations in an effort to stave off the madness.

Visions forced their way into the Ultramarine's mind: the beneficent Emperor, mighty upon his golden throne and the majesty of the Imperial Palace, and Terra, the beacon of enlightenment in a galaxy surrounded by darkness. Then he saw it burning, continents peeling off and red gouts of magma boiling away into space.

He was an Astartes. He was stronger than this.

'Do not give in to madness,' he cried aloud to all who could still listen. 'Hold on and heed the Imperial Truth.'

For a brief moment, it looked like that the warp would engulf them, but then the visions melted away and the screaming ebbed and died. The ship was still again. The *Wrathful* had emerged on the other side.

Cestus breathed hard as the blazing light diminished, leaving a painful afterglow. He adjusted quickly and opened his eyes to see that his brothers were still with him. The shadows came back, too, swallowing the dead. The Ultramarine nodded slowly to Saphrax and

Excelinor and opened up communications through his gorget as he surveyed the carnage around him.

'Admiral, are you still with us?'

There was a pause before the vox-link crackled and Kaminska's voice replied.

'We are through the storm,' she said, similarly breathless. 'Your plan was successful.'

'Medical teams are required at my location as well as fleet morticians,' Cestus informed her.

'Very well.'

'Admiral,' Cestus added, 'as soon as recovery is underway, I request your presence in the conference chamber.'

'Of course, my lord. I shall be there momentarily. Kaminska out.'

HALF AN HOUR later, when the crews began to organise themselves into shifts to recover the bodies and the wounded, Kaminska had Helmsmistress Venkmyer tour the worst-hit sections of the ship and make a report of their losses.

In normal circumstances, Kaminska would have done this herself, demonstrating to the crew that their leader cared about the deaths and the terrible tragedy that had befallen them. More urgent matters pressed for her attention, however, and she was not about to ignore the request of an Astartes.

So, she had made her way to the conference chamber as bidden. Within, the remaining Astartes force awaited her.

'Welcome, admiral,' said Cestus, standing at the edge of the oval table with Saphrax to his right and his other battle-brothers arrayed around him. The Space Wolf, Brynngar, sat opposite with his warriors, but did not acknowledge the admiral's arrival.

'Please sit,' the Ultramarine captain said sternly, despite trying to soften his mood with a small smile.

Now the council was assembled, Cestus surveyed the room, looking into the eyes of each person present.

'It is beyond all doubt,' he began, 'that the Word Bearers are in league with the warp. They are utterly lost.'

Hardened faces returned his gaze as the Ultramarine articulated what they already knew in their hearts.

'With such dark allies at their disposal, together with the *Furious Abyss*, they are a formidable opponent,' Cestus continued, 'but we have a slim hope. I have discovered the nature of the Word Bearers' plan and how it is to be employed.'

Brynngar twitched at the remark. The Space Wolf clearly knew of the methods that the Ultramarine had used to discover the information they needed. He also knew of Mhotep's subsequent revival. The absence of the Thousand Son from the conference spoke volumes as to his demeanour on that matter.

'Make no mistake,' Cestus began, 'what the Word Bearers are planning is audacious in the extreme. In assaulting Macragge, there are several factors that any enemy must consider before committing his forces,' he explained. 'Firstly, the planetary fleet held in high orbit consists of a flotilla of several cruisers and escorts. It would not be easy for any foe, however determined or well-armed, to break through without significant losses. Should he be successful, though, the enemy must then face the static orbital deterrents on the surface: Macragge's battery of defence lasers.'

'And the *Furious Abyss* is supposed to achieve this feat?' scoffed Brynngar. 'Impossible.'

Cestus nodded in agreement.

'Had you asked me the same an hour ago I would have concurred,' the Ultramarine admitted. 'The Word Bearers strategy has two key elements. It all begins at Formaska, which the Word Bearers plan to hit with cyclonic torpedoes to destroy it.'

'I know little of Ultramar,' growled the Wolf Guard, 'but Formaska is a dead moon. Why not use their cyclonics against Macragge directly?'

'A direct assault against Macragge would be suicide. Its defence lasers would cripple their fleet before they made landfall and render any attempt to subdue Guilliman untenable,' he explained. 'The debris from Formaska's destruction will achieve their ends indirectly. The Legion will divert forces to the aid of Macragge caught in the asteroid storm of the moon's demise and the Word Bearers will strike as they are divided and take them utterly by surprise.'

'I've seen it,' said Brynngar, 'on Proxus XII. An asteroid passed too close and came apart. It was a feral planet. Those people thought the world was ending. Fire was falling from the sky. Every impact was like an atomic hit. It won't destroy Macragge, but it'll kill millions.'

'That is not all,' Cestus continued. 'The *Furious Abyss* will then use the debris like a shield, allowing them to get past the warning stations and satellites around Macragge and draw close enough for a viral payload to be effective. Only that ship is powerful enough to weather the inevitable storm of fire from the defence lasers. The death toll from the viral strike will be near-total. Guilliman and the Legion will be divided, some of our forces probably destroyed on Macragge, when the remainder of the Word Bearers' fleet will strike. I do not know whether we could recover from such a blow, should it succeed.'

'What then, is to be done?' the Wolf Guard asked gruffly.

'We are nearing Macragge and soon will be out of the warp,' said the Ultramarine, a nod from Kaminska confirming his words. 'So too are our enemies. It will require discipline, guile and timing.' Cestus paused, and looked around the room again, his gaze ended on Kaminska. 'Most of all it will require sacrifice.'

SPACE RUPTURED AND spat out the *Furious Abyss*, edged hard in the diamond light of Macragge's sun.

Shoals of predators shimmered out alongside it, like sea creatures leaping around the bow of a ship. Caught in the anathema of reality, they coiled in on themselves and seethed out of existence, their psychic essence dissipating without the warp to sustain them.

The *Furious Abyss* looked little worse than it had when it had left Thule. The attack of the escort squadron had destroyed some of the gun batteries on its dorsal and ventral surfaces, and there were countless tiny pockmarks on its hull from the impacts of doomed fighter craft that had crashed into it after their crews had lost their minds. Those scars did nothing to diminish the majesty of the vast scarlet ship, however. It took a full minute to emerge from the warp rift torn before it, and in those moments the warp was full of nothing but slabs of hull plating and engine cowlings all streaming into real space.

Every warning station around Macragge instantly recognised the scale of the ship and demanded its identity. No reply was forthcoming.

THE IMAGE OF Macragge filled the central viewport on the bridge of the *Furious Abyss*. Flanking it were tactical readouts of the system, which were full of early warning stations and military satellites.

'There it is,' said Zadkiel. 'Hateful is it not? Like a boulder squatting in the path of the future.'

Magos Gureod stood beside Zadkiel, mechadendrites clicking like insectoid limbs, withered arms folded across his chest.

'It evokes no emotion,' the magos replied neutrally.

Zadkiel sniffed his mild contempt at the passionless Mechanicum drone.

'As a symbol, it has no equal,' he said. 'The majesty of a stagnant universe. The ignorance of the powerful. The Ultramarines could have done anything with the worlds under their dominion, and they chose to forge this tired echo of a past that never was.'

Gureod remained unmoved. He had come to bear witness to the launching of the torpedoes that would end a world, the unbridled destructive forces yielded by the mech-science of Mars's devotion to the Omnissiah. The magos was standing in the position once occupied by Baelanos, who had fallen at Bakka.

'I take it your presence means that my former assault-captain has been recovered?' Zadkiel snapped, annoyed at Gureod's unwillingness to bask in his self-perceived reflected glory.

'He dreams fitfully, my lord. When the sus-an membrane failed and he roused, somewhat unexpectedly, I was forced to take more drastic methods to secure him,' said the magos.

'See that he does not waken again until the transition is complete. Once Formaska is destroyed, we shall be joining Kor Phaeron's forces on the ground. Baelanos is to be part of that invasion force.'

'Yes, my lord.' Gureod said, showing no fear.

Zadkiel turned his attention back to the viewport.

All was in place now. He would lead the assault that would be remembered forever in history.

A few moments passed. Then the bridge vox-units crackled.

'Awaiting your mark, admiral,' said Kor Phaeron's voice, transmitted across the system from Calth. Even at these relatively short distances, only the most advanced system could allow communication between the two ships without the need for an astropath.

'It shall be forthcoming,' said Zadkiel, turning his attention to another viewscreen. 'Master Malforian,' he intoned, awaiting the grizzled countenance of his weapon master.

The nightmarish visage of the badly injured Word Bearer was forthcoming.

'At your command, my lord,' Malforian responded.

'Open the frontal torpedo apertures and load the first wave of cyclonics,' Zadkiel commanded with relish. 'It begins at Formaska. Let us unleash devastation and bring about a new era of man.'

Sarkorov snapped orders at the bridge crew, and despatched runners as the *Furious Abyss* prepared for battle stations. The navigation crew began orienting the ship towards Formaska, its prow arc aimed like a sniper's sight on his kill.

The moon was on the screen. Deep lava-filled gulleys wormed their way across its continents, broken by boiling seas.

'The primitives of ancient Macragge thought Formaska was the eye of a god, and that it was bloodshot with anger,' Zadkiel said, to himself more than the unappreciative Magos. 'Sometimes, when the lava fields grew, they thought the eye had opened and looked down on them as prey. They prophesied the day when the god would finally decide to reach down and consume them all. That day has arrived,' he concluded.

'Admiral,' the sibilant voice of Chaplain Ikthalon came through on the bridge vox.

'What is it, chaplain?' Zadkiel snapped.

'The supplicants are stirring,' Ikthalon told him. 'There is movement in the warp. It seems that our pursuers have yet to give up the fight.'

'See that they do not interfere,' snarled Kor Phaeron from the long wave vox, before Zadkiel could reply. 'I'm bringing the fleet into an assault pattern. Guilliman knows we are here by now. Fulfil your mission, Zadkiel.'

'So it is written,' replied Zadkiel, 'so it shall be.' He returned to Malforian. 'Your status, weapon master?'

'A few more minutes, my liege,' Malforian replied. 'We are encountering some problems with the torpedo apertures.'

'Inform me as soon as we're ready to fire the cyclonics,' ordered Zadkiel, his tone betraying his impatience at the unforeseen delay.

'My lord,' Helmsmaster Sarkorov interrupted, 'the *Wrathful* is coming abeam. They are priming weapons.'

Zadkiel exhaled his annoyance. He should have excised this thorn from his side long ago.

'Malforian,' he barked into the vox, 'send all targeting solutions to the bridge once the Imperial lap dogs are in our sights. The *Wrathful* does not deserve the honour of dying as a part of this history, but we shall grant them that honour nonetheless.'

The *Wrathful* appeared on the left viewscreen. She had lost half her guns down one side and was followed by a tail of wreckage tumbling out of her ravaged engine and cargo areas. Her hull was weathered and pitted by the lashes of the warp, covered in the tooth marks of empyrean predators.

Zadkiel smiled maliciously when he saw the wrecked ship. He would derive great pleasure from this.

'Let us finish her.'

THE WRATHFUL LIMPED from the warp and went immediately to battle stations. Aft thrusters burning as hot as they were able, the once formidable Imperial vessel drove head on towards the waiting form of the *Furious Abyss*. Diverting power to its port side, the great ship turned grindingly slowly on its aft axis until its still-functioning broadsides were presented to the foe.

Beams of azure light lit up all the way down the *Wrathful's* flank, and in seconds the blazing fury of her lances was unleashed. Explosions rippled down the armoured hull of the *Furious Abyss*, together with the immense blast flares of shield impacts. These wounds were a mere sting to a beast such as this and the Word Bearer vessel responded with a devastating salvo.

As the crimson light rays of the *Furious's* broadside cannons spat out, the *Wrathful* was already moving, trying to bring the enemy vessel's prow abeam of their lances. The shields of the Imperial ship disintegrated against the assault and the aft decks were raked by deadly fire, explosive impacts sending out chunks of debris and spilling swathes of crew. Still, the *Wrathful* endured, its last ditch manoeuvre bringing it away from the deadly barrage. Torpedoes soared from the vessel's prow, followed by a second volley from the lances. Again, the *Furious* was stung and dorsal cannons swung in their mounts to bring their munitions to bear. Incendiaries crumpled against the *Wrathful's* swerving prow, fully extended broadsides punching ragged holes through its hull armour.

Annoyed at the tenacity of this little wasp, the mighty *Furious Abyss* turned to present its full armament against their aggressor. The damage sustained by the *Wrathful* had slowed it, but even still it could have fled if it had wanted to. Instead, the Imperial vessel stood its ground, making a defiant last stand. Lances flashing, the *Wrathful* poured everything it had left at the Word Bearers. It wasn't enough. The *Furious Abyss* had turned, and, now, it unleashed devastation.

ZADKIEL OBSERVED THE short-lived battle from the bridge. The *Wrathful* was in their sights. The might of his ship was at his disposal.

'Crush them,' he snarled.

Malforian replied his affirmation. Light and fire filled the viewscreen a moment later as the *Furious's* guns wrecked the Imperial vessel. Its engines died, and great fissures were rent in its hull as it slowly drifted, pulled by the gravity well of Formaska. As the *Wrathful* fell away, sparks flashed sporadically, rendering it in a grim cast, as vented coolant pipes billowed in hazy plumes.

'I had expected more from a son of Guilliman,' Zadkiel admitted. 'How could such a desperate plan ever succeed? The Ultramarines are deserving of their death warrant.'

'Lord Zadkiel.' It was Sarkorov again.

Zadkiel turned to face him.

'What is it, helmsmaster?' he snapped.

'Shuttles, my liege,' he explained, 'heading for the port side.'

Zadkiel was nonplussed.

'How many?'

'Fifteen, my lord,' Sarkorov replied. 'Too close for lances.'

Zadkiel paused for a moment, still confused as to this latest Imperial gambit. The answer came swiftly.

'They seek to gain entry through the torpedo apertures,' he said.

'Should I give the order to close them, Lord Zadkiel?'

'Do it,' Zadkiel snapped, 'and engage dorsal cannons. Bring them down!'

EIGHTEEN

Gauntlet/Infiltration/Dark dreams

BRYNNGAR SMILED AS the shuttle shuddered, spirals of flak and countermeasures hammering against its hull.

Rujveld and the Blood Claws sat in the tight crew compartment with him. They were strapped down in their shuttle couches, braced across the shoulders, chest and waist. The engines were screaming, and intermittent flashes from the explosions outside threw sharp light into the compartment. The small vessel was armoured, but it wasn't designed to take this punishment. Every bolt and stanchion was straining with the speed.

'Do you hear it, lads?' he roared above the din, utterly at ease.

His Blood Claws, even Rujveld, looked back perplexed.

'It is the call to combat,' he told them proudly. 'Those are the arms of Mother Fenris! That's the embrace of war!'

The Wolf Guard howled and the Blood Claws howled with him.

Beyond the vision slits, it and several other shuttles soared through the void towards the *Furious Abyss*. Deployed before the suicide attack, the *Wrathful*'s feint had given them the time they needed to close the gap. It had provided a chance to reach the gaping apertures of the vessel's torpedo tubes before being scattered into debris by its guns.

DORSAL GUNS PULSED and rocked in their turrets as the *Furious Abyss* sought to obliterate the attacker's force. In the third shuttle, Cestus saw three of his sister vessels explode under a hail of flak. They broke and split apart, their desperate speed abruptly arrested as if they were a sail boat breaking up on the rocks of some ragged cliff line. The bodies of naval armsmen spilled from the crew compartments, frozen in spasms of pain as they were exposed to the void.

Three of his battle-brothers were alongside the Ultramarine captain: Lexinal, Pytaron and Excelinor helping to fill up the compartment with their armoured bulk. They stared impassively into space as the flash of explosions was thrown through the viewports, and the armoured hull shook. Their lips moved as they swore silent Oaths of Moment.

Cestus did the same, watching three more shuttles shredded apart by heavy turret fire.

'Come on,' he urged through gritted teeth, the gaping maw of the torpedo aperture getting ever closer. 'Come on.'

'IMPACT IN ONE minute!' said the vox from the shuttle's pilot.

'One minute from mother's love!' shouted Brynngar, taking a firm grip on Felltooth. Embarkation would need to be swift; there could be enemy forces already in position to repel any boarders. For a moment, he wondered whether or not Cestus had made it through the fusillade. Putting the thought out of his mind, he took up the battle cry once more. They were almost in.

'She's waiting for us there! Mother Fenris, mother of war!'

'Mother of war!' yelled the Blood Claws. 'Mother of war! Mother of hate!'

A few feet from the aperture, a stray round struck the left aerofoil of the shuttle and it spiralled wildly out of control. Exploding shrapnel shattered the front viewing arc; the sound of breaking armourglas could even be heard in the troop compartment. The pilot died with a shard of hot metal in his neck, before the icy cool of space froze him and his desperate co-pilot to their flight couches. Brynngar's shuttle dipped sharply away from the aperture and downward into another void entirely.

A SHUTTLE EXPLODED, its nose sheared off by a shell casing thrown out of the *Furious Abyss*'s gun decks. The remaining craft looped up beneath the battleship's ventral surface, the valleys and peaks of the city-sized ship streaking past.

Cestus saw another vessel explode, the bursting shrapnel shredding much of its frontal arc. It dipped, engines blazing ineffectually, and fell downward until it was lost from view behind a slab of crimson hull.

Ahead, the torpedo apertures were closing.

'More speed!' Cestus roared into his helmet vox.

The blazing shuttle engines screeched even louder.

A snatched glimpse through the viewport showed a third shuttle, banking sharply in an attempt to avoid the flak fire and arrow back towards the battleship. Its retro engines flared as it braked. It didn't slow fast enough and slammed into the hull beside the torpedo aperture. The fat metal body crumpled under the impact and split. Broken bodies were cast into the void. They were wearing the blue armour of the Ultramarines.

Saphrax and Amryx are dead, thought Cestus bitterly.

Twisting sharply, the shuttle found a way through the rapidly diminishing aperture. As the *Furious Abyss* swallowed them, Cestus thought he heard the explosions of the shuttles following them as they crashed against the sealed hull.

'Brace!' yelled the pilot.

Tortured metal boomed. Cestus was thrown against the restraints of his grav-couch and felt them stretch and pull against his cuirass.

A terrible twisting, howling sound, like a metal earthquake, filled the Ultramarine's ears.

'Umbilicals away!' said the pilot's voice.

The hatch in the roof of the passenger compartment slid open. White vapour filled the shuttle. 'Pressurising!' shouted the pilot.

Cestus knew what was next and hammered the icon on his chest that would disengage the harness. It came apart quickly and he was on his feet, his battle-brothers beside him. Excelinor, Pytaron and Lexinal, two with bolters low slung and another carrying a plasma gun: they would have to be enough. Cestus checked the load in his bolt pistol and unsheathed his sword, thumbing the activation stud that sent frantic lines of power coursing through the blade.

'Courage and honour!' he yelled, and his battle-brothers returned the battle cry.

Explosive bolts detonated like gunshots. The second hatch was flung open, and the long dark throat of the torpedo tube opened up above them.

Cestus stormed through the short umbilicus, through the hatch and into the tube. It sloped upwards and was wide enough for an Astartes to walk with his head bowed. Its ribbed metal interior was caked in ice. The shuttle had pumped air into it, and the vapour in that air had frozen instantly.

'Move!' ordered the Ultramarine captain, and headed upwards.

As Cestus led the way up the torpedo tube, the sounds of thundering guns and shell impacts echoed dimly through the structure of the *Furious Abyss*, a terrible chorus welcoming them onto the ship.

Cestus saw light ahead: the fires of a forge. He had his bolt pistol up in front of him, ready to fire. The light was coming through a thick armourglas window in a heavy hatch, sealing the far end of the tube.

'Charges!' he ordered.

Excelinor and Pytaron reacted quickly, planting a cluster of krak grenades around the weak points of the hatch. Charges primed, the Astartes retreated as one. A few feet from the entrance, Cestus bellowed, 'Now!'

A muffled explosion radiated through the tube, echoing off the concave interior, and the hatch fell away in a shower of sparks and fire.

Combat protocols and stratagems learned when he was a neophyte and honed in countless conflicts throughout the Great Crusade cycled through Cestus's battle-attuned mind. Bursting onto the ship, the Ultramarines found themselves amidst the massive workings of an ordnance deck: torpedo cranes, ammunition and fuel hoppers; cavernous spaces criss-crossed with gantries and crowded with gangs of sweating menials were all in abundance.

With tactical precision, the Astartes fanned out. Cestus drove forward with Lexinal, the punch of his battle-brother's plasma gun backing up the ferocity of the Ultramarine captain at close quarters.

A group of deck hands came at them with a clutch of heavy tools. Cestus swept low through their clumsy attacks and rose quickly, cutting through two with a savage criss-cross strike and killing a third with a head-butt. Barking fire from his bolt pistol put paid to two more. An actinic flash sent the temperature warnings in his battle-helm spiking as a beam of plasma ignited a fuel hopper. Fire blossomed in plumes of orange and white, twinned with billowing smoke. A squad of rushing armsmen were incinerated in the blaze and the heavy stubber mount, hastily erected above, was thrown to oblivion.

Left and right, Excelinor and Pytaron let rip with their bolters, creating a deadly crossfire that shredded anything that dared to advance through it. They surged steadily into the deck, despatching targets with brutal efficiency, but these were only ratings and armsmen. Cestus knew that the Astartes of the Word Bearers would be coming. They had to act quickly and disable the cyclonics before the real threat arrived. Without the destruction of Formaska, the Word Bearers could not fulfil their plan and get close enough to Macragge to unleash the viral strain.

His super-advanced mind skipping ahead to the tactical tasking to come, Cestus almost missed the scarred-faced officer flying at him with a power mace.

This one was Astartes, although he wore a half-armour variant of full battle-plate. Most of the bottom half of his face was destroyed and had been replaced with a metal grille. Deep pink scar lines ran like fat veins up his jaw and across his cheek bones.

'Quail before the might of the Word,' he bellowed, voice metallic and resonant through the augmetics.

Cestus parried a deft swing of the mace with his power sword. Arcs of miniature lightning danced across the two weapons as they were locked in a brief, pyrotechnic struggle. The Ultramarine broke away and brought up his bolt pistol, only for the grille-faced Word Bearer to smash it out of his grasp. Pain lanced through Cestus's fingers, even though his armour bore the brunt of the blow, numbing his shoulder.

'Lorgar will guide us to victory,' snarled the Word Bearer, allowing his fervour to fuel his swings, though they dulled his accuracy.

Cestus wove out of the death arc from an overhand smash designed to finish him and brought his blazing blade onto the Word Bearer's bare head. Slicing through flesh, bone and, eventually, armour, he sheared the warrior in two, the corpse flopping on either side of the blow.

'Know that Guilliman is righteous,' Cestus snarled, gritting back the pain to reclaim his fallen pistol. Re-armed, he drove on into the building firestorm, focused on the killing.

'WHERE ARE THEY?' demanded Zadkiel.

'All over the gun decks,' came the reply from one of Malforian's subordinates. In the weapon master's absence, Zadkiel assumed that he was dead or otherwise incapacitated. 'Reports say they're Astartes.'

'They'll be going for the torpedo payload,' said Zadkiel, mainly to himself.

The admiral turned his attentions to his helmsmaster. 'Sarkorov, are we in position to launch?'

'Yes, my lord, but we cannot deploy the torpedoes while the deck is contested.'

Zadkiel swore beneath his breath.

'Reskiel,' he snarled into the throne vox with growing annoyance.

The sergeant-commander responded after a moment's pause.

'I'm calling off the hunt for our interloper. Gather your brethren and head for the ordnance decks at once. Destroy any Astartes you find on that deck. Do you understand?'

Reskiel replied in the affirmative and the vox link died.

'If the attack is to be delayed, I will return to my sanctum,' said Magos Gureod, already blending away into the darkness.

'Do as you must,' Zadkiel muttered, his agitation obvious, the veneer of calm ever slipping. 'Ikthalon,' he snarled into the vox, a plan forming in his mind.

'My lord,' the sibilant voice of the chaplain replied.

'Wake the supplicants.'

THERE WAS NO need to spare the supplicants. The *Furious Abyss* had reached its destination. The mission was over. Their role had been to help with the manipulation of the warp and fend off attacks against the ship. Zadkiel's order meant using them to destruction.

The streams of nutrients were replaced with psychoactive drugs. Restraints snapped apart and cortical stimulators crackled, waking the supplicants from their comatose state to halfway between sleep and waking, where sensations and nightmares alike were real. Some of the supplicants, the ones whose mouths and throats still worked, moaned and mewled as they slithered out of their restraints onto the floor. Some convulsed as unfamiliar impulses flooded their muscles. One or two died, their hearts finally giving out.

As part of his chaplain's attire, Ikthalon drew a heavy scarlet cowl over his battle-helm to prevent excess psychic energy from staining his mind, and moved carefully among the waking supplicants, inspecting readouts and checking for swallowed tongues. One by one, he switched off the inhibitor circuits, the loops of psychoactive material that kept the supplicants' minds from feeding back into the *Furious Abyss*. The cogitators hooked in to the debased creatures' consciousness fed them the image of the ship's prow, the engineering works behind the plasma lance and the ordnance decks below.

Finally, the supply of stupefying narcotics and soothing brain-wave instigators was cut off and the supplicants were given their last silent orders.

CESTUS SPRAYED A gantry with bolter fire. Bodies plummeted and crumpled against his fury. The Ultramarines had gained a foothold on the primary ordnance deck, but Cestus could still see no sign of the Space Wolves. He hoped that they had not shared the same fate as Saphrax. The schematic as witnessed in the vision bestowed upon him by Mhotep filled his eidetic memory. The cluster of cyclonics destined for Formaska was at the end of the deck, doubtless in mid-transit to the torpedo apertures. The viral payload was secured in a drop chamber in the hull. There was no way to get to it.

They would have to hobble the Word Bearers' plan at its first juncture.

Barking fire from a pair of pintle-mounted cannons set up on a loading platform above had the Ultramarines pinned for a moment. Cestus's battle-brothers regrouped behind a pair of empty fuel bowsers and the housing of a torpedo crane.

Lexinal, plasma gun cradled in his gauntlets, slid in beside Cestus.

'What now, captain?' he asked as the barrage above them intensified.

Cestus memorised an open stretch of deck and then the huge metal cliff face of the *Furious Abyss*'s prow, broken by the loading mechanisms and the torpedo tubes. He visualised an industrial tangle on the other side, including giant hoppers stacked with further munitions and the rearing masses of arming chambers where yet more ordnance was stored.

'We have to clear the deck and then get to the munitions store and deploy our melta bombs,' he replied.

'What about Brynngar?' Lexinal asked, using a break in the fusillade to fire off a snap shot that bathed the loading platform in super-heated plasma. The screams died in the raging battle din.

'Once we take out the cyclonics, we link up with whoever is left and do what damage we can,' said Cestus, once Lexinal had resumed cover.

The Ultramarine nodded his understanding.

Cestus relayed the same order through his helmet vox on a discrete frequency in Ultramar battle-cant to Pytaron and Excelinor. The two battle-brothers flanked the captain's position, heavy-duty munitions crates in front of them being chipped apart by persistent fire.

Cestus glanced between the two bowsers. The *Furious*'s crewmen, in dark scarlet overalls and fatigues, had been hit hard by the shock of the assault. Dozens of them lay dead around the torpedo hatches or shot down from the gantries and cranes. The Astartes has exacted a heavy toll, but the enemy were regrouping and reinforcements covered their losses in short order.

There was no time to delay.

'On me,' Cestus cried, 'battle formation theta-epsilon, Macragge in ascendance!'

He vaulted the bowser, bolt pistol flaring and lasgun impacts spattered his cuirass. Cestus held his sword in salute stance, in front of his face and the upright blade deflected energy blasts from his battle-helm. Twin bolters blazed, cross-shaped muzzle flashes glaring, as Excelinor and Pytaron moved in staggered battle formation to Cestus's left. Lexinal took the right flank, firing his plasma gun in controlled bursts to prevent the deadly weapon from overheating.

Towards the last third of the deck, they broke up, each taking a channel into the industrial tangle of machinery. Troops of armsmen had mobilised and came at Cestus with shock mauls and lengths of spiked chain. The Ultramarine captain cut them down, Guilliman's name a mantra on his lips. Amidst the killing, he noticed an access portal to the ordnance deck and wondered why the Word Bearers' Astartes had not yet shown themselves.

'Link up and force through to the cyclonics,' Cestus ordered through his helmet vox as he moved into a labyrinth of munitions.

His battle-brothers obeyed and together they converged on a pair of cyclonics, still harnessed in their mobile racking.

Shots spattered from gantries above, most of the las-bolts and hard rounds smacking into cranes and clusters of machinery. Cestus saw a lucky shot ricochet from Lexinal's breastplate and he staggered. A second burst from a heavy cannon somewhere above them raked his leg greave and he was down. Out of the corner of his eye, Cestus saw a group of armsmen converging on the prone Ultramarine. A las-bolt clipping his pauldron, Cestus twisted as he ran, slamming a fresh magazine in his bolt pistol and discharging a furious burst into the armsmen. Two disappeared in a red haze, another crumpled to the ground nursing the wet crater in his stomach. Cestus didn't see the rest. Lexinal was getting to his feet when a round struck an active fuel bowser. The resulting explosion engulfed the Astartes in coruscating flame, the blast wave throwing him half way across the deck.

The Ultramarine captain averted his gaze, muttering a battle-oath, and refocused ahead.

'Deploy incendiaries,' Cestus ordered when they finally reached the first batch of cyclonics. Pytaron unclipped a melta bomb from his armour, disengaging the magna-clamp that kept it in place. Excelinor provided covering fire with his bolter.

'Brynngar!' Cestus shouted into his helmet vox, crouching beside Excelinor as he desperately tried to make contact. 'Brynngar respond.'

Dead air came back at him. Either the wolf had been killed or he was in another part of the ship where they couldn't reach him.

'Charges deployed,' reported Pytaron. As he turned to his captain, a heavy round struck him in the neck, piercing his gorget. He clutched the wound with one hand, the melta bomb detonator in the other, and fell to one knee as blood streamed down his breastplate.

Larraman cells within Pytaron's body worked hard to slow the bleeding and speed up clotting, but the wound was serious. Even an Astartes enhanced physiology would be unable to save the battle-brother.

'Take it,' Pytaron said, gurgling his words through blood.

Cestus took the detonator, his hands around Pytaron's.

'You will be honoured…' Cestus's voice trailed away as the air around him suddenly turned cold, receptors built into his battle-plate registering a severe drop in temperature. For an awful second, he thought that the deck had de-pressurised and the void would claim them all.

With the cold came screaming: a thousand voices, echoing out from the inside of Cestus's head.

It was not the void, reaching into the ship to freeze them solid. It was something far worse. Prickling talons probing his mental defences like ice blades reminded Cestus of his earlier encounter with Mhotep aboard the *Wrathful*.

'Psyker!' he hissed with sudden realisation. 'Psyker!' he shouted this time to get Excelinor's attention. 'We are under attack.'

One of the *Furious Abyss*'s crewmen stumbled out into the open. He clutched an autogun loosely in one hand, his arm hanging down by his side. With his other hand, he appeared to be trying to tear out his own tongue.

Cestus shot the man in the chest. He bucked violently and fell still against the deck. He then turned and saw Excelinor slowly raise his boltgun to his head.

'No,' Cestus cried, yanking his fellow battle-brother to his senses.

'Voices in my head... I can't stop them,' whispered Excelinor through his vox, still struggling with his bolter.

'Fight it!' Cestus snarled at him, feeling the shreds of his own sanity slowly being devoured by the unseen force of the warp. They had to get out, right now. The Ultramarine captain seized Excelinor's arm, the world starting to blur around him, and hauled him towards the access portal.

'Come on,' Cestus breathed as the floor shifted beneath him and the walls began to melt.

Try as he might, Cestus could not keep himself from falling into madness. The last thing he remembered was his fist closing on the detonator and the rush of fire.

'THEY THINK IT's alive,' breathed Zadkiel, standing before his command throne, 'This ship has been a part of them for so long that the supplicants regard it as an extension of their own bodies. No. It is a host, in which they are parasites. There won't be a mind left intact among them. The enemy will be driven mad long before we kill them.'

'Your orders, admiral?' The voice of Sergeant-Commander Reskiel through the throne vox interrupted Zadkiel's monologue.

'You have gained the area outside of the ordnance deck?' he asked, imagining the warriors of Reskiel looming in the corridor intersections.

'Yes, my lord,' Reskiel answered. Just prior to entering the ordnance deck, the sergeant-commander and his warriors had been ordered to secure the exits, Zadkiel having no desire for his forces to be caught up in the psychic attack.

'Although, a massive detonation destroyed much of the tertiary access points, as yet, we have been unable to break through,' Reskiel added.

'Is it possible that the Astartes escaped the deck?' the irritation in Zadkiel's voice obvious, even through the vox link.

There was a short pause as Reskiel considered his response.

'It is possible, yes.'

'Find them, Reskiel. Do it or do not return to my bridge.' Zadkiel cut the vox link abruptly.

The admiral turned to a secondary force of Word Bearers, who had assembled behind him.

'Secure the ordnance deck, port and starboard access portals. Get in there and recover what is left of our cyclonic payload.'

'Yes, my lord,' said a chorus of voices from the assembled Word Bearers.

'Do so, now!' Zadkiel raged and the clattering sound of booted feet erupted behind him as the Word Bearers deployed.

The infiltrators had to be stopped. Despite the psychic assault, Zadkiel needed to be sure that any further loose ends had been tied up. Nothing must prevent the bombardment against Formaska. Without it, the rest of the plan could not proceed. He would not allow his soul to be forfeit from Kor Phaeron's rage at his failure. Success was inevitable. It had to be. It was written.

MACRAGGE'S NATIVES, THE people who had been there before the Emperor's Great Crusade had rediscovered them, had believed in a hell that was very specific in its cruelties. Its circles each held a certain breed of sinner, all suffering punishments appropriate to their misdeeds. The further in a dead man went, the more horrible and varied his punishments became, until the very worse of the worst – traitors to Macragge's Battle Kings, and those who had betrayed their own families – were held in the very centre in a series of torments that a living mind could not comprehend and upon which the legends refused to speculate.

Those beliefs had survived alongside the Imperial Truth, as folk tales and allegories. Macragge's circles of hell were the subject of epic verse, cautionary tales and colourful curses.

Cestus was, at that moment, in the circle of hell reserved for cowards.

'Run!' shouted the taskmaster. 'You ran from everything! You sacrificed everything to run! Run, now, as you did in life! Never stop!'

Cestus was blinded by tears. His hands and feet screamed at him, cut to tatters. Behind him, a miniature sun rolled towards him, blistering the skin on the back of his torso and legs. It was relentless, never slowing, as it ground its way along the vast circular track, bounded by walls of granite, its light flickering against the stalactites hanging from the cave ceiling overhead.

The floor was covered in blades, swords dropped by failed soldiers as they fled the battlefield. As the ball of fire approached, the sinners fled, tearing themselves on the blades to escape the fire. Their punishment was to flee forever.

Cestus remembered being told of this hell by drill sergeants on Macragge, in the half-remembered time before Guilliman's Legion had taken him from among hundreds of supplicants to be turned into an Ultramarine.

This hell was halfway through the levels of hell, for while cowards were despised on Macragge theirs was a pathetic sin, a sin of failure, and not comparable to the treachery of murder punished closer to hell's heart. It compounded the punishment, not only to suffer, not only to know the weight of failure, but to be reminded that even in sin a coward was lacking.

Cestus stumbled and fell. Steel bit into his hands, his knees and his chest. A blade slid through the softer skin of his lips and he tasted blood. He coughed, desperate for it to end. It felt like he had been there for years, the relentless sun driving him on.

The taskmaster was a drill sergeant of Macragge, the same kind of man who had ordered him to march and fight and strive as a child. Cestus remembered the fear of failure, of letting his betters down. He got to his feet and somehow the flesh was still screaming.

'I am not a coward,' he gasped. 'Please... I am not a coward.'

The taskmaster's whip lashed down. It was a tongue of flame from the sun, scoring a red-black line of agony against Cestus's back. 'You all but murdered your battle-brother because you feared to take his place!' the taskmaster shouted. 'You doomed your fellow warriors because you feared failure! And now you beg for your just punishment to end! What are these but the actions of a coward? And you wore the colours of Guilliman! What shame you have brought to your Legion!'

'I have never run!' yelled Cestus. 'Not once! I never backed down! I never turned from the enemy! Fear never made my choice!'

'Do you deny?' shouted the taskmaster.

'I deny! I deny you! The Imperial Truth has no room for hells! The only hells are those we make for ourselves!'

'Another lifetime, Lysimachus Cestus, and you will break!'

The sun roared closer. It swelled up, angry and orange. Dark spots flared on its surface. Flaming tongues licked out at Cestus, searing the soles of his feet, the backs of his legs. One wrapped around his face and he moaned as it burned through his skin, his cheek and nose, his ear. Cestus fought to escape, but the blades snagged him. One leg was trapped by hooks between the bones and he felt steel scraping along his shin, flaying skin and muscle away. One hand was stuck, too, pierced through by the barbed head of a spear.

'I am not a coward!' yelled Cestus. He tore himself free of the bladed ground. Muscle and blood sloughed away. 'I know no fear!' He turned around and walked on what remained of his feet, into the heart of the sun.

Admiral Kaminska sat in her command throne in front of the blast doors leading to the bridge of the *Wrathful*. The doors were closed, the bridge sealed off against the secondary explosions wracking the ship. Another huge explosion thundered up from the generatoria deep in the stern. The *Wrathful* was breaking up. Formaska's weak gravity well was slowly dragging it into a death spiral. There, upon the barren rock, they would be broken. That was, if a catastrophic reactor collapse didn't destroy the ship completely first.

Kaminska felt curiously calm as they drifted through the void, completely at the whim of gravity. There was still a trace of underlying disquiet at the edge of her senses, however, as if the feeling she had experienced before had remained, but she'd become inured to it.

She had known when Cestus proposed his plan and spoke of sacrifice that this would be her last mission. She wore her full admiral's regalia and had instructed all of her bridge staff to do the same. There would be honour in this final act. They had fought a giant in the form of the *Furious Abyss*, and they had lost, but like the fly irritates the bison, perhaps it would be enough to distract their enemy long enough for the Angels of the Emperor to do what they must.

'Helmsmistress,' said Kaminska, her eyes on the forward viewscreen and space as scattered debris from her ship spiralled slowly past, 'dismiss the bridge crew, yourself included. You are to evacuate the *Wrathful* at once and take the saviour pods. May fortune favour you in the void.'

'I'm sorry, admiral. I cannot speak for the rest of the crew, but I will not obey that order,' answered Venkmyer.

Kaminska whirled in her command throne and fixed her helmsmistress with an icy glare.

'I am your captain, and you will do as I bid,' she said.

'I request to remain onboard the *Wrathful* and go down with the ship,' Venkmyer responded.

For a moment, Kaminska looked as if she were about to erupt into a fit of apoplexy at such insubordination, but the determined expression on her helmsmistress's face made the ice soften and melt.

Kaminska saluted Venkmyer and her bridge crew.

'You do me great honour.' Kaminska was about to smile proudly when the feeling of unease intensified and she realised it was emanating from her helmsmistress.

'No, admiral,' Venkmyer replied, and from the obvious demeanour of the crew around her, they were all in agreement. 'We are honoured.'

Venkmyer raised her hand to return the naval salute when she suddenly clutched her stomach. She grimaced in pain and fell to the deck, convulsing violently.

Helms-mate Kant, standing close by, went immediately to her aid.

'Officer Venkmyer,' shouted Kaminska getting off her throne to go to her helmsmistress's aid. She stopped short when she saw her breath misting in front of her. A profound chill filled the bridge as if it were suddenly converted into a meat locker.

Eyes wide as Venkmyer bucked and thrashed, she drew her naval sidearm.

Armed or not, it wouldn't matter. It was already too late for them all.

Mhotep was meditating in the isolation chamber, his gaze fixed on the reflective surface of the speculum in his wand. Abruptly, his glazed expression bled away and he was at full awareness again.

It was time.

The Thousand Son got to his feet. His gaolers had allowed him to wear his battle-plate and the heavily armoured boots resonated against the metal floor. He approached the locked cell door and raised his hand. Chanting eldritch words in a sibilant tongue, the door dissolved before Mhotep's open palm, disintegrating back into atoms. The Astartes stepped through and was struck immediately by a profound sense of emptiness. The corridors were utterly bereft of life. He knew the *Wrathful* had only a skeleton crew, but this was something else: an absence of existence that smacked of the otherworldly. Mhotep drew the psychic hood over his head, securing it firmly to the scarab-shaped clasps on his gorget. He drew the wand out before him and activated it. The small stave extended into the spear again and a small crackle of energy played down its length as if reacting to the air around it. This ghost ship in which he walked had a phantom. Mhotep knew it for certain.

Calmly, the Thousand Son walked down the narrow passageways that would lead him to the bridge, where he knew his destiny awaited. The lines of fate had been very specific. This was the path he had chosen, despite the efforts of the *other* to try and change his mind, to will him into divine madness.

Mhotep reached the bridge without encountering a single soul. It was as if the crew had been devoured utterly. He moved his hand in a swift chopping motion and the sealed blast doors opened, venting a small cloud of pressure.

Carnage greeted him as the Thousand Son stepped into the chamber. It was as if the bleeding heart of the *Wrathful* had been laid open upon the surgeon's slab.

The heart of the ship, of course, was its crew. Their blood and viscera painted the walls, an incarnadine portrait rendered by an obscene and demented artist. Skin was flayed from bone, organs eviscerated.

A bizarre skeleton ribbed the walls and ceiling, the concomitant elements harvested from the slain crew members, changing the bridge into a macabre ossuary.

Mhotep ignored the abattoir stink assailing his nostrils, even through his battle-helm, the wet redness of the chamber cast starkly in the intermittent flare of warning lamps. He saw Admiral Kaminska, slumped against the floor, a pistol in her hand.

'Get out of her,' she breathed, blood flecking her lips as she spoke.

Standing before them both, an insane grin etched upon her face, was Helmsmistress Venkmyer. She was bloody and her toes, pointing downward in her boots, just scraped the floor as if she were a marionette held limply by its strings.

'Get out!' Kaminska urged again, struggling to stand as she fired her pistol on empty at the abomination that used to be her second-in-command.

The Venkmyer-puppet lashed out, her arm extending as if it were made of clay, and sheared off Kaminska's head with its talon-like fingers. The admiral dead, the creature's arm shrank back into position, glistening with blood.

'You dwell within,' said Mhotep calmly, taking a step forward as he mustered his psychic resolve. 'Come forth.'

The Venkmyer-puppet grinned back at him.

'I am a servant of the crimson eye. I am a vassal of Magnus the all-knowing,' said Mhotep, taking another step as he reaffirmed the grip on his spear. 'Come forth.'

Eerie quiet had descended like a veil and the temperature readings in the Thousand Son's helmet were registering sub-zero. He saw miniature icicles of hoarfrost building on his gauntlets. A faint white patina was emerging slowly on his cuirass as he advanced.

Still, the Venkmyer-puppet did not answer.

'I know you are here!' cried Mhotep, his voice resonating around the bridge. 'You have been here all along! You cannot hide from me. I have the eye of Magnus!' Mhotep levelled his spear at Venkmyer as if she was a wild beast poised to attack.

'Come forth,' he hissed, and the briefest flash of recognition appeared on Venkmyer's face, but was swallowed by agony.

The thing that used to be the helmsmistress opened its mouth and the jaw distended to reveal a hollow maw of deep red. A gush of blood spewed outwards, coating Mhotep in its sickly gore. The Thousand Son did not falter against the crimson tide and held his ground.

The sound of cracking bone filled the air as Venkmyer's spine was ripped out of her back and arced up and over her head like a scorpion's sting. Her neck snapped, and her jaw distended further, tendons severing. Beneath her tarnished uniform, her ribs writhed as a shape fought to free itself from the flesh and bone sack of her body. Convulsions wracked her and the head came apart in a shower of gore and matter.

A shape of raw muscle emerged, unfolding and opening like a bloody flower. Venkmyer's hands became claws and enhanced musculature spread across her ravaged body in a riot. Wet and pink, the muscle swelled until a hard, black carapace formed over it. What had once been Venkmyer, little more than a conduit for something to wrench itself into existence, grew exponentially until it had to crouch to fit into the chamber. The nubs of horns sprouted from a bulbous head from which eyes like pits of tar blinked maliciously. A slit ran across the near-featureless head like the cut from a surgeon's scalpel and a wide mouth opened from it, revealing rows of razor teeth. Talons like scythe blades scraped along the floor from distended, simian-like arms. A long, sinewy tail spilled from its back made of tough muscle-bound vines and twisted spine.

'There you are…' said Mhotep, looking up at the towering abomination, '…Wsoric.'

It was a thing of the warp, a daemon made flesh, and it stared at the Thousand Son, allowing its malign presence to wash over him.

'I am gorged,' the thing gurgled, drooling blood as its mouth deformed to make the words, 'but there is always room for more.'

Mhotep knew then that the beast had been aboard the ship for weeks, devouring souls to gather its strength. It had been the temptation in his head that had almost made him slip into madness. It had fanned the flames of the Space Wolf's enmity against him. It had fostered the madness that had claimed the lives of so many of the crew.

Mhotep brandished his spear and a corona of crackling energy arced over it.

'Feeding time is over,' he promised.

THE SEVENTH CIRCLE of hell, two steps closer to the heart of damnation, was for rebels: those who had cast off the natural order, who had defied their betters or refused to accept their place in the world. In ages past, those who had taken up arms against Macragge's Battle Kings had found themselves here, alongside children who had turned against their parents, and deviants and agitators of every kind.

It was a machine – a vast, complex, endless construction of cogs and steel that churned through the seventh circle. Rebels had failed to realise that they were required to be a part of a larger machine, and so the seventh hell was to educate them in their place. Sinners became a part of that machine, bent and stretched into component parts. The machine never let them alone, always twisting them or thrusting a piston through them, until they gave up their individuality in the hope of ending the pain. The seventh hell was not just a punishment, it was a lesson, and it would break the pupil's spirit in the telling.

Cestus's spine was bent backwards. Spurs of metal were slid in at his wrists, down through the muscle of his arms and into his chest. Metal merged with the back of his skull and snapped it back every few seconds as the teeth of a cog hammered by behind him.

This circle of hell was dark and dripping with blood. Other sinners were everywhere, their bodies so deformed by the machine that they were little more than cogs or cams of gristle and bone, facial features barely discernible. A few others were new and their bodies were still resisting. They screamed, bones poking through their skin and muscles ripping.

'Cestus!' cried someone above him. Cestus tried to look back, grimacing as metal pushed through the skin of his scalp.

It was Antiges. The Ultramarine had been stripped of his armour and was bolted spread-eagled to a cog. His limbs were being forced around to follow the circle of the cog. His shins and forearms were being bent into curves and they looked like they would shatter at any moment. Another, smaller cog inside the larger was fixed to his back, slowly twisting his spine. Already, his torso looked lopsided and his head had been forced down onto one shoulder.

'Antiges!' gasped Cestus. 'I had thought you were lost.'

'I am,' said Antiges, a brief lull in his suffering before the agony returned. 'So are you. Fathers of Macragge, this pain... I cannot suffer it much longer. If only there were some... some new death, some oblivion.'

'This is the hell for rebels,' said Cestus. He felt a note of panic in his mind as the spurs in his forearms and chest began to force apart, drawing his arms behind him. 'We are not rebels. We were always loyal sons of

Macragge! We served the Imperial Truth until the end! Nothing was worth more to us than our duty.'

'Your duties were on Terra,' said Antiges. 'You took a ship and left your post. You took us all on your mission to Macragge, and damned the rest! There was no duty that told you to gather your fleet and abandon Terra. That was your personal crusade, Cestus. That was your rebellion.'

'I had a duty to Macragge and to my battle-brothers. Everything I did, I did because it was demanded of my by my Legion! Loyalty drove me on!'

'Loyalty, Cestus, to yourself.' Antiges threw his head back and screamed. One leg shattered, snapping at the shin. The other one was wrenched apart at the knee. A shoulder followed, the bone torn out of the socket. Skin split and Antiges's arm was held on only by a few tendons. His eyes rolled back and his breathing turned ragged. An Astartes could take pain that would kill a normal man, but even Antiges had his limits.

'Brother!' shouted Cestus. 'Hold on! Do not leave me! Fight!'

Cestus's part of the machine hummed with power diverted to the engines chugging away beneath him. He felt his arms forced back further and a sharp pressure in his back. His head was forced back, too, snapping back and forth as it was ratcheted tight into the top of his spine.

The pressure in his chest was tremendous. An Astartes's ribs were fused into a breastplate of bone, and Cestus could feel them grinding as it made ready to split down the middle. The pain grew and the Ultramarine could feel nothing else, only the awful inevitability of his breaking.

'I am no rebel!' shouted Cestus, drawing resolve from a pit of strength he didn't know he had. 'I only serve! My Legion is my life! I do not belong in this hell of Macragge, and so this hell is not real! I am no rebel! I defy you all!'

Somewhere, a taskmaster turned a rusting wheel and the machine shuddered with power.

Cestus's chest split open. He screamed. Hot air shrieked through his organs. His legs kicked frantically and both his arms snapped. His neck broke, but the pain did not die, and his body was forced to accept the form of the machine.

'I defy you,' gasped Cestus with his last breath.

blur ... the detective was saying ... she would tell ... that would be the end ... no need to ...

... turned to her, ... or being curious, ... would ...

... and Mrs. ... rub a napkin ...

did you see ...

... but Mrs. ... pointed at ... nervously ...

Lester ... with tight ... as where ... the ... through his features. ... he had French ... and then had sobered. His ... over during the ... and all ... the only body was found ... in front ... the ...

... I ... you, there's a ... with her last breath.

NINETEEN

Pack mentality/Wsoric/Reunion

BRYNNGAR STALKED ON all fours amongst the steaming carcasses of the pack. He had rent them apart with tooth and claw, his furred muzzle stained with their blood. They had challenged him and he had proved he was dominant. Upon the snowy, Fenrisian plain, his feral eyes cast across a silver ocean so still that it was like glass. He sniffed the air, the scent of something drifting towards him on the cold breeze. Long wolf ears pricking at the faintest sound of disturbed tundra, he saw a shape above him, moving stealthily up a craggy peak under a shawl of snow.

Another wolf still lived and was stalking him.

Brynngar emitted a baleful howl that echoed across the soaring mountains. Its challenge was met by another.

The hackles rose on Brynngar's back as the other wolf loped into view. He was smaller, but lean and well-muscled. Reddish, brown fur covered his lupine body and he pawed at the ground with blood-red claws.

Brynngar growled at the red wolf's approach, a deep and ululating sound that resonated through his body. The challenger stepped down onto the plain and they began circling each other, the old and venerable grey versus the youthful red. Death was the only outcome. The only thing that was uncertain was whether the duel would claim them both.

Ribbons of wolf flesh still clung to Brynngar's fangs. The blood taste was intoxicating, and the scent set his feral senses aflame. With a roar, he dived at the other wolf, biting and clawing with savage abandon. So furious was the attack that the red wolf was bowled briefly off balance. He twisted in Brynngar's jaws, scraping wildly with his claws and biting down against the grey's back. The wolves broke apart, both bloodied and full of fury. This time the red wolf attacked, launching a swift assault that saw him rake his claws down Brynngar's flank. The old, grey wolf yelped in pain and skidded away across the ice plain on all fours, before regrouping to charge again.

The red wolf slashed a claw across Brynngar's muzzle as he came at him, but the old grey was not to be deterred. Ignoring the pain, Brynngar locked his jaw around the red wolf's neck and bit down. Claws raked his flank as the red wolf's back legs kicked out in desperation. Brynngar could hear his opponent's frantic breathing, and feel the hotness against his fur, the vapour cooling in the cold. With a grunt of effort, he snapped the red wolf's neck. It yelped just before it died, and fell limp in Brynngar's jaw. The old wolf shook the corpse loose and howled in triumph, blood drizzling from his maw as he brandished gory fangs.

The silver ocean was before him once more and Brynngar felt it call to him. Snow spilled across its mirror sheen in fat, white drifts. It fell upon the ground where Brynngar stood, covering up the spilled blood of the slain wolves. The old grey was about to lope off when a shadow fell across the ice plain. He looked up and for a moment could see nothing through the heavy snowfall. Then, slowly, a figure resolved itself. It was a black wolf, easily twice his size, sitting on its haunches watching him calmly. There was no challenge in its posture; Brynngar detected no threat in either its tone or manner. It merely watched. The grey wolf had seen this black furred beast before. He approached it slowly, warily and stopped as the black wolf got up. Its eyes bored into him and it opened its mouth as if to howl.

'Look around you,' said the black wolf, and though it spoke the words of man, Brynngar the grey wolf understood.

'Look around you, Brynngar,' said the giant black wolf again. 'This is not Fenris.'

BRYNNGAR WOKE FROM a dream straight into a nightmare. Rujveld lay dead at his feet. The Blood Claw's throat had been ripped out and vital fluids pooled around his corpse. Brynngar tasted copper in his mouth and knew at once that he had killed him. Out of the corner of his eye, the Wolf Guard saw other grey-armoured forms and realised that he had slain all of his kinsmen. He shut his eyes against the horror, willing it to be his fevered imagination, but when Brynngar opened them again he knew it was not.

The Wolf Guard got unsteadily to his feet. The last thing he remembered was approaching the *Furious Abyss*. Their shuttle had been hit and they'd crashed in a place of darkness. The rest was lost. He had emerged onto what he thought was Fenris. He knew that this was some form of psychic lie. He clenched his fists at the thought of being manipulated by witchcraft. It had cost the lives of his battle-brothers. He had been damned by it.

Senses returning, Brynngar looked around. The chamber was gloomy in the extreme, but felt large and tall. It was some kind of armoury. He stood face-to-face with a suit of dreadnought armour. Startled at first, the Wolf Guard took an instinctive step back and reached for Felltooth. When he realised that the sarcophagus of the mighty war machine was empty and dormant, he relaxed. There was another dreadnought next to it, similarly harnessed, made ready for the warrior who would become entombed within it for all time or until they fell in service to the Legion.

The armoury was vast and well-stocked. There were crates of munitions, stacked in rows. They joined ranks of bolter clips, fuel cells and harnessed grenades. It was the hulking presence of the dreadnoughts, however, that caught the Space Wolf's attention. Next to the second war machine, there was another and another, and another. Brynngar gazed up and across the chamber, his enhanced eyesight adjusting to the darkness. At least a hundred dreadnoughts filled the massive armoury hall, their somnambulant forms held fast in racks and rows. Weapon systems, great piston hammers, power flails, autocannons, heavy bolters, twin-linked flamers and missile pods, were arrayed next to them, waiting to be attached to the dreadnought body. Brynngar balked at the firepower on display and the thought of thousands of these armoured leviathans going to war in Lorgar's name.

Brynngar's ears pricked up; he'd lost his battle-helm at some point he could not recall. A slab of metal slid away from a bare wall in the armoury hall and a shaft of wan red light issued through the gap. A tall, thin shadow was waiting outside and, with the way open, it moved into the room. It was clad in black robes and Brynngar detected the glint of a metal artifice at its back: Mechanicum.

The magos turned when it noticed the Astartes in the armoury. Without preamble, it came at the Space Wolf, a mechadendrite drill emerging from the folds of its robes. Brynngar slashed the mechanical arm of the weapon, oil spilling from the severed metal limb like blood, and brought Felltooth down onto the hapless magos with a roar. The creature gurgled as it died, in what might have been an expression of pain or regret. It twitched for a moment as if its mechanical body was taking time to realise that it was already dead, before at last it lay still.

The red light continued to issue from the portal opened by the magos.

Brynngar had no idea where it led, but perhaps he could find some vulnerable location on the ship and do some damage, making the sacrifice of his Blood Claws and his own terrible act worth something. Maybe even the Ultramarine was still alive and he could find him. These thoughts running through his mind, the Wolf Guard took a step towards the portal, but stopped when he heard the shift of metal in the chamber, followed by the pressure-hiss of a disengaging harness.

Brynngar turned towards the sound, his accentuated hearing pinpointing its location exactly, and paused. He did not have to wait long for the source of the disturbance to reveal itself.

'I serve the Legion eternally,' a scratchy voice, said, emitted from a vox-caster out of the darkness. Heavy metal footfalls like the *thunk* of giant hammers hitting metal, echoed in the armoury as a massive dreadnought emerged from the shadows.

The thing was an abomination, only part-way through the procedure of interment. The armoured sarcophagus hung open revealing a translucent blister pod in which a naked form was surrounded in amniotic fluid. The viscous material clung to the body, casting the enhanced musculature of the entombed Astartes in a dull sheen through the blister.

It walked unsteadily and one of its arms was missing, disconnected cabling flapping like cut veins, doubtless still awaiting the weapons of destruction through which it would express the art of war. The other arm, though, was more than ready, a massive, spiked hammer swinging from it. A faint energy crackle played along its surface, casting stark flashes onto the dreadnought as it primed the deadly weapon subconsciously. A sense of palpable menace came from the metal monster that towered over Brynngar. The old wolf took a step back, swinging Felltooth in readiness. The armour of his opponent looked thick and he hoped that the rune axe could pierce it.

'My enemy,' droned the dreadnought lumbering forward to close off the exit to the armoury as a flare of recognition coloured its tone and demeanour. 'Ultis must die,' it added, pausing for a moment as if suddenly confused, before it refocused on the Space Wolf and continued, 'You will not gain the ship.'

Brynngar knew this warrior. He had killed him once already, at Bakka Triumveron.

'Baelanos...' it said with machine coldness.

The assault-captain.

'Didn't I kill you once, already,' growled the Wolf Guard.

'...Destroy you,' the dreadnought replied, the sarcophagus closing up over the blister.

'Round two,' Brynngar whispered as Baelanos the dreadnought charged.

MHOTEP CRASHED THROUGH the blast doors of the bridge, and skidded across the floor of an adjoining corridor. Fire wreathed his armour and scorch marks tarnished it from where the daemon had burned him with its breath. The force of the blow was such that Mhotep tried to claw at the corridor walls to slow his passage, but the wood veneer and metal tore away in his grasp, revealing bare wiring and fat cables that spat sparks and flame. The Thousand Son struck a bulkhead at the corridor's intersection and crumpled to a halt, pain lancing his back and shoulder.

Heat coiled from the edges of Mhotep's armour. The faceplate of his helmet had taken the worst of the impact and he ripped it away, half-melted, leaving the rest of the headgear intact, together with the psychic hood. Discarding the battle-helm face plate, Mhotep got to his feet. Three claw marks were cut so deep into his cuirass that they bled. The Astartes staggered at first, but drew on his psychic reserves to steel himself. Forcing one foot in front of the other, banishing the pain, he made his way back to the bridge.

Wsoric stepped from the shattered blast doors, metal squealing as the daemon pushed its immense bulk through the ragged hole left by Mhotep. The beast would meet him halfway.

As it got closer, Mhotep saw that the black armour carapace was cracked in places and faintly glowing ichor seeped from minor cuts on its body.

It could be hurt, at least. Mhotep clung to that small sliver of hope as he readied his spear. With a muttered

incantation, he sent an arc of crimson lightning towards
the daemon. The creature shied away at first, using its
muscular forearm to fend off the psychic assault, but
the cerulean energy quickly died and Wsoric emerged
unscathed.

'Like an insect,' said the daemon, its voice accompanied by the slither of muscle and the cracking of bone,
'you are harder to kill than your feeble frame suggests.'

'I am Astartes. I am an avenging angel of the Emperor
of Mankind,' Mhotep challenged, using the brief respite
to marshal his strength. Though he was weak and in
pain, the Thousand Son was careful not to show weakness, not even to contemplate defeat. For if he did, the
daemon would seize upon it and all would be lost.

'I am your doom,' Wsoric promised and came forward
with preternatural speed.

'As I am yours,' Mhotep hissed.

Talons like blades scythed the air and Mhotep's spear
spat golden sparks as he used it to parry the blow. He
was staggered by the force of it and took an involuntary
step back, boots grinding metal. He lunged with his
spear, igniting the tip in an aura of crimson fire, and
pierced Wsoric's side. The daemon's skin felt like iron,
and the resonance of the blow rippled down Mhotep's
forearm and into his shoulder. The effect was numbing
and he nearly dropped the weapon. Wsoric's pain bellow was immense, and the Thousand Son winced
against its intensity before withdrawing.

With the servos in his armour assisting his muscles,
Mhotep leapt backwards, the tattered robes of his
armour flapping like a cloak, and landed, spear in hand,
before the daemon could retaliate.

'You have failed here, spirit,' he said, filling his voice
with absolute certainty. 'Wraith of times past, I name

thee. Native thing of the warp, I shall send you back there. However much you hunger, you are known to me and you will not prevail. You will be banished by the light of the Emperor.'

'You know nothing,' Wsoric sneered, 'of what we are.' The terrible wound in its side was already healing. 'You are misled and you know not of your fate.'

An image flashed briefly in Mhotep's mind, of the spires of Prospero burning and the howling of wolves. It was the same vision he'd seen when Wsoric had first tried to subvert him and it came back like a recurring nightmare to haunt him.

Mhotep focused, determined not to give in, and slowly the image faded away like smoke.

'I am Mhotep, Thousand Son of Magnus the Red. The wisdom of Ahriman flows within me.' The affirmation steeled him and power coursed through his body. Wsoric's body, all muscle and blemished skin like the hide of a diseased corpse, shuddered with what the Thousand Son could only think was laughter. The daemon's bloody lips peeled back from its dog-like skull and its pure black eyes shimmered wetly in sunken sockets of gore. One of Wsoric's hands turned in on itself with a foul sucking sound, forming a wide orifice, which the monster aimed like a gun. The daemon roared with effort and a bolt of purple fire spat from its hand. Mhotep couldn't get out of the way quickly enough and the blast caught his pauldron, hitting him hard enough to throw him, spinning, down the corridor. The Thousand Son was on his feet as soon as he landed, feeling the armour down one side char with the heat and the exposed skin of his face blistering.

Wsoric fired again, a heavy chain of caged fire spitting from his hand. The monster was laughing loudly, a horrendous gurgling sound that sprayed blood from its throat. Mhotep rolled around the intersection, tumbling into another corridor as lances of fire tore through the bulkhead.

The stink of burning metal filled his nostrils and wretched heat plagued his skin, but Mhotep was not about to give up. Once the conflagration had died down, he swung back around the intersection. From his outstretched palm, he sent a boiling mass of crimson fire against the daemon, which coursed over its weapon-arm, searing it shut.

'The Word Bearers will not succeed,' he said, rushing forward with his spear. 'The Emperor knows he is betrayed! Lorgar will not escape his justice!'

'I care nothing for Lorgar's dogs,' roared Wsoric. 'They are beholden to the will of the warp, the ancient ones that dwell in the empyrean. The slave Lorgar is merely a tool in the fashioning of our grand design. Mankind will fall as Old Night returns to the galaxy, shrouding it in a second darkness. You will all be slaves!'

Astartes and daemon clashed. Mhotep ran his spear through Wsoric's side while the daemon swatted him against the corridor wall with a sweep of its gargantuan claws. Before the Thousand Son could recover, it seized upon his skull and started to squeeze. Mhotep could hear the bone cracking inside his head as dark spots flecked his failing vision.

'Your Emperor can plot and cower all he likes,' said Wsoric. 'What has the warp to fear from him?' he taunted, exerting more pressure.

'Knowledge...' hissed Mhotep through clenched teeth, '...is power.' Twin beams of light seared from his eyes, burning Wsoric's face and torso. The daemon recoiled, loosing its grip and Mhotep rammed his spear into its neck. Shrieking in pain, Wsoric let him down and the Thousand Son clattered to the floor, the spear still embedded in the daemon's neck.

With a massive effort, Mhotep got up and threw the daemon off, a mental shield forming in his mind and crystallising in the air before him. Wsoric was angry, its red raw flesh charred and bleeding ichor. The fresh spear wound had not closed.

Wsoric came at the Thousand Son again, tearing through the psychic shield as if it was parchment.

CESTUS FELL FLAT on his face, dry heaving. He couldn't tell which way was up. He was cold, appallingly cold, as if he was wrapped in ice or exposed to the naked void.

The feeling of his body coming apart was an agonising echo in every bone and tendon. To turn like that from a living, breathing man to a piece of mangled meat, to be trapped in that transition, feeling his spine cracking and his chest splitting, had been as obscene as it was tortuous. He felt violated, as if his flesh didn't belong to him any more.

Cestus opened his eyes.

He was in the last circle of hell. It was an endless shaft of blackness, reaching up and down for infinity. Hundreds of long, thin blades penetrated the darkened void, hanging down from above and spearing down forever. On these blades were impaled traitors to Macragge. They slid, centimetre by centimetre, down into the black.

Cestus stood on a thin spur of rock reaching from the wall of this circle of hell. He saw the faces of the condemned, locked in eternal screams as the blades bit slowly through them.

'You have as many circles of sin as hell itself,' said the taskmaster, standing behind Cestus. The Ultramarine

got a good look at him for the first time, as burly as an
Astartes, dressed in tarnished steel armour such as that
worn by Macragge's ancient Battle Kings. He wore a
leather apron stained with blood and sweat. His face
was like a solid slab, features worn down by an eternity
serving in hell. The whip in his hand was as cruel and
ugly a weapon as Cestus had ever seen.

'I'm not a traitor,' said Cestus.

'Neither are these,' said the taskmaster, pointing with
his whip towards the damned souls sliding their way
into eternity. 'They think they are. Theirs is a sin more
of arrogance than treachery. They thought they really
had the capacity to betray their fellow man, but in truth
they are just petty thieves and killers: unremarkable. To
be a true betrayer, you need power to turn against your
brother. Very few ever possess it. That the virtue in
acquiring that very power should be so tainted by the
act of betrayal, that is the truth of the sin. That is what
makes it fouler still than anything else.'

Cestus looked down at his body. His armour was
gone and he wore the deep blue padded armour of an
aspirant of Macragge, with the crest of the Battle Kings
on his chest. It was what he had worn when he had first
stepped up to the Ultramarines' chaplain and declared
that he believed he was ready to join the sons of Guilliman. It was tattered and torn, stained with the blood of
a thousand battles. 'I am no traitor, imagined or otherwise. I have never turned on my brothers.'

'As for you, Lysimachus, where do you really belong?
You are an Astartes, with all the power and brutality that
brings. You're a murderer, too, given all the people and
xenos you have killed, do you truly believe that not one
of them could have been undeserving of their fate?
Think of all those sins, and that is without the mission

you died fighting. You led a whole fleet to its destruction. You allowed your battle-brothers to die in vain. You protected a psyker, knowing full well that he was in breach of the Council of Nikea: all of this to fight your fellow Astartes. Where, captain, do we start with you?'

Cestus looked down over the edge of the precipice. The true heart of hell was there. Something enormous roiled down, barely visible against the darkness. A vast maw ground traitors between its teeth. Thousands of eyes accused them with every flash of pain.

'None of this is real,' said Cestus.

The Ultramarine smiled despite his surroundings as the clarity of understanding washed away all doubt like blue water.

'I am not dead and this is not hell,' he affirmed.

'How can you be sure?' asked the taskmaster.

'Because I may be guilty of everything you have said. I have led men to their deaths, and killed and maimed, and turned on fellow Astartes, but I am no traitor.'

Cestus stepped off the ledge, and fell into the last hell.

PAIN, REAL TANGIBLE pain, slammed into Cestus as he hit the ground. He had escaped. Somehow, through resolve and belief in himself, he had shrugged off the psychic glamour, the cage of his own mind, and emerged intact.

The booming of the big guns hammered at him through the floor and recollection returned.

He was on the *Furious Abyss*. Cynically, he wondered if it might have been more prudent to stay in hell.

Cestus's body ached and he tested himself for injuries. He was bruised and rattled, but otherwise fine and he still had his armour. Getting to his feet, he saw Excelinor beside him. In his fever dream, he must have dragged his battle-brother along with him, although, the Ultramarine captain had no idea where he actually was.

Cestus felt a pang of grief in his heart. Excelinor was dead. It was possible that under the psychic assault the Astartes's sus-an membrane had shut his body down into stasis. It hardly mattered; there would be no waking him.

Cestus crouched over his fallen battle-brother and rested his arms across his chest, placing the short-blade in his grasp in a death salute. The Ultramarine captain could do little more. He stood up again and backed up against a wall, ignoring the throbbing in his head. He felt his armour dispensing painkillers into his system and detected his altered physiognomy at work, enabling him to move and fight.

Scanning his surroundings, Cestus gathered that he was no longer outside the ordnance decks. He had no idea how he had got to this place and assumed that he had staggered through the tunnels of the *Furious Abyss* in a psychic-induced delirium, some innate survival instinct carrying him from immediate danger. It looked like a barracks. He dredged flashes of schematic implanted in his mind by Mhotep. Several dormitories made up the deck and there was temple at the far end. It was the only exit.

Treading cautiously, assuming that the deck must be largely unoccupied or he would've been discovered already, Cestus made for the temple.

The chamber was anathema to everything the Emperor had taught them to believe. It opposed the era of enlightenment that the Great Crusade was meant to usher in for mankind, the banishment of barbarian customs and the value of the empirical over the superstitious. The temple flouted everything the Astartes stood for.

It was a place of worship, but of what craven deities Cestus did not know. An altar sat against one wall and there were pews arranged for prayer. The chamber was dressed with deep scarlet banners with crimson embroidery. The Ultramarine tried to focus on the designs, but found he couldn't as they appeared to squirm and congeal before his eyes.

Several small bloodstained objects stood on the altar. Cestus realised that they were severed fingers, hundreds of them. An image of the *Furious*'s crewmen lining up to mutilate themselves in the name of Lorgar filled his mind. Cestus shook it away and forced himself to focus. His mind was still reeling. He had been to hell. The aftertaste of it was in his mouth and his body remembered the feeling of being wrenched apart.

The sound of footsteps snapped his attention to the present. They were approaching fast: voices barked orders and armoured bodies clattered through a doorway nearby.

Though it rankled to hide, Cestus moved swiftly to the far end of the room where he could disappear into a shadowy alcove. It stank of old blood and decaying flesh. For the span of the *Furious*'s short life, the crew had used it constantly for their devotions. Books were piled up behind the altar nearby, each one with the rune of an eight-pointed star on the cover. Cestus averted his gaze, unwilling to learn of the myriad forms of damnation that awaited him within those pages.

'There! The blood trail's in here. Guns up and execute!' It came from inside the room.

Cestus slid his bolt pistol from his holster and risked a glance around the altar. A squad of five Word Bearers had entered the room and were sweeping every corner with bolters. One wore an open book worked into the breastplate of his armour, words upon it inscribed in gold intaglio. Cestus assumed that he was a Legion veteran given command of the squad.

'Check the barrack rooms,' growled the veteran, with a voice like churning gravel. The Word Bearer cradled a low-slung melta-gun, a short-range weapon that burned through armour and flesh like parchment. It was an Astartes killer, the perfect hunting weapon.

The veteran and two others were left in the temple. The squad fanned out at a silent battle-sign from their leader and were working their way through the pews.

Cestus needed to act, while he still maintained the element of surprise. Unclipping a pair of frag grenades from his belt, he thumbed the activation icon on each and rolled them slowly across the ground.

One of the Word Bearers reacted to the sound and swung his bolter around to fire. Frag exploded in his face before he could pull the trigger, ripping off part of his helmet. A secondary detonation erupted beneath the other Astartes, the impact accentuated in the close confines, and took off his leg at the armour joint.

Spits of flame and a storm of splinters still clouding the air, Cestus was up and drilled a shot through the first Word Bearer, exploiting the fact that his head armour was compromised. A puff of red mist came from the back of the Word Bearer's head before he died.

The Ultramarine heard the telltale whine of the melta-gun powering up and threw himself aside as the Word Bearer veteran discharged the deadly weapon. His sight line was cluttered with debris and the shot burned through the still falling, one-legged Word Bearer, who slumped to the ground with a smoking crater through his torso.

Cestus was up in moments, leaping over the pews and pumping rounds from his bolt pistol. The veteran, the last Word Bearer standing in the temple, saw the Ultramarine, but reacted too slowly. Before he could swing his melta-gun around for a second shot, bolt-rounds punched him in the arm and torso. The veteran spun and bucked with the impacts. As Cestus reached him, he had already drawn his power sword and lopped off the falling veteran's head with a grunt of effort. Ignoring the sanguine gore pouring from the veteran's neck, Cestus pushed on and regained the corridor outside the temple that led to the barrack rooms. A surprised Word Bearer, alerted by the gunfire, emerged from one of the chambers. Cestus shot him through the lens in his battle-helm and the enemy Astartes crumpled with a muffled cry.

A second Word Bearer sensibly employed more caution, using the extended grip of his bolter so that he could reach around the doorway and blindly strafe the corridor. Cestus hugged the wall as the shots streamed past, muzzle flash blazing. An errant bolt-round struck his pauldron armour, sending a chip spinning into Cestus's face. He was without his battle-helm and fought the urge to cry out when the shard cut into his flesh and embedded there. Instead, he rolled his body over the wall, descending into a crouching stance and squeezed his bolt pistol trigger in an attempt to force his aggressor back into the chamber.

The weapon clicked in his grasp. It seemed so loud and final, despite the roar of battle filling Cestus's ears.

The Ultramarine's mouth formed an oath as the Word Bearer, who must have heard the dry shot, came out from his hiding place, laughing.

Instinctively, Cestus hurled his power sword. The blade spun end over end and *thunked* hard through the shocked Word Bearer's gorget, impaling him through the neck. The Astartes staggered, arms splayed at first as he struggled to comprehend what had just happened to him, dark fluid leaking down his breastplate like a flood. Cestus followed the sword's path at a run, smacking the boltgun out of the stricken traitor's hand and wrenching the power sword free, taking the Word Bearer's head with it.

'My brother, my enemy,' Cestus breathed after he took a moment to take stock, regarding the carnage of the dead Word Bearers around him.

Five Astartes slain, albeit traitors, by his hand; a temple devoted to heathen gods; enlightenment and the pragmatism of science and reason abandoned for superstition. Cestus felt the galaxy darkening even as he sheathed his power sword and discarded the Word Bearer's unusable bolter clips. Grimacing, he tugged the ceramite chip from his face and then he pushed on. Somewhere ahead, he knew, was an armoury.

BRYNNGAR LEAPT ASIDE as the power hammer crashed down onto the deck. Rolling to his feet, the Space Wolf could only watch as Baelanos, awesome in his dreadnought armour, wrenched the weapon free from a crater filled with sparking wires and torn metal. Cables ripped out with the hammer head were snarled around the weapon's spikes like intestines.

Baelanos grunted as he righted himself, confusion still warring within him, and charged again.

Brynngar ducked beneath the wild sweep of the hammer this time, the solid metal face whistling past his head like a death knell. The Space Wolf moved in with Felltooth and landed a fearsome blow to Baelanos's armoured flank. The rune axe *spanged* against the reinforced ceramite frame and bit deep, but the Word Bearer dreadnought didn't slow. Baelanos's momentum carried him thundering into the Space Wolf, his machine bulk like a battering ram. Brynngar was smashed aside and lost his grip on Felltooth. He skidded on his front across the deck, friction sparks kicked up from his armour spitting in the Space Wolf's face. Brynngar grimaced and got up, drawing a knife from his belt. The monomolecular blade was honed to beyond razor sharpness and could scythe open power armour with the proper amount of pressure. The only downside was its appalling reach, and Brynngar doubted whether a thrown blade would even irritate his goliath enemy.

Roaring a battle-cry, the old wolf launched himself at Baelanos, who was still turning, flashing in and out of lucidity. With every attack from the Space Wolf, though, the dreadnought's memory was renewed.

Clinging to the Word Bearer machine's weapon arm, Brynngar rammed his knife blade into the armour joint that sealed the sarcophagus in an attempt to prize it open. Baelanos spun hard, armoured feet stomping up and down, and his torso twisting as he sought to dislodge his opponent. Brynngar dug in, wrapping his legs around the dreadnought's shoulder as he pushed the blade two-handed until it reached the hilt.

Baelanos, realising that he couldn't shake the Space Wolf loose, decided to ram the Astartes into the armoury wall and charged headlong into it. Brynngar saw the empty dreadnought suits coming towards him at speed and realised that he was about to be crushed. He swung aside at the last moment, violently thrown clear as Baelanos careered into the dormant armour with a deafening *clang*. Dislodging himself quickly, the

Word Bearer turned and stomped towards the prone Space Wolf, still dazed from his hurried dismount, intending to crush him beneath his feet.

With a groan of pain, Brynngar rolled aside, but Baelanos was getting quicker and caught him a glancing blow with the power hammer as the Space Wolf struggled to rise. White fury filled Brynngar's body and for a moment he was back at Fenris, though now a man, standing upon the shores of the silver-grey ocean. Brynngar ducked a second swipe of the giant hammer that would have shattered his skull and ended the duel then and there. He saw Felltooth in flashes, but couldn't reach the weapon's haft to wrench it free. Brynngar also saw that the sarcophagus had sprung open, the collision forcing it loose with the Space Wolf's knife lodged in the joint. The amniotic blister lay unprotected. Brynngar went for his bolt pistol, but found it wasn't there. He cursed loudly. He must have lost it during the crash or at some point in the psychic fever dream.

Blood drooled from the Space Wolf's mouth and nose, matting in the hair of his beard. His leg felt leaden and unresponsive. His body ached as if stuck with red-hot pins. This was the end. Unarmed and injured, even a warrior of Brynngar's prowess could not hope to hold out against a dreadnought. Baelanos seemed to sense that inevitability and moved in slowly, as if savouring the kill.

The Space Wolf realised that he was laughing. The action of it hurt his chest. The shadow of the dreadnought eclipsed him completely and Brynngar closed his eyes, imaging the ocean.

'Fenris,' he whispered.

A bolter shot, stark and hollow, resounded in the armoury. Brynngar's eyes snapped open to see a

smoking hole in the blister, fracture lines emanating
outwards from the puncture crater. Baelanos was rocked
backwards, a gurgling sound emanating from his vox-
emitter. Viscous, amniotic fluid spilled out from the
crack like brine.

The Space Wolf ran forward, despite a new pain flaring in his leg, and ripped Felltooth free from the
dreadnought's bulk. He carved a line down the blister as
Baelanos flailed in desperation and it cracked apart. The
fluid gushed out, taking the incumbent Astartes inside
with it. Baelanos flopped out of the shattered blister,
half suspended by the circuitry and cables linking him
to the dreadnought armour. A second shot from the still
unseen bolt pistol struck him in the chest and thick
blood oozed from the wound. The dreadnought fell
backwards, hitting the armoury floor with a resounding
clang, and was still. Brynngar crawled on top of it, straddling the machine, and tore into the wasted body of
Baelanos with his rune axe until there was nothing left.

'Try coming back from that,' he breathed savagely.

Resonating footsteps made the Space Wolf turn
around to regard his saviour. Skraal emerged from the
gloom, bolt pistol still smoking in his outstretched fist.

'Thought you were dead,' grunted the old wolf and
promptly collapsed.

MHOTEP FORCED THE end of his arm back into his shoulder joint. The pain didn't mean anything. The grimace
on his face was from frustration that the arm, and with
it his spear, would be weakened. He heaved down a
couple of deep breaths and backed up against a bulkhead.

The battle against Wsoric had passed beyond the corridor outside the bridge and had progressed to the

senior crew quarters, chambers allocated to him before
he'd been confined to isolation. They were relatively
close to the bridge, should an emergency necessitate the
presence of any senior crew. That fact meant little, in the
face of certain death, save that the trail of destruction
left by their battle was short-lived.

As he regarded the collapsed ceiling, the wreckage of
two decks punctuated by a few intact support stan-
chions and columns still smouldering, Mhotep came
to realise that he was the last living being on the command deck. The Thousand Son had lost sight of the
daemon when he'd been smashed through the deck
and landed in the chamber below. Wsoric could be
anywhere. He tasted blood in his mouth and knew the
fused carapace of his ribs was broken. His breathing
was ragged, which indicated a punctured lung and his
shoulder burned.

In truth, the fight was not going as he'd hoped.

'You resisted,' said the daemon. 'I turned your
brothers against you, showed you the path and you
refused it. That was folly.'

Mhotep tried to follow the sound of Wsoric's voice,
but it came from all around him.

'Do you realise how fragile the Emperor's house is?
How easily his sons will war with one another? It took
nothing to make the wolf turn on you and little more
for the puritan captain to abandon your defence.'

Mhotep ignored the goading, and tried to focus. It
was dark in the crew quarters, all power having died on
the *Wrathful* and he closed his eyes, relying instead on
his psy-sight to guide him. Life support was dead too
and the air was growing stagnant without it. Mhotep
kept his breathing steady, so as not to use up too much
oxygen.

'The Imperium will fall,' Wsoric promised, 'and the galaxy will bathe in blood and fire. Humanity's dominance is at an end.'

Mhotep cast about the chamber. His psy-sight showed him a grey, shadow world that was indistinct and grainy. Corpses of the slain officers who had died in their quarters flickered briefly like dimming candles. A voracious life spark, red and angry, got Mhotep's attention. He saw the daemon form. Its skin was like incandescent fire, constantly burning, and ribbed horns curled from its snarling head. A hide of thick, black hair covered its back from where immense, tattered wings extended, and its clawed feet raked the floor.

'I see you,' he whispered and threw his spear.

The daemon roared in agony as the golden spear impaled its neck. Mhotep's eyes snapped open and Wsoric became the fleshy abomination once more, transfixed by his weapon. He ran headlong at the creature, trying to make the most of the small advantage he had gained.

The daemon twisted, enduring the pain it brought as the spear tip tore at its ephemeral flesh. Its gaping maw split open all the way down through its torso and, just as Mhotep reached it, the daemon vomited a hail of burning bone shards. The Thousand Son took a shard in his leg that pierced his battle-plate with ease. Limping backwards, he ripped the spear out of Wsoric's neck, ichor spewing in its wake and thrust again, shredding through the muscle of the daemon's shoulder.

With a lurch of straining steel, the deck collapsed, Astartes and daemon plunging into a dark void below. They landed in a dead space in the hull, separating the crew quarters from the lower industrial decks. A freezing gloom persisted there, criss-crossed with support beams. Mhotep rolled off the creature, which had taken the brunt of the fall, and staggered backwards.

Wsoric rose with the screech of sundered metal. The struts around it were already damaged. The ship was breaking apart. The daemon roared its anger, preparing to vent its wrath when the supports gave way. Together, they tumbled down into the cold blackness.

THE SOUND OF the ocean receded as Brynngar came around. The scarred visage of the World Eater in his battle-helm looked down on him.

'You're a sore sight for my eyes,' grumbled the old wolf and got to his feet. Brynngar's body felt bruised with the effort, and the pain down one leg made him stagger at first before he righted himself. Blood flecked his beard and armour.

'How long was I out?' he asked, aware that they were still in the armoury hall.

'Just a few minutes,' Skraal replied, 'but we've no time to rest. Word Bearers are patrolling the ship looking for us.'

'Been hunting you for a while, eh?' guessed the Space Wolf, taking in the rents and burns on Skraal's armour. He could almost imagine the fevered look in his eyes, the kind of nervous expression that any man on the run might adopt after being chased for long enough. The World Eater was already volatile. Shaken up as he was, he might crack at any moment.

'Several weeks… I think.' The son of Angron came across a little dazed as his time aboard the ship had dulled his sense of what was real and what were merely phantoms of the mind.

'Did anyone else get aboard?' Brynngar asked, swinging Felltooth to better remember the strength of his arm. The old wolf noticed that the red-limned portal was still open.

'I am the only survivor,' Skraal responded curtly and headed for the light.

'You know where that leads?' asked the Wolf Guard, noting the nonchalant way the World Eater approached the doorway.

'The corridor beyond will get us to the engine deck.'

'We need to reach ordnance and destroy the cyclonic payload,' said Brynngar, 'and how do you know that we can reach the engines from there?'

'He knows because I told him,' said a familiar voice from the gloom that sent the hackles on the back of Brynngar's neck rising.

'Destroying the cyclonics is no longer viable,' he added, emerging out of the penumbra.

'Cestus.' Brynngar growled when he said it.

The Ultramarine slammed a fresh clip from the armoury's stores into his bolt pistol and nodded to the Space Wolf.

'There is but one opportunity left to us,' Cestus said. 'The easier course is no longer possible. We must walk the harder road. It is the only one open to us.'

Brynngar's silence held the question.

'We must destroy the ship,' said Cestus.

TWENTY

Contention/Avenge me/Immolation

'DESTROY THE SHIP?' Brynngar laughed as he limped after his battle-brothers. When Cestus went to aid him, he snarled, 'I'm fine,' before continuing.

'This is the single largest and most powerful vessel I have ever seen. A few incendiaries,' the Space Wolf indicated the grenade harness he still carried 'will not see to its ruin.'

'Have you lost your mind as well as your honour, son of Guilliman?'

'Neither,' Cestus replied. 'The *Furious Abyss* can be destroyed. In order to do it, we must reach the engines and the plasma reactor that fuels them. If we can overload them with an incendiary payload of our own the resulting explosion will commence a chain reaction that cannot be averted by the ship's fail safes and redundant systems.'

Brynngar seized Cestus by the shoulder. The Space Wolf's eyes were full of anger.

'You knew this and yet said nothing?'

'It was irrelevant before,' Cestus returned, shaking free of the Wolf Guard's grip. 'Our only way in was through the torpedo tubes, which made the cyclonics our obvious and most immediate target. There was no way of knowing we could've made it this far into the ship for an assault on the main reactor to be even possible.'

'Leaving aside the matter of how you even know this,' snarled the Wolf Guard, 'how do you plan on getting close enough to destroy it? Have you seen the size of this vessel; it will be like a labyrinth in the engineering decks. We might never find it.'

'I can guide us. It will take minutes,' Cestus replied curtly. He was about to head off when Brynngar grabbed his arm again.

'I don't know what pact you have made with the witch that cowers aboard the *Wrathful* and what secrets you may be privy to,' growled the Space Wolf dangerously, 'but know this: I will not abide sorcery in any form. Once we gain the reactor and set this ship burning, our alliance is at an end, Ultramarine.' Brynngar let Cestus go, and stalked away, taking a bolt pistol from the armoury and making ready at the open portal.

'So be it,' said Cestus grimly to himself and went to join his battle-brothers.

THE FURIOUS ABYSS had been forced out of position during the battle with the *Wrathful*. Formaska glowered well to its starboard side, Macragge scarcely less ominous well below it. The planet's local defence fleet was also in sight, lingering above Macragge's upper-atmosphere. With the supplicants dead, the *Furious*'s surveyor-dampening systems, which had allowed it to ambush the *Fist of Macragge* were no longer effective.

Slowly, the vessels were moving into defensive positions. Without knowledge of the Word Bearers' intentions or their defection from the Imperium, though, the Macragge fleet was cautious and had yet to engage. They would try to hail them first. It was all the time that the *Furious Abyss* would need to realign, destroy Formaska and thus cripple the fleet in one stroke. The *Wrathful* was gone from the massive ship's viewscreens, now little more than a chilling tomb of dead lights and lost souls, as it floundered in the void without power. Gravity would claim it.

Orders were relayed down to the *Furious Abyss*'s engine rooms to engage the directional thrusters and orient the ship back towards Formaska. The ordnance decks had been retaken, although the damage done by the enemy' assault was extensive in some areas. The explosive discharge from a rapidly detonated melta bomb cluster had been ill-targeted, but destructive. The repair crews were hard at work clearing debris and expelling corpses into the void, but reaching operational status again would take time. It meant, although the cyclonic payload was intact, the launch would be delayed further.

Zadkiel felt his glory slipping through his grasp even as he listened to the toiling of the ratings on the ordnance deck. He shut down the vox link and closed his eyes, trying to master his anger.

Opening them again, Zadkiel looked at the positional display on one of his command throne's viewscreens. The *Furious* had yet to change its heading and reset the launch vectors for the torpedoes.

'Gureod,' he barked into the vox array.

Silence answered.

'Damn it, magos, why are the engines not engaged?'

Nothing again. Now the magos was just mocking him.

'Reskiel,' snarled Zadkiel, his tone impatient.

'My lord,' said the voice of the sergeant-commander, the thudding retort of gunfire audible in the background.

'Get to engineering and find out why the ship has stalled.'

'My lord,' said Reskiel again, 'we are at engineering. The enemy are here. They move through the ship as if they know every tunnel and access conduit. My squad is moving in to eliminate–'

The sound of a thunderous explosion broke the vox link for a moment. Crackling static reigned for a few seconds before Reskiel returned. 'We have made contact. They are at the edge of the main reactor approach…'

Frantic cries and the screams of Word Bearers punctuated the chorus of bolter fire before the vox link went dead.

Zadkiel clenched his fist, and bit out his next words.

'Ikthalon, lead three squads down to engineering. Seek those curs out and destroy them!' Zadkiel's veneer of calm cracked and fell away completely. He was shaking with apoplectic rage.

Ikthalon had returned to the bridge following the death of the supplicants and had, until now, observed proceedings with silent deference.

'No, my lord,' he responded in his usual sibilant cadence, adding, 'I have endured your ineptitude for long enough. It threatens the glory of Kor Phaeron and our Lord Lorgar.' Zadkiel heard the chaplain draw his bolt pistol from its holster.

'I had thought you impudent, Ikthalon,' said the admiral calmly, his composure returning as he turned to the chaplain. Zadkiel saw that he did indeed have his pistol trained upon him.

'I did not believe you to be stupid.'

The chaplain's posture was neutral and unassuming.

'Stand down,' he said simply, lifting the pistol a fraction to emphasis his point.

Zadkiel bowed his head. In the corner of his eye, he saw Ikthalon start to lower his weapon. It would be the chaplain's last mistake.

Zadkiel moved swiftly to the side, his rapier-like power sword drawn fluidly. The bucking report of the bolt pistol sounded on the bridge, but Ikthalon's shot, confounded by the admiral's sudden movement, missed.

Zadkiel slid the blade through the chaplain's gorget, smacking the bolt pistol from his grasp at the same time.

'Did you think I would leave this bridge, my bridge, to a snake like you?'

Ikthalon could only gurgle in reply.

Zadkiel ripped away the chaplain's battle-helm. Underneath it, Ikthalon was scarred, his face a mass of burn tissue, his ravaged throat a wreck of scabrous flesh. He stared into the chaplain's pink-tinged eyes with intense hate.

'You thought wrong,' he hissed, and pushed Ikthalon off the blade to land with a clang of ceramite on the deck. The chaplain floundered at first, trying to speak, clutching ineffectually at his throat, but was then still, the blood pooling slowly beneath him.

Zadkiel turned to Sarkorov.

'Clean that up and monitor all stations. You have the bridge. As soon as we are in a state of readiness again, inform me at once,' ordered Zadkiel.

Pale-faced at the chaplain's sudden death, the helms-master snapped a ragged salute and gestured to a group of Legion serfs to act as a clean-up crew.

Zadkiel stalked away, wiping the blood off his blade. He would deal with the infiltrators and be damned to ignominy if he was going to let them interfere any further with his plans. Besides, it would not look favourable in the eyes of the arch-commander if he needed his lackeys to deal with their enemies. No, the only way to be sure was to kill them all himself.

RESKIEL WAS PLEASED. Though he had lost several of his squad fighting the loyalists, he had them boxed in, having forced them into a tunnel that he knew was a dead end. The sound of gunfire had abated, but the roar of the primary reactor and all the workings of the ship were still incredibly loud inside his battle-helm.

Using Astartes battle-sign, he signalled for the three warriors with him to descend from the upper stacks where they'd spread out and exploited their vantage point to coral the loyalists into a death trap. For a moment, Reskiel lost sight of two of his warriors as they moved into position.

Reaching the ground floor of the engineering deck, they converged on the tunnel. That was when Reskiel first realised that something was wrong. One of his warriors was missing.

'Where is Vorkan?' he hissed through the helmet vox.

'I lost sight of him as he changed position, sergeant,' one of the others, Karhadax, replied.

Reskiel turned to the second Word Bearer, Eradan.

'I was watching the Space Wolf and the Ultramarine,' he said by way of explanation.

A cold chill ran down Reskiel's spine despite the heat of exertion and the warmth of the engineering deck.

'What of the third? What of the World Eater?'

The hunters had suddenly become the prey.

Eradan's neck and chest exploded outwards in a rain of blood and flesh, the whirring of chain teeth visible through all the gore.

'I'm right here,' said Skraal, his voice dead of all emotion, as the Word Bearer he had slain fell face forward onto the deck. He killed Karhadax next, cutting off his head as he charged. Whatever oath or battle cry the Word Bearer was about to shout died on his lips as his decapitated head hit the ground. Skraal kicked the still-flailing body out of his path and came at Reskiel.

To the sergeant-commander's credit, he did not flinch in the face of the killing machine before him, and even managed to put a bolt round through Skraal's thigh before the World Eater buried his chainaxe into him.

Skraal tore his bloodied weapon out of the still quivering body as Cestus and Brynngar emerged from the tunnel. It was with some degree of satisfaction that the World Eater had killed Reskiel. He had slain Antiges and chased him like a dog through the bowels of the ship. Four other Word Bearers lay within the tunnel nearby, variously punctured with bolter wounds and cleaved by blades. They were the other remnants of Reskiel's hunter squad, despatched by the Astartes.

'Next time, you're the bait,' Brynngar growled at Skraal, who smacked his chainaxe against the deck to dislodge some of the flesh snarled up in its blades.

'There will be more,' said Cestus, ramming a fresh clip that he'd taken from the armoury hall into his bolt pistol.

'There's always more,' growled Brynngar, eager not to linger. 'Lead on.'

Warning klaxons were sounding everywhere as the search for the Astartes saboteurs intensified and found its focus. Red hazard lights flashed with insistent inter- mittence and the shouts of the distant hunters echoed through the metal labyrinth of piping conduits and machinery. Gantries overhead provided only a curtailed view of the maze below, but Cestus instructed them to seek what cover they could whilst moving swiftly.

Determined to inflict as much damage as possible en route to the main reactor, the three Astartes had moved through the secondary reactors, systematically wrecking them as they went. Already reactor three had shut down, several coolant pipes torn free of its side and its crews scythed down with bolter fire at their dead man's handles. Escaped coolant poured down from it in a scalding thunderhead of steam.

Cestus despatched a reactor crewman emerging from a control room with a snap shot from his bolt pistol. Another came from the opposite aisle of conduits. The Ultramarine killed him too.

The death dealing was indiscriminate. Fighting in and amongst the close confines of the pipe-works was like guerrilla warfare. Despite the overwhelming forces arrayed against them, the loyalist Astartes had a chance in this arena. Numerous improvised booby traps, sim- ple frag grenade and tripwire arrangements, had been left in their wake, and the occasional explosion behind them meant that Cestus knew when their enemies were closing. Only the frag and krak grenades were used for traps. They would need the melta bombs for the main reactor. Once they reached it, they would need to infil- trate the protective shielding and plant the explosives into the reactor swell. That was, assuming the reactor's immense radiation didn't kill them first. It was a journey that Cestus planned on making alone and not one he was expecting to come back from.

A fusillade of bolter fire from a gantry above them got the Ultramarine's attention, tearing up sections of piping.

The Word Bearers had found them.

ZADKIEL WATCHED THE Astartes scurry into cover as his squads opened fire from the main access gantry. From his vantage point, he could see the whole reactor section, like an ocean of darkness with the reactors, immense steel islands, connected by a flimsy spider's web of catwalks, coolant pipes and maintenance ladders. He recognised the armour of three Legions amongst the saboteurs, and knew that this was the last of them: the last desperate attempt to try and make a difference.

'It will do you no good,' Zadkiel whispered to himself and turned to his sergeants. 'Grazious, hound them from up here. The rest of us will press on to the main reactor and intercept them.'

The sergeant saluted, snapping an affirmative response as Zadkiel departed.

'Such impudence,' Zadkiel muttered as he headed towards the main reactor.

It would end, here and now, with the death of the Ultramarines.

MHOTEP DRAGGED HIMSELF along the floor of the ordnance deck.

The air was still thick with the stench of death. Dried blood caked the walls and the bulkheads on either side were sealed with super-hot torches.

The Thousand Son rolled onto his back with effort and peered up at the rent in the ceiling far above, through which he'd plummeted. Wsoric had fallen with him. Craning his neck to look down the charnel house gangway, Mhotep saw rotting corpses on either side, prickling with frost as the void penetrated the *Wrathful*'s hull. Breathing was difficult, the air was thinning, and with the life support inoperative it would not replenish itself. Pain kept the Astartes moving. The red hot needles in his body let him know he was alive and still fighting.

He was dying. Mhotep knew this, but death held no fear for him. It was fate, his fate, and he embraced it. Struggling to his feet, the hellish agony intensified, and for a moment, Mhotep thought he might pass out.

Wsoric was a short distance away, squatting over a heap of corpses. They were the remains of the ratings and gang masters that had been sealed in when the deck was quarantined. Already lost to madness, Mhotep could only imagine what they had thought, half frozen from the cold of space, when the daemon approached them. Perhaps they had welcomed it. Perhaps they had forfeited their souls.

Wsoric stood and arched its neck. Distended flesh bulged and writhed as it consumed the last of the survivors in body and in doing so claimed their souls.

The daemon turned, an apparition in the blackness of the abattoir its kind had created, smiling at the Thousand Son's pitiful attempt to escape it.

'I ever hunger, Astartes,' it told him. 'The thirst for souls is never slaked. It is like an eternal keening in my skull upon this plane. You will quiet it for a time,' it promised, heading for Mhotep.

The Thousand Son fell as he went to flee the daemon. Blood was seeping from his cuirass where Wsoric had raked him with its claws. Bloody and battered, the Astartes had been granted a short reprieve when the creature detected the mewling terror from within the deck. It had found the ratings easily, drawn by the scent of their fear. Mhotep had been made to watch as the daemon butchered them.

'I will drink of your hope and bravery until you are hollow,' promised Wsoric.

Mhotep dragged himself up, using his spear as a crutch. He would meet his destruction face-to-face and on his feet. Outstretching his palm, a nimbus of scarlet light played about his finger tips.

Wsoric was almost upon him, and reached out, crushing the Thousand Son's hand in his taloned fist.

Mhotep screamed in agony as his bones were splintered even within his gauntlet. He dropped the spear and sagged, only held up by the strength of the daemon.

'Still you fight, insignificant speck,' it said, mouth forming into a feral sneer. 'To think that one such as you could kill one such as I.'

The daemon's booming laughter flecked caustic spittle and dead blood into Mhotep's face.

'I wasn't trying to kill you,' muttered the Thousand Son, looking up at the beast as he unclipped something from his belt. It was an incendiary grenade.

'What do you intend to do with that, little man?' asked Wsoric with an obscene smile.

'You have tarried here too long,' said Mhotep. 'At any moment you could have swum across the empyrean to the *Furious Abyss*, or back into the immaterium, but your gluttony for reaping souls has undone you warp beast. Look!'

Wsoric's flesh was leaking ichorous fluid as the psychic energy required to keep it in the material universe broke down. Its form was becoming gelatinous and ephemeral. Mhotep had detected the creature weakening all the time he fought it. Every psychic exertion had taken its toll, sloughing away some of the matter that kept it stable and in existence.

'I wasn't trying to kill you,' said Mhotep with his failing breath, 'just to keep you here for long enough.' He thrust his free hand forward, punching through Wsoric's melting skin and releasing the grenade's detonator.

The daemon snarled in rage and sudden fear.

'Puny human, I will feast upon your...'

Mhotep was thrown back by the blast as Wsoric exploded from the inside, destroyed by the dissolution of its corporeal body.

Lying in an expanding pool of his own blood, Mhotep could see through one of the aiming ports in the ordnance deck's starboard wall. Roaring fire burned at the edges of the *Wrathful*'s armoured hull as the ship, caught in the moon's gravity well, hurtled towards Formaska. He imagined the rivers of lava on its barren surface, the crags and mountainous expanses, and smiled, accepting his doom.

THE NOISE OF THE main reactor, even closed off within its housing, was immense. Beyond, Cestus knew there was an approach corridor, designed to enable close maintenance of the reactor when not in use. Beyond that was the incandescent core of energy. To step into it meant certain death. It was a sacrifice he was willing to make.

Using Astartes battle-sign, the Ultramarine indicated for Brynngar to take up position on the opposite side of the armoured hatch that led into the approach corridor. The Space Wolf obeyed swiftly and was about to cleave into the first layer of shielding when a hail of bolter fire rebounded off the metal, forcing him into cover. Cestus followed, Skraal next to him. The Astartes saw a squad of Word Bearers in firing drill formation on a lofted gantry, led by a commander in gilded, crimson armour. So resplendent and arrogant did he look, that Cestus assumed at once that he was the captain of the ship.

'We are honoured,' he said sarcastically, shouting at Skraal to be heard.

The World Eater nodded. He had recognised the captain too, the one he knew to be called Zadkiel: the taunting orator who had tried to twist his loyalty and prey upon his inner weakness. Skraal despised that. Crouching as he ran, he left cover and disappeared for a moment behind a riot of piping. He emerged, bolt pistol blazing. One of the Word Bearers pinning them was pitched off the gantry, clutching his neck. The gilded captain stood his ground at first, but took a step back when a second Word Bearer was spun off his feet, a smoking hole in his chest-plate.

'Skraal, no, it's suicide!' Cestus cried as he watched the World Eater gain the stairway and head straight at the Word Bearers. There was no way he would make it before they perforated him with bolter shells.

'Come on,' Brynngar bellowed, hacking into the armoured hatch with the sudden respite. 'Make his sacrifice worthwhile.'

With the Word Bearers occupied, Skraal had given his comrades the time they needed to cut their way into the reactor and finally end the *Furious Abyss*.

Cestus was on his feet and cleaved into the hatch with his power sword. The metal fell away with a resounding clang as it struck the deck. A backwash of heat flowed from the approach corridor sending the radiation warnings flickering on the Ultramarine's helmet display to critical.

'Bandoleers,' Cestus cried, holding out his hand for the belt of melta bombs that Brynngar carried.

'It's a one way trip,' said the old wolf.

Cestus stared at Brynngar, nonplussed.

'Yes, now hand them over.'

'Not for you,' said the Wolf Guard and punched the Ultramarine hard in the battle-helm.

Cestus fell, half-stunned by the sudden attack, and through his blurring vision he saw Brynngar enter the approach corridor.

'Both of us need not die here. Avenge me,' he heard the Space Wolf say, 'and your Legion.'

SKRAAL TOOK THE gantry steps three at a time. About halfway up his bolt pistol ran dry and he tossed it, focusing instead on his chainaxe. As he emerged into view, the Word Bearers fired. One round tore through his pauldron, another stuck his thigh, a third hit his chest and he staggered, but the fury was upon him and nothing would prevent him from spilling the blood of the enemy. All those weeks fleeing like an animal, caged in the depths of the ship like a... like a slave. That would not be his fate.

Two more shots to the chest and Skraal struck his foes. A Word Bearer came at him with a chainsword. The World Eater swatted the blow aside and carved his enemy in two across the torso. A second went down clutching the ruin of his face where Skraal had caved it in. Another lost an arm and screamed as the World Eater booted him off the gantry to his death below.

Then Skraal faced the gilded captain, standing stock still before him as if at total ease. Bellowing Angron's name, Skraal launched himself at Zadkiel, preparing to dismember him with his chainaxe.

The Word Bearer captain calmly raised his bolt pistol and shot Skraal through the neck. With a last effort, the World Eater lashed out.

Zadkiel screamed in pain as his bolt pistol was cut in two, three of his fingers sheared off with it through the gauntlet.

Smiling beneath his battle-helm, the World Eater felt his leg collapse beneath him. The spinal cord was abruptly severed and a terrible, sudden cold engulfed him, as if he had been plunged into ice.

Vision fogging, he saw Zadkiel standing above, blood dripping from his severed fingers as he drew a long, thin sword.

'I am no slave,' Skraal hissed as the last of his vital fluid pumped out of him freely.

'You have never been anything else,' said Zadkiel savagely, and thrust the blade precisely through Skraal's helmet lens and into the World Eater's eye.

The dead Astartes shuddered for a moment, transfixed on the Word Bearer's sword, before Zadkiel withdrew it with a flourish and Skraal crumpled to the deck. Wiping his blade on the corpse, and with a brief glance at his ruined hand, he turned to his sergeants.

'Now kill the other two.'

CESTUS SHRUGGED OFF his disorientation and went for the hatch, but the barrage of fire resumed, cutting him off from the wolf.

'Damn you, Brynngar,' he bellowed, knowing that it was useless.

Soon the engineering deck would be immolated by fire. The chain reaction that followed after the main

reactor's destruction would be cataclysmic. Cestus
didn't want to be there when that happened. Anger
burned within him at the death of his battle-brothers,
the base treachery of the Word Bearers. He wanted Zadkiel, and although there was little chance of reaching
him on the engineering deck, the Ultramarine knew
where he would find him.

Cestus made his way to the shuttle bay.

BRYNNGAR POWERED THROUGH the access corridor, waves
of radiation washing over him, and tore apart the first
line of shielding that led further into the reactor core
chamber. He pummelled a second bulkhead with his
fists. The sense of descent into the beating heart of the
ship enveloped Brynngar as he crawled on his hands
and knees through the final access conduit.

Ripping away the last barrier of shielding, now several metres below the surface of the engineering deck,
he passed the threshold of the reactor core's inner
chamber. A blast of intense heat struck him at once, his
armour blistering before its fury, and for a moment the
wolf recoiled. A deep cone fell away from a narrow
platform over which the Space Wolf was perched. Hot
wind, boiled up by the lake of liquid fire churning at
the nadir of the cone, whipped his hair. Brynngar felt it
burning, his skin too, as the intense radiation ravaged
his flesh.

Beautiful, he thought as he regarded the glowing reactor mass below: raw, incandescent energy that boiled
and thrashed like a captured thunderhead.

Priming the melta bombs around his waist, the Space
Wolf closed his eyes. It was a hundred-metre drop down
into the reactor core. Its smooth, angled walls were
bathed in light.

Brynngar stepped off the narrow platform and fell. The first explosion was like a thunderclap.

Storms ravaged the platinum sky as Brynngar stood upon the edge of the silver Fenrisian ocean. The tide was high and the waves crashed against the icebergs, shattering the ice-flows with pounding surf. He was dressed in only a loincloth, with his knife tucked into a leather belt and his baleen spear thrust into the hard-packed snow. Out beyond the glowing horizon, there was a keening echo. The great orca was calling to him.

Brynngar took his spear and dived into the ice-cold waters. Light was rising on the horizon, the storm receding. As he swam, he felt a strange sensation. It felt as if he was going home.

THE SUDDEN RELEASE of explosive power rippled through the main reactor. The conical structure ruptured and the plasma roared out. It fell in a massive fountain of fire, drenching the whole reactor section in a monstrous burning rain. Bolts of it punched through machinery and walkways, and through the bodies of Zadkiel's warriors. Secondary explosions tore up from the minor reactors as a terrible chain reaction took hold. There was a deep and sonorous *crump* of force as one of the engines shattered apart with the backwash of energy.

A chunk of reactor housing shot like a missile right through the main chamber of reactor seven, which echoed the explosion with a huge expanding flood of ignited plasma. Emergency systems slammed into place, but there was no way to seal the breach when plasma was free and expanding within the hull.

Reactors two and eight were breached, emptying their plasma into the reactor section's depths. The hapless menials still at work in the labyrinth were devoured in the sudden flood. The level of plasma reached the base of reactor seven, which blew its top, throwing a second burst into the air like a vast azure fountain.

Heat-expanded air ripped bulkheads open. The hull gave way, the inner skins breaching and filling with plasma before the outer hull was finally torn open and a black-red ribbon of vacuum-frozen fuel bubbled out of the *Furious Abyss*'s wounded flank.

Zadkiel crawled away from the destruction as his ship began to destroy itself from within. He reached the portal, sealing it shut before the few survivors of his squad could get through. He watched, curious and detached, as a bolt of plasma fell like a comet and ripped the gantry apart on which they stood. Survival instincts got Zadkiel to his feet. Reaching the vox, he ordered the abandon ship and proceeded to head for the shuttle bays before it was too late.

TWENTY-ONE

Eve of battle/Face-to-face/Still we'll fight

THE BANNERS OF the Word Bearers, deep crimson with the emblems of the Legion's Chapters, barely stirred in the artificial air of the Cloister of Contrition. Kor Phaeron knelt alone in front of the altar, which was crowned with the image of Lorgar, the Prophet of Colchis. The primarch's image, carved from porphyry and marble, was brandishing the book in which he had first written the Word.

The arch-commander was praying. It was this faith that set the Word Bearers apart. They understood its power. Lorgar had been an exemplar of what a man could achieve when he realised his full potential. Indeed, Lorgar had become much more even than that. Each Word Bearer prayed to commune with himself, with the forces of the universe, to discover the means to unlock their latent strength so that they might use it to do the work of Lorgar. On the eve of battle, it was prayer that made the Word Bearers ready.

Footsteps echoed through the cloisters. It was a place of worship large enough to house three Chapters of battle-brothers, or all of the *Infidus Imperator*'s crew, and the echoes lasted for several seconds.

'I am at prayer,' Kor Phaeron told the intruder, the powerful cadence of his deep voice exacerbated by the acoustics of the temple.

'My lord, we have received no signal,' came the disembodied reply.

It was Tenaebron, Chapter Master of the Void.

'Nothing?' asked Kor Phaeron, incredulity masking his anger as he turned to look upon his subordinate.

'The supplicants on the *Furious Abyss* were activated,' replied Tenaebron, 'and some time after, a psychic flare was detected: very powerful.'

'Formaska?'

'Assuredly not, Lord Kor Phaeron.'

The arch-commander stood up. Bareheaded, he was resplendent in his prayer vestments and towered over the Chapter Master. 'You must be certain of this, Tenaebron,' he said, a warning implicit in his tone.

'Formaska still exists,' the Chapter Master replied. Compared to most Astartes he looked old and weak, and some who did not know the Legion's ways might have thought he was a veteran, half-crippled in body, whose role was to advise and lead from afar. In truth, his small wet eyes and sagging, mournful face concealed a warrior's soul, which he could back up with the force staff scabbarded on his back and the inferno pistol at his side. Even that was of little significance compared to the horrible injuries that Tenaebron could inflict on an enemy's mind.

'Zadkiel has failed,' he added unnecessarily.

Kor Phaeron thought for a moment, turning back to the altar as if the statue of Lorgar could advise him.

'Follow,' he said at length, and marched towards the great doors at the far end of the cloister. Kor Phaeron threw them open.

Hundreds of Word Bearers knelt in prayer, by the light of a thousand braziers, filling the cathedral to which the Cloisters of Contrition adjoined. Each one was deep in his prayers, seeking some greater self within him that could win this fight in the name of Lorgar and seal the truth of the Word. Almost the entire muster of the Chapter of the Opening Eye, that which was being transported by the *Infidus Imperator*, was assembled, with Chapter Master Faerskarel in the front row.

Faerskarel stood up and saluted at the arch commander's approach. 'Lord Kor Phaeron,' he said, 'is it time?'

'Zadkiel has failed,' said Kor Phaeron. 'Soon the fleet's presence will be revealed and Calth will be waiting for us. It is time. This will not be the massacre of which we have spoken. This will be a fight to the end, and Calth will not give up its victory easily. We must wrest it from the enemy as we have always done.'

Faerskarel said nothing, but turned to his Word Bearers, who stood to attention as one.

'Word Bearers!' shouted Kor Phaeron. 'To your drop pods and gunships! Now is the time for war, for victory and death! Arm and say your final prayers, for the Ultramarines are waiting!'

CESTUS REACHED THE shuttle bay quickly. In the ensuing panic once the abandon ship had been declared, few enemies opposed him. Those that did were mainly zealous ratings or blood-hungry menials and he despatched them with bolt and blade.

The deck beneath the Ultramarine shuddered and lurched to the side and, for a moment, Cestus struggled to keep his feet. He heard the first of the explosions from the main reactor as they'd ravaged the ship. Now, further internal detonations were erupting across all decks as the chain reaction set in place by Brynngar's sacrifice tore the *Furious Abyss* apart.

The rest of the crew, the cohorts of Word Bearers and the officers of the bridge, had yet to reach the bay. As plumes of fire spat up from the bowels of the ship like white-orange jets through the deck, and the infrastructure of the shuttle bay disintegrated around him, Cestus doubted that they ever would.

Crossing the metal plaza of the bay was like running a gauntlet, as vessels exploded in storms of shrapnel and debris fell like rain. Cestus saw a rating crushed beneath a hunk of fallen arch, the corpse's hand still twitching in its death throes.

Hundreds of small antechambers bled off from the main bay, each housing a quartet of shuttles, racked in a two by two arrangement. Cestus stepped into the first antechamber he could find that wasn't wreathed in fire or sealed shut by wreckage.

Stepping over the threshold, he saw a solitary figure lit up by the warning strobes set into the shuttle runways. It was gloomy in the chamber, but Cestus recognised the livery of the armour before him.

'Word Bearer,' he called out.

The figure turned, about to step into the first shuttle, and regarded the Ultramarine coldly.

'So you are the one who I am to thank for this,' he said calmly, looking around the room as he opened his arms.

Cestus returned the Word Bearer's contempt and drew his power sword. The arcing lightning coursing down the blade lit the Ultramarine in a grim cast.

'You are Zadkiel,' Cestus said as if it were an accusation. 'I thought the captain was meant to go down with his ship.'

'That will not be my destiny,' Zadkiel replied drawing his sword. Energy crackled down its blade too. It was longer and slightly thinner than the Ultramarine's weapon, master crafted by some Martian artificer no doubt, the aesthetic flourishes added by a Legion artisan.

'I have your destiny right here,' Cestus promised him, and thought of Antiges slain in battle, his battle-brothers killed by the warp predators aboard the *Wrathful*; of Saphrax and his warriors smashed against the hull, their honour denied them; of Skraal and Bryn-ngar sacrificed upon the altar of victory and hope. 'This is where your words end.'

'You are a fool, Ultramarine,' snarled Zadkiel, 'ignorant of the power of the galaxy. Gods walk among us, Astartes. Real gods! Not ghosts or ciphers or interloper aliens, but beings of true power, beings who pray back!' Zadkiel's eyes blazed suddenly with fervour.

Cestus knew this was the religiosity for which the Emperor had once scolded Lorgar's Legion. Zadkiel was a fanatic, all the Word Bearers were. It was all they had ever been. How could their duplicity and deception have gone unnoticed for so long?

'We have spoken with them. They hear us!' continued Zadkiel. 'They see the future as we do. The warp is not just a sea for ignorant space-farers to drown in. It is another dimension far more wondrous than real space. Our reality is the shadow of the warp, not the other way around. Lorgar and the intelligences of the warp have the same vision. For the warp and our reality to become one, where the human mind has no limits! True enlightenment, Ultramarine! Can you imagine it?'

'I can,' Cestus said simply. There was pity in his eyes. 'It is a nightmare and one doomed to fail.'

Zadkiel sniffed his contempt.

'You underestimate the power of the Word,' he scoffed.

'Talk is cheap, fanatic,' Cestus snarled, casting aside his helmet so that his enemy could see the face of his slayer, and launched himself at the Word Bearer.

A massive energy flare lit the room in actinic radiation as the two power swords clashed: Cestus's broad-bladed spartha versus Zadkiel's rapier-like weapon.

Sparks cascaded as the two Astartes raked down each other's blades before withdrawing quickly. Cestus let anger fuel his blows and crafted an overhead cut that would cleave into the Word Bearer's shoulder. Zadkiel foresaw the attack, though, and rolled aside, thrusting the tip of his blade into the Ultramarine's thigh. Cestus grimaced as the tip went in and recoiled, swiping downward to force Zadkiel back.

'I am an expert swordsman, Ultramarine,' Zadkiel told him, goading his opponent carefully, 'as martially skilled as any of the sons of Guilliman. You will not best me.'

'Enough words,' Cestus roared. 'Act!' He smashed his blade, two-handed, against Zadkiel's defence. The Word Bearer wove away from the blow, using the Ultramarine's momentum to overbalance him, forging his parry into a riposte that pierced Cestus's shoulder beneath the pauldron. A second stinging blow cut a gash across the Ultramarine's chest and he staggered back.

Breathing hard, using the precious seconds his retreat had given him, Cestus sank into a low fighting posture and went to drive in beneath Zadkiel's guard. The Word

Bearer turned, casually avoiding the Ultramarine's lunge and placing a fierce kick in his guts.

Doubling over, Cestus felt a sharp pain in his side. There was a flash of blazing light, and he felt heat on his exposed skin as Zadkiel's power sword came close. Searing agony filled his world utterly as the Word Bearer plunged the blade deep into the Ultramarine's leg. Cestus fell to one knee, dizzy with pain. Another blow struck him in the chin. It felt like a punch, and he fell over onto his back.

Cestus brought his blade up just in time as Zadkiel launched himself at him, lashing his rapier down against the Ultramarine's improvised guard. It hovered near to Cestus's face, his power sword the only thing preventing it from cutting his head clean off. All the while, the shuttle bay and the *Furious Abyss* disintegrated around them.

'Give it up,' hissed Zadkiel, pressing the blade ever closer to Cestus's throat.

'Never,' the Ultramarine snarled back.

'Calth is dead, Ultramarine!' shouted Zadkiel. 'Your Legion is doomed! Guilliman's head will be mounted on the Crown of Colchis and paraded all the way to Terra! Nowhere is it written that one such as you can change the Word!'

Once, when Cestus was a mere aspirant, one of hundreds drawn from the valleys of Macragge to be judged before the sons of Guilliman, he had scrambled up the steps of the Temple of Hera. He'd defied the whips of the previous year's failed aspirants, who lashed at the youths as they tried to be the first to reach the top. He had hunted through the forests of the Valley of Laponis. He had learned there, not just that the weak gave up and the strong persevered; he had learned that at a far earlier age, or he would never have been considered an aspirant at all. He had learned that perseverance did not just make the difference between success and failure. It could change the test, and create victory where none had been possible. Will alone could change the universe. That was what made a mere man into an Ultramarine.

It was will alone that allowed Cestus to throw off his attacker in the shuttle bay antechamber, crushing the ruin of Zadkiel's severed fingers in his fist to loosen the Word Bearer's hold. It was will alone that brought him to his feet, and will alone that made him cut Zadkiel's sword, hand and all, from his wrist as he hefted it.

Clutching the stump of his arm where Cestus had cleaved it, the Word Bearer got to his knees and bowed his head.

'It means nothing, Ultramarine,' he said with finality. 'It is the beginning of the end for your kind.'

'Yet, still we'll fight,' he said, and with a grunt Cestus cut off Zadkiel's head.

The Word Bearer's lifeless body slid to the ground, as the rest of him rolled across the deck. Cestus sank to one knee beside him and found that he could no longer carry his sword. It clattered to the floor and the Ultramarine pressed his hand against his side. There was blood on his gauntlet. Zadkiel had struck him a mortal blow after all.

Cestus laughed at the ludicrousness of it. It had felt like nothing more than a sting of metal, so innocuous, yet so deadly.

The world was turning to fire around Cestus as he fell bodily beside Zadkiel. The sound of rending metal told him that the integrity of the shuttle antechamber would not hold for much longer.

The *Furious Abyss* was all but destroyed, the plan for it to cripple the Legion in tatters. The thought gave Cestus some solace in the moments before he died. As his cooling blood pooled around him, he thought of Macragge and of glory, and was finally at peace, his duty ended at last in death.

'This conclusion to the Word is no conclusion at all, for it shall go on. The future as it is written is but the merest fraction of the wonders that will be unveiled by my vision. When mankind and the warp are one, when our souls are joined in an endless psychic sea, then the truth of reality will be open to all and we shall enter an aeon where even the most enlightened of us shall be revealed to have been groping in the darkness for some truth to sustain us.

Yes, the wonders I seek are but the beginning, and for our enemies, those who would defy the future and attempt to crush the hopes of our species, the pain is only just beginning, too. Our enemies will fight, and they will lose, and destruction will be visited upon them, for it is written. Even beyond those first battles there is a purgatory of the soul that the most tormented of our foes cannot imagine. Yes, for those who will deny their place in the Word, these hateful birth pangs of the future will be but a splinter of their suffering.'

– The Word of Lorgar

ABOUT THE AUTHOR
Ben Counter is fast becoming one of the Black Library's most popular authors. An Ancient History graduate and avid miniature painter, he lives near Portsmouth, England.

THE HERESY

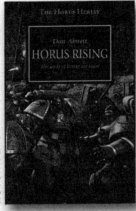

978-1-84416-294-9

978-1-84416-370-0

978-1-84416-393-9

978-1-84416-459-4